His handsome face was very near, his concentration so intense it made her dizzy. "If I thought you could love me, I would make you a widow with this sword!" And as Georgiana recoiled, his brows elevated. "I have gone too fast for you?"

"Nicolas." She tried to steady her voice. "I cannot accept this necklace. Would you please get it off my neck?"

"Perhaps you could hide it?" he suggested wickedly. "Under a ruffle of lace?"

Georgiana stamped her satin slipper in frustration. "Get it off, Nicolas! What would Brett think?"

"He is here to say what he thinks," said a deep voice behind them and they both whirled.

"Brett!" cried Georgiana. "I—I did not expect you so early."

"That"—Brett gave his young bride a wintry smile—"at least is obvious."

Novels by
Valerie Sherwood

This Loving Torment
These Golden Pleasures
This Towering Passion
Her Shining Splendor
Bold Breathless Love
Rash Reckless Love
Wild Willful Love
Rich Radiant Love

Published by
WARNER Books

Valerie Sherwood

Rich Radiant Love

WARNER BOOKS

A Warner Communications Company

WARNING

The reader is hereby specifically warned against using any of the cosmetics or medications mentioned herein. They are included only to give the authentic flavor of the times. For example, ceruse, one of the most popular cosmetics of the day, contained white lead and could well be deadly. Although common sense would normally restrain the reader from using such unappealing items as slaked lime and lye to remove warts, readers are implored to seek the advice of a doctor before undertaking any "experiments" in their use.

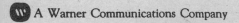

DEDICATION

To beautiful Gold, my enormous and bewitching tomcat, son of Fancy and Spice; Gold, with his winning ways and his singing purr and his soft, amazingly thick fur of brilliant white and golden orange; affectionate, sensitive, intelligent, charming Gold whose huge lamplike golden eyes have such a melting gaze; dear gentle Gold, who loves everyone and who has won a special place in our hearts forever, this book is dedicated.

Author's Note

Fabulous seventeenth-century Bermuda and quaint New Netherland are tormentingly real, but my characters of course are not. Many "great marriages" of the day were strangely fashioned—but none was quite like Georgiana's where unseen hands seemed to reach out across the years to drag her back to far Wey Gat. There was, of course, a "Scottish patroon" but just as Livingston Manor is not Windgate, my "English patroon," Brett Danforth, with his burning desire for one piece of land, is my own invention. And as for Nicolas—there may never have been a rake like Nicolas anywhere.

But that's as may be, for while all the characters and events in this novel are truly fictional and products of my imagination, the backgrounds and fascinating life-styles presented herein are as real and as authentic as I could make them—from Bermuda's wild shores and white cross-shaped houses with their "tray ceilings" and flaring "welcoming arms" front steps to the fascinating world of the patroons of Dutch New Netherland during the third Dutch War, when New York (renamed "New Orange"), although it had been English since Peter Stuyvesant surrendered it to the British in 1664, was briefly Dutch territory once again.

But most important, I have tried to bring to you a world that is gone, yet still seems to flash jewellike in all its beauty and elegance and savagery, for the swashbuckling 1600s were a time of upward mobility, when a man could rise to heights undreamed of and a woman could reach out her arms and encompass the changing world. And since the seventeenth century was also an age of poets, perhaps I can best express in verse what is in my heart:

> *I like to think that words of mine*
> *Will linger on, time out of mind,*
> *Though writers are like moths, I know—*
> *We rise, we shimmer—and we go.*

Valerie Sherwood

Contents

Rich Radiant Love

PROLOGUE

Old New York, February 1672

I

The Adventuress

The devious plan of a devious man
Could sweep her world away
But she's a wily wench herself
And yet may win the day!

It had been snowing all day and now again big snowflakes were floating down through the wintry gray dusk. They festooned the weathervanes and hissed down the tall chimneys of the steep-gabled yellow brick houses and piled up on the clean-scoured front stoops, cleared only this morning from yesterday's heavy snowfall. The thickly falling flakes made it difficult for the driver of the lumbering red-painted coach to see ahead of him as his floundering bays struggled over a narrow snow-covered bridge and came to a halt in front of the cheerful candlelit windows of the Green Lion Inn.

Framed in one of the Green Lion's small-paned windows was a strongly built man attired in handsome honey-tan velvet of a cut almost startlingly fashionable in this New World colony. His saffron-plumed hat was worn rakishly clapped on his head indoors as fashion demanded. The long golden locks that fell to his velvet shoulders, the carefully clipped golden Van Dyke beard that gave his handsome face a slightly satanic look, and the enameled gold snuffbox from which he now delicately took a pinch of snuff all proclaimed him a gentleman. But the slightly aggressive hunch of his shoulders, the scarred basket hilt of his sword (and the nicks along its blade could one but see them) as much as his hard face and cynical expression proclaimed him the adventurer he was.

Triumph lit his blue eyes as the coach's red door was abruptly flung open and he saw that the coach's single occupant, a lady attired in apricot velvets lavishly trimmed in red fox, was the one he had been waiting for.

He had taken a chance that she would come, indeed that she would be at home to receive his note at all, for all New York, it seemed, had been attending the funeral of Peter Stuyvesant, and now that the old Dutch governor with the silver-studded wooden leg had been laid to rest, they had gone home to shovel snow and talk about the old days when New York had been New Amsterdam—before the English had taken over and changed everything.

Erica Hulft, he thought with an inner grin, was not one to waste her time on the funerals of old men—she preferred hers in their prime and fully alive. As he watched, Erica threw her fox-edged hood over her own shining fox-hued hair and gathered the apricot velvet folds of her cloak about her. She stuck her head out and cast a quick surreptitious glance up and down the snowy street. Observing it to be empty, she scorned to await the driver's aid and leaped lightly down from the coach, landing dangerously in the snow on her tall pattens, with a flash of lovely legs. From within, the golden Dutchman watched appreciatively even though the cold expression on the lady's fetching countenance as she swept into the inn along with a blast of windblown snow boded him no good.

"Erica," he said in his warm, rich voice, and strode forward on booted feet to meet her. "I feared you might have gone upriver to Wey Gat—or to Peter Stuyvesant's funeral—and missed receiving my message."

"I did not attend the funeral." Erica's voice, as she paused to shake the snow from her voluminous velvet skirts, held a hint of frost.

Perhaps she had not been invited? he could not help wondering. For funeral invitations, according to Dutch custom, had certainly gone out and black-garbed *aanspreeckers* with their hats trailing long black crape ribbons had gone dolefully from house to house inviting people. Dutch funerals were invitation-only affairs. Erica would be understandably upset if the *aanspreecker* had passed her by.

"Neither did I," he said smoothly. "But then I had a better reason—I was not invited."

"I was, but I chose not to go."

"You probably missed a gift of black gloves," he grinned. "And perhaps a black scarf as well."

"I would not have attended if I had been promised an entire black mourning costume and a brace of jet mourning rings to boot!" Erica gave her skirts a ruthless shake that sent snowflakes flying. "Dead men do not interest me."

"No, I had imagined you would prefer the living." So she had *not* received an invitation and was smarting from the snub. His smile deepened at her obvious irritation.

"Be brief, Nicolas," she said crisply, withdrawing her hand at last from the red fox muff with which she had been beating her skirts, and extending it with a bored gesture. "It's very bad out there." She cast a frowning look at the leaded windowpanes, where the snow was falling faster now.

"So I can see." Nicolas took the dainty peach-gloved hand she proffered him. It was very small in his large one, very delicate, and made him wonder what it would be like to strip away the glove, the cloak, the gown, and carry her in her chemise to the big square bed in his room upstairs. Would the skin of her round bare breasts be as creamy as her throat, glimpsed against the red fox? Or would it be milky white, delicately blue-veined? Would the nipples be petal pink or dusky rose? Would the silken triangle of hair at the base of her hips be the same fox-brush color as the thick shining locks that were now revealed as her fur-trimmed hood fell back? Or would it perhaps be a shade darker, testimony that Erica had aided nature to achieve the bright color of her tresses? And what would be her style . . . in bed, this woman whose escapades were renowned all along the river?

He roused himself from these delightful but distracting thoughts, for Erica was speaking again.

"The coach nearly got stuck coming over the Heere Graft," she told him in annoyance. "And we are like not to make it back at all if I remain here, long." Her purring voice was softly accented with

French, for the lady was a Walloon of aristocratic manners and uncertain antecedents.

Before answering, Nicholas pressed lightly to his lips the small peach-gloved hand she had extended with such indifference. He savored for a moment the glove's faint inviting perfume. When he lifted his head and threw back the thick shock of golden hair that now curled attractively over his shoulders, his smile was ingenuous. He was telling himself that he had judged the wench well. The note he had slipped under her door earlier today had been calculated to bring even the most secure mistress out into deeper snow than this!

I have come into possession of some information, the note had told her cryptically. *It will affect your future—and Danforth's. Perhaps you would care to hear it first, as it concerns a woman.*

He had known *that* would bring her! For Brett Danforth's fox-haired mistress—even if rumor had it that she *had* left him again—was not one to trifle with where her own future was concerned.

"Best you send your driver away," he advised her coolly. "For you will have much to think about after you have heard my story." *And perhaps you will tumble into bed with me when you have heard it,* was the thought unspoken. At least he would be a step closer to bedding her—and there was a future in that!

"Why?" she challenged. "How can you influence my future one way or the other?" And as his smile broadened. "Aside from the obvious—if you ruin Brett."

It amused him to play with her, cat-a-mouse.

"Erica," he said gently. "Perhaps you should best sit down. You are in for a great shock."

"I prefer to stand." Her foot was tapping restlessly; he perceived that she was eager to be gone, back into the snow—away from him.

Very well, let her take the truth standing!

"Verhulst's daughter was not lost at sea after all, as we had all presumed. She lives." He watched her face.

The hand that had gone restlessly to pat the fox-colored hair of the slim apricot velvet figure before him was suddenly stilled like a bird in flight brought down by a hunter's gun. Nothing about her moved for a moment, not even her amber eyes, fixed on the golden Dutchman before her. That tawny gaze had a wary look to it; it measured him, found him wanting.

"I do not believe you, of course," she said carelessly.

The tall Dutchman shrugged. "As you like," he agreed in a calm voice. His brows elevated a bit. "Perhaps you would like to meet her?"

Erica looked startled. "You mean she is *here*?"

The Dutchman shrugged. "We cannot talk here in the door," he pointed out.

Erica moistened her lips. Abruptly she summoned the innkeeper, who had been occupied across the room, supervising the stacking of wine barrels in a corner. She pulled some coins from a velvet purse. "Would you pay my driver and send him away?" she asked with her appealing smile. "I cannot face struggling out to him through the snow."

The innkeeper gave her and the Dutchman a keen look but he nodded and went through the door into the snowy street.

She does not want to risk being seen on the street outside this inn any more than is necessary, Nicolas realized, for he had sported with many a man's mistress and knew all the signs.

Now Erica turned that same melting smile on him.

"Nicolas, dear, would you help me remove my pattens?" she asked. "I cannot enjoy walking on six-inch soles across the room. It makes me feel *gigantic*!"

Hiding a smile that Erica with her delicate build could possibly feel gigantic, and noting with glee the sudden change in her manner toward him from glacial to melting, Nicolas bent to unbuckle her tall pattens, now dripping as the snow melted from them onto the scoured stone floor of the inn. With them off she came barely to his broad shoulder and he escorted her with a flourish to a corner table of the low-beamed common room. There she threw back her fox-trimmed cloak and revealed a gown of matching apricot velvet, surprisingly low cut considering the weather.

The thought crossed Nicolas's mind that a man with a mistress like this one traveled first class, and once again he envied Danforth—as he had so often these months past.

"Some hot buttered rum might warm you," he suggested, and beckoned to a little Dutch serving girl who came into the room wearing a white apron and carrying a big tray of shining pewter tankards. She set the tray down with a clatter and came toward them shyly on her Indian moccasins, for the big Dutchman was so masculine that he intimidated her. Erica watched with amusement how the girl flushed and bridled and pulled on her long fair braids as Nicolas gravely ordered the rum.

When the innkeeper returned, stamping his feet to shake off the snow of the street, he saw facing each other across pewter tankards in one of the deserted common room's darker corners what he considered a rare pair. Like tawny lions, both of them had an extraordinary physical beauty—the man with his golden beard and twinkling blue eyes, the woman with her delicious delicacy, her skin smooth and creamy and her hair the vivid hue of a fox's brush.

The innkeeper gave them both a jaundiced look as he walked over to warm himself at the crackling brick hearth where a round black iron kettle of soup was now bubbling. He knew Erica to be the mistress of the "English patroon," Brett Danforth—and knew too that she often strayed. Indeed, the lady had brought gentlemen here before and he had been well paid to be discreet. But now his curiosity was roused and he wondered what this meeting in the snowy dusk was about, for Nicolas van Rappard was Brett Danforth's sworn enemy.

The landlord would have given a good deal to have heard what was being said in that dark corner but the handsome pair kept their voices pitched so that he could not.

As he watched, the woman shrugged her elegant apricot velvet shoulders and gave the wickedly smiling fellow before her a predatory look from her narrowed amber eyes. "Nicolas," she complained. "Talking with you is like trading with the enemy. I am never sure where I stand."

An audacious grin played over the Dutchman's hard handsome features as he drained his tankard and gestured to the lurking servant girl for a refill before he answered her. When he spoke it was in a caressing voice. "But you know I have only your best interests at heart, my dear Erica."

She laughed. "And how do I know that?"

Nicolas leaned forward, an elegant and impressive figure. "Because I swear it," he said caressingly, and smiled deep into her eyes.

Erica made a slight, disclaiming gesture. "You said the girl was here?"

"I never said she was here. You leaped to that conclusion."

"And you let me do it. . . ." But Erica relaxed, watching him now with catlike amusement. "Perhaps you will stop toying with me,

Nicolas, and tell me why such a great heiress has waited so long to return and claim her inheritance?"

"Because she has thus far no idea of her true identity." He waited to let that sink in and was rewarded by a widening of Erica's amber eyes, a soft catch of breath.

"And where is she?"

Nicolas waited to answer until the little Dutch serving girl— obviously enamored of him, and carrying fresh brimming tankards instead of a pitcher, set them down and retreated with their empty tankards.

"It would seem the woman Elise took her to the Bermudas as a baby. She is living on the island of St. George under an assumed name. My informant said he did not know the name she now goes by."

Those expressive velvet shoulders twitched again. "Then let her stay there! For can she not ruin you both?" As if to mute the sudden petulance in her voice, Erica leaned forward and gave Nicolas a dazzling smile. "What can I do, Nicolas darling, to make you forget you ever heard of this lost chld?" she purred. "The inn is not so crowded that they cannot spare us a room to . . ." She gave him a melting look . . . "discuss it?" Beneath the table her petticoats rustled as her questing velvet knee suddenly brushed tantalizingly against his tawny trouser leg.

Nicolas broke into a low laugh. She was very good at this sort of thing, he thought—almost as good as he. "Not what you have in mind, Erica," he chuckled. "Although a night with you would be well spent!"

Her nostrils flared suddenly with anger and she would have delivered a stinging slap across his face but that he caught her wrist in midair.

"Secrecy is not mine to give," he told her softly. "Your brother Claes has already sold the information."

"Not to . . . Brett?" she whispered.

"No, not to Brett—to me. While drunk." Nicolas dropped the slender wrist that had gone suddenly limp in his grasp.

"Ah-h-h-h, then it was Claes who told you!" The soft exclamation broke from Erica like a wistful sigh and she turned thoughtful, almost melancholy. She toyed absently with the handle of her tankard and her knee drew back almost imperceptibly from its contact with Nicolas's tan-gold trousers. "You should have told me this at once," she reproved him. "A *gentleman* would have." She gave him a resentful look.

"And a *lady* would not have made me such a delightful offer," he countered.

"I made you no offer!" she flashed. Then, with a shrug, "Although one could say that our meeting here *is* somewhat illicit."

"Yes," he said brutally. "Suppose Brett finds out? Do you think he will forgive you?"

If he had hoped to frighten her, the words had no effect. "I have been unfaithful to him before and he has taken me back," she said indifferently.

"I don't doubt it," he muttered, for the skin that showed above her low-cut neckline was petal smooth and her suddenly speculative lazy smile seemed both to strip away their clothing and tell him what it might be like with her in the hot darkness of an upstairs room at the inn, with a fire roaring in the hearth and the sheets rasping softly against their bare bodies and every sense alive to madness and desire.

It maddened him that he must hold himself in check with this tantalizing wench.

"Does Brett love you then so much?" he asked grimly.

"Sometimes I think he does not love me at all," she sighed in one of those flashes of honesty that so intrigued men. "And then again . . ." Her shrug spoke volumes. "Four times I have strayed and always he has taken me back."

"I am surprised that you go back," he said bluntly. "You must have had many other offers. Indeed, better offers!" And as her casual nod acknowledged those other, better offers, "Do you love him then so much?" He felt nettled. And alarmed. For it had been chancy bringing this information to her and he was only too aware that he might live to regret it.

"Love him? I despise him!" she flared. "In fact, I have left him. Again!"

"So I've been told," he murmured. But, then, he reasoned, despite the fact that she had strayed and been taken back four times, mistresses come and go and Danforth was in no way bound to this one. He watched her. "Then it *is* only the money you are after? You wait to be sure he gets it?"

"Oh, he already has it!" Haughtily.

His knuckles showed white but it was the only sign that she had stung him with her answer.

"That he is successful in holding on to it, then? That is why you stay?"

"Of course!" But something in her purring voice gave that the lie. Nicolas watched her keenly. It was difficult to know with her which way the cat would jump, but this elegant fox-haired wench could help him if she would. "I think," he said softly, "that it will occur to Claes, having sold the information to me, that it would be even more profitable to sell that same information to Brett."

And that was why he had sought her out, telling her that he had information that could bring her world—and Brett's—down about their ears.

"Unless," he added, "you find a way to stop Claes."

The hardness in her amber eyes now matched his own.

"And why would I do that?" Silkily.

"Because, as Claes tells it, when he saw her she was a pretty golden-haired child. She might have grown up to be a beautiful woman."

Erica's teeth caught in her soft lower lip and he pressed his advantage.

"Like mother like daughter," he said tranquilly. "I'm told her mother, Imogene, was dazzling."

"Bah! She is still a child!"

"Fourteen this month, by my count. Many girls are wed before that age, as well you know. I myself knew a girl who was married to her second husband before she was fourteen!"

Erica's high-arched brows rose. "Indeed, her first husband must have caught pneumonia on his wedding night and died of it!"

The smiling face of the blond Dutchman opposite her was suddenly very hard. "Marrilee was wed to her first husband against her will. He died suddenly on their wedding trip. By drowning."

Looking at him, her heartbeat quickened. "And were you there, Nicolas?" she asked softly.

"Nearabout." Carelessly.

"And where is Marrilee today?" she wondered. "While her champion converses with me in corners?"

His shrug was completely natural. "I do not concern myself with Marrilee's whereabouts," he admitted frankly. "She must be all of twenty-six by now and since she had an unfortunate tendency to gain weight, she must be as fat as her mother and her aunt!''

"Nicolas, you are a scoundrel!" Erica was reduced to laughter, but she watched him more narrowly.

He made her as deep a bow as table and tankard would permit. "It takes one to know one. Will you have some more rum?"

Not at all offended, Erica rose sinuously. "No, thank you, Nicolas. You have given me something to think about and I feel a sudden need to seek Claes out."

"Tomorrow will be time enough," he told her negligently. "When I left him he was very drunk, sprawled across a table at the tavern down the street. I tossed the tavernkeeper a coin and told him to find Claes a bed upstairs, that either his sister or myself would be back to collect him."

Erica gave him a thoughtful look. Knowing Claes, he would stay there and stay drunk until somebody came for him.

"Besides," added Nicolas, "you have sent your coach away and the snow is now too deep for you to struggle home through it."

"What do you suggest?"

He grinned. "That I tell you my plans and we seal a devil's pact—upstairs in my room, where the chambermaid has already made a fire and put a bed warmer into the featherbed."

"Doubtless in the hope that she herself will soon occupy it?"

"Doubtless," he agreed smoothly. "But I hope that she will be disappointed this night." His long fingers reached out and caressed her gloved hand.

Erica cast a look at the window. In the gathering darkness the world outside was silent and midnight blue. The snow fell softly and steadily, piling up around the windowpanes. There was no need to hasten to see Claes—he would not be stirring from his tavern. Nor would that fast river sloop, the *River Witch*, be likely to voyage downriver in search of her in this weather. She would be safe here, for the landlord was a friend of hers—one well paid for his friendship. And Nicolas was most attractive. She wondered idly, luxuriously, what it would be like to feel his arms around her and what it would be like to run her fingers over his bare chest and feel his muscles tense beneath her teasing. A familiar languor stole over her, making her eyelids feel heavy.

She gave the man across the table a slanted look.

"It *is* drafty here downstairs," she murmured. "Perhaps I *should* warm myself before your upstairs fire before I consider going out into the snow. . . ."

Triumph was etched on the Dutchman's hard countenance. With the utmost decorum he rose, offered her his arm, and led her up the wooden staircase. With a flourish he flung open the door to his bedchamber—and it was, as he had promised, wonderfully warm, with a fire roaring on the hearth and the big square bed with its red quilted coverlet invitingly turned down.

Erica was pulling off her gloves as she entered the room and she flung them onto a cedar chair with a careless gesture. They looked like flowers, he thought. . . . Her cloak and hood followed before he could help her off with them. They slid to the floor and she ignored them. Her amber eyes sparkled like topazes as she tossed back her head, rumpled her hair and turned to him with a low laugh.

"Perhaps I will yet win you to *my* cause," she purred.

"All things are possible." His voice was hoarse with desire and he bent over her, letting one hand run familiarly down her slender velvet back as he pressed a kiss onto her impudently upraised lips. "Perhaps we will find that our interests—converge."

The slim apricot bodice twisted away from him. Her words were a challenge. "I have been told that since coming here, Nicolas van Rappard, you have bedded half the girls in New York."

"Only the pretty ones," he shrugged, advancing on her again.

Again she spun away from him, holding him off with a fragile outstretched hand. "You are in a hurry," she mocked him.

"You fire a man's blood," he muttered.

"And blind him to his destiny?" she suggested, amused.

"That too," he agreed pleasantly, certain that no woman, not even a woman as exciting as Erica Hulft, could ever blind *him* to his destiny. And now he flung his own challenge. "I invite you to try!"

It was the kind of challenge a woman like Erica could not resist. With a low exultant laugh she slipped into his arms, opened her lips invitingly and raked her nails lightly over his cheek as he swept her slight body up against him. *She would give this arrogant Dutchman,* she told herself, *such a night as he would not soon forget! And in his arms she would learn his every plan. . . .*

Their clothes made a ragged trail toward the bed into which they fell like ferrets, holding each other in a death grip—for here were two to whom the game of love was more than a game; it was a deadly serious pursuit with victors and vanquished.

Tumbling, breathless, their naked arms and legs tangled, twining, untwining, bodies clutching, twisting, they made golden promises— forgotten even as they were being whispered. Hot words of love poured out, unheard and only half remembered. The red quilted coverlet had long since slid to the floor and the sheets were a wild rumple as the tawny pair rolled about the bed, each striving for supremacy in this mad, exciting game, each fighting to gain—and hold—the upper hand. Only one man had ever really bested Erica in this sort of encounter—and that man was Brett Danforth. Perhaps that was why, in her own strange way, she loved him.

But tonight—tonight as always during these moments she forgot even his name. Forgot all but the pursuit of pleasure and the man she currently held in her arms. Her every move was exquisite, wanton, enticing. She exulted as Nicolas's passion flared up—and then with marvelous timing she held him back, so that he flamed up again, each time higher, until together they reached exotic fiery peaks.

Although tomorrow she would casually forget him, tonight her body was a frail craft afloat upon a sea of passion—a wild sea that tossed them hither and thither, that whether he guided the boat or she did, brought gasping sobs to her lips and groans of desire and lust from the strong-armed man who held her.

She was—had always been, and had known it since she was eleven—a woman of tinder, of flame. And tonight she proved it once again as Nicolas, driven almost mad by the way she somehow managed to hold him off, while endlessly teasing and tempting and driving him on to bursts of passion, went over the brink with her again and yet again.

Morning found them lying as they had finally fallen apart in exhaustion, with one of her bare legs carelessly thrown over his. And—with the resilience that characterized her—it was Erica who woke first.

She was shivering, for the fire had gone out and the room was cold.

As she contemplated retrieving the quilted coverlet from the floor, there was a discreet knock on the door. Erica sat up. Mindful of the fact that she had not a stitch of clothes on, she pulled the sheet up to cover her bare bosom and called out, "Come in."

The young chambermaid who sidled in had dark circles under her eyes that came from crying. She gave Erica, with her rumpled hair and bare shoulders, in bed with Nicolas, a sullen look.

"I came to make the fire," she muttered.

"Then do so," said Erica. "We are both freezing. But first," she directed carelessly, "bring me that quilt."

The girl bent reluctantly to do as she was bid and gave the sleeping Nicolas a reproachful look as she spread the red quilted coverlet over the bed she had thought herself to occupy. Erica measured her rival with a practiced glance and some amusement. Not much of a face—too puffy, but of course that might come from tears shed over Nicolas—but the wench probably had an excellent figure concealed under the folds of that brown homespun dress. That figure was used to relaxing in this very bed, no doubt. Suddenly the thought irritated Erica, for last night Nicolas had proved to be a remarkable lover whose stamina almost matched her own. Her eyes narrowed as she watched the girl bend over the dead fire, sweeping up the ashes with a short hearth broom into a dustpan.

"If you tell anyone you saw me here, I promise you'll be dismissed," she told the girl in a clear hard voice and was rewarded by a sudden jerk of homespun shoulders.

"I won't tell," said the girl in a muffled voice and Erica gave a low malicious laugh.

"You'd better not," she added warningly. "And you can bring me a bath once you've built up the fire."

The serving girl shuffled out. Nicolas, exhausted from his endeavors, slept peacefully on. He didn't wake until Erica was in her bath and threw a sponge at him. Then he came awake with a start and stared at her, memories of last night curving his mustached mouth into a smile.

"Well, good morning," he said. "When you've finished bathing, come back to bed. It's warm here."

"Perhaps." She gave him a sunny smile, lingered over her bath, holding up first one pretty leg and then the other for inspection.

Let him think she was returning to bed. Let him savor what he thought was soon to be his—and then take it away! For in spite of the fever heat of their passions last night, Nicolas had spoken no word at all of his plans.

She rose at last, standing in the metal tub, and let a last spongeful of water course down her slim delightful body in a display that was wickedly tormenting and made Nicholas's eyes gleam in anticipation. Then:

"I must go find Claes," she said. "He may wander off somewhere and we wouldn't want that."

Nicolas frowned, for he realized the truth of what she said. It was in neither of their interests for Claes to "wander off somewhere." He watched as she toweled herself dry, her naked form emerging and reemerging in tantalizing fashion.

"There's still time . . ." he suggested hopefully.

"Only for breakfast." Her voice was crisp. She was already slipping her sheer bronze lace chemise over her head; it was so gauzy she might have been naked. Erica never planned for cold; her future, like her past, would be full of warm firelit rooms and men to ply her with warming wines and cover her nakedness with lavish velvets and furs. And jewels. Especially jewels.

"Very well." Nicolas sighed and rolled out of bed. He paused to stretch his long arms above his head, to let his strong muscles ripple in a display calculated to entice *her*, to show her what she was missing. He was a little nettled that Erica's gaze passed over him with casual indifference.

"Breakfast here or downstairs?" he asked, padding over toward his smallclothes, leaning down to pick them up from the floor.

"Downstairs," she said, surprisingly, rustling into her apricot silk petticoats, smoothing them down around her. "I think I would like for us to be seen together—in some public place."

He looked up sharply and his dark golden brows lifted. "And why is that?"

"Hurry," she said, not bothering to answer. The apricot velvet gown was already over her head and she was swiftly fastening the invisible hooks. "You can bathe later. I will go downstairs first so that we will not be seen to arrive together. It is best people think I came in off the street."

Nicolas nodded, pulling on his clothes. It was his custom to let the women he brought to his bed leave it in whatever manner they preferred. As he watched Erica run a comb briskly through her gleaming fox-hued hair, he wondered what she was up to. Doubtless she would tell him at breakfast.

Moments later Erica had slipped into her cloak and hood. She brushed by him as if he were some chance-met stranger and opened the door. There was no one about and she went through the door like a shadow, with her tall pattens slung over her arm along with her muff as she pulled on her peach gloves. She walked down the hall and at the head of the staircase she paused, keenly eyeing the room below. Finding it for the moment deserted, she hurried down and seated herself at a table by the window in the low-ceilinged common room.

It was there Nicolas found her, easing out of her fur-trimmed cloak and hood as if she had just arrived. He looked out through the steamy leaded panes and noted that it had stopped snowing and that shovels were busy as thickset men in stocking caps and with woolen scarves pulled up around their ears and noses red from the cold, set to work. At least it was warm in here from the crackling fire on the hearth. He seated himself across from Erica in some amusement.

"There is not much choice this morning," she informed him. "I have ordered you some porridge and—"

"I will take what is offered," he said dryly and sat and grinned at her. Despite this morning's disappointment, Nicolas was feeling quite pleased with himself, for it had long been his intention to bed Brett Danforth's vivacious mistress and he had spent a delightful night with her.

A dark muffled shape went past the window and Erica waved a peach-gloved hand. It was impossible to tell whether the man saw them through the steamy panes or not; at any rate he did not wave back.

"What game are you playing now?" asked Nicolas mildly. "Do you hope by making sure you are seen with me to incite a duel between Danforth and myself? I will tell you now that I do not mind killing him, but it would gain me nothing—there would only be new heirs to be dealt with."

He was silent as their porridge was brought in pewter porringers with the ornate perforated handles so popular with the Dutch.

Erica waited until the serving girl had departed with her tray. Then she said in a quarrelsome voice, "It is not my intent to bring on a duel between you."

"But some jealousy, perhaps?" he interposed smoothly.

"Some jealousy might be welcome," she admitted calmly, toying with her porridge. "But I resent your suggestion that I am playing a game. It is you who are playing a game—with me."

"How can you say it, Erica?" Nicolas's tone was rich and eloquent and bore a note of surprise. "Especially after last night?" His hand dropped lightly to cover her own gloved one on the table.

An ever so slight frown drew Erica's high-arched brows together. "All night you teased me about your plans—without ever telling me what they were. Now I demand to hear them."

Nicolas leaned forward. His wicked blue eyes held a sultry remembered glow as he studied her across the tankards and porringers. "That was not all I teased you with," he murmured. Indeed he had been surprised by Erica's sophistication in bed. And her ardor—which he admitted with inner candor *might* have been faked. Erica was born to be a king's courtesan, he thought—and was not. Just as he was born to be a patroon and was not. And here they both were for reasons of their own in this raw Dutch town on the North American mainland the English had rechristened New York. Adventurer and adventuress—it took one to know one, he ruminated.

"Do not twit me with what I am, Nicolas," she said indifferently. "I cannot help it—any more than you can." But her soft lips parted temptingly and she moistened them with a pink tongue as she spoke, even while her amber gaze challenged him. "It was a lovely night. All of it. But it is over now. Tell me what you intend."

He grinned but he let go of her hand. "But I have already been so generous with my information," he complained. "For which I paid your brother dearly!"

"I am surprised," she said, her eyes narrowing, "that you do not avail yourself of the information to dash to Bermuda and wed the girl yourself. It would make good your claim to the property, would it not? In your view? Not in Brett's, of course."

He acknowledged that with a rueful nod. "Indeed, I'd follow your advice if someone would but advance me the money, for I find I am sore embarrassed for funds. Hardly a florin do I possess, now that your brother's through with me—certainly not enough to carry me all the way to Bermuda and there put up such a show as a man must to win a maid's hand." He paused thoughtfully. "Of course, if we two could strike up a bargain?"

Erica's eyes twinkled. "You are actually suggesting—without quite saying it—that *I* send you to Bermuda?"

"Well, I would be glad to share the proceeds of the venture with you," he declared innocently.

She threw back her head and gave a throaty laugh. It was a very pretty laugh and a man who had just come in the inn door and was stamping the snow off his boots noted it and resolved to regale his friends by telling them how he had seen Erica Hulft in close conversation with Nicolas van Rappard, and wasn't that strange, since everyone knew she was Brett Danforth's mistress, and Danforth and van Rappard were on opposite sides of this quarrel over the land? Which only went to prove that a mare might change riders in midstream.

"Nicolas, I admire your impudence," said Erica, leaning back. "But I would hardly finance you in a venture to impoverish Brett!" Her voice turned malicious as she cocked her head and shot him a look upward through her long reddish lashes. "And, anyway," she shrugged, "how do you know that I will not rush straightaway to Brett and tell him everything you have told me?"

Nicolas sat very still. There was no expression at all on his face. "Because your enlightened self-interest will tell you, Erica, that *he* might rush forthwith to Bermuda and wed the girl himself to ensure his title—and then where would you be?"

"In his bed most likely—if I choose." Erica's tone was contemptuous but he saw her color rising a little in her creamy cheeks and knew he had touched a nerve.

"And besides," he added in a soft deliberate voice, "there is another deterrent."

"And what is that, pray?" she challenged him.

"That I would strangle you with these hands," he told her pleasantly, lifting one of them with a negligent gesture as if he were pointing out something in another part of the room.

The smile in her eyes died. The memory of that story he had told her yesterday was still fresh. Erica had no doubt at all that Nicolas had personally drowned young Marrilee's unfortunate bridegroom. It took one to know one but—Erica had never dealt in murder.

"I will see what I can do to silence Claes," she said in a more distant tone.

"Send him to some far place," advised Nicolas. "Madagascar might be a good choice."

"Claes will refuse to go to Madagascar." Tranquilly.

"Get him drunk enough and he will go."

Erica gave the man across the table a reproving look. "You forget, I have a sisterly affection for Claes. I will not send him out to be murdered by the pirates of Madagascar."

"Well, at least get him away from here," said Nicolas irritably. "Or we may *both* find our applecarts overturned."

As if goaded by his warning, Erica rose suddenly and Nicolas leaped up solicitously to help her on with her cloak and pattens.

"Will you be needing a coach?" he wondered.

"No, I think I can make it as far as the tavern on foot," she said with a trace of irony. "*Au revoir,* Nicolas." She gave him her hand with a delicate gesture. Her expression turned suddenly roguish. "Look me up again," she said blithely. "*If* you win out over Brett—and if you can avoid the hangman's noose!" Her laughter pealed.

"I shall hope to manage both," he told her, brushed her hand with his lips and watched her go. And wished again that he had money enough to go to Bermuda himself and secure his claim beyond question. And there was regret for something else in his face too, for Erica in bed had been wonderfully soft and warm and passionate. She had made his blood race as few women had done—and now, as she said, it was over.

He sighed. Erica Hulft was an expensive wench, and he could not afford her. Again he envied Brett Danforth, and hoped that he had managed by bringing Erica into his confidence to spike any chance that Claes might tell Danforth what he knew and that Danforth might go to Bermuda and ruin in one swoop all of Nicolas's chances to win in the courts what he could not get by other means. Wistfully he fingered the serviceable sword at his side—if only it could be settled *that* way. But if he succeeded in killing Danforth, new claimants would arise out of nowhere, relatives of Danforth's ready to step into his shoes and argue the case for ownership of Windgate with Nicolas van Rappard.

For her part, Erica was already outside, leaning against the strong wind that swept this port town, and making her way with surprising speed on her high pattens along the snowy street. Men tipped their hats as she passed, or tugged at their stocking caps and bowed—and then leaned on their shovels for a moment to watch her as she went, and dream for the moment of being a patroon with a stylish mistress like this one.

Nicolas, still at the table and drumming his fingers as he frowned, was not watching her progress down the snowy street, so he had no way to know how determined she looked. Indeed he might have hurried out without his cloak and caught up to Erica if he had known what was even then going through her mind.

She was thinking that Claes was in no shape to travel anywhere, that he was deeper in his cups each day and that he would undoubtedly—since she had refused to finance his drinking himself into an early grave—go to Brett and try to sell the information as soon as he drank up the money Nicolas had paid him for it. It chilled her a little that Claes had never told *her* about this child growing up in Bermuda with the power to ruin Brett. He *might* have lied to Nicolas in order to extract money from him, but she did not believe Claes was lying, for she knew he had visited Bermuda once or twice—and the first time he had come back with considerable money. She wondered now if he had blackmailed someone for it—possibly the maidservant, Elise.

Well, there was an answer to *her* immediate problem, if not to Nicolas's problem. She would tell Brett boldly about the girl—she would be vague, of course, she would not tell him where she had got her information, she would say only that it *might* be true—and it would be a way to mend things between them, which had been going from bad to worse lately, for was she not looking out for his interests? She would tell him so—and warn Claes that she had told him. And, then, if Brett became curious about the girl, she would get him to send *her* to Bermuda to find the van Rappard heiress. It would be logical enough, for had she not told Brett about the girl's existence in the first place?

And, then, who knew? A lovely smile curved her mouth. Perhaps it was the girl who would be sent to Madagascar! And reports of her "death" could filter north!

Nicolas, of course, had no inkling of what was going on in Erica's agile mind. He left the inn shortly, whistling and cursing his lack of funds, but still feeling that he had done what he could. He glanced up at the big snow-covered windmill that overshadowed the town and hunched his cloak around him against the cold. Behind him came the sound of children's high-pitched laughter, and a pair of sturdy little boys in stocking caps came flying past him carrying ice skates. They were joined up the snowy street by a little girl and her older sister, obviously acting as chaperon.

For a moment Nicolas gave a fleeting thought to the pretty child growing up in Bermuda in ignorance of her vast heritage on the Hudson. He wondered idly if she really had grown up to be a beauty. Then a snowball caught him broadside and he turned with a roar and forgot all about Bermuda and the van Rappard heiress.

If Nicolas could have seen into the future, he would have ignored that sudden rain of pelting snowballs and forthwith strangled Erica Hulft. Or kidnapped her and held her captive—which would have been, all things considered, very pleasant.

But Nicolas could not see into the future and while he warded off the snowballs, Erica Hulft picked her dainty way through the fresh-fallen snow to the tavern and paid her brother's bar bill. Erica had powers of persuasion that Nicolas lacked—she knew all Claes's weaknesses. She had Claes—awake now and singing loudly off-key while he drunkenly waved a bottle of Kill-Devil rum at passersby—loaded into a wheelbarrow and carted off to her home. And once there under the suasion of a hot footbath, hot rum, and sentimental talk of other, better days before he had become a drunk and she a wandering jade, she pried from him a bit of information that Nicolas had not.

She learned from Claes that the van Rappard heiress now went by the name of Anna Smith.

The Bermuda Islands, June 1673

II

The Ingenue

Manors and mansions and vast estates,
Every day dressed for a ball!
Yet to be first in her lover's heart,
Young Anna would trade them all!

With her golden hair tossing like the silver mane of the dancing Arabian mare she rode so effortlessly, young Mistress Anna Smith cantered down the long driveway through dappled sun and shade. She was faultlessly groomed in a dove gray riding habit that fit her slim figure to perfection. A wide-brimmed hat with a silver band, surmounted by tossing gray plumes, shaded burnished gold curls that had been carefully combed and groomed by her personal maid, Doubloon. Her imported gray leather gloves matched her riding habit and a froth of expensive white lace spilled out at her throat and cuffs. Her turquoise eyes, brilliant and deep as the sea off the nearby Bermuda shoreline, were calm and, although only fifteen years old, she bore herself with the self-assurance that became the heiress to mighty Mirabelle Plantation. Behind her down the long drive lay the handsome white stone cross-shaped house over which she had reigned as mistress ever since Mamma Jamison died—and these days, with Papa Jamison away in Jamaica so much, she was effectively the plantation's sole proprietor. Slaves and bond servants, agents and overseers—all of them answered to the girl who was walking her horse in the heat of a Bermuda afternoon down a long green aisle where leafy branches met overhead. Anna loved this driveway and always lingered here, for in this leafy greenness with the big white house behind her she felt there was all the best of Mirabelle—this and the beautiful forest of virgin cedars that lay up the hill. Before her yawned the tall gates that were always open to visitors, for Papa Jamison's hospitality was renowned, and around her stretched the broad reaches of meadow and beach, of cane and cedar, that encompassed Mirabelle.

There was reason for the arrogant way Anna sat her sidesaddle, reason too for the slightly haughty lift to her chin. For Anna's childhood had been spent as the barefoot niece of a bondwoman, Eliza Smith, and now those same hot sands and dusty lanes over which her little feet had scampered were *hers*—or would be hers one day, for had not Papa Jamison promised to leave her Mirabelle?

But it was not wills or money or the power she wielded in ruling Mirabelle that preoccupied Anna that June day or made her clear turquoise eyes gaze so dreamily at the big trees passing by.

It was the thought of a lover.

Of course, all the lads who pursued her had something to offer—and had detractions too:

Lance Talbot had his magnificent horsemanship (he was engaging and flirtatious, but lord, he was more interested in horses than women! And besides, her best friend Sue was madly in love with him, which made him off limits as far as Anna was concerned). Broad-shouldered Ross Wybourne had his father's ships—but any wife *he* brought home would always play second fiddle to the sea. Bumbling Grenfell Adams, who loved her to distraction and was always composing dreadful sonnets to her eyebrows, had his long lineage and his great inheritance to look forward to—but *he* would always have his head in a book, Anna knew. And wild young Flan O'Toole, who beyond doubt would fight any man for her—and probably win!—had his tarnished reputation—since half Bermuda believed he had murdered his betrothed—and his desperate background as a reputed wrecker's son. And Arthur Kincaid had his glamour as a visitor from Boston; indeed the whole island was agog with talk of his wealth there, his enviable position as an only son, what an excellent match he would make for some lucky girl.

Arthur . . .

Anna's turquoise eyes kindled.

Arthur Kincaid attracted her. Perhaps it was his novelty value, for he was different from the other young men she had known. Handsome Arthur dressed like a fop and swore like an Englishman and had a mouth half-cruel, half-smiling. Yes, she decided, Arthur was probably the most interesting of the lot. She would turn her horse's head toward Lilymeade, where Arthur was staying as a guest of his cousins, the Meades. She would be passing by—and find some pretext for stopping.

Beneath their thick lashes her turquoise eyes took on a roguish gleam—she would beat Arthur at chess again! He had been so shocked when she had beaten him before, for had he been so sure he could beat her that he had utterly ignored her warning that she and Papa Jamison had played the game almost nightly since Mamma Jamison had died. Indeed, she had already bested Arthur at cards and bowls, and now—perhaps in retaliation—he had promised to teach her to play tennis, a sport King Charles of England favored, and a sport of which Arthur had assured her he was a master. Perhaps he would win at tennis, she thought carelessly, and that would be a sop to his vanity, for Arthur was certainly most monstrous vain!

Arthur had asked her for her hand, striking a pose and kneeling gracefully on the Turkey carpet in Mirabelle's handsome drawing room—and she had given him a light, offhand answer, not really considering his suit. But so many island lads had asked for her hand that she took proposals of marriage, merrily—and perhaps wisely— as more of a reflection of Mirabelle's undoubted worth than of her own undoubted charms. Now that she was fifteen, the chase had waxed hot—indeed, she was even now riding away from Mirabelle in the hope of eluding one of her suitors, young Grenfell Adams, who persisted in riding over from Great Grenfell every day and boring her with his incessant poetry.

She was running away from a suitor—but not from love. Love had not yet come her way. Her beautiful face as she rode down the long drive on the prancing silver mare, in her smart dove gray riding habit, assumed a pensive expression. Even Arthur Kincaid, for all his glamour and his Boston money and his vaunted accomplishments, was not the answer. Not for her. *Her* lover must be something more.

She had never been able to quite see that lover she was so sure would come. Some days the veil had almost lifted and she had thought she glimpsed him fleetingly in her mind . . . she could never quite see his face, but she could sense what he would be like. She would know him when he did arrive, she was sure of it.

Now, as she often did, she puzzled as to what he would be like. Tall surely, dark probably, for Anna had a penchant for dark-haired men. Above all, he would be manly. His shoulders would be broad—broad enough to carry the world, she thought romantically. His lean body would taper to narrow hips, his step would be light. His voice would carry authority, his gaze would be commanding, his sword lethal. He would stride through life with an arrogant stance and stare down lesser mortals with his cold narrow gaze.

But with her, of course, he would be different—tender, protective, considerate, a tower of strength. She would walk beside him proudly and in all this world she would come first with him.

And that to Anna was burningly important. *To be first.* Not first in his arms—some other girl would long ago have had that honor with the kind of man Anna envisioned—but first in his heart. For Anna had never known affection as a child. She had grown up without ever knowing her real mother—Aunt Eliza had never talked about her, except to say that she was beautiful. Aunt Eliza's homely face mourned at the very mention of her mother, and even a child could see that Aunt Eliza was still grieving for Anna's mother, who had died before Anna was old enough to remember her.

Anna sighed ruefully as she thought of Aunt Eliza, dead these half-dozen years past, whose grave beneath the cedars she often visited. She always thought of her as a cold but kindly woman, unable to give affection. Even now Anna did not understand that poor Aunt Eliza, so much older than her own mother, had feared to give her love to another charming child who would perhaps—like Anna's mother—die and break her heart.

The first warm affection Anna had ever known was frail, comfortable Mamma Jamison's—and even there she had been only a surrogate daughter, replacing little dead Beatrice who had died of the plague in faraway London. Sometimes at her most affectionate

Mamma Jamison had even unknowingly called Anna "Beatrice" and Anna had felt tears gathering and looked away quickly from the fond smile on Mamma Jamison's pale face, and suffered.

After Mamma Jamison's death, Papa Jamison—who had really only tolerated Anna because it made his wife so happy to have a replacement for little Beatrice, and had always been a little offhand with the child—had changed. Their shared grief over sweet Mamma Jamison's loss had brought Anna and Papa Jamison closer together. He had come then to consider Anna as almost a real daughter and had promised to leave her Mirabelle—just as Mamma Jamison had promised her she would have the massive silver candlesticks that dominated the great sideboard at Mirabelle, those candlesticks that had been part of the dowry she had brought to Papa Jamison as a bride back in England. Pleased to have the lighthearted young girl flitting around his big house that seemed to him so empty now that his wife was gone, Papa Jamison had calmly rejected all offers for Anna's hand, insisting the girl would choose for herself soon enough.

Anna had not.

And the reason was not so obvious to the young men who pursued her—else one of them might have overcome it. Blinded by her beauty, sensing perhaps her overwhelming need to be loved, not one of them guessed her blind, unreasoning—and unexpressed—need to be first in the heart of the man who would win her, to be held by him dearer than everyone, *everything*. And although Anna did not herself realize it, she was even now weeding through her prospective suitors one by one, casting aside in her mind first this one and then that one. Not because they did not love her, but because they loved something else *more*.

In her slow progress down the driveway Anna had almost reached the gates. Now as she went through them she brought her thoughts back to the present long enough to turn Floss's silver mane in the direction of Lilymeade and Arthur Kincaid, who was, after all, the best the season had to offer. And her thoughts left that tenuous imagined lover with a crash, for dead ahead was a carriage with a lone woman in it.

The carriage was stopped. It half blocked the road, and Floss, ever of a nervous disposition, reared up on her hind legs and whinnied.

Anna, quick to soothe excitable Floss, saw that the carriage's sole occupant was a stranger, but a stranger who compelled attention. She was elegantly gowned in apricot satin and stroking with peach-gloved hands a little fox-hued Pomeranian dog which she held on her lap. Her gown was trimmed—unseasonably in this climate—with ermine tails, which gave a rich and somehow exotic effect. But it was neither the handsome gown nor the arrestingly beautiful face of the woman that attracted and held Anna's gaze, not even the brilliant red fox color of the woman's massed curls, burning bright against the light. It was the expression on the woman's half-smiling heart-shaped face. Her orange-plumed hat lay beside her on the carriage seat as if she had settled down for a long stay, and her gaze on Anna was so knowing, so mocking, that the girl was struck by it.

As Anna would have eased Floss past the carriage that nearly blocked the narrow road, the woman leaned forward and said something to the driver that Anna could not quite catch. He nodded his head and the woman waved her peach-gloved hand at Anna and asked her if this was the road to Spanish Rock.

Anna reined in Floss, who danced impatiently on her dainty hooves. "No, 'tis a long way," she told the woman. "First you must reach Smith's Parish."

"Ah, then are there not some caverns of note about?" the woman's lazy voice with—was it a French accent?—asked her.

"Yes, many," said Anna courteously. "Crystal Cave and Leamington Cave are the best known."

"And are they worth seeing?"

"Oh, yes!" Anna's turquoise eyes flashed as she remembered exploring those caves with Ross. "They have wonderful ice-cool waterways, all underground with tall stone pyramids rising from the floor and long stone icicles hanging from the roof. Papa Jamison calls them stalactites and stalagmites."

Brightly the woman watched her. Then she raised her peach-gloved hand from the Pomeranian's silky head and lightly lifted and fingered a necklace of pink pearls set with three heavily worked silver links. Her lips were parted as if she would speak again, her fox-colored head inclined alertly toward Anna, as she kept caressing the necklace. It was almost as if she were trying to attract the girl's attention to the necklace.

"And would I reach the caverns by this road?"

"They lie around Harrington Sound. You must reach that by boat."

"Ah, I would not have time for that today, then." The lady sighed and gave her Pomeranian's head a pat. "What a shame!" She did not look at all disappointed. She looked relaxed and happy—as if she was enjoying some vastly amusing private joke. And all the while she was watching Anna with brilliant amber eyes that glowed like a cat's. This burning interest did not subside as she added, "But I was told there are other sights—some unusual rock formations?"

By now Anna had the strange feeling that the woman did not care at all about her answers, that she was instead listening to her voice as if memorizing its diction, its accent. "Cathedral Rocks in Sandys Parish is perhaps the best," Anna told her shortly. "But you would have to reach that by boat also."

"Indeed?" The woman stifled a yawn. "Then I see that I have come all this way for nothing. I shall have to return to St. George." She gave Anna a half-smile and a negligent little wave of her gloved hand and leaned forward and told her driver to take her back to town. As he moved to turn the carriage around, Anna noticed that it was a rental carriage—the sort of conveyance a stranger to these islands might hire. Then she gave Floss her head and they fled by the little carriage like a silvery breath of wind.

She was conscious of the Apricot Woman's stare—for that was how she impulsively thought of her: the orange hair, the orange dog, the orange gown—all the way down the road. Anna could feel that calculating stare boring into her back until she was out of sight of the carriage. That woman had been *appraising* her—but why? She looked back once, compelled by that amber gaze, and saw the swaying orange plumes of the woman's hat as she leaned out of the carriage watching Anna's progress, disappear from view.

As Anna entered a heavy growth of cedars and lost sight at last of the carriage, the words the woman had asked of the driver, which had hovered half heard just below the level of her consciousness, came back to her:

"Is she the one?" the woman had asked.

And the driver had nodded.

It was all very strange. Anna had never laid eyes on the woman in apricot before. She was half tempted to turn and gallop back and ask her bluntly what she wanted but something—perhaps some inner

warning—deterred her. There had been that behind the Apricot
Woman's smiling gaze and brilliant amber eyes that was threatening.
And besides, would she not look a fool dashing off to hurl suspicious questions at a stranger who had only after all asked her for
road directions?

Or . . . she could rein in her horse and sit and wait and watch the
woman go by. Perhaps the woman would stop her carriage and speak
to her again and that puzzling *"Is she the one?"* would be resolved.
Anna told herself she must have misheard that remark, but indecision beset her, and she brought Floss to a walk.

As she sat there undecided, the night Aunt Eliza died came back
to her unbidden. The minister, Mr. Hunt, had been hastily summoned.
There had been hurried discussions that Anna had not been permitted
to hear. And then Samantha Jamison, who had subtly assumed the
role of mother to orphaned Anna, taking over the reins from the
faltering hands of her bondwoman Eliza Smith, who lay dying of
consumption in one of the big bedrooms of Mirabelle, had surged
forward and announced that she would herself take charge of the
child that night. But Anna, sensing something wrong when the
minister had stayed so long with Aunt Eliza, had leaped up and run
out to confront him when she heard his footstep in the hall.

She had stood and stared at him wordlessly, her turquoise eyes big
and frightened. "How is Aunt Eliza?" she had whispered, alarmed
at his dour expression.

Mr. Hunt was not one to mince words.

"Dying," he said shortly and Anna had gasped and collapsed
back against Samantha Jamison's lavender skirts, which had by now
followed the child into the hall.

"Ye should not have broken it to the child in that way, Mr.
Hunt!" Samantha had cried. She clutched Anna's small shuddering
frame protectively to her big billowy body, her taffeta skirts rustling
as she did so. "We'd kept the seriousness of Eliza's illness from
her."

"Then ye should not have," Hunt snapped, his frown deepening.
"For the woman will not last the night." Too late he realized that
the angry face into which he peered was that of the wife of his
richest parishioner. Ah, well, he told himself, he no longer had to
placate this island gentry. He was leaving the island next week for,
hopefully, a better post, and who was he to solve dead mysteries or

make things right for those who didn't deserve it anyway? For Hunt was filled with bitterness. He'd come to this island borne on golden promises and had fully expected to find here a rich and fawning congregation who would bow and scrape before him and beg him to lead them straightaway to heaven. Instead, he was leaving much as he had come, with holes in his socks. His brooding gaze played fleetingly over the indignant mistress of Mirabelle and the golden-haired child she had chosen to make her own—then his thin mouth closed with a snap. Let them work out their own problems here, for had they not rejected his leadership? With a brusque nod, he left them.

That was all that Anna remembered of the incident. Far more important to her had been her last tearful good-bye to Aunt Eliza the next day.

Mr. Hunt had been replaced by Mr. Cartmell the next week and Anna had had no way of knowing, for neither Hunt nor Cartmell had bothered to tell her, that Aunt Eliza had haltingly dictated her life story to the minister the night she died and had entrusted him with that document, signed and sworn to, along with a small journal written in an aristocratic scrawl. Mr. Hunt had carried them both away with him to St. George, sealed in a big packet, sworn not to reveal their contents and to give the packet unopened to Anna on the day she was married.

Annoyed by the trust, which seemed to him just one more irritating duty on an irritating island, Hunt had thrust the packet containing the document and journal into his successor's hand with brusque instructions. And eager young Cartmell, who, unlike Hunt, was overjoyed to be here after the dirty fog of London, had breathed deep of the clean clear air free of the scent of sea coal, interrupted with anxious questions about how the "island gentry" could be expected to receive him—and promptly forgot all about the packet his predecessor entrusted to him.

It had not occurred to him to mention it, not even when Samantha Jamison died and Anna Smith, the barefoot waif of unknown antecedents, became to all intents and purposes mistress of Mirabelle, just as she was reputed to be its heiress.

Anna's mind was still on the day Aunt Eliza died, a day of rain and storm and heavy peals of thunder and great flashes of blue lightning that blinded momentarily the sobbing child by the dying woman's bedside. Had Aunt Eliza's mind wandered in those last hours? she asked herself. For she had seemed to be somewhere else, some place called the Scillies, and then in Amsterdam, which was in Holland, and there she had seemed to be entreating some young girl "not to marry him."

It was all very strange, but it was a puzzle Anna had put out of her mind long ago, and seldom thought about, not even when she visited that lonely grave up in the cedars, for Eliza Smith, a bondwoman, had not rated burial in the stone-fenced family plot at Mirabelle.

Something else stirred in Anna's mind, some memory from long ago, too deep to be easily dredged up, something occasioned by the sight of that fox-haired woman. . . .

She puzzled about it as Floss dawdled down the road, taking her own time, and she might even have decided to whirl about and wait for the woman to come up, but all such thoughts took flight as she looked up and saw to her vexation that Grenfell Adams was riding down the road toward her. Loping along with his popinjay green shoulders hunched, his curly yellow head bent intently over a piece of parchment, his lips mouthing words—another sonnet, no doubt!

Anna would have liked to stamp her foot in irritation, but her booted foot was in a stirrup and she must not disturb excitable Floss. She had not got away early enough; Grenfell had found her after all!

"Mistress Anna!" Grenfell hailed her joyfully. "I was just on my way to Mirabelle."

That was hardly news, thought Anna. *Grenfell's visits to Mirabelle were a daily occurrence!*

"And I've written you some verses!" That wasn't news either. Masking her impatience with a smile, Anna tried to show an interest she didn't really feel.

"This one I've entitled '*To a Goddess*'—that's you, Mistress Anna."

"I don't feel like a goddess, Grenfell, and you will make me a laughingstock if you persist in calling me one!"

"But, Mistress Anna—" Grenfell looked so crestfallen that Anna felt sorry for him.

"It's all right, Grenfell," she sighed. "Read on."

"*I kneel before your dainty knees—*" Grenfell's earnest face flushed suddenly. "I do hope you don't mind my mentioning your *knees*, Mistress Anna? Some might find that a bit forward."

"Not at all. Go ahead and mention them, Grenfell. I have a complete set—two knees." She was half tempted to flirt her skirts so that they showed but decided that would unnerve Grenfell, who was nervous enough already. So she kept her seat calmly on Floss, who was dancing a bit in the dirt of the road, kicking up bits of gravel and dust.

Taking a deep breath, Grenfell began again:

> *"I kneel before your dainty—er—knees,*
> *And fall beneath your spell.*
> *I know I'll never love you less*
> *For I love you now so well!"*

Watching her for effect and seeing that he had made no impression, he added anxiously, "I could say I kneel before your dainty sofa. I mean, you'd be sitting on it. But then it would sound like I was talking about your—" He reddened.

Grenfell's verse—like Grenfell himself—needed seasoning, thought Anna. "I'd stick to the knees, Grenfell," she counseled. "Unless something else occurs to you."

"Something else? What else, Mistress Anna?" A pair of guileless admiring eyes were looking into her sparkling turquoise ones. "Do you mean I should perhaps espouse your eyelashes, the tip of your piquant nose, your dainty chin?"

"Inventories are tiresome, Grenfell. I—look out, there's a carriage coming." She maneuvered Floss to one side. "Move aside, Grenfell, you're blocking the road!"

Grenfell blinked, for as usual he was quite unaware of the physical world about him. But he hastily made way for the carriage that rolled by them with a nod of orange plumes.

"Do you know who that woman is?" Anna asked sharply after the carriage had passed and the dust had subsided.

Grenfell shook his head so emphatically that the tassels on his popinjay green doublet quivered. "I never saw her before, Mistress Anna."

"Neither did I, but her carriage was stopped at Mirabelle's front gates as I came through them just now. She was sitting there as if—as if she was waiting for me to come out."

Grenfell gave her a blank look. "But why wouldn't she just come up to the door and ask for you if she wanted to see you?"

"I—don't know," admitted Anna. "But she gave me a strange feeling, as if—oh, well, never mind. 'Tis a small island. Doubtless I'll see her again." She frowned after the carriage and decided that she would have Mr. Porter, Mirabelle's factor, inquire about this stranger in St. George and find out what she was doing here.

"Come on, Grenfell," she said, irritated that she could not with good grace ride on to St. George herself and ask her own questions, for Grenfell would demur and find some reason not to ride into town—he always wanted to keep Anna to himself. "Let's ride down to the beach. Floss will enjoy a run through the surf and I wouldn't mind dismounting and taking off these boots and running through it myself. Suppose I tuck up my skirts and you pull off your boots and we splash about like fishermen's brats?"

He looked so scandalized that Anna hid a smile. But he followed after her meekly as she whirled Floss about. Lovesick Grenfell would follow wherever spirited Anna led.

They rode wildly down the beach and Grenfell lost his hat, which had been clapped fashionably under one arm. Anna pulled Floss up and laughed at him while he bumbled into the surf after it. But she began to feel friendlier toward Grenfell on the white beach in the dazzling sunshine; his love for her was so childish, but so real, so self-evident in every word and look. She took off her boots and tucked up her skirts and ran through the water, pursued by an awkward but enthusiastic Grenfell.

And afterward, they sat on the sand, gasping and laughing and drying their wet legs in the sun—Grenfell looking both shocked and dazzled at the sight of Mistress Smith's dainty calves, and a glimpse of those white knees to which he wrote enthusiastic sonnets. When Grenfell told her he would not be over tomorrow as he had to squire his mother into St. George to have her new wig fitted since the wigmaker was grown too feeble to ride although he still plied his trade, it occurred to Anna that Grenfell might make inquiries for her even better than the factor, for his mother was a born gossip and attracted all the gossips of St. George to her carriage.

The last thing she said to him when he left her at the gates of Mirabelle was, "See if you can find out who that woman was, Grenfell—the one in the orange-plumed hat."

Grenfell promised cheerfully to inquire, adding, "But you're right, Mistress Anna. On such a small island, you're bound to see her again."

Anna did see the woman again. It was two days later when she rode into town in a carriage with Mr. Porter, Mirabelle's factor, ostensibly to supervise the unloading of the *Marylee*, one of Papa Jamison's little fleet of three ships—the *Marylee*, the *Annalee*, and the *Bettylee*, which sailed throughout the islands, trading. But Anna's real reason for coming along was boredom. Sometimes plantation life, pleasant as it was, palled on her, especially when Papa Jamison was away, and she yearned to see the tall ships maneuvering delicately down the Narrows with reefs to either side, past Five Fathom Hole, to beat their way into St. George's harbor.

Today there was a ship about to leave harbor, the *Dolphin*, and as Anna strolled along the quay in her light blue gown, with little black Boz importantly carrying a silk parasol over her head to protect her complexion from the sun, she looked up and saw the same woman watching her from the railing of the departing ship.

Their eyes locked—and held. *Like two antagonists*, thought Anna, puzzled. Did she imagine it or was there a sudden gleam of menace in those amber eyes? The ship was making way out of the harbor now, her sheets catching the wind, and Anna studied the woman narrowly. She leaned negligently on the rail with the slightly bored stance of one who has taken many voyages and expects nothing new of this one. When she moved, Anna saw that she had a supple narrowness but was yet possessed of a magnificent figure, startlingly displayed in the same apricot satin gown trimmed in ermine tails that had seemed so out of place in the warm climate of Bermuda.

From the quay Anna watched the *Dolphin* depart, blown out to sea on a stiff wind, watched until the Apricot Woman's fox-colored hair blended with the departing ship in the distance. And it was there, standing on the quay as that taunting face faded from view, that the memory that had eluded Anna on the road burst suddenly upon her, and she knew where she had seen hair like that before.

It was when she was seven years old. One afternoon she had accompanied Aunt Eliza on a rare journey into the town of St. George and after Eliza had made her meager purchases they had strolled through the bright sunshine down to the docks. It was on this same quay that she had seen the tall man with the fox-colored hair, exactly the shade of the Apricot Woman's. He was bent over a small keg, disputing its ownership heatedly with a rough-looking fellow. His back was to them, but his fox-colored hair shone orange in the sun.

Beside her, Anna had felt Aunt Eliza suddenly grow tense. At that moment, the fox-haired man suddenly seized the keg, wresting it away from his adversary. The violence of his gesture jerked him half around and brought the child and the older woman into full view.

Anna was almost jerked off her bare feet as Aunt Eliza seized her hand and whirled to run away. Anna was fleetingly aware that he had tossed aside the keg as he roared, "Ho there!" And then she was running down the street, trying desperately to keep up with Aunt Eliza, who had tucked up her homespun skirts in one hand and was moving faster than Anna had ever seen her move.

At that point a team of horses pulling a wagon piled with cedar logs intervened across their path and Anna's bare feet came to a skidding halt. Beside her Aunt Eliza was panting from exertion and the child glanced back to see that the fox-haired man, who had only one leg, but whose strides were long and determined nonetheless, was fast catching up with them.

Eliza would have darted around the wagon but the cedar logs' owner, a planter on a fractious sorrel horse, was right behind his wagon. At her advance the sorrel reared up and Eliza fell back with a cry, slipped, and went down on one hip into the road.

Before she could scramble up, the planter had dismounted, asking anxiously if she was all right. Aunt Eliza was saying "Yes, yes," in a distracted voice as he helped her to her feet. And now the fox-haired man had caught up with them as she stood dusting off her skirts with her big workworn hands while the planter chided her about dashing out into the road without looking. Eventually he finished his lecture, remounted, nudged his sorrel horse with his knee and departed, following his wagon, which was now some distance away.

There was no escaping the fox-haired man now. He had stood by quietly during the planter's tirade, but now he stepped forward. Anna remembered his wooden stump, his one big dusty boot, and his whiskey breath as he bent over her before she turned her head away. His broadcloth trousers had several unmended rips near the knees, and gravy and claret stains marred his handsome fawn velvet doublet.

"Where can we talk?" he had demanded hoarsely.

"I've naught to say to ye, Claes." Eliza, trembling a little from her fall but erect as a poker, had gazed back at him defiantly, and Anna could feel the convulsive pressure of the hand that clutched her own.

"Ah, yes, ye do." Claes's voice became insinuating, and a broad smile lit his face that might once have been handsome before dissolute living had etched it with lines. "I've been quiet these seven years, haven't I?"

"And well paid ye were for your silence." Grimly.

"Aye, but the necklace money is long spent and I've a deep thirst that is hard to slake."

"Then ye might try working for a living—as I do!" snapped Eliza.

"Come, come, Elise, we're not at odds!"

Seven-year-old Anna had looked up sharply. This strange man with the gutteral accent had called her aunt "Elise" and Aunt Eliza had not even seemed to notice. "I only ask some token to help me leave this godforsaken shore where I find myself cast without funds," he said persuasively.

"The necklace was of pink freshwater pearls from Scotland," Eliza had protested. "They should have kept you well for a long time. Even the big wrought silver links were valuable."

He gave her a commiserating nod. Almost he might have been agreeing with her. "But I need a bit more now. For as ye'll note, I lost my leg in a collision on the river—"

"Ye'd already lost it when I gave ye the necklace—which was not really mine to give."

Claes shrugged and his pointed face became sly. "Nothing belongs to the dead, Elise—all belongs to the living."

Torment and futility and rage struggled for mastery on Eliza's worn and honest face. "You've kept my secret?" she asked at last. The child thought she sounded fearful.

Claes nodded, his amber eyes watchful, alert.

"There's a ring," sighed Elise. " 'Tis all I have left. I'd meant it for the child's dowry, heaven help me."

"She could have all the dowry that anyone—"

"No, she could not!" Eliza's voice rose in near hysteria and Anna shrank against her, clinging to the folds of gray homespun that clothed Eliza's long shanks. "I'll bring the ring to you tonight. Where are you staying?"

"At the inn. But there's no need for you to come yourself. The child here can bring it." He reached down with tobacco-stained fingers and touseled Anna's bright hair.

Eliza struck his hand away and her face was white. "So that's your game?" she grated. "You mean to take the child from me?" She backed away from him, dragging Anna with her, and there was panic in her voice.

"No, no!" Claes tried to soothe her.

"There'd be no reward in it for you, Claes," Eliza declared wildly. "You who know so much—d'ye not know they'd not accept her? D'ye not know why? Must I tell ye?"

"Keep your voice down," Claes said uneasily, his gutteral voice with its strange accent becoming upset as he looked around to see if anyone was standing near enough to hear. "I promise ye I've no mind to take the child—I'll not even ask ye where ye're living. Do ye but bring the ring to me tonight, I'll sail away tomorrow and ye'll see me never again. I swear it!"

"Ye swore last time!"

"Aye, and meant it too! And I've kept my part of the bargain, Elise. I've told no one where you and the child are hid." Little Anna was puzzled at that. *They weren't hiding—they'd never hidden. Not from anyone.* She listened intently to Claes's next words. "Ye'd not have seen me this time, Elise, save that the ship chose to stop here for water and I've lost all my money gambling with these local—" he mouthed a foul oath that Anna could not understand and Eliza pulled her sharply away from him, putting her body between Claes and the child.

Anna's last sight of the fox-haired man had been when she looked back as Eliza hurried her away. He had been standing spread-legged in the street, balanced on his wooden leg and his good one, grinning after them.

That night Eliza had climbed up on a wooden table and reached a long arm into the beams and from a roof chink had taken a knotted kerchief. Untied, it had revealed a big gold ring set with a single large sapphire, which she had displayed to Anna.

" 'Twas your mother's," Eliza said as she pressed it mournfully to her lips. "And I'd meant it for you—as a keepsake. But I guess she'll forgive me for the necklace and this too—for I've been faithful in all else."

Little Anna was mystified, and the more so when Eliza took her by the arm. "You're not to go to bed yet, Anna. Tonight—just until I return—I want you to wait for me in the rocks." Eliza's honest face was worried. "I won't be gone long—I hope. If I come back alone, I'll come down there and get you. If I come back with someone, you're to stay where you are no matter how loud I may call to you or what I say. Do you understand?"

The child nodded and felt some of Eliza's deep panic seep into her own heart. She let Eliza position her in a cleft deep in the shadow of the rocks, heard herself cautioned again to stay there. In an unusual show of emotion—for her—Eliza bent down and pressed a kiss on that small upturned trusting face. Anna was surprised to feel tears on Eliza's lined cheek.

"If you don't come back till morning?" she asked in a small voice. "What do I do then?"

Eliza bit her lips. "Wait till well after the sun is up," she said. "And then go up to the big house and tell them something has happened to me and ask them to take you in."

As Eliza took the ring and disappeared into the night, little Anna felt a thrill of fear. She was hiding from the man at the dock, the man named Claes. But why?

It was still dark when Eliza returned. Grim-faced and weary, she had come directly to the place where she had left Anna and taken the tired child back to the little seaside hut they occupied together.

When Anna asked timidly why she had had to hide, Eliza had brushed her question aside without explanation. " 'Tis time enough for ye to know when you're older," she was told tersely. "There's no need to clutter your childish head with old wrongs and old troubles, and matters that cannot be fixed. You'll keep your silence about what you saw and never speak of what you heard today."

Anna had not.

And the very next day, she had wandered up from the beach and down the long leafy drive toward the big white cross-shaped house and seen Samantha Jamison sitting listlessly on the broad veranda, being fanned with a palmetto fan by a little black slave boy.

Samantha had called to her and been enchanted by the golden-haired child. Later she had asked Anna to dinner, and there had been a new dress and a glittering table with a bewildering array of dishes and the servants who worked alongside Aunt Eliza actually serving *her*; and in all the excitement little Anna had forgotten all about the menacing stranger they had run into on the dock. The incident had been pushed far back into her mind, like an unpleasant nightmare—best forgotten.

And if sometimes she had wondered about the incident, and about the man Claes who had been paid for his silence "these seven years" with a necklace, and who had been finally bought off with a sapphire ring that had belonged to her mother, a dangerous man from whom she must hide, she had thought of him as an ogre rising up out of Aunt Eliza's mysterious past, and vanishing along with Aunt Eliza into that quiet grave up in the cedars.

Her own life had flowered as "daughter of the house" at Mirabelle, and these unpleasant echoes of a long-ago past had drifted down and down into her subconscious, like discordant chords of music—forgotten when the beautiful melody rose and soared.

But now as she watched the *Dolphin* disappear over the blue horizon, Anna flayed herself for not remembering earlier the fox-haired man, Claes, and what had been said about a necklace of pink pearls with silver links.

That ornate necklace of pink pearls and silver links—the Apricot Woman had been *showing* it to her, flaunting it, daring her to mention it, perhaps! With her half-malicious smile and glittering amber eyes—eyes exactly the color of the red-rimmed eyes of one-legged Claes in that dusty street so long ago—why, she had been *taunting* Anna with the necklace!

And Anna, caught off guard and years away from her memory of Eliza's confrontation with the stranger, had not made the connection until too late.

It was the woman's fox-colored hair that had brought it all back to her in a rush of memory.

What might that woman not have told her—if only she had known what to ask? What might she not have said if Anna—chancing embarrassment—had bluntly stated, "I recognize that necklace. Where did you get it?"

Had the woman worn a gold and sapphire ring as well? Anna

racked her brain but all she could remember was the peach gloves and the pink pearl necklace with the silver links.

That gold and sapphire ring, like all knowledge of her true origin, she had crammed into the past, as she tried to forget that she was not like other girls who had parents of their own and grandparents and sometimes even great-grandparents.

And now with the *Dolphin* sailing away from her, she had lost her chance to find out.

But as she rode slowly back to Mirabelle, sober now and thoughtful, the encounter set her to wondering about the mother she had never known and the people who would never "accept her." What dark secret had Aunt Eliza kept hidden from her all those years?

She brooded about it for a while, and, Grenfell being no help, she made her own inquiries. But it seemed that the Apricot Woman had not put up at an inn, she had stayed on board the *Dolphin,* which had after all put in only briefly for fresh water and then departed—some said for Jamaica, some for Barbados.

So no past mysteries were unlocked and as life cascaded by her in Bermuda, a life of luxury with every eligible bachelor at her feet, Anna swiftly forgot it. Time passed for her delightfully, with never a care to blot the horizon.

And far away on a ship about to make harbor in an American port—a ship with a Dutch name hastily painted on to obliterate the name *Dolphin* on her hull—a woman whose hair gleamed like a fox's brush in the late afternoon sun held her little reddish-colored Pomeranian close to her tawny velvet breast and leaned over and murmured in French:

"She is too beautiful, is she not, *mon ami*? We will not tell him about her after all. We will let her stay on her island . . . forever."

She gave a little tinkling laugh and the Pomeranian, sighting port, began to bark.

His lustrous mistress held him in one relaxed arm and began to smooth her tawny velvet skirts and to adjust her broad-brimmed hat, afloat with orange plumes, with the other.

The man who would be waiting for her on the dock was all that any woman could ask for. He would ask her bluntly what she had learned—about the girl.

And she would answer blithely—with a lie.

BOOK I
Destiny's Daughter

Daughter of destiny, daughter of fate,
Daughter of passion, daughter of hate,
Daughter to whom the world must bow,
Claim your birthright—do it now!

PART ONE
The Bride In Red Slippers

All that I ask of heaven,
All that I ask of life,
Is that you hold me first in your heart,
Take me and make me your wife!

Aboard The Dame Fortune
Late September 1673

CHAPTER 1

Something brushed her bare leg and Anna stirred in her sleep. A frown creased her smooth young forehead and her head with its great cloud of burnished gold hair moved restlessly on her pillow. She had been smiling in her sleep, for she had been dreaming that she was still in Bermuda, still mistress of the great plantation of Mirabelle with half the island lads dancing attendance on her every whim. Now as she fought her way up from that dream, she decided drowsily that it must be Coral who had wakened her, for the big tortoiseshell cat often leaped in through the open jalousied window beside her bed, sprang onto the embroidered blue and white French coverlet and curled up purring beside her.

Still half asleep she reached out to stroke Coral's soft thick fur. And it came to her, vaguely penetrating her subconscious, that something was wrong.

Slowly her fingers stiffened and her hand went rigid, for what she was touching now was not fur. Neither was it the fine imported linen of the sheets or the embroidery of the coverlet at Mirabelle.

Her hand was wandering along warm bare skin, and beneath that smooth skin were rippling muscles, hard and resilient. It came to

Anna with a shock that snapped her turquoise eyes wide open that her hand was idly caressing a man's lean buttock. That sudden realization made her jerk away with a gasp and simultaneously sit up in bed to stare wildly about her.

A naked man was lying beside her! A well-built, broad-shouldered man with a thick shock of dark hair that fell to his shoulders. Her startled gaze traced the rippling flow of his mighty back muscles, his lean torso, the fluid lines of his narrow hips and long legs as he lay on his side beside her, relaxed in sleep. And she was naked too!

But hardly had that gasp cleared her lips before she realized where she was.

This narrow bunk in its small cabin setting bore no resemblance to the square featherbed four-poster of her big airy bedroom at Mirabelle— or at least the bedroom that had been hers until her foster father's new wife had booted her out of it and reduced her to sleeping in a nearly airless closet off the kitchen, which she was forced to share with the cook! She was not even in Bermuda but on a ship headed north and west toward an American port. Mirabelle was no longer her home—and now it never would be. When Papa Jamison had died, Bernice had snatched it away, along with her clothes and her jewels. She could never go back. Everything had changed for her—even her name. She was no longer Anna Smith, belle of the islands, as she had been when Papa Jamison was alive. Nor was she, as she had been this past summer, Anna Smith, bondwoman and outcast—*she was Anna Danforth now!*

And this long form beside her, looking suddenly so formidable and unfamiliar in the silver wash of moonlight that lit the ship's cabin—this was her bridegroom, Brett Danforth, the man she had met but last night when he had saved her from her attackers on St. George's brawling waterfront—and married in haste this afternoon.

And what an afternoon it had been! With Brett suddenly, mysteriously, producing a special license and rushing her through a hurried ceremony in white lime-washed St. Peter's Church, with its lighthouselike square belfry, that church where she had once dreamed of walking down the aisle a stately bride with all Bermuda's gentry agog at the grandeur of the wedding procession—not scurrying down it as she had in a makeshift gown! And seeing plain in the minister's eyes his disapproval of the whole proceeding!

They had come out of the dim coolness of the church into the blazing afternoon sunlight, their little wedding party of four—no, three, for Brett had lagged behind to pay the minister. Around them the sleepy little port town of St. George lazed as it did on any hot afternoon. Only to Anna it had all looked different suddenly—for she had realized with a sense of shock that she was leaving it. Forever.

She had stood there uncertainly in her makeshift wedding gown of pale yellow voile, and reached up to adjust her wedding circlet. It was not the handsome circlet of seed pearls she had imagined for herself, but a circlet of pink Chain of Love blossoms snatched up from the roadside and hastily woven by her best friend, Sue Waite, on the way to the church. Taffy-haired Sue, always strongly affected by weddings, was crying and hugging her—and then giggling through her tears when Anna confided that the yellow voile dress was practically the only one of her gowns that Bernice had not yet altered to fit her own daughters, and that she had slipped into the unlocked house at Mirabelle only this morning and snatched the dress and the lemon satin petticoat over which it was now draped, and the very chemise she had on plus another, and three pairs of slippers, which were sizes too small for Mirabelle's new occupants and which Bernice had already bagged for shipment to Boston or some other place for sale! Sue had hooted at that and they had both laughed over Anna's unbridelike scarlet slippers that poked out from under the lemon satin petticoat.

"To think that's all you have left out of that huge closet of lovely clothes Tobias Jamison bought you," Sue had sighed. "And your pearls and your coral jewelry and all your other lovely things—it doesn't seem fair that Bernice and her daughters should have all that and you should have nothing!" Sue's sweet face reflected her indignation.

"Oh, it isn't *fair*," laughed Anna—for this was her wedding day and she felt at that moment that all the bad times, the dreadful times, were behind her and that from this day forward the sun would always shine. "But never say that I have nothing! I have Brett now and"—her voice broke a little with emotion—"with him I come first, Sue. It's all I ever asked of life."

"Oh, Anna, I'm so glad for you!" Impulsively Sue kissed her friend's flushed cheek. "I do so hope you'll be happy in America."

"I will," declared Anna confidently. "And I'll make Brett happy too.'' Her turquoise eyes held a soft promising glow that made Sue swallow as she pressed her friend's hand. Sue only hoped that she and Lance would be as happy when *they* got married, and she said so.

And then Brett had joined them, striding tall and confident out of the church. And Lance was shaking his hand and clapping him on the shoulder in congratulation and saying they'd have time to clink a glass at a tavern down the street before the bridal couple sailed!

And so the afternoon had gone, and on the dock Sue had hugged her again and promised Anna faithfully to take care of Coral, Anna's big tortoiseshell cat she'd had to leave behind at Mirabelle. Lance, who had been Anna's suitor in the days when she was an heiress and could finance the stables he dreamed someday of having, but whose affections had shifted easily to Sue, who loved him, had crowded forward to wish her well too. But she could see in his gloomy face that he was seeing trouble ahead—trouble with Arthur Kincaid, to whom this marriage would come as a shock that would rock the islands, for Arthur had never meant to let her go. . . .

All of this flashed through Anna's mind as her startled gaze traced the contours of this long lean naked form beside her.

This was her husband, Brett.

For a wild moment he had seemed a stranger.

Now she relaxed and a smile curved her soft mouth as she remembered what it had been like with Brett last night, that first night before the wedding bells had even pealed, that breathless night that he had come ashore from a ship in the harbor—this very vessel, the *Dame Fortune*—and saved her from two stout freebooters who were in the very act of kidnapping her for who knew what evil purpose. Brett, with his arrogant stride and his easy way with women, who had introduced her to the wonders of love on a moonlit beach in Bermuda—and when she had run away from him, believing him false, it was Brett who had arrived just in time to save her from Arthur Kincaid's wrath the next day.

Her eyes gleamed as she envisioned the scene as it had been: Arthur confronting her with his whip, Arthur dragging her from her horse, Arthur shouting at Brett as he thundered up that he was but chastening his bondwoman as he had every right to do—and, indeed, in the tangled skein she had made of her life, Anna had briefly been his bondwoman. But Brett had cared nothing for that!

Now Anna thrilled at the memory of Brett's sword flashing silver in the sun. How recklessly he had flung himself at Arthur, throwing himself forward into the whip even as Arthur brought it down! Anna had nearly fainted at the sight of Brett allowing that long murderous whip to wrap around him, certain that Arthur would bring him to the ground and cut him to pieces. Instead Brett had jerked a surprised Arthur off his feet by that very whip. Leaping forward he had held the point of his blade to Arthur's throat in the dust and made him sign over—for golden coins contemptuously flung—the rights to Anna's Articles of Indenture and a bill of sale for Floss, Anna's beautiful silver mare that Arthur had threatened to kill if she would not go with him to Boston.

Anna's gaze turned caressing. Surely all her dreams had been answered in this mighty lover, who had sailed out of nowhere to break her bonds and carry her away with him to an unknown future.

Her heart had asked no questions, nor did it now.

Brett was turning over restlessly now, again his lean leg brushed her. He was muttering in his sleep and Anna leaned closer to hear him. It was incoherent at first, then it sounded vaguely like "...find a way to keep it from her." Anna frowned. "She need never know," he muttered. And again, more forcefully, as if he were trying to convince himself, *"She need never know."*

Unaccountably, those muttered words struck cold fear into Anna's heart. Something he had said this afternoon, before he took her to bed this night, came back to haunt her: *I came to Bermuda to marry Anna Smith—only I was under the impression at the time that she was the heiress to Mirabelle.*

He had come to Bermuda to marry an heiress, a girl he had never seen.

But—somewhere along the way he had changed his mind. For he had married her, Anna Smith, fortune or no, had he not? Even though she had lost Mirabelle to Bernice's conniving and had no hope of ever getting it back? *That meant Brett loved her, didn't it?*

So why, then, as she stared at him, lying prone and naked beside her in the warm cabin with the moonlight silvering the long clean lines of his lean body, should she feel so unaccountably afraid? Why had those mumbled words seemed suddenly so cold, so forbidding?

In that moment it came to Anna with force that she had married a man she scarcely knew. A stranger.

Instinctively she moved away from him a few inches and as she did he turned and woke. His gray eyes flickered open and he was instantly fully awake—in the manner of men such as he, she would come to realize. For Brett Danforth was a man whose life had often depended on the length of his sword—and his ability to wield it against odds. He was a man accustomed to danger and to trouble—and accustomed to facing them both frontally without flinching or regret.

Those keen gray eyes were studying her young face in the moonlight.

"You look frightened," he observed. "Is something wrong?"

"No. You—you were talking in your sleep," she murmured, embarrassed. And looked swiftly away from his naked form.

Brett quirked an eyebrow at her, and his rakish expression well hid the sudden tremor of alarm that went through him—for what might he not have said in his sleep? Words too harsh for the ears of this tender young thing who had entrusted her future to him?

"And what did I say? In my sleep?" he drawled, reaching out a lazy arm to seize her smooth naked hips and pull her down toward him across the sheets.

"Nothing," murmured Anna in a choked voice, for the feel of his strong gentle fingers on the silky skin of her hips, the slight rasping of the sheets along her thighs and buttocks and back, the embarrassing fact that she was naked in the probing moonlight, all combined to make her senses swim. She was new to passion, for but last night she had been a virgin, and it seemed to her alarming that this man's very touch should be a sweet fire that reduced her to hot instant confusion. Against her will, for at that moment she wanted desperately to keep cool and judge him, she felt her resolve melting under the very bombardment of his masculinity.

"Are you sure?" His warm lips passed caressingly over her trembling satin-smooth stomach as he dragged her body inexorably downward, and now his lips moved up tinglingly over the delicate white skin of her round breasts, upward over her pale heaving bosom and along the pulsing column of her throat. His level gray eyes were even with hers now, and her own turquoise eyes were wide and the pupils were dilated and dark, for she was suddenly—in spite of the intense physical attraction that almost overpowered her—unsure of him. He was grinning into her face, his strong teeth flashing white in the moonlight. "Perhaps I called out another woman's name in my sleep?" he hazarded in a teasing voice.

"No." She could feel a hot flush rise to her cheeks and she squirmed in his arms as his expert hands roved lightly, teasingly, over her resilient young body, so unused to the ways of men. She gasped as his fingers teased a pink nipple to hardness, then danced as if he were playing a scale on the harpsichord to her other breast and tweaked that nipple to hardness as well.

"What, then?" That easy grasp refused to let her go. He gave the silky hair at the base of her hips a light chiding tweak and Anna felt her tense body give an involuntary jerk. "Come now," he demanded, "What did I say in my sleep that upset you?"

"You said"— Anna told him breathlessly, slapping at his hand and hearing him chuckle—"you said something about—about *'keeping it from her'*—whatever that meant."

Did she detect a sudden stillness in his body? An abrupt hardening of that sardonic expression? The moonlight was treacherous—she could not tell. Certainly she could not fault the lazy voice that answered her.

"Ah, then I know what it must have been," he said suavely. "I must keep it from her—the knowledge that I love her so much, lest she use her power to bend me to her will." He bent his head to nuzzle her bare breasts.

Easy liar, she thought warily, trying to hold him off, for his touch was wickedly seductive and it was her own will that she could feel bending! "How do I know you love me so much as all that?" she challenged.

His head rose and he shook back his dark hair with a grin. Heavy strands of it slid across her breasts and she could feel her breath shorten.

"Does not your common sense tell you? Did I not pursue you like a schoolboy?"

No, she thought, even as white fire pulsed through her veins as his hips moved subtly against hers. *You pursued me ruthlessly, like a man intent on his quarry. And why, Brett? Why me?*

"Hold still," he instructed mildly, cradling her in one hard-muscled arm. "Tell me what you're thinking."

His hawklike face, so hard and masculine, was very near. His dark hair fell across her bare white shoulder and mingled with her own burnished gold hair on the pillow. His very nearness half suffocated her and made her breathless but—tell him what she was thinking? Never!

For she was thinking that perhaps she should not have married him, this man who had swept into her life like a whirlwind, changing everything. Perhaps she should have waited. Known him better. What matter that she had surrendered herself to him on a windswept beach on a night of sighs and promises unspoken? She had felt so secure then in his arms, so sure of herself—and of him. Why could she not feel that way now? Why should she waver?

"Come now," he prodded gently. "What were you thinking? I cannot have you look so troubled."

"I was thinking," she improvised, "that Mirabelle was mine— until Bernice tricked me out of it. It was the only real home I've ever known. And now I'll never see it again." There, there was a grain of truth in that!

Something lost and forlorn in her young voice reached out to him and his strong arm tightened about her. "You'll have a new home, Anna," he promised her huskily. "With me." He was holding her closer now, closer, her body curved to his broad chest, conforming to his flat stomach and hips. His caresses grew ever more insistent, luring her along inviting lovers' paths—but still she hesitated.

"Will I be happy there, Brett?" she asked in a troubled voice. For now abruptly all that had seemed so sure this afternoon seemed less than sure—nothing seemed certain.

"Yes," he assured her firmly. "You will be happy there. It is where you belong."

"Where I belong?" she whispered.

His answer thrilled her, for it was in a rich-timbred voice roughened by emotion. "In the circle of my arms." And then more softly, as she relaxed, giving herself up to his love, to his will, "I will make you happy, Anna, if it is in my power to do it. *That* I promise."

His deep voice had a rich hypnotic quality that went through her like a bar of music, deeply felt. In that moment Anna believed him implicitly. Brett had promised her happiness—and he would make good that promise. Whatever happened. Her face was pressed against the muscles of his neck and she swallowed once, for she had been briefly very close to tears. And clung to him as if she were drowning.

"Anna," he murmured, interpreting the fiery ecstasy of her mood. "Anna . . ."

And then passion claimed them like a driving force, sliding their bodies together as a key fits a lock, hurling them forward into a mad burst of caressing and loving and trembling together upon the brink of fulfillment—until at last with a groan he carried them both over the precipice and the little world of their moonlit cabin seemed bright and shining with its own vibrant glow.

Yesterday morning she had been Anna Smith, thought Anna sleepily as her naked body fell away from Brett's at last, sinking in exhausted fulfillment toward a warm oblivion. But tonight—tonight she was Anna Danforth—Brett Danforth's bride.

It was a lovely thought.

Worn out with the bright torrents of love and emotion that had passed between them, Anna lay beside Brett, her naked hip touching his, her burnished gold hair haloing her pillow. Bermuda and grasping Bernice and vengeful Arthur Kincaid all seemed remote and far away tonight. As if they could never touch her, never again. As Anna drifted off into exhausted sleep, a lovely unruffled future seemed to stretch out before her, as the sails of her honeymoon ship took the wind and carried her onward to her destiny.

PART TWO
The Man From Boston

Some vengeance comes from God himself
And some from hell, deep down,
But none wreak vengeance, high or low,
Like the man from Boston Town!

The Bermuda Islands,
Late September 1673

CHAPTER 2

But although Anna, lying content in her lover's arms, had forgotten about Arthur Kincaid, Arthur had not forgotten about her. He paced the gardens of Waite Hall, glaring out into the hot Bermuda sunshine with a mixture of expressions on his handsome evil face. For him the brilliant blossoms of the bougainvillea went unnoticed, the heady scent of tropical flowers went unsmelled. He was obsessed with but one thing:

Anna Smith.

Her beauty had lanced into him from that first day he had seen her. Her wide skirts had seemed to float as she picked her way daintily through the barrels and kegs along the waterfront in St. George.

Arthur, strolling along in unconcealed boredom beside his cousin, Walter Meade, who was doggedly intent on showing him the town, had come abruptly erect at this vision. His body had leaned forward like a hunting dog scenting a bird. Anna was dressed in a madly bright flowered calico overlaid—and its colors softened by—a light pink silk tissue that drifted on the sea breeze and at the moment Arthur sighted her she was bending down to examine some stalks of yellow bananas. Arthur was quick to recognize how stylish was this girl in the wide-brimmed hat afloat with plumes. He would have been thunderstruck to know that Anna—who was always one to experiment—had had the dress made up herself. Swaying over her pink-plumed hat was a ruffled pink silk parasol carried proudly by little black Boz, who loved these excursions into town. Anna's slim waist was nipped in by the tightest of bodices, her skirts billowed luxuriously, and the spill of expensive white lace at her cuffs was to Arthur's dazzled eyes no whiter than the pearly skin of her breasts, so daringly displayed by her low-cut gown.

At that moment Arthur had thought her the most exquisite thing he had ever seen—and to his dismay he still thought so.

"Who is that?" he had demanded sharply of Walter Meade, and Walter, who'd been squinting to make out the name on the hull of a ship anchored far out, said absently, "Who?"

"The girl in pink." Arthur's lettuce green taffeta-clad elbow gave him a dig in the ribs.

"Oh." Walter got his sights adjusted to matters on the dock. "Why, that's Mistress Anna Smith of Mirabelle Plantation."

Arthur had already heard that Mirabelle was the finest plantation in Bermuda. His cousins at hospitable Lilymeade, where Arthur was a guest, constantly sang its praises.

"Present me to the lady, Walter," he urged, seizing his host by the arm and hurrying him across the dock.

Anna turned as Walter hailed her and smiled as he introduced his houseguest, just arrived from Boston.

Arthur swept her a bow so low his rich dark hair would have brushed the dock had not a practiced flourish of his green-plumed hat held it back. "Mistress Anna," he said fervently. "I'd no idea these dismal islands had anything like *you* to offer."

"So you're from Boston? Where it snows?" Bermuda-bred Anna studied handsome Arthur curiously and with a hint of malice in her turquoise eyes, for she was used to the adulation of the island swains and felt a flash of resentment at Arthur's remark about "these dismal islands" and the superiority of his tone.

"Snows as white as your bosom, Mistress Anna." Arthur's impudent gaze lingered on that breathtaking expanse and he was gratified by her sharp intake of breath that rippled her youthful breasts. "And often as deep as your knees." His hot admiring gaze passed on down her bodice to rest upon her soft outthrust hips, then wandered down to her knees—or the place her knees should be beneath her voluminous skirts.

Anna lifted her eyebrows warily and Walter cleared his throat in embarrassment, for he was uneasy about Arthur's light way with the island ladies. Arthur's remarks did not seem to Walter either proper or called for—especially this calling attention to Mistress Anna's bosom and knees on such short acquaintance and in so public a place.

"As deep as my knees," mused Anna. "Then you must have had a deal of a hard time floundering about in it." She laughed. "And I'll wager in winter your boot tops must always be full of snow!" She nodded toward the wide-topped, fashionably turned down boots that graced Arthur's handsome legs.

"Oh, no, Mistress Anna," said Arthur, delighted at the way her little white teeth flashed in her pretty mouth when she smiled. "When the snow is deep, we wear our boots turned up."

"Oh, really?" Anna's lazy turquoise gaze played over the handsome Bostonian. She was determined to prick his vanity. "And here I thought that in the wilds of Boston, you all wore Indian moccasins!"

That brought Arthur up with a start. *"The wilds of Boston?"* he repeated, stunned, and Anna was quick to catch the chilliness of his tone and be amused by it.

"Yes," she said lightly. "I'm told 'tis not fashionable there as it is in Bermuda and Barbados, and that if one goes there, one should be careful not to take one's lowest-cut gowns lest one attract unfavorable attention. A lady in Barbados, I'm told, sent some old clothes to Boston to be sold and felt obliged to keep all her best and sheerest whisks as they were far too scandalous for such a staid place."

Staid! Unfashionable! Arthur's chest was beginning to expand with anger. Beside him, Walter realized that Anna was punishing this newcomer for his disparagement of the islands. He watched in open amusement as Anna, with the politest manner, poked fun at Arthur.

"Boston is a center of culture and refinement," Arthur declared through clenched teeth. And Walter, frowning now for he saw that Arthur's face had grown pale with wrath, said jovially, "Come now, Walter, can't you see that Mistress Anna is only teasing you?"

Anna's mocking smile refused either to deny or confirm that. "How is your mother, Walter?" she asked graciously.

"Not very well, Mistress Anna." Walter shook his wheat-colored head. "She takes to her bed more frequently now."

"I'm sorry to hear that, Walter. I'll send over some of the fresh citrus we just received on one of Papa Jamison's ships that called at Barbados. Mangoes, lemons, limes, grapefruit, oranges—I know how she loves them."

"Indeed she does, Mistress Anna," agreed Walter. "And most grateful to you we'll all be, for fresh fruit has been none so plentiful this season."

Anna turned to Arthur, who was scowling at her.

"And do you have fresh lemons and oranges in Boston?" she asked with a negligent toss of her burnished gold curls. "Or do they spoil at sea before they can reach Boston harbor?"

"The produce of the *entire world* reaches Boston harbor— unscathed!" declared Arthur ringingly. "Spices from the Orient, dates and figs from the Mediterranean—"

"And buccaneer goods from Tortuga and Port Royal?" she taunted him. "*We* have our choice of those!"

Arthur's jaw was thrust out at a pugnacious angle. "And buccaneer goods as well!"

Anna felt she had punished Arthur enough—besides, he was a guest of the Meades and she liked all the Meades. "You must bring your visiting cousin over to Mirabelle, Walter," she told big Walter in a casual voice. "Since he is so familiar with the goods of the world, he will appreciate the scimitar Papa Jamison brought back from Jamaica on his last voyage. He believes it to be Turkish but Mr. Cartmell insists it's a native weapon from Madagascar."

"What would Cartmell know about it?" scoffed Walter. "A minister's not likely to voyage to Madagascar!"

"True," countered Anna, with her dazzling smile. "But, then, who's to refute the words of a man of God?"

As Walter and Anna wrangled happily over this, Anna insisting that Mr. Cartmell claimed his brother was a missionary who had visited Madagascar in an attempt to convert the heathen there, the brother having claimed he had narrowly escaped death from just such a sword as the one she described, the anger melted slowly from Arthur Kincaid's flashily handsome face. The little minx! She'd been but baiting him—and now she was actually asking him to call upon her at home. Now he understood her thorny attitude toward him—transparent wench, she had been but trying to arouse his interest! He preened himself a bit, tried to stand taller in hope of peering down her bodice, and stared narrowly at her buttocks as she took her leave of them and turned to go. Round and firm they looked to be, if one could but strip away the flowered calico and tissue silk! And he Arthur would find a way to do just that—oh, he had no doubt he would! For Arthur had had his way with many women—sometimes by force—and never doubted that lustrous Anna Smith would be added to his list of conquests and brought to heel like the others.

Those few who'd protested, who'd held him off, even managed to escape his lust, he'd generally made to suffer. Like the chambermaid Ruth, when he was but fourteen. She'd been hired for the upstairs work and the son of the house meant nothing to her—for Ruth had a lover of her own back in Glasgow who meant to come to America and join her. When Arthur had made lewd offers to Ruth, she'd simply turn her head, look blank as if she hadn't heard him, and scurry away. Arthur had had an answer for *that*. He had broken the lock on Ruth's door, which no one got around to fixing. And one dark night after Ruth had been working very hard all day and Arthur was sure she'd be too exhausted to struggle much, he had slipped silently into her cubbyhole of a room. The moon had picked out for him the narrow cot where she lay sleeping heavily with her long dark hair spread out on her pillow.

Without hesitation, Arthur had leaped upon the sleeping girl and stifled her strangled scream with a savage mouth.

But Ruth was strong. She managed to throw Arthur off and in doing so accidentally brought her knee up into his groin with a force that left him writhing in pain on the floor. Uncaring of his gasping moans, she had dragged him from her room and, with a violent slam of her door, left him to recover in the darkness of the hall.

Arthur had crept away, sobbing, vowing revenge.

His chance had come the very next day. He had been hanging around the lower hall waiting for just such an opportunity, when he saw Ruth appear at the head of the stairs staggering under the weight of a heavy laundry basket. She had given Arthur a warning frown as he trotted up the stairs toward her. Looking straight ahead, apparently ignoring her, he was aware of how she hesitated, balancing the heavy basket, at the top.

When the girl saw he was not even looking at her, but staring coldly past her as if he meant to brush on by, she took a cautious step downward—and that was her undoing. For Arthur casually reached out a booted foot and tripped her, sending her hurtling to the bottom of the stairs to land with one leg twisted beneath her, under a pile of laundry.

"Ye'll have to pick all that up, ye know," he had called down callously and gone off whistling down the hall.

But Ruth had not picked up the laundry. She had not been able to lift the basket or indeed to rise at all. Her leg was broken.

Amid an anxious whispered conference held by the servants in the kitchen, it was decided what to do. "His nibs," as they called Arthur's father, would never punish the boy—and Arthur would lie about his part in it, he always did. They put Ruth into a wheelbarrow, for she had no money, and wheeled her through the alleys to her mother's ramshackle house and there deposited her. The leg, set at last, did not heal right and Arthur always took delight later in seeing dark-haired Ruth move unsteadily through Boston's crowded streets, carrying heavy baskets of laundry, for with her new disability she could find no job at all and had to take in public laundry as best she could.

He had punished Ruth, all right!

And that other chambermaid, Sal her name was. She was a buxom girl fresh out of Leeds and she had dared to slap away Arthur's hand the day he pinched her breast in the front hall. And another time she had aimed a halfhearted kick at him when he had slipped up behind her, reached an impudent hand up her skirts and pinched her bare bottom when she was carrying that huge crock and he caused her to drop it. The kick had but grazed him but even that halfhearted kick had marred the brilliance of Arthur's shiny boots.

He had glared from the boots to her for a full minute and Sal, seeing his expression, had slunk away in fear.

Well might she have feared him, for not two days had passed before Arthur found her bending over the hearth, which was full of glowing embers. Arthur pretended to slip and lose his footing, lurched heavily against Sal and sent the girl tumbling into the fireplace. His father heard about *that*, for Sal, writhing in agony—

for she had saved her face only at the expense of a pair of badly burned arms—screamed that Arthur had done it on purpose. But Arthur had sturdily insisted it was an accident and his lie had been believed.

Sal had recovered after long suffering, but she had endured permanent scars and ever after had to wear long sleeves. As soon as she was well enough, she left the Kincaid employ and moved in with a sailor, and after him another and then another. For buxom Sal, her ingenuous dairymaid's face now rouged and painted, maintained to all who would listen that she preferred even the life of a waterfront whore to being Arthur Kincaid's plaything.

After Sal's injury, the female servants in Arthur's Boston home had gone in deadly fear. 'Twas best to submit, they'd whispered, for not to submit brought terrible things down on one's head. The life of those chambermaids was one long nightmare, for Arthur, strong and rested and malicious, waited for the tired girls in dark corners and bent them remorselessly to his purpose. And worst of all, he tried out on his terrified victims all the cruel, sadistic things he'd heard muttered about at school or rumored in the waterfront haunts he sometimes frequented.

More than one housemaid fled the house screaming.

His most unfortunate encounter—from his point of view—was with that trollop of a tavern maid! It was because of her, of course, that he'd left Boston in such a hurry. He'd given her some bad burns and *that*, of course, he did consider an accident, for it was just bad luck that the lighted candelabrum he flung at red-haired Nell when she resisted his advances chanced to ignite the bottle of brandy he'd already thrown at her for the same reason. The splashed brandy had ignited Nell's kirtle and she'd fled the house with her skirts alight and the fire had not been put out till she reached the street, where an alert passerby had flung her summarily into a mud puddle and extinguished the blaze.

Money changing hands in the right places had prevented Arthur's arrest, of course, but Nell had a burly sweetheart, a sailor, and when word had reached Arthur that the sailor intended to pour a whole bucket of brandy—accounts differed as to whether it would be brandy or rum—over Arthur's head and ignite it, Arthur had packed his trunks and left Boston for Bermuda, ostensibly to visit his cousins, the Meades.

The Meades had turned out to be boring provincials, their female servants were all well along in years and built like blockhouses, and Arthur had almost despaired of enjoying his enforced temporary exile in Bermuda until he had seen the lithe young figure of Anna Smith swaying on the dock beneath a pink silk parasol.

The vision faded, and Arthur found himself no longer lost in retrospect of the way the world had wagged that day on the dock but back in the Waites' household with his whole life changed—for the worse.

The wench had toyed with him, goaded him, and then tricked him into marriage—not with herself but with mousy little Mattie Waite! And when Anna had been brought low by Jamison's death and Arthur had managed to maneuver himself into possession of her Articles of Indenture, she had brought that Danforth fellow into his life and Danforth had snatched Anna away and delivered him such a blow as had broken his front teeth for him!

Now Arthur's tongue licked his broken teeth angrily. The pain of them was bad enough—but the sight of himself in a mirror! It sickened him to see his beautiful smile destroyed, and the fact that he had richly merited the blow did nothing to assuage his fury. He had all but stopped smiling, keeping his mouth in a firm straight line that brought out the beauty of his chiseled features, speaking through nearly closed lips. And as if that was not enough, he was now cursed with a permanent lisp. He who was so used to barking orders at his inferiors—and forcing obedience at the toe of a boot—now found air whistling through the space where half his front teeth used to be—he sounded as if he were wheezing!

Most galling of all was the memory of his encounter with Brett Danforth, when he had sought to down Danforth with his whip and Danforth had torn the whip from his hand and stood over him like the Angel of Death with the tip of his naked blade pressed against Arthur's throat. Arthur's heart still lurched in his chest at the appalling memory of that dark, angry, near-demonic face framed with heavy shoulder-length dark hair falling down over a pair of light gray eyes that had murder in them. Arthur's indignant protests that Anna was his bondwoman and he had every right to chastise her had been of no avail. Danforth had contemptuously flung gold at Arthur's feet and forced Arthur at swordpoint to sign a receipt for the wench—and for her horse as well! Arthur's handsome face turned livid at the thought and his mouth formed a snarl. Where had Anna found the fellow? And in such a hurry too!

Hatred of Anna blazed up in him anew. *She* was the cause of all his troubles, she alone! He glared murderously at the house where his wife's face had appeared momentarily in one of the small-paned windows. Repulsively plain she appeared to him, with her dull brown hair and blotchy skin. Their eyes met and for a moment her gaze was reproachful before she quickly cast her eyes down and disappeared from the window. To complain about him to her family no doubt! For although Arthur smarted under the humiliation of his recent encounter with Brett Danforth, he also chafed under the sudden coolness that had come over the Waite family toward him. He read mockery in Sue Waite's eyes, although she tried her best to hide it for Mattie's sake. He even read ridicule in innocent things his young wife Mattie said—and this morning he had slapped her across the room when she asked him if his broken front teeth still pained him.

When Mattie rose from the blow, burst into tears, and fled the room, Arthur had paced about like a caged animal, cursing the heat, Bermuda, everything—and then flung out into the relative coolness of the garden to continue his angry pacing. His temper, never well held in check, was about to devour him. He now habitually snarled at people who tried to be civil to him, and was rapidly becoming shunned even by the senior Waites who, for Mattie's sake, had tried their best to like their unpleasant son-in-law.

Now he struck his balled fist into his palm. He saw before him the pleasant lawns and gardens of Waite Hall but he saw something else too. He saw in his mind visions of beautiful Anna Smith, who had somehow managed to elude his clutches. He saw her crumpled form lying before him on the driveway, when he had finally brought her down from her horse with his whip—and he saw her scramble up and her turquoise eyes glory in triumph as Brett Danforth shoved him backward at the point of his blade and forced him to write out a bill of sale for Anna's Articles of Indenture.

He struck his hand again with his fist and his teeth ground painfully. They were out there somewhere, the two of them, laughing at him! It was Danforth, not he, who was enjoying that lovely body! The hours he had spent imagining Anna naked and in his power, spread out on his bed for himself alone to enjoy, to torment, to ravish, now came back to haunt him. In his fevered mind he saw Anna in beauteous disarray as she had been that day in the cedars when he had fallen off his horse and seized her in fury. He had been near to having his way with her, if that fool of a Walter had not stopped him. And *then* he'd have brought her to heel right enough!

The vision of Anna "brought to heel" coursed over him like a bright flood. He imagined her bare white form down on her knees, groveling, imploring, he could feel her frantic arms clutching his thigh as she begged him not to leave her, to keep her with him, she would do anything, anything—for once back in Boston he had fully intended to frighten her into submission by threatening to rent out her services for part-time work as a scullery maid in the most disreputable places he could find, taverns and inns that were but thinly disguised brothels. Even innocent Anna would have had no doubt what was in store for her when night came and she had finished her chores. First the landlord and then, who knew?

It would have been so easy! He would have had her pliant body under his, her tear-wet face against his own, her soft voice pleading desperately—and then her whole body coming alive to his embraces, thrilling to his touch. His chest expanded at the thought, threatening to burst the buttons from his green silk doublet. He would have been master over her and she his slave!

So Arthur envisioned what might have been, a vein standing out on his forehead from the strain as he glared out across the pleasant gardens of Waite Hall.

And Brett Danforth had robbed him of all this! Yes, and the girl too—she had cheated him! He was past worrying about Sue's and Lance's implication in the plot; a local court would probably do nothing about it anyhow even if he did bring action against them. The wench had reportedly fled with half of Mirabelle's silver—and nothing had been done about that! If he made trouble for Lance and Sue, the Waites would promptly cast him out and he would have to seek less comfortable quarters at the inn in St. George. No, he would forget *their* part in it—it was Brett and Anna he wished to be revenged upon!

He would not go to Boston! He would find the lying wench who had forced him into a preposterous marriage and schemed that he should buy her Articles of Indenture, and then cheated him of her luscious body! He would find her, he would wrest her from Brett

Danforth—or steal her when Danforth was not looking—and he would punish her! He would not use the whip—no, he would find more subtle ways of inflicting pain that would not mar her loveliness, ways of hurting her that would not show up as bruises. Arthur had a fertile imagination and it was filled with visions of the hell he would create for Anna Smith when he caught up with her.

And as for Mattie, he would leave the little fool here! No—his lip curled slyly. Anna was very fond of Mattie. He would take Mattie along—she could come in useful if Anna, in spite of everything, chose to resist his advances. He would discover how much agony softhearted Anna could see Mattie endure without buckling to his will! Ah, yes, Mattie could well be important to his success in this venture—he would take her along.

CHAPTER 3

Driven nearly to frenzy, Arthur went down to see the minister who had performed the ceremony that had united Brett Danforth and Anna Smith. He found him inside the lime-washed white parish church inspecting the work of the sexton.

Mr. Cartmell looked up as Arthur entered. Seeing him only as a silhouette against the harsh sunlight at first, his expression was tranquil. As he recognized that swaggering gait and elegant attire advancing upon him, his mouth formed a straight, disapproving line. Mr. Cartmell had heard unsavory stories about Arthur Kincaid's treatment of his young wife.

"Yes, of course I know where Danforth is going," he told Arthur testily. "But I had it from him privily. You will not have it from me."

Arthur, raging inside, saw he must use guile. He attempted a smile. "I have something of value that Mistress Anna left behind," he said in a somewhat ragged voice. "I would post it to her if I knew where she had gone."

"What is it?" Bluntly. "And how came *you* by it?"

Arthur took a deep breath that strained his tight puce satin doublet. He must tread carefully now; the bait was being considered. "It is a box of things she forgot when she sailed—mementoes, items of that sort. The world may not value them, but Mistress Anna does, my wife assures me. It is on Mattie's behalf that I am here seeking her destination, for Mattie wishes to send the box to her."

It had been on the tip of the minister's tongue to say tartly that there'd be the devil of a time doing that—sending a box to a Dutch colony with Holland at war with England! Still, if young Mattie really did wish to send the box, a way could no doubt be found.

"I suppose it can make no difference," he told Arthur reluctantly, "since 'tis Mattie who asks it. I would not know Danforth's destination myself save that I refused to perform the ceremony until I was told the reason for all this unseemly haste. I insisted that I would not wed the girl to Danforth if his hurry was necessitated by being one jump ahead of the law."

"And you were right to insist!" cried Arthur ringingly.

Cartmell considered Arthur with distaste. He hoped he was doing the right thing. There were some nasty rumors going about concerning Arthur. "Danforth told me that his problem was that he was an Englishman living in a colony that has now gone Dutch, and he must hasten back for he feared for his holdings there. He mentioned the Hudson River and that is all I know about it."

Arthur gave Cartmell a suspicious look. He wondered briefly if the minister had guessed his real intentions and was deliberately sending him off on a wild-goose chase, but dismissed the thought. Cartmell had an open, if disapproving, face and the man had no imagination anyway—that was plain from his sermons, which Arthur had reluctantly fidgeted through in the company of his hosts. No, Cartmell would not invent a lie merely to balk him.

The Hudson River . . . so that was where Danforth had taken her, to a Dutch colony. Somehow that surprised Arthur. He had imagined Danforth to be one of the wild Virginia gentlemen who sometimes came up Boston way and tangled with the hardfisted Yankee traders. Well, now he knew where she was at least!

With a brusque "thank you," Arthur stalked from the church and took himself down to the busy docks. He would find a way to New Netherland even if that way be circuitous!

A ship, the *Mary Louise,* was leaving for Philadelphia the next morning and Arthur—and with him a surprised, unhappy Mattie—were board her when she sailed. The Waites had not guessed Arthur's intentions, for he had not taken Mattie into his confidence about their journey—they thought he was merely eager to get away from Bermuda and since there was no ship for Boston available in all likelihood for some time, that he would transship from Philadelphia to Boston. But from Philadelphia Arthur had no doubt that he could find some adventurous sea dog who'd sail him into New York harbor—into that place the victorious Dutch had renamed New Orange!

Deborah Waite watched her daughter board the *Mary Louise* with some foreboding. Mattie looked so downcast. Even the new gown of blush coral taffeta with its stiff skirts and rustling petticoat had done nothing to cheer her. Watching from the shore, Deborah bit her lip and wondered if she should even now keep Mattie from sailing. But Arthur's deportment during the hours before his departure *had* changed markedly—indeed, he had evinced an almost sunny disposition, despite his newfound lisp due to his broken front teeth, which, quite naturally in her estimation, would anger a man. He had been most civil to Mattie, even suggesting she take an extra trunk to house all her books and gear. Could it be that now beautiful Anna Smith was out of the way, Arthur would see that he had made the right choice of a wife in earnest little Mattie? And if Deborah did pluck Mattie from the ship now on some pretext—as for a moment, looking at her dejected daughter, she had a wild desire to do—might she not be ruining the girl's life? For Deborah doubted that Arthur would ever come back for her. Mattie would live out her life in limbo, neither maiden nor wife, unable to marry even if a man appeared who would fall in love with her.

Deborah sighed. Best, she supposed, to let well enough alone. A wife's place was by her husband.

So Deborah reasoned. So she deceived herself, and waved a

suddenly tearful good-bye as she saw her daughter's figure growing smaller and smaller in the distance on the departing ship.

And so, intent on revenge, Arthur sped north.

Anna would not have slept as soundly in her bridegroom's arms aboard the *Dame Fortune* if she had known what was in Arthur's mind.

Deborah Waite would indeed have wished her daughter back with her in Bermuda had she been able to witness the scene that took place between Mattie and her reluctant bridegroom aboard the *Mary Louise* but half a day out of St. George's harbor en route to Philadelphia.

The sun was beating down upon a sparkling sea, alive with white-capped wavelets. The canvas sails were filled and the ship ran merrily before a brisk wind. This first day out an almost festive air prevailed and passengers strolled the deck whispering that the pair who stood alone by the rail—yes, that handsome unsmiling fellow in scarlet silks and the shy, timorous-looking creature in pink taffeta beside him—were a honeymoon couple, journeying to Boston by way of Philadelphia. Curious glances were tossed their way, but most of the passengers could remember honeymoon journeys of their own and kindly kept their distance.

They would have been astonished had they guessed the tension between this well-dressed pair, for, irritated by Mattie's probing questions about Boston, Arthur had let slip that Boston would not be their immediate destination.

"I realize that we are going first to Philadelphia," said Mattie in an injured tone, for she was ashamed that Arthur should think her so dim. "I only inquired what kind of house we would have in Boston and what your friends are like."

"The house is large," he grated.

Her mother had predicted it would be, but now she had it from Arthur's own lips. "Then we will have plenty of room to entertain," mused Mattie. "Have you a wide circle of friends there, Arthur? Will there be many girls my age? Will your friends hold a reception for us when we arrive?"

Arthur's answer was sharpened by rage that Mattie should be standing there beside him, tied to him, he felt, like a block and chain—for life! Especially since he had already noticed a bright-eyed, black-haired miss who had been giving him mischievous glances and who carelessly flipped her petticoats to show her striped stockings every time she strolled past him on the deck. If it were not for Mattie, he would have left the ship's rail and be strolling after that wench right now. He would be making a great pretense of indifference, and he would have every hope of bedding the wench before the voyage was out. But he had already seen her mother jerk her away and heard her fierce admonishing whisper, "Stop *looking* at him, Millie. I told you, he's *married*!"

That whisper had carried to Arthur even as Mattie spoke. Now he turned on his bride fiercely. "If ye don't stop pestering me with questions, ye'll never see Boston. I'll leave ye in New Orange!"

The moment the words were out, Arthur began to curse inwardly. For Mattie's timid expression changed to one of horror. "New Orange? Ah, you'll not go there!" she beseeched.

"I'll go where I please," said Arthur in a tone that would have shut most women up.

But now that she knew where Arthur's vengeful nature was leading him, Mattie's consternation forced her to protest. "There is no use pursuing her, Arthur."

Arthur jumped as if a pin had stuck him. "Pursuing who?" he demanded with a belligerent frown.

If he expected his fierce demeanor to silence Mattie, he was disappointed. She felt she had to speak, and did so recklessly.

"Your only possible reason for going to New Orange, an enemy port, is Anna Smith—Anna Danforth," Mattie corrected herself hastily. "And it is madness to pursue her, Arthur!"

"She is my bondswoman," he muttered. "I'll not be bilked of my property."

"But she is Danforth's *wife* now." In her anxiety Mattie clutched at his scarlet sleeve. "You *know* he will not let her go!"

"I'll hear no more about it!" shouted Arthur, turning suddenly on his young wife, who was plucking at his sleeve. "My mind is made up!" When Mattie did not immediately release his sleeve he raised his arm in fury and gave her a cuff that sent her sprawling across the deck, to the astonishment of the shocked passengers.

As Mattie, white-faced and frightened and with a red weal across her jaw where Arthur's hand had struck her, scrambled up, the captain strode forward. His own jaw was very set and almost as red with anger as Mattie's was with injury.

"I understand that woman is your wife," he said loudly, confronting Arthur. "At least she is so noted on my passenger list."

Arthur, a little taken aback, admitted this was so. He was massaging his knuckles and realizing with dismay the unwelcome attention he had attracted.

"Then since she is your wife, aboard *my* ship you will pay her the proper respect."

"She was arguing about our destination!" retorted Arthur. "And anyway, *anywhere* a man may beat his wife with a stick as large as his thumb—and I but brushed her with my knuckles."

Captain Rodman regarded Arthur coldly.

"I care not a whit for your landlubber's law," he spat out. "On this ship, *I* am the law and you will answer to me, sir! And I say that if you strike that woman again—indeed, if you so much as raise a finger to her or she is heard to cry out or observed to have a single bruise—that you will spend the rest of the voyage in irons."

"I protest!" cried Arthur. "A man's wife is his property. He may use her any way he pleases!"

"On land perhaps, but if you do not choose to arrive in Philadelphia shackled, you will heed my warning."

The captain turned curtly on his heel and made his way through the staring passengers, many of whom were nodding in approval and giving Arthur black looks, for gentle little Mattie with her shy smile had already made a favorable impression on them and lordly Arthur Kincaid with his haughty manner and unpleasant lisp had not.

"To your cabin, Mattie!" roared Arthur.

"But, Arthur," pleaded Mattie, afraid he would follow her and beat her insensible. "It is so stuffy there and I—I promise not to try to persuade you from going to New Orange!"

"You misunderstood me," said Arthur bitterly, for around him significant glances were being exchanged. England and Holland were at war and there was unfriendly speculation in the passengers' curious gaze as to what his business might be in an enemy city. "We are bound for Boston."

Mattie looked bewildered. She opened her mouth and closed it
again. But she was about to trot obediently to her cabin when the
captain's booming voice again intervened. "The lady will stay on
deck if she chooses," he directed. "And so will you, sir, until your
temper has cooled."

Arthur looked as if he were going to be sick, and Mattie shrank
away from him. Several women left their husbands' sides to rally
round and, despite her aching jaw, she was soon drawn into conversation. A pair of spinsters, the Leighton sisters, homeward bound for
Philadelphia after a vacation visiting a married sister in Jamaica,
joined the group.

"The wind has fallen off. Do you suppose we will be becalmed?"
asked one of them.

"I hope so," said Mattie fervently before she thought, and both
sisters gave her commiserating looks.

Poor little bride, those sympathetic looks said. *At least she is
under the captain's protection now—but anything could happen to
her when they reach Philadelphia*. They were attracted to Mattie the
way they were attracted to lost cats. She was the talk of the ship and
there was much behind-hand talk of "rescuing" her—idle chatter for
the most part; Mattie was but a shipboard diversion for most of the
ladies, to be forgotten even as the ship docked.

Not so with the sisters Leighton, who knew a lost kitten when
they saw one. Before two days were up, when the ship lay becalmed
on a glassy ocean, mirror bright, they had formed a Plan. It was
Sarah Leighton who suggested tentatively to Mattie that Arthur
might have trouble finding a ship in Philadelphia willing to take him
to New Orange.

"Arthur now insists we are not going to New Orange, but to
Boston," mumbled Mattie miserably. "I do not know where we are
going."

"Perhaps he needs time to make up his mind," suggested Penitence consolingly. "When he has had time to think about it, surely
enemy territory will offer little attraction!"

It offered the attraction of lustrous Anna Smith, but Mattie was
too humiliated to tell these kindly ladies about that.

"Yes," echoed Sarah, "and accommodations are very scarce in
Philadelphia. I doubt me he will be able to find a room."

Mattie gave the elder Leighton sister a gloomy look. She was

wondering if Captain Rodman could be persuaded to take her back
to Bermuda with him—if indeed he was voyaging back to Bermuda!

"It might be best, my dear, for you to stay with us while your
husband makes up his mind and finds a ship for you to leave on,"
suggested Sarah. "Our cottage is very small indeed, but there is a
trundle bed in our bedroom that could be pulled out—there would
only be room for you, of course, but your husband would have no
trouble finding shared accommodations in one of the inns catering to
travelers. I'm told the men all pile in together, sometimes three or
four to a bed—sometimes they even sleep by the fire in the common
room."

Mattie looked up alertly. She was being offered refuge from
Arthur, at least for a while! "I would be afraid to mention it to
him," she said slowly. "But perhaps if one of you ladies would
suggest it, he might take kindly to the offer."

The Leighton sisters exchanged triumphant glances. Their offer, if
accepted, would give that young hothead a chance to simmer down
and to realize that it was ridiculous to drag his little bride to
enemy-held New Orange in times like these!

It was Penitence who brought word of Arthur's assent to Mattie.
"He was a bit surly about it," she admitted. "But I really thought
that on the whole he was relieved when I pointed out to him how
crowded were the inns."

Mattie, who had been living under a cloud, afraid to eat, almost
afraid to speak when alone in the cabin with Arthur, brightened.
Arthur was to her a man of mysterious moods and rages, but perhaps
her own admonitions had borne fruit, perhaps Arthur had realized at
last the madness of pursuing Brett Danforth's bride into Dutch-held
territory. Perhaps he had struck her only out of frustration, perhaps
they were really going to Boston after all—and perhaps Arthur,
living temporarily away from her in Philadelphia while he sought
passage, would change, soften. Did not the heroes of the romances
she read do that? Her young brow furrowed as she tried to remember
which ones had.

But Mattie was wrong about Arthur's reason for allowing her to
stay with the Leighton sisters while he put up at an inn. It had
occurred to Arthur that by doing so he could temporarily free
himself from the shackles of marriage. At the inn he could noise it
around that he was single—and rich. Then if there was a handsome

piece of womanflesh about, he would have the better chance of seducing her, for he could fall back on promises of marriage to lure her to bed if all else failed—and in that Mattie would have her uses after all, for at the last minute he could always present her as a barrier to keeping his promises. He was already married! It was a potent defense!

He told Penitence that of course his destination was Boston—Mattie had misunderstood him, as she so often did—that was why he became irritated with her. And Penitence duly conveyed that cheerful information to Mattie who looked doubtful, and then hopeful—and then finally accepted it as true.

But if Mattie believed she was going directly to Boston, she was living in a fool's paradise—Arthur intended to journey to Boston via New Orange even if he had to hire horses and struggle up the coast. And he meant to drag Mattie with him, for he could make use of her there in ways that made his hard eyes glitter, just thinking about it.

Mattie would have fainted if she had guessed the uses for her that Arthur had in mind.

BOOK II
Georgiana

A toast to our island beauty
Adrift on a ship of sighs,
For a man could read fathoms and fathoms
In Anna's turquoise eyes!

PART ONE
The Counterfeit Heiress

The curtain now is ripped aside,
The tragic past's dark veil.
Now she knows why he married her—
And why his plan must fail!

New Orange, New Netherland, 1673

Chapter 4

Northward over brilliant seas swept the *Dame Fortune*. It was a fast voyage for the winds were favorable throughout. But not so fast that Anna did not have time to tell Brett everything about her short life, from her childhood in the beachside hut with her mysterious aunt, Eliza Smith, through the idyllic interval as "daughter of the house" at Mirabelle and all the subsequent troubles that had beset her. He listened intently and held her close, stroked her hair, and if she grew too pensive, remembering, teased her into a laughing excitement that swept all the cobwebs of the past away—and made love to her.

But although Anna, deep in his arms, sometimes asked him muffled questions, he sidestepped them all. He never told her anything about himself.

Anna told herself she did not care. She had a whole lifetime to learn about this man's past, and meantime she was exploring with him all the splendors of love.

By day she found time to comfort Floss, her lovely silver mare, for Floss was bewildered by life on shipboard, and nervous. It was only Anna's soothing voice, Anna's soft loving touch on that silver mane and sleek quivering body that could quiet the excitable Arabian mare.

"I wish I'd brought Coral along," sighed Anna one day.

Brett, who at that moment was lying half across Anna in the bunk with his mouth just then about to nuzzle a pink nipple that peeked at him from her night rail, lifted his head. And then a dark eyebrow. Quizzically.

"Who?"

"Coral. My cat." She ran her fingers combingly through the dark hair that fell down over his face and spilled over her breast like heavy silk.

"Oh. You'll find another. There are plenty of cats at Windgate." His voice was lost as his lips found their originally intended goal.

"Not like Coral," said Anna staunchly. She shivered as Brett's stroking tongue tingled her nipple to hardness. "Coral is beautiful and fluffy—with the daintiest paws."

"Your paws are dainty too," he muttered, turning his attention to her other nipple.

Anna tried unsuccessfully to ignore him. "She has the softest blue green eyes!"

"So have you!" He ran a questing hand down her leg and caused her to catch her breath.

Anna felt a gurgle of laughter well up in her. "You're outrageous! We're talking about my *cat*." She wriggled, for Brett's playful assaults were causing little tremors of feeling to cascade through her body. "She has a lovely waving tail and—"

"Well, we must investigate the similarity!"

"Brett!" Anna was laughing but her palm was fitted over his naked left chest in a mock effort to hold him off. Beneath the sheets their legs skirmished joyously. "Coral is—special," she managed to gasp.

With his strong fingers clasped firmly around her slender squirming hips, Brett lifted his lips enough to say, "Then if Coral is so special, why didn't you bring her along? You brought your horse!"

Anna felt his long leg slide by and gave a playful lurch to avoid for the moment his masculine hardness. She was fast learning that anticipation worked wonders. "I suppose," she admitted in a gasping uneven voice, "it was because I was afraid to go back to Mirabelle—after stealing the clothes."

That brought him upright, his grasp on her soft hips suddenly released. His gray eyes were very level.

Looking into that suddenly grave face, Anna was glad she had not added "and the candlesticks," as she had been about to. "Sue promised to come and get Coral and take her to Waite Hall and take care of her," she volunteered in an attempt to divert him. But he was not to be diverted.

"Clothes?" he demanded frostily. "Tell me what clothes you stole!"

"Well, the clothes were mine," she hastened to assure him. "*Had* been mine, anyway. All things Papa Jamison had bought me, Bernice—I told you about Papa Jamison's new wife who took everything from me after he had his stroke and couldn't stop her—was altering all my clothes to fit her two daughters. But I managed to snatch a dress to be married in—and two chemises and a yellow satin petticoat and two pairs of slippers. Otherwise," she added plaintively, "I'd have had to be married in homespun and torn lace!"

Above her that long body relaxed. Brett wouldn't have liked being married to a thief. At times he had—fleetingly—considered being married to a wanton, for Erica Hulft at her best was an entrancing wench, not lightly to be put aside—but a thief would have been too much.

He smiled down at the girl he had married in such haste. A lovely thing she was, lying there with her bright hair spread out gloriously around her piquant face. A pulse beat rapidly at the base of her white throat and her turquoise eyes were wide and sparkling and riveted to his. His gaze roved up and down her naked form, enchantingly displayed before him. She looked so young, so vulnerable lying there, with her lovely face—indeed her whole body—flushing rosily at his calm inspection. Lovely and untouched and innocent—and perhaps going to be hurt.

But not yet! Today and tomorrow he could shield her from that hurt—perhaps for many tomorrows. He sank slowly back upon her yielding softness, pressed a gentle kiss upon her softly parted expectant lips, and gathered her into his arms with such a fierce tenderness that Anna was shaken by it. Shaken and made starry-eyed by the love, the passion, the burning desire that transmitted itself to her thrillingly, wordlessly, as Brett swept her along with him on a bright wild river of desire, to deposit her at last on the golden shores of fulfillment and content.

For Anna, locked in her bridegroom's embraces, this long voyage north on the *Dame Fortune* was a dream of love—a delightful dream from which she waked abruptly when the ship docked in New Orange and she saw the rectangular fort and the big windmill that dominated the landscape and the whole panorama of the crowded Dutch town spread out before her.

"To think," she murmured, "that such a short time ago it was English! I am afraid I will forget and call it New York."

"Do not do so," Brett cautioned her. "For I am considered a probable traitor already. Any small spark might ignite a fire which could blow Windgate and all my holdings right out from under me."

Anna knew that Windgate was the name of his estate on the Hudson. "I will be careful," she promised. "Is wampum really the coinage here?" She felt curious about a land where strings of beads could pass for money.

"For small transactions only. This is a busy market town and there is not enough coin to go around. Barter is as common as paying for goods in coin."

"It will be fun to browse in the shops, for you tell me goods come here from everywhere—even the Far East."

"Aye, the East India merchantmen."

"I will buy me a rug from China!" she laughed.

"There are several already at Windgate," he told her.

Anna opened her eyes in surprise. Rugs from China were rare and nearly priceless. She had been but joking when she had said she would purchase one.

To her surprise, Brett did not take rooms for them at an inn. Instead he told her his fast river sloop was waiting for them. Scarce had they unloaded Floss—and Anna insisted on seeing to that herself, for she did not want the dainty mare to be frightened by strangers—than they were both hurried directly on board the *River Witch*, where a big Dutchman swept her a delighted bow and said in a deep baritone, *"Welkom aan boord!"* But Anna had little time to respond to his greeting, for the crew were already loading on their baggage and Brett was motioning to her impatiently, asking her what items she would like brought to their cabin.

"Are we then to go immediately upriver?" asked Anna, when the luggage had been stowed where she wanted it. Her voice was wistful, for she had hoped to give Floss a chance to try her "land legs" and for herself she had wanted to explore New Orange. She could see that it was far larger than St. George and wonderfully different with its clusters of huddled yellow brick houses that sported steep step gables and interesting weathervanes. The town, she had noticed, had a fascinating jumble of shops, and streets where Brett told her canals had once run when the Dutch ruled it before. On her way to the sloop she had heard the languages of many nations spoken and observed with delight some tall buckskinned Indians mingling with the crowd.

"No, not immediately, but we will make our home on board the sloop. Its accommodations are more comfortable than those at the inn."

"Oh, I'm glad we aren't leaving right away!" Anna turned a bright face to him, tossed her hat on the bunk and ran her fingers through her hair luxuriously. "Wait till I comb my hair and you can take me sightseeing!"

"Not today. I am going ashore and I will send back a cobbler with a selection of slippers and shoes. You will need shoes and pattens and boots, for the winters are cold at Windgate."

"Oh, but can't that wait until tomorrow?"

He shook his head. "I will also be bringing a seamstress who will speak only Dutch—you will have to let me translate."

"A seamstress? Oh, you mean for the clothes you brought to Bermuda to woo your unknown bride?" Anna laughed. "That can wait until we reach Windgate. Surely there will be some woman who sews tolerably well who can alter them there."

"There are several in my employ who sew better than tolerably well."

"Well, then?"

"The alterations I speak of must be done at once. I realize the gown is both too wide in the waist and perhaps also too long—you will have noticed that dresses are worn rather short here among the sophisticated Dutch."

Anna had indeed noticed a far greater display of ankle in New

Orange than was generally on view in St. George. "What alterations need to be done in such a hurry?" she wondered.

For answer Brett strode across the room and opened a small, brass-fitted trunk that had been waiting for them in the cabin when their luggage was brought in.

She had assumed it contained Brett's clothing, which he wore when making the journey up and down the river.

He held up a gown and Anna came forward, marveling. It was of elaborate white satin brocade, stiff with embroidery and garnished with seed pearls, the whole of it overlaid by sheer white lace, almost tissue thin. She could see a petticoat of shimmering white silk lying in the chest.

"There is also a chemise," he told her. "The finest I could procure in New Orange. But for shoes and stockings and gloves, I had no idea of the size. I will send the cobbler around and you will choose—whatever else you select—a pair of white satin slippers that will fit you, whilst I pick up some white silk stockings and white kid gloves. You will love the gloves of New Orange, for the Dutch pride themselves on wearing beautiful gloves. I promise to bring you the most elaborate pair of white gloves I can find—oh, and wear these in your hair." He took something from his doublet. "The Dutch are extravagant when it comes to dress; they will appreciate them." He handed her some little gold brilliants to wear in her hair.

Anna, who had been so taken aback that she had not spoken, now found her voice. "But—but this is a wedding gown, Brett," she protested. "And we—"

"Are already married, you are about to say?"

"Yes."

"But we will be wed again, no later than this afternoon if I can make the arrangements."

"Married? *Again*?"

"A Dutch wedding this time—we have spoken our vows under the English flag, now we will do the same beneath Dutch colors."

"I do not understand, Brett."

He shrugged. "We live under Dutch law here." And when Anna still looked mystified, he elaborated. "I wish all to know this is a legal marriage. Having another ceremony here in New Orange will proclaim it."

A legal marriage? But that made no sense. People got married wherever they chose—they did not repeat the ceremony when they changed locations! Unless . . . unless Brett had had other loves— indeed he had mentioned one! Perhaps some other woman had lived here as "wife" to the "English patroon." . . .

Anna's clear turquoise gaze played over him. "Tell me the truth, Brett. Am I the first woman to live aboard the *River Witch*?"

"Yes." His voice roughened. "Don't ask so many questions, Anna. I haven't time for it. Believe me, I'm only doing what's best for us. Stay in the cabin until I return."

He turned on a booted heel and was gone. Like a woman in a dream, Anna went over to the small brass-fitted chest and lifted out the items in it one by one. There was even a wedding circlet made, not of real flowers, but of simulated ones made of white silk and seed pearls.

What, she asked herself, troubled, *had Brett not told her?*

She looked up from her worrying. The cobbler had arrived. He was a short fellow in baggy pants who came bustling in, smiling. In voluble Dutch, of which Anna understood nothing, he described the wares he spread out before her. After he had gone Anna sat and stared at the white satin bridal slippers she had selected.

When Brett arrived with a little birdlike woman in a starched apron who helped Anna into the wedding gown, Anna gave Brett a grave look. She was standing stiffly while the little woman knelt on the floor with a mouthful of pins, pinning up the skirt. "Tell her I do not want it too short," she said. "A bridal gown should sweep the floor."

"As you like," Brett shrugged. He leaned over and spoke to the woman in Dutch, who protested but began pinning all over again.

When the pinning up was completed, Brett left them again while the stitching up was done. Anna watched the needle flying deftly through the cloth, propelled by experienced fingers. She felt helpless and adrift.

Their second wedding ceremony took place that afternoon. Holding up her white satin skirts to keep them from getting dusty, Anna was escorted through the streets of New Orange with everyone staring. Her face flamed at all this unwelcome attention, for she felt like a fool, but Brett seemed to relish it. He was dressed with unusual care in dull gray satin with a brocaded doublet and a great wealth of Venetian lace at his throat. His wide-brimmed gray hat was loaded with silver plumes caught with an ornament of flashing jewels and the middle finger of his right hand sported an enormous ruby.

Anna's eyes widened at sight of that ruby. She herself was wearing the elaborate white beaded gloves Brett had bought her, as became a bride. Her ankles were encased in the white silk stockings he had bought in the town. And around her bright hair, shining in the sunlight, was not the circlet of pink Chain of Love blossoms, hurriedly woven, that she had worn in St. Peter's church in Bermuda, but a graceful circlet of seed pearls and brilliants and a misty veil of gossamer lace. It was almost the wedding gown she had dreamed of long ago—but not in this place, not with these staring people.

"I can see from your ring that we are still solvent," she murmured with an attempt at humor as she picked her way along, managing to avoid an aproned woman in a lace-trimmed cap who shouldered her way through the street carrying a brace of live ducks.

"Just barely," Brett told her in an undertone. "It's glass." And swept a deep bow to a lady in black who looked at him coldly but returned his greeting.

Anna, startled at this admission, almost lost her footing. She would have lurched into a buckskinned Indian, moving silently along on moccasined feet, save that Brett caught her elbow and steadied her.

"And the jewels on the hat?" she whispered.

"Glass also," he muttered. "Smile. Look prosperous."

Anna swallowed, wondering what game they were playing, dressed to the teeth and making their way through the crowded narrow streets of this unfamiliar Dutch town. She was dying to ask him, but she did not dare. She had expected Brett to introduce her to those he met—and he was obviously acquainted with almost everyone—but instead he bowed gravely to people he knew, and they moved aside to let them pass when he told them they were indeed in a great hurry, for they were already late for their own wedding!

And then she was standing in a strange church beside Brett, once again facing a preacher.

Once again only a handful were in attendance—but that handful was a scattering of polite Dutch burghers dressed in rich black with frosty white linen collars, and wearing heavy gold chains about their necks, and beside them their richly clad Dutch-speaking wives adorned with gold and silver girdle chains and jingling gold necklaces.

Anna guessed these were local merchants with whom Brett did business. They greeted Anna with great earnestness, but she was sure she would never remember any of their faces later, for just before the ceremony Brett leaned over and whispered, "Everything will be in Dutch—I will tell you what to say and you will repeat it exactly as I tell you. And do not worry about the names—if my name were Henry, here they would call me Hendrik."

As if that had not been enough to upset her, Anna was not able to identify even her own name in the ceremony. It seemed to her that the domine was calling her "Georgiana"—could that be Dutch for Anna?

And afterward, when the guests crowded around and she and Brett accepted smiling congratulations, she was certain from the disappointed look on one or two faces that they had been offered hospitality which was regretfully turned down, after which she was hurried from the church.

"I am surprised you did not wait to have the ceremony until we were at Windgate," she told him as they were walking back to the sloop and being stared at once again, "where you could invite some of your friends."

"I am not sure of my friends anymore," he muttered, guiding her past a man carrying a large wicker basket full of live chickens. "Things are changing rapidly in this colony. Smile, Anna. Remember, you are a bride and happy about it!"

Hastily, Anna turned her brilliant smile on all comers. The pink in her cheeks deepened as they passed a knot of giggling Dutch girls, one of whom pointed at the length of Anna's bridal skirts and snickered. Anna cast a scornful look at their short quilted petticoats that displayed to advantage their high-heeled shoes and their trim ankles in red and green and blue worsted stockings decorated with parti-colored clocks. Such short bright petticoats would have been totally out of fashion in Bermuda, she told herself wrathfully. But it was a shock to her to see the exuberant ostentation of the town. These wide-breeched Dutchmen wore handsome hats of beaver, and sometimes caps of taffeta or fur. And their lace-capped women sported gold and silver girdle chains and heavy gold necklaces. Their linens were snowy—she was to learn that every household had numerous spinning wheels for flax and wool, and many sported looms as well. So hope chests were brimming with home-fashioned items, hand-loomed, hand-sewn, and hand-embroidered—and the owners of those hope chests could poke fun at a stranger from Bermuda whose skirts were too long by New Orange standards!

"I don't know why I'm doing this," she muttered darkly to Brett, for she felt resentful that she—clad in her dream of a bridal gown—should be made to feel foolish merely because of its length by these women with their sophisticated scoffing glances. "Parading through the town as if I'm on display!" She hopped aside to avoid collision with a buxom serving maid determinedly surging through the crowd carrying a pair of leathern buckets slung on a wooden brace over her fat shoulders. Even that serving wench, Anna noted wrathfully, with her home-dyed blue skirts and her steel-and-glass bead necklace, lifted her brows at the sight of Anna's trailing skirts!

"Trust me," was all Brett said, and nodded briefly to acknowledge the greeting of yet another passerby, this one a heavyset man in buff plush trousers who bowed scrupulously low to the English patroon.

Perhaps that bow was *too* low, thought Anna. Could there have been scorn in it? Slyness in the look he gave her?

She wondered if Brett had noticed as they made their way through a chattering group carrying baskets of fish, and a party of silent Indians unconcernedly munching on large fresh-baked cakes as they strolled about. Brett maneuvered her through them all adroitly and they were face to face with another group of short-skirted women staring pointedly at the hem of Anna's bridal gown.

Anna, her burnished gold head erect under her now tossed-back bridal veil, swept on.

"Are we supposed to have increased your popularity with this charade of a wedding?" she demanded indignantly as they climbed back aboard the sloop.

"Perhaps." Brett's tone was noncommittal. "Having a pretty girl in tow is apt to increase any man's popularity! Observe my crew—they are overcome by your splendor!''

Anna sniffed at this sally and stalked in her white satin slippers back to their cabin. "I'll wager Floss is as tired of boats as I am," she flung over her shoulder as she went through the door. "And as anxious to be ashore!''

"You'll feel better," Brett chuckled, closing the door behind him, "after we've shared a glass of wine to toast our second nuptials!"

"I am surprised your Dutch-speaking friends did not bear us away to a reception after the ceremony!" she said tartly.

"Oh, they wanted to." Brett's smile was urbane. "But I explained that we had not the time.''

" '*Had not the time?*' " Anna turned to face him. "But what was our hurry?''

The gray eyes above that steady smile had turned steely. "I told them we had to return to the sloop.''

"Surely the sloop would have waited for us no matter how long we took!''

"Oh, yes, the sloop would have waited," he said easily. She would learn soon enough, he told himself with an inward wince, that he had chosen his wedding guests with care—all Dutch-speaking so that his English-speaking bride could ask no questions and get no answers. And when she did learn—and learn the reason for it—that knowledge might well destroy their happiness.

Anna gave him a bewildered look. Surely he was not planning to keep her cooped up on the *River Witch* with all of New Orange out there to explore! She would have preferred a few explanations to wine and she took only a sip of the rich red port he poured into a pair of chased silver goblets before she tossed off her misty veil and glittering wedding circlet.

"I do not feel like sitting around a small cabin in this dress, Brett," she complained. "I feel I should be out dancing in it—or receiving guests. If we are not going ashore, then at least let us get into something more comfortable!''

The tall man in gray satin complied with alacrity. Brett was more than glad to help Anna out of her wedding finery!

After he had lifted the magnificent dress over her head, he pushed down the neckline of her chemise, and the palms of his big hands rested lingeringly on the cool firm roundness of her bare shoulders. He sighed as his caressing fingers slid downward over her warm breasts and his hands cupped them lovingly.

"God, you're beautiful," he murmured. "You drive a man mad, Anna."

Anna, her irritation over this strange second wedding ceremony driven from her mind, exulted against him, pressing her smooth cheek against the heavy gray brocade of his doublet, thrilling as she felt his hands gently knead her throbbing breasts through material thin as gauze, so delicate it hardly seemed to be there at all.

"I think we will not stay in New Orange this night," he said hoarsely. Anna, looking up, saw something driven and tormented in his gaze, something she did not understand. "Anything you desire to buy can be sent upriver for your approval. I will go tell Kryn to cast off."

He dropped his hands from her breasts, leaving her trembling. His face was again a cool mask as he went out on deck to give the order to up-anchor.

Anna watched him go, feeling outraged. She quickly pulled on her yellow voile dress over her shimmering wedding petticoat and with half the hooks still unfastened, hurried out on deck. She did not want this last sight of New Orange to escape her, for who knew when they would venture downriver again from Brett's distant stronghold?

They were already pulling away from the dock and Anna was made sharply aware of her half-hooked bodice by a golden-haired Dutchman who was arriving at the dock on the run. At the end of the dock he came to a halt, his hot gaze roved over the *River Witch* and came to rest on Anna. Anna was suddenly uncomfortably aware of the gaps in her bodice and put up her hands to shield them from his gaze.

She saw his wide face split into a grin and heard him laugh, a wicked and delighted laugh that rippled his long golden mustache and his pointed Van Dyke beard. He propped a booted foot upon a wooden cask, set a gauntleted hand upon his knee, pushed back his broad-brimmed, gold-plumed hat and stared at her. He was a resplendent figure in his honey-colored satin doublet and buff velvet trousers. A gold chain swung from his throat. Anna stared back at him, hypnotized.

"Is he not a gorgeous sight, a veritable peacock?" muttered Brett's ironic voice behind her.

"Who is he?" she wondered, seeing the man on shore sweep off his hat with a deep bow to her that swept the dock with golden plumes.

"Nicolas van Rappard, claimant to Windgate."

Claimant to Windgate! Anna gave Brett a startled look, turned as the Dutchman on the dock called to them in perfect, if slightly accented, English. "I came to pay my respects to the van Rappard heiress, Danforth, but I see you are already beating a retreat!"

"I have pressing business elsewhere, Nicolas," called the man behind her. He put an arm around Anna's waist and drew her toward him. "You can pay your respects at Windgate."

"Aye, you'll be seeing me—at Wey Gat!" was the blithe response.

"Wey Gat?" wondered Anna, turning her face up to Brett's.

"Dutch for Windgate," said Brett briefly. His body had gone suddenly still.

"What is it?" asked Anna. She turned back to look at the dock and stiffened. A woman in peachbloom velvet and a large hat afloat with apricot plumes had just joined the golden Dutchman. She took his arm and he turned away from the departing sloop with a jaunty wave of one gauntlet glove.

"I see the wolves are gathering," Brett murmured.

But Anna hardly heard him. She was straining forward. "Brett, who is that woman?"

"No one important." His tone was unconcerned—*too* unconcerned. "Her name is Erica Hulft."

They were gaining distance now as their sails took the wind. Gulls screamed overhead and Anna squinted her eyes across the glittering water to see better. That woman in peachbloom velvet with hair like a fox's brush—she looked like same woman who had sat in a carriage just outside Mirabelle and waited for Anna to come out! So she could view her!

The Voyage Upriver,
1673

CHAPTER 5

Anna seized Brett's arm.

"That woman, Erica Hulft," she gasped. "I—I have seen her in Bermuda."

It seemed a long time before he answered her. Above them the sea gulls swooped and screamed and the sloop gained speed as they left New Orange behind them. When he did speak his voice was heavy with irony.

"I don't doubt it," he said, and the gaze he turned on her was unfathomable. "She is known on many shores. What name was she calling herself there?"

"I—I don't know." Anna's head was whirling. "I saw her but twice: once when she sat in her carriage—oh, she was obviously waiting for me to ride out of the driveway and through the gates of Mirabelle. She promptly engaged me in conversation but I had the feeling that she did not care about what I was saying, that she only wanted to hear my voice. She did not tell me who she was and I did not ask her. The next time I saw her was on a departing ship as it was leaving the harbor in St. George—she stared at me then too. I made inquiries but I could not find out who she was."

"Ah," said Brett softly. "So that was the way it was. . . ."

Anna, frowning as she tried to remember, missed that. "I remember she was fingering a necklace of pink pearls with big

106

silver links as she sat in the carriage—she seemed to be flaunting it at me.''

"No doubt she was, if she seemed to be," said Brett gravely. "Erica is subtle only when she thinks it will serve her purpose."

Anna, caught up in her memories, rushed on. "That necklace—it was the necklace made me remember something that happened years ago when Aunt Eliza was alive. There was a tall man with the same fox-colored hair, and a wooden leg, that Aunt Eliza tried to run away from in St. George, but he caught up with us. She called him Claes and she was afraid of him. He wanted money from her. I remember Aunt Eliza protesting that the necklace of pink freshwater pearls from Scotland with the big silver links should have kept him well, but he said he had gambled—and then she said she had only one thing left to give him, a ring that she had been keeping for my dowry. He promised to sail away and never bother her again if she gave him the ring—and he did. But before she took it to him, Aunt Eliza showed me the ring. It was of gold set with a single sapphire. She said it had belonged to my mother.''

Brett was gazing at her with a very set look on his face.

"What else did she tell you?"

"Nothing. Brett, who was that man, the one who took the ring? I can see from your face that you know."

"He was Erica Hulft's brother." He fished in his gray satin sleeve, brought out something. "Is this the ring, Georgiana?"

With widening eyes Anna stared down at the blue sapphire winking back at her from its big gold setting.

"Where did you get this?" she whispered.

"Claes Hulft led me to it just before he died. You will wear it at Windgate. You will say it belonged to your mother and was given to you by the woman who brought you up.'' He leaned toward her intensely. "You will do this for me, Georgiana."

Anna's face went very still. "Georgiana," she repeated. "You have called me that twice. And that was the name that was used today in the marriage ceremony, wasn't it? Georgiana—and something else, something I can't remember."

"Georgiana van Rappard. That is your name, Anna. Not Anna— Georgiana."

She stared up at him, stunned. The ring slipped from her nerveless fingers and Brett bent to sweep it up in his big hand. "Then—*I* am the van Rappard heiress, as the man on the dock said?'' Her world was whirling.

"Come to the cabin," he said. "I have something to show you."

She followed him, past speech.

In the cabin he unlocked a little box and took from it a packet. He seemed to be loath to give it to her. "I had hoped we would have a few more days of bliss before all this came out." There was an underlying sadness in his voice. He reached out and touched her hair wistfully. She felt almost that he was leaving her.

"Georgiana," he said in a low voice, "do not let this make a difference between us."

Anna stared down at the packet, without touching it.

"What is in the packet?" she asked in a troubled voice as he pressed it into her hand. She was almost afraid to open it.

"Read it for yourself. I have not opened it. It was given to me in Bermuda by the minister who married us, who in turn had it from his predecessor. Elise Meggs—whom you knew as Eliza Smith— gave it to *him* on her deathbed with instructions that you be given this packet on your wedding day. This is your true wedding day, Georgiana, for today you were married before the eyes of the world under your real name." His voice was gentle. "I will leave you to read it alone and after you have done, I will answer any questions you care to ask me."

He left her and Anna broke the wax seal and slowly took out a parchment.

I, Elise Meggs, who for some time now have gone by the name Eliza Smith, she read in the minister's precise handwriting, *being fully aware that I am near to death, do wish to say that I was born in the Scilly Isles at the south of England and there was nurse and later maidservant to young Mistress Imogene Wells, who had lost her parents. I loved Imogene like my own daughter. There was trouble for her in England, for the man Imogene loved killed her betrothed and Imogene's guardian sent her to Amsterdam to save her life. I went along. While there, she heard her lover was dead and she married the Dutch patroon, Verhulst van Rappard. She was seventeen when he took her to America, to his great estate of Wey Gat.*

Wey Gat—Windgate! Anna read avidly on.

But the patroon could have no children—indeed, he came not to my lady's bed, and so when the child Georgiana was born, he knew it was not his. But for a time he seemed to accept her, and my lady was content. Then he grew cruel and threatened to send the child away to Holland. It was then my lady learned that her lover—little Georgiana's father—was still alive. His name was Stephen Linnington and he wrote to her when he learned of her trouble, and did try to save her.

It was all there in the letter: how Stephen Linnington had come for Imogene in an iceboat, and Verhulst, who had discovered the plot, had shot him. How Stephen and Imogene had both died in New Amsterdam, while Elise had taken little Georgiana and escaped aboard the *Wilhelmina*, a Jamaica-bound ship, fleeing Verhulst van Rappard's vengeance.

But aboard the Wilhelmina, *as luck would have it, there was a Dutch woman who remembered seeing me at Wey Gat. She told the captain and I knew he would never let us land at Jamaica, but would take us back to New Netherland, where the patroon would pay him a handsome reward for our return. I feared he would kill us both. So when the ship made an unscheduled stop at Bermuda to take on fresh water, since the water casks taken on in New Amsterdam were of green wood and the water was fouled, I arranged with a fellow passenger, one Claes Hulft—here Anna gave a start—to smuggle me ashore for the price of a valuable necklace of pink freshwater Scottish pearls with heavy silver links. I had a few coins and at this time did not know my lady was dead, so I put up at an inn and kept asking the news of ships' officers who docked at Bermuda. I learned that it was a lucky thing we had left the ship when we did, for word soon reached us that the* Wilhelmina *had been attacked by a Spanish warship and sunk with all hands. When I heard that a stone had been erected at Wey Gat to my lady, I knew that she was dead. I feared to try to contact anyone for aid, for the patroon was a dangerous man—I always thought him mad. So I bound myself to the owner of Mirabelle Plantation and later the new owners, the Jamisons, who bought up my Articles of Indenture along with the plantation, took a fancy to little Georgiana, whom I had told everyone was my niece Anna Smith, and now I see that she will be treated well here and so I am not afraid to die. I have told little Georgiana nothing of this, for I am still afraid of the patroon's vengeance—I do not know what he would do to her if he found her.*

But when she marries, Georgiana will have a husband to protect her from the patroon—on that day she will read this and understand why I feared to tell her this lest it wreck her future.

It was witnessed by the minister and sworn to, and signed with a scraggly *X* and below it, in the minister's firm hand, "Elise Meggs/Eliza Smith."

The other object in the packet, Anna saw, was a small journal written in a hurried scrawl that grew more cramped as she turned the pages. As she opened it she saw the words, *Since I do not expect to survive the winter if Verhulst has his way, now that he has found out that Georgiana's real father is still alive, though I had thought him dead*—so her mother had kept a diary! There were tears on Anna's lashes as she put it down. She would read it later. But now—now there were questions to be answered.

She went on deck and joined Brett at the rail. Like the curtain wall of a frowning stone castle, the ramparts of the Hudson's towering Palisades were flying by on her right as the sloop skimmed upriver. She gave them not even a glance.

"Brett," she said, eyeing the crew uneasily, "does anyone else on board speak English?"

He gave his head a somber shake. "No. I realize there is much you will want to ask me, Georgiana."

She winced. It was going to take time for her to get used to that name. Not Anna—*Georgiana*.

"And perhaps I was wrong," he mused, "not to tell you from the first that you were Verhulst van Rappard's daughter—"

Anna's mouth opened—and closed again.

"And therefore, now that he is dead, the heiress to Windgate."

So Brett did not know that she was *not* really Verhulst van Rappard's daughter? Only Elise Meggs had known that! Anna shivered, realizing suddenly the value of the packet Brett had given her unopened.

"My mother—ran away from him," she said woodenly.

"He was a difficult man," said Brett in a moody voice. "Nobody understood him, it seems."

"Did you ever meet him?"

"No. I was far away and occupied with other matters at the time. But there is a portrait of him at Windgate, which I am told is a perfect likeness—as well as a portrait of your mother, Imogene. She is very beautiful."

Anna felt a burst of pride that her mother had been beautiful. But beauty, she reminded herself, had not brought Imogene happiness.

"They had—quarreled?" she asked, wondering how much the world knew.

Brett sighed. "I had hoped you would have learnt that from the packet Elise Meggs left you."

"I learnt why Elise fled New Amsterdam. She was afraid the patroon would take vengeance on her—and me."

"I doubt he would have harmed *you*," said Brett. "But I do not know what he would have done to Elise, for she had helped your mother to run away with her English lover."

"Is that what she did?" asked Anna steadily.

"Yes, Georgiana. The patroon shot the lover as he picked up Imogene in an iceboat. She was badly hurt because the iceboat had crashed into her as she ran from the patroon. The patroon and his men pursued them downriver. They believed the iceboat had sunk and all on board had drowned. Van Rappard held a funeral for Imogene such as had not been seen on the river and erected tombstones to all of you—even her lover. And killed himself—so the story goes."

Wide-eyed, Anna was drinking this in.

"Van Rappard had left a strange will instructing that the manor house be completed and his possessions kept intact until it was done. His only relations were in Holland and none could be found. In the meantime, matters at Wey Gat fell into a sorry state, the place was ruinously in debt, the English had taken over the colony from the Dutch, New Netherland had become New York— I bought Wey Gat when the house was completed and paid off the debts. It took all that I had and more—I had to borrow. I am still heavily in debt to moneylenders in London, but I have got my mill erected and by next year, God willing, the property should pay a handsome profit."

"How did you find me?" asked Anna in a small troubled voice. "*Why* did you look for me, Brett?"

He gave her an almost sorrowing look, as if he knew he had to hurt her. "After I bought Windgate, a claimant showed up who says he is the nephew and only living heir of Verhulst van Rappard. You saw him on the dock." *The golden Dutchman!* she thought. "Shortly after that, Erica Hulft, the fox-haired woman you saw on the dock with Nicolas, came to me with a story that you were alive, that you had survived the tragedy and were living in Bermuda. At the time I brushed the information aside, for, although Nicolas van Rappard was still pressing his claim, I felt the English courts would see my side of it. Then word reached us that Charles II was turning his back on his Dutch allies, that he had made a secret deal with the French. I realized that I was in a colony basically Dutch and one that could be Dutch again if the war heated up. When my worst fears were realized, and the Dutch fleet sailed in and took the colony by force, I knew that I would now be under Dutch law and that Nicolas van Rappard had not only made friends in the colony, he was one of them. A Hollander like themselves. Thinking I might need more than a bill of sale to stand against Nicolas in court, I sent Erica to Bermuda to find you and tell me what you were like. She came back and told me she could find no trace of you." His lip curled. "I should have known better than to trust her!"

Anna gasped. A mix-up indeed! But why had the fox-haired woman lied?

"You will understand," he said slowly, "my choice of messengers was poor. It seemed the lady herself intended to be mistress of Windgate."

So she had been right. That woman—that vixen who had given her that predatory stare outside the gates of Mirabelle had meant to ride her down, to keep her buried in Bermuda and ignorant of her heritage on the Hudson.

"I had thought I could trust Erica but something happened to make me less sure."

"What? What happened?"

"I found her in Nicolas van Rappard's arms," he said grimly.

"Oh," said Anna in a small voice. It sounded inadequate.

"It occurred to me then that she might have tricked me. I reasoned that since Erica had never been in Bermuda before, but her brother Claes had, she had had her information from him. I contacted Claes, who was then staggering out his life in drunkenness, and for the price of a few drinks he led me to this ring, which he had sold to a tavernkeeper, and I bought it from him. Claes told me that Elise Meggs had become a bond servant in Bermuda although he did not know to whom she was indentured or precisely where. He said he had seen you as a child and had no reason to believe you were not still alive. I was in haste now, for I realized that Erica and Nicolas were plotting against me, and Erica's plots have been known to bear fruit. So I sent a man I trusted to Bermuda—Alexander Timmons. Timmons could not write so I gave him a brass button in an envelope addressed to me and told him to send it to me when he had located you. When I received the button, I set out for Bermuda on board the *Haarlemmer,* which cast anchor, rechristened as the *Dame Fortune,* in St. George's harbor. But when I reached Timmons, I found him in bad case—shot and dying. He could gasp out only the name you went by—Anna Smith—and the name of Mirabelle Plantation, to which he claimed you were the heiress." *Heiress to Mirabelle,* thought Anna. *Brett had told her in Bermuda that he had come to marry the heiress to Mirabelle—and later he had said he came to marry* her. *He had believed Anna Smith to be the heiress to Mirabelle!* "I stayed with Timmons until he died," Brett added morosely, "and gave the doctor money for his burial. On my way back to the inn in St. George that night I found you being abducted."

"And so you had no idea who I was?"

"No. Timmons was too far gone to give me a description. He gasped out that you were the heiress to Mirabelle Plantation and I suppose he would have told me more but death overtook him. I did not learn who you were until I called at Mirabelle and saw your portrait on the wall. The woman there told me that was a portrait of Anna Smith and for a few pounds gave me written permission to marry you."

"She cheated you," said Anna wryly. "For she thought me gone, run away. Arthur had told her so earlier that morning."

Brett nodded, giving her a sober look. He seemed to be waiting. She sensed the tension in him.

And now it must be asked, the great question.

Anna took a deep ragged breath. The wind blew against her hot cheeks. "As a man of honor, Brett, I ask you this." Her steady gaze held his. "Having met me, having spent the night with me, if the van Rappard heiress had turned out to be not myself but one of Bernice's daughters, would you have asked for *her* hand in marriage?"

The tall man before her squared his shoulders and stood straighter. There was agony in his face.

"The truth!" she cried.

"Yes," he said in a strangled voice. "I would have asked for her. That is the truth."

Anna felt those words crash in on her, like heavy stones falling. She felt them strike her, one by one.

I would have asked for her. . . . She had it from his own lips. For a moment she felt that her heart would break. She turned blindly and fled from him, slammed the cabin door, latched it with trembling fingers and threw herself upon the bed.

She was not first with him, as in her lovesick state she had believed. She had never been first. She had deluded herself. She was but second in his life—a house, a piece of land named Windgate came first! And to keep his grip on that piece of land, he would have wed another woman—even after spending a moonlit night in her arms.

Georgiana bent her head and wept.

On the Hudson River,
1673

CHAPTER 6

Hours had passed. Hours in which Georgiana had sat silent as stone, staring at nothing. The first heartbroken weeping had passed and her eyes were dry and empty. All the need she had to be loved—all the need she had always had—was clawing at her unmercifully. She wanted to get up and run out and hurl herself overboard, lose herself in this terrible river where the world believed her mother had died.

"Georgiana." Brett was knocking on the cabin door. "Georgiana, it's late. Let me in."

"Go away," she said tonelessly.

"Georgiana." His voice grew more level; instinctively she knew that from him that sound was dangerous. "If you force me to break down this door, there will be talk. It will be surmised that perhaps I forced you into this marriage."

"And that might endanger your chances of holding on to Windgate?" she said with heavy irony. "How unfortunate!"

His answer was cool. "It would also be a lie. Say to me, if you can, that you did not wish to marry me—that I forced you."

Georgiana's hands clenched. "You know that I cannot say that!" she choked.

"Then stop acting the fool and open the door. What is done is done!"

He was right. What was done was done. Moving as heavily as an old woman, Georgiana rose and started for the door. Suddenly her gaze fell upon the parchment and the journal, which still lay where she had left them when she had gone to join Brett on deck. They were incriminating documents involving her mother, they could bring shame to her and death to Brett's hopes! Acting purely from instinct—although she told herself she cared nothing for his hopes, he could lose Windgate for all she cared!—she snatched them both up, replaced them in the packet, and stuffed them deep into the chest Brett had given her to hold her belongings—and closed the lid. She would not let him see them!

"Georgiana!" He was becoming impatient.

"I am coming."

Silently she threw open the door.

"I am glad you have come to your senses," he sighed, closing the door behind him. "My crewmen are loyal but they have eyes and ears, they talk—and they are not above repeating a juicy bit of scandal like a wedding trip where the bride locks out the groom!"

Georgiana went over and picked up a shawl. The face she turned to the man in gray satin was a stony one. "I will not lock you out, Brett. Indeed, I will do better—I will give you the whole cabin to enjoy alone. It is my intention to spend the night on deck beneath the stars. With Floss."

"No, by God, that you will not do!" He reached out and his detaining hand closed over her wrist like a vise. "My crew could understand many things—but not a bride who prefers to spend her wedding night sleeping beside a tethered horse on deck rather than in bed with her lawful bridegroom!"

She gave her arm a jerk that caused her silk shawl to slide from her shoulders to the floor, but Brett did not stoop to pick it up. He kept his hold on her.

"Brett, let me go!" Her turquoise eyes flashed and her voice held a warning. But she was alarmed too for she knew that when she had threatened to sleep on deck she had touched his honor. He would not be made a fool of before his men!

He studied her mutinous face intently and a crooked smile crossed his dark countenance. Still gripping her wrist, he moved toward the door. "Since you yearn to spend the night outdoors beneath the stars, we will put in to shore and you shall have your chance! My men will doubtless consider the notion romantic!" He gave a mirthless laugh.

Georgiana gazed up at him, affronted and alarmed. Through the cabin window, across a ribbon of water, she could see a strange wild shore gliding by in the darkness. Heavily forested and with never a light or a house, it looked dark and furtive and unfriendly.

"Come," he taunted when she hesitated. "We will test your courage."

Georgiana pulled back. She felt panic mounting in her. "I said I would sleep on deck with Floss. I do not wish to go ashore."

He paused and his dark brows lifted derisively. "Yet you were eager enough to go ashore this afternoon. Why do you hesitate now? It is a fine night."

"*That* was in New Orange," she said through her teeth. "I heard wolves howling out there just now!"

Brett gave an indifferent shrug. She could not help noticing the breadth of his chest in his brocaded doublet. "Wild dogs probably." He would have urged her forward but that she pulled back.

"And a great snarl like a large cat," she insisted.

He gave a short laugh. "This country used to be full of big cats—indeed the Catskills were named for them—but they are long gone, hunted down and driven off. You imagined it. Come." He gave her wrist a tug.

"I **will** not stir a step from this cabin," she said desperately, hanging back.

"Indeed I am glad to hear it," said Brett coolly. He released her wrist and went over and latched the cabin door. "We will spend the night here, then. Together."

"No!" The word was ripped from her violently. She could not bear the thought of his flesh just now. That a man who had just broken her heart should caress her—it was too much!

"Take your choice, Georgiana," he said quietly. "Here or on land. Either way, I will be with you."

His gaze on her was very steady. Many a man would have quailed before it. Georgiana did not. She tried to dart around him but he stepped in front of her, blocking the way. She spun around so that her back was to him. Her teeth were clenched.

He came up behind her, stood very close, not touching her. "I know that I have hurt you, Georgiana, and for that I am sorry." He sounded troubled and he reached out to caress her shoulder.

She twitched her shoulder angrily away from him. "Why could you not have told me the truth? That you were marrying me because you believed me to be the van Rappard heiress?"

"Would you have married me if I had?" he countered.

"No!" she flashed.

"You see?" He spun her around to face him and although his lips were smiling, his hard gray eyes were not. "You have said with your own tongue that deception was the only way I could have you. Ah, I judged you well!"

"And deceived me well!"

"That too," he said calmly. "I admit it. But not to your disadvantage." Before the fury in her face he inclined his dark head thoughtfully. "Think on it this way, Georgiana," he mused. "Would your life have been so much better if I had not come into it?"

Georgiana winced. He was plainly reminding her how he had saved her from that pair of ruffians in Bermuda when they were in the act of carrying her off.

"That isn't fair," she cried hotly. "And besides, any man alive would say you were paid in full for rescuing me—with my virginity!"

"That is true." He inclined his head with gravity. "And after that, what did I offer you?"

"Second place!" Her voice was filled with heartfelt bitterness.

He studied her, frowning. "All I knew of you then was that I had rescued a pretty waif who had given herself to me willingly. I told you that under other circumstances I would have asked you to wife—which was true enough—but since I could not, I offered you my protection."

"*Could not?*" she said bitterly. "Say rather, *would not!*"

"As you like. I still offered you my protection."

"A life as your mistress?" she scoffed.

"Others have not objected," he pointed out.

"I am not '*others*'!" she flashed.

"No, I can see that," he said slowly. "You are more spoiled. 'Tis easy to see that Bernice and all the hardships you endured under her rule did not break your spirit."

"*Nothing* will break my spirit!"

He sighed. "I believe you are right," he agreed, with a tinge of humor. "Not to digress, I will ask you what happened then? You flung away from me and when next I saw you, you were again in need of saving. Indeed you had just been flung to the ground by a whip and were about to endure a lashing. Did you ask me to depart and leave you to your fate?"

Her face flushed scarlet. "You are twisting words. Of course I was glad to see you—I would have been glad to see anyone. Arthur was about to tear me to pieces with that whip!"

"We both know," he said, each word flicking her like a light tap on a bruise, "that Arthur would have been easily persuaded from doing that. In fact, 'tis doubtful he would so much as have marred your flesh—that flesh he so desired that it was driving him to a ridiculous course of action. You had only to say 'Arthur, I am sorry' and he would have desisted. *Do we not both know that?*"

"I would never have said it!"

"Perhaps not. But you were delighted when I rid you of him. And to all your desires, I acquiesced. We were married in the church of your choice. I bought the Articles of Indenture you had, in a moment of madness, signed. I bought your horse, which is even now tethered on the deck."

Floss—for the moment she had forgotten Floss. Gentle, trusting Floss had stood the trip well; Georgiana had meant at the very least to go on deck and give Floss a good-night hug. "Has she been fed? Watered?" she asked anxiously.

"Of course. Stop trying to change the subject."

Georgiana gave him an angry look. "Yes, you have done much for me—I admit it. But you still deceived me."

He leaned closer, a heady nearness that interfered with her breathing. She could smell the light pleasant scent of Virginia tobacco, feel his breath warm upon her cheek, feel the pressure of his overpowering masculinity driving her forward along a course *he* chose. Her heart gave an uneven lurch and it was difficult to hold her expression taut, to keep from trembling.

"Tell me, Georgiana," he asked softly, "do you not find happiness in my arms? Don't clamp your lips together like that. There is no shame in enjoying a man's caresses."

She turned her face away sharply, for she could not meet his probing gaze. "You know the answer to that," she mumbled bitterly.

"Yes," he agreed in that deep resonant voice that seemed to go right through her. "I know the answer to that." And drew her unprotesting body toward him with confidence.

Trembling from the mixed emotions that surged through her slight frame, Georgiana looked up into his rapt face. Her gaze was tormented. "Do you love me, Brett?"

"Don't you know I do, Georgiana?"

"I want to hear you say it," she whispered.

"Very well. I do love you—more than I ever thought I could love a woman." His voice was rich and soft and his warm lips were brushing her ear. She could feel his hot breath blowing tendrils of her hair. It was growing harder every second to resist him, to keep her slender body stiff and unyielding in his embrace. And why *should* she resist him? Had he not said he loved her more than he ever thought he could love a woman? And was not love all that counted? Oh, yes—the rest was worthless!

She let him take her then, melted into his arms, tried to forget her hurtful thoughts. And as his hands played expertly over her slender body, bringing it to tingling desire, she *did* forget and was swept away on a tide of feeling that welded them together as if their quarrel had never been.

Their clothes were strewn around the room where they had been hastily discarded—a shoe kicked off here, a stocking pulled from a graceful leg there, a belt hurriedly unbuckled and lying where it had been flung. Over here Brett's doublet fallen atop Georgiana's yellow voile dress, over there Brett's trousers and a shimmering pile that was her wedding petticoat. And lying intimately beside his shirt and smallclothes, fragile and only slightly torn, Georgiana's lace-trimmed chemise.

They were on the bunk now, rapt and clinging. The sparks of their quarrel had ignited the banked fires within them and the flames now leaped up and became a raging conflagration.

"I love you, I love you," Georgiana was murmuring brokenly against Brett's straining shoulder. Her voice was a sob of surrender as passion flamed within her. His every touch was sweet madness and although she was crushed against him, she could not hold him close enough. His passion was her passion, his will her will. He was lover, husband—everything. He was all she wanted from life!

Borne on the wings of that passion, they soared like gods. Their bodies rose and fell like gaint waves cresting, and the storm that shook them carried them both away, carried them in a kind of beautiful desperation somewhere beyond imagined delights and in a last burst of frenzy over the brink of the world, a high and lovely place from whence they seemed to float down like feathers from a great height, to find themselves mortal again.

For a time they lay there, still breathing unevenly, lying side by side on their naked backs, bathed in the warm afterglow of remembered ecstasy. And then Brett rose on one strong arm and passed a tender caressing hand over her naked body that responded with sweet submission to his touch.

"Now that we are friends again," he said calmly. "I would ask that you satisfy my curiosity. I have been waiting for you to tell me what the long objects are that you have wrapped in damask table-cloths and passed off as pokers and tongs. They are indeed heavy and not of a shape to be worn or consumed."

Georgiana gave him a dazzling smile. "They are the big candle-sticks from Mirabelle," she told him with a calm that matched his own. "I filched them shortly before you found me at Waite Hall, along with the clothes I wore to be married in, in St. George." At his blank astonishment, she added defiantly, "The clothes were my own which Bernice had taken from me and the candlesticks had been promised to me as part of my dowry when I married, by Mamma Jamison herself."

"And you did not intend to leave the island undowered," he concluded wonderingly.

"I think I was striking out at a world that had hurt me," she said ruefully, giving him a thoughtful look. "The clothes were my own, of course, and I needed them But the candlesticks—to me they were a symbol of Mirabelle, of home. Doubtless you would have stopped me from taking them, had you known—that is why I told you they were popcorn poppers and such. But since you have brought them along, you can consider them a dowry. They are very valuable—'a buccaneer's treasure' the minister used to call them."

Brett struck his bare thigh with his open palm, threw back his head and laughed. "Had I known what contraband I carried, I'd have been in an even greater hurry to leave Bermuda! 'Tis plain, Georgiana, we can never go there again. There'll be a warrant out for your arrest!"

"It doesn't matter." Georgiana's shoulders rippled in a careless shrug. "I'm never going back."

"Really?" He ruffled her bright tangled hair with a gentle hand. "For a little while tonight, I was afraid you were considering it. Afraid you would return to Bermuda and leave me to my fate." His tone was whimsical.

She gave him a troubled look, for his words had brought back to her all the searing turbulence of this night's discoveries, all the knife-edged thoughts that had cut at her before. Pensive now, she tried to smile and his arms went round her tenderly, protectively, as if he would save her once again from all the hurts of life. But this time when his arms went round her there was not the joy in her face that there had been when he had clasped her aboard the *Dame Fortune*.

It is my misfortune to love him, she admitted now to herself. *But does he really love me? Will I ever know?*

What a strange life she had lived! From rags to riches and back to rags again—and now, suddenly an heiress again, she had unwittingly fallen into the trap that so often befell the rich and the fortunate—never to know if one was loved for one's self or for one's great possessions.

The eyes of the girl who clasped Brett Danforth to her, the girl who looked up over his broad shoulder at the stars that twinkled through the cabin window, were dark with doubt.

Perhaps I am wrong, she told herself as she lay against him. *Perhaps he does love me after all. God grant that I am wrong and that he married me for love, and not because—mistakenly—he believes me to be the rightful heiress to Windgate.*

Now that their "Pandora's box" had been opened, now that there was truth between them at last, Brett told her much about himself. About his boyhood in Devon, about his first romance.

"She was very pretty and I thought myself madly in love with her," he told Georgiana. "But she chose to marry an earl instead of a younger son without prospects. She thought to keep me around lapping up, like a dog, the crumbs of her affection. I ran away to sea instead."

"And forgot her?" Georgiana asked on a breathless note.

"In a month," he said absently.

He omitted telling her of the other women he had known—although that was what Georgiana most desired to hear. But he did skim over some of the hard times he had known, and how he had come by this passion for Windgate.

"I was trading far upriver for furs," he told her. "Up in the Mohawk country. I got caught in a battle between rival tribes and an arrow pierced my back. I went down like a stone and when I came to myself, the battle had raged on past me and the fighting was some distance away. I could hear war cries, and screams of the dying through the trees. Somehow I made it back to my canoe and shoved off, but the wound festered—I bear the scar of it still."

Georgiana nodded raptly. She had seen the deep scar on his back.

"A farmer found me when my canoe became tangled in some drifting tree branches and came ashore. He cut out the arrowhead, which was deep embedded, and he nursed me through fever—and he told me of Wey Gat. Vast and rich and beautiful, he said, but cursed, for all its owners since the house was first begun had died violent deaths. He aroused my curiosity. I had not much time to get downriver, for my ship would soon sail, but I paused at Wey Gat and studied it. I wandered across its lands. Never had I seen such beauty. . . ." His voice had a deep resonance like some stringed instrument. It made her see, feel, a little of what he had felt then—awe of the high-flung virgin forests, delight in the meadows and sparkling rivulets flowing down from the heights to the broad Hudson far below.

"I determined then that I would buy it," he said softly. "Even though it was far beyond my reach. And it was being harmed, for although the great house was being kept up and even desultorily completed under the terms of Verhulst van Rappard's will, the rest of it was being allowed to run down. Owning Windgate became an obsession with me that blotted out everything else. I *would* have it."

There was a ruthlessness in his voice now that swept Georgiana along. She began to understand how it was with him and the direct, arrowlike thrust of his purpose.

"The next season I went back again into the Mohawk country. And I made a discovery. It seems that in the battle that near cost me my life I had saved a young boy—a chief's son. 'Twas no great thing, the lad was being overpowered by two stout warriors and I cut them down before they could finish him. Lying on the ground, the lad saw me take the arrow before he ran away. His father the chief had looked for me to thank me for saving his firstborn, but my body had disappeared—indeed I had staggered away to my canoe and floated downriver, but they did not know that. Since it was thought my wound was mortal— I had been seen to die, as they put it—and since I now returned to them in perfect health, that was considered a miracle. My return was a good omen. In gratitude, I received the fur concession for the whole Mohawk Valley from that chief. It made me rich—but not rich enough to buy Windgate. *That* took all that I had and all that I could borrow from the moneylenders in London as well."

"But you still have the concession for furs, have you not?"

He shook his head. "That chief was killed last year and his son with him. His successor does not favor me and has warned me off the Mohawk River."

"And the farmer, the one who nursed you back to health?"

"When I came back to reward him the next season, I found him
dead of a tomahawk wound. And scalped."

Georgiana shivered. Outside was a land of shadows—and death.

Windgate,
1673

CHAPTER 7

Upriver sped the *River Witch*. Forests and rounded hills were flying
by in the sunlight as the wind whipped the sails and carried them on
to Windgate.

But Georgiana, like her mother before her, was unprepared for the
sight of the tall frowning castle that rose on the bluff to her right.
Completed now, the Great Plan of its builder had become a reality.
The building of it had spanned two generations, for the great stone
edifice had been begun by Verhulst van Rappard's father and
completed years after the young patroon's death. The house, she
saw, would have a commanding view of the Hudson and all the river
traffic, but from the river looking up it seemed a jumbled mass of
stone wings and gables, of high-pointed Gothic windows and steep
slate roofs that sprouted a forest of tall chimneys, magnificent,
disdainful, aloof.

"This is Windgate," Brett told her.

She nodded. "I know."

Brett smiled down at her teasingly. "How did you know?"

"You said it was the finest house on the river and—it takes my
breath away."

She could feel the pride in him well up. "Is it not all that I said?"

"All that you said—and more," she told him soberly, for she had been unprepared for such grandeur. This house had no outflung "welcoming arms" like Mirabelle. Its massive pile reared up awesomely before you, flinging down a challenge to all who plied the river. Those gray stone walls silently proclaimed that this was a baronial holding and any man rash enough to cross the lord of this stronghold did so at his peril.

Georgiana felt all that sink in on her as Brett went to speak to the *schipper*, for they would soon be making fast at the long wooden dock that stuck out into the river.

At least, she told herself ruefully, it is a house and land and not some other woman that he puts before me! Another woman—*that* I could not stand! For Georgiana had discovered something new about herself. She who had never felt any twinge of jealousy of any man before was wildly jealous of Brett. On shipboard, she had been the only woman, but once in New Orange she had felt tension mount inside her every time a passing woman on the street looked at Brett—and a violent twist of her heart every time he looked back!

Here at Windgate, at least, she would have no rival save Windgate itself! Smiling as they tied up at the pier, she gave Brett her hand and together they walked up the grassy bluff toward the big gray stone house that was to be her home. Behind her, tethered on the *River Witch*'s capacious deck, Floss gave a soft approving whinny as she sniffed the air from the meadows behind the house.

The servants were lined up in the hall to greet them but that did not daunt Georgiana—as former mistress of Mirabelle, she was used to being in command! But accustomed as she was to the much smaller houses of Bermuda, Georgiana did find herself awed by the enormous heavy front doors of thick black oak, by the great entrance hall stretching dimly away, by the wide heavily carved stairway that seemed to lead endlessly up, and by the magnificent wallpaper with its hunting scenes of lords and ladies riding to hounds, which rose above the intricately carved wainscoting.

"This hall is lovely by night when the moonlight streams through that window," Brett remarked with a careless nod of his head toward a Gothic window set high above them. Georgiana noted the richness of his tone. *He loves it here,* she thought wistfully. *So I must learn to love it too!*

Proudly, he took her on a grand tour of the house. He led her through the handsome drawing room with its furniture of rare

Oriental woods and large gold Chinese rug that seemed to glow softly where the sun struck it, on into the adjoining ballroom with its several dozen matched gilt chairs, which lined the ornately paneled walls, through all the main bedrooms with their views of the Hudson and the opposite bluffs that took her breath away—and at last they reached the office, where a tall thronelike chair of black oak, heavily carved, frowned from behind a massive oaken table. Both pieces of furniture dwarfed the small beamed room.

"That chair looks like—a throne," she blurted.

Brett frowned. "I know. I think that was what my predecessor intended, but I don't use it myself." He paused and glanced at her uneasily as it came to him that his lightly referred to "predecessor" was Georgiana's father, but she seemed not to notice. Nevertheless, he thought it best to explain. "I generally see my tenants out in the fields, in their *bouweries*—no need to drag them all the way in here when I make the rounds anyway."

Brett is kind to his tenants, she thought, turning to smile at him. And had a sudden chilling view of what it must have been like when Windgate was Wey Gat and a violent young Dutch patroon lorded it over the land from that oaken throne. She had had time to read her mother's journal now and it had made her shudder. She envisioned Verhulst as hard-faced, leaning across that enormous table and meting out justice—she had no view of the tormented man Imogene had known, a man whose thin body had been dwarfed by that massive chair, who had seemed diminished rather than enobled by it.

But it was the dining room that disturbed her most of all. For at one end of the long handsome room, facing the light, was a portrait of Imogene, looking incredibly young and beautiful and light of heart.

"Your mother," Brett told her gently. "I understand Verhulst van Rappard had it painted in Amsterdam. And that"—he turned to nod at a haughty painted face above a frothing white lace collar and black velvet doublet that frowned down from another gilt frame—"is your father."

Tears filled Georgiana's eyes and sparkled on her lashes as she studied that carefree young likeness of Imogene, her lost lovely mother. The sunlight struck the golden hair of the woman in the portrait, caressed the peachbloom of her delicate skin—but here was more than beauty; here was spirit, here was pride. Those delft blue eyes were alight in a reckless face—and she had a heartbreaking smile.

Georgiana dashed the tears from her lashes and recoiled as she turned to consider, opposite, the portrait of Verhulst. A pair of dark, almost fanatical, eyes gazed scathingly back at her from that sallow, oversensitive face. His dark hair gleamed as if it had been waxed, every hair precisely in place, and there was a cruel look to that thin patrician mouth. The artist had done his job well, he had captured on canvas those characteristics of the young patroon that had made him feared throughout Wey Gat.

Georgiana stared fiercely at the painting. Her heart was pounding so loudly she feared Brett must hear it. *This* was the man who had driven her mother to her doom, who had set dogs on her that terrible night on the ice!

"I wish you would take it down!" she cried in a choked voice.

Brett looked startled. Quickly Georgiana realized what she had said, how strange it must have sounded for a daughter upon arrival in the home her father had built instantly to demand that his picture be torn from the wall.

"I mean," she amended lamely, "I think it looks—gloomy here. His portrait. After all, this is the dining room and he is so thin I cannot think he could have cared much for food—I think he would be far happier hung opposite that big throne chair he must have been so proud of."

Her husband's dark brows elevated. He shot a look at Verhulst's dark portrait—and opposite, Imogene's, that woman of light. "As you like." He sounded mystified. "After all, they are *your* parents; you may do what you please with their likenesses—as with the other furnishings here."

Georgiana yearned to tell him this man was not her father, but she forbore. Someday perhaps—but not now, not when as a new bride and great heiress she was his checkmate to Nicolas van Rappard's claim to the property.

"I think I would like to change my dress for dinner now," she said in a muffled voice.

"I have had prepared for you the bedchamber they told me was your mother's," Brett told her as they climbed the wide carved stairway. "It is the loveliest room in the house. Imogene selected all of the furnishings herself, I understand, in Amsterdam."

It was not always her bedroom, thought Georgiana bitterly, remembering Imogene's journal. Sometimes she was locked away on the other side of the house, away from her baby, away from her only friend—Elise. It was from a room on that other side of the house that Imogene had made her tragic escape, a room that overlooked the fields and forests stretching away toward Connecticut. The last entry in the journal—the last entry made on the very night she died—had told Georgiana that. But Brett was not to know that—not now, perhaps not ever.

But upset as she was, Georgiana could not help being enchanted by the big bedroom with its delicate blue and white French wallpaper and blue drapes and fluffy white cambric curtains. Her toes tested and sank in the thick blue Chinese rug and she smiled, thinking that this room was a perfect example of what money and taste could do when brought together. What a pity they could not have loved each other, Imogene and Verhulst—they had had such an idyllic setting for it.

Supper was an event. Although Brett explained that it was but a hastily prepared feast to welcome the patroon and his bride, Georgiana exclaimed that she had never seen such gigantic oysters, and the size of the river eels amazed her.

"We dine well here at Windgate," Brett told her, leaning back expansively over his wine at the end of the long table after they had finished. "You grace this table well, Georgiana."

That name, she felt, would ever be strange to her, but she was trying to become accustomed to it.

"My mother sat here," she said, looking down the table's long polished surface and imagining the terrible dinners Imogene had so vividly described in her journal—dinners when her young husband had taunted and threatened and frightened her.

"And she gazes over this board still." Brett smiled at the beautiful portrait smiling down from the wall.

"Yes, she does," said Georgiana soberly. "I wonder what she thinks of us, Brett."

"I hope she approves." His tone was jaunty. "You're a credit to her and soon, I don't doubt, will be the toast of the river, for we're invited to a ball this coming Friday at the ten Haers'. They're our neighbors to the south. You remarked their house as we passed it."

"*Rychie* ten Haer?" Georgiana was somehow surprised that

Imogene's old enemy, who had been described at length in the journal, should invite them to a ball.

"Yes. How did you know her name? I don't remember mentioning it."

Georgiana caught her breath. "You must have," she said hurriedly. "Else how would I have known it?" And not to show too much knowledge, "Does she live there alone?"

"No, she is married to her cousin, Huygens ten Haer, a decent enough fellow who has proved to be a good neighbor." He chuckled. "She browbeats him."

"Do they have a family?" wondered Georgiana.

"One daughter—Katrina." He spoke the name very cautiously and Georgiana gave him a sharp look.

"And what is Katrina ten Haer to you?" she asked tartly.

Brett's laugh was a little uncomfortable. "You'll hear rumors about her, so I may as well tell you now. All the river gossips had us married off."

"Was there any truth to the rumors?"

"Some," he admitted reluctantly.

"You mean you were betrothed?"

"No, it never got that far. I never asked for her, but she's a determined wench, is Katrina ten Haer. She may be a little cold to you at first."

That, thought Georgiana, was probably putting it mildly. Katrina ten Haer would undoubtedly hate her. "What does Katrina look like?" she asked.

"Ah, she's a showy piece. She has her mother's coloring but a little less blatant. They're a striking pair, with their saffron hair and bright blue eyes—the older version and the younger."

A showy piece...striking.... Georgiana felt jealousy surge through her like the twist of a knife. "I doubt if I'll see much of her," she told Brett airily. "I can see that I'll have more than enough to occupy me here at Windgate."

"Well, you'll certainly run across her at every ball we attend, for Huygens is a patroon and invited everywhere, and Katrina is very fond of dancing."

She'll dance to another tune if she tries again for Brett! Georgiana promised herself grimly. She set her glass down with rather more force than was necessary. Brett watched her narrowly over his wine.

"There's no reason to be jealous of Katrina," he said.

Georgiana flushed to the roots of her golden hair. "I'm not jealous!" she protested.

He shrugged. "Anyway, I tell you now about the ball because I'm sure you'll want time to plan what to wear and I'll be leaving before you're awake tomorrow. I must see to the mill upriver and have a look around the outlying *bouweries*. Gerrit tells me there's some talk of Indian trouble there. I'll be away three or four days but," he grinned, "don't worry, I'll be back in plenty of time to take you to the ten Haers' ball!"

"Oh, no, Brett—take me with you!"

He shook his dark head. "If there's really Indian trouble—and I hope there is not—then I wouldn't want you with me. Here at Windgate you're as safe as anywhere on the river and there are strong men to guard the house. I won't expose you to any narrow Indian trails leading up into the tamaracks."

Although she argued, she could not shake him. They strolled outside on the bluff and stood under one of the big chestnut trees that dotted the lawn, looking out over the broad expanse of shimmering water that flowed past them from the high Adirondacks down to the sea.

"I can understand your loving it here, Brett," she told him soberly. "I think I've never seen anything so beautiful as this river."

He looked about him and she could feel his air of proud proprietorship. "I'd never thought to settle down," he murmured, "until I saw Windgate. I saw it and suddenly I wanted to raise my sons here—the sons we'll have together, Georgiana. This is the land I want to leave them when I die."

"Oh, Brett . . ." her fingers gently caressed his forearm at this confidence. "There may be daughters too. What will you leave *them*?" she asked teasingly.

"Some other great estate—for I've my eye on several along this river. And with the mill going—and other mills I'll build, with the ships I mean to have one day that will carry my goods overseas, there'll be more than enough for daughters, no matter how many you give me, Georgiana! And now it's time for bed."

He swept her up and carried her, laughing, over the dark lawns, back up the bluff. A smiling servant, who must have been watching their progress, threw open the big front door.

"You can lock up now, Wouter," Brett flung over his shoulder.

"My lady and I are for bed. But mind you wake me early in the morning, for I'll need to spend all day at the mill."

"I don't like having separate rooms," Georgiana protested as Brett carried her into her big square bedroom. "Even if they do adjoin!"

"You'll grow to like it, for I'll be getting up earlier than you do and you wouldn't like being disturbed. Most mornings I'll join you for breakfast."

"In bed?" She was curling herself luxuriously into his arms as she spoke, feeling the buttons of his doublet bite into her soft breasts and trying to settle herself more comfortably against him. She felt wonderfully relaxed after their stroll. She felt she would like to spend her life in those arms.

"Anywhere you like," he said in a soft rich voice, and his ardent mouth clamped down on hers. She was thrilling to the hard masculine feel of him through his doublet as he laid her gently down on the big square bed.

He caressed her hair for a moment and then straightened up, smiling down at her. "Undress now," he said. "I'll be back in a minute. My nightshirts aren't unpacked."

She gave him a bold enticing smile, and stretched. "It's too warm for a nightshirt."

"So it is. I'd forgotten that Wouter built a fire in the fireplace earlier to knock the damp off the room." He went over and latched the door, began stripping off doublet and shirt.

Georgiana kicked off her shoes, hurriedly rid herself of garters and hose and let her petticoat fall in a careless heap around her ankles. As she hurried out of her dress and chemise, she stole a look at Brett. What a handsome animal he was! Lithe as a sword blade, strong and light-footed, possessed of a magnificent physique. Had she fallen in love with him for that? No, it was for something she sensed in him, something she could not quite define that made her his. . . .

Now she was divested of her clothing and she saw that he stood across the room from her, a naked giant, hands on hips, studying her with admiration in his gray gaze. She blushed and reached for her night rail. But before she could put it on, in two strides he had reached her. Gently he took the night rail from her and as she looked up wordlessly, he reached out and ruffled her hair, ran his hand from the top of her head down her shivering spine all the way to its base, cupped one buttock in his hand and grinned down at her.

"Brett—my night rail." She reached out for it.

But he held it beyond her reach, tossed it away. "Ye'll not be needing this tonight," he said carelessly.

"Brett!" she protested.

" 'Tis plain you're not in such a hurry as I am," he chuckled. "Perhaps I can entice you to bed by these methods!"

She squirmed and struck laughingly at his hand as he tweaked her breasts and patted her bottom, urging her toward the big four-poster. "Anyone would think I were your doxy instead of a respectable married woman," she protested. "And that you were in a hurry to bed me because you must needs be shortly gone!"

"You *are* my doxy, wife or no!" Brett gave her a boost that tossed her breathless onto the big bed, to sink deep into the feather mattress that threatened to close over her naked body. "And 'tis true I've little enough time for loving, if I'm to catch any sleep—for if I'm to do any good at the mill tomorrow, I'll indeed be shortly gone!"

Georgiana laughed and tried to evade him as he plunged toward her. She was half turned over, near suffocated by the enveloping feather mattress that seemed to have swallowed her up, when she felt his big warm body close over hers and felt her blood race at the contact.

It was the most playful night they had ever spent together: a night of whispers and sighs, of ticklings and mock tormented groans and tumbling about. Georgiana's long hair got tangled around his arm, and between them, they could hardly extricate her. And once, with her slender legs trapped between his strong ones like a vise, she made a mock lunge to evade him and ended up with her head entirely enclosed by the deep goose-down mattress, crying to him in a muffled voice that she was smothering. Brett rescued her with alacrity, releasing her legs from between his own and turning her back to face him, grazing her naked breasts with his lightly furred forearm as he did so.

"So you seek to escape me, wench?" he demanded with mock ferocity. "Ah, but in this bed I promise you I'll find you!"

Georgiana, "saved" from being smothered by the mattress, collapsed against him, laughing until she was weak.

It was then he took her, exciting her to frenzy with his skillful fingers, holding her close as they rolled over and over and back again in the mattress's downy depths. Their hair tangled and twined and spilled over their faces and got into their mouths as they exchanged wild laughing kisses. And Georgiana felt her passions shiver and mount as her body was moved skillfully up and down so that her flesh rasped sweetly against him and a thousand little soft explosions of feeling seemed to assault her all at once.

And then abruptly she was his, welded to his body, her back arching, hidden wells bubbling up inside her, reckless thoughts filling her mind, hot blood coursing through her veins.

"I fear me you'll think me as hot as any trollop," she gasped when it was over. She was leaning on one elbow, studying him with sparkling turquoise eyes as he lay on his back. One of his outflung arms pinioned her soft hip.

"Then, thank God for trollops," sighed Brett and rolled over, sat up. " 'Tis plain I'll get me no sleep here, my girl. I'm off to my own room." He bent and pressed a kiss on her smooth stomach, chuckled as her muscles sharply recoiled.

Smiling, he slid a gentle hand down her legs, feeling the soft skin of her inner thighs. "Sleep well," he sighed. "For any more of you and I'd ne'er make it to the mill—I'd sleep long after cock crow!"

With her body still glowing from their last fiery contact, Georgiana lay on her elbow and watched him go, a tall form dark against the moon's pale light. His dark hair was gilded for a moment as he passed through the door into the adjoining room.

"Leave the door open," she called.

"No, I'll not let Wouter, when he comes to wake me, see you sleeping." Firmly he closed the door.

At least, she told herself, giving her pillow a blow with her fist, he had not latched it!

Wakeful now, she waited, pouting, annoyed that he had left her side. Perhaps he would come back!

When he did not, she got up and put on her night rail. Silently she padded over the soft carpet to the door that separated them. She opened it without a sound and glided to Brett's bed and stood looking down at him. He had not even thrown back the covers, but lay atop them fast asleep.

For a long time she stood there, a bride with a guilty secret and a desperate need for love, staring down at the man who had thrown himself down upon the coverlet and now lay there sleeping heavily.

He is tired and must be up early, she thought fondly, giving that strong determined face a tender glance. A doubting glance too, for in spite of all his playful lovemaking and disturbing passion, she felt she would never be sure of him. Suppose some other girl had been heiress to Windgate? Who would then be lying in his arms?

Suppose, suppose . . .

After a while Georgiana tiptoed away and cautiously shut the door behind her. She stood looking around her in the moonlight at the lovely room her mother had decorated so long ago.

Suddenly she knew what she wanted to do. She wanted to go downstairs and study in absolute privacy, without the feeling that Brett or the servants might wander in, the features of the woman who had smiled back at her from a gold-leaf framed portrait on a thick plastered wall—a woman of light and air, breathtakingly lovely, and young as Georgiana was young—her mother.

Soundlessly, and with that sense of urgency still upon her, Georgiana stole downstairs, down that broad stairway lit by moonlight from the high Gothic window overhead. She made her way by moonlight into the long dining room where Verhulst's and Imogene's portraits were hung. Tall Gothic windows spilled a moonpath straight across the room and gave Imogene's portrait a sudden ethereal life.

Swiftly Georgiana padded across the long room and stood motionless in her white night rail staring up at the portrait. So young her mother looked! Imogene must have been about Georgiana's age when this was painted. So young and so—carefree.

Reluctantly she turned from the painting and her brooding gaze scanned this handsome room where Imogene's jealous husband had grasped his wife by her long fair hair and reached for a carving knife on the dining room table. Murder had almost been done here, she realized with a shiver. All the terrible misfortunes she had learned from Imogene's journal spilled over Georgiana in a wave, and a sob caught in her throat as she turned again to her contemplation of the warm, lovely woman in the portrait. This was the mother she had never known, whose love she had missed all these long years, a woman whose personal tragedy had marked her daughter as well as herself.

And suddenly all of her being seemed to converge in one great long inner wail. *"Oh, Mother,"* she whispered to Imogene's painted likeness, *"why couldn't it all have been different? Why couldn't you be here to advise me?"*

PART TWO
The Carolina Lady

The shadowy wings of the future
That flit o'er the present's pain
And remind one at last of all that is past....
Will it ever return again?

Longview Plantation, The Carolinas, 1673

CHAPTER 8

In a frowning mansion on the Hudson, Georgiana whispered what was in her heart to a portrait, called to that painted likeness on the wall.

And far away in the Carolinas, the woman who had sat for that portrait—Imogene herself, a woman the world thought dead, roused with a sudden start from her sleep and threw back her embroidered coverlet. She cast a swift look at the long lean body of the sleeping man beside her, but he did not stir. She threw one long lovely leg over the side of the bed and got up in a froth of expensive Venetian lace. With a light toss of her head she threw back the tumbled gold hair that cascaded over her white shoulders—she had meant to braid it neatly but in the torrential heat of their lovemaking before they went to sleep she had quite forgot and as usual it had covered her pillow like a shining golden shower, making it difficult to comb in the morning.

But it was not morning. . . . A cold white moon shone through the windows of her bedchamber, brilliant against the black velvet night.

She shook her head as if to clear it.

"I thought—I thought someone called my name," she murmured to herself in confusion.

So strong was her conviction that she moved to the windows, her bare feet silently crossing the thick red Turkey carpet, the only sound in the room the steady breathing of the dark-haired man on the bed and the slight rustle of her silken night rail.

She stood there brooding, looking out, listening.

Before her was spread out the whole panorama of the front lawns of Longview Plantation, sloping down to the wide silvery expanse of the Cooper River, winding its way majestically to the sea.

Something must have disturbed her—but what?

I was dreaming we were back in Tortuga, she thought, puzzled. *That I was in my bedchamber and there was a noise in the courtyard below and Arne was speaking to someone and—I thought someone called my name.*

She looked about, half expecting to see below her a figure waving and gesturing, trying to attract her attention.

But of course that was ridiculous. Newly arrived guests at Longview would not be shouting from the yard, they would be banging the big brass knocker designed like a ship in full sail—and would be let in by sleepy-eyed servants.

She looked up sharply as a flight of birds obscured the moon, flying south down the Great Eastern Flyway to winter in summer islands basking in the sun.

She herself was a daughter of the summer isles—but hers were far away now and far back in her memory. Her own summer islands had been the Scillies at England's southern tip, and she had been born Imogene Wells, loveliest daughter of those "fortunate isles" and destined for a turbulent life of shattering passion and wild remorse and now—at last—happiness.

She glanced north whence the birds had come. Here in the Carolinas the weather was still fine and fair, but along the wild banks of the Hudson River it would be snowing soon—and she was suddenly reminded that she had once been Imogene van Rappard, wife of the young patroon of Wey Gat.

And it was at Wey Gat that she had borne Georgiana, her beautiful baby—only to lose her to the guns of a Spanish man-of-war somewhere off the Great Bahama Bank.

She shivered and a pain seemed to pierce her heart. So many tears she had shed for Georgiana—and waked screaming from so many nightmares in which Verhulst van Rappard's dogs chased her over the ice. *Georgiana* . . . again a spasm shook her delicate frame. And then she straightened. All that was behind her now, lost somewhere in her past.

She had another life now, another last name.

Her gaze flew to the man whose gleaming dark hair was spread out on the pillow of the bed she had so recently quitted—van Ryker, the wild buccaneer who had snatched her back from death, made her live again and filled her days with splendor and joy. There were wings of gray along his temples now and in the wash of moonlight they shone like the silver flash of his ever-dangerous sword. Her delft blue gaze traced that calm sardonic visage looking so young and so relaxed in sleep, caressed his mighty wingspread of shoulder and his broad chest that moved rhythmically with his steady even breathing.

She smiled at him tenderly. It was a comfort for her to see him so, to know that he would be there when she waked—for there had been other, more desperate days when she had watched his tall ship sail away, uncertain that he would ever return.

Without him, she felt she had been like a rudderless ship, that with him she had cast anchor and in his arms found her safe harbor.

She turned back to the garden again, for surely she had heard *something*, some sound that had waked her. But around her the sleeping house was silent and the stubborn thought stayed with her that the sound must have come from outside.

The white moon still drifted over the low-hanging clouds, and shadows came and went over the gardens she herself had planted, reclaiming them from the palmetto clumps and luxuriant undergrowth native to the Carolinas. For a moment her lovely face with its frame of thick luxuriant fair hair studied those gardens intently, the big live oak trees, the boxwood hedges, the shrubs imported from half a dozen countries. All of it lay spread out before her in beauty, but in the silent moonlight nothing moved.

Imogene leaned dreamily on the sill, remembering the old days, the wild rebellious days when the man asleep on the bed had been the notorious and feared Captain Ruprecht van Ryker and she his buccaneer bride. For buccaneer he had been—never a pirate. Indeed he had fought only the ships of Spain and had been always chivalrous and helpful to the ships of other countries. A privateer was what they should have called him, she thought idly, but in the wild West Indies men like van Ryker were called buccaneers. . . .

She sighed. They had changed of course.

Gone were the days when van Ryker had stormed through the Caribbean on his great ship, the *Sea Rover*, striking fear into the hearts of the Spaniards, seizing the Spanish treasure fleet entire. Gone were the hot nights in buccaneer Tortuga when, in the bedchamber of a white-plastered house overlooking blue Cayona Bay, that same van Ryker had claimed his golden bride, the lustrous Imogene. Gone—but not forgotten.

Now Imogene climbed into the window seat and sat with her chin on her knees, her arms clasped about her slender white legs, letting her light silk night rail cascade down to pile up like foam on the thick boards of the random-width cypress flooring. She looked thoughtfully out at those lovely gardens the planting of which she herself had supervised.

None of their Carolina neighbors knew of their wild past. Van Ryker, pardoned by the king, was using his real name of Branch Ryder at last and her own turbulent past was well cloaked. She was no longer the English bride of a Dutch buccaneer, but an aristocratic lady of colonial America, the elegant wife of the distinguished landgrave of Longview Plantation, whose forty-eight thousand acres stretched along the broad banks of the Cooper River and whose gracious white-pillared home rose majestically to be reflected along with the magnolias and live oaks on the river's shining surface.

In the great double drawing rooms of the floor below, where graceful French doors opened to the cooling breezes from the sea, she entertained colonial governors and burgesses and their ladies. Distinguished visitors made a point of stopping by, for not only were the food and hospitality at Longview renowned but the landgrave was a man to be reckoned with and his charming, golden-haired wife was famous for her beauty. Invitations were eagerly sought for the balls Imogene gave—and not only by the far-flung gentry of the Carolinas. People came from as far away as Virginia and Philadelphia to attend these balls and came away singing the praises of their host and hostess. *England's loss was America's gain*, they said— and went away never dreaming that the gracious host at whose carved walnut table they had just dined had once been the terror of the Caribbean, or that the elegant lady who had just shown them her rose garden and beaten them at whist had once been the toast of lawless Tortuga.

It was vaguely understood that the landgrave had inherited his family home back in England and that the Ryders sometimes went back there for short periods. And even more vaguely understood that he had some holdings in the West Indies—but that was not too unusual, many of the Carolina planters had come here from Barbados and some still had holdings there.

But the guests who strolled the handsome halls of Longview and trod a measure to the tinkle of the rosewood harpsichord in the elegant ballroom would have been startled to learn that some of these trips home to England were made roundabout by way of Amsterdam, where van Ryker had a fortune in gold earning interest in Dutch banks. And astonished to discover that Branch Ryder had indeed reclaimed his family home of Ryderwood—but only by dint of repurchasing it when it was almost a ruin, that he and Imogene seldom went there and that he had restored the hall to its former elegance only out of sentiment. Stunned they would have been to learn that a handsome townhouse on one of the best streets in London awaited this Carolina landgrave's pleasure, completely staffed and ready even to fine satin gowns and jewels for the landgrave's lady—although it too was for the most part vacant, for the former buccaneer favored life in the New World to life in the Old, and fretted when he was too long away from the Carolinas.

But most of all they would have been amazed to learn that the landgrave's handsome vessel, the *Victorious,* which rode at anchor at the mouth of the Cooper River, had once been the notorious *Sea Rover* and still voyaged every year or so to cast anchor in an unnamed Jamaica bay. In Jamaica the striking couple who appeared out of nowhere to occupy Gale Force plantation for brief periods were reputed to be from Devonshire, where it was rumored they had some great estate. It was said this particular gentleman, whose first name nobody knew at all, had inherited the Jamaica plantation from a brother who had passed on. Nobody ever saw them at balls, for they stayed to themselves at beautiful Gale Force, coming into Spanish Town only to call on the governor, who was reputed to be an old crony of theirs, supposedly from his London days. Their name was vaguely known in Spanish Town to be Ryder, and weren't they some relation to the Carolina Ryders? Different coloring of course, for the Carolina landgrave was known to be tall and dark and his lady, a great beauty, was a dazzling blond, and these Devonshire folk were just the opposite—the lady dark, the gentleman fair. Which was true enough, for when the former Captain van Ryker and his lustrous Imogene rode into Spanish Town—and most especially when they rode into Port Royal, which was still largely a buccaneer stronghold and where they might well be recognized—they wore enormously fashionable enveloping wigs, the lady's black as a raven's wing, the gentleman's of a sandy hue. At those times the master of Gale Force sported a foppish, almost French elegance of dress and a tall silver-handled cane adorned with a ribboned rosette that always seemed to come loose and demand his attention, causing him to bend over whenever someone he might once have known came too close. In similar fashion, his lady affected both a large silk parasol and an intricately carved ivory fan, which—at the right moments—effectively obscured her beautiful features. At all these foibles, the governor of Jamaica, who had known them in the old days and enjoyed keeping their secret, cocked a knowing eye.

"Your lady's as ravishing a brunette as she is a blonde, van Ryker," he was wont to say when they were alone, toying with gem-studded goblets of wine on the wide balcony overlooking his tropical garden. "And to think," he had once added softly in an aside to Imogene, "you could have been the consort of a governor and you chose instead to be wife to this great hulk of a Carolinian!"

"Your tongue is as blandishing as ever, Darnwell," Imogene had responded with a swiftly caught breath. Her delft blue eyes challenged the handsome governor. "Why do you not take a wife, Darnwell, and fill the empty rooms of this 'governor's palace' with children?"

Van Ryker, who knew that just before their arrival the governor must have cleared out the three mistresses who kept these rooms from being empty, gave Lord Marr, the governor of Jamaica, an innocent smile over Imogene's raven-wigged head. "Yes, why don't you, Darnwell?" he asked softly.

The governor cleared his throat. "It might become—overcrowded here," he maintained. "After all, this governor's residence—'palace' as you politely call it—is none so large." He hoped sincerely that none of his "women" would come sauntering in half-dressed, for he did not wish the elegant Imogene to know that he kept a disreputable household; he preferred her to think he still pined away for her—as indeed he still did at times.

"Overcrowding. Yes, there is that to consider," agreed van Ryker gravely.

Lord Marr gave him an irritable look. This damned buccaneer was poking fun at him! His gaze fell on the jeweled goblets, gift of this same "damned buccaneer," and philosophically he took a pinch of snuff from a gold snuffbox. "If I have children, I think I'd prefer launching them in some English hall," he told van Ryker frankly. "Rather than marry here and send my offspring on a dangerous voyage back to England—" He had been about to add "to be educated" but he stopped abruptly and looked stricken, for he had belatedly remembered that Imogene had lost a daughter to a "dangerous voyage."

In the awkward pause that followed, before van Ryker swiftly led the conversation down another track, Imogene winced. For her old suitor, the governor of Jamaica, had recalled to her the memory of Georgiana, the daughter she had lost. Van Ryker, noting that wince, plunged abruptly into a discussion of life in the Carolinas, which kept the governor attentive as he sipped his port.

"How is it you're never recognized, van Ryker?" he asked cheerfully. "I know you're supposed to be dead, I've heard the stories, but surely *someone* should recognize you."

"We are different people there, Darnwell," Imogene assured him demurely. "So respectable." She made herself laugh to brush the shadows away. "None there think to associate us with our old life."

Now as she looked down into her Carolina garden, all those years away from that conversation in the governor's palace in Spanish Town, she thought how true that was. Nothing of the old buccaneering life remained—except taciturn Arne, who had one day unexpectedly joined them, arriving unannounced to assume his old duties of keeper of the door just as he had at their house on Tortuga. Arne had exchanged his leathern buccaneer breeches for a suit of handsome broadcloth in deference to his new position, but he still sported his worn cutlass and his ways had not changed—he still beat the servants out of their wages at cards and dice, although Imogene did her best to restrain him. And Arne could be counted on never to speak of the past to anyone; he was close-mouthed, stomping about

purposefully on his silver-studded wooden leg. When visitors sometimes remarked in his hearing that he looked like an old pirate, Arne
would spit disgustedly and stomp away—and they took this to mean
that he scorned pirates, as indeed he did, for buccaneers were a cut
above. They were not pirates at all, actually, but unlicensed priva-
teers, some of them even going so far as to carry letters of marque
from the French governor of Tortuga. Van Ryker had never bothered
with that, believing rightly that if the Spaniards ever caught him they
would hang him high with the letters of marque hung derisively
around his neck as a lesson to others.

Arne could have told these visitors much—of how the buccaneer
van Ryker had taken the Spanish treasure *flota*, and how he had lost
Imogene and found her again, of how she had left him in anger and
been reunited with him on the Cornish coast—but he never did. He
even kept his silence the night a planter named James Scofield
passed by him in the front hall of Longview, Scofield casually
regaling his host and hostess with the tale of how the buccaneer van
Ryker and his "woman" had died on a cliff in Cornwall.

The landgrave and his lady had exchanged glances.

"And were they never found?" asked Imogene carelessly.

"Oh, yes. Their bodies were later washed ashore and identified.
A pity that he should have died, don't you think, Branch? For,
surely, by capturing the Spanish treasure fleet entire, no man did
more to break the power of Spain in this hemisphere and so secure
the Indies. From my view, he should have been knighted for it!"

His tall host looked on him rather more fondly. "Doubtless you're
right, Scofield," he agreed. "Doubtless." And Imogene warmly
agreed.

Scofield's angular wife sighed and fingered her less than regal jet
and shell necklace set in silver—they had not been able to afford a
pearl necklace, for the money had gone to buy seed and labor for the
spring planting on their large acreage. "Imagine taking the Spanish
treasure fleet!" she murmured dreamily. "I wonder what he did with
all that gold?"

Her host—he who had once been himself the notorious Captain
van Ryker—cast an amused look around him at the lavish appoint-
ments of this colonial barony over which he now reigned, and at the
gold lace and gold-shot satin of the new gown his wife was sporting
this night.

"I imagine he found a use for it," he murmured, and Imogene's glance reproved him.

"Just think what he might have done if he had lived," murmured Madam Scofield. She turned to her husband. "What do *you* think he would have done with it, James?"

Her husband, a hardworking planter, meditated a moment and chewed at his mustache. "From the tales I've heard of him, I shouldn't think he'd have wanted to do like some of those fellows when they made a great haul, and take off for Tangier or some other barbarous place," he said. "Decent sort of chap, from what I've heard—he'd want to live among his own sort, I wouldn't doubt. Most likely he'd have changed his name, emigrated to some place where nobody knew him and set himself up like a lord. Some place like you have here, Branch," he added jovially.

This was getting too close for comfort. "Let me show you my new rose garden by moonlight," Imogene interposed hastily. "I planted it only last year and with all the musk roses and damask roses, it's a magical place after dark. The roses were all sent out from England, and they survived the journey magnificently. The scent is heavenly. Just come and smell the blooms!"

Now, years later on another night in the Carolinas, she was breathing the fragrance of those same roses, for it was a long lazy fall all along the East Coast that year and roses still bloomed on the banks of the Cooper River.

With her chin on her knees, Imogene sat soberly reviewing her life—and thinking treacherously of Georgiana, the child she had lost, and who of latter years had been pushed back into memory.

If Georgiana had lived, she would be a young lady now, attracting suitors, thinking on marriage, dancing at balls, swirling with lightsome laughter through the wide corridors of Longview. She would know the whole story of her reckless mother—and forgive her. Yes, of course Georgiana would forgive her, Imogene told herself, for her Georgiana would have a generous heart. If Georgiana had lived, she would be sleeping in one of the big bedrooms down the hall right now with the moonlight silvering her burnished gold hair.

Such a yearning went through Imogene at that moment as to be actual physical pain. *If only Georgiana had lived. . . .*

"Imogene." The man on the bed had waked and noted her sitting crouched in the window seat with her head bent and her chin on her knees. "What's the matter? Can't you sleep?"

"No." Imogene turned to look at him. Her eyes were wet, but silhouetted against the moonlight he could not see that. "Go back to sleep, van Ryker," she said in a muffled voice, calling him by the name that she had so long trained herself not to use. "I'll be there soon."

Sensing something was wrong—for van Ryker had always been able to sense how she felt, her change of moods—he got up and his long naked form gleamed formidably in the moonlight as he moved toward her, leaned down and encircled her lightly with his sinewy arms.

" 'Tis good there's no one outside to see us," she murmured ruefully. "Else surely we'd become a scandal, embracing in windows!"

Van Ryker chuckled, but he had discovered when his hawklike face brushed hers that her cheeks were wet with tears. "Come now," he said in a cajoling voice, "what's troubling you? Are you regretting that you've invited so many people to visit that we probably won't get to Jamaica this year?"

"No." Imogene shook her head, burrowing into his deep comforting chest. "I love filling the house with people. And Gale Force will be just as beautiful next year."

"And Jamaica's governor—" he teased.

"Will be just as feisty," she said with a wistful smile.

"And just as much in love with you as ever," he added, seeking to cheer her up.

Imogene shrugged that off but her spirits rose. "Nonsense. He got over that long ago."

But they both knew that wasn't true. And van Ryker, looking down on her pale silky head in the moonlight, feeling her soft lovely body in his arms, thought of the dauntless spirit and fire of this woman and knew in his heart that no man who had loved her ever quite got over Imogene. Not fully.

"Then what is it that keeps you from sleeping?" he asked, letting his hand slide lightly, tinglingly, down her back.

Imogene moved restively. She didn't want to bring up Georgiana's name again—she had suffered so much over that already, and van Ryker had endured it all, helped her through it when the world seemed blackest.

"Oh," she hedged, "I was just wondering if our neighbors, the Scofields, ever figured out what the buccaneer van Ryker could have done with his gold? 'Tis a favorite subject of theirs!"

"He'd have given it to a woman of gold," said van Ryker huskily, letting his lips wander over her fair hair, down her smooth forehead, across her cheeks. "And tried his life long to make her happy with it. *Have* I made you happy, Imogene?"

Her body surged against him in a sweet silent rush that gave him his answer. Completely.

"Oh, yes, van Ryker," she breathed fervently against his chest. "I have been *so* happy with you. . . ."

With two fingers he lifted her chin so that her tearstained face came under the inspection of those keen gray eyes.

"Then why were you crying?" he asked bluntly.

Imogene looked up at him, feeling as ever the compelling pressure of his masculinity, feeling too the hopelessness of her situation—for all her tears could not bring Georgiana back.

"I woke because I thought—I thought someone called my name. And it seemed to me"—she looked away from him, stricken—"it seemed to me somehow that it was Georgiana's voice."

"You were dreaming," he said roughly, for he could not bear for anything to hurt this lovely lady of his—not even her own bitter memories. "Come back to bed." He swept her up in strong arms and Imogene, lying relaxed against his chest, was very submissive as he deposited her upon the linen sheets.

Lying there beside her, he held her silently for a while, letting her rest in the shelter of his arms, for he understood the hurt that was deep within her, the hurt that would never entirely heal. And then his gentle hands began subtly, expertly, to explore her woman's body, playing upon it as a great musician might upon a delicate musical instrument, as he lured her from thoughts of death to thoughts of life.

And Imogene, feeling her passions waked, clung to him, grateful to a heaven that had sent him her way, grateful for all the years that he had loved her.

Dreams, like dust, were brushed away as their bodies fitted together in silent communion. To van Ryker, Imogene's nearness was—had always been—heady wine. And Imogene knew the sinewy arms that held her would always be the right arms, the *only* arms.

They touched and murmured and laughed a little, for they were not
only lovers—they were friends as well. But every touch, every
murmur, every drifting sigh aroused within them further passions
and drove them on to new delights until their tumultous ardor
seemed to have a pulsing rhythm of its own that tossed them this
way and that, a throbbing beat that filled their ears and their world
like the deep resonant thrumming of far-off drums, coming closer,
ever closer, as their bodies strove toward the heights—and reaching
a crashing crescendo of delight as their passions peaked, their bodies
melded, and they drifted earthward through golden showers of
ecstasy.

And the golden haze lingered until she fell away from her lover at
last and sank into a restless, exhausted sleep.

Imogene, sleeping fitfully this night in the Carolinas, would have
been thunderstruck to know that the daughter she had long since
given up as lost when the *Wilhelmina* was sunk off the Great
Bahama Bank now occupied her old four-poster in Windgate on the
Hudson.

Chapter 9

True to his word, Brett was gone before she waked. Georgiana woke
and padded into the next room to find him gone. His big square bed
had already been made up by the industrious, early-rising, upstairs
maid. She felt a ridiculous sense of loss—he might have waked her
to tell her he was going, she told herself crossly.

She could not know that he had walked softly into her room by
the dawn's first light, before putting on his boots. That he had
stood smiling down at the lovely young girl on the bed. His gaze
had traced tenderly her slender outflung arms and her lacy white
cambric night rail, hastily donned for her excursion downstairs last
night, open at the throat and revealing a snowy expanse of breast

and a peeking pink nipple. She only stirred in her sleep when he bent to plant a light kiss on that winking nipple, but the little protesting noise she made in her throat was so childish and sweet that it caught at his heart. With a sigh he strode from the room to tug on his boots and depart for his difficult journey, first to the mill and then around the *bouweries*. He would not even get to them all, he knew, so vast was the estate. But he would cover the potential trouble spots at least—that much he could do in the time he had allotted.

For Georgiana, this first day in her new home was a day of exploration. She prowled the big rooms looking out the windows, at the huge walnut and chestnut trees that graced lawns fragrant with junipers, down the bluff to the Hudson River flowing by on its way to Storm King and the Palisades and eventually the sea. It glittered in the sunlight—half as long as the Rhine, unique and lovely, flowing down from its source in the high Adirondacks. Brett had told her the Mohawks had named this river the *Oigue*, which meant "Beautiful River." Studying the breathtaking view from Windgate's tall windows, it was easy to understand why. This was lovely country—different from the soft semitropical landscape that she had known in Bermuda—but in its way even more enchanting: rugged, picturesque, wild.

Although she had met the staff last night, it had been a hasty meeting. Today she set out to get to know them.

She found it a surprisingly international household. Although Wouter, Brett's personal servant, and Maryje the stout cook and her daughter Annekje, who assisted her, were all Dutch, the grooms and the scullery maids were Scandinavian, and the two little upstairs maids, Linnet and Belle, both fresh-faced lasses with excellent robust figures, were from Yorkshire.

"You can be my personal maid," Georgiana told Linnet impulsively when she found the girl staggering under an almost unmanageable feather mattress she was attempting to turn over. "Here, I'll help you."

Red-haired Linnet blinked, then beamed with delight as together, giggling, they managed to turn the mattress over.

"The last ones as lived here would never have done that—helped me, I mean," she told Georgiana.

"The last ones? And who were they, Linnet?" The smile froze on

Georgiana's face, for she felt she was about to hear a denunciation of her mother.

"Why, them as took over the house afore it was sold to Mr. Danforth—I mean the patroon." The girl dimpled and tucked back a lock of red hair behind her ear. "They was Dutch and court-appointed and I hear things were bad here then."

Georgiana relaxed. Not a slur on her mother, then. She had felt herself go tense. "Were they here long?"

"Oh, lor', yes." Linnet nodded her head vigorously. "For years, so they say. And it's *thought*"—she inclined her face toward Georgiana with the characteristic pose of the natural gossip and lowered her voice conspiratorially—"that they'd planned to steal everything before they left, all the silver and everything, but then—" She stopped abruptly.

Georgiana gave her a curious look. "Who were they?"

"Why, Huygens ten Haer and that mustard-haired wife of his!"

"Rychie ten Haer?" Georgiana voiced her astonishment. "But why would a patroon's daughter—?"

"They do tell a story about her. They say that Rychie ten Haer meant to marry the patroon here at Windgate all along, only they quarreled or something and he went to Amsterdam and married this other lady—your mother." Hastily. "And this Rychie was jealous and couldn't stand having another woman get ahead of her here on the river, and when they all died—I mean, your parents, ma'am—Rychie got her husband court-appointed and they lived here for a long time. *She* says now she moved away because the house was too big and gloomy, but everybody *else* says it was because the place was heavy in debt and she and Huygens, even with her father backing her, couldn't raise the money to buy it. So when her father, old Hendrik ten Haer, died, she moved back to Haerwyck, where her husband could be patroon 'cause it was plain as day he wasn't never going to be patroon here at Windgate!"

"You say they were planning to steal the silver?"

The Yorkshire girl's face reddened. "I ought not to have said that," she mumbled.

"Oh, come now! Do tell me. I can't have a maid who won't confide in me, now can I?"

Thus goaded, Linnet burst out reluctantly, "Well, they do say that when Mr. Danforth offered to pay off the debts and buy Windgate, ma'am, that Rychie was mighty happy and she said she'd just leave everything intact because her daughter Katrina was the best-looking girl on the river, same as she'd been in her day, and Katrina was sure to get it all anyway!'' Linnet laughed.

"So Rychie thought Brett would marry her daughter?''

"She was counting on Katrina's looks, I guess. Katrina's mighty striking.''

Brett had said she was striking too. Georgiana considered that a bad sign.

"Did any of the ten Haers ever come here—to visit, that is, after Brett took over?'' she asked cautiously.

Linnet frowned with concentration, trying to remember. "No-o-o, I don't think so. Of course, I haven't been here that long—just a year. I'm indentured." She dimpled at Georgiana. "When my term is out, I expect to have earned a dowry and I'll marry." She stated it as a fact.

"Oh?'' Georgiana was amused at such foresight. "And have you already picked out your young man?''

Linnet shook her heavy head of hair vigorously. "I'll wait and see what's offered. But I can tell you this, ma'am—it won't be one of those bottom-pinching sailors who swagger about New Orange!''

Georgiana felt like hooting with laughter. "And have you had much experience with sailors, then, Linnet?''

"Enough! I was black and blue, coming over here on the ship!''

Georgiana hid her mirth. "Have any balls been held here since Brett took over?''

"Not as I know of, ma'am—I don't think so. Things was very grand here when your mother was alive, they do say. Loads of silver and enough dishes for a banquet every night for supper and the servants all tuckered out. And the two of them just eating alone, and her all decked out in satin and diamonds and them stormin' at each other—'' Her face reddened. "I'm sorry,'' she said lamely. "I didn't think.''

"It's all right,'' said Georgiana firmly. "They didn't get along.'' *That much all the world knew!*

"Would you like to see where she's buried, ma'am?''

"Yes, I would. Just point the way to me, I'll go alone.''

The path Linnet pointed out to her led her to the walled family burying ground. Ivy had grown over the stones, but she tore it free and read the names on the stones. She swallowed as she read the name "Imogene van Rappard" and "Lost to the River." And beside it, amazingly, carved onto a stone was the name of Georgiana's real father, "Stephen Linnington, gentleman of Devon" and the date and a Dutch word the cook later told her meant "Tomorrow."

How strange of Verhulst van Rappard to have such a thing engraved onto a stone in his family plot, after having driven Imogene and her lover to their death!

And then on Imogene's other side was a stone the servants at Wey Gat had raised to their patroon. And it too said "Tomorrow."

Georgiana returned to the big house feeling sad. She was beginning to feel that her mother had not understood her young husband, and that if she had, everything might have been different—she, Georgiana, might have had a home and a family.

Of course, she *had* had a home and family for a while—the Jamisons. But she had only been a counterfeit daughter there, just as now she was a counterfeit heiress here.

With a rueful grimace, she went to look up Floss, who could use exercise after her long grueling confinement on shipboard.

Floss, in her stall in one of the big stone stables with their peaked slate roofs, nuzzled her delightedly.

"You look a little thin and your coat has lost its luster," Georgiana told Floss. "Fresh hay and sunshine and romping in the pasture will do wonders for that—and most of all a ride with me!" She hugged that strong silvery neck and felt Floss's tossing mane mingle with her own fair hair. When she mounted, the mare danced impatiently, eager to be off and away.

With a chuckle, Georgiana gave Floss her head and let her roam where she pleased. Together they raced through the fragrant meadows of fall, beneath trees gone red and crimson and gold. Floss was as delighted as her mistress with this tour of exploration of the Hudson River country. Georgiana indulged the mare, allowing her to stop whenever she liked to nibble the vegetation and daintily munch a bit of succulent grass here, nip a tasty weed there.

They had been riding for some time and the air was freshening with a hint of rain in it when Floss crested a little rise and Georgiana saw below her a low Dutch farmhouse.

"Well, Floss, we'll just inspect a *bouwerie!*" she told the horse merrily, and together they thundered down upon it.

The soft thud of hooves must have alerted those within, for the door flew open and a man stuck his head out. The head was as quickly withdrawn and as Georgiana neared the farmhouse she saw a mounted man, with his hat jammed down over his head and a mass of blond hair spilling out from beneath his hat, ride away fast from the back of the house and disappear into the woods without looking in her direction.

Intrigued by that, Georgiana rode in and dismounted at the farmhouse door, leaving Floss's reins dragging, for she had no fear that well-trained Floss would run away.

Before she could knock, the door opened and a heavyset black-bearded man said, "Afternoon. What's wanted?"

Somewhat daunted by his gruff tone, but mindful of the days when she had run Mirabelle single-handed, Georgiana said, in her straightfoward way, "I am Georgiana Danforth."

"Yes, ma'am," he said without inflection. "I know who you are." His hard gaze bored into hers without expression.

Surprised at that answer—news certainly must spread fast along the river!—Georgiana gave him a winning smile and asked if he was happy here and if his crops were doing well.

"Well enough," was the laconic answer.

She had half expected him to offer her a glass of homemade cider or home-brewed beer but he did not. He waited patiently while she made small talk. "The patroon's not with you?" he asked, scanning the empty landscape behind her.

"No, he's off to the mill and to inspect the *bouweries*. I thought he might have dropped by here this morning?"

"No, ma'am. Hasn't been here. I'll be wantin' to ask him when he wants the use of my horse and wagon—I be owin' him three days' use of my horse and wagon as part of my contract."

It was plain black-beard wasn't going to ask her in. Something in his gruff manner made Georgiana feel she was being dismissed. Oh, well, doubtless he had work to do and was anxious to get on with it! She was mounting Floss even as she said, "I'm sure he'll be back by Friday. If he hasn't stopped by in the meantime, I'll ask him for you then when he'll be needing your horse and wagon."

She thought she saw a flicker of satisfaction in his hard eyes as she turned Floss about, gave him a rather cold "good day" and turned to go. When she looked back from the crest of the low rise, she could see the black-bearded man was still standing there watching her.

It occurred to her then that she had seen no woman about the place nor any sign of one. That was odd. Why would a man shut himself away from the world on a lonely *bouwerie* without a woman to keep him company? How would he spend the long shut-in winter that must surely come to this northern land?

Thoughtful now, she rode home beneath lowering skies. Once, a white-tailed doe crossed her path like a bird in flight and Floss reared up. It reminded Georgiana how pleasantly wild this country was, how full of living things.

When she got home she told Linnet where she had been and was informed that the man's name was Jack Belter and that he came from Lincoln. "He pays no attention to anyone, Jack doesn't," Linnet added with a sniff. "Haughty, that's what—and no reason for it that I can see!"

"There was someone visiting him, a strongly built fellow with yellow hair. He was too far away for me to see him well, but he had the look of a gentleman about him."

Linnet looked surprised. "Jack don't mix with no one," she insisted. "Just keeps to hisself. Whoever 'twas, must have been a stranger asking the way to somewhere's else."

Yet he took flight at my appearance, mused Georgiana, and decided to ride over to Jack Belter's *bouwerie* again one day.

The rest of the day she spent inspecting the kitchen and the stores in the capacious cellars. She marveled at the extent of the preserving as she passed countless crocks of jams and jellies—gooseberry, currant, blueberry, strawberry—and saw the big crocks of brandied peaches, preserved plums, and apple butter. Deep bins held potatoes, parsnips and fragrant apples. She almost tripped over a keg of pigs' feet and gasped as she saw the great array of cheeses and the shelves of spiced fruit. There were hogsheads of corned beef and great quantities of salt pork. And would she like to see the smokehouse? Linnet, her guide, wondered. It was crammed with meat and fish. And there'd be more, for the day after the first frost was "hog-killing day" and there'd be fresh pork and sausage and then they'd cure the big hams and hang them up and smoke them.

Georgiana could see that this was basically a Dutch household— even to the "table carpet," a lightweight Oriental rug that graced the long dining table when it was not in use. She was very content to leave it so, for Dutch ways were gracious ways and based on a life of plenty.

It was lonely but grand when Georgiana sat down to her solitary dinner, facing down a long snowy cloth toward Brett's richly carved empty chair. Her heart rebelled that he should be gone but—perhaps it was better so. Now she would have time to get to know the house and the servants really well before he got back. She began to feel he might have planned it that way. . . .

The next day she did not ride out, for the sky threatened rain and she felt that Floss, still in delicate condition from her long tiresome journey, might be a little tired from yesterday's long ride. Instead she had Linnet guide her all over the house, poking into bedroom closets and seeing the big feather "puffs" that were tossed over the thick feather mattresses when the weather grew cold. The servants slept in the big attics on straw mattresses that were thick and, Linnet assured her cheerfully, quite comfortable.

"Would you want to marry a man on one of the *bouweries*?" Georgiana asked the girl curiously. "Or don't you fancy farm life?"

Linnet hesitated. " 'Tis a hard life on the *bouweries*. Although 'tis easier, I am told, under this new master. The old contracts called for a tenth of the produce and five hundred guilders' rent, which is a great sum—and two fathoms of firewood cut for the patroon and brought to the water's edge and also ten pieces of fir or oak. And besides that each *bouwerie* must furnish the patroon with twenty-five pounds of butter, two bushels of wheat, and two pairs of fowls as quit rent, and they must keep up the roads and repair the buildings and—"

"Anf furnish three days' service with horse and wagon—I know," sighed Georgiana. "It is so much I do not see how they find time to do it all. I am going to speak to Brett about it."

"Even so, I *might* marry a man on one of the *bouweries* if he were good to look at and caught my fancy. Of course, I would *prefer* a gentleman!"

Georgiana gave Linnet an indulgent look. She liked the little Yorkshire girl and determined that if and when Linnet married, she would not go to her groom clad in homespun. Linnet would have a proper wedding dress—*she* would provide it!

Which brought to mind her own dowry—that dowry she had

snatched from Mirabelle! Georgiana went downstairs, noting as she did so that the great hall had gone dark and rain was pouring down outside. There she supervised the unpacking and polishing of the two enormous candlesticks that meant so much to her, placed them prominently on the big sideboard in the dining room and stood back proudly to survey them.

"They're wonderful!" gasped Linnet. And added ingenuously, "You must have been very rich in Bermuda."

Georgiana gave her a rueful look. It had been an on-again, off-again life. From pauper to princess and back again. From surrogate princess to counterfeit heiress. Who knew what the future held?

"It was awful your not being found for so long," went on Linnet. "How did it happen you didn't come back?"

Georgiana decided not to satisfy gossipy Linnet's curiosity. They were treading on dangerous ground. "It's a long story," she said. "Come, I want to check the linens in that big chest."

"Cook calls it a *kas*," giggled Linnet. "That's a Dutch word."

"Very well," smiled Georgiana. "I want to check the linens in the *kas,* and by then it will be time for dinner."

She dressed slowly for dinner, rather overcome by how much there was to learn here. So many things were done differently from the way they were done in Bermuda—for one thing, there was so much preparation against the bitter cold to come. Listening to the rain beat down, she trailed down to dinner in one of the gowns Brett had brought to Bermuda in the big sea chest: a simply cut copper velvet that had been hastily altered to fit her. It was vastly becoming with its big detachable sleeves laced with gold, from which spilled a torrent of white lace, and its deep-cut neckline edged in copper lace.

She had hardly sat down to dinner before the heavy brass knocker on the front door sounded. Surprised that anyone should be calling at this hour and in this weather, she followed Wouter to the door, where he let in a dripping gentleman from whose hat a whole teacup of water seemed to cascade as he made her a low sweeping bow. His thick golden hair was wet too and splashed little droplets of water at her as his head came up from that bow.

"A thousand pardons," he beamed at her. "But 'tis so wet I can't ride home, for my horse is up to his fetlocks in mud! And I wondered if Windgate could give me shelter for the night?"

Startled, Georgiana realized that she was looking into the face of Nicolas van Rappard, claimant to Windgate. Nicolas, the golden Dutchman who had hailed them from the dock as they left New Orange.

BOOK III
Windgate's Mistress

From the turmoil of her past,
Where her future was forecast,
Will she win to wealth and fame?
All the river know her name?

PART ONE
The Golden Dutchman

His lips are hot and tempting....
Dare she follow where he leads?
Will she end up lost and lonely,
Victim of his reckless deeds?

CHAPTER 10

If Georgiana was daunted by the sight of Nicolas van Rappard standing on her doorstep in the rain, she was determined not to show it. Her heart was pounding but she was well aware that the custom of the day made automatic welcome to passing travelers on obligation. Had Brett been here, she knew he would promptly have extended the hospitality of Windgate to Nicolas, and she would do no less!

Her elegant copper velvet skirts swirled in a curtsy as formal as had been Nicolas's sweeping bow.

"Indeed you are most welcome," she said graciously, rising to face him—although she could not look him squarely in the eye, he was so much taller. "Come in out of the weather. We will do our best to make you comfortable, Mynheer van Rappard."

"You remember me!" he exclaimed in delight.

"I could hardly *not* remember you," she told him in a rueful tone. "Since you scandalously accused my husband of beating a retreat from you when you could plainly see his sloop had already left the dock before you hailed us! Wouter, take the gentleman's cloak, it is dripping a river on the carpet. Come, mynheer, you are just in time for dinner."

"How fortunate!" Nicolas sounded overjoyed. "For I lost my way in the woods, what with sopping branches slapping me in the face and my horse slipping and sliding on wet leaves. I missed lunch—indeed, I am weak from hunger."

He did not look weak, thought his hostess, from hunger or anything else. Now that his sodden cloak was off, she could see how resplendent were his garments—the same he had worn that day on the dock, she thought, of a becoming honey tan velvet adorned with—could his lace be ever so slightly shabby? Certainly any shabbiness was entirely overshadowed by the personality of the man. Tall and jaunty and well-formed, her golden-haired guest headed toward the dining room with a springy step. It was obvious that he knew the way. He offered her a damp velvet arm and they went in rather grandly to find another plate already set. Georgiana looked at the extra plate in surprise and met Wouter's eyes. He grinned at her and Georgiana smiled back. Word would get around that things ran smoothly at Windgate under the regime of the new bride!

Nicolas pulled back her chair with regal ceremony and they sat down, Georgiana gingerly arranging her copper velvet skirts and watching her unwelcome guest warily. Nicolas was lavish in his praise of the food.

"Windgate has flowered under your dainty hands," he told her effusively as he launched into the excellent baked capon.

"The last time I saw you, you called it Wey Gat," she challenged.

"Ah, but that was before I had time to drink in the beauty of Wey Gat's heiress." Nicolas's blue eyes twinkled at her. "Henceforth, in your honor—since you are English—I shall call it Windgate." His voice was merry.

Had he given up the effort to seize the patroonship, then? she asked bluntly.

"Oh—you understand there may yet be some little business in the courts." He shrugged, his manner noncommittal. "Nothing, I am sure that need concern you."

"Any change of ownership of Windgate would indeed concern me," Georgiana pointed out dryly.

Another merry smile split his handsome golden mustaches, drew attention to his clipped—and carefully brushed—Van Dyke beard gleaming gold in the candlelight. "That's as may be," he shrugged. "Legal things once started are hard to stop."

"I should think it would be very easy to withdraw a challenge to ownership," said Georgiana, nettled.

"Who knows?" he said airily. "But in any event we must not let such things interfere with our friendship. After all, we are, for a time at least, neighbors."

"Really?" That did surprise her. "And where is your home? Brett had not told me that you had purchased land in the vicinity."

"Touché!" He wagged an admonishing finger at her. *"Home* at the moment is at the hospitable ten Haers', who have kindly given me shelter. I assume you'll be attending their ball next week?"

"Neither Brett nor I would miss it," she assured him grimly.

"Ah, yes, Brett. Where *is* Danforth?" Nicolas looked about him as if he had just noticed her husband's absence.

"Gone to his mill and to inspect the *bouweries*."

"The new mill—of course, I had forgotten. Your husband is an enterprising man, mevrouw."

"Very." Having Nicolas captive at her table, Georgiana decided she would find out some things she wanted to know. "May I ask why it was so many years before you discovered yourself to be an heir? Surely you must have heard of Verhulst van Rappard's death long before you appeared on Windgate's doorstep!" She would have to watch herself, she realized. She had spoken of Windgate's former *patroon* as if he were a stranger, yet all the world considered him her father!

Nicolas had been polishing off the capon with relish but her question arrested him in mid-bite.

"A good question, mevrouw." The blue eyes twinkled again. "I was aboard an East Indiaman when a storm came up and I was washed overboard. Fortunately, I managed to hold on to a piece of planking and eventually came ashore on a small island. It was three years before I managed to make my way back aboard another East Indiaman. On arrival back in Holland I was told that my family had perished of the plague—which indeed was still raging in my home city of Leyden. Faced with this grim news, I chose not to return to Leyden but instead took ship for Curaçao, where I spent some years as an inter-island trader. It was by sheerest chance that I learned—so tardily, as you point out—of my Cousin Verhulst's death. And I was told, of course, that he had no surviving relatives save myself—we did not know about you then.''

Georgiana ignored that. She stared down at her untouched capon. ''You have led a venturesome life, mynheer.''

''True,'' he acknowledged carelessly, again attacking the capon with gusto. ''And a roving one. You, I understand, are from Bermuda?''

''Yes,'' said Georgiana warily. She had been toying with her food, watching him, but now she felt herself go tense.

''I have heard your story of course—as by now all on the river have heard it: how the maidservant Elise Meggs fled with you, somehow escaping death on the ice, and managed to keep your identity a secret even from you. A romantic story.'' His gaze rested on her mildly.

''I suppose it *is* a romantic story to one who did not live it,'' Georgiana agreed shortly. ''But I was too young to know what was happening. All I remember is growing up in Bermuda.''

His alert eyes held a flash of understanding. ''Yes, many events seem romantic to those who do not have to experience them.'' He sighed. ''I had hoped to hear the story from your own lips?''

Georgiana's mouth closed rather tightly. Instinctively—although his manner was kindly enough to lure her into trustfulness—she was afraid of Nicolas.

Wouter came and went from the dining room. A little maidservant brought more rolls. Outside, the rain beat down, chattering against the windowpanes.

Across the table Nicolas's pensive voice goaded her. ''Perhaps, if I heard it as you would tell it, you could even persuade me to withdraw my suit?''

''I doubt I could persuade you to do that,'' said Georgiana bitterly. ''The lavishness of this house and the extent of Windgate's land must be a tremendous incentive to lay claim!''

''You are a woman of rare understanding,'' Nicolas admitted, and she realized suddenly that his leisurely gaze was traveling rather more intently than seemed justified over the bare expanse of her white neck and bosom, that he was studying the depth of her neckline and the tempting cleavage there with fascination.

Under that hot caressing gaze, Georgiana moved restlessly. ''Perhaps I am speaking too plainly, mynheer. It is not hospitable of me. You must forgive my lapse.''

"Hospitality you have already given," he said with a magnanimous gesture. "Truth would be an even greater gift."

Was there an implied threat in his words? Certainly his tone was mild and there was no change in his bland expression.

"And what truth do you seek, mynheer?" she asked bluntly.

Nicolas leaned forward. The candlelight made his blue eyes brilliant—and hard. She had not before realized how hard. "I seek to know a little more of the lady who vanquishes me. Is that so difficult to understand?"

No, she supposed it was very natural. In his place, she might have felt the same way. She tried to relax. "What is it you wish to know, mynheer?"

"Just that you tell me of your early life so that I will understand how you—a patroon's daughter—came to be lost for so long."

"*I* was not washed overboard," she told him ironically. "I was presumed drowned when the *Wilhelmina* was fired on by a Spanish warship, burned to the waterline and sank. Nobody in New Netherland knew at the time, I suppose, that the ship had made an unscheduled stop in Bermuda to take on fresh water. It was there Elise Meggs— whom I knew as Eliza Smith—brought me ashore."

"All that I knew already. And this Eliza called you—what? 'Georgiana van Rappard'?"

"No, she called me 'Anna Smith' and passed me off as her niece."

"I see. Why would she do that? Did she not realize that the patroon your father would pay a large price to have you back?"

"I think she felt the patroon would have her head for taking me away from him," said Georgiana slowly. "For she was my mother's old nurse and when my mother—" she hesitated.

"Ran away with her lover," Nicolas prodded in a soft voice.

Georgiana stiffened. "If you have come here to insult my mother—" she began hotly.

"Forgive me, I meant no offense." He raised a hand laughingly to fend her off. "But all along the river know the story of how the lovers fled together by iceboat and were drowned when the ice gave way beneath them. Indeed, there was an eyewitness—one Schroon, who gasped out the account with an Indian arrow draining away his life.''

Georgiana had not known about Schroon. "An eyewitness who saw the iceboat go down?" she faltered.

Nicolas nodded. "I am wondering how Elise—this Eliza Smith who brought you up—managed to make her escape when the others died.''

"I do not know," said Georgiana truthfully. "She never told me."

"Then *how*"—he leaned forward—"did you discover you were daughter to the patroon of Wey Gat?"

Neither noticed that he had slipped back into calling Windgate "Wey Gat." Both were rapt in concentration.

"I learnt it from—from my husband." Georgiana's voice trembled.

"Ah-h-h-h. . . . I see. You learnt it from a fortune hunter. Then the woman who brought you up never told you any of this?"

Fury washed over Georgiana. "I also learnt it from a letter she left me!" she flashed. "And how dare you call Brett a fortune hunter?" Too late she realized what she had said. She caught her breath as across the table Nicolas van Rappard's smile deepened. He looked positively cherubic.

"Ah, so now we get to it! There is a *letter*! Excellent! Might one be permitted to see it?"

That incriminating document! Anna cursed herself for having thrown caution to the winds as she spoke out in defense of Brett. That letter could well destroy his chances!

"I have misplaced it," she said coldly. "It may have been lost in the hurried packing for the journey north. But I assure you there is a letter and it names me as Imogene van Rappard's daughter—and none could know better, for Eliza—Elise as you call her—was there when the baby—when I—was delivered. She nursed me as a child even as she had nursed my mother back in England in the Scilly Isles. Eliza kept all this from me because she feared—" *No, she could not say Eliza feared some harm would come to her, Georgiana. What harm would a man do his own long-lost child?* "She feared what might happen to her for having aided my mother in her flight," she finished.

"And so poor Elise lived in abject terror of my Cousin Verhulst all those years," Nicolas mused. "Well, I am told he was a man to be feared."

"Obviously."

"But"—his gaze was tranquil—"at some point she did sit down and write it all down for you?"

Georgiana swallowed for she saw the trap Nicolas was laying for her. "No, she did not. She dictated her story as she lay dying. Someone else wrote it down for her and she made her mark to sign it."

"Who wrote it down?"

Georgiana shrugged irritably. "Some minister—long gone. I was a small child at the time. Do not ask me to remember these things very clearly for I cannot."

That genial smile played over her again. "I had heard Elise Meggs could neither read nor write," he admitted.

Cold hands seemed to caress her. She must tread warily with Nicolas. Suppose she had tried to brush him off by simply agreeing when he asked if Elise had written it down? He would have trapped her neatly!

"What kind soul did you say wrote it down for her?" he wondered.

"The minister. His name I've forgotten. He took down what she said on her deathbed and witnessed it."

Nicolas looked pensive. "A deathbed statement—yes, that would have some force. And when she died, you rummaged among her things and found it?"

"No," choked Georgiana.

"No," he agreed. "For Elise Meggs died while you were still a child and if you had known of your great inheritance then while you were penniless you would certainly have told someone, would you not?"

He knew too much! Erica Hulft must have made exhaustive inquiries about Anna Smith in Bermuda—she must have discovered all these things and told Nicolas!

"She entrusted her dying words to the minister who witnessed the paper and instructed that it be delivered to me on my wedding day!" snapped Georgiana defensively.

"And why did *he* not apprise you at once of the contents, since it was obvious you would be a great heiress once the facts were known?"

"He was sworn to secrecy!" cried Georgiana. "Eliza had made him take oath on it and he honored that oath!"

Nicolas, who had been leaning forward, fell back and cast a mystified look at the ceiling. "Now why would Eliza do that?" he puzzled. "The woman was dying, Verhulst could not hurt her, he was long dead—"

"Eliza did not know he was dead!"

"All right, granted she did not know Verhulst was dead. That is almost worse. Since her death would put her beyond Verhulst's reach, why would she not at that point have returned you to him so that you could assume your rightful place in the world?"

His logic could not be faulted. Georgiana felt smothered. "Remember, Eliza was dying," she said steadily. "She had lived in fear of him for so long she may not have thought of that."

"H'mm," he said thoughtfully. "So this minister who witnessed the document gave it to you?"

"No, he had left the island. It was his successor."

"His successor?"

"Mr. Cartmell, the minister of St. Peter's Church in St. George."

"And Cartmell gave you the letter in advance, knowing that you were to be married in New Orange?"

Georgiana had the uneasy feeling that all of this was going to be checked. "Brett and I had an earlier wedding ceremony in St. Peter's Church," she admitted. "Mr. Cartmell officiated. Afterward he gave the letter to Brett. There are witnesses who saw Brett leave with the packet!" she finished in exasperation.

"The *packet*?" Nicolas looked fascinated.

"Packet," she repeated woodenly. "I am neglecting my duties as a hostess, mynheer. Will you not have some more of the capon? Or some of this river shad? I am sure you will find it very tasty." She had let her own food grow cold but she went hurriedly on, urging on him ham and rolls and vegetables—anything to keep him from interrogating her further, for she felt she was getting mired in deeper and deeper. Nicolas seemed to sense her reluctance and desisted. He took ample helpings of everything she offered and ate thoughtfully.

Suddenly he looked up. "You have set my mind at rest on many things, mevrouw, but I am still perplexed about one thing. How did you live, all these years in Bermuda? Was this Elise Meggs—this Eliza Smith as you knew her—independently wealthy?"

Georgiana stiffened. "You know as well as I do that Eliza Smith was a servant," she told him haughtily. "She supported herself in Bermuda as any servant must—she took employment."

"Employment?" he echoed.

"She bound herself."

"So you were supported in Bermuda by a bondswoman, and yet a story has reached me that you were wealthy there, that you wore fine clothes and cut a dashing figure on your horse. You were accepted as the daughter of the house on a plantation called Mirabelle."

Erica Hulft had undoubtedly told him that!

"That is true. The Jamisons of Mirabelle had lost their only child. They brought me up after Eliza died and treated me as their own daughter."

"Then you are twice an heiress?" he murmured.

Georgiana shrugged and urged on him more wine. She had no doubt that even now a ship was hurrying to Bermuda to find out all about Anna Smith's recent past—and they would learn much! But *she* at least did not have to supply the information.

"These candlesticks that you see on my sideboard were a gift from Samantha Jamison for my dowry," she told him ironically, and had the grim satisfaction of seeing Nicolas's eyes widen.

"A lavish gift," he commented. "They must be worth a king's ransom!"

"I don't think of them in terms of money," said Georgiana quellingly. "They are dear to me because they were at Mirabelle and had been part of Samantha Jamison's dowry when *she* was wed."

"Will we be seeing something of these Jamisons?" wondered Nicolas.

Georgiana wished she had not spoken. "No, they are both dead."

"Then you have already inherited from them?"

"Mynheer, you ask too many questions," said Georgiana crisply. She wished in her heart that she had cut off this conversation long before this. "Guest or no, this inquisition is beginning to weary me. You see the candlesticks before you, I have told you my story. Let us make an end of it."

"True, you have told me your story." He gave her an indulgent smile. "But, then, Brett is such a resourceful fellow, and a man of such wealth as might sway others to—" He let the words drift off, leaving the subtle implication that Brett might have purchased the witness, purchased the candlesticks.

White-faced at his implication, his hostess rose. "Stay where you are," she told him menacingly. "I will settle this conversation in a way that even *you* will find hard to refute, mynheer!"

She left him looking mildly astonished and went upstairs. When she returned she was wearing the gold and sapphire ring that had belonged to Imogene.

"With your thoroughness, mynheer, I am sure you must have not only a list of all the furnishings and linens in this house but certainly a list of the jewels Verhulst van Rappard gave his wife!"

Nicolas gave a pained, deprecating shrug, indicating that this might be so.

"Then I think you will recognize this," she said ruthlessly, flashing the stone at him. "It was my mother's. But in case you do not, I suggest you read the inscription." She tore off the ring and tossed it onto the table.

Nicolas caught it as it bounced. "You are careless with a valuable stone, mevrouw!" He was turning the ring over in his hand.

"My patience is at an end," she cried. "Read the inscription!"

Nicolas held up the ring and squinted his eyes to read the inscription by the light of the candles. *"To Imogene, my golden bird of Amsterdam,"* he read.

"There is one other word you have omitted from the inscription," Georgiana told him in a chilly voice. "That word is *'Verhulst.' This* was in the packet!"

Nicolas looked again, squinting. When he looked up his gaze was suddenly very sharp, very penetrating. "This is but one of her jewels," he said in an altered voice. "Cousin Verhulst showered his bride with gems."

"I know." The journal had mentioned that, bewailing a man who would give gifts of gems but never the gifts of trust, of comradeship, of confident abiding love.

Nicholas leaned forward, his blue eyes intent upon her face. "You mean *you* have the van Rappard diamonds?" he demanded incredulously. "It was presumed they went down when the iceboat sank into the Hudson!"

That brought Georgiana up short. Her mother had been vague about the jewels Verhulst had given her, as if they did not much matter to her—or as if other things mattered so much more. She had never once mentioned the van Rappard diamonds. She would have to tread more carefully, she saw.

"You are to presume what you like," she said loftily. "I only brought you this ring as proof because you claimed kinship with me!"

"But you *do* have them?" he prodded.

Georgiana thought it safer to stick to the truth. "No, I had only some lesser pieces my mother had given Elise," she said honestly.

Some of the tension seemed to go out of the man before her. Silently he handed her back the ring. "I think I owe you an apology, mevrouw." His voice was bland; she did not trust it.

"I think you do! But in any case you have given me a headache. I will bid you good night, mynheer."

"Nicolas," he corrected her imperturbably.

Georgiana brushed that aside. She did not feel she had arrived at a first name relationship with this irritating Dutchman. "Linnet, my maid, will show you to your room," she said stiffly. "I trust you will rest well. A hot bath will be brought up to you shortly. And breakfast will be brought to your room in the morning—myself, I do not rise till noon." A lie, but a useful one for she did not want to see Nicolas van Rappard on the morrow. If tonight was any sample of his zeal, he would have a whole new batch of probing questions for her then!

Nicolas saw he was being dismissed. He rose with alacrity. "I am sure I will be most comfortable, mevrouw. Although I wish," he added plaintively, "that you would call me Nicolas and let me call you Georgiana, since it seems we are blood cousins."

Georgiana gave him a baleful look. "It will take time for me to feel close to you, mynheer," she said in a cutting voice. "Perhaps a lifetime!" Her velvet skirts swirled as she turned to take her leave.

"Nevertheless, I bid you good night—Georgiana," he called after her. "It is my hope that we shall be good friends." He sounded quite happy. "Perhaps the weather will be so inclement that I will not be able to ride back?" he added hopefully, inclining his head to listen to the patter of the rain as he followed her to the stairs. "Then we might enjoy lunch together?"

On the stairway Georgiana turned regally. "If the weather be foul or too muddy for you to attempt the ride downriver, you will be delivered to the ten Haers' by sloop, mynheer—I shall leave word with the *schipper* of the *River Witch* that it be done!''

"Dismissed, dismissed," he chuckled, his admiring gaze enfolding her like a blanket. "And dismissed by such a beautiful lady. I could imagine you clad in gossamer silk—"

"*Good night*, mynheer," she told him firmly.

"Good night. Until the ten Haers' ball, Georgiana!"

Georgiana ground her teeth as she fled up the stairs. She hoped she had seen the last of Nicolas. Still, insufferable as he was, there had been an appreciation of womanflesh gleaming from those sparkling blue eyes and merry devils danced invitingly in his smile. A man who might sway many a woman—not such a one as herself, of course!

Chapter 11

Georgiana had a hard time falling asleep, for the harrowing thought occurred to her as she got into the big square bed that she should not have told Nicolas that the ring was in the packet, for Brett had acquired that ring thorough Erica Hulft's brother and might not Erica have known about it—and told Nicolas? If so, she must invent some new lie and brazen it out!

She awoke with the whole thing preying on her mind and saw that the rain had stopped and the sun rode high in the heavens. A deep sense of relief stole over her—her unwelcome guest would now be gone, either by horse or, if the terrain was too muddy, the *River Witch* would have taken him away.

She sat up in bed with a gasp. She had forgotten to send word to the *schipper*! Would he perhaps have taken it upon himself to transport Nicolas back to the ten Haers'? Not likely! She got up and ran to the window. The *River Witch* was not in sight.

She frowned—and then realized what in her excitement she had forgotten: that Brett must have taken the *Witch*. He must have sailed to the mill—not ridden as she had supposed. And he could have taken a horse with him, or picked up a horse at one of the *bouweries* for his ride "into the tamaracks."

All of which meant that the dangerous golden Dutchman was still at Windgate. Waiting for her, downstairs.

Hastily she donned a turquoise velvet riding habit that had been among the things in the sea chest. It was smartly tailored and had a rakish look to it—exactly the way she wanted Nicolas to view her: sophisticated, worldly—not some simple maid he could cozen! Her small chin was carried very high as she clattered down the broad front stairway in her riding boots. Breakfast could be got through—somehow. And after that she meant to speed her unwelcome guest on his way, even if it meant mounting Floss and showing him the way home herself!

Nicolas was waiting for her in the big drawing room, standing before one of the tall windows, looking out at the miraculous view of the river and the opposite bluffs. His hair spilled thick and golden onto his shoulders, mingling with the heavy point lace of his white linen collar. A fresh one from his saddlebags, no doubt! She guessed irritably that last night Nicolas had timed his arrival well, that he had had every intention of spending the night at Windgate.

He stood at his ease and in the bright sunlight she could see him better than she had last night by flickering candlelight. The deep honey tan of his cut-velvet doublet and trousers went well with his coloring, she noted critically. Their excellent cut and fit showed to advantage his robust masculine figure. Looking at his broad jaunty back, Georgiana wished suddenly that Brett cared more for clothes. All *his* money had been poured into Windgate and the big press where he kept his clothes was practically bare. Except for the dull gray satin trousers and brocaded doublet he had worn on the occasion of their second wedding ceremony in New Orange—and closer inspection had revealed both to be quite worn and the Venetian lace he had worn at his throat much mended, although snowily white; he had nothing suitable to wear to a ball or reception. He was still wearing the same russet cloth suit he had worn in Bermuda and she supposed he would wear the gray to the ten Haers' ball.

She sighed and Nicolas swung around.

Although he could hardly have missed hearing her clattering descent down the stairs, Nicolas had waited until Georgiana was well in the room before he turned about. It was as if he wanted her to have time to study him as he posed there before the window with the shining river behind him so she could observe what a dashing figure he cut, she thought crossly. At sight of her his golden brows shot up, a smile of delight lit his broad face, and he swept her a bow that would have done credit to a courtier at any court in Europe.

"Ravishing!" he pronounced. "I have not seen a riding habit cut so well since I was at the French court."

"And when was that?" wondered Georgiana, taken aback.

"Oh, a few years ago."

"But I thought you had spent all your recent years in Curaçao and the West Indies—or being washed overboard in the Far East?" She sounded a bit sharper than she meant to.

He gave her a tolerant look of pure amusement and her cheeks grew hot. Of course it was all a pack of lies! He had been God knew where all those years—perhaps even in Bermuda! No—surely she would have seen him if he had been in Bermuda. Such a figure as he cut was hard to miss!

"I am even more amazed at your determination," he added, his puzzled gaze passing down her tight riding habit and up again.

"Determination? What determination, mynheer?"

"To clatter down the stairs dressed for riding when your horse is sure to sink in mud up to her fetlocks. Did you not hear it raining late last night? It was heaviest at dawn."

"No, I must have slept through it."

"That bespeaks a clear conscience!" he laughed.

"When I woke and looked out the window, I could see it was damp out but—is it really so very muddy?"

"Through the window I have been watching one of your servants trudge across the lawn carrying a pail. He has slipped and dropped it twice. Even on the lawn his feet are sinking."

Georgiana's heart sank even deeper. Plainly she would have Nicolas on her hands for another day. One could not turn a guest out without reason and hers would seem flimsy enough to anyone who did not know the whole truth—even Brett would not countenance it.

"Besides," he added genially, "as you can also see by the window, it is clouding up to rain again."

More rain. That was all she needed!

"Perhaps Brett will abandon his plan to visit the outlying *bouweries* and come home early," she suggested, her turquoise eyes sending off warning sparks.

"More likely he is bogged down like the rest of us," declared Nicolas cheerfully. "Indeed, if this weather keeps up, I may be the one to escort you to the ten Haers' ball rather than your husband!" His blue eyes sparkled at the thought.

"If the weather is so soggy as you would suggest," she told him coldly, "neither one of us could get to the ball because the *River Witch* is upriver with Brett and I have no intention of arriving at the ten Haers' in a rowboat."

"Yes, I wondered last night if you had not noticed the *Witch*'s absence," he murmured. "When you told me so regally that I should leave aboard her."

Georgiana felt a flush creeping into her cheeks. "I had forgot Brett took the *Witch*."

"Of course." He smiled wickedly. "And then too you were excited. I had the feeling I had somehow upset you."

Georgiana drew a deep breath—and wished she hadn't, for Nicolas's admiring gaze was riveted on the sudden strain of the turquoise material of her bodice.

"Shall we go in to breakfast?" she asked menacingly.

"By all means." Gallantly he extended his velvet arm and she took it, fuming. "But we would have no need to attend the ball in a rowboat. If I am not back by Friday, the ten Haers will send a sloop upriver to see what has happened to me, we will hail it from the pier and arrive at the ball in good style."

"Why would they wait till then?" she wondered. "Since you were on your way back yesterday, I would expect them to be worried *now* and think something had happened to you."

"Oh, no," he said casually. "I often wander away for a few days. They assume I am wenching." He grinned.

She felt that last was meant for her and gave him a warning look. "I hope you like pancakes, mynheer, for that is what we are having."

"And a few other dishes also, I see," he said, scanning the loaded table. "Yes, I am fortunate to like pancakes and most other foods. I can do justice to a second breakfast!" His manner was blithe. He held out her chair and, once they were both seated, embarked on a roster of the exotic dishes he had sampled in various parts of the world. As he ate, he threw in careless remarks like: "The native girl who shared that dish with me wept when I left but what could I do? The ship was sailing within the hour!" And "I could have had not only the steamed oysters there, but a large plantation as well, had I been willing to wed and bed my host's daughter! But enticing as was her bustline and wicked as were her green eyes, my foot has always tended to wander." And "Now, at the Court of St. James's they flavor it differently."

Georgiana, eating silently and listening to her voluble guest, realized she was being charmed, impressed, rallied, and withal vastly entertained by an experienced man of the world. She wondered what had wrought this miraculous change in Nicolas. Yesterday he had been her clever adversary—today he seemed more like a suitor! She began to believe that Erica's brother had died without ever telling Erica about the ring. If Nicolas had known the ring could not possibly have been in the packet, as she had claimed last night, certainly by now he would have charged her with it! That he had not, made her spirits rise.

After breakfast, Nicolas insisted on teaching her to play chess. That he could point out exactly which cupboard housed the chess set showed her precisely how conversant with this house Nicolas was. Of course, he might have found it this morning, he might have been poking about as he waited for her to come down to breakfast but . . . suddenly Brett's words floated back to her: *It seemed the lady herself intended to be mistress of Windgate. . . .*

Erica!

And Brett had said he'd thought he could trust Erica until he found her *in Nicolas van Rappard's arms*. Could that have happened *here*? The thought made Georgiana's eyes sparkle, for if it was Nicolas who had removed the lustrous Erica from Brett Danforth's field of vision, then Nicolas was of some use after all! She resolved to be more gracious to him.

They enjoyed a long leisurely lunch, idly picking at roast pheasant and wild duck and half a dozen other dishes. Listening raptly to the handsome Dutchman's witty stories, Georgiana wondered how he had come to speak English so well—so far Nicolas had told her at least three versions, all of which she doubted! So thoroughly did she enjoy his droll company, now that he had abandoned—permanently, it seemed—the subject of her doubtful inheritance, that she did not even notice as the afternoon wore on that the weather, changeable in the morning, was clearing up.

When at last he rose and suggested doubtfully that his horse might be able to make it back to Haerwyck now, Georgiana wouldn't hear of it.

"You must stay to supper," she told him warmly. "And the night as well. I am sure the ground is still very soft."

Nicolas's gaze on her was very soft too.

"I should like that, Georgiana," he said in a low timbred voice.

Georgiana breathed a little faster. She went out to confer with cook about dinner.

Cook was a big energetic woman, much given to the use of herbs and spices. She sang off-key at her work, and around her thick neck hung, conspicuously, a string of Job's tears, which Linnet had whispered was a cure-all fruit much favored by the Dutch.

"But cook looks so healthy!" Georgiana had protested.

"Never sick a day," grinned Linnet. "She wears it to *ward off* what might come!" Her laughter had pealed.

Now, looking at that necklace, and cook's round, honest, perspiring face as she bent over to sample with a long spoon some broth from a black iron pot that hung suspended above the flames of the hearth, Georgiana smiled. At cook's behest, she tasted the broth, agreed it could use a mite more parsley and yes, indeed, some bay leaves might help.

"Where did you get your necklace?" she wondered, hoping cook would tell her some fabulous tale of a peddler with exotic promises.

"Well, I—" for a moment cook's honest face looked confused. "It was give to me," she muttered. "By a gentleman."

Georgiana blithely imagined some stout Dutchman in voluminous breeches solemnly calling on cook. "And do you find Job's tears effective in maintaining your health?" she asked gravely.

"Indeed I do!" Cook bobbed her head emphatically. "I haven't been sick a day since this necklace was give to me!" She considered a moment. "I know where you could get one."

Georgiana was touched, but she turned down cook's offer with a light heart. It occurred to her suddenly that she was feeling awfully good today. Surely everything was going to be all right! That her newfound optimism might be due to Nicolas's influence did not occur to her. When cook solemnly assured her that they had a batch of fresh-caught eels, enough for a feast, Georgiana went back to the drawing room and asked Nicolas if he liked eels.

"Well, not as close traveling companions!" he responded with a grin. "Did I tell you how I got up to propose an after-dinner toast and fell off the ten Haers' sloop into the river along with a bucket of eels?"

"No, you didn't," laughed Georgiana, "although I can see that you're going to! But I wasn't asking you to dine *with* eels, Nicolas— just *on* them!"

Nicolas asserted that he was very fond of eels, but added softly, "Indeed, sweet cousin, I doubt I shall taste anything at your board, for the spice of your presence overshadows all!"

"You are given to extravagant compliments, sir!"

"Only when the lady is extravagantly beautiful," he asserted sturdily.

"Nonsense." Georgiana gave him a demure look. "I am sure you would do justice to cook's eels were I not even here! She prepares them masterfully."

"Yes," said Nicolas thoughtfully. "I remember."

For a moment that brought Georgiana up short. Nicolas *remembered*? He remembered the cooking, he knew the way to the dining room, he had moved directly to the chess set.

"Nicolas, has Brett entertained you here?" she asked blankly.

"Never," he said promptly.

"Then how—?" She gave him a mystified look.

Nicolas was grinning at her. "I have dined here," he amended. "But not with the master." With perfect aplomb, he added, "I dined in the servants' wing."

Nothing could have surprised Georgiana more. Her jaw dropped. *"In the servants' wing?"* she gasped.

Nicolas nodded airily. "And they were delighted to show a stranger around—especially one who was cousin to the builder."

"Did Brett know of this?" she asked, fascinated.

Nicolas shrugged. "I doubt it." And in response to the mixture of expressions on her face, "Come now, Georgiana," he said plaintively. "I had just landed, I was new to the river, I knew no one. I was understandably anxious to see my inheritance without delay. Brett was away somewhere and his household staff graciously gave me hospitality.''

"Wouter must have been away too," she said quietly. She could not imagine Wouter letting a stranger wander through these rooms, rummaging through cupboards.

"Yes, I believe Wouter was confined to his bed with a cold," acknowledged Nicolas. "Anyway, you will be glad to know that I paid for my supper. I gave cook a necklace of Job's tears to cure all her ills.''

Georgiana sat staring. Then she broke into wild laughter.

"*You*?" she cried incredulously. "*You* are the 'gentleman' who gave her the necklace? Oh, Nicolas, you *are* a scoundrel! She is healthy as a horse!"

"And doubtless the necklace will keep her so!" He looked very pleased with himself.

Georgiana doubled up with laughter.

Dinner, as she had expected, was a rollicking meal, with Nicolas recounting droll stories and proving himself once again a mighty trencherman, devouring enough eels to please even cook, who believed all mortals to be on the verge of collapse if they were not stuffed like a Christmas goose. When the servants were out of earshot, Georgiana merrily teased him about ingratiating himself with cook and Nicolas took it all in good part, plainly enjoying the raillery as much as she did. And afterward, over the fine wines—for Georgiana was serving him the best from Windgate's cellars—he sat across from her lazily enjoying the view.

That view was very good, for Georgiana had dressed with exceeding care tonight for a guest who—now that he had left off baiting her—she now made most welcome. Her gown of peachbloom velvet was cut dashingly low and just a hint of gold lace barely protected her pink nipples from peeping out. The sleeves were huge and slashed and lined with matching peachbloom satin embroidered with gold threads. A special chemise had come with this dress—the loveliest in the sea chest of garments Brett had bestowed on her—and it was of a deeper peach cambric. Its fluffy sleeves poured fashionably out of the larger oversleeves and just below the elbow spilled a torrent of gold lace like a waterfall over her slender arms. The tight bodice swept down into a V below the waist and the peachbloom velvet overskirt was split down the front and caught up

in great billowing panniers at the sides to reveal her best petticoat—
of gold satin so heavily embroidered with roses stitched of glittering
gold threads that the effect was a golden shimmer as she moved.

"You should wear that gown Friday night at the ten Haers' ball,"
Nicolas exclaimed. "You will be a sensation in it!"

Georgiana flushed with pleasure. This was indeed the gown she
intended to wear to the ball. The best seamstress at Windgate had
spent the last two days making careful alterations to sleeves and skirt
and bodice. No matter that there were still a few pins left in it—in
fact one of them was sticking her right now—she had worn it tonight
to "try it out" on this experienced courtier to see what impression it
would make on him. Apparently it was a success!

"You should wear your hair that way also," he added critically.
"Those little gold ornaments catch the candlelight and sparkle like
fireflies whenever you turn your head."

Georgiana could not help but be pleased, for she had dressed her
hair with great care in the latest fashion and the impression of a swirl
of golden hair lit with moving fireflies was exactly the impression
she had intended to give.

"In Peru," he told her negligently, "the ladies of Spain wear real
fireflies caught up in their hair and attend balls looking as if dozens
of tiny candles are caught in their curls."

"You have been to Peru?" This was really impressive, for Peru
was Spanish. For a Dutchman to have been there must mark him
either as a spy or an adventurer who counted his life for little.

"Oh, yes, I have been to Peru." Although he was still wearing
the same honey-tone velvet suit, he had brought an abundance of
fresh linen in his saddlebags and looked very fit. Fresh lace-point
boothose spilled over the tops of his wide-topped boots and a
cascade of cambric and heavy white point lace spilled out from
beneath his heavy and slightly wavy golden hair. He looked dauntingly
splendid across the table. Georgiana felt wickedly that any girl along
the river would envy her her handsome guest. "Indeed I have been
to Peru more than once," he told her, lifting his wineglass lazily to
study its ruby light. "I was once in the service of a Spanish
grandee." He laughed at her startled look. "Of course he was
somewhat deceived—he thought me a minor nobleman of Valencia,
one José de Garcia. My Spanish is excellent, Georgiana."

"Indeed it must be!" Like his other stories, she doubted this one,

but she listened with delight as he brought to her a far-flung world of
glamour and danger, of languorous South American nights spent
with a variety of beautiful women—he skimmed over those, telling
her just enough to tantalize her. "My hands could span her waist,"
he would say. "And she had a delicious habit of nibbling on my ear
whenever her husband was not about!" Or "Her father never
guessed that she spent those hours in my arms." Or "She was a
passionate wench—I beg your pardon, Georgiana, but she is one of
my favorite memories!"

Georgiana was kept laughing and gasping by his revelations. Had
he really seduced the Spanish grandee's daughter? she asked herself.
Had the unlikely combination of an enamored chambermaid and a
housekeeper who had been duped into believing him her long-dead
son, really joined forces to help him escape the dungeons?

It was another magical evening.

CHAPTER 12

When they had finished their after-dinner wine, they went into the
drawing room. Nicolas sat down at the small rectangular virginal
and ran his fingers lightly, expertly, across the keys and sang to her
in his throaty masculine voice the love songs of half a dozen nations.
Georgiana leaned on a peachbloom satin arm with gold lace spilling
over the polished rosewood of the virginal and asked herself dreamily if Verhulst van Rappard had only been like his Cousin Nicolas,
what might life at Wey Gat have been like? Certainly Imogene
would have sung for joy in the mornings, and instead of steadfastly
refusing to learn to play this delicate virginal that Verhulst had gone
to so much trouble to import for her—this she knew from Imogene's
journal—she would have dazzled the night with the tinkling keys
and sung love songs without end.

"You should be wearing jewels, Georgiana." Nicolas had stopped playing. Now he sounded one last plaintive chord as he gazed pointedly at the white column of her neck. "A necklace at the least."

"Oh, I—" Georgiana had almost said "Bernice took them all" but she remembered in time and said, "I brought no jewelry with me from Bermuda."

If that seemed strange to him, he did not remark on it. Instead he frowned. "Has Danforth given you no jewels?"

He had given her the gold and sapphire ring that she now wore on her finger, but she could not tell Nicolas that, having already claimed she had had it from the packet Elise left for her.

"He will," she said. "In time. Of course, I have this ring." She flashed it deliberately for him to see, hoping that if he did know its origin he would speak now.

"Yes, you showed that to me yesterday." He was still frowning. "You are like a peach in that gown, Georgiana, a beautiful ripe peach, but any lovely peach deserves a frosting of dew and *you* deserve a frosting of diamonds."

Georgiana's laughter pealed. " 'Tis plain you made your way well at court, Nicolas." She had fallen into the habit of calling him Nicolas just as he now called her Georgiana. "In whatever country you found yourself!"

"Ah, but I am serious, Georgiana. Your gown needs but that one last touch to make you ravishing!"

"Then I shall have to go unravished," she told him, amused. "For I have no 'frosting of diamonds' to wear!"

"I hope you will not think me overbold," he murmured, and rose, reaching into his pocket. "But I cannot let such a luscious peach be brought into so public a view without at least a small frosting of dew."

He brought out a delicate necklace of intricately wrought gold that flashed in shiny points like the tiny golden ornaments in her hair—and from the necklace was suspended a pendant, a small teardrop of a diamond.

"The drop of dew I spoke of," he said softly, and reached out to clasp the necklace around her throat.

So stunned was she by this unexpected gift that he had closed the clasp before she found voice to protest, "But I cannot accept such a gift from you, Nicolas!" She sounded shocked.

"Why not? It is but a trifle."

"It is valuable and you know it!"

Nicolas shrugged. "Value is a relative thing. About *your* delicate throat it does appear to have great value. On *my* sinewy neck it would fade into insignificance."

"Not *your* neck, Nicolas," she laughed. "Your lady's!"

"But I have no lady to wear it! Perhaps if I lent it to you just for the evening?" He gave her a wistful look.

"No, not even that. Brett would be furious!"

"Ah, yes—Brett." He made the name sound distasteful. "A patroon who gives his wife no jewels."

"Give him time, Nicolas—I am but a bride!"

"*My* bride," he said, his body seeming to move slightly toward her, "would have jewels on her wedding day. I would see to that!"

His nearness was heady wine. He was a handsome male animal, a vigorous man in his prime, and he desired her. That much was plain. *And he had come to Windgate carrying with him a diamond necklace....*

"A man does not carry a diamond necklace with him on idle jaunts about the country," she said breathlessly.

"No, he does not." He was inching closer, she could feel his strong masculine presence closing in on her.

"You did not merely happen by and get caught in a drenching rain, Nicolas. Windgate was your destination!"

"True," he smiled. "Although the rain made me arrive late."

"*You* were the man who rode away from Jack Belter's *bouwerie* day before yesterday," she accused. Her eyes widened. "You knew Brett had gone upriver!"

"He passed by me on the *River Witch*."

"And yet the next day you came on to Windgate."

He nodded and his smile deepened.

"To see me?" It was a whisper.

"To see you, Georgiana. I had glimpsed you from the dock, and on board the *River Witch* you looked very enticing and very lovely. I could not wait for the ten Haers' ball—I had to see you again."

She was startled.

"Then the ten Haers know where you are?" she exclaimed.

"Oh, yes."

"And you told them to send a sloop for you if you were not back by Friday?"

Again he nodded.

She could hardly believe it. "But you surely could not have expected it to rain until then?"

"I had hoped for a flood," he said plaintively. "To be trapped here with you, surrounded by an impassable sea of mud."

Georgiana gasped, not sure whether to laugh or be angry with him. This was all going too fast for her. Last night's inquisition, today's right-about-face, and now this blatant admission that it had all been *planned*! "I don't know what you expected to gain by it," she said, trying to move away from him.

He caught her by the shoulders. His voice was low and intense. "Georgiana, can you not believe that a man can fall in love with a woman on first sight?"

"No." She shook her head to clear it. "No, you were not in love with me when you came here yesterday. Do not pretend that you were. You played a cat and mouse game with me then. What game is it you are playing with me now?"

"I had to make certain that you were really Verhulst's daughter," he said with a frankness that startled her. "And not some light wench Danforth had hired for the occasion."

Her look of blank shock seemed to amuse him.

"I see they preserve innocence in Bermuda," he said whimsically. "It must be a delightful place!"

"But"—she recoiled from him—"you couldn't think that of Brett, that he would do such a thing!"

His eloquent shrug spoke volumes. "In my less than sheltered life, I have seen worse done—and for far less. Be fair, now. In my place would you not have wished to make certain that the heiress to Wey Gat was truly who she claimed to be?"

"Then all of those things you said yesterday—"

"Were to test you. And you passed that test. Ah, Georgiana," He shook his head and his heavy golden hair moved luxuriously on his broad velvet shoulders and his face was wistful. His voice deepened, grew richer. "Believe me when I say this: I have roved the world and never anywhere have I met a woman so desirable as you. I did not come here to question your claim to Wey Gat—only to ascertain that you were in truth Verhulst van Rappard's daughter. And you are—the ring proved it beyond doubt. For it fit your story—how else could you have come by it? Indeed, I hope that you will be mistress here forever!''

Georgiana blinked. These revelations were coming too fast for her.

"I only wish I had met you first—instead of Danforth," he sighed. "Ah, Georgiana''—he reached out to caress her hair with light fingers—"you do not know what you do to me."

He did not know what he did to her either! she thought uneasily. Her heart was thumping in her chest and she jumped, and jerked her head away as his questing fingers touched her earlobe.

"I would put jewels on those lovely ears," he said softly. "I would encrust your neck and arms with sparkling gems. I would take you to Paris and London and Amsterdam."

"Nicolas," she cried in bewilderment. "You are talking to me as if I were some young girl in need of a husband!"

"And so you are." He stated it flatly. "You are in need of a husband who will stay by your side and protect you from such as I! A husband who will marry you not for gold or land but for the turquoise depths of your eyes!"

"You don't seem to understand, Nicolas. Brett and I are *legally married*."

"Yes." Calmly. "Twice."

"Then you should consider me doubly wed!"

"I consider you"—his hand left her hair and passed down her shoulder, down her arm, for he surged forward even as she tried to back away—"the most gorgeous, the most desirable woman in the world, Georgiana. If I thought you could love me, I would make you a widow with this sword!" With a sudden violent gesture he touched his sword hilt.

She recoiled. "I don't believe this! I hardly know you! You are a guest in my home and now suddenly you declare your love and threaten to kill my husband?"

His face was very near, his concentration so intense that she felt dizzy. "I have gone too fast for you?" His voice was pleading. "Think on it, Georgiana. As you come to know me better, perhaps you will find some pity in your heart for my plight."

It was on the tip of her tongue to tell Nicolas that she would have little chance to know him better, for she would probably be snowbound here at Windgate during the long winter and he would be similarly snowbound at Haerwyck, but she was almost afraid to say anything for clever Nicolas had a way of twisting everything to his advantage. Nicolas van Rappard was more attractive than a man should be, he had a glib tongue, he was without principles or morals—and she would not listen to any more of this.

"I thank you for the thought, Nicolas," she said in as steady a voice as she could muster, "but would you please get this necklace off my neck?"

"Its clasp was made in China," he said, stepping back from her with a smile, and his bright blue eyes seemed suddenly hooded, as if his golden lashes had dropped a shutter over them. "It is a true Chinese puzzle making it come unfastened."

"Well, take all the time you need but be about it. I cannot accept your pretty bauble, Nicolas. Somehow you must get it off!"

But although Nicolas worked diligently for at least ten minutes, the clasp refused to budge.

"Perhaps I can pull it off over your head," he offered, and tried that without success. "No, it will not go over your chin." Regretfully.

"Nicolas," Georgiana wailed. "I cannot go through life in this necklace!"

So intent were they on their task that neither of them noticed that a man had come through the front door and into the hall and now was standing squarely in the door of the drawing room with his booted legs spread wide apart, frowning as he surveyed the scene before him.

"Perhaps you could hide it?" suggested Nicolas wickedly. "Under a ruffle of lace?"

Georgiana stamped her satin slipper in frustration. "Get it *off*, Nicolas! What would Brett think?"

"He is here to say what he thinks," said a deep voice and they both whirled to see Brett standing there frowning at them.

"Brett!" cried Georgiana in confusion. "I—I did not expect you home so early."

It was the wrong thing to have said. *"That,"* he gave her a wintry smile, "at least is obvious."

Georgiana tried to get herself together. "We have a guest, Brett—Nicolas van Rappard."

"I am aware who the gentleman is. What I would like to have

explained to me is what he is doing in my house trying to remove a necklace of price from my wife's neck—a necklace that *I* did not give her!"

"The necklace was offered only as an appreciation of beauty," drawled Nicolas, his hand dropping lazily to his sword hilt. "It was refused."

"And it won't come off!" wailed Georgiana. "I was so startled when Nicolas put it around my neck that I let the clasp close before I thought to stop him—and now neither one of us can get it off!"

"Really? Perhaps I can rectify that." In four strides Brett had crossed the room. He would have run over Nicolas had not Nicolas stepped hastily back out of his way. Georgiana gasped as she was whirled around with such force that her peachbloom velvet skirts described a wide arc. She made a little ineffectual gesture of protest as Brett's strong fingers twined themselves in the necklace and it burst apart, losing a link in the process. Silently Brett held the glittering necklace out to Nicolas van Rappard. "I find it breaks more readily than a wedding band," he said evenly.

Nicolas accepted the necklace that was dropped into his hand and took two wary steps backward from his host, who seemed to have gained in stature and looked exceedingly formidable. He flashed a winning smile at Brett. "Faith, I hadn't thought of that way of removing it," he murmured. "Doubtless it would have come to me in time."

"Doubtless," said Brett ironically.

"Oh, you broke it," wailed Georgiana. "How could you, Brett? It's such a lovely thing."

"The necklace can be repaired," Brett told her with a frown. He turned to Nicolas. "You may send the bill to me, van Rappard."

Nicolas's golden brows elevated but his hand strayed away from his sword hilt. "A stylish offer!" he murmured.

"We live a very stylish life here at Windgate—but not quite so stylish as *you* seem to believe. We have not yet adopted the manner or morals of the court!"

Nicolas sighed. "I take it you are angry with me?" he said plaintively.

Brett gave him a disbelieving look. "First you would seize my home, now my wife! Are you suggesting I should *not* be angry?"

Georgiana stepped between them. "Oh, no, Brett, you misjudge

Nicolas. He has given that up. He is not going to pursue the Windgate matter any further—are you, Nicolas?''

Brett shot a look at Nicolas, whose smile never wavered.

"I believe your wife to be all that she appears to be," he said enigmatically.

"There—you see?" Georgiana turned an appealing face to Brett. "Nicolas accepts my claim—he has told you so himself."

"So it's Nicolas now, is it?" Brett's face was grim.

"Well, after all," cried Georgiana, telling herself that surely one who had told such large lies would be forgiven a small one, "we *are* cousins. On the van Rappard side."

"And how long has *Cousin* Nicolas been here?"

"I arrived yesterday—in the rain," supplied the smiling blond Dutchman. "My horse was sinking to his fetlocks in the mud."

"As I recall, last time you arrived in the rain too," said Brett grimly.

"A coincidence only." Nicolas's engaging smile flashed.

"May I suggest that the next time it rains you turn your horse's head in some direction other than Windgate?"

"I'll do that," agreed Nicolas brightly.

Georgiana was frowning. This interchange was going on above her head. What other time were they talking about? There was a violent undercurrent here as if Brett might at any moment launch himself at Nicolas, and Nicolas's stance—lazy but ready—showed he half expected it to happen.

"Nicolas begged shelter for the night and I gave it to him," she said hastily. "I could hardly send anyone away on such a night!"

"And he is still here." It was a statement, baldly made. "The rain has long since stopped but I take it he was not to be sent away tonight either?"

The color deepened in Georgiana's cheeks. A sense of panic washed over her. All of this was being terribly misunderstood. She turned to Nicolas for help.

"It is my fault," the Dutchman said softly. "I taught your lady to play chess and we kept at it longer than we realized. I will take my leave."

Brett stared at him and back to Georgiana, who was looking mutinous. He had no real belief that anything untoward had transpired here, but it was irritating to return home to find one's wife trying to struggle out of a diamond necklace another man—and a damnably attractive one—had placed around her neck. Shafts of unwanted jealousy were coursing through him. Nicolas van Rappard was not only good-looking, he had the wild look of the adventurer about him—such a man as could turn a young girl's head. And Georgiana, for all her beauty and charm, was after all a very young and inexperienced girl.

It occurred to Brett Danforth that it would be very bad form to turn a guest out at this time of night. Not only might Huygens ten Haer—who so far had been neutral toward the "English patroon" —take exception to it, but it might make Nicolas assume an aura of importance in Georgiana's eyes that he did not wish Nicolas to acquire.

"I will not turn you out in the night, van Rappard," he said curtly. "You are welcome to remain till morning as *my* guest." He emphasized that word "my" and Nicolas hid a grin. Brett turned to Georgiana. "I haven't supped."

"Oh, I'll have cold meats and wine set out at once." Georgiana's relief showed in her voice.

"Perhaps you will share them with me, Georgiana." He turned to Nicolas with stiff courtesy. "And you, sir, you are welcome to join us."

Nicolas realized that he had been fortunate to come through this encounter with the formidable Englishman unscathed and chose not to chance another this night. "I'm to bed," he said easily. "For with the ground as wet as it is I have a hard ride ahead of me tomorrow."

"The *River Witch* can take you home," offered Brett carelessly.

"Faith, I may avail me of that offer," said Nicolas with a grin. "For my horse barely carried me up here. Whether he's up to the return trip is anybody's guess!"

He bowed and left them together and Georgiana was alone with her husband. He stood studying her and she waited tensely for him to speak.

"I'm starved," he said, and headed for the dining room, where food was being hastily set out on the long board, for Wouter had seen the master ride in.

After the servants had gone, Georgiana closed the door. "Brett, in spite of what you may think, I didn't encourage Nicolas."

He cast a look at her sumptuous peachbloom velvet gown. "That dress, I suppose, was not designed to encourage him?" he asked dryly.

"I meant to wear it to the ten Haers' ball" and—her words came out in a rush—"I *did* so want to try it out on someone first and see what was said about it. I admit it was silly of me but there you have it!"

So naively feminine was this answer that Brett, looking at Georgiana in some amazement, accepted it for what it was—the truth. "So you see, he was just riding by and—"

"Are you telling me that the man rode north carrying a diamond necklace and did not have something in mind?" Brett cut in, setting upon the cold meats with the zeal of a starving man.

Georgiana took a deep breath. The truth would bring on a duel and she did not want that. She certainly didn't want Brett hurt and—she now admitted it to herself—she didn't want the smiling Dutchman hurt either. "I think the necklace was in the nature of a peace offering," she said hurriedly. "After all, we are cousins and he has been trying to wrest your estates from you and that could hardly be deemed civil!"

"No, it could not," Brett agreed with raised eyebrows.

"And so Nicolas wanted to make it up to us—how could he know you were not home?" She was involved in a web of lies now, for she knew very well how Nicolas knew, but she dared not let Brett know that.

"He might have guessed me absent, since he could see the *River Witch* was missing from the pier."

"Ah, but he was already here by then, and anyway you often send her on errands, do you not? Does she not ply up and down the river at your bidding?"

"That is true." Wine and meat were getting to him, he was feeling more expansive and very indulgent of the beautiful woman who faced him so earnestly, trying to explain away the scene he had just witnessed.

"So Nicolas arrived and it was raining, and although I did not want to, I felt obliged to give him a night's lodging. And he was charming to me and taught me to play chess—so you should be grateful to him," she added ingenuously, "for he has added to my accomplishments."

Brett looked squarely at his golden-haired wife. She looked

exceptionally beautiful tonight, he thought, flushed-faced and with those little sparkling things in her hair. His heart softened but he kept his voice firm.

"I would be just as grateful if other men did not add to your accomplishments," he said dryly, holding out his glass for her to pour more wine.

Georgiana was pouting. "You came in at the only moment that could have made trouble between us." There had been a couple more such moments but she chose to forget them. "I think you should look at it from my point of view, Brett. Here I was alone in this big echoing house with everything strange to me—I'd have been glad to see the devil himself. And probably asked him to stay to dinner to boot!"

Brett laughed. Whatever her misdemeanor, he had forgiven her. And Nicolas van Rappard would be returned to the ten Haers' tomorrow morning via the river—he would see to that personally. And there was little likelihood that their paths would cross frequently in the future, even if Nicolas van Rappard now chose to pay court to the ten Haer heiress, Katrina, for Katrina would probably nourish a grudge against them and would not seek them out, and although there were occasional balls and parties at the big houses along the river, their lives were busy ones and, in the main, isolated.

When he rose from the table, he threw an arm around Georgiana. "You look like a peach tonight," he told her. "With that dress and your coloring."

Georgiana refrained from saying that Nicolas had told her the same thing—and with somewhat more heat.

"But"—Brett leaned his dark head down and his lips brushed the silky skin of her upper breast—"I prefer you with it off." His head came up and his gray eyes smiled into hers. "Shall we go upstairs and do something about that?"

He lifted her up in his arms and carried her like a bride up the grand stairway. And later, when the peachbloom velvet gown was a pufflike heap on the blue Chinese rug, and all their clothing lay scattered about the room where they had flung it in their haste, Georgiana fell backward into the big featherbed and stretched luxuriously, watching with delight the fiery flicker her every shrug or stretch brought forth in the eyes of the naked man who watched her.

"Beguiling wench!" he muttered. "Don't think you can trap *me* with your witching ways. I know you were only amusing yourself with van Rappard but that's a dangerous game and you're not to play it!"

Georgiana laughed recklessly. "The only games I care to play are with you, Brett!" She held out her arms enticingly and he went into them. Georgiana sank beneath him with a sigh and abandoned herself to all the desires of the flesh.

PART TWO
The Gorgeous Rival

To love him? Or leave him and try to forget?
She asks herself, which is the worst?
If she who yearns for a love returned
Ever must hunger and thirst?

Windgate On The Hudson,
1673

CHAPTER 13

Nicolas van Rappard was not the only uninvited guest to appear at Windgate that week. Another arrived by river sloop on the evening of Nicolas's departure—and at sight of this one Georgiana caught her breath.

For the woman who disembarked and walked in leisurely fashion down the long wooden pier—walked as if her feet would know the way in the dark to the main house—was Erica Hulft.

From the tall windows of the great house they had watched the sloop sailing toward the pier.

" 'Tis Govert Steendam's sloop," Brett told her in surprise. "I wonder why he sails upriver? Come, Georgiana, we will go down to greet him."

Govert Steendam. . . . Georgiana recognized the name as belonging to one of New Orange's wealthy burghers. She wished she had not been working hard all day at supervising the rearrangement of the basement stores. The Dutch burgher had surprised her in her housedress!

Halfway down the slope, they saw a woman clad in fiery tangerine velvet and copper lace disembark. Beside her, Brett missed a stride and stiffened. Casting a glance at him, Georgiana saw his hawklike face harden to watchfulness.

A moment later she realized that beneath that wide-brimmed plumed hat the new arrival had hair like a fox's brush.

Erica Hulft was moving sinuously toward them.

"I wonder what *she* wants," muttered Georgiana.

Brett did not answer. His stride picked up speed and Georgiana was hard pressed to keep up with him down the steep slope.

"Brett!" Erica held out a creamy-gloved hand in greeting and gave Brett a lazy look through copper lashes. Such was her manner, thought Georgiana irritably, that it might well be Erica who was welcoming *them* to Windgate instead of the other way around!

Brett took that outstretched hand, carried it lightly to his lips.

"Erica, I believe you have not met my wife. Georgiana, this is Erica Hulft. Of New Orange—and other places."

If his last words had been intended to nettle Erica, they did not have the desired effect. "Yes, *many* other places indeed," she agreed instantly, giving him a dazzling smile.

Georgiana gave Erica a stiff little nod.

"We have not met but—I have seen you, of course." Erica turned her winsome smile on Georgiana. "From the dock in New Orange, I believe it was."

"You have seen me twice," Georgiana corrected her clearly. "Once in New Orange and once in Bermuda. I seem to recall that you sat in a carriage and waited for me outside the entrance of Mirabelle."

"Really?" Erica's copper lashes fluttered, but her light voice with its slightly French inflection was unperturbed. "Your memory is better than mine, but of course it is possible." Her negligent tone said *anything* was possible.

"But you *have* been to Bermuda, have you not?" pursued Georgiana ruthlessly.

"But of course!" Erica's deprecating little laugh said one had been everywhere—naturally!

"You must pardon me, Erica," Brett cut in with a glance back at the sails. "But I keep expecting to see Govert Steendam disembark."

"Ah, you have noted that this is his sloop!" laughed Erica. "No, Govert is not with me. He sent me on ahead."

Georgiana was quick to note that "*sent me on ahead*." She

wondered what it meant, and what transactions Erica Hulft had with Govert Steendam.

"You are journeying upriver alone, then?" Brett asked.

"Yes, to look at some land south of the van Rensselaer holding."

"Then you will of course sup and stay the night with us?"

It was a common enough invitation; any patroon along the river would have invited the aristocratic-looking lady sailing upriver on Govert Steendam's sloop to stay the night, but Erica seized on it joyfully as if it were something quite out of the ordinary.

"But I would *love* to!" she purred. "It will be so nice to visit Windgate again and"— she turned her smile on Georgiana—"to see all the changes the new bride has made in the different rooms."

She is telling me neatly that she is familiar with every room in the house, Georgiana thought hotly. *She wants me to know where I stand!* "I have not had time to make many changes," she announced in a cool voice. "Nor yet to plan parties."

"Oh, I do hope Govert and I will be invited when you do give a party." Erica took Brett's arm as if she owned it and began moving gracefully up the slope, holding up her voluminous velvet skirts with her other hand. The deep gold satin linings of her slashed sleeves flashed as she moved, emphasizing the richness of her gown.

"You and Govert?" asked Georgiana in a blank voice. Abruptly she took Brett's other arm. With every step she hated herself for letting Erica catch her in a hastily stitched up linsey-woolsey housedress. True, it's wide gray blue skirts swung attractively around her trim ankles, for it was short in the Dutch style, and the bodice was a marvelous fit for her slim figure—but it was no match at all for the elegant garb of the woman beside her.

"Oh, I forgot you didn't know," that careless voice went on. "Govert Steendam and I are to be married."

Did she imagine it, wondered Georgiana, or did a slight ripple go through the arm she was holding so tightly? Brett's voice, when he spoke, could not have been calmer. It was precise, almost formal.

"I didn't know you and Govert were so close, Erica."

Erica shrugged and the tangerine plumes of her wide-brimmed hat rippled seductively. Georgiana yearned to tear them off and push her unwelcome guest back on to the boat that had brought her, and cut it adrift. She tensed at Erica's murmured, "The association is recent—

I admit it. Those abandoned"—Erica had tilted her head so that she was looking up directly into Brett's eyes—"fall into other hands."

This was strong stuff. Georgiana had a sudden wild desire to bring it all out into the open. "*Who* abandoned you?" she asked recklessly—and was instantly sorry she'd asked.

"My lover," said Erica, still in that careless voice. Her gaze, Georgiana saw, had never left Brett's face. She was watching him intently.

"I do not think you were ever abandoned, Erica." Brett sounded grave and chiding. "Rather that you chose to roam."

"Ah, yes, I was ever a rover—you always said so!" Laughter bubbled up in Erica. "Ah, here we are at last at your front door! It takes strength to climb the steep slope to your door, Brett—only the strong should attempt it!" Her amused gaze slid over Georgiana.

"Fortunately I am young and strong," pointed out Georgiana stiffly and they all went into the dim wide hall.

Although her bubbly guest would have been delighted to settle her tangerine skirts in the big drawing room, Georgiana left Brett downstairs and ruthlessly escorted Erica to one of the big guest rooms. "To freshen up after your tiresome journey upriver," she told Erica sweetly. Their passage was constantly interrupted by Erica's light comments: "How I always loved that picture!" Or "This rug was always lovely underfoot."

"I take it you have spent some time at Windgate?" Feeling forced to comment on the obvious, Georgiana flung wide the guest room door. "Your luggage will be brought up directly," she added. "I heard Brett calling to one of the men to bring it."

"Oh, no need to bother about my luggage. I've only an overnight bag anyway. I'll just freshen up a bit—I don't intend to change for dinner."

No, you don't need to, thought Georgiana bitterly. *You came ashore dressed for dinner! And you were careful not to announce your arrival in advance. You meant to find me dressed in some serviceable rag like this one, so Brett couldn't fail to notice the difference between my dowdiness and your elegance!*

She forced her thoughts away. Erica was speaking again.

"Yes, I've spent a bit of time here." Nonchalantly. "Ah, I see you have not changed the curtains in this room—I'd thought you might. Fifi chewed that one at the corner—just there."

Georgiana stared at the corner of the curtain. It *did* look a bit chewed.

"Fifi?" she asked blankly.

"My puppy."

Now Georgiana remembered. In Bermuda, Erica had been carrying a silky little Pomeranian.

"And do you have him with you, Erica?" She tried to laugh. "We could let him chew up the other curtain so they would match!"

Erica sighed as she drew off her gloves. "Unfortunately not. Fifi fell overboard and drowned on the way here. It was my fault—I was not watching. Things—have a way of slipping through my fingers. But no matter," she added cheerfully. "I always replace them!" *As I have replaced Brett,* was the plain implication.

"I should think it would be hard to replace a pet you loved," frowned Georgiana, marveling at Erica's hardness of heart.

"Not so difficult," said Erica coolly. "Govert will buy me a dozen Pomeranians."

But not Windgate . . . and not Brett, thought Georgiana. *Those you have come to take for yourself!* She had begun to feel suffocated and longed to be free of her unwelcome guest.

"Dinner will be served as soon as you come down." Firmly, she closed the door on Erica and hurried back to change into something more aggressive. She would need all of her finery to equal Erica's copper elegance.

"Wear something simple," Brett advised, watching her as she tore frantically through her wardrobe, tossing gowns to right and left. "For contrast."

"Why?" demanded Georgiana through her teeth. "I have no wish to be overshadowed by that woman!"

He gave her an indulgent smile. "There's no chance of that, Georgiana." He was thinking how young she looked with her face flushed and her turquoise eyes snapping.

In her anxiety over choosing a gown, Georgiana did not catch the caressing note in his voice. "I will wear the lemon silk shot with gold threads," she decided in a rebellious voice. "*That* surely should be simple enough to please you. And my best gold petticoat."

"Here, I will help you with your hooks," Brett offered as she pulled the gown willy-nilly over her head. Suddenly his arms enfolded her and he gave her a small reassuring hug. "*She* is copper," he murmured against her shining hair. "*You* are gold."

It was just what Georgiana needed. She smoothed down her silken skirts, gave Brett a flashing smile, and seized her silver hairbrush.

"Shall I wait for you?" he asked.

For a moment her heart lurched, but she could not begin her marriage *by not trusting him*. For a moment the silver brush wavered in the air. Then: "No," she said bravely. "Go on down and entertain our guest."

Minutes later a slightly breathless Georgiana burst into the drawing room and found them companionably sharing a glass of wine before one of the front windows. They looked, she thought with a pang, as if they belonged together.

Erica turned blithely as Georgiana entered. "I was just telling Brett that the ten Haers have postponed their ball for another week. I do not know why—probably because Katrina's face has broken out again and her mother wants to give her time to look presentable."

"Again?" Georgiana was fascinated. She urged more wine on Erica. "Is she plagued this way often?"

"Often." Erica nodded. "Every time Katrina goes into a rage her face breaks out. It infuriates Rychie—her mother."

"And what caused Katrina's rage this time?" wondered Georgiana.

Erica laughed. "Tell her, Brett!"

"I wil leave that to you," Brett frowned.

Erica turned with laughter still bubbling on her lips. "Katrina went into fits of rage when she learned Brett had married you, Georgiana. Oh, don't look at me that way, Brett. Georgiana could have heard it from anyone on the river."

"Nicolas did not speak of it," Georgiana said coolly. "And he's their houseguest."

"Nicolas?" Erica shot her a fascinated glance. "You've seen Nicolas? Here at Windgate?"

"He was with us for several days," said Georgiana airily. "You just missed him. He left this morning."

Brett's amused glance told her she was carrying off a difficult situation rather well, but Georgiana was still alarmed by the formidable beauty and wily mind of the woman before her.

Erica did most of the talking at dinner, and her host and hostess watched her across the long board—for neither of them believed for a moment that it was a "piece of land" that drew her to Windgate.

Erica, seemingly unaware of their burning curiosity, continued her lightsome chatter. It was rumored, she told them, that the king of England—Charles himself—was going to storm the colony and take it back. Had they heard it? No? Well, most rumors were lies anyway. Still . . . here her feline amber gaze rested lazily on Brett . . . if it did happen, she told them merrily, if New Orange became New York once again, *she* would throw herself on the king's mercy and perhaps Brett, an Englishman, would speak for her?

"I am sure none could speak for you better than yourself, Erica," said Brett dryly.

Erica laughed. "He is wont to say such droll things, your new husband," she told Georgiana with a charming gesture of deprecation. "But surely *I* would not have survived save for his sword arm."

Georgiana felt her features tighten; she too had survived by that same sword arm. "Tell me about it," she said in a wooden voice.

"Oh, 'tis a long story," shrugged Erica. "Some other day. . . ."

"Perhaps Brett will tell it to me," countered Georgiana, nettled.

"I happened by when Erica was in an intolerable situation," explained Brett. "Fortunately I was able to give her some aid."

"Yes." Georgiana's voice was a dry wisp. "I seem to remember that you are given to helping maidens in distress."

Erica's laughter pealed. "I was hardly a maiden! I had buried two husbands, but then I was a child bride, of course. I was but sixteen—well, a *trifle* over"—this as Brett's brows elevated—"when Brett discovered me at an inn in New York weeping over the loss of my luggage, which was indeed all I had in the world."

"And what did Brett do about that?" Georgiana hated herself for asking.

Erica's answer took her breath away. "Brett realized I had nowhere to go and so he kindly escorted me to Windgate."

On her lap, concealed by the heavy white damask tablecloth, Georgiana felt her nails bite into her palms. Well, it was out in the open now! She hated that beautiful taunting face before her. Erica was *baiting* her! "While you made your arrangements?" she said coolly.

Erica's little shrug of her velvet shoulders spoke volumes. "The swordplay came later," she murmured.

"Erica told me she wished to marry well," Brett interposed with a frown. "She needed a protector while she made her choice."

"And now she has chosen." Georgiana's voice was brittle. "How nice."

"Yes, isn't it?" cooed Erica. "Govert Steendam is the wealthiest merchant in all New Netherland. He has told me he will build a castle for me on the river. Even now I am looking for a site."

And you have found it, thought Georgiana bitterly. *Right here at Windgate! You don't want to build—you want to move in!* She felt a sudden pity for Govert Steendam if he married this prowling female.

But Erica had turned coolly to Brett.

"I was thinking of that land for sale south of the Van Rensselaer holding—the same land you were considering, Brett. Before you realized the extent of Windgate's debts." (*She is telling me she knows that too!* though Georgiana hotly. *That we are deep in debt and likely to be so for a long time to come! And twitting us with how rich she will be when she marries Govert Steendam!*) Erica picked thoughtfully at her food. "Perhaps you could accompany me there, Brett, and point out its boundaries?" She turned hastily to Georgiana as if she had just remembered her hostess. "Perhaps you could *both* accompany me?"

Georgiana drew a deep ragged breath and leaned forward. The thought of accompanying Erica upriver made the blood rush to her head.

Brett caught her wrathful expression and the shadow of a frown flickered over his face, but his voice was imperturbable. "I regret I must decline for us both," he told Erica firmly. "Georgiana is new to this country, she is still getting her bearings. And as for me, estate matters are too pressing, Erica."

Before Erica could think of some new way to persuade him, Georgiana cut in recklessly. "What kind of man is Nicolas?" she demanded, disregarding Brett's sudden warning frown. She wanted to hear her rival speak on that subject.

"Nicolas?" Erica looked startled—then her laughter pealed again. "Nicolas is a wonderful liar and"—she gave Brett a wicked glance from beneath demurely lowered lashes—"if reports are to be believed, a wonderful lover! I have advised him to marry Katrina ten

Haer now that she is again available—for she is certainly the best catch on the river.''

"And you are interested in assuring his future?" Georgiana asked softly.

Erica gave her a smile of pure astonishment. "Is not *every* woman interested in assuring the future of a fascinating man? Come, Georgiana," she challenged, "can you tell me truthfully that you did *not* find Nicolas fascinating?"

Georgiana could not. Her color had risen rather high. Brett was looking at her; she could not read his inscrutable gaze. She told herself she must try to find her way out of this maze before Erica boxed her in. "And do you think Katrina will accept Nicolas?" she asked, ignoring Erica's pointed question.

"Certainly," cried Erica. "Who would not accept Nicolas if he offered?"

Brett leaned forward. There was amusement in the steely gray eyes that considered his pretty guest. "You sound as if *you* would accept Nicolas if he offered for you, Erica."

Erica gave a regretful sigh. "You know as well as I do, Brett, that I cannot *afford* a man like Nicolas. Nor, as matters stand, can he afford me." Her shrug included Georgiana. "You see, unfortunately, beggars had best not become lovers." And then her smile turned roguish and her amber gaze played over Brett. "Of course if I were certain Nicolas would win his suit against you, Brett, *then* I might accept him! And become mistress of Windgate in the bargain!"

She had flung out a challenge. Georgiana was aware of it. She felt her skin prickle.

But Brett's amusement only deepened. He leaned back in his chair and considered his guest amiably. "What a pity for you, my dear, that that is impossible. For I am doubly owner of Windgate—not only did I purchase it, but I have married the lady who had the prior claim."

A false claim, thought Georgiana in panic. And someday perhaps it would be proved false!

"True," sighed Erica, giving Brett a slanted look. "Windgate is indeed a prize any woman would seek even"—a taunting smile played around her pretty mouth—"even with such an ogre as you, Brett, as master of it!"

"*I* do not find Brett an ogre," interposed Georgiana stiffly.

"Give him time!" laughed Erica. "You have much to learn of him!"

Somehow dinner was got through, somehow they drank their wine and Erica ran careless fingers over the harpsichord that Georgiana's mother had hated so.

"I used to envy the golden lady in the dining room portrait," Erica told Imogene frankly.

"My mother?" Georgiana was startled. "Why did you envy her? She led a tragic life and was cut down in her youth!"

"But, then, she was mistress of all this!" Erica ran a tinkling scale with deft rapidity. "And surely that was worth *something*."

Georgiana gave her a wooden look and Erica's clever fingers came to a halt with a single crashing chord. But, thought Georgiana reluctantly, there was truth in what Erica had said. She supposed it *had* been worth something, even to Imogene, being mistress of Windgate. Wealth and position . . . her gaze wandered to Brett, looking so urbane, so sure of himself, as he leaned negligently against the harpsichord, watching them. She had married him not knowing of Windgate, she had loved the man. She loved him still but now she felt she walked along a knife edge, for if Brett were to find out that she was not in truth Verhulst van Rappard's daughter, and therefore not heiress to Windgate, would he continue to love her?

A little chill went through her and she turned quickly away lest Erica Hulft see the tormented expression that had passed over her face. She was glad when Brett spoke.

"When do you and Govert marry, Erica?"

"We have not yet set the date. That is up to me." Erica's tilted face, looking up into Brett's, said as clearly as words, *That is up to you*.

Georgiana felt that unspoken appeal knife through her and shivered inwardly. Brett had felt something for this woman—perhaps he still did. And Erica was beautiful and conniving and soon she would be the wife of this colony's wealthiest merchant, a woman to be reckoned with, a woman who could harm Brett if she chose.

"Perhaps you will change your mind, Erica," she said in a brittle voice when Brett did not comment. "And decide to take Nicolas away from Katrina ten Haer after all."

Again Erica's laughter trilled but there was chagrin in her face as she turned away from Brett, for she had seen no answering light in those steely gray eyes. "That *would* be fun," she admitted. "If only to see Rychie ten Haer sizzle and burn! Rychie," she added lightly, "has no love for me."

"And why is that?"

Erica hesitated. "I am not quite sure," she admitted. "Unless it is because she could not bear to see any other woman living at Windgate. Even briefly. You see, Georgiana, Rychie has always considered Windgate to be rightfully hers. Verhulst—your father—proposed to her, you know, and she rejected him and married her Cousin Huygens instead. But Huygens did not make the great fortune Rychie had expected and Verhulst, of course, married your mother and I suppose he must have lorded it over Rychie."

"Then she will dislike me as well?"

"Oh, yes, of course—for that and other reasons. You and your mother have both been great thorns in Rychie's flesh, Georgiana. First your mother married Rychie's lost suitor, then you took away Rychie's daughter's intended! I am surprised Rychie invited you to her ball at all."

"We are her neighbors," pointed out Brett blandly. "Even though on the river distances are long."

"Yes," echoed Erica. "Distances on the river are very long indeed and land adjoining the Van Rensselaer's holdings would be *very* far from New Orange and *very* isolated in winter. Tell me, Brett, do you not have some river lands you would part with?"

Georgiana held her breath. *This* was why Erica had come, to cajole Brett out of some land on Govert Steendam's behalf!

"Some lands to the south, possibly?" Erica rushed on. "Govert and I would make a lovely barrier between you and your spiteful neighbors to the south—especially if Katrina ten Haer marries Nicolas van Rappard! Their eyes would ever be turned enviously to the north to the heritage they all believed to be rightfully theirs!"

She means to get close! thought Georgiana in fright and leaned forward tensely to hear Brett's answer.

"A lovely barrier you would make indeed, Erica," he agreed. "But I will somehow manage to fend off whatever comes against me. Even without your aid."

Erica's look of sudden desperate longing entreated him not to fend *her* off. Georgiana found herself clenching her hands at that look.

"If the ten Haers postpone their ball long enough," she said, quickly throwing a new thought into the tensions of the room, "I will have time to have a new ballgown stitched up for it. Have you decided what you will wear, Erica?"

"Something Brett chose for me once," murmured Erica, and Georgiana felt she would explode with fury..

Brett must have felt the tingling electricity in that room for he rose suddenly. "It is time for bed, Georgiana," he said. "We have much to do tomorrow and I am sure our lovely guest will wish to be off early if the winds are favorable."

"Yes," said Georgiana, speaking for Erica. "I am sure she will and, judging by today, tomorrow bids fair to have favorable winds."

"Not only a lovely child but a prophet," murmured Erica on a note of distaste. "Ah, well, sleep is just what we all need, I am sure, to face the morrow!"

Georgiana couldn't have agreed more. Anything to get Brett away from that beautiful worldly face and that seductive body and all those shared experiences that must inevitably be drawing them back together. She tried to tell herself that Erica had *not* been Brett's mistress, that she was just a waif he had helped—and failed miserably. It had never occurred to her, when she had flung herself recklessly into marriage, that there would be so many former loves to contend with: first Katrina ten Haer, now Erica Hulft—it seemed to her suddenly that the rounded hills that sloped down to the Hudson were full of prowling females with all their interest centered on Brett.

Silently she went up to bed, to be held and comforted by Brett's arms. She clung to him, finding no words.

CHAPTER 14

Why Georgiana woke, she never knew. But she reached out an arm and found herself alone in the great bed. Then, as a white moon, drifting over scudding clouds, illuminated the big square room, she saw that Brett was not in the room at all. She leaped up, barefoot, and—without realizing just why she did it but with a confused sense of urgency—checked the adjoining room.

He was not there either.

Moving cautiously, since she had no candle—for in her hurry she had not bothered to light one—Georgiana moved down the dark hall toward Erica's room. She hated herself for doing this, but *she had to know: Was Brett with Erica?*

Heart pounding, she paused outside Erica's door. It would be irrevocable, she told herself, if she found them here together. There would be no going back to the way they had been before—ever. She was half tempted to flee, to run on swift silent feet back to her room and not discover, now or ever, what lay behind that door. Shaken by indecision, her trembling fingers reached for the latch—then fell away again.

On a sudden rush of courage she seized the latch. It was cold in her fingers, as if silently bidding her to leave, to keep her illusions. *But she must know!* her feelings screamed at her.

Dreading every moment she pushed the door open and turned her gaze toward the bed. It was difficult to see, for the branches of a tree outside obscured the moonlight and the room seemed full of moving shadows. She tensed, half expecting Brett to spring up from that big square bed and confront her—or Erica to bounce up with a sudden scream of fright. And what would happen then?

Moonlight, wavering through the branches, illuminated the attractive room.

There was nobody in it.

Georgiana leaned dizzily against the wall. She had been so sure she would find—them. Together.

Now she asked herself, *where was Erica? Where was Brett, for that matter?*

Puzzled now as well as worried, Georgiana made her silent way downstairs. The wind had come up; it whistled through the chimneys and moaned around the panes like a living thing. But Georgiana was grateful for that wind for its wail obscured any light footfall of hers and she had a sense of dread that she might stumble upon Brett and Erica embracing in some dark corner. How irrational that would be in a house fairly bursting with comfortable bedrooms with doors that could be latched against prying eyes did not at that moment occur to her. Borne forward on wings of alarm, she padded softly through the semidarkness into the wide reaches of the lower hall. Candlelight reached her from the dining room and she moved like a wraith toward it.

Now she could see the big table, and on it a silver tray with a glass of milk and some cold meats.

For a moment she felt relief. Erica, having only picked at her food at dinner, had come down for a midnight snack.

But then a man's tall shadow wavered across the dining room wall. Capriciously the wind stilled and she heard Brett's low voice saying, "You must realize that things have changed."

And Erica's passionate answer. "*Nothing* has changed! Oh, Brett, this marriage need make no difference between us!"

"Which marriage?" he asked dryly. "Yours or mine?"

"Neither one! Oh, do you not see, it is the perfect answer—I will make a friend of this child bride of yours. She will see me with Govert, she will not suspect!"

"Erica, you have already all but flung our affair in her face! How could she *not* suspect you?"

"That will pass, she will forget." Erica sounded strained, tormented. "Ah, Brett, for me there has never been anyone but you—"

A shutter banged as the wind shrieked again and Brett said sharply, "Be quiet. We may awaken Georgiana."

In the stillness that followed, broken only by the low moan of the wind, Georgiana beat a hasty and silent retreat up the stairs. She heard Brett's footsteps, realized she could not make the top landing without being seen, and whirled to face him just as he emerged into the hall, making it appear that she was just coming downstairs.

"I woke up and found you gone," she said, eyeing him, hoping the candlelight from below would not show her upset expression. "And I was hungry so I came down to get something to eat."

"Hunger seems to have struck us all," said Brett. There was a grim note in his voice. "I heard a noise downstairs and came down to investigate and found Erica pouring herself some milk in the kitchen."

As if called, Erica came gliding out from behind Brett. "And then we found some cold meats." Her calm voice in no way betrayed the emotion that had swept her but moments ago; *she* might have been the hostess and Georgiana the guest. Georgiana envied her that aplomb. "Won't you join us, Georgiana?" Graciously, Erica gestured toward the table.

Georgiana managed a muffled answer and her reluctant feet carried her downstairs again. She never knew what she ate, seated at the long dining table in her nightdress, facing Erica. Erica in a dainty orange satin robe seeming more hostess than she! But after she was back in her bed, staring at the ceiling in the moonlight, she knew a bright burning jealousy.

They had all come upstairs together after their snack, with Erica lighting their way with a candle held high. Erica had lighted the way to Georgiana's room and would have waited while Georgiana entered, to light Brett to his, but that Brett said quietly, "I'm stopping off here, Erica."

If there was a double meaning in his words, Erica appeared not to catch it. She was gone, on down the hall, tossing them a blithe "Good night" over her shoulder.

Georgiana half expected Brett to go on through the connecting door to his own room, but he did not. He stood watching her.

"I think I'll sleep in your room tonight," he murmured, for he had noted the torment in his bride's eyes and guessed that Georgiana's suspicions might have been aroused by the midnight rendezvous in the dining room that she had chanced upon.

Staying in her room, was he? Georgiana's senses quivered, but any yearning she felt was overcome by a sense of indignation that he had been trysting with Erica downstairs while his wife presumably slept!

"As you like," she said indifferently. She crossed the moonlit carpet and flung herself into bed, turning her back on him. "Good night," she said, her voice muffled by the pillow.

"Good night?" he echoed, and to her annoyance he sounded amused. His voice grew caressing. "I had thought your late night snack might make you wakeful?"

"Well, it hasn't." She tried to sound sleepy, and managed only to sound childishly resentful.

"No? Well, I'll just sleep here tonight anyway," he said companionably, sliding into the bed beside her.

Georgiana was very aware of his long body, only a breath away. She hardened her heart.

"Good night," she said again. Firmly. Before he could gather her into his arms, before he could begin making love to her, before he could work his magic to still her wild thoughts. She felt shaken, bruised by what she had seen and heard, but at the moment being held in Brett's arms would not reassure her. She lay beside him, stiff and still, until the sound of his even breathing assured her he was asleep.

After that, she tossed and turned. Every word she had heard spoken downstairs was grinding and searing through her mind. Erica's passionate: *Nothing has changed . . . this marriage need make no difference between us!* It gnawed at her.

When Brett had had time to think about it, what would his answer be?

There was no sleep for the island beauty that night and she rose restlessly as dawn was breaking.

Brett, who had waked as she left the bed, was lying on his back with his hands clasped behind his head, watching her.

"You're rising very early," was his mild comment.

"I have a guest to speed on her way!" snapped Georgiana.

Brett made no rejoinder. Instead he watched her with a steady gaze as she flung things about, muttered angrily when she could not find the petticoat she wanted and finally, in a rare temper, threw her shoes across the room.

"Jealousy of what's past will avail nothing," he said at last.

She turned on him, barefoot and trembling with anger. "How can I know it's past?"

That steady gaze now held a steely light. "Because I tell you so, Georgiana."

She bit back the words that rushed to her lips, words to accuse, to condemn. "I must go downstairs and supervise breakfast," she said in a muffled voice, found her shoes and left the room.

At the top of the stairwell she heard a light step behind her and turned to see Erica, fully dressed and wearing a sweeping hat decorated with orange plumes that were outrageously close to the color of her fox-burnished hair. Unlike her hostess, who was a trifle pale and grim, Erica seemed blithe as the morning. In her gold-laced orange brocade gown, which fit her enticing figure as if a man's hands clasped it, a gown that swirled out into rustling brocade skirts over a burnished gold satin petticoat, she was a sight to turn any man's head.

Looking at Erica, Georgiana regretted having dressed so hastily.

"I did not dream you would be astir so early, Erica," she said with forced politeness.

"I am equally astonished to find *you* up," smiled Erica, "since brides have a habit of sleeping late." She was drawing a pair of orange kid gloves over her slender hands as she spoke. "Indeed, I had thought that Brett, who rises early, might be up to bid me Godspeed—but *this* is more than I had hoped for."

The subtle irony of her tone brought a flash to Georgiana's turquoise eyes. "Well, since we are both up, you must stay to breakfast," she told Erica crisply. "I am sure Brett will be down shortly—to bid you Godspeed." The irony of her tone matched Erica's and Erica's brows shot up. Making a great effort to be civil, she added, "Your sloop's *schipper* will no doubt be glad of the respite."

"Seylns, our *schipper*, is a dour man," sighed Erica. "He eats alone." She dimpled for she had been about to add, "He sleeps alone too now that his teenage mistress is no longer our stowaway—that is why he is so dour!" And what would this virginal bride from the islands think about *that*?

"Well, this morning Seylns may share our breakfast."

"How kind of you," murmured Erica, rustling downstairs beside her hostess. "But I doubt Seylns will accept. I imagine he will already have broken his fast."

But Seylns did accept. With alacrity. Having missed dinner last night in Windgate's big kitchen on orders from his employer's intended bride to stay aboard at all costs, she might be leaving suddenly, he relished the thought of sugared cinnamon pancakes and fat sizzling sausages in the big dining room at Windgate—the glories of which he had heard. He hurried up the slope, all smiles, refuting Erica's comment that he was dour.

Georgiana, still clad in the simple blue gown she considered a most unfortunate choice against Erica's startling finery—but a gown that brought out the turquoise of her wide dark-fringed eyes and complemented the heavenly gold of her hair in a way that made Erica study her irritably—presided over her long table with grace. Seylns, Govert's *schipper*, was enchanted by her. He sat back expansively, filled with pancakes and good will, and spun her sea stories while Erica raised her brows in annoyance.

Brett could barely conceal his amusement and prodded the fat *schipper* into further endeavors. Georgiana listened politely, her mind but half on what Seylns was saying, but Erica gave Brett a black look.

They were about to rise from the table when a messenger arrived. Brett spoke to him in the hall. When he came back to the dining room, his face was grave.

"It seems there has been a murder in one of our northern *bouweries*," he said. "The neighbors accuse the wife of complicity and say her lover did the deed. The wife pleads innocence and claims a passing Indian fell into a quarrel with her husband. I had best look into it."

That meant he would be sailing north alongside Erica's sloop!

"Can you not send for the sheriff?" cried Georgiana.

"Doubtless I will send for the *schout* soon enough. But first I owe it to the dead man, Michaelius, who was my tenant, to look into the matter myself. I may be away two or three days, Georgiana."

He was moving toward the stairs as he spoke and Georgiana threw down her napkin and hurried after him. She was conscious as she passed of the convulsed amusement Erica Hulft was hiding behind a gloved hand.

In the bedroom, where Brett was preparing rapidly for his journey north, Georgiana confronted him. Hands on hips, both feet planted, and full of suspicions that he had somehow *contrived* this so that he might be alone with Erica on the river, she cried, "*Must* you sail north with that woman?"

He seemed surprised and looked up from pulling on his boots. "I will not be aboard Govert's sloop, Georgiana. I am taking the *River Witch* north."

"It is the same thing! Sloops pull up easily along riverbanks and exchange their passengers!"

Brett gave her a long slow look and stood up. He seemed to tower over her and his answering tone was hard. "You may come along if you like, Georgiana, although you are like to find it an unpleasant journey, full of briers and thorns once we leave the sloop and turn inland."

Blazing with jealousy, she yet refused herself the comfort of going along to make sure that, once out of sight, the sloops did not pull alongside so that Brett might sweep Erica over the side of the *River Witch* into his arms.

She would maintain at least a semblance of dignity!

"I have too much to do here," she said loftily. "I wish you joy of your journey!"

"Doubtless I shall have it," said Brett ironically. "Although what joy there will be in comforting a weeping woman and trying to learn whether or not she killed her husband, I'd not be knowing!"

He tossed a russet cloak over his shoulders, stuck a couple of pistols into his belt and strode away downstairs. Georgiana, feeling angry and rebuffed, followed the clatter of boots in his wake.

She walked down the steep slope with them, for she told herself that it would be the height of rudeness not to tell her unwanted guest good-bye at the landing—but she knew in her heart that she was making sure that Erica did not somehow depart on the wrong sloop!

The two craft departed at almost the same time, for Brett's cheerful Dutch *schipper* was always in readiness and kept the *River Witch* at the ready for his master's whims.

Once before, just as she had in Bermuda, Erica Hulft was looking at her from a departing ship, with triumph written all over her beautiful face.

Georgiana waved to Brett from the wooden pier and watched the two sloops pacing each other upriver until they disappeared. Then, blindly, she turned and ran back up the slope to the big empty house, up to her bedroom where she threw herself on the bed in a paroxysm of weeping.

Brett was gone, making his way upriver with tempting Erica within easy reach. *Gone a couple of days*, he'd said. *Anything* could happen in a couple of days, she told herself passionately.

Lying there in tears, she felt betrayed.

But being the kind of woman she was, she did not lie there long. She jumped up and rubbed a kerchief across her wet cheeks and stared out the window at the beautiful Hudson, the river the Indians had called The River that Flows Two Ways.

Did Brett's heart, like this river, flow two ways? Toward Erica Hulft in one direction and toward herself in another? And if so, was not the answer to make Brett jealous? Why should not her own heart bend two ways—toward Brett her husband *and* toward debonair Nicolas van Rappard?

And she would see Nicolas at the ten Haers' ball!

With anger sparkling in her turquoise eyes, Georgiana made her plans.

But each day's passage was irksomely slow with Brett gone. Georgiana tried to learn Dutch ways and Dutch words, she consulted with the seamstress who was trying with some difficulty to remake a heavy velvet dress from the sea trunk Brett had given her aboard the *Dame Fortune*, she supervised the cleaning and making up of the bedchambers in case they should have unexpected guests—and she moved the furniture about.

"We must clean behind each piece," she insisted. "Heaven knows when it was last done!"

"Even *that*?" They were standing in Georgiana's bedchamber and Linnet looked in awe at the seven-foot-wide armoire of solid cedar that rose to towering heights above them.

Somewhat daunted, Georgiana stared at the armoire. Since most of the furnishings were heavy and carved, she had already enlisted the services of a straining Wouter and one of the stableboys but the weight of this gargantuan piece looked to be beyond them.

At that moment a moth chose to fly out from behind it.

"Even that," she said firmly.

" 'Tis a massive piece," sighed Wouter when she told him she wanted it moved to the other side of the room. And enlisted the aid of yet another stableboy.

With maddening slowness, the three of them moved the heavy piece, for they had no doubt of its value and since it was not only richly carved but gleaming and polished, they knew they must take exceeding care.

And to everybody's surprise, once the armoire was moved a door was uncovered—a door that not even Wouter had known was there. When Georgiana opened it, another shock met her. It was, she saw, an anteroom. Elise must have slept here in the days when this had been Imogene's bedchamber. But now it was full of trunks and when the trunks were opened, they revealed women's clothes.

Looking at the rich laces, the gleaming satins and velvets, the gold and silver tissue and stiff brocades—all of it heavily scented with lavender—Georgiana marveled. This trove must have belonged to her mother—to Imogene! Verhulst must have put them in here to get them out of his sight, all these reminders of his golden woman— and he had barricaded the door with that great heavy wardrobe lest in his grief he be tempted to seek again the things she had worn and touched.

How he must have loved her, Georgiana thought, awed. And for the first time she pitied the young patroon who had held her mother prisoner in this big echoing house, and who had not long survived her.

She felt tears sting her eyelids as she bent over these things that her mother's fingers had touched, these rich and delicate fabrics she had chosen, these elegant clothes she must have loved—and for a long, sighing moment Georgiana felt that Imogene, the wild young mother she had never known, was there beside her.

"I think we have moved enough furniture now," she told Linnet hoarsely. "Thank Wouter and the stableboys and tell them cook has a big pasty waiting for them to share in the kitchen."

She was still bending over the trunks, bemused, as the men's footsteps died away.

"Help me bring all these things into the bedchamber, Linnet," she told the girl when she came back. "I want to try them on and see if I can wear any of them."

As it turned out, she could wear them all. Although she was about two inches shorter than her mother, so that the gowns now swept the floor, they fit her figure admirably. Some, she realized regretfully as she paraded before the tall pier glass while Linnet marveled, were quite out of style now. But some with only the slightest alteration could be worn.

She tried on all but the wedding gown. *That* she touched with reverence and laid away to rest in its white, lavender-scented loveliness. Her turquoise eyes were brooding as they fingered the elaborate white satin brocade encrusted with seed pearls, the petticoat of shimmering white silk, the delicate gloves. Her mother had been as young as she when she had worn this—and as filled with dreams.

She would not disturb those dreams now. Silently she laid the dress away.

"I'll wager if Erica Hulft had known these things were here, they wouldn't be here now!'' Linnet's cheerful voice broke in on her moody thoughts.

Erica...in the excitement of finding her mother's things, Georgiana had forgotten Erica.

"I don't doubt you're right," she agreed dryly. And, then, to banish Erica from this day of discovery, she pointed out to Linnet one of the loveliest of her mother's collection of ball gowns. "I think this one would be perfect for the ten Haers' ball, don't you?"

"Oh, yes," sighed Linnet, stroking the heavy Chinese gold satin of the dress Georgiana had chosen. Although neither of them knew it, this was one of the dresses that had made Verhulst van Rappard call Imogene his "golden bird of Amsterdam."

With its heavily embroidered lemon satin petticoat and the special chemise, obviously meant to be worn with it, made of fragile white lawn with big puffed sleeves that spilled a spidery web of white lace caught up with golden ribands, it was dreamily beautiful. Georgiana, trying it on and marveling, could almost feel she was touching her lovely doomed young mother, who had worn this dress before her.

But in the back of her mind hovered the thought that if she wore this gown to the ten Haers' ball, even sumptuous Erica Hulft would not outshine her!

Brett returned and Georgiana, who had spied his sails from the window, promptly retired to the kitchen to consult with cook until she was sure he must have reached the house. She did not intend to run out and meet him, she would not run out to meet any man who had left with his sloop pacing Erica's!

When she could not find him downstairs, she went up to her bedchamber, intending to act surprised at seeing him. She found him standing in the newfound door to the anteroom. He whirled as she entered.

"What's this?" he demanded.

"We found it when I had the armoire moved over there." She nodded toward its new place, bitterly conscious that he had given her no real greeting.

Brett was looking about the anteroom, puzzled. "Verhulst must have blocked it," he muttered. "I wonder why? What did you find in here?"

"Nothing but those trunks of clothes," said Georgiana, coming up behind him. "They belonged to my mother and I think he must have walled them up because he couldn't bear to look at them after she was drowned—they reminded him of her. I imagine Elise slept in here—it's large enough. You can look inside the trunks if you like.''

"No, I'll leave that to you," said Brett restlessly. He ran his fingers through his hair. "Georgiana—" he began, and stopped.

She looked at him inquiringly.

"Is supper ready?" he asked. "I'm starved."

She was sure that was not what he had meant to say, and said "almost ready" and waited, but he did not enlighten her. She did not ask, for she was half afraid that what he had to say concerned Erica. It made her manner toward him cold at supper but Brett did not seem to notice. He was reserved, distant, preoccupied.

No sooner had the dishes been cleared from the table than Georgiana announced that she had a headache and went upstairs to bed. Brett did not follow her. He stood moodily, staring at the fireplace. She was not even sure he heard her crisp "Good night."

Once in bed, Georgiana waited tensely for the sound of his footsteps in the hall. When at last she heard them, she hastily pretended sleep. She noted that he paused at her door before going on into his own room. He had "looked in on her," no doubt! But he had not—as she was sure he would have before Erica Hulft's visit—come in and quietly joined her in the big bed.

Silently Georgiana wept into her pillow and told herself she did not care.

From that day there was a new coolness between them. A coolness that lasted right through to the ten Haers' ball. When Georgiana had asked Brett about his trip, he had frowned. "I believe the Michaelius woman to be innocent of her husband's death. Her neighbors of course do not share my view. They insist that she and Kray killed him."

"Kray is her lover, then?"

"Reputed to be."

"Why? Why do you who never really knew her believe her to be innocent when those who know her well are so convinced of her guilt?"

He turned toward her, frowning, and tossed back a lock of dark hair that had fallen over his eyes. "I don't know exactly. But there was something in her face, in her voice when she spoke of him . . . something *lost*. But there is much evidence against her.'' He sighed. ''I have sent for the *schout*.''

''Is she beautiful?''

He nodded. ''In a dark, sensuous way. Hers is a face to stir men—I think that may be why the women are so set against her.''

Georgiana's lip curled. Beautiful . . . *that* was the reason Brett believed the Michaelius woman to be innocent! Erica Hulft had beauty too. . . .

''It may be true about Kray having an affair with her, Georgiana, but I cannot believe she had any part in her husband's murder. I have learnt more about Jan Michaelius, the murdered man. It seems that he treated his young wife with great brutality. She was seldom without bruises. Once he broke her arm. Perhaps she had reason to kill him.'' He looked moody.

Georgiana could not resist asking, ''Did Erica decide on the site for her castle?''

''I don't know. I stopped at the place nearest the Michaelius *bouwerie* and set out to reach it overland. Erica sailed on; I do not know what she has decided.''

Georgiana moistened her lips with her tongue. ''Then she did not stop when you did?''

A look of anger passed over Brett's dark face. It gave him suddenly an evil look and she would have shrunk back from him had not jealousy urged her on.

''Georgiana,'' he said quietly, spacing his words. ''I will not tolerate these long tiresome inquisitions. Be direct. Ask me what you want to know.''

''Did she not stop when you did?'' repeated Georgiana stubbornly.

Brett passed a restless hand through his hair. ''Yes, damn it, she did! Her sloop had fouled its rudder with a drifting log and my crew helped clear it.''

So Erica had stepped ashore with Brett. They had been alone together, the fox-haired minx and the tall man who had once loved her, perhaps loved her still. Alone in the virgin wilderness. The great chestnut trees had sighed above their heads and they had walked through a primeval Eden together. . . . She had asked him and he had told her—and now Georgiana wished she had not asked at all. A clock was ticking very loud in the stillness of the room. Georgiana drew a long shaky breath.

"Now," he continued—and she felt the sting of contempt in his voice, "ask me what you really want to know. *Did I sleep with her?*"

Georgiana's hands were clenched so tightly she felt the bones of her fingers must break from the pressure, but she kept her mouth tightly shut as she glared at him.

'*Ask!*'' His tone was rough and peremptory.

"How dare you use that tone with me?" she cried wildly. "I am your wife—I have a right to know where you are and with whom!"

"Very well, I was with Erica Hulft—but briefly, for her sloop sped on as soon as we had cleared the rudder."

She stared at him in an agony of doubt, for she was not sure she believed him. She had been asking herself strange questions all the time he had been gone: If he chose to keep a mistress, would she even know about it? If he chose to renew his old relationship with Erica, would she know when they met or where? Would she know when they clasped each other close, what they murmured, what promises were made?

No, she told herself miserably, she would *not* know. Marriage was based on trust and she was beginning not to trust this tall determined fellow she had married.

"I am telling you the truth, Georgiana," Brett said quietly. "I have always told you the unvarnished truth."

She looked back at him, wondering, doubting. True, he had before this told her bitter truths. He had said that if one of Bernice's homely daughters had been heiress to Windgate, he would have married *her*. Why, then, should she doubt him now?

In her heart she knew it was the blazing vision of Erica herself that stood between them. A sumptuous woman, sophisticated, worldly, adorned in the latest fashion with jewels sparkling at her ears and throat. A woman who would stop at nothing.

She was desperately afraid of Erica. For Erica, she felt, could destroy her.

"I don't wish to discuss it," she said hoarsely and stumbled from the room. In the hall outside she leaned against the wall and felt her whole body shake with spent emotion. Beautiful Erica, twining her coils around Brett again—*what could Erica not do to her life*?

That night Georgiana locked her door. Brett tried it once—but not again.

The coolness between them increased.

As she dressed for the ten Haers' ball, her face flamed again at the memory of that humiliating conversation with Brett. She had not locked her door after that night, but to her distress he had not again tried her door. He had slept in his own room. She did not know quite what to do about that, for she had always known he was a man who would not plead—he would accept or he would take, nothing in between.

And she was too proud to make the overtures.

It was only too clear that she had alienated him. He seemed hardly to see her, to be absorbed in the affairs of the estate.

Whether that indifference was real or imagined on her part, she told herself she could not be sure. Brett was a strange, complex man, she did not even pretend to understand him. He had one love—Windgate. And after that, did anything else really count?

To Georgiana, the girl who so desperately needed to be first, it was a galling realization.

Linnet was dressing her. One by one, with maddening slowness, Linnet's fingers fastened the myriad hooks that held the tight bodice of Georgiana's beautiful Chinese gold satin gown.

"This color goes wonderful with your hair," Linnet observed. "But 'tis a pity to hide this lovely petticoat." She touched the embroidered lemon satin reverently.

"You can pull the overskirt back into fluffed panniers when we get there," Georgiana promised her indulgently. "And then the petticoat will show nicely. Come, you must wear something nice too, Linnet. What about that blue kirtle I gave you? And the doublet with the slashed sleeves lined in gold?"

It had been almost her favorite costume around the house but Linnet had admired it so, Georgiana had given it to the girl.

Linnet brightened. "I was afraid you'd think it was above my station," she admitted honestly. "I was so glad you were taking me along, I was going to wear my homespun!"

"All the ladies will bring their maids along. Wear the blue, it becomes you. Who knows, perhaps one of the footmen will fall in love with you!"

Or perhaps one of the male guests might fancy her! thought Linnet joyfully, and hurried away to dress herself in her best.

Georgiana cast a wistful look after her. If only her heart were as light as Linnet's!

BOOK IV
The Notorious Rake

What will he remember, when his life is spent?
Gold that trickled through his fingers? Where it went?
No, he'll remember turquoise eyes that smiled into his own
A lilting laugh and fair white arms—that could have brought
*   him home....*

PART ONE:
The Handsome Schemer

What a choice he now must face
Here at the ten Haers' ball....
The lady or the great estate?
Faith, he would have them all!

Haerwyck On The Hudson,
1673

CHAPTER 15

Clad in a gown that made her seem—like her mother before her—a woman of gold, Georgiana boarded the *River Witch* along with Brett and an excited Linnet, for the short sail to Haerwyck. Just before leaving she reread the part about Rychie ten Haer in her mother's journal:

It is plain Rychie hates me. And she is envious too, for she once turned down Verhulst's offer of marriage and apparently she expected him to languish forever! So although the ten Haers are our nearest neighbors downriver, I can expect no help there. If only I could reach Vrouw Berghem who was so kind to me in New Amsterdam!

And now Rychie's daughter, Katrina, had expected to marry Brett, and Imogene's daughter had cut her out! Georgiana thought wryly that *she* could expect no help there either!

The trip downriver was uneventful, punctuated by Linnet's bright chatter and Brett's deep-toned answers. He was very kind to Linnet, Georgiana thought, troubling to explain to her that the mighty Hudson on which they traveled was only half as long as the Rhine but much deeper.

" 'Tis said that in places it's bottomless!'' Linnet said in awe.

Brett laughed. "No river is bottomless, else it would flow into the ground and be lost, but I suppose the Hudson is as deep as any. It cuts a deep gorge down to the sea." Georgiana leaned against the rail, watching the water and listening idly in the dusk, with the dark shapes of the rounded hills rising up about them in grandeur. The sky was a mellow gold and shadowy blue as the sun set and above them a narrow rind of pale moon was rising. The wind blew her hair and from the shore came the sleepy night sounds of birds chirping a last good night, and all the little creatures of the night beginning to stir. There was a nip in the breeze tonight that told her the soft days were waning and the harsh northern winter was soon to come.

"I still don't understand how a river can flow two ways," Linnet was insisting. She was having a wonderful time, sitting there in her blue kirtle and slashed sleeves, talking to the patroon!

"Well, that's because the tide comes upriver and meets the waters cascading down from the Adirondacks," Brett explained indulgently.

"But don't they meet in a big swash?"

He laughed. "No, they flow over each other. Sometimes it will hold a boat back. Ask our *schipper* to tell you about it. He waxes voluble on the subject!"

"I don't speak enough Dutch to do that and, besides, the only time I ever spoke to the *schipper* he pinched me," pouted Linnet.

"He must have drunk too much Kill-Devil," Brett chuckled, using the local name for Barbados rum. He was in a very good mood tonight, thought Georgiana, even though they had not exchanged more than two words in the last day and a half. He had eyed her gown with approval as she boarded. She had half expected him to comment on it, but he had not. Oh, well, she was sure Nicolas would comment on it—and hopefully in Brett's hearing!

"But you've got more than pinching to worry about," Brett was telling Linnet with mock seriousness. "I hear they're counterfeiting wampum now in New Orange."

"Oh, no!" cried Linnet in real distress, for she had been hoarding the black wampum beads, three of which were worth about a stiver, in the belief that they were getting scarce and she would double her money.

Georgiana, who knew about Linnet's secret hoard, was about to tell Brett to stop teasing Linnet when there was a cry from the other side of the sloop. A whale had been sighted, swimming majestically upriver. They watched the great beast in awe, saw water spray up suddenly from its snout.

"That's a rare sight," Brett told them gravely. "And it well may be the last whale you'll see on the river. When I first came here it was fairly common to see a whale."

"Civilization," sighed Georgiana whimsically, joining in the conversation at last. "It's creeping in everywhere. The big wild cats are gone, and now the whales. What will be next?"

"The trees, I imagine," said Brett.

"The *trees*?" She was fascinated, for on all sides all she could see was virgin forest.

"Some of them at least. I'm referring to the tanners. I can see it becoming a great industry here. They'll strip the trees of bark and the trees will die." He sighed. "That's progress, I'm afraid."

And with his words Georgiana was wistfully reminded how very much Brett loved this country—more than he could ever love any woman. She shivered and pulled her silk shawl around her although the night was not cold.

She tensed as their sloop docked at the ten Haers' wooden pier, identical to the one at Windgate only not quite so long. Another sloop was just docking as they gained the dock but Georgiana's gaze was focused elsewhere.

"Isn't that Jack Belter?" she asked, peering at the big black-bearded man who was just then striding up the pier.

Brett's dark head swung around to look. "So it is," he murmured. "I didn't know you'd met him. He keeps to himself mostly."

"I rode by his *bouwerie* once. . . . What do you think he's doing here? He can't have been invited!"

"No, I doubt the ten Haers would invite him." He grinned. "Maybe Belter's having an affair with one of the chambermaids!"

She would have made him a tart rejoinder but at that moment the party from the other sloop that had just docked spilled over and Jack Belter was forgotten as Brett introduced the patroon of Rensselaerwyck and his family. All of them swept in together.

From the outside, Georgiana had had an impression of an over-grown Dutch farmhouse but inside she was impressed by Haerwyck's handsome furnishings. The small deep-silled windows held Chinese vases and articles of cloisonné and chased silver. On the wide scoured boards of the floors—except for the big living room, which was cleared for dancing—lay thick Turkey carpets, and the chairs and tables were of exotic woods: teak and sandalwood and other woods from the Far East—a reminder to Georgiana that Holland was a seafaring nation and New Netherland was her colony. Tall-masted East Indiamen had brought across the oceans the blue-and-white China plates that were so proudly displayed on the curtained mantels.

Icily correct, her saffron-haired hostess, vividly gowned in scarlet overgown and yellow petticoat, greeted her. She was a tall buxom woman, was Rychie, with large powerful features. How well her mother had described her, thought Georgiana: *Rychie is overpowering. She flashes her big white teeth like a wolf and shakes all that startling hair to gain attention. Men are attracted to her but they are also afraid of her, I think. Afraid she may devour them.*

Now Imogene's daughter, staring into Rychie's brilliant blue eyes, hard as China plates, had the same impression.

Now it was Rychie's daughter who was welcoming her and Georgiana's heart quickened as she viewed her other rival.

Katrina ten Haer's manner could not have been more correct. She smiled winsomely at Georgiana. Like her mother she was big and showy. She had her mother's large white teeth and thick saffron hair, but from her father's side she had inherited large expressive brown eyes as melting as a spaniel's and a more slender graceful figure than Rychie had ever possessed. Despite Erica's spiteful comments, Georgiana saw that Katrina had a complexion as smooth as cream. The sun and wind of the Hudson River country had kissed her skin to gold and she was wearing a wide-skirted gown of saffron velvet with huge puffed sleeves slashed with brown satin and laced with wide brown velvet strips the color of her eyes. Her petticoat was a rippling brown satin embroidered in gold and almost as handsome as Georgiana's. Her neckline seemed to plunge down forever toward her voluptuous rounded breasts as though to an abyss, and her cleavage was fantastic.

Georgiana drew in a quick breath. *Here* was competition.

"We are so glad you could come," Katrina was saying in her lightly accented English. Her smiling gaze passed over Georgiana to rest lazily on Brett.

Georgiana was suddenly uncomfortably aware that she was in very fashionable company. She had had the passing impression of a farmhouse—and it was not. She had expected these people to be basically simple country folk—and they were not. Her gown, which she had taken up only a little, for she hated to spoil the long sweep of it, was unfashionably long here. The sophisticated Dutch ladies all wore their dresses daringly short, displaying excellent ankles. She wished she had had her gown hemmed up more deeply before leaving Windgate, but it was too late now!

Her gaze focused suddenly on the delicate necklace Katrina ten Haer was wearing around her sun-kissed throat. Gold links and a diamond pendant—why, it was the exact same necklace that Nicolas had given to *her* with such protestations of infatuation, the one Brett had torn from her throat, that had almost caused a duel between them! Nicolas must have had it repaired in a hurry to give it to Katrina, she thought with a little rush of indignation at this sign of his fickleness.

She came back to the world. Katrina ten Haer was speaking to her.

"Are you happy in your new home, in Windgate?" Katrina inquired in a bored voice, as a chattering group swished by.

"Oh, yes, very happy," said Georgiana mechanically, stepping a little to the side to let the group pass. She thought she might escape then, but it was not to be. Katrina's voice—as penetrating as her mother's—found her, pinned her.

"You do not find it strange here? This northern landscape when you are used to balmy weather and palm trees?"

"No, it is very beautiful here," said Georgiana truthfully. "And very wild," she added. She had been about to say "savage" but thought better of it. This spaniel-eyed girl with the commanding features would certainly respond unfavorably to *that*!

"And the house," persisted Katrina. "Does it please you?"

"It astonishes me," admitted Georgiana. "I did not expect anything half so grand."

"Indeed?" A little coldness crept into those melting brown eyes. "But then we Dutch do things on a grand scale." Her lofty manner seemed to diminish the wife of the "English patroon," to point out that, after all, Windgate with all its glories had been built by a Dutchman.

"I am sure you do." Georgiana was mindful she must be polite to her hostess.

"But are you not lonely in such a large house?" persisted

Katrina. She wafted an ivory fan decorated with brown ostrich plumes, although the night, even in this packed house, was scarcely warm enough to warrant it. Georgiana decided Katrina wanted to display the rippling brown satin lining of her enormous enveloping sleeves and the amethysts set in silver, which seemed to hold the brown ostrich plumes to her fan.

"I find things to do."

"Of course. And perhaps you will not be so lonely after all, for there will be Erica Hulft from time to time to keep you company—or has she not been there yet to call upon you?"

Katrina's barb had gone home. Georgiana felt hot color rise to her cheeks. Behind her, Brett's face went stony.

"I doubt we will see much of Erica, Katrina," he cut in before Georgiana could answer. "Now that she is marrying Govert Steendam. She will be living downriver in New Orange."

The saffron brows raised slightly. "Is she indeed? I did not know. But then I suppose such women are never faithful. . . ." A shrug of her big velvet sleeves dismissed Erica's moral character. "But of course you *have* met her?" She was watching Georgiana keenly. "Nicolas told me she was going upriver. She must have stopped by?"

No chance to lie now and say she had never laid eyes on Erica. This time Brett did not help her. Georgiana felt she might suffocate.

"Erica stopped by on her way to view some property Govert proposes to buy near Rensselaerwyck," she said carefully.

Katrina's smile was malicious. "Near Rensselaerwyck? So if they buy it, she will be constantly on the move, up and down the river, pausing to visit you each time she journeys. When she 'dropped in,' she stayed the night, I'll be bound!"

"Of course," said Georgiana steadily. "We could not be so inhospitable as *not* to invite her to spend the night."

"Of course you could not!" Katrina's smile deepened. "Brett was ever hospitable." Her penetrating voice raked over Georgiana's raw feelings like a claw. "And her sloop paced Brett's upriver, I'll be bound—until hers fouled its rudder and they had to land."

Georgiana gasped. How could Katrina know that? News surely traveled fast along the river!

"Was it a happy landing?" Katrina turned doe eyes to Brett.

"It was brief," he said evenly. "My crew helped clear her rudder and the lady went on north while I struck out toward the east overland to the Michaelius *bouwerie*."

"Ah, yes, the Michaelius woman who killed her husband," murmured Katrina. "I heard about that. . . ." But her bright wicked smile told him she did not believe a word he was saying.

Huygens ten Haer came up and clapped Brett jovially on the shoulder—he was obviously trying to demonstrate that although the "English patroon" might have difficulties with some of those along the river, his nearest neighbor was not one of them. He bore Brett away with him, and Georgiana, wishing she were anywhere else, asked, "Will Erica be here tonight?"

Katrina shrugged. When she did answer, Georgiana thought her voice unnaturally loud. "If Govert brings her, she will be here. *He* was invited of course and my father says Govert's betrothed must be made welcome." So she *had* known of Erica's betrothal! She continued to regard Georgiana with those large spaniel-like brown eyes, so at odds with what Georgiana considered rather hard features. "If *I* were mistress of Windgate and Erica Hulft arrived at my front door, I would throw her out, no matter what Brett said about it!"

Georgiana, looking at this big Dutch girl with her flashing eyes, little doubted it. Bodily, she would imagine. She could picture the scene—both woman screeching and kicking, gloved fingers locked alike in fox-brush hair and saffron.

"But then *you* are not mistress of Windgate," she observed softly. The shot went home.

"No—thank God," said Katrina crushingly. "I consider it a narrow escape, for I well might have been. Brett will never relinquish Erica, you must know that. If you do not, I tell you so now. That woman is a vulture. She gets her talons hooked into a man and she never lets go. Did you know that Lodowyck Verplanck blew out his brains with a pistol when Erica left him for Brett?"

"No." Georgiana was taken aback. "I did not know it!"

Katrina gave her a distant, pitying look. "You have much to learn. And before that there was Wilbruch Hendrickson, who gambled away his fortune to please her. And before that"—she made a small deprecating gesture that shook her big puffed velvet sleeves—"so many others. But"—her eyes shone maliciously—"there was always Brett hovering in the background. Brett had only to snap his fingers and Erica would desert her latest paramour and return to him. I see you have much to learn at Windgate.''

Georgiana managed to control her inner fury. "Apparently I have,'' she told Katrina sweetly, and then delivered a crusher of her own: "but I have only to come to Haerwyck to learn all about it!''

"Georgiana, what nonsense is our madcap Katrina filling your pretty head with?'' It was Nicolas, coming up behind Katrina to smile over her saffron head at Georgiana. A splendid Nicolas in brown velvet the exact shade of Katrina's eyes—and of Katrina's petticoat and ribands as well, so fine a match that Georgiana was sure they must have planned it together. Nicolas's doublet was so heavily laced in gold that he seemed to gleam. His blue eyes too gleamed wickedly as Katrina turned with a bright smile. Her gaze on Nicolas was possessive, caressing. "I had forgot that you two know each other,'' she said carelessly.

It was Georgiana's turn to needle. "Oh, yes,'' she said airily. "In the short time I have been at Windgate, I have not lacked for callers. There was Erica, who stayed overnight, and Nicolas, who stayed longer and taught me to play chess and told me so much about the life here on the river. How are you, Nicolas? It is good to see you again.''

Katrina's smile grew a little fixed. "You taught Georgiana to play chess?''

Nicolas grinned. "Yes. I might have taught her to play tennis, which the English king so admires—''

"But that I already play!'' Georgiana cut in laughingly.

"But we could not play outdoor games,'' he continued ruefully, "for it was raining. We were confined to indoor sports.'' His hot gaze caressed Georgiana, slid down her throat to rest on the daring sweep of her décolletage, for this was a gown that Imogene had once worn, and Imogene had worn her necklines cut *low*.

"Indoor sports?'' echoed Katrina. There was indignation in her tone. She gave Georgiana a black look. Plainly Katrina considered that Nicolas belonged to her.

After the drubbing she had taken about Erica, Georgiana was eager to return the favor. She laughed. "Nicolas played—and sang to me.'' Her voice grew lazy, languourous. "It was all very—pleasant.''

Plainly her hostess did not consider it so pleasant. Bright spots of color appeared on Katrina's hard-featured face and she wielded her plumed fan with uncalled-for briskness.

"I see," she said stiffly.

"I like your necklace," drawled Georgiana, with a sidewise glance at Nicolas.

Nicolas came alert.

Katrina touched the necklace with some hauteur. "Nicolas gave it to me."

"Somehow I guessed that," murmured Georgiana.

Nicolas gave her an uneasy look.

Katrina's big white teeth snapped together. There was an undercurrent here that she neither understood nor trusted. "Nicolas," she said stiffly. "I would speak with you in private. Will you excuse us, Georgiana?"

"Of course." Reflectively, Georgiana watched them go, melt into the crowd around the dancers. As golden a pair as could be found on the river, she'd wager. But Nicolas van Rappard was in for a tongue-lashing—that too, she'd wager. For there was certainly nothing subtle about Katrina!

CHAPTER 16

"There you are!" caroled a voice and Georgiana turned to find a stout elderly lady, with enormous panniers of green brocade trimmed in black lace, bearing down on her. "Why, I would know you anywhere—you look exactly like your mother!" The stout lady grasped Georgiana by the arms and peered up earnestly into her face. "No, not quite like her. Her eyes were blue and yours are—blue green, I think."

"Turquoise," supplied Georgiana, bewildered. "But who—"

"And your hair's not quite the same, a bit more coppery, and I think you may be shorter—but you're wondering who I am! I'm Vrouw Berghem.''

"Of course,'' cried Georgiana delightedly. "My mother—'' No, she could not say "spoke of you so often in her journal,'' for that would be to admit she had the journal. "My mother's friend,'' she substituted quickly.

"Her friend indeed! I was there the night Captain van Ryker near stole her from the Governor's Ball!'' Vrouw Berghem's throaty laughter pealed. "Verhulst challenged him to a duel, but there was a fire and after the fire Captain van Ryker sailed away. I hear he was seen in New Amsterdam once since then—I wonder why? He used to come there so often. But, then, perhaps he has,'' she added merrily, "for all my news is secondhand. I have been living with my eldest daughter in Holland these years past—can you imagine, she has two sets of twins? And I have only just returned this past month to sell my house. Poor thing, it has been sitting vacant all these years. I found it covered with dust—indeed, I have been hard put to get the floor white-scoured and the fireplace tiles shining and a new mantel curtain up—for it must look nice, you know, if it is to fetch a good price.''

With Vrouw Berghem's fast-skipping comments swirling about her head, Georgiana let the old lady drag her to a quiet corner. She smiled warmly and tried to answer all the buxom Dutch vrouw's questions, for running through her mind were the words in her mother's journal, that heartfelt *If only I could reach Vrouw Berghem.* . . .

"You must come back with us to Windgate and pay us a long visit,'' she told the older woman warmly.

"Ah, I would, I would, but I am due back in New Amsterdam—I cannot remember to call it New Orange, just as I never could remember to call it New York! I should not even be here tonight, for day after tomorrow in the afternoon I have an appointment to show my house. And it is not presentable, not presentable at all! There is so much to do, more than I can manage.'' She shook her head helplessly.

"Perhaps Govert Steendam will buy it,'' hazarded Georgiana. "I understand he is to marry Erica Hulft.''

Vrouw Berghem looked at her sharply. "Govert Steendam already has a fine house of his own in New Amsterdam. And I can see from your face that you have heard stories. But you are not to listen to them! Brett Danforth is not the man the gossips would make him out to be. It is that Hulft woman who makes men crazy. She with her hair like a fox's tail! I have been hearing about her ever since I arrived back in New Amsterdam.''

"What—do the gossips say, Vrouw Berghem?'' asked Georgiana diffidently. "People hint but they never tell me. I ak you because I know you will tell me the truth, for you were my mother's true friend.''

Vrouw Berghem drew in her breath and exhaled it again before she spoke. "Well,'' she said uncertainly. "You are a new bride and new brides have no trouble holding on to their husbands. I should not think you would need to know anything.''

"But I do. Erica Hulft has already spent a night in my house. When she left, my husband's sloop paced hers upriver. Her rudder became fouled and so they went ashore.''

"Ah-h-h, I see.'' Vrouw Berghem sucked in her breath through her teeth. It made a whistling sound. "So Erica does not plan to let go?''

Georgiana was glad there was no one standing nearby.

"I do not think she does,'' she admitted in a hurried voice.

"Then that *is* a problem.'' Vrouw Berghem's brows drew together thoughtfully.

"Katrina has just told me that if she were in my place, she would throw Erica out bodily.''

"And I am sure she would do it,'' said Vrouw Berghem energetically. "And possibly drive her husband right into Erica's arms! For I have met your husband, Georgiana, and he is not a man to let some woman tell him what to do or not do. It would never have done for him to marry Katrina ten Haer. She is too like Rychie. Do you notice how Huygens ten Haer ducks his head whenever he goes near his wife? It is an unconscious gesture, but to me it looks as if he is used to her words raining down on him like blows!''

Georgiana laughed. She had not noticed that, but now she certainly would. "Then you advise me to do nothing?''

"It takes two to dance a measure,'' said Vrouw Berghem frankly. "And if one refuses, the other may jump about but nothing will come of it.''

Georgiana bit her lip. "Katrina ten Haer tells me that Erica Hulft has had many lovers but always returns to Brett.''

"And that should tell you something!" exclaimed the older woman triumphantly. "Is it not plain that Brett relinquishes her to anyone who will take her? He is not trying to hold on to her, is he?"

No, but perhaps he does not have to. Perhaps he knows his power over Erica.

"Also," added Vrouw Berghem with a frown, "you are forgetting Govert Steendam. He is a dour man who will not let his wife go cavorting about falling into bed with anyone she pleases. He will keep Erica in line!"

But he had not kept her from pursuing Brett upriver . . . thought Georgiana. "I am sure you are right, Vrouw Berghem," she said mechanically. "I have nothing to worry about."

"That's right, put a good face on it." Vrouw Berghem gave Georgiana's arm a jolly punch. "Remember, you're prettier than Erica, and younger. *You* wear his ring, *you'll* bear his children."

And every day my enemy grows older. . . . But there was cold comfort in that, thought Georgiana ruefully, for growing old could take a very long time.

The music struck up.

"Ah, we are going to dance again!" cried Vrouw Berghem, looking about joyfully for a partner.

Georgiana turned and waved imperiously to Brett. He came over to them, smiling.

"Vrouw Berghem." He acknowledged the older lady's presence. "I think my bride wishes me to lead her out upon the floor, if you will excuse us."

"No," said Georgiana impulsively. "I wish you to lead Vrouw Berghem out upon the floor, for she was my mother's true friend and I would like you to do her honor and dance your first dance with her."

Vrouw Berghem looked delighted. She bounced up, flushed-faced and smiling. Brett gave his bride an approving look and whirled the stout lady in green out among the dancers. Across the room Georgiana saw that Katrina ten Haer had noted this little tableau and her saffron brows shot up.

"Now that we are so cleverly rid of the husband, let us not waste this music!" It was Nicolas's wicked voice behind her. Georgiana turned and Nicolas took that opportunity to seize her hand and whirl her out upon the floor.

"You take long chances," laughed Georgiana.

Nicolas, who danced very elegantly, made a handsome turn and smiled down at her. "Oh, I do not think Danforth would run me through merely for claiming a dance," he said carelessly.

"No, but *she* might!" Georgiana nodded her dancing curls toward Katrina ten Haer across the room. Katrina had seen them and was looking stormy.

"Ah, yes, *she* might." The golden-bearded face split into a grin. "But, then, women were ever dangerous. It is part of their attraction. Tell me, Georgiana, what concealed weapons do *you* carry?" His significant gaze fell to her round breasts, rising and falling with the slight exertion of the dance.

Georgiana gave him a wary look. "Nicolas, you are a rake indeed! You scheme to scoop my very home out from under me and yet you pay me court like any gallant!"

"There would be no reason for you to leave Windgate if I were to win my claim," he said coolly.

Georgiana blinked. "You are saying you would allow us to remain?" she demanded incredulously. "I can hardly credit it, Nicolas! That would be generosity indeed!"

His head inclined lazily toward hers as if he might kiss her on the mouth, and their bright hair almost tangled as they made a sharp turn on the dance floor. His lazy blue eyes held flickering lights, devil lights. "I did not say Brett could stay," he amended softly. "I said *you* could."

Georgiana stiffened. Instinctively she flinched back. Here was effrontery indeed. She would have drawn away from him but his grip was inexorable. She was abruptly aware that they were attracting attention—not merely because Nicolas was an excellent dancer but because he held her far too close and he was bending dangerously near her face.

"What you suggest is ridiculous," she snapped. "And you know it as well as I."

"No, I don't know it!" was the irrepressible answer. "Just what makes it so ridiculous?"

"Because I'm *married*!"

"Ah, yes—that." He sounded bored.

"Yes, *that*!" snapped Georgiana. "And kindly keep your distance. You are holding me so close that people are beginning to stare."

"You must be used to that," he said equably. "With beauty like yours, people must stare wherever you go."

"And I resent the way you keep treating me as if I were a loose woman. Brett leave and I remain, indeed!"

He leaned toward her lazily. The eyes that gazed down on her were hypnotic; they had lured many a woman from her lawful spouse. "A beautiful woman is like a treasure ship, Georgiana," he told her. "Many hands reach out to her. Only the strongest take her—and hold her."

His voice was caressing, fraught with meaning. Georgiana felt a little ripple of feeling assault her tense nerves.

She was fascinated by this irritating golden Dutchman. And determined not to let him know it. She lifted her chin haughtily and looked past him, making clear that she was ignoring everything he said.

"Your indignation does you credit," he laughed, executing a difficult step with the grace of a dancing master. "And it makes your turquoise eyes turn green as emeralds. I see you now as a golden vision, richly garbed as any queen. Are you telling me you yearn to be a goose girl? I think not. You married a man of wealth and power—not some clerk or stableboy! This is the life you want— admit it!"

Georgiana's head was whirling, but out of it emerged one thing— truth. "In Bermuda," she told him stiffly, "I had many suitors. But with none of them was I truly first. One loved horses, one loved ships, and one loved learning. Not one of them loved me best of all. I do not think any woman will ever be first with *you*, Nicolas. You love adventure, grandiose schemes. God knows where you will end up!"

"In some duchess's bedchamber, doubtless," was his wicked rejoinder. "But you are right, Georgiana, you read me well. I am as other men, I am mad for the thing of the moment—I burn for it, I fight for it! But in that I think we are akin. You were young, untried. Your gaze fell on Brett Danforth—and, granted, he's a man to reckon with. You desired him, you wanted him under your spell. But do you think you're first with him beside that piece of land? If you were on one end of the scales and Windgate balanced on the other, which do you think he'd choose?"

He'd choose Windgate, she thought unhappily. *Nicolas is right.*

But she wasn't going to admit that, not to this smiling Dutchman who was looking at her so keenly!

"Brett would choose *me*, of course!" she said haughtily—and proved how little he had ruffled her by executing an intricate dance step as handily as he.

Nicolas lifted his golden head and laughed. "Spoken like an infatuated child! Here where skirts are worn short and a man is known by the beauty of the mistresses he keeps, you will learn that there are other ways of thinking!"

So he had noticed that her dress was too long! She felt humiliated.

"I do not believe what you say about the morals here," she said hotly.

"You do not? Look at that heavyset fellow over there—the meek-looking one with the long clay pipe who is just now speaking to your husband. That fellow's wife thinks he plays at bowls four evenings a week, but in truth he has two mistresses across town from each other and he visits them on alternate days. That is why he looks so sleepy. And all of them are married—his mistresses' husbands actually play at bowls unaware of what their wives are doing in their absence!"

Georgiana stared over Nicolas's shoulder at the placid face of the man with the clay pipe. He looked so *ordinary*! She could hardly believe Nicolas's story.

"And that fellow just now leading the woman in pink ruffles out on the floor," continued Nicolas, determined to shock her. "*He* was a clerk in a warehouse until he married the owner's widow. When she died, he married a shipowner's widow. He is fast trading up. Who knows, if this one dies, he may marry the owner of a warehouse in some other port and so consolidate his enterprise! And the pale gentleman taking snuff by the door, I know for a fact that *he* has an affair going with every new housemaid his wife employs— she cannot get rid of them fast enough but that he brings in another one! And that sea captain there, the one with the rolling gait and stiff whiskers just now bowing to Vrouw Berghem—he has a 'cabin boy' who is really a girl in boy's clothing. She sleeps in his cabin and attends his needs. His crew looks the other way, I'm told, and dare not bring it to the attention of his wife, who is daughter to the ship's owner. I know it for a fact—I was there one day when the 'cabin boy' dived over the side and bathed in the river. A real mermaid she was, all silvery and blushing with surprise that she had dived in beside me!"

"Come now," said Georgiana crossly. "I think you're making it all up. This is not Paris or London. It is an outlying colony peopled with hard-working fellows and their wives who have neither the time nor the strength for all the dalliance you suggest!"

"Look hardest at these dull communities that seem to be all work and no play," Nicolas advised her with a sage wag of his head. "For these men need *divertissement*—and they will find it!"

"With women like Erica Hulft, no doubt—don't pretend you don't know her, Nicolas, for I saw her standing beside you when our sloop pulled away from the dock in New Orange."

"Ah, yes, Erica," he said reflectively. "Everyone knows Erica, I suppose."

"And what is that supposed to mean?"

"Anything you care to read into it." His lazy glance was alive with meaning. "'Tis women like Erica make the world more delightful for men."

"Especially the roving kind. Like you," she said rudely.

"Yes, the roving kind—like myself, for instance."

Georgiana sniffed.

His sunny smile played over her. "And like your husband," he added softly.

Georgiana stiffened. "Please do not equate yourself with Brett!"

"And why not?" he challenged her humorously. "All that he owns may one day belong to me!"

"Not *all*!" She gave him a dangerous look. "Never *all*, Nicolas. Whatever happens to Windgate, *I* do not go with it—I will not be part of your prize."

"I wonder . . ." he said thoughtfully.

She could have slapped his handsome face!

"Then cease to wonder," she snapped. "For I assure you that it will not come to pass!"

"You say that now." His smile was lazy, knowing. "I will ask you again when you have come to know Erica Hulft better."

Ah, how that stung! How transparent she must be, Georgiana thought miserably, that Nicolas could pin down so exactly how she felt about provocative Erica! Her senses revolted, but before she could fling away from him—for he must have guessed her intention—

he had whirled her through the open door that led out upon the empty terrace. And in a dizzy whirl, holding her with a grip she could not break, around and around with her golden skirts billowing out so that she seemed like some vivid satin-winged butterfly fluttering across the grass. Swirling around they went, over the gray stones of the terrace, out onto the deep green grass, until they ended up breathless beneath the shadow of a huge chestnut tree.

"Georgiana, Georgiana," Nicolas murmured raptly. "Could you not find it in your heart to love me?"

CHAPTER 17

Before Georgiana could gasp out, *No, I could not love you, Nicolas,* his golden head had bent, his thick heavy hair had tumbled down over her satin shoulder to mingle in a shower of gold with her own silken tresses, and his warm mouth was on hers with a yearning pressure that would not be gainsaid. Silently, thrillingly, insistently, those lips made their own demands. Georgiana's struggles were of no avail. Her slight body was clasped hard to his. Through the gold satin of her tight bodice that held back her straining young breasts, through the brown velvet of his gold-encrusted doublet that covered his deep chest, she could feel the strong beating of his heart—a reckless heart to seize her thus, hold her thus! She felt the soft impetuous tickle of his golden mustaches against her face, his carefully clipped golden beard was pressed like a soft fur piece against her upraised throat, lightly abrading her skin in a way that turned her flesh to goosebumps. She tried to speak and could not, tried to move and could not, tried to resist the dangerous animal magnetism of this man, to stand rigid and unyielding as a statue in his arms—and could not. Before his sweet assault her body quivered. One of his powerful arms was clutched hard around her waist, holding her immobilized while his hand groped for her pulsing breast. His other big firm hand held her head cupped viselike as he explored her lips—and then she felt with a quiver his tongue impudently pushing back her soft lips, parting them, pushing through them past her pearly teeth to quest negligently beyond.

Georgiana's whole body was tense as a coiled spring. She was intimately aware of every brush of her chemise against her soft flesh, of every pressure that Nicolas's strong masculinity exerted. Her mind too was awhirl. Nicolas was a rakehell, an interloper, a fortune hunter, a cheat—he was no good, all the world knew it. Even now he was deceiving her. All this she told herself, but for a moment there beneath the stars that shone down upon the Hudson and made magic of its shores, she believed none of it. His questing tongue was a hot flame of desire that licked at her senses, his hard body a usurper that took her breath away. With her will battered, half crushed by the enthralling pressure of his maleness, Georgiana felt herself slipping, slipping, as if she were being pulled inexorably toward some vast abyss, as if she were adrift upon a broad river and could hear ahead the roar of mighty falls but was powerless to resist the river's swift current, sweeping her ever onward. For a treacherous moment her warm woman's body was seduced into a thrill of acceptance and she melted against Nicolas sinuously, returning kiss for kiss.

Encouraged by her response, his arm went round her the tighter, holding her in a grip that held her breathless.

Instinctively Georgiana had closed her eyes as she lost herself in the magic of his kiss, and now as they flickered open the very stars seemed to dazzle and blind her. Nicolas's eyes were dark pools so close she could lose herself in their burning blue depths. He had wrenched himself away from her mouth at last, allowing her to gasp for air. But his lips even now were but a breath away and his hoarse whisper was felt as much as heard: *"Georgiana, together we would be wonderful..."*

Every word went right through her, piercing her to the heart. *Together we would be wonderful....* It was wicked but it was true. Nicolas's arms were made to hold a woman, every inch of his long masculine body was designed to tempt a woman, to lure her into indiscretions from which there would be no going back.

With a valiant effort, Georgiana got control of her feelings and—almost—of her voice. It still held a slight tremor as she whispered, "Nicolas, I never said—"

"You did not have to. Your body gave you away."

"Then my body lied." She pushed him violently away from her. "I love my husband!"

"That will pass," he said with urbanity. "You who yearn to be first will tire of being second—possibly third—in his heart. Hear me, Georgiana, hear me well. For you I would change. I never thought it possible that I would say that to any woman and mean it. But, for you, I would change. I would become whatever you want me to be."

So intent was his expression, so intense his voice that Georgiana felt in her quaking heart that he was speaking the truth. Nicolas—Nicolas the rakehell, the seducer—was offering her a new life. Indeed, he was offering her a new Nicolas! She wondered wildly if it were possible for a man to change that much.

"What do you mean 'third in his heart'?" she demanded, trying desperately to change the subject, for Nicolas had caught her wrists as he spoke and still held her captive. At any moment some of the other guests might stroll out upon the terrace and what would they think to see Nicolas holding her captive like this?

Every word he said flicked a raw wound. "First with Brett comes Windgate." Contemptuously. "*But not with me*, Georgiana, never with me!" His voice was resonant as music. "If you would love me, Georgiana, if you would run away with me, I would forget my claim, I would leave Brett to enjoy Windgate."

"You can't mean that!" she gasped.

"Before God, I swear it." There could be no doubting the controlled passion in his voice. "There's a sloop at the landing. I would take you away now, tonight!"

She stared at him dizzily, cut adrift from reality by his forcefulness, and caught by something deep within him that seemed to be calling to her, begging her to want him, to love him. And all of this from Nicolas the Rake!

"You cannot have thought this out," she cried. "We would be disgraced! On what would we live?"

She was considering it! Nicolas gave a low triumphant laugh. "The world is wide. We could live at Mirabelle, if you like."

"Ah, yes," she said in a flat voice. "Mirabelle. Let go of my wrists, Nicolas."

"Or you could sell Mirabelle and we would be off and away!" he amended hastily. "I would show you Paris, London—"

"And Amsterdam," she said bitterly. *That was where my mother went wrong!* Nicolas had loosed her wrists but he was advancing on her again. She pushed him away with unsteady hands. "You are very eloquent, Nicolas," she said ruefully. "You almost made me forget that I am a married woman, sworn to a man I love better than you—that I will always love better than you."

He took the blow of her words stolidly, his handsome face a mask, but she heard a tiny regretful sigh as he drew in his breath.

"Then you will spend your life as third in your husband's heart," he told her evenly, brutally. "For Brett Danforth already has a mistress of the heart—one he will never divorce. Her name is Erica Hulft and no matter what her amorous crimes, he always takes her back."

"That was before I came along," scoffed Georgiana.

It was his turn to smile. "Turn your head, Georgiana," he commanded lazily. "Look down toward the river. Do you not see a new sloop there? It belongs to Govert Steendam. Perhaps you have seen it before when it docked at Windgate's pier?"

Georgiana's head swung around and she felt the cool breeze from the river whip her hair. There below her was the handsome sloop that had brought Erica Hulft to Windgate.

Nicolas had caught her arm as she whirled, lest she run away from him. "That sloop's occupants came through the front door just as I whirled you out here—Erica and Govert."

She tried to wrench away. "I am surprised the ten Haers invited them," she said bitterly. "Katrina ten Haer sounded as if she hated Erica."

Nicolas kept a firm grip on her. "And so she does—even as you do. But Katrina's father will not offend a man as powerful and as wealthy as Govert Steendam. Nor will Danforth. You will find yourself inviting them to Windgate whenever you give a ball, welcoming Erica to your home whenever she chooses to call."

"Never!"

"You say that now, but you will do it when Danforth explains his reasons. They will be excellent reasons indeed and you will see the folly of not heeding them. Katrina hates Erica—but Erica is here, attending the ball. And she will be at Windgate too.''

"I will not listen to you!" cried Georgiana. "Let me go, I am going back inside.''

His fingers loosened and she slipped through them like water, ran toward the door. Looking toward the house, she thanked God that there was no one on the terrace, no one who had observed the scene with Nicolas.

At the door she paused, not wanting to attract attention by catapulting through the door as if she were escaping from Nicolas.

"Observe," he remarked, looking about him as they entered the room together. "Your husband is nowhere in sight.''

"He has probably gone looking for me," she flashed.

"And Erica Hulft," he added softly, "is not in view either.''

Georgiana's swift glance swept the room. It was true, neither of them was visible.

"I wonder where they are?" he murmured. "Together, perhaps? Closeted upstairs? Outside beneath the trees?''

Georgiana gave him an angry look. She opened her mouth to denounce him but closed it again as her host, Huygens ten Haer, came up to claim her for a dance.

"We are delighted to have Verhulst van Rappard's daughter home at last at Wey Gat," he said in his gutteral English.

Georgiana, impatient to be off looking for Brett, fearful that Nicolas's innuendoes were all too true, answered mechanically, "It is good to be back in my mother's house.''

"Your father's," he corrected, a little coldness creeping into his tone.

"Yes, of course," she agreed hastily. "I never knew either of them, you see. I was just a baby when—when they died.''

Huygens accepted that, she could see from his mollified expression. She reminded herself that it was important not to offend Huygens ten Haer. Brett had told her he was a magistrate, would be one of those called upon to hear Nicolas's charges, if they were ever brought. She forced a brilliant smile onto her face. "I feel as if I have always lived here," she said insincerely. "Perhaps this lovely river, this Hudson, is in my blood.''

He nodded. "The North River is in all our blood." He called the Hudson by the name the Dutch called it. "Even if you feel strange here now"—his keen eyes searched her face—"you will come to call it home."

Georgiana's color rose. Huygens had seen through her. He might have a harpy for a wife and a vixen for a daughter, but this big Dutchman was no fool. In confusion she looked away from him and caught sight again of Nicolas. He was looking at her fixedly and she could not read his expression, but for a moment, surprisingly, she thought he looked sad. She told herself she must be wrong. That hard, handsome face had never known sadness.

Georgiana would have been touched indeed if she had known what Nicolas was thinking, for a whole new world was flitting through Nicolas's fevered mind: a world in which he would become a changed man, suddenly possessed of virtues he had never had, a world in which he could offer Georgiana a love as true as she deserved, a heart that would never falter. Before him stretched a dazzling future in which he and his golden girl would linger in distant unattainable Mirabelle as in some vanished Eden. Never had a woman affected him so. Nicolas, the carefree rake, was astonished at himself.

With a rueful laugh, he turned to claim Katrina ten Haer for the next dance, for she had managed to position herself artfully near him with that in mind, and he had guessed her intention. As he swung her out on to the floor he told himself that the idyllic life he had envisioned for Georgiana and himself was unattainable, had always been unattainable. He told himself roughly that he was acting the part of the bedazzled swain, that having won her, he would tire of her—as he had tired of other women. But as he gazed thoughtfully at lovely Georgiana, dancing now with the patroon of Rensselaerwyck, he knew himself for a liar. Could he but win her, he would never tire of her. Never.

Now Nicolas's blue eyes lit with dark humor, for across the room he could see Brett Danforth and Erica Hulft just strolling in from the hall. Brett was frowning but Erica, gorgeous in burnt orange velvet highlighted with black and copper lace and sporting the carnelian and diamond brooch that was Govert Steendam's most recent gift to her, looked wickedly triumphant. Then his gaze fled to Georgiana and he saw with irony that angry, baffled look she gave them before her face went back to its polite frozen smile as she replied to something van Rennselaer had said.

"What were you two doing?" she demanded in a furious undertone of Brett when he claimed her for a dance.

"I might ask the same of you," he drawled. "For weren't you just now outside with Nicolas?"

Georgiana's face was stained red at the truth of his accusation and a little tremor went through her at the memory of Nicolas's kiss and how foolishly she had reacted. "He had hold of me and he danced me through the door," she defended, almost missing a step as she prayed Brett had not glimpsed her through the windows! "I could either go where he led me or make a scene—I chose not to make a scene."

"Very commendable of you." Brett's voice was ironic as he whirled her deftly around. "I went with Erica for the same reason."

So Erica would have made a stormy scene if Brett had not gone with her! Georgiana felt a little mollified. "Where did she take you?"

"Into Huygen's office." And to her bewildered look. "It is on the other side of the house." He nodded his head in a direction away from the terrace.

Thank God it was in the other direction—he could not have seen her from the windows! Georgiana breathed easier. "But why did she take you there?" she wondered.

"She wished to consult a map there and show me the land Govert Steendam has bought just south or Rensselaerwyck. She wanted to discuss a deal between Steendam and myself, a joint venture on a mill there. Who knows, it might work."

"And Govert Steendam is a magistrate," Georgiana said bitterly. "He will be one of those who will decide Windgate's ownership if it ever comes to court."

"We would have to wait until that battle is over, of course, lest there be a charge of self-interest on his part."

"Of course." Georgiana shot an angry look across the room at Erica and got a serene look in return before the dancers whirled between them and obscured her view. Erica was sure of her ground now. She was planning to shackle Brett to her with chains of gold—mercantile ties he could not get out of. "But you told me you planned to develop your own mill as near Rensselaerwyck as you could. I thought you planned to develop your own mills."

"A partnership with Steendam might be better in the long run,"

Brett said thoughtfully. "Govert is Dutch and I will remind you that this is a Dutch colony once again. And Govert has vast influence in New Orange."

And Govert Steendam would be unlikely to decide so important a legal matter as the ownership of Windgate *against* the man who was to be his future partner! Ah, it was all very neatly thought out, handsomely packaged, and tied with riband! Erica had done her work well! Georgiana gave her rival a bitter look and was answered by a lighthearted wave of a lace kerchief—her enemy blithely acknowledging her presence. "I wish we had never come to this ball!" she said through her teeth.

"Why?" Brett was startled. "You have seemed to be enjoying yourself, you charmed Vrouw Berghem—and certainly Nicolas van Rappard has been paying you court. Not a person in the room but has noticed it."

"I did not invite his attentions," she said hotly. "And besides, I would think you would want to know what is brewing in that direction."

"Oh, I do, I do." His voice was laced with irony. "But I am not about to share my wife with Nicolas, Georgiana, no matter what he may think. In the courts of kings a man may turn his back upon his wife's dalliance, look the other way and become rich—I am not such a man, Georgiana, so make no deals with Nicolas!"

The warning on his sardonic hawklike face was clear and unmistakable. He had guessed what Nicolas was about and he was warning her.

She tossed her head and in making a turn stepped back with such abandon that she almost crashed into someone. Deftly Brett averted the collision. "And what makes you think I would consider making a deal with Nicolas?" she demanded airily.

"Something reckless in your bearing tonight," Brett told her silkily. "For 'tis a quality I well remember—in myself."

"We are nothing alike, you and I," she scoffed. "Doubtless you made *your* way at the point of a rapier!"

"And you with other points just as potent." His significant gaze swept across the white expanse of her heaving breast, sumptuously displayed in her low-cut gown. Georgiana glared at him and he chuckled. "Come now, shall we forget our differences and enjoy the evening? For there will be few parties on the river when the snow flies.''

It was on the tip of Georgiana's tongue to retort that neither Nicolas nor Erica were apt to allow themselves to be forgotten, when the full significance of her husband's words sank in on her: *few parties on the river when the snow flies. . . .*

''Do you mean boats will not ply the river in the snow?'' she demanded.

''I mean that when the icy cold sweeps down from Canada, the Hudson may well freeze solid from bank to bank—it has done so in the past.'' *Yes, Imogene's journal had told her that.* ''And then the river traffic will come to a crashing halt.''

And Erica Hulft and her new husband would be stuck downriver in New Orange! Georgiana's turquoise eyes sparkled. ''But surely sleighs and ice skates will bring neighbors together?'' she protested, almost skipping.

''Oh, yes, there'll be ice dances and bonfires on the snowy banks and a certain amount of merrymaking, but few large balls such as this.''

Georgiana gave him her sweetest smile and when the music ended, she stepped away from him and suddenly clapped her hands.

''Your attention, everyone!'' she cried. ''For I have an announcement to make.''

Brett's head swung around in surprise and he frowned down at her. Reckless she was, and ever would be so, this girl he had married. He could only hope her jealousy would not lead her into excesses from which he could not extricate her.

Georgiana's voice rang out merrily, floating above the throng. ''We at Windgate would offer all of you our hospitality. When the first snows fall, bring your sleighs across the ice to Windgate and warm yourselves at our hearth. And wear your masks, for we will give a masquerade ball—with ice dancing—to usher in the winter season!''

Startled murmurs greeted this announcement.

''Too vague,'' Brett muttered, and added his voice to hers. ''We will send invitations to all we can reach, weather permitting,'' he said smoothly. ''And we would appreciate your guest list, Huygens, that we may not miss anyone.''

There was a light dusting of applause, but many of the Dutch guests had no love for the "English patroon" who, they felt, had usurped Nicolas van Rappard's rightful inheritance. Still, there was this suddenly produced daughter of Verhulst van Rappard. Warily, they turned to each other, murmuring that they would come—weather permitting. It gave them leeway, was the unspoken agreement between them.

Katrina ten Haer looked daggers at Georgiana, who had thus managed to steal the limelight. But across the room, Erica Hulft moved her burnt orange skirts restlessly in this crush and bit her lips. Would she be able, she wondered, to get Govert to undertake the perilous journey up the frozen Hudson for a ball? Her pretty face hardened. If not, she must arrange to go herself—alone.

But Nicolas, who had just had his glass filled with golden Canary wine, lifted that glass in tribute to Georgiana's impulsive invitation and downed it as he would a toast. With lazy interest, he studied the lovely lady of Windgate. And told himself that he would somehow find a way to capitalize on her desperate throw of the dice.

CHAPTER 18

"If you are suffering van Rappard's attentions in a mistaken effort to aid me, disabuse yourself," said Brett bluntly. "For now that I've married you, he cannot fail to see the folly of pursuing his claim to Windgate. He allows it to hang fire to save face, but he'll not bring it to court."

Georgiana turned her face away, glad to have the darkness hide the guilty color that must be rising there. For although that had been her original intention, to try to divert Nicolas from his attempt to claim Windgate, her interest in Nicolas had subtly changed, evolved into something else. Something she refused to give a name.

They were back on board the *River Witch* and that shallow draft sloop with its red painted hull was carrying them fast upriver away from the festivities, for the house at Haerwyck was crowded and the Danforths had elected not to stay the night but to sail back to Windgate. Nobody was near them on the wide deck, so they could speak freely without being heard. A pale moon glazed the river's dark surface but gave no hint of the brilliant autumn colors that garnished the rounded hills about them. Tonight those hills seemed like the round backs of giant sleeping turtles clustered at the water's edge. There was a little splash as a raccoon broke the surface and swam toward a low-lying branch that scraped the water, climbed upon it. Georgiana was silent, watching him as they sailed past. He clung tightly to the tree with his tiny feet, his russet furry body leaning comfortably in a crook of the branch, looking at them with bright interested eyes.

He was free, she thought, not—as they were—chained to a piece of land. Windgate.

Brett mistook her silence for sullenness.

"If you are angry because I shared a plate with Erica Hulft," he began, "it was Steendam who asked me to do it. It was he who enjoined me to take care of her whilst he conducted some business with Huygens. I could hardly refuse."

"Of course—you could hardly refuse," she echoed him mechanically. "Whilst I shared my portion with Vrouw Berghem, who told me that in Holland, when her grandson was born, her daughter hung a red pincushion trimmed with lace on the door latch to announce it. If it had been a girl, the pincushion would have been lace-trimmed white! Even the poorest sort in Holland hang strings or ribands to the door latch to announce the arrival of a child."

He frowned down at her. "I am glad you found Vrouw Berghem so entertaining."

"Oh, I did! And were you equally entertained—with Erica?"

He stiffened. "Oh, yes," he drawled. "Erica entertained me by inviting my attention to this and that—for instance, who it was who brought those heaped-up plates to Vrouw Berghem and yourself."

"It was Nicolas," said Georgiana carelessly. "You must not be so jealous of him, Brett."

Her tall husband seized her by the shoulders and spun her around to face him. "Have I cause to be?" he demanded, and she could see angry lights dancing in his gray eyes.

Georgiana shook her shoulders to free herself of his grasp. His grip relaxed and he let her go, stood watching her intently.

"For a man who spent his evening dancing attendance on Erica Hulft," she said evenly, "it seems to me you have no cause to complain." She turned abruptly away from him, again considered the shining river flowing down from the Adirondacks to the sea. "Vrouw Berghem was telling me that to make her house more desirable for sale she was having a lot of fresh white sand thrown onto the floor and swept into a fancy design. It seemed very odd to me."

Her voice drifted to a halt, for it had occurred to her with a sudden pang that it had been rather splendid of Nicolas to offer to throw away everything for her, to forsake his claim to Windgate, to disappear—if only she would share his exile with him. While in contrast, Brett—she cast a sudden resentful glance at that dark hawklike face hovering so near her own—even after knowing her, loving her, Brett would still have married someone else to make fast his holding! She could not forget that—and it rankled. And sharpened her voice as she began again, unwilling to tackle him on the main issue. "Vrouw Berghem says the designs in the sand are—"

"Stop making conversation, Georgiana," said Brett in a quiet voice. "Neither of us cares a hoot whether Vrouw Berghem sweeps her sand into designs or tosses it into the East River! Let us talk about our differences."

"Our differences?" Georgiana essayed a yawn. "I didn't know we had any," she said coolly.

Brett restrained a violent desire to shake her. She was so lovely, so irritating—and so near. Her very nearness set his blood to racing.

"Nicolas van Rappard's attentions to you were observed by all the company," he told her in a hard voice. "I saw heads turn and tongues wag."

"I suppose the tongues have already wagged about you and Erica until they are tired and must have something new to keep them going?"

"Erica means nothing to me!" he exploded. "*You* are my wife."

"Keep your voice down," she advised in a low tone. "You have told me you do not care for your men to hear us quarreling. Nor do I care for Linnet to hear us and carry tales about us to the kitchen!"

She distinctly heard his teeth grate.

"Georgiana," he said coldly. "I did not take you for a fool."

"Nor am I one," she flashed.

"Then for once observe with your eyes and not your heart. Did you actually *see* one single thing transpire between Erica and myself at Haerwyck that could give rise to gossip?"

Georgiana was about to reply "Yes, you not only ate with her, you disappeared from the party with her!" when she realized that not only had she eaten with Nicolas and Vrouw Berghem, she too had disappeared from the party—with Nicolas. Deprived of that retort, she took a new avenue to show her resentment. "And when you were not dancing attendance on Erica Hulft," she accused, "you were pursuing Katrina ten Haer!"

"God give me strength!" Brett rolled his eyes toward the moon and Georgiana could almost feel the tautness of his muscles.

But perversely she continued to torment him. She peered down at her hands. "I seem to have lost a glove. I must have left it with Vrouw Berghem when we supped together. Ah, well"—she turned to give Brett the full brilliance of her smile—"Nicolas may find it and return it."

She saw sudden anger darken her husband's face and knew with fright that she had gone too far. He seized her arm in an ungentle grip and she saw his eyes flash.

What would have happened then they were never to know, for abruptly the sloop seemed to shudder, then sidle. Simultaneously there was a shout from the *schipper* and a scream from Linnet, some distance down the deck.

A ripple went through Brett's frame and he released his grip on her half-numbed arm with a low curse.

"What the devil—?" he demanded and strode forward, toward the commotion.

"Have we struck something?" cried Georgiana. She hurried along behind him.

"I think we've fouled the rudder," he flung over his shoulder.

Fury had warmed her but now the night chill struck her as suddenly as the sight that rose before her.

The entire crew was clustered together at the rail, and Linnet too was leaning over it, staring down. Someone was wielding a pole—

one of those with an iron hook on it, made to clear floating debris away from the rudder.

"Oh, it's horrible, horrible!" Linnet cowered away from whatever the men were looking at, down in the water.

Brett brushed by the moaning girl and was abruptly silent. Georgiana came to stand beside him and looked over the rail to see what everybody was staring at.

There, lit by the moon's pale light, was a woman's face, open eyes staring upward, long dark hair streaming out into the water. A drowned face.

"It's the Michaelius woman," Brett said in an altered voice. "Here, get her aboard—careful with that hook, she may yet be alive."

Beside Georgiana, Linnet whimpered, as the men, under Brett's supervision, brought the Michaelius woman over the side with exceeding care. But there was no reviving her, she must have been dead for hours.

"How could she have floated so long?" marveled Georgiana, standing well back from that limp wet form on the deck. She looked very fragile lying there, the Michaelius woman, and there was a dark bruise along her jaw.

"Her dress was caught on that floating log that fouled our rudder," said Brett, running a hand through his dark hair. "Did you not see it? 'Twas what caused the *Witch* to shudder and when the men rushed to free it—they found her."

"I did not see the log," mumbled Georgiana. "I saw only the woman."

Only that tragic young face with its spreading tangle of coal black hair. "Oh, Brett, how terrible!" Her voice quavered. "Do you think she drowned herself?"

His arm went round her shoulders protectively and she was glad to seek the comfort of contact with his warm body. "We may never know. Perhaps Kray will know something—even if he does, he may not tell us. Come inside, Georgiana, you're shivering. The men can take care of her and Linnet's here to do anything a woman should do." He was urging her toward their cabin as he spoke. "We'll take her body back to Windgate and give her decent burial there."

A sob escaped Georgiana as they went through the cabin door. "My mother—drowned in this river," she managed to get out.

"I know," he said. "I know." He reached back and closed the cabin door with his foot.

"Just—hold me," she whispered.

But even with Brett's arms warm and comforting around her, Georgiana could not seem to stop shaking. Her beautiful fair-haired mother who had swept all before her had lost her life in this cold wild river, this Hudson, and that drowned face she had just seen with its staring eyes and wet ribands of black shining hair had brought it all back to her.

And at that very moment, the mother Georgiana had long thought drowned was working by candlelight over the books of Longview, her Carolina plantation. She made a beautiful picture there, the elegant fair-haired woman in her gown of sapphire silk, just this month imported from Paris. She had chosen the gown for its sky blue color, which was van Ryker's favorite, and it was cunningly trimmed in point lace rosettes, its deep square neckline outlined, as were the full puffed sleeves, slashed and lined in pale violet silk, with ice blue satiny ribands. The night was cool, her violet silk petticoat thin, and Imogene had thrown an embroidered lavender silk shawl carelessly across her shoulders as she frowned over the books. In the candlelight that gilded her golden hair as she worked, she seemed to shimmer like a moth in moonlight.

She sighed, for van Ryker was off up the Cooper seeing to the clearing of additional acreage that would be planted to tobacco, and he had been talking about planting rice as well. Downriver toward the coast, on the west bank of the Ashley, Albemarle Point had been renamed Charles Town in honor of the dissolute English king and last year a more defensible walled town had been laid out six miles away. New people were streaming in; the lonely days when she would see nobody but plantation personnel for weeks were fast drawing to a close. Well, at least she would have the plantation's books in good order before van Ryker returned! It was a job she had taken on herself, for their excellent factor was away visiting his relatives in Scotland. The books had fallen sadly behind in his absence and Imogene meant to rectify that, for who knew when he would return, sea voyages being what they were!

Something soft and furry brushed her skirts and made them rustle. She glanced down to see that Nicodemas had joined her and was rubbing his thick black fur against her legs, looking up at her with big trusting green eyes, and kneading the Turkey carpet with his white paws.

Imogene smiled down at the cat and bent to stroke his soft fur. Nicodemas arched his back and purred loudly. Longview was well supplied with cats of Nicodemas's characteristics now, for several pussycats had jumped ship in the Cooper, preferring the lazy freedom of plantation life to the more austere diet and restricted quarters of life at sea—and Nicodemas had made the most of his opportunities. He had a handsome harem now and his great-great-grand-kittens, many as coal black and white-pawed as he, strolled through the rose gardens at Longview, slept under its hedges and beside its sundial, and caught mice in its big attics and rats in its capacious cellars. Imogene, who was fond of cats, loved them all, but the original Nicodemas, who had befriended her on shipboard when he had seemed for a while her *only* friend, would always be her favorite. He was growing old now, was Nicodemas, and he moved a little stiffly sometimes as he jumped down from his special velvet pillow on a low cedar stool beside the hearth, but he still carried himself with the same debonair swagger he had sported when she had met him aboard the ill-fated *Goodspeed* so long ago.

Dear Nicodemas, friend of a terrible shipwreck that had not crossed her mind for years. She thought of how he had looked that night, silhouetted against the jagged rocks of the Scillies, terrified, ears flattened, half drowned and clinging for dear life to the ropes that bound a little cask as she somehow propelled him through the wild water to the shore.

"We'll find you a piece of cold chicken in the kitchen," she promised the cat affectionately. "As soon as I'm finished with these books. They won't seem to balance—I think it's all that ironstone ware we imported that somehow didn't get marked down—oh, and perhaps that shipment of Sheffield plate as well!" she exclaimed, and forgot Nicodemas as she went back to poring over the books.

The cat seemed to understand. He curled up on the hem of her sapphire silk skirt and stretched luxuriously. Imogene went on with her work, her ringed hand moving swiftly over the parchment. She dipped her turkey quill pen into the India ink and looked up at the wild cry of a night bird.

Quill poised in air, she thought unbidden of Georgiana, the lovely child she had lost so long ago. Wistful and dreaming, she put the pen down upon the little writing desk's polished rosewood surface, closed eyes that smarted suddenly, and wished with all her heart that it could all have been different.

But life was like that, Imogene told herself bitterly there in the Carolina moonlight. *It tore you from the arms you loved and cast you on other shores.* She got up and walked nervously about, the skirts of her ivory satin dressing gown swishing about legs as young and lovely as ever. How often she had told herself she must forget but—how could she forget what had been all her fault? If she had lived her life differently, little Georgiana would not have gone down aboard the *Wilhelmina.* She bent her head as if beneath blows—so often had she rained down recriminations upon herself.

"*Georgiana, Georgiana,*" she whispered. "*I gave you life— and caused your death.*" She rested her face in her hands, feeling tears wet upon her cheeks. It was an old wound, Georgiana's death, but it had struck her afresh. As if something stirred . . . out there beyond her vision.

And even as Imogene suffered in Carolina, the daughter she thought she had lost shuddered in Brett's arms in that sloop upon the Hudson as she imagined her mother—that haunting face from the portrait at Windgate—floating in the dark water, drowned.

"They never found my mother's body," she whispered painfully to Brett. "One of the servants told me that. Verhulst van Rappard put up a memorial stone to her, but my mother—there was no body in the coffin beneath the stone. It was an empty coffin he buried."

Again she had said "Verhulst van Rappard" and not "father." Brett frowned down on her shining hair, and stroked its gleaming surface affectionately. Georgiana said "mother" easily enough, but the word "father" came hard to her lips. He wondered if she had something against her dead father. Grim man Verhulst might have been, but surely he had been within his rights to take exception to a wife who fled him with her lover! And if the story told was a true one, van Rappard had had no part in killing his young wife— although he *had* fired a shot into her lover's chest.

Brett Danforth looked down on that fair head, cradled against his chest. His gaze was puzzled. Did Georgiana know something about these people that he did not know, for all her insistence that she did not? Had there been something in those papers, that packet the minister had thrust upon him in Bermuda, that had made her sheer off from her father's memory and take her mother's side so passionately?

"Georgiana," he sighed, toying with a lock of her fair hair. "Can you not accept the fact that I love you? Must you ever doubt me?"

"Oh, Brett, I don't doubt you!" cried Georgiana. And at that moment she did not. Brett's strong frame seemed the only anchor to her wildly careening emotions and she clung to him desperately.

Silently he swept her up and carried her to bed, silently made love to her. And it was indeed a night of sighs and splendor, for that nearness to death had made Georgiana see her world in a new light, had made her realize anew that life was fleeting, that Brett could be wrested from her, that anything could happen. She must seize and cherish this moment out of time, for there might never be another. . . .

But for all its silent intensity, there was an unspoken commitment in the tempestuous joining that they shared that night and Brett Danforth held his lady close and kissed her tears away and promised himself grimly that in future she should have no cause to doubt him.

And so in the dawn they returned to Windgate with their sad burden.

Kray was duly notified, and he turned up on their doorstep, distraught and gaunt, looking as if he had not slept for a month. Georgiana met him in silence and in pity and led him to the room where the Michaelius woman lay, awaiting the building of her rude coffin.

"Kristin! Oh, my Kristin!" Kray gulped out the woman's given name and went down on his knees beside her body, heaving with sobs.

There could be no doubt that he had been her lover. Georgiana would have withdrawn, leaving him alone with her, but that he turned a suddenly fierce countenance toward her—a countenance so forbidding that she took a step backward.

"Kristin killed no one!" he cried in a muffled voice. " 'Twas I who killed Jan Michaelius, when I found him beating her! I thought he was like to kill her and I felled him with an ax—and I'm glad he's dead, but poor Kristin, she feared the hangman's noose for she'd seen her father hanged. Such a little neck. . . ." He turned and his fingers gently touched her cold white flesh. "My Kristin . . . she said she'd drown herself if she thought they were going to take her in custody and now she's done it. God help me, I never thought she would. I only killed her husband to save her life, for I was sure his next blow would be the last of her.'' He collapsed upon her slight body, sobbing.

"Kray." Georgiana's voice trembled as she spoke. "You have put your life in my hands by saying to me what you just said. But I am not your judge—nor yet your jailer. I have already forgotten your words. And—I think you have been punished enough. Say what you will to the authorities—I will not reveal what you have just spoken to me."

She closed the door on his mumbled thanks and met Brett just coming up the hall.

"Is Kray there?" he asked. "I heard he was here."

She nodded. "The *schout* brought him."

"Is he in there too?"

"No. He's strolling with cook in the woods behind the house." Brett quirked a quizzical eyebrow at his wife.

"She had told me he was an old beau of hers," said Georgiana demurely. "So I gave her the afternoon off. I think she wanted to renew the acquaintance."

"Then Kray is alone in there?"

"Yes.

"I'd best see to him. He may try to escape and the *schout* will hold me responsible."

Georgiana laid a detaining hand on her husband's arm. "I wouldn't disturb Kray right now, Brett. He's not thinking of escape—he's mourning her loss. He must have loved her very much."

"It's true, then," he mused. "Kray *was* her lover."

"I am sure of it, but whatever happened at that lonely *bouwerie*, let it rest. Two people are dead, enough blood has been shed."

"Spoken like a woman," said Brett impatiently. "It is my duty as patroon to bring justice here."

"Then do not listen to the ravings of a man half mad with grief," she cried, matching his impatience with her own. "Allow him to be alone with her—this last hour."

"Very well, I will set a guard on the door."

They left Kray alone with his lady all the afternoon. Alone in his misery, with the death of all his hopes and dreams. Finally, Brett became restive and muttered that he would go and see if the man was ill, since he had not come out. Uneasy herself, Georgiana followed him.

Brett dismissed the guard but when he opened the door, they both saw that Kray's long gaunt figure was lying half across the fragile body of Kristin Michaelius. Brett strode across the room and quickly lifted him up by the shoulders, but it was too late. He could see the knife hilt-deep in Kray's chest.

Georgiana cried out and Kray's lids fluttered open. His face was gray but his lips moved.

" 'Twas none of it Kristin's fault," he mumbled. "She was only pretty and young and wed to the wrong man. *I* killed Jan Michaelius—I alone. But I'll not hang for it."

"No," said Brett thoughtfully. "You'll not hang for it, Kray. Of that you can be certain." Even as he spoke, the tall man's body went limp in his arms. Kray had spoken his last words and made his dying confession.

"You knew," Brett accused, turning his gaze on Georgiana as he lowered Kray's body gently to the floor. "You knew he did it."

"Yes. He told me he killed Michaelius." The words, *She was only pretty and young and wed to the wrong man,* rang in her ears.

"And yet you did not tell me," he murmured.

"Why should I? So you could save him for the hangman? Remember how near you were to killing Arthur that day he attacked me in Bermuda!"

"Aye, I was that," he agreed, his eyes kindling. "And might have done it, had he shown more fight!"

"And they would have hanged you for it!"

"But Arthur," he pointed out quite rationally, "was not your husband."

"No, but I was at that moment his bond servant—and the world would have called him justified in chastising me, for I had run away from him and caused him to miss his ship to Boston!"

Brett Danforth's brooding gaze was on his excited young wife. She looked very beautiful standing there, challenging him. Confronted by that appealing young face, he had not the heart to point out that there was a vast difference in the world's view between a husband and a bondmaster.

"So you wanted to give Kray his chance for an honorable end," he said quietly.

"Yes!" Her staunch demeanor challenged him to say she had been wrong. "He loved Kristin and she was gone, and he had nothing but a noose to look forward to."

"Perhaps you are right, Georgiana." Brett sighed heavily but he looked on his bride with affection. "We will tell the *schout* that he confessed."

Turquoise eyes looked soberly into gray.

"He loved her and it brought him to this," said Georgiana softly. "I wonder how it started between them—perhaps with just a little thing, a word, a sigh. Their eyes met—and they fell in love."

Brett rumpled her bright hair. "They were walking on dangerous ground, Georgiana."

"And they slipped. . . ."

Brett nodded. He could not know that his young wife was not thinking of Kray and his drowned beloved, but of herself and Nicolas van Rappard. There had been a moment there at the ten Haers' ball when she herself had so nearly slipped. . . .

PART TWO
The Jealous Mistress

A moon of honey, a moon of gold,
A love so fragile and fair. . . .
Yet many dark nights will still unfold. . . .
Then will she find him there?

Windgate On The Hudson,
1673

Chapter 19

It was strange but this double suicide of the lovers had somehow brought Brett and Georgiana together in a closeness they had not known before. Their next days were idyllic, a golden time of strolls together in long-shadowed afternoons beneath the tall chestnut and walnut trees that guarded the bluff, a time of smiling wordless glances across their long gleaming board as they sat at dinner, a time of yearning heartfelt embraces on the soft feather mattress of Georgiana's big square four-poster.

Perhaps the high point of that time was the excursion they took aboard the *River Witch*. Brett broached the idea at breakfast.

"There's a beauty spot upriver I want to show you," he told her, smiling across the table. "And make love to you there before the weather's too cold for it outdoors!" he whispered roguishly as Wouter left the room.

Georgiana's heart quickened for Brett had indeed been a masterful lover last night and it was exhilarating to think that he so yearned for a return engagement that he would forsake even Windgate's pressing problems to do it!

"Will we be riding?" she asked, carefully sprinkling sugared cinnamon onto her pancakes from the big silver *ooma*. "Floss could use the exercise—every time I go near the stable she looks at me reproachfully, she thinks I'm neglecting her."

He shook his massive head. "Let Floss trot around the pasture for her exercise today. You can ride her after we return. We'll take the *Witch*. 'Tis faster—and safer.''

"What is this wonderful place we're going to see?"

" 'Tis only a glade," he said carelessly. "But I would show it to you, Georgiana. I think you'll appreciate it. We'll leave as soon as you've finished." He laid down his napkin, for Brett ate faster than she did. He rose and called to Wouter to have the *schipper* make ready the *Witch*.

"Will we be gone overnight?" she wondered. "Because cook—"

"Yes, but only the one night. Your household duties won't suffer. And between them, Wouter and cook know well how to run this house."

"Better than I do, I don't doubt," admitted Georgiana. "Still I must be about, if I'm to learn how to do it. Cook might leave us—Wouter too. And then where would we be?"

"In the market for experienced help," he said sardonically.

She chose to ignore his raillery. "Since we'll be picnicking out, I'll take Linnet," she decided. "She can fetch and carry while I attend to—other things." She gave him a witching look.

Brett laughed. "I see you're slipping into lazy Bermuda ways, Georgiana. Surely you don't need a lady's maid for a night spent in the brush?"

"No—well, it isn't that I need her," admitted Georgiana frankly. "Linnet's moping about. She stands there wool-gathering, she drops things, she looks as if she's lost her last friend, she laughs—and then suddenly bursts into tears for no reason. She's been that way ever since we attended the ten Haers' ball."

"Maybe it was seeing the Michaelius woman drowned that upset her?"

"Perhaps," said Georgiana hesitantly. In her heart she didn't really think that was what was bothering Linnet.

"I hope nobody at the ball was unkind to her. I had let her dress up and she looked so pretty, she far outshone the other ladies' maids. They could have been envious."

Brett gave his lady an indulgent look. She was kind to those about her, he thought affectionately—sometimes kinder than they deserved. "Of course you can take Linnet," he said. "Although I draw the line at her going ashore with us. She went into hysterics when we found the Michaelius woman in the river—I'd hate to think what she'd do if we encountered a bear."

Georgiana hated to think what she herself would do if they encountered a bear. "We aren't likely to run across one, do you think?" she asked nervously.

"No, of course not. But Linnet's sure to imagine bears every time she hears a raccoon or a rabbit scuffling in the bushes."

"Yes, she does tend to exaggerate things," agreed Georgiana with a laugh. But she was glad they would be taking Linnet with them. It would give the girl an outing and perhaps—who knew?—she might take a fancy to one of the rakish crew members, out there on the romantic river's shining surface.

But one thing after another delayed them so that it was almost dusk before they set out.

It was a different Hudson on which they embarked from the Hudson whose waters they had negotiated in warmer weather. Brilliant leaves had fallen everywhere, carpeting the earth in rich browns and red and gold. Only the beeches and hickories still seemed in full leaf. The sounds of chirping insects were absent and all the fish had run downstream—passing the trout, which were surging upstream to spawn. Georgiana saw them flashing by the sloop in the last of the sunlight, brilliant as maple leaves. The work of the busy muskrats and beavers was nearly complete now and soon the curious raccoons with their comical faces would no longer peer down from the trees but would seek winter quarters in rocky dens. Fat winter birds fluttered by against the waning sun, their feathered bodies storehouses layered with fat to endure the hard northern winter.

The *River Witch* plunged south into the Hudson Highlands. For a while they lost the wind and to keep the tide sweeping upriver from carrying the sloop backward they had to use the long oars or "sweeps," but when the wind picked up again they glided south.

"Along here in the spring," Brett indicated the steep eastern bank with a wave of his hand, "there will be a solid blaze of strawberries. And just ahead I've often seen the rigging filled with fireflies." He stopped abruptly and his gray eyes narrowed as he studied three long birchbark canoes that were sliding silently along the opposite shore. "Now what would that many Iroquois be doing so far from their territory?" he asked of nobody in particular.

"Perhaps they aren't Iroquois."

"Perhaps," he said in an absent voice. "Let's see what our *schipper* thinks."

Georgiana had seen but one Iroquois. Incredibly tall and with a bone structure that would have done credit to an ox. His voice had seemed to emerge hollowly as from the depths of a cavern. No wonder the local Indians were afraid of this northern breed, she had thought. Now as Brett strode forward to confer with his *schipper* she leaned forward to look, but in the shadows of the trees on the opposite bank she could not see these canoe-borne warriors as different from any other Indians. To her they seemed but dark shapes in the night, distant, unreal.

"At least they've passed Windgate on their way south," she said when Brett came back. "We won't be bothered with them."

"Yes." He did not seem inclined to talk about it, but she noted that every man aboard had turned watchful and constantly scanned the shoreline. It gave her an uneasy feeling.

"They may just be going south to the fair," she suggested. "*Kermis*, I think cook called it. Anyway, she said there was some kind of Dutch fair going on in New Orange."

"Perhaps," he agreed. "But I think we'll have our outing another day. The wind is against us but if we turn about now we can make it back by morning."

She knew then with a cold feeling that he thought there might be other canoes gliding down from the northern reaches. War canoes, with this party but the advance guard.

"But no need to spoil our holiday," he said jauntily. "The crew have fiercer drinks to warm them—Kill-Devil and Bride's Tears, but we'll share a bottle of fine Canary, and Linnet can spread out a linen cloth for us here on the deck and we'll have the picnic you mentioned. By moonlight."

"Not yet," she said wistfully, unwilling to leave the rail. Shapes of the mountains shadowed the wild shores beyond this silver river. A glamorous landscape.

"Yes," he said, his mellow mood matching her own. "It is lovely, isn't it?" He leaned down, his hand lightly caressing her hair, and breathed deep of its lemony scent, for it was not the night that had captured him but the woman.

"Lovely..." she echoed dreamily, her eyes on that distant shoreline. She put the thought of Indians and tomahawks from her.

" 'Tis too cold anyway for sleeping out ashore," he said casually. He sniffed the air. "The wind is fair but it smacks of snow. You may be giving your masquerade ball sooner than you had planned. Are you ready for it?" he challenged.

Georgiana lifted her head and faced him. If he wanted to ignore the Indians and talk about trivialities, so would she. "I will be ready for it. The servants at Windgate are well trained and we have infinite supplies of stores. And enough wine in the cellars to float the *River Witch* to Bermuda!"

Brett sighed. "I realize we have enough wine, but music must be provided for dancing, rooms must be made ready to bed down a great number of guests, the kitchen staff must work for a week or more making sweetmeats and cakes—such is the custom here along the river. And," he added, "at least one of your servants appears to be moonstruck." He was looking at Linnet, some distance away and leaning pensively on the rail. "Or seasick," he added critically.

"She is neither," laughed Georgiana. "Linnet is in love. She has at last admitted it—whispered it to me just as we came aboard."

"Who is it she's taken a fancy to, do you know?"

"She wouldn't tell me—set her jaw. She's very stubborn, you know. All she would tell me—and I quote her—is that he is 'a most wondrous gentleman' and that she met him at the ten Haers' ball."

"A *gentleman*?" Brett was startled. "I'd assumed she was enamored of some lackey."

"Well, gentlemen have wandering eyes too," pointed out Georgiana, her own eyes dancing.

"But that could mean trouble, for most of the men at the ball were married. Get her to tell you his name."

"I doubt she will. She says she is sworn to secrecy but that he has promised to visit her soon."

"Married," sighed Brett. "Else why swear her to secrecy?"

"Let us hope not—and there could be other reasons. He could be young and his family might not approve of his courting a serving wench."

Brett's skeptical shrug gave her back a cynical answer.

"In any case, I wish her joy," said Georgiana quietly. "She has had a cruel, hard life and I intend to give her another dress that she may parade before him—whoever he is. Something in soft orange, I think, to complement her rich brown hair."

"You would make a lady of the wench because you like her but—you may come to regret it," warned Brett. "For you know not who this gentleman may be."

Later Georgiana would realize sadly how true that was.

But for now she tossed her head scoffingly. "Linnet is like me," she told him. "She gives her heart away suddenly—and follows where it leads her."

"That too," said Brett, eyeing her with more tenderness, "can be dangerous. Look where it has led you."

"Yes," sighed Georgiana, swaying against him, feeling the pistol he had thrust into his belt cut into her soft flesh. "Look where it has led me." The moon had come out and she gave him a winsome smile, her teeth flashing white in the moonlight. Here in the magic night, with the wind billowing the sloop's sails and sending them skimming over the Hudson's silver surface, here with the great rounded hulks of the mountains rising majestically like sea monsters from the deep, here with the wind blowing fresh and fair, and Brett's arm about her, she could believe herself capable of anything. She could make Erica fly away, she could forget Nicolas's claim to Windgate—and his disturbing presence—she could toss her cares into the river and forget them.

Tonight, this magic night, she was Brett Danforth's woman!

"Let's go to our cabin," she said softly. "We can eat later and, after all, if there's a chance of Indian trouble ahead, you'll need your rest."

He gave a low laugh. "Rest, my lady, is not what you have in mind."

Her winning smile told him that was true indeed.

Abruptly he swept her up in his arms and carried her to the cabin. As he passed the *schipper*, the big Dutchman raised a "blackjack" leathern tankard of Kill-Devil in salute. Down the sloop's rail Linnet turned enviously to look. Her own eyes grew starry as she watched the lovers disappear into the cabin, shut the door. Someday, she told herself dreamily, someday that could be her and her gentleman drifting with the tide upriver, forgetful of all but love. . . .

Linnet was a hopeless romantic but, unlike Georgiana, she was not set on an even keel. Just now she was listing badly, for the handsome fellow who had kissed her so briefly at the ten Haers' ball—lord, there had not been time for more than that although Linnet would have been glad to give her all—had almost capsized her emotions. She would do anything for her gentleman, she told herself tensely, *anything*!

From her place by the rail, with the heavily wooded landscape flying by, Linnet yearningly imagined the scene in that cabin. They were both so handsome, Georgiana and Brett—beautiful people. He would be laying her down gently on the bed right now and Georgiana would cling to him, not wanting him to take his arms away—not even to undress!

Linnet pulled her shawl around her shoulders for the night had turned cold and the fresh breeze with its hint of snow was chilling her to the bone. She warmed herself with the thought of that warm bed where the naked lovers were locked in a hot embrace.

She sighed. So it would be one day for her, when her wondrous newfound gentleman came to claim her. She leaned on the rail, daydreaming about him, wondering how soon he would come to Windgate—for he would come, as he had promised. Of that she was certain from his hot beguiling whispers in her ears, from his questing hand that had wandered delightfully along her heaving bosom and pinched and fondled her ripe breasts. He would come for her and then—and then—Linnet felt her whole body go weak at the thought and her legs began to tremble. He'd said nothing about marriage, of course—there was too much difference between their stations in life for that, she knew with a flash of honesty, but—*to be a mistress to a man like that*! The very thought dazzled her.

And such a man! A man who could have Erica Hulft at a snap of his fingers, or Katrina ten Haer, or even her mistress, the glorious Georgiana—for such was what Linnet naively believed.

The man of her dreams who would one day "come for her," of course was Nicolas. He had come upon her in the dark hall at Haerwyck, where she had retreated on hearing footsteps coming— for she was not sure that haughty Rychie ten Haer would relish having a serving wench, no matter how handsomely decked out, get too close to the crowded ballroom. He had in fact been momentarily blinded by the blazing candlelight he had so recently left, and had crashed into her and instinctively closed his arms around the warm yielding body with which he had collided.

"Well!" His voice was appreciative—the more so because he was still smarting from Georgiana's rejection of him and some harsh words from Katrina ten Haer. "And what lovely creature do we have here? Do I know you, Juffrouw?"

Young lady! He had called her *young lady*! He must think her to be one of the invited guests! Linnet felt suffocated by excitement, for she had instantly recognized the voice of the tall man who had reached out to catch her as she was knocked off-balance, and whose mustaches were even now tickling her ear.

"You—you saw me at Windgate, sir," she faltered. "I'm Linnet, maid to the mistress."

"Ah, yes, maid to the mistress." Nicolas did not release his hold on her. Instead he kept her close against him, amused that he could feel her heart pound through the thin material of her bodice. Those were soft round breasts that were pressing so tight against him, and now he recalled her although at first he had not. A luscious piece, even though a trifle obvious. "But maids have a way of *becoming* mistresses, Linnet," he said whimsically, and bent to steal a kiss.

It meant nothing to him, that stolen kiss in the dark hallway at Haerwyck, but it stunned Linnet. Her response was immediate and violent. She flung herself against Nicolas with all her strength and when he would have let her go, pulled his golden head down to hers and kissed him passionately. All the pent-up frustration of her manless life, all the scorching dreams of a lover that she had never confided to anyone were in that kiss.

"Well, well," murmured Nicolas, sensing a lass ripe for bedding. His impudent fingers toyed idly with her breasts. "Perhaps we could find an unoccupied corner of this manse and pursue this matter further?"

Linnet was agog at the suggestion. In her mind Nicolas had the same standing as a patroon—for might he yet not be the patroon of Windgate? Linnet had heard and savored the gossip, indeed there was little else to occupy her mind at isolated Windgate. That Nicolas should favor her was almost more than her full heart could bear.

But it was not to be.

"Linnet? Linnet, where are you?" It was Georgiana's voice, calling her.

To keep her from answering—and therefore disappoint Georgiana, who had disappointed him—Nicolas pressed his lips down firmly again upon Linnet's mouth that had just opened to speak. "Don't answer," he said, speaking softly into her throat. "I've only just found you."

Linnet thrilled to such obvious interest. "But I was always there," she gasped, breaking away. "You just didn't *see* me."

It was true enough but Nicolas's next words swept the past away. "I see you now," he whispered. "And I like what I see."

Her clothes! thought Linnet joyously. It was her wonderful blue kirtle and her sleeves slashed in gold that had made Nicolas notice her! How irrational that was in the semidark did not even occur to her. Her spirit was leaping forward on wings of joy at his touch, at the bold impudence of his words.

"I—I like you too, sir," she quavered.

"Enough?" His hand was questing down inside the cleavage of her thin doublet. "Do you like me *enough*, Linnet?"

"Oh, yes, sir!" Responding to his touch, all her senses racing, Linnet felt as if she would faint. "I've always liked you," she added with complete honesty. "Even when you didn't notice me."

"Linnet, we are going now!" called Georgiana. "The house is crowded, there is no room for us. Linnet." She was beginning to sound exasperated. "Linnet, where are you?"

"I must answer her, sir!" Linnet broke away. Her voice trembled as she called, "I'm here—I'm coming, my lady."

With obvious reluctance, her new admirer let her go.

"I'm sorry," whispered Linnet, with real tears in her voice. "I wish I could stay. . . ."

She sounded so desperate that Nicolas's good humor was solidly restored. "I'll come and visit you at Windgate," he told her wickedly, half intending to keep that promise—it would serve the lofty Georgiana right to find him seducing her maid! His eyes gleamed. "Till next we meet," he said gallantly, and planted a kiss directly on her heaving cleavage.

On wings of joy, Linnet ran out to find her frowning mistress.

"Wherever had you got to, Linnet? I've been searching the house for you. Brett is waiting for us at the landing."

Linnet said the first thing that came into her head. Her fertile imagination came to her rescue. "I was in the dark hall dancing by myself," she confided. "And I bumped my head against the wall and it must have stunned me."

"You do look a bit dazed," observed Georgiana critically.

Delighted with the success of her lie, Linnet rushed on to embroider it further. "And then I realized I'd burst my doublet and something might pop out, and so I ran back to stitch it up and when I came back down the hall, I heard you calling me and I answered."

Linnet's explanation sounded a bit confused but Georgiana had no reason to doubt its veracity. "Come along," she said crisply. "We've already bade our host and hostess good-bye, and bursted bodice or no, we mustn't keep Brett waiting."

Down the uneven moonlit slope, Linnet could hardly keep her feet from dancing. If the mistress knew who her lover was, wouldn't she be surprised?

The thought had stayed with her, teased her, as they cast off from the ten Haers' dock and made their way out into the main current. The wind whipped the *Witch*'s sails and blew her red curls into her eyes but she hardly saw the dark shoreline sweeping by. All she could see was the gleam of Nicolas's eyes shining down on hers in the darkened hall, all she could feel was Nicolas's warm lips and impudent questing hands, all she could hear was his beguiling voice.

What wonders lay in store for her!

That Nicolas had forgotten her the moment she was out of sight and returned to his ardent pursuit of Katrina ten Haer—and Katrina ten Haer's fortune—never even occurred to seething Linnet.

Back at Windgate, Linnet had alternated between almost hysterical gaiety, which caused cook to look askance at her, and fits of depression that worried Georgiana. The thought of Nicolas coming to call—and by now Linnet had persuaded herself that he would not only call, he would sweep her up and take her away with him—sent her soaring to the heights, but as the days passed and her lover did not put in an appearance, she fell into a deep dejection that was lifted only slightly by this unexpected downriver outing with her master and mistress.

Linnet had seen the Indian canoes pass by but had paid them no attention. Her thoughts were all centered on Nicolas—when he would come, what he would say, what she would say, and—she shivered just thinking of it—what they would do when they were alone and shedding their clothing in some delightfully dark and private place. An inn perhaps downriver in New Orange—for Nicolas was a gentleman, he would take her somewhere grand! And some serving wench would struggle upstairs with bathwater and a metal tub—ah, how marvelous her handsome Dutchman would look in his bath!

She would scrub his back, she thought raptly. And then pour fresh warm water from a pitcher down over his shoulders to rinse away the soapsuds, admiring the strong rippling muscles that emerged from the foam. And then he would rise up dripping, magnificent animal that he was. His loins would gleam wetly and he would smile at her—the same way she had seen him smile at Georgiana. Exactly the same! And she would seize a fresh linen cloth and towel him dry. She would be—naked, of course, and very fetching. He would not be able to keep his eyes off her. She would work the towel down over the golden fur of his broad chest and over his taut stomach muscles. And when the towel reached his hips she would be giggling and playful and by then he would be overcome with passion and he would tear the towel from her grip and toss it away, and with his legs still gleaming with droplets he would sweep her up and stride with her to the featherbed and plunge upon it, unmindful of dampening the sheets. He would stroke her body with those hands that had so briefly thrilled her the night of the ten Haers' ball. And he would lower his long length onto hers and he would—

" 'Tis cold. Would ye fancy a sip of Kill-Devil?" Big Kryn, the *schipper,* was offering her his black leathern tankard.

Linnet jumped and blushed. She felt that what she'd been thinking must show on her scarlet face.

"No, thank you," she said crisply, waving away his outstretched hand. "I don't drink Kill-Devil. 'Tis too strong." She was surprised that the *schipper* was speaking English. Usually he spoke only Dutch.

Crestfallen at her rejection, Kryn mumbled something in Dutch that ended in "juffrouw." But Linnet, intent on her thoughts of Nicolas, was not listening. She could not know that Kryn had learned those few words of English just to please her, for he had long fancied the pretty serving girl but never before had the courage to speak to her. She always went by with her pretty nose in the air, ignoring the likes of him. But tonight the familiar sloop, the silver river, the romantic darkness had conspired to make him bolder.

Suffering inwardly at being ignored by the lady of his choice, Kryn stood for a moment, awkward and baffled, then he took a long draught from the leathern tankard and went back to the more friendly company of the crew.

Linnet did not even notice his going. She stood by the rail, looking pensively at the cabin door that had closed behind Georgiana and Brett. She was wishing with all her heart that by some miracle the ten Haers' sloop, with Nicolas aboard, would sweep up the silent river and hail them.

But for all her fruitless dreaming about Nicolas, Linnet had imagined well the scene behind that closed door on the *River Witch*, for there Georgiana clung with desperate urgency to her husband's strong frame. Whatever tomorrow brought—be it Indian wars, or heartbreak from sleek fox-haired Erica, or ruin from Nicolas's connivings—they would have tonight.

And so she burrowed into Brett's arms as if she would nest there, and stroked his face with tender fingers and murmured endearments in a manner so intense that Brett lifted his head and looked at her keenly, even though she was only a blurred shape in the darkness of the cabin.

"Faith, what's got into you tonight?" he wondered. "For ye're in a devil of a hurry!"

"No." Her voice was barely a sigh and she brought his face down lovingly to rub her cheek against his again. "I'm but holding on to what is mine. I want these moments to last and last and last forever." There was a little catch in her voice as she said "forever" and she clung to him.

"Georgiana," he murmured, and from the way he spoke her name she could tell how moved he was.

He might have said more, but that she was smothering him with kisses and—passionate lover that he was—this once he let her lead the way and marveled, as he always did, at her seductive sweetness. He felt privileged to hold her thus, privileged that she should let him love her and love him so completely in return. But it would never do to let her know it—for that would give the wench unbounded power over him!

And then he forgot everything else, as did Georgiana, in the miracle of love as they clasped each other close and forgot the world in ecstasy.

"I'll not let the Indians have you," he promised her humorously when, passion spent at last, he came up for air, "even though you weaken me down to half my strength with these exertions!"

"Oh, Brett." It was a little cry from the heart as she nuzzled against him, warm and tingling in the afterglow. "I wasn't thinking about Indians."

He chuckled. " 'Tis plain that you weren't." He ruffled her hair tenderly. "Catch a wink of sleep now, for we'll soon be arriving."

But once Windgate was hailed and she dressed hastily and accompanied him out on deck, her viewpoint changed mercurially.

"You see, there was no reason to come back," she scoffed as they stepped ashore. "There have been no Indian troubles here or Wouter would be racing down the bluff to meet us."

His gaze rested on her a bit wearily as he strode up the hill. "But there *could* have been, Georgiana, and we'd have been outnumbered even by a small war party, caught away from our stronghold, leaving it with no strong hand at the helm."

For all her airy bravado, she was abashed. For his words had brought it home to her clearly: at Windgate, as on any other savage frontier, the price of life itself was continual vigilance.

"I'm sorry," she said abruptly and gave him a stricken look from wide turquoise eyes.

"Don't be." Brett reached out and drew her along with him, slackened his long stride to accommodate her shorter one. "This is a new way of life for you here, different from Bermuda. It takes time to learn a new way of thinking."

"Do you think I will learn it?" she asked a trifle bitterly. *Doubtless Erica Hulft was well versed already and Katrina ten Haer had been brought up in this way of life.*

"Of course you will learn," he said easily. "In fact, I think you already have. You could have protested our change of plans on the sloop—but you did not."

"No, I did not," she said softly, and went into the house a happy woman.

CHAPTER 20

No Indian war party arrived, but an alarming message did, for a passing river trader told them that the cattle on one of the distant *bouweries* were dying of a mysterious plague "and the tenant, I'm told, refuses to discuss it!" That same river trader imparted the welcome information that the Indian canoes they had seen were seeking a runaway squaw rather than white men's scalps. This cheerful news left Brett free to leave Windgate to Wouter's care, with Georgiana as chatelaine.

"I'd best head north," he told Georgiana restlessly. "If there's some kind of scourge besetting the cattle on one of our *bouweries*, we'd best be advised of it—we may need to take measures."

Georgiana did not ask what those measures would be. "But what about the Indians?" she demanded in an attempt to head him off, for she wanted these blissful days to linger.

Brett shrugged. "The Indians will have found their woman by now and be dragging her back. No business of ours. There'll be many an Indian scare here that comes to naught, Georgiana. 'Tis a constant shadow that hangs over all our heads in this wilderness. Guns are always being run upriver to the Iroquois. But meantime the cattle must be thought of."

And he was off, over her protests, on a three-day excursion into the forested countryside—and his going marked the end of their extended honeymoon in New Netherland's red and gold autumn.

Georgiana sighed to see him go, his stalwart straight-backed form in its sturdy leather doublet and soft buckskin breeches riding off atop his big black stallion. She yearned to hike up her calico skirts and leap on Floss's silver back and go with him, riding up into the tamaracks and firs to drink from the cold rushing mountain streams that silvered down from the heights, and eat at hastily built camp-fires, and lie on her back on cushions of spruce branches with her lover and look up through the crisp night air at the stars, shining brilliant in the clear mountain air.

Her soft gaze followed that erect masculine figure until it vanished into the trees, and she turned away with a sigh. She knew she would have loved him if he had brought her to a hovel instead of a mansion and she must rub her fingers raw at the spinning wheel and carding wool instead of airily directing the operations of a nearly self-sufficient manor. Her heart rode with her lord up into the tamaracks but—her body must stay housebound. For there was a chill in the winelike air these days and cook—who was an authority on such things—had told Georgiana importantly that there would be frost any day now and frost meant butchering. And Georgiana knew she must be there to learn how things were done here, so she could properly supervise in future the curing and salting of the meat.

So Georgiana sighed and controlled her urge to run after Brett as she watched him go, reminding herself sternly that she could not be off in the tamaracks if she was to get a grip on this place, this northern climate. For New Netherland's ways were not Bermuda's ways, as she was learning afresh every day, and she who had been so sure of herself and so in command as mistress of Mirabelle Plantation in Bermuda often felt helpless as mistress of Windgate on the Hudson.

Cook was right. The warm days had lingered unusually long, but that very night the first frost of the season made lacework of the small panes of the windows and silvered the grass down the bluff. The brilliant autumn colors would go now, the leaves come rustling down in a thick carpet that would soon be covered with snow and the white snowy expanse would become a road map with the little tracks of furry animals leading across the banks and into the forest glades and down to the frozen river.

Georgiana woke to a flurry of activity. For this was "hog-killing day," which meant for the household that all those hams and pork shoulders must be salted and cured eventually to hang in the big smokehouse. Next would come the sausage making and the render-ing of the lard to be stored in big earthenware crocks in the cool cellars of Windgate.

Georgiana put on a huge enveloping white apron over her trim

slate blue housedress with its snowy collar and tucked back her
fetching curls. She was dashing by the dining room windows on her
way to the kitchen when she saw the ten Haers' familiar sloop
sailing up to the pier.

Oh, no, not Rychie and Katrina! she thought with a sinking heart.
Not on butchering day. Not when I look like this!

But it was Nicolas who stepped ashore. With a little unbidden
quiver in her breast, she watched him alight and walk with that
slight swagger she remembered so well down the long wooden pier.
Nicolas was a jaunty sight with his wavy golden hair spilling down
over the shoulders of a fashionable short brown velvet cloak trimmed
in gold braid and lined in gold satin that gleamed in the sun as the
wind that rippled the surface of the Hudson blew it back from his
broad chest. That cloak was just the shade of Katrina ten Haer's
deep brown velvet eyes, she thought cynically—just as the saffron
plumes that dipped from his broad-brimmed sand-colored hat were
just the shade of Katrina's thick shining hair. Nicolas's trousers were
the same sandy color as his hat and his wide-topped russet leather
boots had a high polish. Against his smiling sun-browned face, the
frosty white of his linen collar shone as brilliantly as did the white
lace points of his boothose. He was wearing tan leather gloves and a
sword swung carelessly at his side. Ah, it was indeed a dandy that
was striding up the steep slope toward her!

Georgiana frowned. The double tragedy of the lovers had somehow exorcised the glamorous shadows of Erica and Nicolas from her
mind. She had left her brief turbulent feelings about Nicolas back at
the ten Haers'—she wanted them left there. Forever. But now here
he was, swaggering toward the massive front door of Windgate!

Her lips compressed. Well, she would seize this opportunity to
make it blindingly clear to Nicolas that there could never be
anything between them. With that in mind she lifted her chin and
went out to receive him, swung open the massive oaken door before
his hand could reach the heavy knocker, and greeted her smiling
guest standing in the wide doorway with the great hall yawning
behind her.

"You've been watching for me!" cried Nicolas delightedly.
"Watching for my sails! You knew I'd come," he added roguishly,
and the saffron plumes of his hat swept low in greeting as he made a
leg to the lady.

Georgiana opened her mouth and closed it again. Somehow that unexpected greeting had nonplussed her.

"Don't be ridiculous, Nicolas," she said, returning his bow with an automatic curtsy. "You find me in my housedress about to supervise the butchering. You can hardly think I was *waiting* for you. I merely happened to pass by the window and saw your sloop arrive at the pier."

Nicolas had risen from his bow and now he surveyed her with a wicked grin. "You do protest too much!" he said cheerfully, wagging a gloved finger in her direction. "I am tempted to believe you have been peering out the windows ever since your return from the ten Haers' ball, wondering when I would come to visit."

At this bland assertion, hot color rose unbidden to stain Georgiana's cheeks. "Indeed I have not, and this is certainly no time to visit. The whole household is in an uproar with all this meat to be salted and cured."

"Your cook's an old hand at it. Leave it to her," Nicolas advised, steeping into the hall and letting her lead him into the drawing room. "Faith, you're a lovely sight, Georgiana," he sighed, letting his eyes rove over her trim figure in the gray housedress. "You set a man to dreaming." His gaze lingered speculatively on her round breasts, rising and falling a bit rapidly, for Georgiana's breath had grown short at sight of Nicolas. Before she could contradict him, "I came to return this to you." He held out the glove she had left behind at the ball.

"I am surprised you did not dash upriver with the glove at once," she murmured humorously. "Such an important item, how could I have survived without it?"

He refused to be laughed at. "I thought to give you a little time to reconsider the joys of marriage with the patroon of Windgate," he said loftily.

"And should I reconsider them?" she challenged.

"You know you should, Georgiana." He leaned forward, his voice of a sudden gone deep and caressing. "You will come to grief here. With me you could be happy. We both know it."

Perhaps it was his wicked smile, the intense blue of his eyes. In any event, Georgiana's heart had begun to pound uncomfortably. She felt uneasily that she had invited this conversation—worse, she was enjoying it!

"Nicolas, you are a scoundrel." She took the glove gingerly, being careful not to touch the strong hand that held it, for she knew his touch—even in those handsome leather gauntlets—to be too exhilarating for comfort. She escorted him into the drawing room, dropped the glove upon a table. "You need not have bothered," she said carelessly, waving him to a chair. "You could have sent it along on any sloop that was passing by."

"Ah, but the ten Haers' sloop *is* just passing by," Nicolas chuckled, seating himself on one of the gilded chairs that had been made in France and had reached Windgate by way of a tall-masted ship from Amsterdam. "For I am off on a mission for Huygens ten Haer that will perhaps annoy your husband." His blue eyes danced.

Georgiana's brows lifted. She settled her slate blue skirts and made a gigantic effort to sound bored—and didn't quite manage it. "And what is that mission, pray, that my husband would find so annoying?"

"Don't look so worried," he teased. "I am off to Rensselaerwyck to see if the patroon there will perhaps not part with a tiny bit of land just north of that which Govert Steendam is purchasing."

"How did you know about that?" she asked sharply, for Brett had told her Steendam's transaction was still a secret.

"A lady told me," he grinned.

Erica! Not yet married to Govert and already betraying him! Georgiana's lip curled scornfully. "And what would Huygens ten Haer want with this 'tiny piece of land'?" she asked, although she had already guessed.

"He wishes to construct a mill."

"Did the lady not also tell you what Govert Steendam plans for his land?"

"Oh, yes. Steendam plans to construct a mill—along with a manor house." His blue eyes watched her brightly.

"But two mills cannot be supported so close together," said Georgiana sharply. *Of course there would be no second mill if she had her way, for she meant to influence Brett against this partnership with Steendam that would shackle him to capricious Erica's whims.*

"So I told Huygens," said Nicolas in a suave tone. "But he persists in considering it a good idea. Indeed, it would seem he has sent me as his ambassador to the patroon of Rensselaerwyck to offer him a partnership in the enterprise. Van Rensselaer puts up the land—ten Haer puts up the money."

"And you no doubt will supervise the mill's construction and thus have a share in the enterprise."

"No doubt."

"I wonder who thought that up," said Georgiana coldly. "Erica?"

"I shouldn't wonder." His reply was careless. "Certainly not Katrina," he chuckled. "She would be tearing out her yellow hair by the handfuls if she thought her father was about to embark on an enterprise that would send me sailing constantly back and forth upriver past Windgate."

So Katrina was jealous of her. . . . Perversely, that pleased Georgiana. "You had best not risk offending the ten Haer heiress," she warned. "For as Huygens's only child, she is your best chance of a patroonship—now that Windgate is lost to you."

"Oh?" His voice was a mere breath on the wind although his blue eyes had hardened. "And is Windgate lost to me, Georgiana?" he asked softly.

"Of course."

"I told you on what terms I would give up my claim—if you were to leave Danforth and sail away with me."

She felt suffocated. "That's impossible, and you know it!" she flashed.

"No, I don't know it." He looked about him. "I do not see the English patroon about. You are always alone when I find you."

"Brett is visiting one of the outlying *bouweries*," she said, and her voice softened as she spoke his name. She was suddenly stabbed by the thought that she was sitting here making idle talk with a rogue like Nicolas while her husband, her strong wonderful husband, was far away among the tamaracks. It made her wistful.

"He leaves you much alone," criticized Nicolas.

"Yes," she sighed. "I miss him."

Nicolas was looking at her as she spoke and those three simple words struck him like separate stones. He was struck with envy at the glorious light that filled Georgiana's eyes when she spoke Danforth's name. She had never spoken *his* name like that and he guessed glumly that she never would.

He rose abruptly. "I cannot stay, Georgiana—much as I would like to do Danforth's homework for him." His wistful smile played over her face. "I must be off on mine host's business to Rensselaerwyck."

"I am beholden for the glove." Georgiana rose and made her guest a stiff curtsy. From her formal manner the scene at the ten Haers' ball might never have happened. Nicolas might never have held her in his arms and she might never have trembled and looked up at him in an agony of doubt.

"The pleasure was mine—in seeing you again," said Nicolas bitterly. "Be about your household duties, Georgiana. I can let myself out."

"I wouldn't think of it," said Georgiana, loftily correct. She accompanied him to the door, saw him through it and bid him a last good-bye out upon the green lawn before the house. Her heart quickened as he brushed her hand with his lips and then strode down the bluff to the waiting sloop—a shade less jauntily than he had strode up it.

She watched him step aboard and turned to go back to the house when she saw Linnet catapult through the front door. She raced toward Georgiana with skirts flying. Surprised, Georgiana stepped back or she might have collided with the girl. Linnet bent to pick something up and then fled on down the slope.

"Mynheer van Rappard!" Georgiana heard her calling. "Mynheer, wait!" Her voice trailed back to Georgiana, who watched in astonishment as Linnet, with her skirts hitched up, pursued their departing guest all the way to the dock.

But Linnet was too late. The sloop had already cast off and Nicolas waved debonairly to those on shore as he departed. Georgiana lifted a hand to him and then waited for Linnet, who came back up the hill looking defeated.

"I was looking out the front bedroom window," she panted with a defensive look at Georgiana. (*Spying on me,* thought Georgiana in some amusement, knowing how gossipy Linnet's mind ran.) "And when Mynheer van Rappard told you good-bye I saw him drop his snuffbox. I could see it shining there, gold in the grass."

"And you came running down at breakneck speed to restore it to him?" Georgiana's brows rose. "Really, Linnet!"

"Well, I—I knew you would not wish him to use it as an excuse to return," faltered Linnet. She studied Georgiana anxiously, hoping her mistress would not sense the real reason she had pursued Nicolas so wildly down the slope. And when Georgiana did not answer, "I called to you through the window, but you did not hear me through the glass," she added defensively.

"No, I didn't," admitted Georgiana. *Probably because my mind was on other things . . . I was concentrating on Nicolas, for all I tried to tell myself I was not!*

Ruefully, she took the snuffbox that Linnet proffered.

"Doubtless he will return for it," Georgiana told the crestfallen girl with a sigh. "It seems we are always strewing things about, Nicolas and I—he a snuffbox, I my glove." *But not our hearts,* she thought. *We are more careful with those. Nicolas's heart is held fast to a dream of gold and as for me—I love my husband.*

She gave Linnet's drooping shoulder a pat, tucked the gold snuffbox into the capacious pocket of her white apron, and went off to find cook.

Fascinated by Dutch ways, and absorbed by cook's intricate method of making pickled pigs' feet, Georgiana gave little thought to Nicolas. She was unaware of how much her apparent disinterest had nettled him. She would have been startled to have seen his grim face, staring at the riverbanks flashing by as the ten Haers' sloop, with wind and tide in her favor, fled fast upriver toward Rensselaerwyck.

Wild thoughts flew through his mind. His nearness to Georgiana had disturbed him more than he cared to admit. How enchanting she had looked in that prim slate blue housedress with the white collar only serving to emphasize the peachbloom of her skin and the tight bodice outlining a figure a man itched to hold in his arms! He had been honest in his offer to her—it surprised him now to admit it. He *would* promptly have abandoned his claim to Windgate and taken ship for Bermuda—if she would have gone away with him. They would have lived on love, he thought with a twisted grin—and Georgiana's money.

For the thought that Georgiana might have no private fortune had never entered Nicolas's mind. Her beautiful silver mare, which he had seen for himself in Windgate's stables, was as valuable as any horse on the river—Arabian blood, he knew what that was worth. And had not Erica's cryptic description of Mirabelle Plantation also described Georgiana as heiress apparent? Nor had Georgiana herself denied it. And to top it all off, those massive silver candlesticks that she had brought with her from Bermuda looked as if they belonged in a palace—no, Nicolas van Rappard had no doubts about Georgiana's personal fortune.

Drumming his knuckles irritably on the rail as the sloop made speed upriver, he asked himself suddenly if Georgiana herself would be enough—without the money. He had a treacherous feeling that she would be, that he would be willing to settle down to making a living in some decent respectable way if only he knew she were waiting for him—with that glory in her eyes that had been there when she mentioned Danforth's name.

He shook his head to clear it. These were strange thoughts that occupied his roiling mind as the forested shoreline swept by.

He refused to admit even to himself that he was in love with Georgiana. Instead he wondered if she had found the gold snuffbox he had so carefully let drop when he kissed her hand in farewell. It never occurred to him that that was what Linnet was calling to him about from the shore; he had assumed it was something else, some personal wail to resume a relationship that had not yet even flowered—a relationship Nicolas had decided to let drop as carelessly as he had dropped his snuffbox. Whatever the girl had been calling could have been of no importance, but the gold snuffbox, ah, that was his perfect excuse to see Georgiana again. With difficulty Nicolas wrenched his thoughts from her and began to speculate on what arguments he would use to convince the patroon of Rensselaerwyck that it would be wise for him to part with a small parcel of riverfront property.

CHAPTER 21

At Windgate, the butchering had proved so monumental a task—for some forty hogs were being slaughtered this day to fill the big smokehouses with hams and pork shoulders and the huge crocks with lard—that even the house servants who normally had no kitchen duties were being called upon to help.

Georgiana stayed well away from the actual killing ground, which sickened her and which was staffed entirely by men. She wandered about watching cook bawling orders and stomping around in great glee. Cook was in her element when acting as a "straw boss"; she loved ordering others around. Georgiana almost protested when cook stuck a large butcher knife in Linnet's hand, aimed her at a side of pork and gave her an impatient push. But, then, she told herself, the other house servants were helping, and Linnet might well incur their dislike and eventual retribution if she were excluded.

But Linnet was still downhearted and all thumbs. Working listlessly and paying little attention to what she was doing, she promptly slashed her arm with the heavy knife and gave an anguished cry so piercing that cook nearly dropped a boiling pot she was carrying. Trumpeting her rage, cook promptly ordered the sobbing girl out, and Georgiana, with a reproving look at cook, withdrew her and cleansed and bandaged the wound herself.

"There now, you'll be all right," she said as she finished—and Linnet burst into a fresh shower of tears. Since the wound had turned out to be superficial, Georgiana was astonished by so much grief and could not help asking herself if Linnet was not perhaps crying over something else—some cut that went deeper. "Come along," she said, feeling sorry for the girl. "We could both use a respite from all that noise and the smell of blood. Why don't you take me on a tour of the garrets? Somehow I missed them when I went through the house."

Swallowing, Linnet wiped her eyes and quavered that she'd be glad to lead the way.

Georgiana was amazed at how huge they were. Windgate's roofs were so steep that there were two stories of garrets—an upper and a lower. Linnet explained that when the weather was warm and wet, clothes were hung in the upper garrets to dry—and indeed Georgiana could imagine it would be stifling there in summer. But mostly the upper garrets were just used to store things, mainly flax for spinning, which would become a major occupation during the long winter months. She then escorted Georgiana through the lower garrets where most of the servants slept, for beneath Windgate's high gables—as in the step-roofed houses in Dutch New Orange, the lower garrets were used for servants' quarters. Georgiana exclaimed at their capaciousness, remarked that the servants must be provided with more wool blankets against the cold, and led Linnet back downstairs.

"'Tis only my arm I cut—not my hand." Linnet turned forlornly to face her. "I could go back and help with the butchering."

Georgiana thought of cook's angry howl of "Get out and stay out!" when she had so nearly dropped the boiling pot.

"No, I think you might do some mending instead," she suggested, smoothly finding a way to evade Linnet's handsome offer. "For you're deft with a needle." She thought for a moment. "The guest room Erica stayed in when she was here—she showed me a place at a corner of the drapes that her little dog had chewed. Do you think you could mend it?"

Linnet brightened a little. She liked to sew.

"And when you finish, you might unstring the black and white beads of the wampum belt Brett left for me. You'll find it lying on a chest in my bedchamber. You could fill my little plum velvet purse with them so I'll have small change handy. And, Linnet," she added kindly, for she knew how Linnet stored wampum in a personal horde, "if the little velvet purse won't hold them all, you can have the overflow." Her eyes twinkled for she knew there'd be extra beads.

That offer brought Linnet to life. She was speculating in wampum, sure that it would soon increase in value, for how could the Indians, busy trapping every animal that moved, have time to grind all those shells into beads? "Can I keep some black ones too?" she cried breathlessly, for she knew that while the white wampum made from periwinkle shells were more prevalent, the black wampum ground from the clam shells' blue hearts were more valuable.

"Of course you may," laughed Georgiana. "And if your arm starts bleeding again—stop, come down, and we'll have another look at it."

She left Linnet dashing away, and went back downstairs humming, this time to pitch in and take Linnet's place, for she told herself all hands were needed. Nightfall found her too tired to eat and she fell into bed to sleep dreamlessly till Linnet woke her, reminding her cheerfully that she had asked to be roused at dawn.

Georgiana groaned, stumbled into her clothes and went down half awake to find that energetic cook was already marshalling her forces. And so the time passed until Georgiana, deeply immersed in sausage rendering and perspiring before the heat of the fire around the iron pots, heard someone call, "The patroon is back!"

She dropped the ladle with which she had been skimming the contents of the pot and rushed out to meet him. She got there just as he swung down from the big black stallion.

"You're home early," she cried, and her voice sang with joy at his return.

Brett swung her up into his arms and kissed her hot face.

"Faith, your skin burns me," he murmured.

"I've been near a fire," she laughed, pushing back a lock of damp golden hair from her perspiring forehead. "You will have to content yourself with fresh pork and succotash and suppawn tonight," she told him happily. "For we are still busy with the butchering and have no time for fancy dinners!"

Brett set her down. "Well, many's the time I've made do with Indian meal porridge alone," he commented, but his swift smile approved his wife's sudden wave of domesticity. "We'll make you a Dutch housewife yet," he laughed. "Making duffel cloth and sauerkraut, and pickling oysters, and with a knitting bag hung from your belt!"

Georgiana shook her head ruefully. "I doubt it. I cannot even get used to these high shallow fireplaces and today cook scolded me for forgetting to order the servants to take down the cloth ruffles across the top on Saturday to launder them for the Sabbath! We did not have fireplace ruffles in Bermuda! Cook is in a rare temper—she kept muttering something in Dutch I couldn't quite catch about the upstairs maids."

"Called them scatterbrained flibbertigibbets," laughed Brett, swinging his saddlebags over his shoulder and heading toward the house with Georgiana almost running beside him to keep up with his long stride.

"However did you know that?" marveled Georgiana.

"Because it's what she always calls them," Brett chuckled. "And I see she's taken a liking to you, since she's instructing you in Dutch ways. She's a woman who loves to dominate. Don't let her bully you, Georgiana. Learn from her, but keep the upper hand." He ruffled her hair affectionately.

"Have done," she said breathlessly, pulling away. "It's tangled enough. I don't doubt I'll break the teeth of my comb, combing it!"

To distract him, she asked, "Did you find out why the cattle were dying?" For that had been the reason for his journey.

"Mismanagement, I think," he told her frankly. "Two calves had died. Mulvaney, the tenant, met us half drunk, startled to see us. I had a feeling he'd drunk himself into a stupor one evening and left the calves shut out of the barn all night and wolves had gotten them. He must have waked at the noise and driven the wolves off but the bodies were half eaten. Mulvaney claims it was done after they died, but I could find no sign of disease."

"You think the Irishman lied?"

"Yes. But—" he hesitated. "It's lonely up there and Mulvaney has no wife, and it could be this was a warning to him and the only time he'll forget about the stock. If he keeps on in this way, he won't make it. He'll get drunk at the table and fall across it and his fire will go out and he'll freeze to death some cold night."

Georgiana shivered, but she did not want to think on death just now—she wanted to think on life, and all it meant to her.

"Is he good-looking?"

"Who? Mulvaney?"

"Of course, who else?"

"I suppose so. Wild-looking and unkempt because—"

"Because there's no woman to set him straight," she smiled.

"Undoubtedly." His features relaxed into a grin.

"Perhaps we should have sent Linnet up there with you," she suggested pertly. "She seems to be pining away over something and she has a marked predilection for handsome men!"

"I'll remember that next time," he said ironically. "If there is a next time."

They had reached the house now and as they went inside, Brett tossed his saddlebags to Wouter and picked Georgiana up in his arms again. "It's good to be home," he said indistinctly as he nuzzled her throat.

"Put me down," gasped Georgiana, wriggling in his grasp. "It's undignified. Wouter—"

"Has tactfully disappeared," said Brett. "See for yourself."

A glance around the hall told her that this was so.

"But there are other servants who might pass by and see!"

"Let them see," he said calmly. "For I've been gone these two days past and I've missed my wife and I've a mind to take a nap before dinner—with my wife. In fact, it's all I've thought of for the past hour!'' He was striding down the long hall toward the stairs with her as he spoke. "What's happened while I've been gone—aside from the butchering?''

"Oh, nothing much. The trammel broke''—she was speaking of the chain that held pots suspended over the fire—''and cook near had apoplexy until the blacksmith fixed it. Two Indians came by with a brace of turkeys apiece and I paid them in wampum—I can't get used to it, using beads for money. And we fed them crullers and they went away happy. Which reminds me, there's cold turkey in the larder. Would you like a bite? What with rendering the lard, supper will be late, I'm afraid.''

"Don't try to distract me from my purpose." He leaned down and rubbed his stubbled chin playfully against her cheek, causing her to start in his arms as he took the stairs two at a time.

"You should shave first!'' protested Georgiana in mock horror, putting her hand over her cheek and looking up roguishly into his eyes.

Brett grinned. "Indeed I'll shave first—and take a bath too. Wouter!'' Brett turned his head and called down the stairs to the manservant who had come into the hall at the sound of his master's voice and was looking up at them rather wistfully. "Have a bath sent up.''

"I'll need a bath sent up too, Wouter,'' called Georgiana.

Wouter nodded affably but the smile he gave them held a trace of sadness. He was remembering what it had been like to be a bridegroom—with his first wife, not the second. His first wife had been a sweet little thing who had expired in childbirth and the baby along with her. His second had proved to be a harpy and he had left her in Delft and emigrated from Holland, never to return.

"You won't need a bath sent up—you can join me in mine,'' Brett told Georgiana as he swept through the door of her bedchamber.

Her cheeks pinked at that. "Even *your* big hip tub is far too small to hold us both,'' she protested.

"You can sit on my lap.''

"I will not!''

"Look what you'll be missing,'' he chided. "I'd bounce you on my wet knee and scrub your back for you and we could splash together!'' He gave her a little spank on the rump as he set her down.

Georgiana went over and threw herself upon the bed, rested herself on her elbows and kicked her heels as she watched him undress. First went the serviceable sword and the pistol. He had left his long gun in the hallway below. Next he divested himself of his heavy leathern doublet.

''It's too cold for you to take a bath in here,'' he said, and strode to the door. ''Wouter!'' he bellowed. ''Make a fire for my lady!''

Georgiana lay there and beamed at him. She had forgotten Erica, forgotten her jealousy even of Windgate. These last days since the ten Haers' ball had been wonderful, interrupted only by his brief jaunt to an outlying *bouwerie*, and now they were back together again in their personal Eden. In perfect happiness she watched Wouter make the fire, watched the two baths brought and set before a half-stripped Brett.

By now the servants had gone, the fire was crackling on the hearth, the room was warm and Georgiana watched Brett strip off the last of his clothing and plunge his big body into the steaming hip tub.

Now at last she rose lazily from the bed and stood there smiling at him. She took her time about undressing, turning about from time to time for his approval. First the white apron and the slate blue housedress moved with leisurely assurance over her head of tangled hair and were tossed carelessly onto a chair. Then, as Brett watched from the hip tub with kindling eyes, her stiff white petticoat departed her body and joined the blue dress on the chair. With elaborate care she removed her shoes and stockings, making sure to present her dainty legs to best advantage.

Down now to her sheer chemise—and fully conscious of the pretty picture she made with the late afternoon sunlight streaming through the window and the crackling flames from the hearth sending sparkling highlights along her burnished gold hair—she walked casually to her dressing table and picked up a comb.

''I really must do something about this mop,'' she murmured, frowning at her curls in the mirror. She gave it a comb or two, then idly, almost absentmindedly, tugged at the ribbon that held her chemise at the neck. She loosed it only a little so that somehow the sheer white lawn rippled down seductively over one bare shoulder and displayed a wide expanse of smooth back. While Brett watched appreciatively, she made a great thing of combing and pinning up her bright hair—and every time her arm went up, her chemise slipped a bit more until finally it fell to her waist, held up only by her softly rounded hips.

"Venus rising from the foam," murmured Brett, gazing at the elegant puff of near-transparent material from which his young wife seemed to be rising. "Come here." He reached out a hand for her.

"Not Venus," smiled Georgiana, holding her ground. "Eve. For I'm about to tempt you with an apple. Here—catch." She reached into a bowl of ruddy apples on a low stool beside her dressing table and tossed him one, which he reached out and caught handily with a wet hand. "You must be starving, Brett. For cook said, when someone cried out that you were coming, that you must have made a forced march to get home this early, and you were undoubtedly looking forward to a good meal."

"Cook's a perceptive woman." He took a bite out of the apple but his eyes never left Georgiana's lovely form, so provocatively displayed for his gaze. "But she can't have been so simple-minded as to think it was her cooking that brought me home early. And if you're Eve, you must know what I'm talking about. Here, take a bite yourself."

He tossed her the apple and in reaching up to catch it Georgiana's chemise billowed down to land in a white puff around her slim ankles.

Naked now in all the glory of her youthful femininity, Georgiana stood smiling at him and took a dainty bite out of the apple. "There," she said, and her turquoise eyes seemed to sparkle with mysterious lights. "Now we've tasted the same forbidden fruit."

"Don't move," he said raptly, and she was caught by a pulsing undertone in his timbred voice, like a distant onrushing waterfall. "The firelight plays over your body and the evening sun gilds your hair. I want always to remember you like this."

Sure of herself and happy, Georgiana stood a moment more posing elegantly for his enchantment. Then she stepped daintily out of the mound of sheer material. It collapsed softly to the floor as she stepped into her own steaming hip bath and settled herself luxuriously into the water.

"We wouldn't have had all this hot water ready if we weren't butchering,'' she said contentedly, wriggling her hips down into the tub. ''I expect cook is swearing at all the servants right now and making them carry pail after pail from the well!''

''Join me, Georgiana.'' Brett's voice was husky as he extended his hand toward her again.

''Not till I scrub this grime off,'' she insisted, seizing a sponge and soaping it and covering her round breasts with suds. ''I've been working around steaming pots all day!''

''A pity to conceal all that beauty with soapsuds,'' he sighed.

Georgiana laughed and squeezed a spongeful of water down over her breasts. The suds disappeared and in their place her round breasts gleamed wet and the pink nipples held drops of water that caught the light like diamonds.

''I don't know whether I like you better wet or dry,'' Brett observed whimsically and rose from his tub.

She guessed his intention.

''Brett,'' she said breathlessly, holding up her sponge as if to ward him off. ''I'm not finished bathing—and you haven't shaved. You've an awful stubble on your chin. You near sanded my cheek with it. Go on—shave. And then you can scrub my back and towel me dry and—''

''And *I'll* think of something to do after that,'' he promised with a grin, drying his big handsome body with a towel as he watched her.

She bathed leisurely, feeling the water swirling warm about her legs and hips as she sat in the tub and watched him shave. So expertly did he strop his razor, so precisely scrape off his beard . . . she marveled that he did not cut himself.

''You sound like you've had a dull time of it,'' he tossed over his naked shoulder, staring into the mirror as the razor grazed deftly over his chin. ''If all that's happened while I was gone is that the hearth-chain broke and some Indians chanced by!''

''Oh, Nicolas came by—to return my glove,'' said Georgiana carelessly. She was rising from the tub as she spoke and was surprised to see Brett's big head swing around sharply.

''He did?'' he asked softly. ''And when was that?''

''Yesterday.''

''And did you invite Nicolas to stay the night?''

Georgiana felt suddenly very naked standing there. Her wet body was under her husband's fierce inspection as if he would glean the truth from its gleaming surface—but his gaze upon that body was not friendly. Possessive but not friendly.

"No, I did not," she said defensively.

"You entertained him for a meal perhaps?"

"Not even that." She reached for a towel, held it up before her as if to shield herself from his hard gaze. "Nicolas arrived as we began the butchering, and he stayed but a minute. He could see that I was very busy."

Something in the man across from her relaxed. The keen gray eyes that had been searching her face softened into amusement. "That must have annoyed him," he murmured.

"Why should it?" she demanded tartly.

The big head swung back toward the mirror. "Well, if you don't know, I won't tell you." Calmly, he continued shaving.

"Nicolas had other things to do," she said sharply. She decided not to tell him *what* things—since he was so suspicious, let him find out for himself! And perhaps, a small thought nudged her, when he found out it would be too late for him to form a partnership with Govert Steendam and fall again under Erica's spell. "Nicolas merely returned the glove and went on his way," she said airily.

"He probably filched the glove when you set it down at Haerwyck and held on to it to give him an excuse to come up here to see you."

"Nonsense!" But she was glad he was not looking at her just then, for her face flamed.

"And then you sent him on his way without even a cruller? You did more than that for the Indians!" Brett wiped his razor on the towel and turned to grin at her. "Mind you, I like your style. And you're very pretty, flushed and indignant like that. Which reminds me—I didn't soap your back!"

"It's already done," said Georgiana hastily. "I did it while you were shaving, and rinsed off the soap too."

"Well, then let me help you dry yourself." He tossed the razor away and strode toward her.

Georgiana had stepped out of the tub and was bent over toweling her feet and legs. "That's done too."

She would have tossed the towel aside but for Brett's laughing, "Come now, there must be *some* places that aren't quite dry!" He seized the damp towel and began to tickle her with it, lightly scraping her breasts, passing the towel naughtily between her thighs and causing her to jump and protest and giggle.

And, then, as if the silken touch of her had been too much for him, he dropped the towel and the laughter and the teasing, and smothered his face in her perfumed hair. Georgiana clung to him, responding ardently to his change of mood.

"I've missed you," he muttered, and swooped her up and carried her over to the big bed and made love to her with fierce intensity there atop the quilted coverlet.

Georgiana lost herself in those protective arms, lost herself in the wild winds of love that bore her on, lost herself in time and place as she abandoned herself to passion. *These*, she told herself fiercely, were the only arms that counted, *this* the only man worth having.

Downstairs, cook bustled about, taking time out from the butchering to prepare what she called a "monstrous fine supper," and in her attic hiding place Linnet secreted—and counted yet again—her store of wampum, so full of black beads! And out in the chilly meadow Floss danced and romped and whinnied and cast a wistful look at the house that contained her young mistress. In the wide shining river the fish fled south, passing the flashing trout on their way upriver to spawn. And all the little furry creatures of meadow and woods made haste to finish up their winter quarters against the coming freeze.

But the "English patroon" and his lady were happily oblivious of all that. Locked in loving embrace there in the big warm room with the fire crackling merrily on the hearth and their naked bodies glowing in its light, they thrilled and touched and shared all the joys of earthlings, and Georgiana, happy and content, wished herself no better fate ever as she thrilled beneath her husband's long, ardent body there on the wide Dutch bed.

CHAPTER 22

Nicolas stopped by Windgate on his return trip downriver. Georgiana was walking about the lawn and paused as she saw the ten Haers' sloop tie up at their pier. She waved as she saw Nicolas alight and hurry up the slope toward her and he waved back, a wide grin on his handsome face.

They met almost at the front door. He swept her an exaggerated bow that grazed the grass stems.

"I clean forgot," he said urbanely, "that I was carrying a letter for you along with the packet of mail I escorted upriver."

"Nicolas!" cried Georgiana reproachfully, for letters for her were rare indeed in this isolated Dutch world—indeed this would be the first. "Do let me have it at once!"

Nicolas produced the letter.

"I did truly forget it," he said with engaging frankness. " 'Tis the effect you have on me, Georgiana!" He gave her a rueful look, very attractive as his white teeth flashed against his carefully trimmed golden beard and mustaches. "I was told by the captain of the sloop that brought it as far as Haerwyck that it came by way of Philadelphia," he added.

Georgiana bade Nicolas come in and snatched the letter.

" 'Tis from Bermuda!" she cried in delight. "It will be from Sue."

Nicolas followed her into the drawing room and sat down before the tall windows, facing Georgiana. He had chosen the spot carefully so the afternoon sunlight blazing in through the windows would gild his golden locks and halo the saffron plumes of his hat, which he wore fashionably clapped on his head indoors. This ploy was lost

301

on Georgiana, who was rapt in speculation over what Sue might have to tell her.

"I am burning to read my letter, Nicolas," she said without looking up. "Will you excuse me?"

"Certainly. I only stopped by to ask if you had found my snuffbox—and then I remembered the letter."

"The snuffbox?" Georgiana was already breaking the wax seal. "Oh, it's over there on the table. Linnet saw you drop it and ran down the slope to return it to you but your sloop was already departing."

So that was why Linnet had been waving so frantically from the shore, he thought wryly. *And he had presumed her excitement came from a desire to see him again!* The thought piqued him as he leaned over to pick up the snuffbox. "And where is your bright-eyed little maid?" he drawled. "I'd like to thank her."

"I don't know. Probably wandering about somewhere." Georgiana was absorbed in Sue's letter. "I'll tell her you said thank you."

Nicolas took a pinch of snuff and leaned back on the carved overstuffed sofa. He watched Georgiana with jaded eyes as she perused the letter and wished again that she were his. . . .

We all miss you, Sue wrote, *but there is much news. Bernice claims to have found a will. It leaves Mirabelle, everything, to her. I hear it is to be probated but I do not know how long it will take. It would seem that Mr. Jamison had a solicitor in Jamaica as well as one in London.* (But he didn't! thought Georgiana indignantly. He would have told me! It is another of Bernice's tricks!) *So it is good that you did not stay in Bermuda as there is nothing for you here with Mirabelle gone and Arthur laying claim to you in his obnoxious way. He still beats poor Mattie and I am sure she thoroughly regrets having married him, for all she was so eager to do it at the time. They are off tomorrow for Boston—by a roundabout way, they will have to journey by way of Philadelphia. Mattie pleads to stay but mother will not hear of it and Arthur was—for him—fairly civil to Mattie yesterday, I will say. He even said she could take an extra trunk to hold her books and trinkets—imagine, with all his trunks of clothes, peacock that he is, Mattie can take one extra trunk! Poor Mattie!*

There was more: how much Sue missed her, how well Coral the cat was doing—and then Sue's big news.

Georgiana turned engagingly to Nicolas, and he thought how fetching she looked in her striped tabby gown with its handsome slashed sleeves and those gathered great ruffles at the elbows. An edging of Flanders lace caressed her low-cut neckline, looking stiff and starched against the delicate skin. And her olive taffeta petticoat rustled delightfully. He wondered if beneath that petticoat she was wearing striped stockings like Katrina ten Haer and cast an inquiring glance down to find out. But Georgiana's gown was still not as short as the sophisticated Dutch girls affected, and not until she moved her feet as she turned impulsively to speak to him did he glimpse her trim ankles clad in fragile green silk.

He sighed. So much more to his taste, silk. Just as the dainty ankles that the green silk encased appealed to him so much more than did Katrina ten Haer's sturdier ones.

"Sue writes me that by the time this reaches me she and Lance will be married," Georgiana told him, smiling.

"And who is Sue?" he wondered.

"Oh, she's my very best friend." She scanned Sue's next words: *We are going to live with Lance's family temporarily although Mother says that will not do in the long run, that we must have an establishment of our own.* "And she says that Lance's favorite mare is about to foal and that is all he can think of—that he does not hear half what is said to him." She looked up at Nicolas with laughing eyes, and again he envied Danforth. "I only hope that Lance will be as excited about his own offspring when they come, but I am sure he will not. Lance is surely half horse! He used to propose to me twice weekly at Mirabelle, always explaining the advantage of combining our stables!"

Nicolas's blue eyes narrowed appraisingly. "You had excellent stables at Mirabelle, I take it?"

"Oh, yes, excellent." Georgiana led him on with glee. "Lance had the best stallion on the island—and I had the best mare." She gave him a wide-eyed innocent look. "You must have seen her, Nicolas—Floss, my silver mare. She's an Arabian."

Nicolas's brows shot up and his gaze flew to the massive silver candlesticks, which could be viewed through the open doorway into the dining room. Wickedly, Georgiana could guess what he was thinking: *Plate fit for royalty and Arabian horses!* It amused her to

depict herself—she, the dispossessed waif of the islands—as a
Bermuda heiress and watch Nicolas's blue eyes gleam with avarice.

"Danforth is a lucky man," he muttered, frowning. "On several
counts."

"I hope Brett shares your view," laughed Georgiana. "But I am
afraid he considers me a handful."

"One I would gladly take off his hands," murmured Nicolas.

"Spoken like a court gallant!" declared Georgiana, watching him
with sparkling turquoise eyes. "Katrina ten Haer would *strangle* you
for saying it! Tell me, Nicolas," she added roguishly, "how does
your courting go?"

He looked uncomfortable. "I am not courting Katrina ten Haer,"
he insisted.

"No? But you gave her a diamond necklace, did you not? I seem
to recall seeing it around her neck."

"She has already lost it," he said hastily. "Things have a way of
slipping through Katrina's fingers."

"And men too, I don't doubt," said Georgiana, amused.

"Yes. She considers herself unlucky in that respect," he said
shortly.

Georgiana wondered if he had come upriver not so much to aid
Huygens as because he had suffered some rebuff from the ten Haer
heiress. Possibly he was trying to make Katrina jealous by paying
court to Georgiana?

"Why, Nicolas," she teased, "I was expecting you to sing
Katrina's praises and tell me how wonderful she is in all ways, and
how you intend to have an entire saffron suit made for yourself, just
to match her yellow hair, and how you would be wedding her before
Christmas is past!"

He sighed. "You can stop making sport of me," he told her. "It
is bad enough that you ignore me whilst you read your mail, must
you poke fun at me too?"

She was instantly contrite, for he had been very patient. "Oh,
Nicolas, you know I did not mean it," she said, for she really liked
this big smiling Dutchman in spite of his bad character and the
danger he posed to her and Brett. "But do you really think you
could live at Haerwyck with a mother-in-law like Rychie? And with
Katrina growing more like her every day, for she's just a brown-eyed
Rychie, you know!"

"You sound as if you know Katrina very well." It was his turn to jest. "And her mother too. Yet I could swear that you had met them but once!"

Georgiana realized she must be careful, for her knowledge of Rychie ten Haer had been gleaned from her mother's journal. "I have my sources," she said airily. Let him think it was all servants' gossip!

"Still," he said softly, leaning forward, "your own husband stood ready once to chance the dangers of Rychie ten Haer as a mother-in-law!"

That barb went home. Georgiana caught her breath. "I am sure he never seriously considered marrying Katrina."

Nicolas cocked a knowing eye at her. "You think not? Not to hear Katrina tell it!"

"Oh, I am sure *she* maintains he asked for her hand on bended knee—repeatedly!" scoffed Georgiana.

"No, she maintains he asked her but once. Very clearly. She regards herself as having been jilted—although her father prefers to glaze it over for the sake of peace on the river."

Georgiana tossed her head and her golden curls bounced. "Then no doubt Katrina won't care to attend my masquerade ball!"

"Don't get your hopes up," laughed Nicolas. "I am sure nothing would keep her away!"

Or Erica either, that merry glance told her. She felt suddenly angry with Nicolas, who felt he could predict her future.

"Will *you* be there?" she shot at him.

"Of course—if only to watch you," he grinned. "I am sure all your rivals will be skating about *en masque* at your ball. By the way, do you skate?"

"No," said Georgiana airily. "But by then I will have learned. The edge of the pond is beginning to ice up and Linnet tells me it will soon freeze over and be strong enough to support us."

"By then you will have learned?" he echoed, and she caught a shade of laughter in his voice, hastily covered up. "I must tell you, Georgiana, that both Katrina and Erica have skated all their lives and are superior skaters—especially Erica, who is the soul of grace. As you glide out among your guests, tottering on your shaking ankles, you must remember that I warned you."

"I have said I will *learn*," said Georgiana, nettled.

"So you did," he chuckled. "And has Danforth assured you that skating is an art you can master in a day or two?"

"We have not discussed it." Georgiana dismissed the matter as trivial. "In any event, you will be there to gloat if I fall on my face!"

"More likely I'd catch you and keep you wavering but erect!" he corrected humorously. "By the way, where *is* the lord of the manor? Away on his rounds? I always seem to miss him."

"Brett is spending the day in the forest, supervising the felling of great trees. We are building a new stable and it seems the span of the roof will require enormous beams."

"I am glad to hear he is making improvements," said Nicolas urbanely. " 'Tis good of him to keep the place up." *For me,* was the wickedly unspoken implication.

Georgiana stiffened. "You must stay to sup with us," she said coldly. "Brett would not wish me to let you go without offering you a meal."

"Would he not?" murmured Nicolas, amused. "But I am afraid I must decline, for the sloop awaits me and her captain is eager to push on downriver to Haerwyck." He rose and gave her a roguish look. "His eagerness leads me to believe there must be a willing bedfellow waiting for him there among the servants."

"Or perhaps he aims a bit higher?" suggested Georgiana sweetly.

Nicolas laughed aloud. "He may *aim* but I doubt if he'd *land,* for he's a dour fellow pushing sixty—a bit old for either Rychie's or Katrina's taste!"

"And was your trip to Rensselaerwyck successful?" she asked as she accompanied him down the slope toward the sloop.

Nicholas shrugged. "Van Rensselaer says neither yes nor no. He takes it under advisement." They had reached the pier now and he leaned down, watching her. "And *that* bothers you, Georgiana, for you had hoped with all your heart that I would succeed."

Georgiana missed a step. "And why would I do that?" she demanded breathlessly. "Since you are well aware that Brett plans to construct a mill at almost precisely the same place?"

"But you wish him no luck with the venture!" laughed Nicolas. "For that would bring him into partnership with Govert Steendam and you do not want him mixed up with Erica!"

Georgiana glared up at him. "I never said so!"

"You did not need to." The tall Dutchman gave her a caressing look. "You are a jealous woman, Georgiana—and Danforth will give you cause, never doubt it." He paused thoughtfully. "Are you *sure* your husband will be back tonight?

"Of course I'm sure!"

"Too bad," he said regretfully. "You could have sworn the servants to secrecy and I could have spent the night here—and ridden off south in the morning with none the wiser." His hot gaze rested on her with bright speculation; she felt restive under that gaze. "You will come to that sort of thing eventually, Georgiana." His voice was cool, even, hypnotic. "Your own pride will drive you to it. If only to get revenge."

"Oh, be off!" she cried impatiently, stamping her foot. "You are insufferable!"

Suddenly his arm encircled her waist and his fiery lips brushed her own. Almost before she could sort out her wits enough to struggle, he let her go—and she guessed it was in deference to a shout from near the house. His golden head lifted and he gazed intently at the speaker, who was only calling something to the sloop's captain, who bellowed a reply.

"Faith, I thought it was your husband," Nicolas muttered.

"Thank God it was not," gasped Georgiana, falling away from him. "What came over you, Nicolas? Do you desire to die young?"

The tall Dutchman gave her a crooked grin. "I might risk it," he murmured. "In the right cause. Till we meet again, Georgiana. Oh—my regards to Danforth." He left her, laughing, swaggering down the pier toward the sloop.

Georgiana watched the sloop depart with mixed feelings. Her heart was still beating fast as she retraced her steps to the house.

On her way to the kitchen she ran into Linnet, who was surreptitiously stuffing a hot *olykoek* into her mouth.

"Well, Linnet, the gold snuffbox has been returned, and Mynheer van Rappard sends you his thanks for finding it." Georgiana tried to sound blithe.

Linnet's expression was ludicrous. Almost without volition, her teeth closed on the *olykoek*. "Has he gone?" she asked indistinctly.

"Yes, the sloop has left," sighed Georgiana. "And this time I followed Mynheer van Rappard to the pier to make sure he didn't drop anything that would require his return!"

Linnet tried to swallow. She choked and went into a fit of coughing.

Alarmed, Georgiana slapped her on the back and when that didn't work, she ran to get a tankard of water. When she came back with the water, Linnet's face was purple and large tears had formed in her eyes and were spilling down her cheeks. At last she managed to swallow and Georgiana, worn out between Nicolas's exhortations and Linnet's unexpected behavior, thrust the glass of water impatiently at Linnet, advised, "Don't take such large mouthfuls!" and swept on to the kitchen to see cook about supper.

She would have been astonished had she seen what Linnet did when she was gone. With no one about, Linnet threw herself face down upon the sofa Nicolas had so recently quitted and sobbed silently and beat upon the cushions with her fists. Her wild anger brought on another fit of coughing that made her sit up again, gasping for air.

Nicolas had been here—again! And again she had missed him! Oh, if only she had not found those two black wampum beads and slipped up the back stairs to add them to her attic store! Twice he had been here and both times she had been unavailable. So dejected was she that she pleaded a headache and went upstairs without supper; she did not want to face anyone just now. Wakeful and distraught, she lay in her bed and prayed in a whisper to a God she believed in absolutely to make Nicolas come back again to Windgate.

Downstairs, Georgiana was having her own problems.

Brett had come in tired and frowning. He had spoken hardly two words to her and now he watched her narrowly over their repast of stewed sweet turnips served with fish, fresh pork with carrots, and shellfish turnovers dripping with sweet sauce. For them it was a simple meal, so decreed by Georgiana because she knew how exhausted the kitchen help was from the butchering. She had begun to wonder if it was perhaps *too* simple a meal when Brett remained frowningly silent throughout.

"I had a letter from Bermuda today," she volunteered. "Sue is getting married."

"Who brought the letter? I didn't see a sloop at the landing."

"Oh, it didn't stay."

"What sloop was it?"

"The ten Haers'," said Georgiana hurriedly, and then to distract him: "I told cook my best friend was getting married and she asked me if I'd be going to Bermuda to attend the ceremony. I told her no, it was too far away. It seems strange to realize I might never see Sue again." She sounded pensive, for she was thinking wistfully of Sue and her lost girlhood. Both seemed impossibly far away. It was as if years had passed in the short time since the *Dame Fortune* had cleared St. George's harbor.

But Brett was not to be distracted. "Did Huygens bring the letter?"

"No, it was Nicolas. He just stopped by to deliver it on his way back downriver. The letter had been brought to Haerwyck and entrusted to him—but he had forgotten it on the way up."

Brett snorted. "Forgot!" he scoffed. "Like he 'forgot' his snuffbox."

"Well, he's a forgetful man," she said reasonably, busying herself with her shellfish turnover.

"I don't doubt it." The servants had gone now and Georgiana looked up to see that Brett was eyeing her ruthlessly across the table as he sipped his wine. His gray eyes were very cold. "I'm told you saw him to the sloop."

"As far as the pier, yes," said Georgiana nervously, for she guessed where this was leading.

"Teunis stepped out of the kitchen to call a message to the sloop's captain as he left."

"Yes. I saw him."

"He reported that you kissed Nicolas good-bye."

"I'll remember that Teunis carries tales!" she flashed.

"Is it true?" he asked inexorably.

"No—although I'll admit it may have *looked* so," she said with as frank a look as she could manage. "A sudden gust near took his hat and we collided as we tried to keep it from going into the river."

"*Collided,*" murmured Brett. He sounded amazed at her inventiveness.

Georgiana colored. "I most certainly did *not* kiss Nicolas!" she told him stormily. And she hadn't, she told herself. Of course she had not been able to stop *him* from kissing *her* but there was a very large difference—she had not responded to his kiss. What might have happened if he had held her a few moments more she refused to think about. She could feel her heart pounding in alarm.

Across the table her husband was studying her thoughtfully. She could not read his expression but he looked grim. "See less of Nicolas," he advised bluntly.

Georgiana's breast rose and fell rapidly. It was a delightful sight but at the moment it did not seem to tempt her husband. "I only offered him the most ordinary hospitality!" she protested. "I told him you would wish him to stay and sup and he declined!"

"Wise of him," grated Brett. "I'd have been tempted to slap his teeth for him."

"That's ridiculous!" Georgiana found she was shaking. "I was very cold to him and I followed him down to the pier lest he conveniently lose something else and use it as an excuse to rush back!"

"Next time, find reason not to receive him. Say you are indisposed."

"You must learn to trust me!" said Georgiana sharply.

"Oh, I trust *you*," said Brett. "It is Nicolas I do not trust."

"Well, I can't see—"

"Nevertheless, whether you see or not, you will oblige me in this." His tone was inexorable. "I will not have you spending time alone with Nicolas van Rappard."

Resentment at this cavalier treatment washed over her. "And am I to understand that *you* will spend no time alone with Erica Hulft?" she countered.

"You are to understand so, yes."

"Except perhaps at night when you think I am asleep?" she said bitterly.

Across the table Brett stared at her. "So you heard . . . that night?" he said softly.

"Yes! I heard everything! I heard her tell you nothing had changed between you, that she would enchant the 'child bride', that she—"

He sat back, his eyes hooded. "Then you must also have heard what I told her," he interrupted impatiently, "that it is over between us."

"Erica didn't think it was over!"

"She will come round to thinking it!"

"And meantime you twit me about Nicolas!"

"I only said, see less of him."

She lifted her chin. "You must learn to trust me, Brett. There are many attractive men in the world!"

"But only one Nicolas van Rappard. Stay away from him."

Georgiana's delicate jaw was set. Her face was flushed and stormy. "Yet we will continue to receive Erica, I take it, while denying Nicolas common courtesy?"

Her husband gave her a weary look. "I said nothing about common courtesy. I said do not be alone with him. And Erica is to marry Govert Steendam. It will make her a force on the river. Of course we will receive her."

Nicolas had been right, Georgiana thought bitterly. He had said Brett's arguments would be logical, his reasoning overpowering. He had said—

Sudden fury overcame her and she half rose from the table.

"So I am asked to trust *you* with Erica, yet we all know what you have been to each other—*what you still may be*!"

She had not meant to say that, and having said it she would have given much to unsay it—but pride would not let her take it back.

Brett's broad shoulders had hunched and his face had gone white with anger. He rose from the table, knocking over his chair, and stomped out.

Nicolas was right that she was a jealous woman—and she felt that, as Nicolas had surmised, Brett had given her cause. Confused and filled with guilt laced with indignation—for surely her behavior with Nicolas had not been enough to warrant Brett's edict not to see him again—she went upstairs to bed. And found Brett's door solidly closed against her.

Too proud to ask his forgiveness, Georgiana slept alone. And wept alone.

It was the beginning of a rift between them.

BOOK V
The Seducer

Promises made in the light of the moon
May wither in light of day
And the words that he said as he lured you to bed
Vanish fast away!

PART ONE
The Innocent

The heart is a dreamer, it loves to take flight
But dreams are soon gone, like a thief in the night
And the promises whispered all through the long night
Are gone with the morning, are lost with the light...

New Orange, New Netherland, 1673

CHAPTER 23

The ball at Haerwyck, and the revelations it had brought him about himself and his feelings for Brett Danforth's beautiful bride—and now her obvious indifference on his last two brief visits—had made Nicolas van Rappard restive. Hardly had the ten Haers' sloop carried him back to Haerwyck before Nicolas was again on the move. Irritated by Rychie's and Katrina's incessant discussion of the Danforths and by Katrina's furious outbursts when he failed to agree with her passionate denouncement of Georgiana, Nicolas took passage aboard the first river sloop to dock at Haerwyck and was carried downstream to New Orange.

His freshly clipped pointy Van Dyke beard was just as golden, his elegant clothes and saffron-plumed hat just as handsome, but his usually cheerful expression was gloomy, his step less jaunty than usual as he strode past a collection of the step-gabled yellow brick houses with their divided Dutch doors and scrupulously clean low front stoops. Several wide-breeched Dutchmen bowed to him affably, for Nicolas van Rappard was known to be a contender for the vast patroonship of Windgate and if he won, he would become a power in the community. But Nicolas was too downhearted to more than nod in reply. He went past a tobacconist's shop and at the doorway almost collided with a pink-cheeked boy carrying a basket, who cried *"Pypen en tabac?"* Nicolas was low on tobacco but he was even lower on funds. He shook his head at the boy grimly and marched on, dodging a waddling country woman in a lace cap who was carrying a brace of ducks, and a group of lean buckskin-fringed woodsmen who padded by on Indian moccasins, carrying long muskets.

He might have called on Erica Hulft—and created some excitement if Govert Steendam happened to be there—but his heart was not in it. He passed a saddlemaker's, an apothecary, a candlemaker's and a tinsmith's, and turned into the familiar Green Lion. He was a bit too late for tiffin but he had had a snack on the sloop just before docking. In his present mood he was more interested in serious drinking, so he swung wide the door and prepared to join a gathering of tall-hatted, pipe-smoking gentlemen in the common room.

But his progress was abruptly arrested by a dandified young gentleman in green satin who dashed from the common room, intent on the door to the street just as Nicolas was entering—and collided, cursing, with Nicolas, ricocheted off the Dutchman's sturdy form, and barked his shin painfully against a nearby bench.

"Damme, ye were in the way!" cried the stranger, hopping around on one polished boot and clasping a shinbone resplendent in green silk stockings. His handsome young face reflected both rage and pain.

Nicolas, who had been knocked offstride by the clumsy stranger who had blundered into his scabbard and had nearly lost his hat in the process, was not in a mood to be charitable. His hard gaze raked his adversary. A veritable peacock the fellow was, with red satin lining his full slashed green sleeves, expensive Brussels lace at his throat, and frosty point lace edging the white lawn boothose of that leg he was hopping about on. *New* that lace looked to be—whilst he, Nicolas, was having to rely exclusively on starched and carefully mended *old* boothose! And this dainty fellow wanted *him* to give ground? "If ye brush me again," he warned the stranger in a menacing voice, "I'll crack that shinbone for ye with my boot!" His blue eyes narrowed and his weight shifted to one foot as he considered taking that route on the instant.

"Have done, young sirs! No need to be brawling!" The stout

elderly Dutch innkeeper hurried over as fast as his girth would permit him.

The gentleman in green satin gave Nicolas an angry look, marred by a pair of broken front teeth. The effect was sinister but it seemed not to impress the golden fellow who confronted him. He was tempted to unsheathe the dress sword he carried and slash the golden fellow to pieces here and now for his insolence but he bethought himself in time that this was not Boston, he had no powerful friends in this Dutch town, and the glint in those hard blue eyes no less than the serviceable look of that sword were such as to inspire caution even in such a hothead as himself. He was even a bit glad when the stout innkeeper bustled between them.

"Now, then, gentleman, no harm done," cried the innkeeper cheerfully. "I'm sure this gentleman who just bumped into you, Mynheer van Rappard, meant you no offense. He is in haste to get him to Wey Gat." His gaze on Nicolas was bland. "It would seem he has business there with the English patroon."

Nicolas's weight shifted abruptly to both feet. He gave Klaus, the innkeeper, a sharp glance. Klaus was in his pay for any information to be gleaned that might help his cause—and Klaus was trying to tell him something.

"Wey Gat, you say?" Nicolas turned a genial smile onto the newcomer.

"I know nothing of Wey Gat," snapped the green satin fellow, who was still hopping about on one foot, gingerly holding his bruised shin. "I am seeking a bastard named Brett Danforth and this fellow here"—he indicated the innkeeper with a nod of his head—"has told me he lives upriver." Arthur had been so relieved to have this verified that he had been dashing out to make arrangements to sail upriver, when he had crashed into Nicolas.

"I like your choice of words," murmured Nicolas, warming to any man who would openly call Brett Danforth a bastard. "Here, have I hurt you?" He was all solicitude now, peering anxiously down at the shinbone he had so lately threatened to break. "Come, the least you can do is to let me make reparations! A tankard of ale? Or do you prefer wine?"

"Well." Ungraciously. "I have not all that much time, for I must make arrangements with some riverboat to take me upriver."

"Perhaps I can help you with that. I am well acquainted here, am I not, Klaus?"

Klaus beamed an assent tempered with relief that these two tindery gentlemen had not come to blows in his front door, thereby interfering with the passage of customers coming to drink deep of his stock of wine, bought cheap from the buccaneers.

Nicolas overrode Arthur's protests and even as he spoke he was shepherding his newfound friend, now limping slightly, to a table in the corner, farthest from the tall-hatted group, all of whom were showing interest in this tableau.

"Sit you down, sir," he said heartily. "I am Nicolas van Rappard. Who do I have the honor of addressing?"

"Arthur Kincaid of Boston," said the newcomer sulkily, allowing himself to be propelled almost forcibly onto a bench. "And I will take a glass of wine—if any here be drinkable," he added in a disagreeable voice.

The innkeeper, who had been following along, stiffened upon overhearing that remark but Nicolas grinned and winked at him. "Two glasses of your best port, Klaus," he said, and as the innkeeper grunted and shuffled away, he turned back to Arthur with a winning smile. "And what quarrel have you with the English patroon, may I ask?"

"I do not know him for a patroon," declared Arthur in a loud blustering voice, for he remembered only too well how he had been herded along humiliatingly at the point of Danforth's blade. "I know him for a *poltroon*!"

"Brave words," murmured Nicolas, aware of raised brows and attentive ears among the pipe-smoking gentlemen to whom that remark had carried. "And that sword you carry, I take it, fits your hand well enough that you can back them up?"

It was a bland statement but it brought Arthur up short. "I expect to haul Danforth before a magistrate," he announced haughtily. "For stealing my property from me."

His property? For a moment Nicolas, so used to thinking of the property at Windgate as *his* property—likewise stolen by Danforth, as he liked to think, froze to stillness and his blue gaze turned frosty. But hot on the heels of that thought came the realization that it must be some other property Kincaid was talking about.

"Aye, Danforth's known for his taking ways," he agreed affably, as the innkeeper, whose barmaid was off sick, banged two black-jacks and a bottle down. Nicolas poured a generous portion of port into Arthur's black leather tankard and one for himself before asking, "And what did he steal from you, sir?"

"A woman!"

Nicolas nearly choked on his wine. "The devil you say!" His blue eyes began to sparkle. "Your betrothed, was she?"

"My bondswoman!" Despite his lisp, fury made Arthur's voice crackle.

"Ah—a bondswoman." This was not as interesting as Nicolas had hoped. He would have preferred the lady in question to have been aristocratic and—married. Something he could have called merrily to Georgiana's attention. He sighed and took another drink.

"And he had the gall to *marry* her!" Arthur's lisping voice cracked with rage.

Nicolas's wine went down the wrong way. Choking, he regarded Arthur Kincaid with blue eyes gone round with shock. "He *married* her, you say?" he gasped as soon as he could manage any words at all.

"Aye!"

"And what would this lady's name be?"

"Anna Smith is her name and Danforth married her without my permission!"

"Did he now?" Nicolas was fascinated. Was Danforth then a bigamist? Had he married some other woman in Boston? If he had, then Georgiana was not legally tied to him and would turn her back on him as soon as she heard, no doubt! He leaned forward, concentrating on this surprising fellow from Boston. "And when did all this happen?" he asked.

"A few weeks ago in Bermuda."

Nicolas almost choked again. *In Bermuda!* But the new bride of Windgate was from Bermuda!

"Faith, he's a man of parts," he muttered. "Marrying two Bermuda brides almost simultaneously!"

"I know not what you're talking about," said Arthur, vexed. "*Two* Bermuda brides? I know of but one."

"Well, Danforth has on the premises a Bermuda bride he married right here in New Orange some weeks past."

"Bah," said Arthur. "It could not be. He would not have been so bold!"

"Oh, I assure you he *did* marry her. A number of wealthy burghers were in attendance on that occasion. I don't doubt one or two of them are in this very room." He swung his head around to have a look.

Arthur was dumbfounded at this calm assertion. If Danforth had married recently in New Orange, then surely Anna must have died on the voyage! For one could not imagine a spirited wench like Anna countenancing bigamous nuptials! A new thought occurred to him.

"What does she look like?" he asked in an altered voice.

He had come to the right place for a description.

"She is a most lustrous lady," Nicolas sighed. "Having once seen her, none could possibly mistake her. She has golden hair as fine as spun silk—so silky a man can scarce resist running his hands through it, and luminous turquoise eyes, and a waist a man could span with his hands—"

" 'Tis the same," interrupted Arthur.

"I think not. *This* lady calls herself Georgiana van Rappard—not Anna Smith."

Arthur shook his head irritably. "I care not what name she now calls herself. She is Anna Smith of Mirabelle Plantation."

"Of Mirabelle Plantation, you say? Then assuredly she must be the right one, for this lady claims to be the heiress to Mirabelle."

Arthur spat out a bitter laugh. "Heiress? She is no heiress! She was a bondswoman's niece who was taken in and treated as a daughter of the house at Mirabelle, to be sure, but when Jamison died he left the property to his new wife, who has two daughters of her own."

So regal Georgiana van Rappard was actually Anna Smith, bondswoman. Stunned as he was, Nicolas was still forced to admire the cleverness with which she had fooled him, toyed with him. How she must have been laughing at him! He squirmed at the thought.

"Have you proof," he murmured, "to back up your claim that Danforth's wife is your bondswoman?"

"Of course." Arthur's hauteur was somewhat marred by his lisp. "I have her Articles of Indenture in my trunk and with her own signature affixed!"

Signed by her! Nicolas made a slight gesture as if to brush away cobwebs. He was having difficulty imagining the elegant mistress of Windgate as anybody's bondswoman, least of all this arrogant lisping dandy who sat opposite.

He sat back and considered the handsome young man before him. Well dressed he certainly was, and truculent in manner. His story had a kind of wild sincerity . . . almost the ring of truth. But true or not, it was hard to imagine this strutting popinjay going up against the lean forceful patroon of Wey Gat.

"And how," he asked bluntly, "do you propose to get her back?"

"I don't propose to do it myself at all," said Arthur in a lofty voice. "I merely propose to go upriver and discover if she is still cohabiting with him and, if so, to let the courts deal with the matter."

"Oh, I can assure you she is still cohabiting," chuckled Nicolas, enjoying Arthur's choice of words. He was suddenly engulfed with amusement by a vision of Arthur Kincaid confronting the patroon of Windgate in his upriver lair. "I have recently spoken with the lady." And at Arthur's outraged look, he explained, "The lady's husband is not too fond of me. On a recent visit he was so eager to speed me on my way, he furnished the sloop to help me depart!"

"I don't understand."

"I am a guest of Danforth's neighbors, the ten Haers," elucidated Nicolas. "And I have some litigation pending with the English patroon."

"Litigation?" demanded a puzzled Arthur.

"Yes—but not half so interesting as yours. Tell me just how you propose to wrest a man's wife away from him, for I must admit the idea fascinates me."

"She married without my permission, in the face of my strong opposition—and she has seven years yet to go as my bondswoman!"

"Yes, I realize an indentured servant cannot marry without her master's permission, but still—the deed is done. You cannot undo it."

"I can take the girl away with me, for the papers Danforth forced me to sign—"

"Papers?" Nicolas came alert.

"He forced me to sell him the wench. Under duress it was, at the point of a sword! Any court in the land would call it duress!"

"Some might even call it love. Of a desperate nature, of course," murmured Nicolas, whose good spirits had been entirely restored by this rejuvenating conversation. "Still, he has papers, you say?"

Arthur's handsome face reddened. "He flung some money at me and forced me to sign a receipt for her and for the horse."

So Danforth had bought the silver mare too! God's teeth, what a judge of horseflesh and womanflesh he was! Nicolas was forced to admire him almost as much as Georgiana. Buccaneering ways suited his adventurous nature far better than this litigation he was forced to go through to gain his ends.

"I am surprised that he did not demand the original Articles of Indenture," he remarked.

"Oh, he did, but I told him that they were not at hand."

"And he took your word?" Nicolas was astonished.

Arthur flushed again uncomfortably. "I told him I had torn them up in rage that she had run away from me."

Nicolas inclined his head. "A clever lie," he agreed.

" 'Twas then that he made me write it out that I had sold her Articles to him."

"Perhaps you would be better off to claim the papers you were forced to sign are a forgery," suggested Nicolas, smiling. "And that you did not sign them at all."

Arthur gave him a startled glance. "No-o-o, I cannot do that," he admitted. "They were witnessed by Sue."

"Sue?"

"My sister-in-law. She and Anna are old friends." He was about to allude bitterly to the way Sue had helped Anna elude him when Nicolas murmured, "Ah, yes, Sue . . . I carried Georgiana a letter from Sue recently."

Arthur's countenance grew livid. Sue's letter had managed to precede him! It suddenly occurred to him that Sue's letter must have been entrusted to the captain of the very ship that had brought him and Mattie to Philadelphia, and been handed on by him to some captain who had made a faster voyage! He almost choked with the inequity of it. "Those papers I was forced to write under duress are not valid," he snarled. "They will not hold, I say!"

Nicolas tried to imagine a Dutch court—even one at odds with the English patroon—ordering the forced breakup of a marriage celebrated with such solemnity in New Orange—and could not. It would never happen, whatever this tense young man thought about it.

"Mynheer," he said softly. "A word of warning. You step into a hornet's nest if you go to Windgate—for that is Danforth's stronghold. He will never let you take her—court order or no." And at Arthur's angry ejaculation, he raised a negligent hand. "But I think, mynheer, that there might be a way. Klaus," he called, "do you have a private dining room available? My friend here and I have some matters to talk over."

Klaus, the innkeeper, was silent as he ushered the two gentlemen into the one small private dining room his establishment boasted. He would have given his day's profit to know what they were talking about in there, but after that first loud remark about a "poltroon," Arthur had kept his voice as low as Nicolas's and the clay-pipe-smoking gentlemen had satisfied their curiosity no more than he. The pair of them talked for a long time in there and came out the best of friends, clapping each other heartily on the back.

Arthur Kincaid signaled the landlord with a regal gesture and took two rooms. "Your best," he directed haughtily. "For my wife and myself."

Nicolas's golden brows elevated. "From the way you spoke about Mistress Anna Smith," he muttered in surprise as the landlord went out to call someone to make the rooms ready, "I had somehow not imagined that you had brought your wife along."

"Mattie is still aboard ship," sighed Arthur. "She has been seasick the whole voyage. And that is another thing I lay at Anna Smith's door," he burst out. "She connived to force a distasteful marriage upon me—and then departed!"

Escaped, amended Nicolas silently. He knew nothing about what had transpired between her and Arthur, but he was certain that the beautiful bride of Windgate would never waste herself on such a petulant fellow as this!

"Then we are agreed on our course of action, mynheer?" Nicolas asked smoothly, successfully shielding his true opinion of Arthur. "Granted, 'twill take some contriving and you should bide here in New Orange whilst I look into what's possible to be done, but if we pool our resources, we might both achieve our goals handily, do you not agree?"

Arthur agreed. He winced, for his boots hurt his feet. "I must to the ship," he muttered, "to disembark Mattie and get her settled.

And then to buy me a new pair of boots. This cursed pair has worn blisters on my heels.''

"I'll to the ship with you," offered his newfound friend. "And I'll be delighted to take your lady in tow and get her settled at the inn whilst you shop for boots, for the shops will be closing soon."

"Closing? Oh, yes, I hadn't noticed the time." Arthur consulted a large expensive watch that drew an envious glance from Nicolas. "That is, if Mattie won't be too much trouble?"

It was on the tip of Nicolas's wicked tongue to say that other men's wives were always some trouble but—on the whole—worth it, but he had the good sense to keep silent. If Arthur Kincaid wanted to believe that entertaining his young wife would be trouble-some to Nicolas—so be it!

CHAPTER 24

It was with amazement that Nicolas viewed Arthur's young wife when she stepped off the ship. She saw Arthur and waved. Her face brightened for as time had worn on since he left the ship, she had been half afraid that he had deserted her. In Bermuda that would have pleased her no end, but the captain and crew that had brought them here to this Dutch town were of a sort that made her flesh crawl. Arthur had been weeks making the arrangements and he had been charged a pretty penny for this voyage—he had even been made to pay for the painting of a Dutch name on the ship's hull. Mattie had had plenty of time on board during a gale-swept voyage to resign herself to the fact that she was, willy-nilly, en route to New Orange, and now in sheer relief she left the vessel to step on this foreign shore with all the exuberance of a schoolgirl on holiday.

Somehow from Arthur's deprecating tone and inflection when he spoke of his young wife, Nicolas had imagined Mattie to be hideously ugly, ungainly of figure, devoid of grace and charm—at the very least a shrew. Nothing could have been further from the truth.

Mattie's friends would barely have recognized her. Her plump figure seemed to have undergone a sea change—she was almost thin, for she had been so worried back home in Bermuda that she had been unable to eat, and so terrified of Arthur on the voyage aboard the *Mary Louise*—although he had not dared to lay a finger on her after that first attack on deck—that she had been able to hold nothing down. In Philadelphia Arthur had left her scrupulously alone while he spent his evenings with bawds and chambermaids, and Mattie had had a grand time visiting the elderly Leighton sisters, although she had been shocked by their poverty. They had scrimped for years to make this voyage and their table was so sparsely set, their diet so poor that Mattie had felt ashamed to eat up their food and had done little more than nibble, insisting she was not hungry. Had she had any money of her own, she would certainly have spent it on delicacies for the Leighton sisters, but her mother had sent her off with only the new pink dress and good wishes and Arthur never bothered to give her any allowance. So Mattie starved herself and on departure gave the sisters, who were loath to see her go, her two best petticoats and her best shawl.

She had expected to eat heartily on the voyage to New Orange— even ship's biscuit would have been welcome—but they were barely out of Philadelphia harbor before they ran into a gale. Mattie was promptly and violently seasick. When Arthur decided of a sudden to exercise his marital rights, she retched all over him. Yelping that she had ruined his doublet, he had in fury knocked her across the room—but the humiliating incident had also, she thanked God, made him keep his distance lest he sully his fine clothes again. Mattie learned fast. She had pretended seasickness for the remainder of the voyage—and it had kept Arthur away from her. It had also kept food away from her and now her once plump figure was almost willowy.

Lack of her usual rich diet had cleared up Mattie's mottled complexion and her skin was now as clear and smooth as a peach blossom. The sea breeze had added color to her cheeks, and her big brown eyes, echoing her excitement at embarking on this new life—for youth is resilient and Mattie had had several respites from Arthur—looked wide and scared and sparkling and vividly alive.

Even her mousy hair seemed to have achieved a richer shade of brown—which probably had to do with her diet.

Mattie had never looked so well in her life, and the rose petal silk gown she was wearing (a hand-me-down from her mother and now sizes too large for her slender figure), by its very ill fit gave her slim body a delicacy, a fragility that it had never before possessed. As if she were a little girl—dainty, slightly awkward and embarrassed but excited withall, dressed up in her mother's clothes. Fearing that she might have been deserted, her frightened gaze had only scanned the busy waterfront. Now she looked up at the big Dutch windmill with its wide sails that dominated the town and her soft mouth formed a silent round O. It was an appealing childish mannerism and somehow it touched the sophisticated Dutchman's heart.

"This is your wife coming toward us?" he murmured, trying to keep the astonishment out of his voice.

Arthur, having already made up his mind about Mattie's complete undesirability, and preoccupied with desperate plots and schemes, had noticed no change in her.

"Yes, that's Mattie," he said in a tone of complete indifference. "Come. If she stops gawking about, I'll present you."

Nicolas found Mattie's "gawking about" very fetching, since it consisted of swift shy glances at everything about her and then quickly looking away as if she dared not be noticed. He was smiling when they rounded a pile of kegs, and Mattie, who was daintily stepping over some coils of rope, reached them.

"This is my wife, Mattie," said Arthur in an offhand way as if he were making known some upper servant. "Mynheer van Rappard."

"A water sprite," murmured Nicolas—and would have said more but that he reminded himself that he was in the presence of the lady's husband and contented himself with making a most elegant leg to Mattie and brushing the back of her gloved hand with his lips.

Shy Mattie was instantly bedazzled. She raised those large brown eyes toward him and he realized with shock that she was sporting the remnants of a black eye concealed beneath a hastily applied layer of ceruse. Somehow the bruise below her fluttering lashes made her seem all the younger and more vulnerable, all the more lost and appealing.

"My name is Mathilde, mynheer," corrected Mattie softly, for she had made a firm decision the day she left Bermuda that she would no longer be called by her hated nickname Mattie.

Arthur snorted. He shared his wife's dislike of the name and for that reason felt it suited her—he intended to call her Mattie until the day she died. "I must leave you now," he said. "Go with Mynheer van Rappard, Mattie. He'll escort you to the inn and I will join you there later. Oh, and see to the luggage."

"It's already on deck," said Mattie timidly and Nicolas could see from her manner how afraid of Arthur she was.

"Well, have it brought to the inn," said Arthur irritably, and took himself off.

"Mevrouw," Nicolas said in a timbred voice and gallantly offered her a tawny velvet arm. He smiled into her eyes—his best smile, a flash of white teeth, a flash of wicked blue eyes, a jaunty gleam of golden mustaches and beard. Mattie looked up into that face and went weak. The saffron plumes that had near swept the dock when he bowed seemed to sway dizzily overhead. There was freedom in his reckless gaze—the same freedom the sea gulls knew, circling overhead in the endless blue . . . the same endless blue of those eyes gazing down at her.

"M-mynheer," she faltered, certain he must hear the loud thumping of her heart.

"Your husband bids me escort you to the inn," Nicolas said gravely and offered her his arm.

No one—not even Arthur in the days when he was trying to impress the Waites—had ever bowed to Mattie with such courtliness. And no one *ever* had gazed on her like that. As if she were—beautiful, desirable, someone to be treasured.

"But—but the luggage," she said breathlessly. "I must stay and make sure it is all unloaded properly."

"Nonsense. Point it out to me."

Moments later, to Mattie's unbounded joy—for she had expected to spend a vexing hour or more on the task—a masterful Nicolas had requisitioned half a dozen burly men from the docks, and their trunks and boxes were being speedily removed from ship to dock.

"Should I not check it out?" wondered Mattie vaguely. "There might be something missing, some box I have overlooked."

Nicolas was allowing himself to admire her eyelashes and the depths of her large brown eyes—so much softer than Katrina's. "I am sure you have overlooked nothing," he said in a caressing voice.

"But Arthur will be so *angry* with me if anything is lost."

"We will check out every last box at the inn. Come, my lady." Again he offered her that tawny velvet arm.

Torn between a fear of Arthur so great it threatened to suffocate her and a mad desire to seize that arm and cling to it and let it take her anywhere it chose, Mattie made a sudden momentous decision. With surprising strength, she seized the proffered arm and marched beside Nicolas with a springy step to the inn.

On the way there Nicolas amused Mattie with odd bits of information about the colony: one paid for things here with beaver skins or wampum but one expressed their *value* in guilders or stivers. Lawyers were practically unknown and much disliked by the Dutch—some had arrived with British rule, but now under Dutch rule again New Orange had gone back to its old lawyerless ways— oh, there was no shortage of court cases, to be sure. Slander especially was quite a common charge—the Dutch had a way of speaking their minds!

Mattie countered by commenting ingenuously on the number of Indian moccasins being worn ("Cheap," explained Nicolas, laughing); and the lace-trimmed Dutch caps on so many female heads ("Ah, that's Holland for you," he sighed. "Industrious vrouwen, they make their own lace. And sell it for pin money," he added casually.) She mentioned the shockingly short skirts she saw about and the brilliance of the well-displayed petticoats.

"They look like bawds to your conservative Bermuda eyes, don't they?" said Nicolas wickedly and Mattie colored to the roots of her hair.

"I—I did not say that," she corrected breathlessly.

"No, but you thought it," he grinned. "Everything you think shows on your face. Your thoughts pass over it like a mirror."

"Oh, *dear*," said Mattie, distressed, hoping he had not read her excited assessment of *him* on her countenance. From the triumphant gleam in his eyes she rather thought he had!

They made a grand entry into the Green Lion "at the head of their men" as Mattie romantically put it to herself. Certainly they created a small stir, with a straggle of burly followers sweating under a motley collection of trunks and boxes. Heads turned to watch them from the common room as they made their way up the stairs.

Mattie, on learning that Arthur had taken not one but two rooms at the inn ("He must be as rich as Mamma says!" was her first startled thought), quickly recovered. "The second room is for the trunks and boxes," she decided sensibly.

"Better to distribute them evenly between the two rooms," suggested Nicolas. "And not block access to either bed. Then, if one of you should be sleepless, tossing in a strange bed, you can always steal out to the other room."

Mattie gave him a big-eyed look. If Arthur should be sleepless and restive, she knew that she would cling to the edge of the mattress throughout the night and pray that one of his threshing arms or legs would not collide with her trembling body—for that would doubtless cause him to knock her out of bed and she would spend the night shivering on the floor, as she had done more than once in Bermuda. As for herself, she would not dare to be restive; she would lie there stiffly even though her body ached, and fight off sleep until morning to avoid retribution, no matter how dark the circles under her eyes became.

Well aware that she might be spending the night on the bare floor instead of in the soft featherbed with its bright green quilted coverlet, she called for an extra quilt and laid it carefully, still folded up, upon the room's single large chest.

"It will not be cold enough for an extra quilt surely," objected Nicolas. "There will be a fire built to ward off the evening chill."

"Still—I may need it," said Mattie evasively. The men had gone now—to be paid by the innkeeper and the amount added to Arthur's bill—and she was standing rather uncertainly in the center of the square low-ceilinged room with her back to the one small window. She felt forlorn standing there in her ill-fitting pink silk dress facing the only man who had ever paid any attention to her—and now he would go away and there would be nothing to do but to sit and wait for Arthur's arrival.

But Nicolas had other plans for her afternoon. Now that they had dispatched the luggage so handily, he said, why skulk about here? Could she not join him in a walk about the town? He would show her the sights. There were so few of them, it would take no time at all!

Mattie yearned to go with him. "I would so love to see New York—I mean New Orange." She blushed uncomfortably at her slip of the tongue but the golden Dutchman did not seem to mind. "But Arthur will be angry if I am not waiting for him when he returns," she explained, twisting her hands together nervously.

"Then could I not coax you into sharing a glass of cider with me?" wondered Nicolas. And when she hesitated, "No, not in the common room. I can see you feel your husband might object to that, but this inn provides a small private dining room where we might sip a glass of wine unobserved, and Klaus, the innkeeper, will notify us if your husband arrives early."

Mattie's resolve was weakening. "Well," she said. "Perhaps a glass of cider."

. They repaired straightaway to the private dining room, where Nicolas consumed a bottle of fine Malaga while Mattie, who found she could not eat much after her long fast, sipped her cider and nibbled at a snack of cheese and little cakes.

Sitting across the oaken table from her with his back to the big gumwood *kas* that dominated the small room, Nicolas drew her out. What had it been like living in Bermuda? he wondered.

Mattie was glad to tell him. Headily aware that she was sitting across from a most attractive—and attentive—male, she never realized how adroitly Nicolas guided the conversation. Was she aware why her husband had come to these shores?

Mattie looked frightened. She set down her piece of cheese and unconsciously clenched her hands together, but she kept her mouth stubbornly closed.

"Come," coaxed Nicolas with his engaging grin. "I think we both know why. He seeks one—Anna Smith, does he not?"

"Yes," said Mattie with bitter emphasis. "And I wish he did *not* seek her. For there will be nothing but trouble if he finds her. Brett Danforth bested him in Bermuda and this time he might well kill Arthur."

"Ah?" Nicolas's golden brows shot up. His blue gaze was focused squarely on Mattie's ceruse-concealed black eye. "Am I to presume, then, that you are worried about your husband?" he asked softly.

Mattie hesitated. She had always been truthful and, in truth, she was not sure how she felt about Arthur now. She had been absolutely overwhelmed by his manly beauty when first she had laid eyes on him. If Walter Meade had not interrupted that day when she had been swept from her horse by a low-hanging branch, if Arthur, bending over her to see if she was hurt, had actually made advances to her, she knew she would have responded to him. Indeed it would never have occurred to Mattie not to let Arthur have his way with her, for wasn't that but a prelude to marriage in the exciting books she read? And wasn't she a "good" girl who had never permitted any man to take liberties with her (not that any liberties had ever been attempted) and an island aristocrat to boot? No man, she had reasoned innocently, not even a stranger from Boston like Arthur, unused to island ways, would dare to lay a finger on Mathilde Waite unless he intended marriage—and marriage to handsome Arthur had seemed to Mattie at the time a golden unreachable dream.

That Arthur Kincaid considered Bermuda barbaric and its aristocrats little better than savages, Mattie had yet to learn that day when she had been struck from her horse and Walter Meade had dragged Arthur back to Waite Hall and accused Arthur of attempting to rape Mattie. Weeping, Mattie had been appalled to discover that Arthur's intentions were a good deal less than honorable—he had told Amanda Waite that he had no intention of marrying her daughter. And Mattie had felt deep galling shame that Arthur had to be threatened into taking her to the altar.

Still, she had asked herself—even with her heart pounding with apprehension as she and Arthur were escorted by burly Walter and Mattie's glowering father into the parish church in St. George—was not this what was meant by "an exciting life"? Would not Arthur, once brought to earth, capitulate and love her forever and ever?

So it would happen with Arthur, Mattie had reassured her palpitating heart.

It had not worked out quite that way.

Mattie had survived a disastrous wedding night—when a fuming Arthur had wreaked his vengeance against the excited young girl he had been forced to marry—and waked up to realize with despair that she had married a brute.

Arthur bullied Mattie. He pushed her roughly aside when she got in his way, which was often for Arthur had a disconcerting habit of turning about halfway and suddenly striking out in the opposite direction. He derided her taste in clothes, which he called dowdy and provincial, her carriage ("stooped"), her figure ("fat"), her coiffure ("ugly"), even her unshakable affinity for pink, which he told her with brutal candor made her look even more sallow.

In bed he often reduced her to tears by leaping off her and pushing her violently to the far side of the bed—or even off it—and telling her in a steely contemptuous voice that she was stiff and cold and totally undesirable. When in desperation she tried to please him, he would take her with a careless brutality that left her flesh bruised and her spirit cowed and her mind in a seething panic that she was—as she honestly believed, for had not worldly, experienced Arthur said so?—utterly deficient in womanly attributes.

It might have helped had she known that Arthur's experiences with the opposite sex—except for those he had raped outright—had so far only encompassed slatterns and charwomen and such unfortunates as could be cheaply had. But Mattie of course did not know that. In matters of sex, in her innocence, she considered Arthur an oracle, akin to gods and devils, and no matter how badly he treated her, when she found herself unable to respond as ordered, she humbly believed his every pronouncement of her ineptitude.

Arthur was experienced; she was a novice—and she had proved unworthy.

Time and a few hard cuffs and two ocean voyages and the agonizing realization that Arthur preferred Anna Smith to her, indeed that they were hot on Anna's trail, had wrought a subtle change in her feelings toward Arthur, but Mattie was not yet ready to admit it.

In point of fact, she had learned to hate Arthur. She wanted impotently to strike at him—for wounding her innocence, for destroying her dreams. She wanted to strike at him—but she did not know how.

And now a smiling stranger, the best-looking man she had ever seen, was staring raptly into her eyes and his glance was—her heart gave a little lurch—admiring. And he was asking her, was she worried about Arthur?

Mattie swallowed. "No," she said rather vaguely. "I am not worried about Arthur."

Nicolas considered that answer amusing—and perhaps justified coming from a demure little bride who was sporting a black eye.

"Mevrouw," he said suavely. "Mathilde—may I call you Mathilde? It is such a lovely name."

"Oh, yes," breathed Mattie, who rejoiced just to hear someone call her by that name. "Please do!"

"I do feel that we are going to be good friends, don't you?"

"Mattie forgot all about eating. This splendid fellow wanted to be her friend! "Oh, yes. Yes, I do," she agreed earnestly.

"What is Anna Smith really like?" Nicolas asked suddenly. For if he could avoid a vituperative tirade—such as a similar question might have evoked from Katrina—he might glean a key to Georgiana's character from this lost wistful child who had known her in the old days.

To his surprise, Mattie was all too willing to describe her beautiful rival. "Anna is very kind and very generous," she admitted with the honesty that was characteristic of her. "She gave Sue a beautiful blue gown—and Lance fell in love with her in it. In case you have not seen Anna," Mattie rushed on, "you will have no difficulty in recognizing her. For she has a face people turn in the street to look at and a smile that makes strong men weak. And as if that were not enough, she has a stunning figure and a great sense of style and masses of shining fair hair. And beautiful turquoise eyes that—that sort of challenge you."

Too well Nicolas remembered the challenge in those haunting turquoise eyes, but he was amazed that Mattie, who he presumed to be competing with Georgiana for Arthur's affections, should render such an unbiased assessment of her rival. He gave a slight start as Mattie finished dismally, "I haven't a chance beside her."

"Of course you have," he was astonished to hear himself say.

"What?" Mattie was looking at him, startled. "What—did you say?" she faltered.

"I said you have every chance. You are young and lovely and desirable," he rushed on recklessly. "Your eyes are like brown velvet and you have skin that would do credit to a peach." Such flattery came easily to Nicolas. Words of love rolled off his rakish tongue as readily. He checked himself suddenly and felt ashamed.

The object of his attentions was sitting up straight and looking at him with round astonished eyes in which adoration was just beginning to appear. Her lips were softly parted and her breast rose and fell with sudden rapidity.

Nicolas told himself he was a bastard. This frightened child was not for him.

"I have been less than honest with you, mevrouw," he said slowly. "I am well acquainted with Anna Smith."

"Then if you know her," cried Mattie, "you must get word to her. Tell her she must go away—anywhere, that Arthur is looking for her and I do not know what trick he will try!"

Nicolas gave her a pitying look. "I will convey your message, of course, mevrouw," he said smoothly, never once intending to do it. "But you need have no fear for the lady. She came to these shores saying she bore the great name of Georgiana van Rappard and she is the wife of the English patroon."

"English patroon?" faltered Mattie.

"Yes. An Englishman who bought up my patrimony, a place called Windgate. We have some litigation about it."

Mattie's puzzled face told him she knew nothing of these intrigues.

"Georgiana is the talk of the river," he told her, leaning back and fondling his glass. "I am told there is quite a story to her early life. Perhaps you will apprise me of it?"

"Arthur will be getting back," said Mattie uneasily.

"Oh, your husband won't be back for some time," he laughed. And at Mattie's questioning look, "You've married a suspicious fellow, Mathilde. He'll want to do some checking up on me, I don't doubt. And since I am Dutch and he is not, he'll be suspicious of a Dutch town backing me up, so he'll go from place to place asking questions. It will take time."

Mattie didn't understand what he was talking about, or why Arthur should go about asking questions about a chance acquaintance, but suddenly she didn't care. The Dutchman's rich caressing voice was lulling her and his golden hair seemed to halo a wickedly enticing face. She relaxed and lost herself in the vivid blue of his eyes, smiling at her across the rim of his glass. And under the pressure of that smiling hypnotic gaze that made her feel that she was every inch desirable and made for love, Mattie told Nicolas breathlessly what she knew of Georgiana's life in Bermuda, ending ingenuously with, "And so all of us, even Anna, believed she was the heiress to Mirabelle. That is, until Bernice turned her out."

"So that was the way it happened," murmured Nicolas thoughtfully. "Strange . . . it would seem from what you tell me that Anna Smith never knew of her heritage as Georgiana van Rappard. You say she never spoke of it. Then, am I to assume that she was not aware of her great expectations until she married Brett Danforth?''

Mattie felt called upon to protest the sardonic irony of his tone. "I think the only inheritance Anna ever expected was Mirabelle," she said uncertainly. "And of course, Bernice got that away from her.''

"And so she merely moved over and took someone else's inheritance.'' Nicolas smiled lazily. "As soon as someone pointed it out to her.''

"Oh, no, I don't believe Anna would do anything *wrong*,'' Mattie interjected hastily. "You should have seen the way she attacked Arthur for trying to burn up Mamma's saddle horse! I mean"—her cheeks burned—"she *accused* him of doing it.''

Tried to set a horse alight, had he? Nicolas felt distaste for his newfound accomplice rising in him with every revelation. "And did he accomplish his goal?'' He tried to sound casual.

"Oh, no, Anna stopped him—I mean, she *said* she did. Mamma didn't believe Anna's story, of course.''

"But you believe it, don't you, mevrouw?'' asked Nicolas quietly.

Mattie's suddenly ducked head and the uneasy way she plucked at her skirt was answer enough.

Nicolas bethought him of the time. Arthur should have worn himself out asking questions by now!

He set down his glass and rose to his full height in a single fluid gesture. Mattie looked up and the sight of him standing there in his tawny velvets smiling down at her was so splendid that it made her dizzy. "Mathilde,'' he said gently. "You have a husband who'll come limping in any minute now in new boots and it might be best for both of us if he didn't know we'd had this conversation. Come, I'll escort you back to your room—he'll never know you left it.''

Mattie's deep sigh of relief and sudden look of brimming gratitude made him feel suddenly abashed. He refused to admit even to himself that it had been her story about Arthur trying to set the horse alight that had made him suddenly so careful of this frail child before him.

In silence he escorted an enchanted Mattie back to her room.

CHAPTER 25

"Will we see you at dinner?" Mattie asked Nicolas wistfully as they reached her door.

"Perhaps." He bent low and brushed her hand with his lips. Mattie shut the door behind her and leaned against it with her eyes closed. A soft ragged sigh escaped her lips. She wondered if she would ever see the golden Dutchman again.

She did. At supper. He came in late and smiling and joined them at their table in a corner of the common room. Arthur had had an earful of gossip about Nicolas van Rappard's prospects this afternoon and looked at Nicolas with vastly more respect. And to think, he had thought him but a common adventurer!

Mattie felt this change in the atmosphere and reveled in it. She was (she considered) most fetchingly gowned in the beruffled blush coral taffeta creation in which she had left Bermuda. Its enormous sleeves fairly dwarfed her newly slender arms and in desperation she had tied a rosy riband around the waist in an attempt to make it fit better—but all to no avail. With her sparkling eyes and hairdo that would not stay quite neat, she looked like a mischievous little girl dressed up in her mother's clothes and Nicolas's hard blue eyes softened as he looked at her.

"You look very elegant tonight, mevrouw," he said gravely, and caused Mattie to blush to the roots of her less than elegantly got-up brown hair.

To cover that guilty blush, Nicolas turned smoothly to Arthur. "Did you try the bootmaker I recommended?"

"Aye," sighed Arthur. "And the new boots are well made, as you said they would be. But as to the fit, my heel is so raw from wearing the others that I can't tell whether these will rub or not."

338

Nicolas, smiling benignly on him, remembered the tale Mattie had told him about the horse and fervently hoped that the new boots rubbed Arthur till he bled.

"I have bought us a bottle of fine Canary, brought up from the Caribbean by the buccaneers," he said, producing it.

"Will the innkeeper allow you to bring in your own wine and drink it here in his common room?" marveled Arthur.

Klaus will let me do anything I like," replied Nicolas easily, but his lazy smile was for Mattie. She could feel her very flesh prickle under the warmth of that smile.

In point of fact Nicolas had not five minutes ago bought the bottle from Klaus, although he wished Arthur to think he had come by it elsewhere. Now he signaled the innkeeper for fresh glasses, and poured it himself, bending over it with great ceremony and handing Mattie and Arthur their glasses with a flourish.

"To the venture," he said, looking Arthur straight in the eye.

"To the venture." Arthur drained his glass.

Their words, their toasts, went by Mattie in a dream. She lifted her glass to her lips and drank some but she never really tasted it. Although he sat beside her at the table, Arthur and his moods were temporarily forgotten, for she saw but one person at the table: Nicolas. And when that tawny velvet arm reached out to fill her glass again, Mattie, who never drank anything stronger than cider, dreamily allowed it to be refilled and tossed it down as if she had been drinking deep all her life.

Nicolas, watching her, gave an inward chuckle. Arthur, he thought contemptuously, was a fool and worse.

From across the room Klaus the innkeeper watched the trio curiously, for he had had an interesting conversation with Nicolas just before Nicolas had joined Arthur and his bride. Nicolas, he told himself, was up to his usual tricks.

For Mattie it was a wonderful evening and all too short. But it was ended rapidly, for Arthur, his speech thickened with drink, lurched to his feet and told her to come along, that he was for bed.

Mattie scrambled up before Nicolas could pull out her chair, but she walked on air all the way up the stairs beside a wavering Arthur and turned on the landing to give a last lingering look to their dinner companion. She would have blown him a kiss, had she dared.

Arthur went to sleep that night so suddenly that Mattie was

amazed. He had stumbled around taking off his clothes and had scarce got undressed and into bed before he was fast asleep. Mattie lay beside him listening to his heavy even breathing and was wondering if she dared to fall asleep herself—or would Arthur rouse suddenly and pummel her—when there was a soft knock on the door.

Thinking it must be a servant girl sent to stir up the fire or bringing another long brass bed warmer, Mattie padded to the door, hastily donning her flowered dressing gown over her white night rail as she went.

She opened the door a crack and found herself looking into the golden Dutchman's smiling face.

"What—what are you doing here?" she gasped. "Arthur is asleep. If we wake him—"

"Oh, no chance of that," he said easily. "I put something in his wine."

"Why?" faltered Mattie.

"So you would get a good night's sleep for a change. I was right that you do not get those too often, was I not?" he guessed shrewdly.

"Thank you," whispered Mattie. There were tears in her soft brown eyes.

"And I came also to ask a favor. Your husband preempted the innkeeper's last two rooms. I find myself without a bed."

"Oh, my goodness," said Mattie in consternation. "I'm sure Arthur wouldn't mind your sleeping in the other one. You can enter it from the hall."

"No, I'm sure he wouldn't mind," agreed Nicolas, not stirring from the doorway. "But the night has grown colder than I thought it would and the maids are all busy downstairs—I don't like to disturb them to build me a fire."

"Oh, if you want to borrow some fire from our hearth, there are plenty of hot coals," said Mattie eagerly.

"Good," said Nicolas. "If I might just step in and get some?"

Mattie saw that he had brought with him a small hearth shovel for the purpose, and swung wide the door. She gave the sleeping Arthur a frightened look, but his even breathing continued without a break.

"And now if you would just follow along and make sure that I do not strew sparks on the floor and set the inn alight?" suggested

Nicolas, and Mattie stole along beside him and watched while he made a fire in the second bedchamber. White moonlight, streaming in through the small-paned window, made it almost as light as day. Mattie felt awkward and exposed standing there in her dressing gown and thin night rail.

"Well, I suppose you are all right now," she said rather helplessly as the fire flamed up, for even though the room was still cold, it was somehow warmer than the room she had just left. "I'll be going back."

"Oh, it may be a bit chilly yet before morning." Nicolas, kneeling by the fire, flung over his shoulder. "Would you mind bringing me that extra quilt you got, for there's none on this bed?"

"Of course I will." Mattie hurried back to get the quilt and returned to find Nicolas standing up and pouring out two goblets of wine from a bottle that had miraculously appeared.

"To warm you," he said engagingly and held one out for her.

Mattie knew she should go back. Her every woman's instinct warned her she should leave at once, go back to her own room and latch the door. Against this tall compelling stranger. Against her own wildly beating heart. Against these wild feelings and hot desires that were drifting through her as she looked into his kindling eyes in the moonlight.

Instead she held out a steady hand and took the goblet Nicolas proferred, took an experimental sip. It was delicious. It seemed to her that it had an extra flavor, something exhilarating that she had never tasted before. Her hand began to shake a little now, for she thought she saw something unexpected in the intent gaze of the man before her: rescue. Rescue from this awful life with Arthur.

In a sudden wave of revulsion against the strength of her own feelings, she pulled her robe tightly around her and looked about for a place to sit down.

"I'm afraid we'll have to sit on the bed," said Nicolas cheerfully, spreading out the red comforter Mattie had brought, with a careless hand. "This is a small room and the only chair seems to be occupied with a large heavy box that looks as if it ought not be disturbed."

Mattie giggled. The box was her own and it was full of delightful romances by her favorite authors. She had managed to smuggle it on board while Arthur was not looking. And now all those elegant heroines could envy *her,* for she was having an adventure as exciting and clandestine as any of theirs! But—she was nervous. She sat down gingerly on the edge of the bed, knees pressed tightly together.

Nicolas took that giggle as a good sign. "Drink up," he advised, holding the bottle in readiness. " 'Tis still chilly in here and we don't want you catching cold."

The unaccustomed wine, on top of what she had already drunk at dinner, was warming Mattie's whole body. Indeed she felt slightly dizzy. She finished her glass and silently held it out to be refilled. What did she care if she got drunk? She was in better company than she had ever been before in her life!

But Nicolas quietly took the empty glass from her.

"No, Mathilde," he said softly. "You have drunk enough wine. It is time you drank deep of other wine—the wine of life."

Cymbals seemed to clash in Mattie's head, a wild jumble of music, all of it sweet. Nicolas had caught hold of her wrist but she hung back, too shy to look at him.

"Come," he coaxed. "Look at me. For in me you have found a friend. That bruise beneath your left eye, how did you come by it?"

"I—I bumped into something aboard ship," she mumbled.

"Your husband's fist, no doubt?"

Mattie swallowed and nodded.

"And it is not the first time?"

She shook her head miserably.

Nicolas was studying her bowed head keenly. He could not imagine why he, a man who had always pursued women more than able to take care of themselves, should feel such a rush of sympathy for this forlorn waif before him. "Why?" he wondered. "Why does he beat you?"

"He didn't want to marry me," Mattie blurted. All of a sudden, under the influence of the wine and Nicolas's sympathetic manner, words came gushing out. "It was all a misunderstanding but my father made him marry me, and he blames Anna for it, and he swears he will get even. Oh"—tears of self-pity spilled over her lashes—"My life is so *awful*. I am afraid to sleep, afraid to wake!"

Nicolas let his big warm hand drop over her small clenched one, lazily caressed her arm beneath her big enveloping sleeve. He was rewarded with a tremor as she looked up, startled, through her tears.

"And is this husband who was thrust upon you so forcibly

successful as a lover?'' he murmured. His fingers were fondling her elbow now, creeping up toward her shoulder.

Mattie swallowed. To this newfound friend who was so gently caressing her, she could not bring herself to lie. "*Arthur* is successful," she got out in a quavering voice 'but I—I am very deficient, to hear him tell it." Her face was woebegone. "He goads me, he instructs me, he pushes me about this way and that, but he says that I am as stiff as a post and like one frozen—and I fear it is true because I am frozen with fear of him. I know not what he will do next and he hurts me so often that I—I cannot enjoy being married to him or yet *be* enjoyed," she finished lamely, her voice fading away even as the flush on her face deepened.

Nicolas, whose fingers were delicately toying with her bare shoulder now, under cover of the big enveloping sleeve, traced the column of her throat with his other hand and studied her. Poor child, she had known only bestial treatment! He yearned to get Kincaid on the toe of his boot—he'd boot him right out of the colony! No, he remembered abruptly why he couldn't do that, there was too much at stake. But there *was* something he could do about Kincaid's unhappy young wife.

"Mathilde," he said gently, holding Mattie's pulsing throat in a gentle hand and bending down just a kiss away from her parted lips, "what say you we latch this door? For there's time and to spare to teach you the difference here and now between a man and a brute."

"But Arthur," said Mattie shakily. "Arthur is in the next room!"

"You have nothing to fear from your husband tonight," Nicolas told her calmly. "He will sleep for many hours—through tomorrow noon probably."

Mattie stared at him, dazed. His gentle touch was wearing down her resistance. "But the—the servants," she protested weakly. "*They* might discover . . ." And, then, more sensibly, "They are in your pay, aren't they?"

"Not exactly. But Klaus, the innkeeper, is a friend of mine. His servants are aware of that friendship. They will do nothing that might bring retribution down upon their heads."

"No, I—I couldn't," said Mattie in a strangled voice. But she sat helpless with her trembling hands clutched in her lap as this wicked gentleman she had met but a few hours before rose and leisurely latched the door, divested himself of his hat, which he had worn fashionably indoors, tossed aside his sword, and returned to lean down over her.

"Just think how all your life you'll regret not having tried it," he coaxed wickedly, and as he bent down his golden hair fell in a bright shower over her shoulders. She could feel it brush her throat like tendrils of fire. Now his hands were moving impudently, easing back her dressing down from her shoulders, teasing the riband that held up her night rail until it came undone. Mattie gave an instinctive, convulsive movement. He was toying with her breasts!

I should resist him! she told herself wildly. *I should tell him to go away, that I've taken marriage vows, that I belong to Arthur. I should escape!* But she knew in her heart that she had no wish to escape, and that she would never truly belong to Arthur, for Arthur did not want her, had not wanted her from the start. She sat, unable to move, unable to speak, as if in a trance. But she was tinglingly, inescapably aware of what was happening to her. The tall Dutchman's hands—so gentle, so teasing, so totally unlike Arthur's rude grasp—were inside her night rail now and she found herself taking short ragged breaths and tingling with a totally unfamiliar pleasure.

"There are *no* women unable to learn," Nicolas murmured tantalizingly in her ear. "There are only men who are unable to teach!"

Sighing now as he pulled her gently to him, Mattie believed every word. For this Dutchman who held her transfixed and melting was infinitely more worldly than Arthur—anyone could see that—and infinitely more qualified to teach. She could already feel herself turning into a pliant sinuous thing—not the stiff frightened woman Arthur mauled and violated. Sophisticated Nicolas would impart to her secrets she needed desperately to know. What had he called them—"the wine of life"?

And as he whispered now urgently, "Mathilde, Mathilde, don't be afraid, don't hold back, *let me teach you what it is to love,*" Mattie felt a sense of revelation. He had certainly found the right word. Nicolas, she told herself righteously, would be able to teach her what Arthur had been unable to impart. Arthur had found her deficient, unable to learn, but here in Nicolas she had found an adroit teacher, full of warmth and gentleness. In his arms, she would learn to be a woman. In his arms, she would learn to be all the things that Arthur complained she was not.

Nicolas would teach her. Ah, that was the key word: *Teach.* She needed this instruction, she told herself righteously, and Nicolas was so willing to instruct! How could it be wrong, since Arthur would ultimately benefit? He would not know about his benefit, of course, how he had come by it, but that would not matter for the benefit would be there. Oh, yes, it was right, right that she should do this!

"Teach me," she whispered. *"Oh, teach me, Nicolas!"*

With a tenderness he had not felt in his life before, the lean Dutchman drew the unhappy waif into his arms. She fit as if she belonged there. At his every touch she quivered and when he kissed her, he could feel as well as hear her little heartfelt moan.

"Lovely lady of Bermuda," he murmured, and Mattie felt the words whir dazzlingly through her brain. No one—*no one* had ever called her lovely before. Not even her mother, who loved her. And certainly not Arthur, who daily disparaged her face, her figure, her walk, everything about her.

"Oh, Nicolas," she whispered desperately, "do not say things you do not mean."

"I mean every word," he insisted. He was slipping off her dressing gown as he spoke and easing down her night rail. He ran his hand lightly down her bare back as the soft material rippled downward. "Every word, Mathilde."

A little sob broke from Mattie's throat and she flung herself against him. "Oh, Nicolas," she whispered, "do not let me fall in love with you. Please do not let me fall in love with you, for it can never be—it can never, never be. You know that."

Not since he was seventeen and had bedded a chambermaid who kept calling him ludicrously "my one true love"—ludicrous, since she'd already slept with half the county—had Nicolas heard so foolish a comment. But somehow, coming from this honest little girl in her billowy, ill-fitting night clothes, it went straight to his heart.

"Fall in love with me, Mathilde," he urged, managing to wrench up her night rail until it rode around her hips. "Don't be afraid to let yourself go—if you fall, I'll catch you."

Nothing like this had ever happened to Mattie. The slight rasping of her cambric night rail seemed to burn her thighs, her buttocks, his every touch seemed to set her afire. She gasped for air—and did not care if she never breathed again. She moved in splendor and shut her eyes against the dazzle. She was half naked in his arms, clasped firmly to his body, and he was thrusting within her now with a delicacy and command such as she had never known from Arthur's rough embraces. She held her breath. This was—magic. She had become a pliant thing in these new strong arms that held her, trusting, swaying, yearning, moving toward him and then sinuously back again. She felt transported, swept skyward by vast emotions such as she had never before encountered. Marveling at each new sensation, her senses lurching wildly with his every touch, her closed eyes alight with nameless splendors, she soared with Nicolas across a shining sea. Her back arched like a purring kitten's, strange soft sounds broke from her parted lips. She was one with him, arching, loving, soft and supple—his whole being seemed to encompass her, to swallow her up until she felt very small but very much alive. She felt—beautiful. And *wanted*.

Nicolas, who had thought only to amuse himself with the waif in his arms, was startled by the desperate urgency that coursed through him, sending fire through his veins. Had it been so long since he had held a woman? Three days at most, for Nicolas always lived off the country, foraging—when ladies were not available—for chambermaids and tavern maids and bright-eyed laundresses.

Now this slip of a girl with her bruised eye had caught—not his fancy, but his heart. He felt born to woo her; her supple body fitted against his lean length as one of his palms fitted the other. He knew for her a sympathy he had never felt for Georgiana. He took her to the heights and soared there with her. And heard with a kind of triumph the little cry that broke from her lips as together they went over the brink.

"Mattie," he whispered as she lay trembling in his arms in the aftermath of lovemaking, her eyes closed, lashes fluttering spasmodically. "Lovely, lovely Mattie."

Hearing it spoken so, with that soft inflection, Mattie knew that she would never again hate her own name. Because Nicolas had spoken it—and made it beautiful.

She breathed a little ragged sigh of contentment and pillowed her head on his shoulder, let him toy idly with her body in the warm afterglow of passion, let him stroke her and tease her and tempt her until finally in a little rush of emotion she turned toward him and murmured breathlessly, "I do not feel I have learned well enough, Nicolas—I feel the need of more instruction."

Nicolas felt a chuckle course through him. "A novice but insatiable!" he teased, tweaking a pink nipple and being rewarded by a small scuffle.

But this time it was a new Mattie who gave a long shuddering sigh of release and went like a leaf carried on the tide into Nicolas van Rappard's ready arms. For Arthur had, unbeknownst, awakened desires in Mattie that she had not thought herself capable of fulfilling. Arthur had awakened desires—but he had never satisfied them—not even once. Nicolas van Rappard was a talented lover. In his arms, Mattie had found desire, escape, fulfillment. And now she sought those arms again. For Mattie was ripe for romance, ripe for a lover.

She threw caution to the winds—just as in Bermuda she had thrown caution to the winds with Arthur. Romance was here and she would seize it—no matter what the ending.

Nicolas, who had considered shy Mattie a rather tepid personality and had been extraordinarily gentle with her, was amazed and delighted at her enthusiasm for this sort of thing. Her pure joy in being embraced by him, made love to by him, did much to restore his damaged ego, which had been buffeted about most cruelly by Georgiana's blithe unconcern.

Mattie had a charming body, he had discovered, under all those layers of ill-fitting material.

"Arthur might—awaken," she said dreamily, running her nails lightly—with exhilarating effect—along his groin.

"If he does, I promise to run him through with my sword," Nicolas promised recklessly, and clasped her to him.

Mattie, usually so gentle and averse to bloodshed, did not even protest. She lay back with a luxurious sigh in Nicolas's arms, and let passion take her where it would.

"This is really very bad of me," she murmured happily, afterward, wriggling as Nicolas lazily caressed her bare thigh.

"How so?" a sated Nicolas demanded with some truculence, for how could a woman go wrong in *his* arms?

Mattie was smiling and now she traced the contours of his golden mustaches lovingly, laughed as he nipped at her fingers. "Because I'm married, of course."

"But to a fool," he shrugged.

"No," she sighed. "To a monster. To a man I can never

love—could never have loved." She sat up and regarded Nicolas gravely. "I was confused before but—now I know the difference. Between—men." She flushed under Nicolas's bright regard. "I—Nicolas, help me get my night rail on properly. I am all thumbs."

And, then, as in obedience to her demand he held up the night rail for Mattie to thrust her arms through, she suddenly flung herself against him, crushing her soft bare breasts against his hard chest. "Oh, Nicolas, I do thank you. I never—never guessed it could be so wonderful. I will never, never forget."

And Nicolas, who had known endlessly more beautiful women and possessed many, was so touched he could not speak. He bent down and planted a gentle kiss on the pink-crested nipple of one trembling breast. "There is no need to forget me, Mattie," he said simply. "For I will be around."

"But I—we couldn't. I mean, we were overcome by the moment, by the wine, but now—" She sought for words, did not find them.

"You have only to call," he said, kissing lightly the palm of her hand. "And I will find a way."

"Oh!" Mattie was breathless and ecstatic. She could not speak as Nicolas drew her night rail on, smoothed it down around her pulsing young body, carefully tied the riband at the top, and pushed back her tumbled brown hair gently from her shoulders.

"Why do we not stay here the rest of the night?" he murmured.

" 'Twould be a risk," she said hesitantly.

"A risk," he agreed in a lazy voice.

"For we cannot be sure when Arthur will wake. . . ."

"No, we cannot." But his blue eyes held amusement for he sensed the change in her, the unexpected recklessness.

High color still stained Mattie's cheeks. Her whole being was aglow. "Yet a risk worth taking," she murmured in a soft rich voice. "And"—she sank against him "you *will* remember to leave early in the morning before Arthur wakes?"

Nicolas nodded, burying his face in the smooth column of her neck. His voice came to her muffled, "I've already asked Klaus to have me wakened at cockcrow."

"Wicked," she said in a breathless voice. "You knew I'd want you to stay."

"Hoped. Only hoped."

"And stay you shall," she said with that bright new confidence. She, who had never felt even passably pretty, felt beautiful this night. She, who had never before felt she had a man to call her own—no, not even though she wore a wedding ring—was suffused with confidence and hope, elated, bursting with self-esteem and pride. Breathlessly, even as Nicolas's warm hands and lips caressed her body, she hugged the realization to her—she had taken a lover! A wonderful, handsome fellow who called her "lovely" and said she had only to call and he would be there!

"Nicolas," she said softly. "I want to remember us always—just as we are at this moment."

"But I told you I am not going anywhere."

"I know, I know." Her voice was soft and slurred and she did not quite meet his eyes in the firelight. How could she tell him from her fluttering heart that she *expected* him to vanish, for surely this was all too wonderful to last? "But could I—could I have some token, a lock of your hair to remember you by? If"—she stumbled over the words—"if life should separate us? Just a small snip of your hair—you'd never miss it—to braid into a locket and wear around my neck?"

To wear around her neck to remember him by.... Nicolas, who was given to handsome gestures, gave Mattie a startled look. Many baubles he had given away in his careless life but of all the lustrous ladies he had known—and many had coaxed from him some valuable trinket "to remember him by"—none had asked for a piece of himself. This sweet wistful child cuddled up beside him in her night rail wanted as her token only a snip of his hair to smile upon and touch.

"I can do better than that, Mattie," he said, and leaning over, produced from the sleeve of his tawny velvet doublet the dainty diamond pendant that had caused so much excitement that night at Windgate.

"Better you wear this to remember me by," he said jauntily, and Mattie clasped her hands together in delight and her mouth formed a round breathless O.

Thoroughly enjoying sweeping Mattie off her feet with the magnificence of his gift, Nicolas fingered the diamond pendant and smiled. It had been through a lot with him, this pendant. Originally it had been the gift of a contessa in Rome, who had urged it upon him in memory of a night of stars and sighs—and had been swiftly spirited away by the conte when that worthy discovered a pair of strange boots in his young wife's bedchamber (Nicolas, the owner of those boots, had gone headfirst out the window into a rosebush at the first sound of footsteps along the gallery). The contessa's irate husband had taken his beautiful wife forthwith from their Roman villa to the provinces and before leaving she had sealed the diamond pendant into a letter and sent it around to Nicolas's apartments with the terse words, "You will find another neck to clasp this around."

And indeed he had. The necklace had jaunted with him half across Europe. Most recently he had given it to Georgiana—and actually intended for her to keep it, but Danforth had snatched it from her neck and returned it to him. Then he had roguishly given it to Katrina ten Haer—and filched it back from her, letting her think she had lost it.

The necklace—generally—reposed round the throat of Nicolas's latest light of love. And now it was going to decorate the neck of this shy romantic child who gazed at him in the firelight with her heart shining in her brown eyes.

He rather thought he would let it stay there.

"Oh-h-h-h," breathed Mattie, who felt she had never seen anything so beautiful.

With a slight swagger to his tawny shoulders Nicolas clasped the diamond pendant lightly around Mattie's white neck and felt the pulsations of her throat with caressing fingers. The gold chain glittered in the firelight and the diamond pendant looked like a single tear about to fall.

"*This* you will wear," he said softly, "to remember the giver."

"Oh, I will," whispered Mattie ardently, impetuously covering his strong hand with kisses. "I'll never take it off." Fingering the pendant's golden chain, she leaned back with a luxurious sigh. Then suddenly she sat up straight, her expression more than a little wild. "Oh, yes, I will!" she cried in alarm. "You must get it off right now, Nicolas. Arthur knows I don't possess such a necklace, he might guess how I had come by it. Oh, he would kill me, he would break my bones!" She shivered, and clawed at the necklace, her soft brown eyes gone big and black with fear.

"Then we must by all means get the necklace off." Nicolas made haste to do so.

"But I—I will hide it," Mattie said dreamily, letting the glittering chain trickle through her hands like running water, touching the tear-shaped diamond with light, experimental fingers. Nicolas had already given her the most beautiful night of her life—and now he had made her a gift of this lovely necklace, tangible symbol of his esteem, for remembrance. "I will treasure it always," she sighed.

"No." Firmly, Nicolas removed the necklace from her fingers. "You must not. Not if your husband would take such violent measures against you. I had not thought about that."

"Oh, but I could hide it well!" cried Mattie.

"I wouldn't think of letting you take the risk." Coolly, Nicolas stashed the necklace back in his velvet sleeve. "Someday"—he brushed her pale forehead with his lips—"I will return the pendant to you. Someday when we can be—*safe*. I will not have you take unnecessary risks on my behalf."

It was a romantic suggestion and Mattie gazed at him adoringly.

Before the blinding sweetness of that look, Nicolas felt his gaze fall away. Looking down at the pendant, he felt fleetingly ashamed of himself. For he had not removed the necklace from Mattie's reluctant fingers for the reason he had given her. A new and startling use for the pendant had just occurred to him and he was eager to put it into effect. By the Lord Harry, he would set about it the very next day!

But first, through the long night, he would hold a rapturous Mattie in his arms.

His mind churning with plans, Nicolas was still not asleep when the serving girl scratched lightly on the door to tell him it was time to rise. But Mattie, worn out with lovemaking, long since had drifted off. She lay blissfully in his arms, as limp as a rag doll, and she did not wake—only made a small, childish, protesting motion when he carefully put her from him.

Swiftly he dressed—it was an easy business since, in order not to frighten shy Mattie, he had worn most of his clothing to bed. Mostly a matter of donning boots and blade and saffron-plumed hat.

Having clapped on his hat, he lingered, considering the young girl on the bed. So trustingly she lay there in the dawn's first pinkish light. He must remember to tell Klaus to have her waked in an hour or two, so that if Arthur recovered earlier than expected from last night's drugged wine, he would find Mattie beside him and never suspect in whose arms she had spent the night. He considered waking her himself and giving her what was left of the powder he had put into Arthur's drink last night, so that she might use it on Arthur again to gain a night's peaceful sleep the next time Arthur turned nasty. But he decided, on thinking about it, that Mattie would not use it, she would not risk hurting anyone—not even a vicious brute like Arthur. She was too gentle for that.

He frowned. It hurt him to think that he was returning her to Arthur, but return her he must.

He cast a last look about him, making sure he had not left anything that would incriminate Mattie if Arthur should later check out the room. It occurred to him of a sudden that this was the same room in which he had seduced—or been seduced by?—Erica Hulft the night he had told her about the existence in Bermuda of the van Rappard heiress. That might even be the same red quilt that covered the bed. But it never occurred to Nicolas to compare Mattie's shy ardent warmth with Erica's worldly passion.

He smiled gently at Mattie. She was sleeping like a baby, curled up in a childish crouch, with one arm outflung and her long thick hair spread out like a skein of rippling brown silk across the creamy linen of the pillowcase. The hem of her night rail had ridden up around her neck—that neck that had worn so briefly his diamond pendant—like a ruff. An inch or so of bare skin showed between the tumbled white froth of her night rail and the red quilt, which he had drawn around her against the cold. She looked small and helpless and vulnerable and very, very young.

He picked up her flowered dressing gown, which had fallen unheeded to the floor, and laid it carefully across the foot of the bed, and for a wild moment he wished he could stay with her—pick a quarrel with her young husband, run him through with his blade, and scoop up Mattie and take her with him. The thought died aborning. This night of sighs had been a totally new experience for him, but Nicolas van Rappard had other fish to fry upriver.

He gave a last lingering tender look to the girl on the bed and stole out, softly shutting the door behind him. But he was thoughtful as he left, clattering downstairs into the common room that was just coming awake as sleepy servants scuttled about carrying mops and pails and trays of fresh tankards.

Georgiana had awakened his gallantry, his sense of a better life waiting for him out there somewhere. But this brief bittersweet interlude with little Mattie had given him an inkling of what it might be like not only to win a woman but to love her, really love her. Forever, without a thought of self.

Nicolas did not tarry in New Orange that wintry morning, but made his way quickly upriver by the first sloop that would take him, to resume his stay at the ten Haers' handsome Dutch farmhouse. And if a pair of soft brown eyes had haunted his journey up the Hudson, he shook off their influence the moment that Haerwyck was sighted. He arrived at the pier his usual jaunty and confident self and swung off the sloop smiling broadly at all about him, for now he felt that he had stumbled upon the right weapon to win for him possession of Windgate.

Her name was Linnet.

PART TWO
The Naive

It is a sad heartbreaking joke
That words of love were all he spoke
When all the time, if truth be told
His thoughts unswerving were on gold!

Windgate on the Hudson, Winter 1673

CHAPTER 26

Winter had closed in on the Hudson River Valley. The trees that graced the bluff at Windgate were barren now of leaves; only a few hickories behind the house kept a tattered remnant of their summer foliage against the bleak gray sky. The woodchucks had burrowed into the hillsides to sleep the winter away and the beaver were cozy in their winter quarters in the quiet already ice-laden ponds and cold streams, even the raccoons had left the big trees for their rocky dens. Even the odd snapping sound of the wood borers at work in the trees had slowed to a stop in the winter chill.

The first snow had fallen on the valley and all at Windgate were in a fever of preparation for the costume ball that was to be held on Thursday. Invitations via river sloop had gone out to all those on the ten Haers' guest list and many besides, and feather mattresses were being shaken and fluffed and trundle beds rolled out in preparation for the large crowd that would descend on Windgate two days hence.

In a shallow pond behind the house the ice had hardened smooth as glass and several of the servants had been out to try it on wooden skates. Brett had offered Georgiana a pair with handsome metal runners and she had accepted them in some trepidation, for ice skating was an accomplishment she could hardly have been expected to pick up in sunny Bermuda.

Plainly he expected her to learn.

Georgiana waited until he was occupied in the office and went out and tried it. With Linnet to spur her on—and indeed to lean upon for she found her ankles, unaccustomed to ice skating, were weak and tended to collapse—she gamely made it across the pond to collapse, panting, on the snowy opposite bank.

"And to think I promised them ice dancing!" she wailed. "There'll be no hope of my joining them. And I thought it would be so easy—like any other kind of dancing!"

"It is easy," insisted Linnet, who hailed from Yorkshire and had skated since she was a tot. Her mother had been the best skater on the River Swale and had taken joy in instructing her small daughter—and Linnet had profited by it and become a flying butterfly on skates. Now, on a pair of skates carved out of bone, she whirled away from Georgiana into a perfect figure eight, swooped backward across the ice with one foot raised in the air and made a graceful recovery with a sweeping curtsy before her astonished mistress.

"I can hardly believe it," said Georgiana, her breath making a white fog before her in the cold air. "Linnet, you are a wonderful skater!"

"I won a pair of earbobs for best skater in my village the time we held the frost fair, " admitted Linnet, flushed with pride at Georgiana's wonderment. For a moment her eyes were haunted by the remembered flash of skates on English ice, and the wild and beautiful country of the North Riding flashed through her mind. It was on a day like today that she had won her earbobs at the frost fair. She had been fifteen and apple-cheeked and deliriously happy at winning. And a young gentleman in scarlet—at least she had thought him to be a gentleman at the time; he had turned out to be something less, a roving gambler from Lincoln but one step ahead of the law—had scooped up the exultant winner as *his* prize and dazzled her with his wicked laugh and merry sallies. He had swooped her away to an inn where she had drunk deep of unfamiliar rum "to warm her" and waked alone and confused in a big bed minus her virginity, with a constable dragging away the protesting gentleman in scarlet and with the frowning innkeeper demanding she pay him for the night's use of the room "now that her lover had gone." In the ensuing scandal,

Linnet's betrothed, the young son of a dairy farmer on the Swale, had promptly broken their engagement, her stern Puritan employers had dismissed her, her angry father had turned her out—and Linnet had ever since instantly distrusted any man garbed in scarlet; she felt they were deceivers all. Homeless, angry, confused, without money, Linnet had drifted to the coast, worked at odd jobs for poor pay, drifted southward. She had been working as a tavern maid in Kingston upon Hull when a Newcastle trader, his ship blown into the mouth of the Humber during a gale on its way to the colonies, had seen her bright face smiling at him over his tankard of ale. Expansive and drunk and wanting to impress her, he had told the rosy-cheeked Yorkshire girl of the glories of New York, "a veritable London with palaces rising." Linnet had listened scoffingly, but she was tired of tavern life with its rough talk and surreptitious pinches on the bottom. She had signed Articles of Indenture with the trader so that she might emigrate. Sold and resold in New York, she had eventually arrived at Windgate on the Hudson, far, far from home.

But now her young mistress was talking to her. Linnet collected her wits. "I always loved to skate," she mumbled in a rather melancholy voice.

"I can see you must have!" Georgiana was at a loss to understand the shadow that had passed over Linnet's usually bright face. "I can't imagine anyone skating better than you!"

"There's some as do," sighed Linnet. "And perhaps I'd have been better off if I hadn't skated so good. I might have been..." She stopped and looked away, up toward the wild Adirondacks stretching far away.

"Why?" teased Georgiana, imagining some embarrassing spill in front of spectators, with petticoats riding up and striped woolen legs spread out awkwardly on the ice. "What would you have been if you hadn't been such a good skater?"

"I'd have been wife to a dairyman in Yorkshire," murmured Linnet, "with a thatched-roof cottage and children of my own about me...." She shook her head as if to clear away cobwebs and turned with determination to Georgiana. "I can tell that you will be a good skater too, my lady. But I fear you will not have time to learn before a party that is only two days away. You had best stay off the ice."

"You are right to warn me. And indeed I will stay away from the ice before my guests, Linnet, lest I land in an undignified fashion on my backside!'' Georgiana remembered smartingly the hint of laughter in Nicolas's voice when she had briskly informed him that by the time the masquerade ball was held she would have learned to skate! He had told her something else as well—that both Katrina and Erica were excellent skaters.

"I suppose Katrina ten Haer can be counted on to bring her skates,'' she said moodily, imagining the statuesque saffron-haired Katrina making her elegant way across the ice.

Linnet nodded. "And Erica Hulft too. She is very fond of skating. And better at it even than Katrina.''

"Perhaps Erica will not favor us with her presence,'' countered Georgiana sharply. "Now that she is betrothed to marry an older man who will probably prefer smoking his pipe in comfort to gliding over the ice.''

"I think she will be here,'' said Linnet. "The river is not yet frozen over, the channel is open all the way to Rensselaerwyck—I heard Lars say it. It is hard to believe that Erica Hulft will allow herself to miss the greatest ball of the season!''

Linnet spoke with a knowledge of Erica, Georgiana realized bitterly, acquired firsthand—right here at Windgate. "Is Erica as good a skater as you are?'' she asked suddenly.

Linnet thought about that. "I do not believe so,'' she ventured. "I can do leaps and turns that I have not seen her do—and I can do them *faster*, which impresses people.'' She sighed. "I had a fine pair of skates in Yorkshire, but now I have only these carved bone things, which are not reliable and indeed may break under me.'' She cast a discouraged look down at her skates.

Yes, Linnet's skating was very flashy, Georgiana had to admit. She had hoped to shine in Brett's eyes by giving this ball with a sure and practiced hand, leading out the masked dancers onto the ice, but now she saw how impossible that was. Brett of course must have known it from the first—and had not warned her. So now she was faced with the unpleasant fact that Erica Hulft—if she came—would certainly outshine her.

Linnet, watching the play of emotions over Georgiana's expressive face, guessed what she was thinking. "You will learn to skate,'' she volunteered. "I will teach you.''

"But not in time.''

"No,'' echoed Linnet honestly. "Not in time for the ball.''

"And you are right." Georgiana's voice was energetic, for she was determined to put her rivals out of her mind. "You do deserve better skates than those." She gave the girl's woolen mitten a pat with her fur-lined glove. "And you shall *have* better, Linnet. Here"—she began to unfasten her skates—"I will give you these. I can get others later when I have time to learn."

Linnet flushed at the unexpected offer of so handsome a gift. Georgiana was by far the kindest mistress Linnet had ever had and she adored her. "I don't deserve them," she said, looking upset.

"Nonsense," shushed Georgiana. "Of course you do! I'm sure your skating puts everyone on the river to shame!"

It was not skating that Linnet had in mind. She hesitated. "Then, "I—I have a suggestion," she said in a hurried voice. Georgiana, looking up into Linnet's anxious face, could not know that the girl's anxiety came from something she had done, something about which she felt very guilty.

"And what is that, Linnet?" she asked, finally freeing the last skate strap.

Linnet sank down beside her in the snow. Her eyes looked dark and enormous and her voice was exceedingly earnest—almost pleading. "Well, I was just thinking that we are the same height and almost the same size and it will be a masked ball. If you were to wear something that concealed your hair—a flowing costume of some kind, you could announce that you would skate for us. Alone. With everybody gathered round watching." She swallowed and hurried on. "But it would be *me* doing the skating, for I would have taken your place. I would be wearing *your* costume, and none would be the wiser. And by next season you would have learned to skate, for I would teach you, and you could make excuses and not try the harder things until you are able to do them for yourself!"

"Oh, I—I couldn't do that, Linnet." Georgiana shook her head firmly.

"Why not?" cried Linnet. She sounded quite desperate. "For if you do not, then surely everybody will be looking at Erica Hulft and Katrina ten Haer, for they are the best skaters on the Hudson!"

Best skaters on the Hudson . . . the words rang cold as the clash of skates on ice in Georgiana's ears. They would be out there, her rivals, dancing on the ice, swooping about gracefully—and Brett would be out there skating with them, while his wife moped about on shore! It was very tempting to imagine herself giving a dazzling display on skates—and outshining both her rivals!

"Oh, but I couldn't," she demurred, rising to brush the snow off her gray linsey-woolsey skirts. "For even if no one recognized me while I was skating alone on the ice, the moment there was general ice dancing, Brett would be sure to seek me out and—he would know the difference between us, Linnet."

"But you could tell *him* ahead of time," cried Linnet.

"Others would know the difference between us too," said Gerogiana dryly. She was thinking of Nicolas and the color deepened in her cheeks. "You would be out there, trapped on the ice with people who wanted to crowd around and talk—and our voices are nothing alike. It wouldn't work."

But Linnet had an answer for that too.

"When I finish, I could skate to the far side of the pond," she said earnestly. "Away from the house, where there wouldn't be anybody. There are trees there and I could take off my skates and trade places with you and you could say—oh, that you turned your ankle a bit—you might even manage a graceful hobble or two, and everyone would understand, for their minds would be filled with the beauty of your ice dancing." She stopped abruptly, for she had used a phrase that the gentleman in scarlet had used years ago when he had lured her to the inn. He had said his mind was "filled with the beauty of her ice dancing." She gave her mistress a suddenly bleak look, almost of panic.

The brushing motions of her fur-lined gloves ceased as Georgiana looked at Linnet thoughtfully. The idea appealed to her reckless nature. She could imagine Brett frowning at the very thought and mentally tossed her head in disdain. *He* of course would point out how embarrassed she would be if she were found out. But as Linnet described it, she felt they could brazen it through without being discovered.

In the gray overcast skies an eagle soared overhead.

"It *would* be fun," Georgiana admitted with a little laugh, "to outshine Erica out there on the ice where you say she is so sure of herself." *And Erica deserves a rebuff*, her wayward heart insisted. *And my "performance" would so astonish Brett it would take his mind off Erica entirely. . . . That* was certainly in its favor!

"I would be glad to do it," urged Linnet. "And I am sure we

could carry it off. We could change places right before my performance, and I would dash away right after. Perhaps some friend of yours would pick me up and carry me away to remove my skates and we could swiftly change places!''

Georgiana sighed. "I have no friends among this crowd that's coming—at least none who'll be out there skating on the ice." She was thinking of Vrouw Berghem, who had befriended her mother.

"Your husband, then?"

Georgiana gave her a wry look. "Brett would never do it. He is not devious. He takes all his objectives frontally. But . . ." her eyes gleamed suddenly. "Nicolas would do it!"

So enchanted was she with the idea that she did not notice the slight start of Linnet's shoulders beneath her brown cloak or the strained expression on the girl's face.

"Nicolas is game for anything, Linnet," she laughed. "A complete rake—and I am sure he will come, aren't you?"

"Oh, yes," agreed Linnet in a stifled voice. "I am sure he will come." In point of fact, she was absolutely certain Nicolas would come, for she had seen him but two short hours before. In a rare appearance, dour Jack Belter had come by the house on horseback. Linnet had seen him from the kitchen window where she was munching doughnutlike *olykoeks*. A big black-bearded man, he was sitting there studying the house while his gray horse stamped and blew clouds of steam into the cold air. His eyes narrowed as he saw her face peering out and he took a quick look around, then beckoned to her, a swift surreptitious gesture. Puzzled, Linnet had stared at him through the frosted panes for a moment, wondering why Jack Belter should be beckoning to her, for she had scarce said two words to him ever. But curiosity overcame her and she swallowed the rest of the *olykoek*, rubbed the grease from her hands and went outside, lifting her flannel skirts carefully as she stepped into the snow.

Jack Belter had abruptly dismounted and muttered that Nicolas van Rappard was waiting for her at his *bouwerie*, that she could ride there behind him on his horse if she chose, and to meet him behind the stables if she wanted to go. In her excitement Linnet had promptly choked on her last bite of *olykoek* and been unable to reply. But Jack Belter had taken her reply for granted. He had brushed on by the gasping, choking girl with the purple face and entered the kitchen, saying in a surly voice that he was out of maple sugar and had come to borrow some, for a man needed sweetening on his hot cakes these cold mornings.

When she got her breath back, Linnet had made a quick excuse to Georgiana, who was so busy with cook making final decisions on the sweetmeats for the party that she had hardly noticed the girl's leaving. Snatching up her cloak and hood and pulling on her mittens, Linnet had stolen out to the stables and ridden away behind Jack on the big gray horse.

Her heart was beating wildly as she rode, and she was almost afraid to think. Her patroon (for in her romantic imagination that was how she characterized Nicolas) had not forgotten her after all. Twice thwarted in his attempts to see her (for now she innocently believed that the last two times Nicolas had stopped by Windgate it had really been to see her), he was trying again. And he had made sure this time, by sending big Jack Belter to fetch her.

Linnet's heart sang. Nicolas van Rappard of the golden beard and the wicked smile had come upriver again—to see *her*! And of course he would expect—Linnet's breath came short in the cold air and her cheeks flamed even though no one could see—a warm welcome. *And would have one*, she thought ecstatically, glad beyond measure that she had only this morning put on all fresh underthings. *And* taken a bath last night despite cook's gloomy warning that she would catch her death.

All the things she had ever heard tavern maids say about being bedded by gentlemen raced through her mind as the gray horse skidded and floundered through soft places in the snow. And Belter cursed as low branches switched his face, and jerked the horse's head up, cruelly sawing on the reins.

Let's see, there had been demure little Dora, who was a great favorite with sailors and who'd sighed and said if she could have a gentleman to her bed just *once*, she'd die happy! And blowsy Lou, who'd said dryly that men were all alike—some just dressed better. And frowning Tippie, who'd said the only gentlemen she knew were the kind who got you pregnant—and then left for the colonies!

Nicolas, Linnet told herself righteously, was not like that. Not like that at all.

A red fox dashed across their path and the gray horse reared up, nearly unseating Jack. Linnet clutched Jack Belter's iron-hard middle for dear life and screeched as she almost fell off. The fox streaked off into the low brush, leaving dainty tracks across the snow as Jack Belter bellowed, "Damme, wench, hang on!"

Linnet clung the tighter, shivering in the cold, glad that Jack Belter's *bouwerie* was but a short ride away—although it might have been in the far reaches of the Adirondacks for all they ever saw of Jack. She flexed her cold fingers in their green woolen mittens and reminded herself that there'd been lots of weather colder than this in Yorkshire, and it hadn't stopped her from going out skating on frozen ponds and rivers of the North Riding.

A gentleman . . . she had a gentleman waiting for her! Something her grandmother had once said to her came back to her and she smiled. Her grandmother had been a wicked old lady, not local—she had hailed from London. In her cups she had claimed to have been the fourteen-year-old mistress of the earl of Essex and to have fled London when Queen Elizabeth I (she always called her vengefully "the old Queen") had him beheaded. "And had it not been for that one great slash on the chopping block, you'd have been born a lady!" she had wailed once, on a drunken crying jag, to Linnet.

The child had loved her stories. Listening, Linnet could almost hear the sighing of the ax as it severed the head of the luckless earl.

"Remember now," her grandmother had urged her tipsily. "Remember what I told you, Linnet, if you ever meet a gentleman." She had wagged a gnarled finger at Linnet and her toothless face had split into a waggish smile, for Gramma was terribly old and only drank, so Mamma said, because her old bones ached so. "Remember to tell him how near you were to being born a lady!"

"Would he really have married you, Gramma?" demanded Linnet, enthralled. "The earl?"

"Who knows?" hiccupped Gramma. "Who knows?" She thought about that, owlishly. "Well—of course he would. Eventually. For he said I had the best legs and the best—" She checked herself, realizing belatedly that she was speaking to a child. "But if you ever get a chance to have you a gentleman, Linnet, my girl," she finished roguishly, "Take it! Mayhap he'll carry you away to a palace the way Essex might have done me if 'the old Queen' hadn't cut his hair for him!" She subsided into a drunken resentful mutter.

But curled up beside Gramma's coarse linsey-woolsey skirts, the child dreamed. A gentleman—oh, yes, she would grow up and have herself a gentleman! That was for sure!

But the chances for Linnet to garner herself a gentleman in the North Riding had seemed slim indeed. Indeed, all her family had marveled at Linnet's good luck when she had caught the eye of the son of a well-to do dairy farmer whose meadows sloped down to the River Swale. "Have a good life, Linnet," her once carefree but now workworn and shattered mother had whispered on her deathbed but two days after the betrothal had been celebrated. "I'm glad you're marrying well—you won't have to work so hard as I have."

And Linnet's tears had watered her grave right up to the time they froze on her face when her father cast her out.

Now as she clung to Jack Belter's firm middle while the horse's hooves pounded the snowy earth, Linnet's young face with its cold red nose hardened. She would take Gramma's advice, she would have herself a gentleman! And that gentleman would be Nicolas van Rappard!

CHAPTER 27

The gray horse missed its footing, staggered and almost lost his riders. Belter was cursing in earnest now, a steady stream of invective. It came to Linnet suddenly that she was riding away with a man she had scarcely ever said two words to—and no one at Windgate knew she had gone away with him. True, he had said Nicolas was waiting for her but—suppose he wasn't? Suppose it was a trick? Suppose it was only Jack Belter who was waiting? Waiting to get his hands on her in the privacy of his isolated little farmhouse?

Linnet's eyes widened in fright. In vain she reminded herself that Jack Belter's *bouwerie* really wasn't such an isolated place after all. His land stretched right along the Hudson and his low Dutch farmhouse was a lot closer to the water than was the frowning mansion of Windgate. Boats would come by, people would come by—Jack would never dare. And besides, who was to say that someone hadn't seen her slip away? Now she hoped fervently that someone had.

She was not only cold, she had frightened herself weak with her fancies by the time the big, black-bearded man drew up in his own front yard, said tersely, "He's waiting inside for you," let her off and went away to feed and stable his winded animal.

Standing in the snow by the front door, Linnet hesitated, about to take flight. Still . . . Jack's manner had been reassuringly gruff and if he'd been kidnapping her, wouldn't he have tried to lull her fears and make her feel safe?

Of course! Her courage restored, Linnet, with her skirts held well up from the snow, picked her way carefully toward the house. Her breath was coming short and fast in expectation and she was wearing her brightest smile when the door swung open—for their approach had been noted from inside—and Nicolas himself, looking jaunty as ever, stood facing her.

The smile froze on Linnet's face, wavered and was gone.

Nicolas was wearing red. Around his broad shoulders was draped— a scarlet cloak. Red. All Linnet's distrust of gentlemen in scarlet came back to her in a bright wave and she almost turned and ran.

Nicolas, seeing her wild expression, came forward laughing. He was tossing the cloak aside as he came.

"I was catching forty winks while Belter went to fetch you," he said, reaching out to take Linnet's mittened hand. Debonair as always, he led her through the divided Dutch door into the single large room that constituted the cottage. "This will warm your bones," he said conversationally, seizing a tankard and filling it with hot rum. He held it out to her. "Faith, your nose is red as a cherry in this cold! Come over here by the hearth, Linnet. You're shivering so—you must be near frozen. Have you no warmer cloak than that?"

Linnet's whirling world settled down. This was Nicolas, her "patroon"—and he looked his charming self again now that he had discarded the red cloak. For a moment there she had seen him as a red devil, bringing disaster down upon her.

"'Tis my only cloak," admitted Linnet breathlessly, taking the leathern tankard in her cold mittened fingers and letting the hot liquid cascade down her throat. "But my dress is warm. 'Tis flannel."

"Drink some more," he urged. "'Twill warm you."

Linnet drank some more, pulled off her mittens and looked around her.

A Dutch family had occupied this place before Belter and there were still evidences of their occupation in the beehive oven used for making bread, which was set into the side wall of the big stone fireplace, and in the battered gumwood *kas* that sat forlornly against one wall, but Linnet could see that it had been a long time since this room had known a woman's touch. Everywhere were evidences of neglect. A big straw broom stood in the corner but ashes from Belter's long clay pipe were scattered helter-skelter about the packed-earth floor. The hearth—on which a fire was burning merrily—had ashes piled up around it. The curtains hung in forlorn tatters in the gray winter light and in one corner stood a cupboard with sagging broken hinges. Belter's clothes and some pots and pans hung from nails driven at random into the walls and a large slop jar reposed conspicuously beside the cupboard.

She half expected to be pounced upon and plumped immediately into the big featherbed, which was the only really comfortable piece of furniture in Belter's bleak farmhouse—indeed she would have made no objection had Nicolas seized her at once. But instead her "patroon" took her cloak with some ceremony, got her seated on a wooden bench at the hearth and insisted she prop her cold feet up on the battered iron hearth rail. Once she was settled he dropped onto a bench opposite her, lounging at his ease.

It was like being courted, she told herself rapturously. Nicolas was treating her like—a lady!

"Are you hungry?" he asked. "I can offer you some *hutspot*. I'm afraid it's all there is in the house to eat except some tough cold venison; there was some *rood kool* but I just finished it off."

Linnet didn't care for *rood kool* anyway—spiced red cabbage had never appealed to her. But like everyone else at Windgate she was very fond of *hutspot*, which was a delicious dish of carrots, onions and potatoes cooked together.

"No, thank you. I had a bowl of *erwten* and some *olykoeks* just before I left." She cast a doubtful glance at the jumble of pewter dishes piled unwashed on the rude wooden table in the center of the room.

Nicolas followed the direction of her gaze and laughed. "Oh, it's all right," he said easily. "I brought the *hutspot* and the *rood kool* both up from Haerwyck with me. Belter's a good enough cook when it comes to wild game"—he indicated with a nod the long spit for turning meat above the hearth—"but there his domestic talents cease. Jack needs a wife."

Linnet hitched up her skirts a little so the fire could warm her cold, striped-stockinged legs. She let her hood fall back and shook out her red hair so that it was displayed to advantage.

"I doubt any girl would marry a man who looked so fierce," she said with a nervous laugh.

"That's what I told him. 'Shave off that beard, Jack,' I said. 'It makes you look a demon!' "

They both laughed, Linnet drank some more rum and Nicolas went on making small talk, feeling his way, for he must ease into his subject carefully. Linnet, never guessing his purpose in inviting her here, was utterly charmed that her "patroon" should take so much time to court her. She looked at his long relaxed figure lounging there in tawny velvets and felt her heart pound.

"When the river freezes over, I could skate up here often," she told Nicolas eagerly. "If—if you could meet me, sir?"

"Nothing would please me more than to see more of you, Linnet."

She blushed with pleasure. " 'Twould be no trouble for me to skate here and back," she added wistfully. "I'm from Yorkshire, you know, where we have lots of ice."

"Are you?" asked Nicolas absently, drumming his fingers. He wanted information and he was still trying to formulate a plan. Best to let the girl talk, he told himself. Then, when he launched into questions, it would all seem more natural. "You could skate all the way up to this *bouwerie*, you say?"

"Oh, easy, sir! I won a pair of earbobs, I did, for skating at the frost fair!"

Nicolas felt boredom stealing over him. The fire's warmth was making him relax. He repressed a yawn. "You can do figure eights, then, I take it?"

"Oh, yes—and more. I can take great leaps and turn in the air and whirl around and skate backwards and twirl like a top. I once took a flying leap over four barrels!"

"And did not land on your head, I take it?" Nicolas was impressed. "So you dance on ice, Linnet?"

Proudly, Linnet bobbed her auburn head and let Nicolas pour more hot rum into her tankard. "I skate like a bird, they say." Her voice was growing a little slurred.

Nicolas frowned. He would have to be careful not to get the girl drunk. Questions might be asked about where she got the liquor. But a plan was forming in his mind, a plan that might work—if Linnet could be talked into it.

"Well, you *are* an accomplished wench," he said, leaning back and toying with his drink. He smiled into her eyes. She gave him back a dizzy look.

Warm now and with her tongue loosened by the hot rum, Linnet responded easily to Nicolas's smooth flow of questions. He wanted to know what Windgate's bride had brought with her from Bermuda and listened intently as Linnet faithfully described the few belongings that had arrived with Georgiana.

"The great candlesticks . . ." he mused, frowning, when Linnet mentioned them. They were a puzzle to him. Surely Georgiana would not have had the temerity to steal them? Were they then a gift from Brett Danforth, who sought to establish for his bride a credible past? "Were there any papers that you can remember?" he shot at her. "A packet of papers perhaps?" He was thinking of the letter from Elise, whose existence Georgiana had blurted out.

Linnet's reddish brows furrowed. "Only the packet she keeps hidden in the big wardrobe beneath her clothes."

So there *was* a packet! What secrets might it not reveal? With difficulty Nicolas managed not to show the surge of excitement that swept through his big frame.

"Why do you want to know, sir?" Linnet was asking him in a troubled voice.

Nicolas shrugged his tawny shoulders. "I am as curious as a cat, Linnet. 'Tis something you will learn about me when you come to know me better." His voice stroked her, lulled her. "And what does this packet contain?"

When she came to know him better. . . . To Linnet's blurred mind that sounded like a promise.

"I—I do not read, sir," she admitted.

"Good," he said bluntly. "I do not care overmuch for learned women."

Linnet, who had not been expecting that answer, dimpled. Basking now in the glow of the lean Dutchman's approbation, she was eager to provide more information. "But there is a parchment in it that she takes out and reads sometimes and looks sad. And there's a leather-bound book in the packet too."

"A book?" asked Nicolas sharply. "What kind of book?"

" 'Tis handwrit and I've seen her cry when she reads it, but always she tucks it away when I come into the room. She does not know I know where she hides it, but I have seen her put the packet away when she did not know I was watching. I think it might be something her mother had writ, sir, because I once saw her get up from reading the little book and go downstairs and stand for a long time looking at her mother's portrait."

"A journal," mused Nicolas. *"Imogene van Rappard's journal!* Faith, I'd give a deal to know what it says!" He turned his wicked smile on Linnet, stripping her with his eyes, and watched her melt. "D'you think you could borrow it for me without the mistress knowing?"

Linnet recoiled. "Oh, sir, I couldn't!"

"Ah, now, why couldn't you?" wheedled Nicolas. "I don't want to keep it—I want to borrow it only and none would be the wiser. Why, you could lift it for me and slip the packet to me at the ball and I'd read it and return it to you—she'd never know you did it."

Linnet gave him a frightened look. "Suppose someone caught me? And anyway, 'tis wrong—oh, no, sir, I couldn't do that, not even for you."

Nicolas leaned over and caressed her arm. His voice was very coaxing. "I only tell you this because you are so important to me," he said—and felt that arm quiver. "The courts are going to decide my claim of ownership to Windgate and—"

"But I thought—I mean my lady said—"

"That I had given up my claim? Never!" He laughed and let her arm slide away from him as he leaned back expansively. He had never looked more handsome. "And I'm sure the courts will decide justly Linnet."

Linnet bobbed her head; she had vast respect for courts.

Nicolas's handsome face had taken on a moody expression. He seemed to ponder. "But my problem is, I know not what I face." He saw she was watching him, full of sympathy. He heaved a deep sigh.

"I do not know what documents Danforth has to prove his wife's claim to be Verhulst van Rappard's daughter."

Linnet's eyes grew round. "You mean you *doubt* her, sir?"

His quizzical look and raised brows spoke volumes. "Where vast sums of money are concerned, I doubt everything, Linnet. Once I arrived on the scene to challenge his claim to Windgate, it was to Brett Danforth's advantage to find himself the van Rappard heiress—and presto! He found her and married her. Do you not think his timing most remarkable? Why, he might as well have pulled her out of a hat!"

Linnet could see that. She listened intently as Nicolas held forth on the subject. "And besides," he finished, "I have just learned that in Bermuda our Georgiana was not an heiress at all but a bond-servant—and a runaway bondservant at that."

"Oh, sir!" cried Linnet, shocked into protest. "I can't believe it. The mistress is a lady born, anyone can see that!"

"Perhaps *you* can, Linnet," sighed Nicolas. "But the courts may not be as astute. It is entirely possible that our lovely Georgiana is an impostor, playing a part conceived and guided by Brett Danforth. Do you think it fair that I should be deprived of my rightful inheritance by a lie?"

"Oh, no, of course not, but the patroon did buy the estate, I'm told, and—"

"But not from me. I am the rightful heir, Linnet."

Linnet swallowed. "I won't do nothing to hurt my lady," she said rebelliously.

Nicolas saw that he would have to regroup. Linnet was proving to be more difficult than he had expected.

"You won't be hurting her, Linnet," he said earnestly. "I guess I didn't tell you, but there's a man searching for her—I met him in New Orange. He's come all the way from Bermuda to find her."

"Why?" asked Linnet, looking apprehensive.

"To expose her, to find her and bring her back to Bermuda, where she'll no doubt get twenty lashes as a runaway bondservant," improvised Nicolas, watching Linnet for the effect it had on her.

The effect was immediate and explosive. "Then I must tell her," cried Linnet, springing up. "So she can watch out for him. The folks at Windgate won't let her be taken, you'll see!"

In some alarm at the havoc he'd created, Nicolas seized Linnet's shoulders, kneaded them gently with his big hands as he pushed her back down. "Now, now," he soothed. "No need to go off half-cocked! Let me tell you the rest." He regarded her with some unease. The wench had her teeth caught in her lower lip and was watching him from beneath lowering brows. She was attracted to him, yes, but it was easy to see how deep was her affection for her lovely young mistress. He began again. "Linnet," he said carefully, "I am as fond of Georgiana as you are."

Linnet's stormy gaze told him she doubted it.

"This stranger approached me in New Orange. He was asking about her, where he could find her. It seems she used a different name in Bermuda—Anna Smith."

"You see?" cried Linnet in triumph. "It isn't her at all he's looking for. It's someone else!"

"No, Linnet." Nicolas's golden head shook decisively. "The description he gave fit her perfectly and it seems that Danforth married this same Anna Smith in Bermuda."

"And then married her again *here*?" Linnet was stupefied. "Why'd he do that?"

"He married her under the new name to shore up his claim, Linnet. You see, as Anna Smith she was married to Danforth without proper permission. Her Articles of Indenture were still in force."

"But—but they can't take her away from her husband!" cried Linnet. And at Nicolas's grim expression, "Can they?" she faltered.

Nicolas sighed. "I'm afraid they can."

"Then I must go warn her!" Linnet was on her feet again but this time Nicolas was expecting it. He caught her wrist in a firm hand, imprisoned it.

"No, you must not!" he said sharply. "She'd be humiliated to have us or anyone know about her lowly beginnings, for she's been treated as a lady here and she's loving it!" There was some truth in what he said, he thought with satisfaction, and that made it sound all the more convincing.

Linnet sank back, confused. Her mind, befuddled by drink, refused to grasp all this.

"Nothing is going to happen to Georgiana right away," Nicolas assured the despondent girl before him. "The man hasn't located her yet, *but he will*, Linnet. He will."

"That's why I must warn her," declared Linnet argumentatively.

Nicolas sighed and passed a hand across his forehead in a manner that said, *Give me strength!* "This man isn't going to dash up to Windgate and take her by force, Linnet. He's going to find out where she is and send the *schout* for her."

The sheriff? Linnet recoiled. Her nose had gone from red to pale.

"The *schout* will come with whatever force is necessary and seize her and ship her away to Bermuda and none of us will ever see her again." Nicolas leaned forward, fixing Linnet with his hard blue gaze. "*Do you want that to happen?*"

"No, of course I don't, whimpered Linnet. She was shivering again—and not from cold. Like a rabbit cornered by a dog.

"Then listen to me. If I could but read what is in that packet, I would know how to proceed. I believe that there is something in Georgiana's past—something that she will not tell us, yet something that can be used in her favor. Perhaps she is ashamed of it, afraid her husband will find out—I don't know."

Linnet was regarding him with fascination. Nicolas went on:

"There is a great plantation in Bermuda, Linnet; its name is Mirabelle—I am sure you have heard Georgiana mention it. *I* believe it to be rightfully hers. And if it *is* hers, I believe that I can show that she was sold into bondage illegally *and save her,* Linnet."

"How?" gasped Linnet.

Nicolas leaned forward impressively. "I believe Georgiana to be *not* the long-lost daughter of Verhulst van Rappard but the illegitimate daughter of the dead owner of Mirabelle Plantation."

Linnet's jaw dropped.

"And therefore heiress to Mirabelle. Now do you understand?"

Linnet did not understand but Nicolas's portentous manner had so cowed her that she bobbed her head humbly. She sat there confused, with the heat from the fire scorching her toes, as Nicolas went on.

"I believe that I can negotiate with Danforth, Linnet, that we can reach an agreement whereby he will trade his claim to Windgate for Georgiana's claim to Mirabelle—*but only if I have access to that packet*!"

Now Nicolas leaned forward and put his hand on Linnet's knee. He was about to play his trump card. His voice was rich, vibrant, timbred—and his concentration on the girl before him was so intense that she felt pinned by it, like a helpless butterfly being pinned to a parchment. "And if you help me, Linnet"—he smiled caressingly—

"and if I am right, you could well end up beside me, wife to a patroon and mistress of Windgate."

Linnet swallowed—and then again. She felt dizzy and unreal—and not from wine. "I—I can't believe it, sir," she breathed. "You want to *marry* me?"

Having made that startling proposal, Nicolas stiffened and his voice harshened. "I'll marry no one, Linnet, unless I can prove my claim to Windgate," he declared ringingly. "I've no mind to be an impoverished bridegroom with a bride who must scrub and fetch and carry. Has it occurred to you that I'm not treating you like a light woman,"—hastily he removed his hand from her knee—"that I've made no advances, that I'm courting you as properly as if you were the daughter of an earl?"

"Granddaughter, sir," interposed Linnet eagerly.

"What?" Nicolas looked as if he had not heard aright.

"I mean I *might* have been," explained Linnet apologetically. "My old Gramma was mistress to the late earl of Essex, him that lost his head on the block."

"But that was in Queen Elizabeth's time!"

Linnet nodded her head vigorously. "She was fourteen then, and he'd have married her, to hear her tell it. And if he *had*, then I'd have been granddaughter to an earl!"

Nicolas regarded Linnet in true amazement. Whatever he had expected to hear from her lips in answer to his proposal, it had certainly not been this! He fought back a wild desire to laugh, kept his expression grave. "So you see," he managed disapprovingly, bent on impressing it on her, "I'm not treating you like a strumpet or a lightskirt—you have noticed that, have you not?"

"Oh, yes, I have, sir," stammered Linnet, enchanted by his words. "But—" She was about to say that lifting her chemise for *him* wouldn't make her a lightskirt, but her voice trailed off as she looked at the elegant Nicolas, lounging back and frowning at her so forcefully. She couldn't believe he'd actually asked her! *Her husband*—oh, it was too good to think upon!

Nicolas could have asked Linnet to do anything for him at that moment—anything. He was fleetingly, almost regretfully, aware of that fact. He checked the thought aborning, and told himself there was no time for dalliance now—there was more to his plan that involved Linnet.

Linnet, lost in her dreamworld, found her rapturous train of

thought interrupted not by Nicolas's strong arms but by his voice—
he was speaking again.

"I am truly fond of Georgiana," he told her with ingenuous
frankness. "And I realize now that you are too."

"Oh, yes," she mumbled, her eyes fixed on him adoringly.

"So now let me tell you there is a way that you can oblige both
me *and* your mistress."

Linnet's eyes lost a little of their adoration. She gave Nicolas a
doubtful look.

Nicolas was equal to the situation. He hitched his bench closer so
that his velvet-breeched knee carelessly brushed Linnet's thigh and
was rewarded by a little tremor from the girl.

"Your mistress is very jealous of Erica Hulft—as well she should
be."

"That she is!" Linnet bobbed her auburn head energetically.
"And Erica is a bad one. She lorded it over us all something terrible
when she was running things at Windgate."

"I don't doubt it," said Nicolas in a sympathetic tone. He
drummed his fingers and frowned. "For reasons of my own, I'd like
to humble Erica."

Linnet swallowed apprehensively. She'd heard stories about Nicolas
and the glamorous Erica. She'd overheard Lars telling cook how
he'd seen Erica going upstairs with Nicolas at the Green Lion—and
many were the tales that had drifted upriver about him slipping into
her house at dusk and leaving at cockcrow. Knowing how haughty
Katrina ten Haer must burn to hear them, those stories had amused
Linnet—once. Not any more.

"Erica won't bother us none," she told Nicolas hastily, hoping it
would prove true for—like Georgiana—Linnet feared Erica's wildness,
her worldliness, her way with men.

"No, she won't bother us, Linnet," agreed Nicolas, and she felt a
sense of relief. He put his hands together pontifically, appeared to
study them. "I've been thinking about it. Now that the pond at
Windgate is frozen over and Georgiana has promised us ice dancing,
Erica is sure to give an exhibition of her skating at the masquerade
ball—she wouldn't miss such a golden opportunity to have all eyes
centered on her."

Linnet was sure she wouldn't. Miserably she mumbled her agreement.

"Tell me, Linnet," he shot at her, "do you think you can dance on the ice as well as Erica?"

Linnet drew herself up in surprise. "Better, sir!" she exclaimed. "I haven't seen nobody in this whole colony that skates as good as me!"

"Then here is what you must do," said Nicolas gravely. And outlined the plan for Linnet to switch places with her costumed mistress.

"It might work," the girl agreed doubtfully. "If the costumes was right. We're near the same size."

"Oh, your mistress will make it work if she likes the plan," Nicolas assured her with a laugh. "It's up to you to present it. Linnet—will you do this for me?"

He was very near and gazing raptly into her eyes. Linnet, quite carried away, agreed as if mesmerized. "I'll do it, sir. Can't do no harm to suggest it, can it?"

"Of course not, Linnet. Indeed, you'll be helping Georgiana." His voice rang with sincerity as he smiled down fondly at the girl. He'd have liked to seduce her, for she was a pretty little thing with her big round befuddled eyes staring up at him like that, and her voice so breathless, and her bodice heaving, but—he gave an inward sigh and told himself regretfully there wasn't time. Every minute Linnet spent away from the house was dangerous and might bring on suspicion.

"If ye want to marry me, Linnet, and become mistress of Windgate," he said softly, rising and bending over to take her chin between thumb and forefinger and press a kiss upon the girl's trembling lips, "then do what I ask. Slip the packet to me the night of the ball. Hide it in your skirts and I'll slip it into my doublet and read it and return it—none will be the wiser."

"Oh, I'll do it, sir," babbled Linnet. "I'll do—whatever you want, sir." Her gaze turned yearningly toward the big bed, and her body sagged toward him.

Nicolas sighed. " 'Tis time Jack takes you back," he said ruefully, pushing her gently away from him. "For it must not be known that we've had this little conversation."

"Is—is he to be trusted, sir?"

"Not with information. Tell him nothing. He's in my pay, but when a man's for sale to the highest bidder—who knows?" Nicolas, who knew all about being for sale to the highest bidder, shrugged. "Oh, I almost forgot." His voice was elaborately casual. "I have a little gift for you—a betrothal gift." He brought out the delicate necklace of intricately wrought gold links with its tear-shaped diamond pendant that he had given in turn to Georgiana and to Katrina ten Haer. Now he was offering it to Linnet.

Linnet stared dazedly at the necklace. Never very bright, her few wits deserted her entirely at sight of this lavish and totally unexpected gift. She was almost afraid to touch it and shuddered convulsively as Nicolas's warm fingers put it around her neck. Just short of clasping it, he hesitated. "Perhaps I should keep it for you," he mulled. "If it is seen, it would cause questions and we must be careful yet a while."

"Oh, no, sir!" wailed Linnet, stung at the thought of losing her new gift before she had had a chance to enjoy it. Her fingers clamped down on the golden links in panic and refused to be dislodged even when Nicolas applied gentle pressure. "I'll wear it round my neck underneath my collar," she gabbled. "I won't take it off *never*! And I won't let no one see it neither, I promise!"

Faced with rising hysteria, Nicolas capitulated.

"Very well then, Linnet." With an indulgent smile, Nicolas clasped the necklace and stepped back to consider how she looked. It would be well worth a dozen necklaces if his scheme—of which Linnet was so integral a part—worked.

He had to admit the girl looked pretty, standing there proud and beaming at him in her flannel dress with the firelight setting her auburn hair aflame. "You're a lovely thing, Linnet," he said in a new, softer voice.

"Thank you, sir." Linnet made him a mock curtsy and added wistfully, with another glance at the bed in the corner. "Are you sure you don't want nothing more of me? Everyone's so busy at the big house, they won't miss me for hours."

Nicolas's sigh rose from his boots. His easily stirred blood was already running hot and it was hard to turn down such an eager lass. Almost involuntarily, perhaps out of sheer habit, he reached out a questing arm, meaning to encircle her yielding waist and sweep her up and carry her over to the bed—and then, suddenly, he did not know what was wrong with him but he had no desire to bed her.

Every time he looked into her face a pair of shy trusting brown eyes got in the way. . . .

He shook his head as if clearing away cobwebs and impatiently brushed his thoughts of Mattie aside. That had been a pleasant bit of dalliance, he told himself firmly, but that was all it was—dalliance. Mattie was a poor girl, penniless save for what Arthur gave her, which was little. She could not afford him. No—he gave an unconscious sigh—he must forget poor little Mattie. His future lay elsewhere.

And he was determined to make it a bright future. He fixed Linnet with his intent blue gaze and saw her eyes dazzle. She would be like butter in his hands this one, to be shaped and patted into whatever design he wished. But—he would not make love to her. At least not today. He forced himself to put the thought away.

"This necklace will be our bond, Linnet," he said with hearty insincerity. "Until I can replace it with a wedding ring."

"Oh, you mustn't never replace it, sir," cried Linnet. "Not even when you give me a ring! I want to keep this—always." Her fingers were still wound firmly into the links as if to emphasize the point.

"And keep it you shall," he said hastily. "I never meant to take it away from you. But remember how important it is that you do all that I ask—remember how important it is to our future, yours and mine."

"I will, I will," breathed Linnet. Her voice was prayerful. She had never murmured anything half so intense in church. "You can count on me, sir."

"And you must stop calling me 'sir.' My name is Nicolas—at least in private."

"Nicolas," she whispered on a note of wonder. "Nicolas."

He could see that it was time to get rid of her. She was at exactly the right point—desperate to please him, lured by glamour and avarice, with a world opening up before her such as she had never imagined she might reach. She would do his bidding without question now—do it eagerly, do it well. She would suppress the pangs of conscience, she would not look too deeply into *why* he had asked her to do these things, for she would not want to risk losing her chance at the dazzling future he had dangled before her: *wife to a patroon*!

"We must wait, Linnet. We must bide our time," he said fondly.

"Oh, sir—oh, sir!" Linnet's voice broke as she let go of the necklace and hurled herself violently into his arms, almost crashed into him. "I can't believe it's happened!" She began to cry, tears streaming down her face from sheer happiness.

Nicolas stood his ground manfully before this onslaught. Only slightly staggered by Linnet's catapulting form, he enfolded her in his arms and pressed on her eager mouth a long, slow, delightful kiss such as set his own hot blood to stirring again.

But then that pair of reproachful remembered brown eyes intervened and Nicolas held Linnet off from him and stared at her for a long moment. He reached out and tenderly dried her cheeks with his fingers.

"There'll be another day for us, Linnet," he said softly, for he could see that kiss had shaken her clear to her toes. Abruptly he strode to the door. "Jack," he called loudly, and when there was no response he stuck his head out and shouted, "Jack, 'tis time to take my lady back now."

Not "wench" but "my lady." As he came to the door, Jack lifted his heavy brows and looked at Linnet with new respect. His surprised gaze caught the flash of gold and diamond as Linnet hastily tucked the necklace beneath her white collar and then stuffed it farther down under her high-necked chemise. She had been truthful with Nicolas—no one would see the necklace. Linnet intended to sleep in that chemise and not take it off unless her bedchamber door was well and truly latched.

"Have you got a fresh horse, Jack?" Nicolas asked and Belter gave a surly nod.

With a cynical look on his handsome face, Nicolas watched Linnet ride away behind dour Jack Belter. Both of them were in his pay, he reasoned. Linnet's price was just a little higher, but then she was going to deliver Georgiana to him.

And as soon as Belter returned, Nicolas would have another errand. He must go downriver as fast as a sloop would take him and collect Arthur Kincaid, for Arthur too was a part of the plan he had formed while talking to Linnet. And there was a sloop waiting for him just beyond the trees, out of sight of this farmhouse—he had not wanted Linnet to see it. Now he strolled out the door, meaning to make his way down the riverbank to have a word with her captain.

Jack's mare was just cresting the hill that would take them beyond view of the farmhouse as Nicolas came out. Linnet, clinging to Belter's middle with one arm, turned and gave him a last wave with a green-mittened hand. Her brown cloak was blowing in the wind. Her hood had fallen back and her bright hair spilled out of it. For a moment he saw them there, horse and riders etched stark against the pallid wintry sky. Then they were over the hill and out of sight, and Nicolas turned away to consider the details of the devious plan that he truly believed would deliver to him both Windgate—and Windgate's bride.

When Belter returned from dropping off Linnet, he asked Nicolas, "Will the wench help us?"

Nicolas nodded absently. He had been standing at the window staring out into the late afternoon light, watching the shadows grow long and blue upon the snow. "She'll do what I say, Jack."

And he was sure she would. Over and over again he had gone over in his mind what had been said—and what had not been said. It was unlike him, he realized, to have behaved so well. The old Nicolas would have bedded the wench, urged her "to do this little thing for love of him" and forgotten her before the day was out. What had deterred him, he wondered? Why had he taken all that tiresome time in argument when he could have had his way quicker and easier by way of a torn chemise? It did not occur to him that breathless Linnet, in that moment by the fire when she had first looked up at him, had had something childlike and trusting in her gaze that had reminded him of Mattie, a trust this new more fastidious Nicolas would not wish to violate.

Nicolas never thought of that. Instead he wondered uneasily if he was getting old.

CHAPTER 28

Linnet rode home from her rendezvous with her mind awhirl with thoughts of a glamorous future. Clutching Jack Belter's firm middle, she forgot the cold as she hugged to herself every word, every glance Nicolas had given her. *And, Gramma*—she cast a smiling wicked glance at the sky as a hawk flew over—*she had remembered to tell her gentleman how—except for a whim of fate and the flash of the headsman's ax—she would have been born a lady!* And now she was going to be the wife of a patroon! Linnet gave such a deep ecstatic sigh that Belter was moved to swing his big head around.

"Are ye sick?" he demanded sharply, for now that Nicolas had had his way with the wench (as he firmly believed), now that she was "in it" with them (as she must be although she hadn't said so), he was concerned with her well-being—at least until whatever part she played in this game (and Nicolas hadn't enlightened him as to that) was over.

"No, I'm fine," murmured Linnet to that bristly black beard—so different from Nicolas's fine gleaming golden beard that had brushed her face like a skein of lustrous silk. How his mustaches had tickled! She giggled suddenly and Belter's frown deepened. Mad, that's what she was. He hoped not too much of the plan depended on her!

He let her off at Windgate, wheeled his horse and departed.

Linnet let herself in through a side door that was left unlocked by day, and put her things away. Having done that, she began to wander dreamily through the big rooms, deserted now since—with so many guests about to descend on them—all the servants had been pressed into temporary service in the kitchen. She was viewing everything she saw in an entirely new light. She might one day be mistress here! She could imagine herself prancing down to the big kitchen and giving cook her orders—no, she'd just let cook come to *her,* and waddle off some of that fat! And if someone came to the door she didn't want to see, she would regally instruct Wouter to "turn the fellow away," she wasn't receiving! She saw herself refusing entrance to Erica Hulft, snubbing that stuck-up Katrina ten Haer, wearing clothes as beautiful as Georgiana's—and twice as much jewelry, gorging herself on sweets, and sleeping blissfully beside Nicolas in the big square bed in Georgiana's bedchamber.

She shivered with anticipation. It was a dream that might not come true, she knew, for the English patroon had a hold like an eagle's claws on this bank of the Hudson, but, she told herself with a slight pout, it couldn't hurt to dream. And—she gave a little skip as she went into the drawing room—even if Nicolas gave up his claim and went away, he would still take her with him into some other bright future.

She was just deciding how she would rearrange the furniture in this room and what color drapes would replace the present ones when she jumped—for she had heard her name called.

"Linnet, wherever have you been?" Georgiana, dressed in the sensible gray tight-bodiced linsey-woolsey dress she wore when she was supervising household chores, was just coming through the door, wiping her wet hands on her enveloping white linen apron. "I've been looking all over for you. And why are you standing there holding that chair?"

Linnet dropped the little straight chair she was holding as if it were hot. She had been so carried away with deciding how she would rearrange the furniture that she had actually picked up the chair and been carrying it across the room when Georgiana arrived.

Georgiana gave Linnet a penetrating look that caused Linnet to shift her feet uncomfortably. "Cook said she thought she saw you riding in with Jack Belter."

Linnet's face crimsoned. "Well, I—I might have done," she stammered. She felt almost ashamed to face Georgiana, after having calmly discussed matters this afternoon that would mean turning her out!

Georgiana looked at the girl in amazement. Of all the men in the world to pique Linnet's interest, the last one she would have expected to have done so was fierce-looking Jack Belter. Suddenly she remembered having seen him on the dock at Haerwyck as they had stepped ashore for the ball, and how dour and forbidding he had seemed to her. She remembered remarking on his presence in surprise, and Brett saying, "Maybe Belter's having an affair with one of the chambermaids!" *Could the chambermaid Belter fancied have been Linnet? Could he have guessed she'd be at Haerwyck like the other ladies' maids, and have pursued her there?* And she'd had trouble finding Linnet that night when she wanted to leave. *Could the girl have been closeted with Jack Belter somewhere, perhaps locked in fierce embrace, kissing him?* If so, it would certainly explain Linnet's odd unpredictable behavior ever since the ball.

But—*Jack Belter!* And to have described him as "a gentleman"! Georgiana reminded herself wryly that love struck in odd places. And made people act most peculiar. And perhaps now that her secret was out, Linnet would settle down, for she had been very flighty lately, given to sudden sulks and even bursts of tears.

"And here I thought you were so set on saving yourself for a gentleman!" she teased, for Linnet had confided to her that story about Gramma and the earl of Essex.

Linnet jumped as if a pin had stuck her. "Oh, I've forgot all about that," she said quickly. Her voice dropped to a mumble. "Jack's good enough for me." Having said it, she brightened, relieved to find this easy way out of her predicament. And, besides, seeming to be having a romantic affair with Jack would explain Her visiting his cottage at some future date—to meet Nicolas.

"Well, I'm glad you've found someone." Georgiana gave the girl an impulsive hug that made Linnet feel suddenly very guilty. But even through that stab of contrition, she reminded herself that Nicolas—golden wonderful Nicolas—was counting on her, and she must not let him down. *That* was the thought she must hold on to if she was to get through all these devious connivings he had embroiled her in.

"I'm—glad too," she managed.

"Come along," Georgiana told her gaily. "Brett is in his office consulting with one of his long-winded tenants who'll keep him there for at least another hour. And while he's in there I've a mind to try out my new ice skates. I've been determined to find a moment when he wasn't looking—in case I fall flat on my face."

"Oh, you'll fall—more than once," Linnet assured her cheerfully, remembering some of the many nasty spills she'd taken herself back on Yorkshire ice.

Georgiana untied her apron and they donned their cloaks. Georgiana pulled on fur-lined leather gloves and Linnet the green mittens she had taken off such a short time before. They left the house by the same side door through which Linnet had entered and set off on high pattens for the pond, carrying their skates.

"You'd best tuck your skirts up," Linnet advised her.

Georgiana looked around. The pond, while near the house, was quite isolated actually, its snowy banks ringed by trees and brush. It might have been set in a woodland far from any house. There was nobody to see. She tucked her gray linsey-woolsey skirts up and let Linnet adjust her skate straps for her. She flexed her ankles, trying to get the feel of them. Linnet did a fast little turn before her. It looked easy.

Determined to learn and learn fast, she let Linnet help her up and, then, scorning further aid, she made her first sally out onto the ice. The ice on the pond was smooth and firm—and hard, as she discovered when her ankles seemed immediately to give way, her feet promptly flew out from under her and she crashed down hard on her bottom.

"That's not the way to do it," said Linnet.

"I can see that," said Georgiana ruefully, struggling up with Linnet's help.

Half an hour later she was still wavering, still falling. Feeling frustrated and ridiculous and not a little sore, she sank down, panting, on the opposite bank and acknowledged defeat—at least for now.

That was when Linnet had unveiled her tempting plan to switch places with her and confound Erica Hulft with a dazzling exhibition on the ice.

At first it had seemed mad and unworkable, but the more Georgiana thought about it, the more attractive it became. And with Nicolas to help—and she had no doubt he would, he was sure to find it all vastly amusing—they could probably carry it off.

"What are those tracks in the snow?" Georgiana asked idly as they shouldered their skates and prepared to walk back through the trees.

"Fox tracks, I think," said Linnet, peering down.

Foxes . . . Georgiana was suddenly reminded of the reddish fox's brush color of Erica's hair. It hardened her resolve.

"Come along, Linnet," she said briskly. "We'll see what we can do about a costume for you."

Brett met them in the hall as they were removing their tall pattens and shaking the snow from their wide skirts.

"Well, I see you've tried it," he observed, eyeing the skates.

"Yes," said Georgiana shortly, for there was still that coolness between them.

"How do you like skating?" he asked mildly. "Or have you fallen down so often you're too numb to tell?"

She gave him a look of feigned astonishment. "Fallen?" she scoffed. "I didn't *fall*. I'm quite good at it already. Linnet says I have a natural aptitude for skating. Perhaps it comes from having danced so much."

He gave her a sardonic look. "We must take a turn around the ice tomorrow and test this new proficiency of yours."

"I'm much too busy for that." Georgiana's voice was crisp. "With all I have to do. I will get in what practice I can at odd moments, for I intend to be dancing on the ice with the others."

Brett raised his dark brows at this bit of bravado, but he said nothing as she swished past him herding Linnet before her. His thoughtful gaze followed their progress up the stairs. Then he strode out the door and they heard it shut behind him.

"What do you think he thought, Linnet?" asked Georgiana in a worried voice.

"He thought you were a liar," said Linnet bleakly and Georgiana gave a short mirthless laugh.

"Yes," she sighed. "Brett's good at seeing through people." *All except one—Erica Hulft.*

Accompanying Georgiana into her big square bedchamber, Linnet was having her own problems. Now that Georgiana had assented to the plan, she was suddenly terribly troubled by what she had promised to do. Georgiana, she reminded herself, had been kind to her—far kinder than any mistress she had ever had in her young life. Had not Georgiana given her the lovely clothes she had worn the night of the ten Haers' ball? Why, where would she be now without the mistress?

Still, a girl had to look out for herself and she now had Nicolas's interests to think of.

But consideration of Nicolas's interests did not keep her from giving Georgiana a stricken look. "I—I wouldn't want to do anything to hurt you," she blurted. "If you think we'll be found out?"

Georgiana, searching for her costume among the clothes in her big press, took that to mean that Linnet was afraid this charade, if discovered, would cause trouble between herself and Brett. Well, suppose it did drive a further wedge between them? Georgiana asked herself bitterly. Wasn't it worth taking the chance? For Erica Hulft would be after Brett at the ball and Georgiana as hostess would be too busy to be ever watchful. If she could just best Erica in this one thing, this exhibition on the ice, might not Erica in pique (sensing that she had been downed unfairly) become angry and offensive and thus alienate Brett? Georgiana's delicate jaw hardened. "I think it's an excellent idea," she said in a new steely voice. "I'm only surprised I didn't think of it myself."

Linnet, both glad and sorry, felt a sense of relief.

"There." Georgiana pulled out the dainty blue and white shepherdess costume she intended to wear, spread it out on the big square bed. She studied it, shaking her head. "There's really no way this can be duplicated for you, Linnet," she sighed. "The seamstress might have time to stitch up another but there are only a few scraps of this blue silk left and even if we sent downriver, there's no guarantee that a proper match could be found." Indeed, the material was old. She had found it, just the proper length to make a dress, in the anteroom with Imogene's other things, left behind before her wild ride down the frozen river. It had probably come from Amsterdam or Paris and it would be hard to duplicate that exact color and sheen. She frowned, studying the neckline. "Anyway, this neckline is very low cut and revealing and your bustline is heavier and lower than mine. My waist is slimmer than yours and your legs are heavier. No, it was a wonderful idea but I don't see how we can work it out."

Linnet saw all her plans going out the window. "No one's seen your legs in your long dresses," she pointed out eagerly. "So if my skirts fly up, they'll never know whose striped stockings they're looking at!"

Striped stockings. . . . That gave Georgiana an idea. She never wore striped stockings herself, preferring sheer plain color silks, but they were very popular, especially here in this Dutch colony, where the women fancied brilliant red petticoats and short dresses to show off their stockings.

"They'll have seen my ankles," she murmured.

"Who notices ankles?" scoffed Linnet.

Brett and Nicolas do! she was tempted to reply, but instead she shot a question at Linnet. "Do you own two pairs of striped stockings exactly alike?"

Linnet blinked. "No, I don't, but cook's daughter does—she got them for her birthday and hasn't worn them yet. She's waiting for the holidays. Red-and-white-striped wool, they are."

"See if you can borrow them. I'll make it up to her. And there's a lot of yellow wool yarn in the sewing room. Bring it to me, and bring the seamstress with all the ginghams and calicos she can find—we're going to be a pair of rag dolls, Linnet!"

"But your beautiful shepherdess costume!" wailed Linnet, who had yearned to wear one like that and prance before Nicolas across the ice—because of course *he* would know who was doing the skating!

"Oh, I'll wear the shepherdess costume," Georgiana laughed. "And then I'll change for the skating exhibition and the ice dancing—only of course there won't be any ice dancing for me because I'll pretend I hurt my ankle at the end of the skating exhibition."

"I'll end it by jumping over some barrels," offered Linnet, sensing a new way to look spectacular in Nicolas's watching eyes. "And after I land I'll stagger and make it look like I was hurt."

"Well, not too exaggerated a stagger—and be sure not to fall," cautioned Georgiana. "For that would bring Brett on the run and we might be found out." She was mentally certain that no cleverness of costume was going to fool Brett at close quarters. "Are you sure you can jump over *barrels*?" she asked uneasily.

"Oh, yes, I've done it often! Jumped over four barrels, I have!"

"Three will be quite enough," sighed Georgiana.

The seamstress was confused but—sworn to secrecy—she warmed to the idea and made up two matching ruffled costumes and two matching ruffled dust caps and white silk face masks to which were affixed long fat braids, which Georgiana and a willing Linnet fashioned from the yellow wool knitting yarn. The bodice of each was of checked gingham, the left side green and white checks, the right side red and white, and the huge full puffed sleeves were the same colors in reverse with enormous yellow-and-white-checked gingham ruffles that spilled from the elbows.

Georgiana had wanted a big ruff to conceal the neck but Linnet had protested, "I can't skate in one of them great wheel things—'twould get in my way!" They had compromised on a flowing white linen collar to which the ends of the silk face mask would be attached by a few stitches after the costume was on, so the mask could not fly up during one of Linnet's flying leaps and reveal her features.

The wide gingham skirts were of alternate yellow and red and green checks and the whole thing was elaborately patched in bright swatches of flowered calico. The costumes were deliberately made loose and flowing so that Linnet's heavier figure could be concealed by a confusion of bright patches and gingham ruffles and calico puffs. The enormous sleeves completely enveloped Linnet's heavier arms and the plain white billowing petticoats were conveniently made out of old sheets. The heavy red and white striped stockings had been duly borrowed from cook's mystified daughter, whom Georgiana had delighted with a gift of a new red flannel petticoat that even Linnet envied. The stockings were so thick and of so uneven a texture that Georgiana decided the difference in their legs would pass even Brett's and Nicolas's sharp eyes unnoticed.

Shoes had been a problem—Linnet's feet were two sizes larger than Georgiana's. This was solved by creating a kind of mock boot of black felt to be worn over the shoes—the two pairs were exactly the same size, only Georgiana's were destined to be stuffed with yarn to make them fit.

"These skirts are shocking short," protested the seamstress, biting off the thread as she finished and holding up the almost mid-calf-length skirt before her.

"So a bit more stocking will show," said Georgiana coolly. "Linnet has to have her skirts short enough so there's no chance of her catching her skates and falling."

The seamstress looked doubtful, obviously thinking a bit more decorum on the ice would be in order, but Linnet giggled. She'd be glad to show the full length of her stockings—and more besides—

out there on the ice with Nicolas watching. And indeed she might, with the great leaps she'd be taking.

The same makeshift technique used to cover their variance in shoe sizes was applied to gloves to cover their variance in hand sizes—for Linnet's were considerably larger than Georgiana's. This was solved by covering round bulky mittens with black felt and adding long black gauntlets, which completely concealed any forearm that might be shown when the sleeve ruffles blew back.

When both girls were dressed in their bright costumes, complete to red-and-white-striped stockings and the white silk masks that covered their faces, leaving only long slits for the eyes and with round patches of pink silk appliqued to simulate rosy cheeks, they stood side by side before Georgiana's dressing mirror and the seamstress burst out laughing.

"As alike as two peas in a pod!" she declared proudly, turning her head to one side and standing back to look at them. "Ye could pass for twins now, for all that the mistress is slimmer!"

Turning about, Georgiana studied her reflection critically—and decreed that in the time that remained, brilliants should be sewn at strategic places on both costumes.

She wanted to sparkle out there on the ice!

BOOK VI
Masquerade on Ice

A little west of loving, a little east of sin,
A little south of innocence—oh, where do I begin?
Somewhere across a plain of doubt, high on a cliff of pride
This foolish troubled woman's heart must find a place to hide!

Windgate on the Hudson,
Winter 1673

CHAPTER 29

Georgiana had originally wanted to wait until the Hudson itself was frozen over (as Linnet had assured her would soon be the case if the cold weather held) but Brett had been adamant. She had announced to the world the night of the ten Haers' ball that they would be giving their own masquerade ball with the first snowfall—and so it would be done.

So the invitations had gone out, and Georgiana had had to bite her tongue to keep from telling Brett *why* she had wanted to wait—so Erica Hulft would be stuck in New Orange and unable to make the journey upriver.

If he guessed her reason, he gave no sign. His expression was stern.

The invitations went out a week before the ball and Georgiana kept hoping for a sudden freeze, something that would confine the guests to neighbors who could make the journey conveniently, but although the pond was hard-frozen now, the river remained flowing.

Georgiana looked out at the river, that beautiful damnable stream that flowed two ways—as her mother's heart had done. And perhaps—although she did not want to face it—her own. No, she told herself sharply, she loved Brett, despite this temporary estrangement, but she could not—she *would not* share him with Erica Hulft.

Erica arrived a day early. Georgiana could hardly believe it when Govert's sloop—it was easily remarked for its hull was painted red—sailed up to the landing and made fast. She and Brett were at breakfast when vaguely in the distance they heard the sloop hailed. She ran to the drawing room windows and looked out, wondering who it could be—surely not guests for the ball; *they* would not come until tomorrow.

She caught her breath as she recognized the sloop.

Brett had risen from the table and now he joined her at the window.

"Govert Steendam's sloop," he said in an expressionless voice. "And apparently"—he watched as a woman in an apricot velvet cloak lavished with red fox furs that matched her brilliant fox-brush hair alighted alone—"it carries only Erica."

Georgiana stared indignantly at the sloop, at the elegant figure just now alighting from it. "How does that woman have the effrontery to come here alone—again?" she muttered under her breath.

Brett gave her a sharp look. "You will be civil to her," he said. "Steendam and I may become partners in a mill near Rensselaerwyck, remember."

Goaded by his recent coldness, by the unexpected appearance of her rival, by the splendor of Erica's garb while she herself was running about in her slate blue housedress, supervising fevered last-minute preparations, Georgiana turned on her husband.

"A mill?" Her voice rang out scornfully. "And a partnership with Govert Steendam. . . . It all seems very important to you, doesn't it?" When he was silent she continued to glower at him. "Oh, don't you see?" she burst out at last. "It is all part of her contriving! Erica's using you, maneuvering you! She wants this partnership with Steendam to come about because then she will have the whip hand. She will have you just where she wants you then. You will jump when she snaps her fingers, for you will know that if you do not, she will whisper into Steendam's ear on her pillow that you and she were lovers, and he will withdraw his aid, and by then you will be in too deep to recover and he will ruin you! *Erica* will ruin you!"

"You misunderstand Erica," Brett said coldly. "And since you know nothing of Steendam or the way things are here, I will tell you about it. Govert Steendam came here from Leyden twenty years ago with all his savings. He was in love with Annekje Maarten, a Leyden beauty of great fortune and he worked desperately to amass enough money so that her father would accept him as a suitor for his daughter. His friends have told me that Govert would have walked barefoot through the snow from New York to Albany, could he have brought Annekje here. But Maarten threw away Govert's frantic letters begging him to wait; he gave Annekje to a man old enough to be her grandfather. She wrote to Govert, broken-hearted, and told him of her betrothal. Like a madman, Govert dropped all that he was doing, took ship and sailed for Holland. He arrived in Leyden three days after the wedding and, I'm told, did not have a sober day for six months. Then one day quite by chance he ran across Annekje in the main street of Leyden and they both stopped dead and stared at each other. Her face had gone white and she looked about to faint and he helped her into a tavern. There, in tears, she pleaded with Govert, she told him that she had been forced into this marriage, but that if Govert would but go back to America and wait for her, she would yet be his for her elderly husband was in his dotage and very ill and could not live much longer."

"Why did she allow herself to be forced into a marriage with an old man she did not love?" burst out Georgiana indignantly. "Why did she not run away?"

"Undoubtedly *you* would have done so," said Brett. "But it seems that Annekje had not your courage. And remember, when the wedding took place, she still believed Govert to be far away across the sea, too far to aid her. Annekje chose to wait, hoping death would resolve her situation. Govert, moved by Annekje's pleading, agreed to wait, accepted the situation, again embarked for America and plunged with renewed vigor into his business. It flourished. The years dragged by, while he lived on occasional letters from Annekje. And then one day he received word from a friend in Holland that Annekje, his Annekje, had died in childbirth. Her elderly husband, not in his dotage after all, it seems, had survived her. Govert turned gray in the face when he read the letter and turned his face to the wall. His housekeeper—we have the story from her for she read his mail and observed his actions—thought he would die of grief, for he spoke to no one and ate almost nothing for two long months. At the end of that time, he got up and went about his business, as gray and cold as ever.''

"And then Erica came along," breathed Georgiana.

"Yes, then Erica came his way—and someone who once saw Annekje in Leyden told the housekeeper that Erica bears a striking resemblance to Govert's lost Annekje."

Georgiana cast a look down the slope at Erica, who was in animated conversation with the sloop's *schipper* on the pier. "If so," she said rudely, "I've little doubt that the father of her child was not the old man in his dotage she claimed him to be but some more virile lover—I'll wager Annekje fooled Govert Steendam with this tale! If she was anything like Erica, she probably wanted to keep them both!"

Brett gave her a reproving look. "Steendam turned to Erica as to Annekje reborn," he said shortly. "She is the lodestar of his life just now. If you would have the heart to deprive him of her, at least I have not! So since Erica is shortly to become his wife, I would hope that you could manage to be civil to her. Why indeed can you not become friends? Govert Steendam is perhaps the most powerful man in New Orange right now and we may yet be in sore need of powerful friends in this Dutch colony!"

Friends! She and Erica Hulft—*friends!* It was not to be imagined.

"Ah, but there's another reason besides business for us to become 'friends,' isn't there?" she cried bitterly, venting her anger at the suggestion on Brett. "A more potent one? Why don't you admit it?"

The answer was like a bucket of ice water thrown in her face.

"I do admit it," he said coldly. "Erica and I go back a long way. She once wanted—yes, *expected* although I gave her no grounds to expect it—to become my wife. She has made many mistakes, but it would take a large one indeed to make me turn my back on her."

Georgiana felt as if her head would burst. She turned away from him, plunging toward the doorway. "You may greet your former mistress alone!" she flung over her shoulder. "I shall be too busy to receive her!"

But of course Erica was not to be ignored. Later in the day as she busied herself with checking out the guest rooms with Linnet, she looked out the window and saw Brett strolling with Erica across the lawns. Erica said something that made him laugh. She could see him throw his head back. And then Erica tossed her fox-brush head prettily and bridled and took his arm and leaned upon it.

Georgiana could hear her own teeth grinding. So angry she felt physically sick, she whirled away from the window and clutched a chairback, held on to it as if to anchor herself in the room. Every feminine instinct she had urged her to go down and take a broomstick to Erica. Every grain of common sense told her to hold her fire, to say nothing, to wait. Sooner or later Erica would make a mistake and she would pounce upon it. And if she did not—there was always the ice dancing exhibition to prod Erica into making a false move. Reasoning thus with her own wild nature, Georgiana clung to the chair until she felt calmer.

She even managed to be gracious to Erica at supper, although it cost her a deal.

She had taken the time to dress properly before greeting her guest. The pale lemon damask of her gown was complemented by wide gold velvet ribands caught cunningly at the elbows of her big full sleeves, from which spilled the dainty white lawn ruffles of her chemise. Her wide skirts were most carefully tucked up to display her gold satin petticoat. Having arranged her burnished gold hair in a most becoming fashion, she had looked with satisfaction in the mirror and gone down to meet Erica.

Erica and Brett were waiting for her in the wide front hall. They were deep in conversation, laughing into each other's eyes when Georgiana caught sight of them below her. She almost missed the top step.

Erica looked *stunning*. The sleek copper satin of her gown outlined a lissome figure and was cut even lower than Georgiana's, which displayed a snowy expanse of bosom. Glittering copper lace spilled from Erica's big slashed sleeves, which were richly lined with black velvet set cleverly here and there with brilliants that flashed as she moved. Her satin skirts were gathered up into enormous panniers to display a velvet petticoat, black as night, and there were copper lace rosettes on her black velvet slippers.

Looking at this vision, Georgiana felt suddenly like a pretty provincial lass brought to court for the first time and watching in baffled wonderment as an elegant courtesan swept by. It was no wonder, she realized, that Brett had been attracted to Erica and . . . still was.

Erica looked up and saw her watching.

"Why, Georgiana," she cried in a warm light voice, sounding somehow surprised to see her—and this Georgiana's own house. "How lovely you look!" And came forward to greet her with both hands extended in a charming gesture, even as she turned to say something over her shoulder to Brett.

Georgiana felt she was interrupting their conversation, which continued to swirl about her as they drifted into the long dining room. She felt left out of it, and her turquoise eyes were snapping as she coolly warned her guest that with all the great preparations underfoot, cook had balked at preparing more than suppawn and *hutspot* and cold meats for tonight's supper.

"I don't mind," laughed Erica. "Brett and I have supped often enough on Indian meal porridge and *hutspot* when cook flew into one of her tempers over something the servants had done!" Brett frowned at her and she looked momentarily distressed, her long lashes fluttering against her creamy cheeks, but when her gaze flew to Georgiana—her host and hostess were seated appropriately at the long board and Erica was seated, appropriately, between them—her silky and slightly malevolent expression told Georgiana that the slip had been deliberate. It was Erica's way of telling the new bride how much time she and Brett had spent in this house together when *she* had been mistress here. Georgiana managed to keep her fork steady and hoped the resentment she felt did not show on her face.

Conversation lagged while Brett expertly carved a haunch of venison. When he had finished, he smiled at Georgiana. An impersonal smile, she told herself hotly. She might have been a guest!

"Erica is an excellent skater. You should ask her to teach you," he suggested.

"Thank you, I have already learned," said Georgiana distantly.

Brett managed to conceal his astonishment, for he had imagined that Linnet must have had to drag her across the glassy surface of the pond, holding her up. "Indeed?" he murmured. "I am glad to hear it."

"I am amazed to hear it," said Erica. "Coming from Bermuda, where there is no ice."

"I have been skating but a short time," Georgiana told her frostily, "but—I have natural aptitude."

Erica's skeptical amber eyes mirrored her disbelief. "Perhaps we could do a few turns about the ice tomorrow?" she suggested. "Before your guests start arriving?"

"I am sorry, I will be much too busy."

"Perhaps even tonight?" Erica's smile was malicious. "The sky is so clear. When the moon comes up, it will be like day."

"I am afraid I must decline," said Georgiana in what she hoped was a bored voice. "I have had an exhausting day." She decided to take the offensive. "I believe I have not asked you." She gazed at her guest with a fixed expression. "Why did not your husband accompany you?"

"Oh, you mean Govert? We aren't married yet." Erica laughed and put up a hand as if to brush away cobwebs. It was a light, delicate gesture and flashed her rings to advantage. "Govert keeps importuning me but—I keep putting off the day." Her face turned to Brett and her gaze rested on him softly. "Do *you* think I should marry Govert?" she asked wistfully.

Brett studied her with some amusement. "I think he would suit you admirably. He has a deep purse and no heirs and he is not young—you should outlive him."

"Yes, I have thought of that," said Erica frankly. "And of course *that* part appeals to me, but when one has known other, more desirable men...." She let her voice trail off significantly.

Down the table her hostess flushed and leaned forward. "But if those men are *already taken*"—she tried to keep the anger out of her voice—"might you not be wise to make the best of what is left?"

"It is what I keep telling myself," said Erica with another negligent gesture. "But, then, I am so hard to *convince*." She batted her lashes at Brett again and he grinned widely.

At that moment Georgiana could cheerfully have killed them both.

"Sometimes one marries and finds she has made a mistake—that there is a better man available," she tossed recklessly into the conversation.

"Indeed?" Erica turned to consider her. "I find that very interesting. Could you be more specific?"

"Suitors come and suitors go," shrugged Georgiana, glad to take this dig at Brett, whose brows had drawn together as he considered his rash young bride. "One is always curious what differences in one's life a change could make."

Erica's delicate brows shot up. "Your bride has hidden depths," she remarked to Brett. "Indeed, *I* might have made that comment but I am surprised indeed to hear it from Georgiana's lips."

"So" said Brett in a level voice, "am I. Perhaps you would care to be more specific, Georgiana?"

It was a direct challenge. They were both looking at her—Erica with lively curiosity, Brett with a lowering look. Georgiana, who had not meant to go this far, felt cornered—but she was still angry and she had no intention of backing down.

"No," she said flippantly. "I would not. Old friends, new friends—I suppose one must find some way to while away the idle hours."

Erica laughed behind her napkin, obviously amused by this interchange between Georgiana and Brett. "I see you have your hands full," she told him in a low voice as Georgiana led them into the drawing room after supper. "Nicolas must have been here."

Georgiana overheard that remark and turned around angrily with a swirl of yellow damask skirts. "Nicolas has indeed been here. *I* found him very charming."

"Beware," cautioned Erica. She waved a mocking finger. "He has broken many hearts, has Nicolas!"

"Oh? Is yours one of them?" demanded Georgiana rudely.

"Georgiana did not realize you were but jesting, Erica," interposed Brett smoothly, and before Georgiana could interrupt to say indignantly, "Because she was not!" he turned to her and there was a note of warning in his tone. "Perhaps you will play a tune for us on the virginal, Georgiana?"

"Oh, yes, do," cried Erica. "And I will sing for you."

Brett had taken her hand firmly and was urging her toward the virginal, with Erica in her finery bringing up the rear. Unhappily, Georgiana sat down upon the round stool before the small legless gilt and rosewood spinet that had given her mother so little joy and found herself with unsteady fingers accompanying Erica in a love song, which Erica sang flirtatiously, with stage gestures. She ended by running over to Brett and making him a deep curtsy.

"There," she cried, leaning over and ruffling his dark hair. "Just like the old days!"

"Not quite," said Georgiana, rising from the virginal's stool. "He has a *wife* now."

"Oh, but of course I did not mean—" Erica's voice was deprecating, but with her back to Brett her half-smile challenged Georgiana.

"I think we both know what you meant!" Georgiana stormed from the room.

Brett caught her halfway up the stairs. "Come back," he said in a low voice. "Control that violent temper of yours. You are making much out of little. Erica meant nothing by what she said."

"*You* may call it nothing," flashed Georgiana, struggling to free her arm. "But I consider that your former mistress has come here to challenge me in my own house and that you are abetting her!"

Brett's grasp on her arm tightened. "Control yourself." His tone harshened. "She is listening from the hall. Do you want the whole river to know that you have made a fool of yourself?"

"I have already done that by marrying you!" cried Georgiana in fury. "Erica is *your* guest—*you* entertain her. I am going to bed!"

"Very well, you may go to bed." Brett released her abruptly. "I will make your excuses to Erica, I will say that you are unwell—it may help to excuse your bad temper."

"Don't bother!" stormed Georgiana. "She is aware of how I feel about her!"

"But in the morning," he went on, his manner inexorable, "I will expect to find you in better temper. If not, we had best cancel the masquerade ball."

"Oh!" cried Georgiana on a wave of indignation. "You wouldn't! Not after all this hard work by the whole household!"

"It might be best if you cannot control yourself. If you continue in this vein, even a mask will not conceal your feelings and you will indeed become an amusing story along the river."

"I am already an amusing story along the river," cried Georgiana. "I don't doubt wagers are being taken as to who will replace me in your bed—Katrina ten Haer or Erica Hulft!" She was trembling now. "I warn you, Brett, not to parade your mistress before me! If you do, I will leave you—there are other arms besides yours!"

From the hallway came faint mocking applause.

Brett looked upset. He reached out to Georgiana—perhaps a conciliatory gesture—and caught her wrist lightly. But for Georgiana it was all too much. She broke free with a sob and ran up the stairs away from him—to throw herself on the big square bed in her bedchamber and sob the night away.

Brett did not join her.

Sleepless, feeling feverish, she wondered if he was sleeping with Erica. By 2:00 A.M. she could stand it no longer and crept to the door of the adjoining room and peered in. The moonlight showed her his long masculine figure in bed—alone. And sound asleep.

With a deep shuddering sigh, she eased the door shut and went back to bed—and at last to sleep.

In the morning Erica apologized. With ease and grace. "I behaved very badly last night, Georgiana," she said, coming forward gracefully to clasp Georgiana's hand. "I do hope you will forgive me."

Georgiana looked at her guest, elegantly gowned in amber velvet with row on row of burnt orange satin ribands flashing around the hem of her skirts and the deep ruffles of her voluminous sleeves as she moved. That gown eclipsed her own tailored blue gray woolen edged in black braid in which she intended to greet her guests, for she would change later into her shepherdess costume for the ball— but no matter, she told herself. One thing at least she had last night decided: she was not going to behave like a child, full of tempers and tantrums, egged on by a malicious Erica.

"Of course I forgive you," she said distantly.

"My behavior is often outrageous." Erica spread her hands and made a wide gesture that seemed to encompass the Hudson, indeed the whole world. "Few can find it in their hearts to forgive me." She gave a deep, heartrending sigh.

"Georgiana has a kind heart," said Brett, smiling at his wife. "I am sure she will."

Georgiana gave him a mutinous look. This day and the masquerade ball must be got through somehow, but if he thought she was going to let this sort of thing go on and on—! "Shall we have breakfast?" she asked, cutting off the discussion.

They went in to breakfast on waffles sprinkled with sugared cinnamon from the big silver *ooma*, and delicious little sausages, but Georgiana found she could hardly swallow. Her whole being was seething. She felt betrayed and angry with Brett.

He does not want to give her up, she thought, stabbing at the untasted food on her plate. *He does not realize it, he thinks he is being gallant—but that is not the real reason. She has been his for a long time—his whenever he wanted her. And she will be his again* *whenever he wants her, she has made that abundantly clear. And he* *does not want to give her up.*

The thought was galling. And painful.

Somehow the meal was got through. Georgiana was coldly civil to both Brett and Erica and she kept her eyes mainly upon her plate. She was paler than usual.

Linnet passed by the dining room door and gave her mistress a compassionate look. *Forced to sit there like that with Erica Hulft!* she thought on a note of rising indignation. *No wonder she looks downcast!*

But on the whole, Linnet had thought very little about Georgiana and her problems. For Linnet was holding in her heart a secret love and, like other forbidden pleasures, she took all the more joy in it because she could not speak of it openly.

Poor lady, she thought of Georgiana, when she thought of her at all. *So soon to be dispossessed!* For Linnet was every hour filled with more confidence in Nicolas and his destiny. She had walked casually by the dining room door to make sure they were all still at breakfast—it would give her a perfect opportunity to slip into Georgiana's room and rummage about and find the packet Nicolas wanted. She felt she would be quite safe in doing that, for Georgiana, with a houseful of guests, would hardly take time out to read the journal and papers she had so carefully secreted. And before she looked for them again, Linnet would have returned them. But when Linnet stole into Georgiana's room and took away the packet with its, to her, unreadable—for she was illiterate—journal and parchment, she felt a pang of guilt and made herself a promise: *If Windgate is taken away from her, I will take her into my service and be kind to her—as she has been to me. Nicolas—*Linnet caressed the thought of her golden Dutchman, her patroon—*would want me to do that.*

What she would do with Brett in such a case, she had no idea. Nor had she given thought to the unlikelihood that proud Georgiana would accept such a position. But fancies like those somehow comforted Linnet, who had never before done anything dishonest or disloyal.

Linnet's wild dreams would have awakened scorn in Georgiana

had she been able to divine them. Fortunately for Linnet she was not.

Yesterday they had gone through a last rehearsal of their plans.

"We are agreed how we will make the switch, then," Georgiana had told Linnet. "I will come down the main stairway in my rag doll costume but without my mask. I will put on the mask and headdress in full view of whoever is there. And *you* will go down the back stairway and be waiting for me in the thickest part of that clump of trees out back."

"I can go all the way to the pond under cover of the brush," offered Linnet, "for the undergrowth is very thick there. Even though the leaves are all gone, the snow on the branches gives plenty of cover."

"I will meet you halfway," decided Georgiana. "You will be waiting behind that big bush where you showed me a stitching of mouse tracks across the snow. We will trade places there. People will have seen me, carrying ice skates, dressed as a rag doll, go into the bushes—they will see *you*, carrying ice skates, dressed as a rag doll, come out. I will wait there while everybody watches you dance upon the ice. After you have made your last spectacular leap—over the barrels, and *do* be careful—you will bow and wave to your audience and suddenly dash up the bank. When you reach the big bush, you will take off your skates—and we will trade places again. You will hide in the bushes until you can safely slip into the house and get rid of your costume—hide it well, Linnet. And I will come limping out, carrying my skates and claiming that I turned my ankle in my reckless dash up the snowy bank."

"You could come out leaning upon Mynheer van Rappard's arm."

"No, we will not need Nicolas—and better perhaps that we don't take him into our confidence. Let Erica Hulft puzzle forever how I leaned to skate so well in Bermuda! She will never find out!"

"I think she is dangerous," said Linnet soberly.

"How so?"

"I do not like the way she looks at you when you are not looking."

Georgiana did not care how Erica looked at her. She did not like the way Erica looked at Brett. Or the tolerant smile of camaraderie in his eyes when he looked back at Erica. Georgiana was young and jealous. She did not realize that a man might tolerate much in a mistress that he would not brook in a wife.

"One more day to go," Georgiana had sighed. "And then the party will be upon us, people will be arriving." And the next day, hopefully Erica would go home! Now that Erica was here, Georgiana hoped fervently that the river would not freeze over—Erica might use that as an excuse to stay until the spring thaw if Brett let her! She wondered what Govert Steendam must think about Erica dashing off upriver to a ball without him. Erica had said vaguely that "pressing business matters" were keeping him in New Orange, but it would not have surprised Georgiana to learn that Erica had taken the sloop without Govert's permission, lied to the *schipper,* a self-effacing man who had elected to stay aboard his sloop "the better to see that the crew does not get into mischief." He might better have addressed himself to the mischief that Erica might get into! thought Georgiana.

But now the day of the ball was upon them and at any minute sloops carrying guests might start arriving.

Right after their silent breakfast Erica managed to find Georgiana alone.

"I think we must have a talk," she said, smiling.

"And what have we to talk about?" wondered Georgiana, who was at the moment making a last count of the number of table napkins, which suddenly seemed to her in short supply.

"Your husband." Erica, with her usual directness, came instantly to the point.

The large dining room with its massive furniture seemed suddenly very empty, the world of the river far away.

Georgiana put down the stack of linen napkins she was holding. The count number had departed her mind as Erica spoke. "I do not wish to discuss him with you," she said bluntly.

"Ah, but it is important that we do discuss him, for we will see much of each other, you and I, if Govert and Brett go into business together."

"If you're speaking of the mill, that will be but a small part of Brett's operations here." Georgiana's careless shrug was a rebuff in itself. "I don't attach much importance to it." As if to dismiss Erica, she began her count again.

"But it will be more than just a mill," insisted Erica. "It will be—what is the word? A coalition, a joining of forces. Govert controls many ships, his warehouses are full of the world's goods, or didn't you know that? Brett longs for such a coalition, for it would make him rich beyond his wildest dreams.''

Georgiana lost count. Erica went on.

"You see, Georgiana, Brett is in an awkward position as an English patroon in Dutch-held territory. Govert is a powerful man in New Netherland. With Govert's ships to carry his goods, Brett can enter into the fur trade in a large way. He might even open up the Mohawk Valley. He might—''

Georgiana set down the stack of napkins she was holding. She turned to stare her rival full in the face. "What are you trying to tell me, Erica? That I must tolerate any kind of behavior between you and my husband in order to advance him? Let me tell you now that I don't intend to do it. Money just isn't that important to me.''

"Ah, but it is to Brett," purred Erica. "Windgate is an old dream of his, but it is part of a larger dream. Hasn't he told you?'' Her tone was mocking. "If he has not, you must ask him.''

Standing stiffly by the gleaming dining room table, Georgiana studied Erica. Suddenly she was seeing her as she must have been with Brett—once. When she had first met him. A slip of a girl. Winsome, willing, desirable—perhaps even with a kind of inno-cence. She was seeing Erica through Brett's eyes, seeing that graceful small-boned figure free of its corset and stays, willowy, winning. Seeing Erica's slanted-lashed smiling look as she slipped naked into Brett's waiting arms.

Her cheeks grew hot at her own thoughts.

"Come, Georgiana.'' Erica had a damnable way of reading her mind. "You must not ponder on the past. Whatever Brett and I had is—over long ago.'' There was a note of insincerity in her tone as she said that and it gave Georgiana hope—perhaps Erica had not been as successful with Brett this time as she had hoped to be, perhaps he was being more polite than loving.

"Erica,'' she said bluntly. "Feeling as you do about Brett, I am surprised you did not marry him while you had the chance.''

To her surprise, the woman before her winced. "But I did not have the chance,'' Erica smiled. "*I* was not heiress to Windgate. He was saving himself for you, Georgiana.''

Georgiana's face went wooden. Any sympathy she might have felt for Erica went out the window with that remark. "It might surprise you to know," she told Erica with heavy irony, "that Brett fell in love with me *before he knew* that I was heiress to Windgate."

For a moment Erica looked taken aback, but her aplomb was restored immediately. She wore it jauntily, like a fashionable hat. "*That* would indeed surprise me," she agreed airily. "For Windgate comes first with Brett—he loves this land like a woman. No, his love for Windgate is more than that—more like the love of a mortal for a goddess."

Sadly, Georgiana acknowledged the truth of that statement.

"Windgate," Erica reminded her softly, "will always come first with Brett. Wife or mistress—*they* will always come second."

"Exactly what is it you want me to do, Erica?" demanded Georgiana.

"Accept me," supplied Erica promptly.

"*Accept* you?"

"Yes, accept me for what I am. When I marry Govert Steendam—and I have decided now that I will do it—I will become very important in Brett's scheme of things, for I will be able to influence my husband for or against Brett's interests." At Georgiana's indignant expression, she added with a wicked smile, "What is thought to have been gained by day is often lost in the bedroom by night—between different combatants. Govert Steendam is fiercely jealous of me. If I were so much as to murmur that Brett sought to reclaim me, it would ruin Brett in his eyes."

Blackmail, thought Georgiana, with a sinking heart. Wily Erica was bent on finding a way to manage them all!

"I will think on it," she said coldly.

"Do so." Erica's voice was suddenly crisp. "I think you will find that we can come to an amicable understanding." When Georgiana remained silent, she turned and strolled from the dining room into the empty drawing room, moved restlessly to the window. "Ah, I see Brett walking down the bluff," she called over her shoulder to Georgiana. "A sloop full of guests must be arriving."

Georgiana came into the drawing room to see for herself.

"I think I will go down and join him," said Erica. She turned at the door, her expression bland. "Won't you come along, Georgiana? After all, they are *your* guests."

My guests—but *you* might be giving the ball! thought Georgiana resentfully. With compressed lips, she accompanied a smiling Erica down to the pier to greet her guests, who turned out to be the Van Rensselaers from upriver. They had arrived, belatedly bearing wedding gifts for the patroon's new bride. Georgiana liked the Van Rensselaers, she thanked them warmly for their gifts—and it gave her a respite from Erica, who seemed bent on welcoming the arriving guests as if she were still the chatelaine of Windgate.

Georgiana had linked arms with the Dutch patroon's lady and was chatting with her as they strolled up the bluff toward the house when Van Rensselaer, who was walking just ahead of them, flanked by Brett and a laughing Erica, turned jovially to say something to his hostess, cast a keen look downriver and came to a sudden stop.

"What sloop is that?" he wondered, peering southward, and the entire party came to a halt and stood, watching the sloop sail upriver and tie up at the wooden pier. "Why, that's Govert Steendam," he cried, and turned to Georgiana. "I thought you said he wasn't coming?"

"He must have changed his mind," murmured Georgiana, stifling a sudden burst of mirth as she and Brett excused themselves and went down to greet this new arrival. Her turquoise eyes were dancing as Erica detached herself from the group and hurried ahead of them down the slope to meet Govert.

Erica would have to abandon her role of chatelaine now, thought Georgiana gleefully, and concentrate on the gray-haired, stoop-shouldered Dutchman whose eyes lit up at sight of her, and who greeted her in such a possessive fashion. She would have to stay by his side at least for a seemly interval and leave Georgiana to do her own hostessing. Lest she lose ground with her wealthy betrothed, who was pivotal to all her devious plottings.

New Orange, New Netherland, 1673

CHAPTER 30

Nothing in Mattie's short life had prepared her for Nicolas's enticing seduction, his skillful flattery, the pressure of his overpowering masculine charms. Fresh from the lash of Arthur's continual sharp criticism, bowed from his contempt, bruised by his hard fists, Mattie had instantly flowered under Nicolas's lighthearted wooing, her petals opening like a rose on a dewy summer morning.

It had all seemed beautifully unreal to her, made of substance and moonbeams—not wrong, surely.

She had felt herself to be exactly like a long-ago ancestress who her mother boasted had made a dizzying upward march as mistress in swift succession to five minor noblemen, ending up at the altar—in Canterbury Cathedral no less—bride to a belted earl. Nicolas—who was almost a patroon in Mattie's excited fancy—was miles above Arthur, who was only rich and bad-mannered. But she did not even think of that.

She was entirely carried away and knew for the first time a rich and engulfing bliss.

A man—and such a man!—had taken her in his arms gently, beguilingly, and made love to her for pure joy.

Mattie's openhearted nature had responded buoyantly. In Nicolas's enticing arms she had forgotten Arthur and all the times he had hurt and humiliated her, forgotten him as if he had never been.

Not till after it was over did she really remember him.

409

And then it hit her like an iron-shod hoof right between the eyes. She had committed adultery! She had become a strumpet! She would, in her sudden tragic view, be drummed out of the human race.

In her agitation, after Nicolas had gone and she was back in her room beside a heavily sleeping Arthur, Mattie sat up in bed hugging her shivering body with her arms and castigating herself for all her sins—especially this last, overwhelming one. Her head was bowed and tears coursed down her pale cheeks. Dawn came and still Arthur had not awakened. The sun poured through the small-paned windows and yet he slept as heavily.

Mattie could stand the inaction no longer.

She jumped up and dressed, intending to go for a walk before breakfast. Nicolas had said Arthur might not wake till noon. She must be calm and collected by then.

In her haste to leave she tripped over one of Arthur's carelessly shed boots as she went out the door—and from the bed Arthur gave a snort. With her nerves in an uproar, Mattie swung around so violently that she lost her balance and her jaw collided painfully with the door jamb. She fell away from it with a little cry, only to stand trembling in silent horror, clutching her jaw, watching with dilated eyes that form on the bed.

But Arthur had only made a noise in his sleep. He was as dead to the world as ever.

With her jaw aching, Mattie closed the door and leaned against it for a moment with her eyes closed. Then she hurried downstairs and out of the inn, brushing by in succession with downcast eyes and humble manner (for she felt herself brought low): a smiling chambermaid who had borne five children out of wedlock fathered by five different men (but all of them Dutchmen and religious, the girl was prone to assert piously); the innkeeper's swaggering broad-hipped daughter who had only last week been wed at the point of a musket to a lad so frightened he could not find the voice to explain that he had not been the one who seduced her; and the innkeeper's blowsy loose-lipped wife, who owed her laces and fine petticoats to the favor of traveling gentlemen with whom she nipped upstairs for a swift surreptitious romp while her husband was busy pouring out ale below. Past all of these women Mattie scuttled in abject misery with her head hanging, for she felt herself beneath their contempt.

Having enjoyed the deed, Mattie was now suffering additional agonies because she had *enjoyed* it. If only it had been distasteful, or if she had fought bravely and been overpowered, she might have squared it with her suddenly refocused conscience. But she had *loved* it, all of it—every sigh, every touch, every scorching embrace. Indeed she was still tingling with the wonderful remembered glow of Nicolas's long body hot against her own. All she could think of was when she would see him again.

It was *wrong*. She knew without a doubt that she would burn in hell for it.

And besides she was Arthur's wife and what she had done was an inexcusable affront to Arthur, who was still her husband, no matter how badly he had treated her.

So reasoned Mattie as—trying blindly to escape her own thoughts, her own deeds—she hurried down New Orange's waterfront, dodging small children and women laden with ducks and geese and food-stuffs, and occasionally crashing into a tipsy sailor who laughed loudly as his arms closed around her and then guffawed as she fought free.

Halfway down the dock she tripped over a piece of loose lumber and collided with a sailor who did not let her go, but held on to her arms and looked down at her in amazement and said as if he could not believe it, "Why, 'tis little Mattie Waite! What brings you to New Orange, Mattie?"

Flustered and startled, Mattie found herself looking into a familiar and surprised Bermuda face—the face of Flan O'Toole, who had set all the girls' hearts aflutter in St. George.

But it was a new and transformed Flan O'Toole, Mattie saw as she stepped back. For he now swaggered along sporting a dangerous-looking cutlass, and a brace of pistols were stuck in his belt. He had a red scarf wrapped round his sunny yellow head beneath a new-bought (or stolen) plumed hat and one big gold earring swayed jauntily from his left ear. There had been wild stories circulating about him in Bermuda, where it was whispered that he was "the wrecker's son"—but he had never looked like this. Piratical. Mattie regarded him in amazement.

"Why, I—" For a moment Mattie was so rattled that she couldn't for the life of her think what she was doing here in this faraway Dutch colony. "What are *you* doing here, Flan?" she cried. "Don't you know there's a war on between England and Holland, and yet you're standing in this strange place wearing all the pistols in the world?''

"Not quite all," corrected Flan, his dark eyes dancing. "Look about you. And our crew is welcome enough in port. Look behind you," he laughed. "You'll see our ship, the *Swan*, is flying the Dutch flag!"

"I can't believe it," cried Mattie, scandalized. "You're a traitor, Flan, you've gone over to the other side!"

"Nothing of the kind." Wide-booted legs spread apart, he stood solidly before her with the sunshine gold upon his hacked-off yellow hair, and flexed his broad shoulders with a slight swagger. A stooped elderly man carrying a basket of fish tried to squeeze between Flan and a stack of kegs; Flan did not give ground. The old man sighed and went around. Mattie did not notice. Her gaze was fixed on Flan accusingly, and he saw that in her eyes he was most reprehensible.

"We've only just docked," he told her easily, anxious to get that look off her face, for whatever he was now, he had danced in her father's house and drunk his wine and flirted with his daughters. "We're trading here, Mattie." His voice had gone low and conspiratorial so that it would not carry to a clot of nearby black-clad burghers. He gave her a smiling wink.

The impact of his words struck Mattie like a slap. "You've become a pirate!" she breathed, staring at him while a flight of seabirds wheeled overhead, clamoring after the man with the basket of fish.

Flan gave her an uncomfortable look. That sort of gossip—and he hardly thought Mattie would keep her opinion of him to herself— would not stand him in good stead in Bermuda when he got back there. In point of fact, the *Swan* was carrying wreckers' loot taken in Bermuda to whatever ports currently paid the highest price and wealthy New Orange, as New York was now called, was always a good port of call for such as they.

"Oh, nothing so romantic," he protested, lowering his voice a little as two wide-breeched gentlemen with gold money chains swinging from their lace-collared necks brushed by. " 'Tis only honest trade and the high prices these Dutch burghers will pay for goods that's led us here." Being chased off course by a prowling Spanish warship and then caught in the teeth of an Atlantic gale had also led them here, but Flan saw no reason to enlighten Mattie about that.

"Oh." Mattie didn't know whether to be glad or sorry. It would have been exciting to believe that Flan O'Toole had become a pirate—or a buccaneer; she wasn't quite sure what the difference was. But what had come to her suddenly was that here in the person of Flan O'Toole was salvation.

"Oh, Flan," she blurted out, ignoring the painted dockside whore who was just sidling by and who had captured Flan's admiring attention. "I have to get back to Bermuda. Can you take me back aboard your ship?"

Flan turned tardily from his hot inspection of the woman, who had paused and given him an arch look. She was now posing seductively with one striped satin-clad hip outthrust and her arms akimbo, displaying her majestic bosom. Flan, deciding that the bawd's face beneath its layers of ceruse and Spanish paper rouge was older than he'd thought—he was looking for someone young and kittenish to play with—hastily got back to what Mattie was saying. "Why, Mattie, what's amiss?"

"It's Arthur," admitted Mattie, her face reddening with shame. "He—he beats me, Flan."

The dockside whore heard that and gave a contemptuous snort. With a shake of her hennaed head she sidled on, past boxes and barrels, to confront a group of disembarking sailors with her broad hips and generous bust. Flan had already forgotten her.

He was digesting Mattie's remark slowly, and now he focused his attention on her more closely. There certainly was an ugly new bruise on Mattie's jaw and an older yellowing one beneath her right eye—and her eyes were red and swollen as if she might have been crying. "And you a bride," he muttered, shaking his head.

Mattie nodded miserably.

Flan remembered suddenly some of the things an overwrought Anna Smith had told him the day he sailed—about Arthur. "But what's Arthur Kincaid doing here?" he demanded, for there must be more to this. "I thought he'd be taking you to Boston?"

Mattie shivered. "He's still after Anna."

"Anna?" Flan's jaw dropped. "But Anna's in Bermuda!"

"No, she married right after you left. She lives in New Netherland now."

Anna—*married*! Flan felt rocked to his foundations. Used to being careless with things, with people, it had never occurred to him that Anna would not wait for him—after all he'd promised her he'd come back rich! "Who'd she marry?" he demanded harshly.

"You don't know him—his name is Danforth."

Flan shook his head. "Never heard of him," he said in a surly voice.

"Oh, you will if you stay here! He's a patroon with a great estate somewhere upriver."

A look of chagrin flashed over Flan's hard face. Chagrin, for he had for a wild moment hoped to come charging in and save Anna from Arthur and with that one bold stroke—win her back. But Anna, it seemed, was held in strong hands. "Rich, is he?" he growled, well aware that such as he could hardly expect to lure away a rich man's wife.

"Yes. Oh, Flan, I'm so afraid of Arthur—I'm afraid he'll kill me!" That this blinding new fear came from Mattie's guilty knowledge that she had cuckholded her husband, Flan had no way of knowing. But the very real terror in Mattie's voice reached him.

"We couldn't take you on the *Swan*," he reflected, remembering uneasily the kind of men who manned her—not the kind of men timid little Mattie could deal with. Nor would he, he knew with honesty, be able to protect her from them. "And, anyway, we'll be here three weeks and more, for we're determined to get the best prices we can and that takes time—and we made a slow voyage, the crew is tired and needs rest." What he meant—although he didn't say it to this hurt-looking child-woman in her frumpy pink gown— was that the crew were entirely delighted with New Orange's motley collection of dockside whores and it would probably be a month before their money had run out and they could be persuaded to face their trade again. "But"—so great was Mattie's disappointment, so accusing her big brown eyes that he found himself shuffling his feet and feeling as if he'd struck her himself—"it might be I could find you passage on some other ship, Mattie." He looked doubtful.

"Oh, any ship at all," cried Mattie. "And I don't care how roundabout she sails, just so long as I can get back home, away from Arthur!" She was hanging on to his flowing coarse cotton sleeve in her desperation.

"Have ye not tried to find passage yourself?"

"Oh, no, I'm afraid to. If Arthur found out—!"

Flan reached up under his hat brim and scratched his head. The gesture freed him from Mattie's clutching hand. "It's possible there'd be a ship sailing for one of the Dutch islands in the Caribbean that might be willing to stop and let you off at Bermuda—not St. George, perhaps, but somewhere along the coast, maybe Sandys or one of the smaller islands where fishermen would find you."

"Oh, that would be fine—just so I could get back home, Flan!"

"But—" Flan's face grew solemn. "It will take money, Mattie, for they'd be taking a chance that some British warship might blow them out of the water."

"I'll have the money," promised Mattie bravely. Her mind was casting about wildly for just *how* she could get it. From Arthur's strongbox, that was it! She knew he carried a little metal strongbox nestled in the bottom of his heavy round-topped leathern chest—for she'd seen it. One night he'd taken the key—which he wore on a chain around his neck underneath his doublet—and gotten out some money and pocketed it. There were a number of coins in the box, gold coins. Some of them, she thought bitterly, were part of the meager dowry her parents had been able to thrust into Arthur's greedy hands before they left. Well, that money would now take her back to Bermuda and into her parents' arms! Unused to coping with life, it never occurred to her to ask Nicolas for help. Terrified Mattie was running back home, back to her dull humdrum life, back to safety. "I'll have the money," she repeated more firmly.

"All right." Flan nodded is head thoughtfully. "Where are you staying?"

"The Green Lion."

Flan smiled down at her. His was a light nature and he had already partially recovered from the shock of Anna's marriage. "Just hang on," he told Mattie. "It may take a while but we'll get you home."

"Arthur—Arthur mustn't know," cautioned Mattie in a frightened voice.

"Nor will he," promised Flan, and took his leave with a bow, swaggering away from her, past barrels and ropes and produce and people, down the dock.

Mattie felt a sinking feeling steal over her as she watched him go. Would he do it? She'd never known him very well—it was Anna he cared for. For a moment she stood there in the bright sunshine of the dock biting her lip. Arthur cared for Anna too. . . .

Then she took a deep breath and lifted her chin, looking out to sea. Somewhere out there was Bermuda—she'd see it again. Of course, Flan would do it! Everybody said Flan O'Toole's people were wreckers, and no doubt part of the money she'd give him for ship's passage would stick to his fingers—but he'd do it, all right! Because there was money in it. . . .

Shy little Mattie was learning the ways of the world.

But time dragged by and Flan brought her no word.

Arthur spent most of his hours away from her. That was a blessing because Mattie had come to realize bitterly that her husband disliked her, would always dislike her. Only the nights were terrible, for it was then that Arthur staggered up the stairs drunk and took her with the same callous disregard he showed for the New Orange whores—whose company he much preferred.

The daylight hours passed pleasantly enough, for Mattie wandered about the narrow streets and picked over the merchandise that was offered for sale in the shops. She bought nothing, for Arthur kept strict control of the purse, but her smiling face was welcome in the shops, and smiles came her way when she strolled across the Heere Graft, or around the fort, looking up at the belfry of St. Nicolas Church, the top of which could be seen rising above the walls of the fort. Sometimes she studied with awe the great windmill, which seemed to be the town's main feature. And once or twice when she ate sizzling *rolliches*, savoring the delicious fried diced beef, or snacked on tasty *olykoeks*, or watched some smiling Dutch matron shooing her towheaded children from the immaculate stoop through the divided Dutch doors into one of the cheerful yellow brick step-gabled houses, she found herself wishing New Orange was New York again, and that she had come here under British rule and without Arthur, but with some better man, someone like—Nicolas, for she felt she could have been happy in this busy, friendly city.

Nicolas had sent her no word, she had not seen him again—nor did she now expect to. And that too would be a blessing, she told herself bleakly, because naught could come of such an affair.

Just when she had given up hope, she again ran into Flan, swaggering toward her inn. "I've news," he hailed her. "There's a ship, the *Gudrun*, that will be leaving soon for Curacao and her captain has promised that he will drop ye ashore somewhere in the Bermudas, no questions asked!''

"Oh, thank God," said Mattie fervently, for she had had a particularly difficult bout with Arthur last night. She had protested something he did and he had literally kicked her out of bed. Her bottom was still painful to sit upon and she had eaten her breakfast standing up.

"So if ye'll just give me the money, I'll pay for your passage." Smiling, Flan named a staggering sum; he was quite offhand about it, for was not Arthur known to be well-to-do? Flan assumed that Mattie would pay in gold, or at least that her jewels and pin money would fetch the price of passage.

Mattie recoiled at the price. "I'll—have it for you later," she told him hurriedly.

"Well, don't wait too long," he cautioned. "For although the *Gudrun*'s captain means what he says, he'll hold his ship in port no longer than he has to, to get unloaded and take on a new cargo."

"I won't," promised Mattie, feeling panic steal over her.

She went back to the inn with her feet dragging. It was going to be terribly difficult to get the key to Arthur's strongbox away from him. He slept with it around his neck and she was always afraid to touch him, for any touch merited a cuff and a full awakening meant she would be subjected again to his brutal carnal passions.

She need not have worried about it, for she was not destined to give Flan the contents of Arthur's strongbox.

When she returned to the Green Lion, Arthur was waiting. And with him her heart nearly lurched from her chest at sight of him and her face paled—Nicolas. A tawny-suited Nicolas who gave her a bland smile and a low courtly bow and said, "How soon can you be ready, mevrouw?"

"Ready for what?" faltered Mattie.

"Van Rappard here has come to fetch us upriver," explained Arthur tersely. "We are leaving within the hour."

Mattie turned with a look of frightened appeal to Nicolas.

"I have a sloop waiting for us," he told her, smiling. "We go upriver. There is no need to worry, mevrouw, it will be but a short voyage."

And so Mattie lost her chance to escape. But now that Nicolas was here she was not so sure she wanted to escape.

Windgate on the Hudson,
Winter 1673

CHAPTER 31

At Windgate the masquerade ball that would open the winter season
along the river—and truly it would be *the* event of the year, for
Windgate was a glamorous place that would inevitably be gossiped
about and no parties had been held there for a long time—was in full
swing.

The guests were wearing masks now, those who had arrived
earlier and changed into their costumes in the spacious upstairs
rooms (the ladies with the help of their maids, who were excited by
this great event), as well as those late-arriving guests who were
disembarking steadily from the fast river sloops that the Dutch
settlers boasted were the fastest river transportation in the world. A
variety of costumes greeted Georgiana's eyes and, beside her, as
they stood to welcome their guests, Brett murmured to her the names
of those he recognized.

That black bear there, limping slightly as he leaned upon his cane,
was Dr. Pos—he would come in handy if any of the guests ate or
drank too much. That elegantly dressed pair in black velvet were the
Van Rensselaers—the Dutch patroon had asked him if he didn't
think he looked a fool in that outmoded ruff his wife had forced on
him, insisting that if she could cope with an enormous wheel
farthingale, *he* could cope with a ruff! He had congratulated Brett on
his good sense in declining to wear a costume, saying that as host he
had no need to. Georgiana, at odds with him of late, had not

protested, and he looked dignified and forceful in the same clothes he had worn to the ten Haers' ball.

A late-arriving foursome swept in from their sloop. Georgiana had no need to have *them* identified for her; they were undeniably the ten Haers and with them Nicolas. Rychie and Huygens were resplendent in red satin trimmed in wide black velvet scallops. Both of them sported wide black hats laden with scarlet plumes and scarlet masks—but their identity was given away by the distinctive color of Rychie's heavy sweep of saffron hair. The same held true of Katrina, whose saffron hair was heavily adorned with brilliants and who was even more violently attired in saffron satin and black velvet stitched into a domino design, her black mask bejeweled and her huge sweeping hat laden with saffron plumes.

Nicolas lounged in beside Katrina. He was wearing—surprisingly— not the tawny velvets and saffron plumes he usually affected but a plain black suit above his wide spurred boots. Indeed he was hardly in costume at all. But he had tied a black silk scarf across the lower part of his face and stuck a brace of pistols in his belt, which gave him the look of a brigand—which she supposed he was emulating. His short black cloak was worn rakishly over one shoulder but he hardly stood out in a gathering where wreathed heads and Roman togas rubbed elbows with pirate captains sporting a single gold earring and a brace of cutlasses—there was even one fairly good replica of the French king in pink and coral satins.

Even had not his merry blue eyes and the obsessive proximity of Katrina ten Haer given him away, Georgiana would still have recognized Nicolas instantly from his distinctive swagger and from the golden hair that cascaded down to his shoulders from beneath his plain black hat. He was having some kind of argument with Katrina as they approached and her saffron head was turned, the better to castigate him. From snatches of the argument that reached her, Georgiana gathered that Nicolas must have arrived on some other sloop (probably chasing some pretty girl, she guessed in amusement) and that Katrina had feared she would have no escort. Katrina's flow of invective ceased abruptly when she thought she had come within earshot of her hostess and she closed her mouth with a snap.

Greeting them, Georgiana had an urge to ask Nicolas what had quenched his spirits that he should be so soberly garbed among the resplendent guests, but she did not. Brett was watching her closely and she was certain he would not approve of such levity on her part with a man who was bent on taking the very roof from over their heads.

But if Katrina ten Haer hoped to outshine the other guests, she would have difficulty, thought Georgiana. For most of the ladies had chosen to wear their best and add only a mask to complete their costumes—the rooms were filled with satin and damask and rich velvets and laces and the scent of musk and lavender. And there was a scattering of wildly overdressed imitation gypsy lasses, a flamenco dancer or two, and even one Far Eastern costume complete with turban and multicolored veils.

She saw Katrina start, saw her deep brown eyes widen, and turned to see Erica Hulft trailing down the wide stairway.

Erica was elegantly gowned in tangerine velvet trimmed with clusters of ermine tails and brilliants at the shoulders of her big puffed virago sleeves. A spiderweb of delicate black lace spilled from the cleavage of her breathlessly low décolletage. She entirely eclipsed poor Govert Steendam, who followed her meekly down the stairs looking—for all his gray hair and dignity—like an elderly lackey who might have gained his stooped shoulders and stiff walk in her family's service. Georgiana wondered if Erica had deliberately contrived this effect, for she had added a dull maroon doublet to Govert's rich black velvets and the effect was strangely like livery. Erica herself was wearing the smallest mask in the room—a black lace mask so tiny that no one could fail to know that this elegant lady was Erica Hulft. She had powdered her fox-brush hair in imitation of the ladies of the French court and added a black court plaster beauty spot to one peachbloom cheek. Her cheeks were slightly flushed and her amber eyes sparkled. The effect might have been achieved by rouging with Spanish paper, but however she had achieved it, she looked wonderful. Georgiana hated her.

She herself might have stood elegantly gowned beside her tall husband to receive her guests, but instead Georgiana had chosen— she who had stood out from all the others as a woman of gold the colorful ball at Haerwyck—to wear the simplest gown in the room.

She was dressed as a shepherdess—a slightly unreal shepherdess with voluminous skirts of heavenly blue silk, a breathtaking décolletage that just skirted her nipples with taut folds of delicate white cambric barely managing to conceal her round breasts. Her big white puffed virago sleeves were caught at the elbows with sky blue silk ribands and spilled a foam of white ruffles at the elbows that cascaded down over her slender forearms. A dark blue V-shaped "corselet" was laced in front to further emphasize her slender waist and delightful figure, and her wide blue skirts were gathered up into matched panniers at each side to reveal full white ruffled petticoats shorter than anybody's in the room, that displayed her sheer blue silk-stockinged ankles and dainty slippers. Her burnished gold hair was caught up artfully with sky blue silk ribands and she carried a long shepherd's crook with a large blue silk bow tied onto it.

"All you need now is a sheep," said Katrina ten Haer spitefully as she greeted her hostess.

Georgiana laughed indulgently, as if Katrina had paid her a compliment. She was delighted at Katrina's chagrin and felt she had done the right thing, for once again her shepherdess costume was the most outstanding in the room—at the ten Haers' her gown had stood out for its color, this time it stood out for its graceful simplicity.

"Perhaps Nicolas will play woolly lamb to my shepherdess and let me guide him around the floor with my shepherd's crook?" she suggested lazily to annoy Katrina.

Nicolas laughed and Georgiana could hear Katrina berating him as they were swept away from her by newly arriving guests, this time a pair of green-clad foresters accompanied by a blue-eyed young girl wearing a beaded white buckskin Indian bridal costume, and dangling necklaces of wampum.

But the new arrivals were dwindling away now; Brett had entered into deep discussion with Huygens ten Haer some distance away. Nicolas (escaping from Katrina's tongue-lashing, Georgiana thought in amusement) had made his way back to her.

"Did you know your shepherdess costume is a favorite of Nell Gwyn's?" he murmured. "And I've heard 'tis King Charles's favorite to *see* her wear—next to dressing her as a boy in doublet and hose and showing her pretty legs to the hips. Tell me, will you be wearing something like that at the next masquerade ball you give? For I will be sure to attend!"

"You do get around, Nicolas," laughed Georgiana, glad of this respite from meeting strangers—and those who only looked like strangers in their outlandish costumes. "First the French court and now the English! And you are so conversant with kings' mistresses that you even know their favorite gowns! No, I will *not* be wearing doublet and hose to any parties—Brett would disown me and every lady in the place would turn their backs on me as a loose woman!''

"A pity." He gave her a wicked smile—she could tell from the way his blue eyes crinkled even though she could not see his mouth with that black silk kerchief obscuring his face. " 'Tis my belief your legs would outshine Nellie's."

"You're not apt to find out," she told him merrily. "And you'd best stop this discussion of my legs before Brett turns from talking to Huygens and hears you! I think he'd take it amiss—especially after walking in unannounced and finding you draping me in diamonds! By the way, I notice Katrina isn't wearing her necklace. Are you two at outs again? I heard her snarling at you as you arrived."

"Katrina has misplaced the necklace—or lost it altogether," he told her blandly. "She strews things about as badly as her mother."

"She must be brokenhearted, since 'twas you that gave it to her," Georgiana rallied him. "Perhaps she was urging you to replace it and that was the nature of your argument?" she teased.

"She was angry because I have been sojourning downriver in New Orange and chose to catch a ride in another sloop rather than accompany Katrina and her family here."

"But you came in with them," objected Georgiana.

"I waited on the pier till they arrived," he admitted. "Else Katrina might have seized one of these pistols which mainly constitute my costume and shot me dead with it!"

They both laughed.

"If you could resist answering my sallies in kind and manage *not* to be amused when I suggest your role as woolly lamb to my shepherdess, Katrina might be kinder to you!"

Nicolas gave a deep theatrical sigh. "My heart is in the right place," he insisted with mock melancholy. " 'Tis only my devil's tongue that's out of order sometimes."

"I can well believe it," she said, her eyes dancing. "You're so somber tonight, Nicolas," she teased, "with those black clothes. Surely you must have borrowed them, for they certainly aren't your usual style and give far too sober an effect to suit your disposition! Or can it be you've suffered some tragedy of which we haven't been apprised? A devoted mistress has left you for another, perhaps?"

Brett, having finished his discussion with Huygens, caught the tail end of Georgiana's outrageous remark and gave her a warning look. He was faultlessly dressed in dove gray velvet and looked every inch the patroon he was, Georgiana thought with a pang. But she was still very angry with him, for nothing had been resolved about Erica Hulft. Indeed Erica might get rid of Govert on some pretext and remain as their guest until the river—or hell—froze over, for all she knew. She gave Brett an airy look and turned to smile fondly at Nicolas, hoping that would make him jealous.

It did. With a black frown, Brett turned to answer a question put to him by Dr. Pos, perspiring in his bearskins.

"You'd best get lost among the crowd," Georgiana whispered.

"I do agree." Nicolas's blue eyes crinkled and she knew that he was giving her a sunny smile, flashing below his black kerchief. In point of fact he had worn this black garb so he would be less visible in the dark—he would sink into the shadow of trees, for instance, without notice. Georgiana would not have been smiling had she known the real reason behind Nicolas's somber costume.

The music struck up. It was provided by the smiling daughter of one of the downriver Dutch burghers, who was proficient on the spinet, and the wailing strings of one of the house servants who had practiced by night in the attic servants' quarters on the viola. Brett claimed Georgiana to lead out the dancers and Nicolas went off to look for Linnet.

She was not hard to find. She was lurking in the hall watching for him.

"Did you succeed in making the arrangements I asked you to make?" he asked her.

Big-eyed, Linnet nodded. She wondered what would happen if she were to walk into that drawing room the moment the music stopped, step out onto the floor and dramatically announce her betrothal to Nicolas. She put the thought away. Nicolas had asked her for secrecy and she would keep their secret.

"Good. And do you have the packet for me?"

Linnet nodded again and gulped. The diamond pendant around her throat, well hidden by her chemise and collar, felt suddenly cold against her skin. She did not know why she should feel so but she felt *bought*. She pushed the thought away from her. Nicolas was her betrothed, even though the world did not yet know it; she owed him unswerving loyalty—even against her better judgment, even against her conscience.

"I have it," she whispered, stiffening as a couple dressed as dominos danced out into the hall. "Here." She leaned against the wall and managed to slip him the packet with a quick flirt of her skirt to hide the gesture. Instantly his swift fingers slid the packet inside his doublet. He would read its contents later.

"You have done well," he murmured, "but the most important part is yet to come. Meet me in the upstairs hall in five minutes and explain exactly what you and Georgiana have arranged."

Linnet was upstairs in four minutes. In five more she had told him all she knew.

Nicolas was content. He could not have bettered Georgiana's plan himself.

"What—what do you intend to do?" Linnet asked timidly, for she did not like the wolfish gleam in his blue eyes.

"That is not for you to know," he said sternly. "Just remember this: whatever happens, you must keep a close mouth about it, do not involve me in anything. Remember, *our future depends upon it*!"

Linnet gave him back an unhappy look. She yearned to insist upon an answer but she did not dare. Nicolas was gentry and affianced bride or no, she found it hard to step over the barrier between master and servant. He gave orders, she followed them. So it had been all her life. And tonight—even though curiosity and guilt both ate at her—was no exception. She subsided.

"And now we won't see each other again for a few days," Nicolas told her.

"But—" She would have protested, so disappointed was she, but the sudden flash of anger in his blue eyes forbade it.

"I will be back for you," he said testily. "If you doubt it, consider where you are—Windgate. Do you think I will go away and forget Wey Gat?"

No, she did not think so. She cast her eyes down. "I will do as you bid," she mumbled.

"Good." Satisfied she would obey him, Nicolas gave her rump a quick familiar pat. "That's a good girl. Mouth tight shut, don't believe anything you hear, and I'll see you in a week or two."

Thoroughly unhappy now, Linnet watched him go, swinging

jauntily down the shadowy upstairs corridor toward the main stairway. He had left her without even a kiss! When all the time she had been hoping—yes, even planning!—that he would sweep her into one of the guest bedrooms and latch the door and they would try out the featherbed before those who were supposed to sleep in it this night got the chance!

Suddenly it came to her that he had said he would be gone a week or more, but had said nothing about returning the packet—Georgiana might miss it, there would be an uproar, she might be blamed! She ran down the corridor after Nicolas.

He heard her feet pattering after him and stopped, turned about. "What now?"

"The packet," she gasped. "What about the packet?"

"I will return it to you before I leave," he told her smoothly. "Do not worry about it. Just show us what a magnificent skater you are and remember—I will be watching."

Somewhat mollified, Linnet stood and watched him turn the corner to go downstairs. After Nicolas had seen her skate, she told herself confidently, he would be so thrilled he'd want to return to her at once; perhaps he'd even spend the night with her in the servants' quarters, slipping in through the darkness. For she was sure to shine on the ice. Her life long, she'd been known as a glorious skater. Daydreaming, she leaned against the wall until a group of chattering ladies sailed by looking for their maids.

Nicolas, meanwhile, had gone downstairs; there was someone he must see.

Almost everyone was dancing now, with the exception of some of the older guests like Govert Steendam and Dr. Pos. Erica Hulft was being whirled around the floor by an energetic Dutch schoolmaster who was overjoyed to be dancing with her, but her gaze was on Brett, now dancing with a pouting Katrina ten Haer. Georgiana had excused herself to go and speak to cook, for after the ice dancing there was to be a late supper, and now that she was back in the drawing room her gaze drifted over the dancers. The many candles from the chandelier and wall tapers picked out a variegated crowd. Some of the costumes were beautiful, some garish, some—like Dr. Pos's bearskin—rather unpleasant. And one—her gaze focused suddenly on a black hood of coarse material with only slits for the eyes that fell down over the shoulders, and she shivered. That was an executioner's hood. Looking at it one could almost hear the whisper of the axe. Impossible to tell who was wearing it; its owner was wearing a long black cloak that swept the floor and black gauntlet gloves. She wondered who the executioner was; certainly she and Brett had not greeted anyone garbed like that. Probably some late arrival who had come while they were dancing. Conscious of the executioner's glittering eyes watching her through the slits in that black hood, she moved toward him like a dutiful hostess, meaning— in spite of her revulsion for his costume—to welcome him to Windgate. He moved on through the crowd. Somehow there were always people between them. She decided not to chase him around the room. Allowing herself another slight shudder of revulsion at his costume, she turned back to her other guests.

The eyes of the executioner followed her malevolently as she turned away, for those eyes belonged to Arthur Kincaid, who had managed to slip into the house by mingling with a group of late arrivals who had come in during the dancing. He had to conceal a tremor of rage as he watched Georgiana strolling through the crowd across the room, a dainty picture in her blue and white shepherdess costume. Nearby a lady tapped him with her fan and said something. To her casual pleasantry Arthur muttered something inaudible and brusquely went his way, for he was shaken again by Georgiana's beauty, which he had not remembered as so dazzling by half, even though he had alternately raped her or beaten her every night in his dreams ever since he left Bermuda.

He had been amazed at the size and magnificence of Windgate— but that made no difference. Damnable wench, he *would* tame her! This marriage of hers was nothing—a sham. He'd not given his consent to it, and she was *his* bondswoman. True, he'd been forced to sign her over but any court in the land would promptly rectify that, seeing plainly it had been done under duress—certainly any Boston court would and that was where he meant to take her.

Detaching himself from the crush of milling guests, he leaned against the wall and imagined himself tearing that shepherdess dress from her luscious body. First he would jerk open that blue ribbon that held that dark blue corselet thing about her ribcage. The corselet would fall free; in his imagination he could see it strike the floor. Then he would insert his fingers in that breathtakingly low neckline, not minding if his nails left a red weal on those snowy breasts—his breath came faster for he yearned to feel her wince beneath his rough handling. As the material came away, tearing alike her bodice and the light chemise beneath it, she would scream—he licked his lips at the thought. But if she resisted—ah, if she resisted and she *would* resist—he would slap her cheeks until they were red as apples, knocking her head from side to side like a pendulum. He would seize that fetching mass of burnished gold hair, coming free from its pins and falling down about her shoulders under this treatment, and he would jerk her around by that hair to face him when she tried to run away; the blue ribands would fall out, sliding down her white shoulders and heaving bare breasts to tangle themselves in her tumbled skirts.

He would then address himself to those skirts, grasping them by the hem in one strong authoritative hand and tossing the whole of them violently over her head, where he would pinion her struggling arms with them—oh, he had it all worked out, every step. He had thought of little else these past weeks.

And then her flailing white legs—he was trembling all over now as in his imagination he went at them.

"Faith, have ye the ague?" muttered a familiar voice in his ear. "Ye're not sick, are ye?"

Arthur, half overcome with his violent visions and wanting to scream his disappointment at the speaker who had interrupted, for he had just begun his imaginary rape and wanted to bring it to a properly dramatic conclusion, came up out of the mists of fancy and realized that Nicolas was speaking to him.

"No, I'm not sick," he said in a muffled voice.

"Then come into a corner of the room where we can talk more freely under cover of all this hubbub."

Arthur followed, listened silently as Nicolas in an undertone outlined what Linnet had told him and how he proposed to proceed.

"You understand?" he asked impatiently when Arthur still did not say anything.

"Perfectly," mumbled Arthur in a sullen voice. He was still angry at having his lascivious musings interrupted.

Nicolas frowned at his sullen cohort. He wished unhappily that he could deal with someone less obnoxious than Arthur in this matter. But his sigh was lightened by a sudden cheerful thought—Arthur, unpleasant as he was, was the perfect person to shift the blame upon. And disliking Arthur as he did, it would be a joy to do it!

But contempt for Arthur's treatment of Mattie had made Nicolas underestimate Arthur. For all his bad manners and violent temper, Arthur was nobody's fool. All the way upriver he had been thinking deeply about what Nicolas proposed to do and he had come to the inescapable conclusion that Nicolas was planning to get what he wanted, disengage himself from the enterprise and let Arthur take the blame for whatever happened—in case something should go wrong.

With that in mind, he had come prepared for such an eventuality.

After Nicolas left him, he made his way to a back stairway. It was an easy thing with so many of the servants out front, to slip up them on silent feet and make his way to Georgiana's bedchamber. He found it by the simple expedient of heading toward the majestic front of the house and trying all the doors. The one in which he found her clothes would be hers, of course—and he knew he would have no difficulty in recognizing it by the sumptuous gowns it contained.

When he found it, he was aghast at its opulence. The gall of the woman—*his* bondswoman living in a luxury that he himself could not afford! A delicate night rail, so sheer he could have read print through it, lay casually tossed across a chair. The thought of Anna's pale tempting body encased in that half-transparent garment sent his nostrils flaring.

He finished his business and left.

The evening wore on. Ice dancing by moonlight had been promised and many of the younger guests and even some of the hardier older ones had brought their skates. Although the river was as yet unfrozen, many of them were familiar with the beautiful pond in the wooded area near the house. Some had seen the torches that were even now being set up to throw vivid light upon the scene, for the moon was proving unreliable, scudding back and forth behind the clouds and some of the more apprehensive guests were already muttering that it might become "a wild night with sleet and snow coming down from the north" and maybe they'd best cut their stay short and sail home before the river became a raging torrent that tossed sloops about like toy sailboats.

Amid the whirl of dancers and the pouring of wine, Erica Hulft had been drinking rather more than was good for her. Brett had rebuffed her, telling her that she was mad to risk alienating Govert Steendam by seeking him out so publicly, and in her anger she had prowled upstairs and clawed about in her things to find a certain piece of jewelry. Having found it, she stood smiling with wicked malice down upon it, before she clasped it around her neck. Then she picked up her fur-trimmed velvet cloak about her shoulders. She would go down and confront Brett, she told herself recklessly. She would insist that he stroll out across the snow with her—and Georgiana would miss him, and perhaps look out and see them together. . . . Or someone might tell her where Brett had gone and with whom—Katrina ten Haer could be counted on to do that. And she and Brett would return, laughing, out of the snow to find the child bride (for that was how Erica thought of Georgiana) standing in the hall in impotent fury, watching them make their entrance. Perhaps Georgiana would even make a scene, burst into tears, shout. Still smarting under Brett's rebuff, Erica relished the thought.

Downstairs, Georgiana decided that it was time for the ice dancing. The weather was looking unpredictable—they had best begin. She signaled to Linnet to join her and started upstairs—and met Erica Hulft on her way down.

Erica was a breathtaking sight in her fox-lavished apricot velvet cloak with her white powdered hair and that black court plaster beauty spot to show off the pallor of her sheer complexion. When Georgiana would have brushed on by, Erica stepped deliberately in front of her, blocking her way.

"Go on upstairs, Linnet," said Georgiana in irritation. "I'll be up in a minute. One of my guests"—her voice had an edge to it—"seems to require my attention."

Standing on a step above looking down at her, Erica laughed. "I had thought you'd be dressed in more queenly garb and wearing the van Rappard diamonds to down us all," she said with a slight curl to her lip. "And yet here you are—a mere shepherdess." She lifted her brows and looked bored.

"What do *you* know of the van Rappard diamonds?" demanded Georgiana, gone suddenly cold.

"Oh, I know a great deal about you, Georgiana." Erica shrugged aside her elegant furs for a moment and revealed about her neck, complementing the tangerine velvet of her gown, a necklace of pink fresh water pearls with heavy wrought silver links.

Georgiana drew in her breath. She had seen that necklace before—in Bermuda. And Erica had chosen to wear it here, in *her* house.

"I think you are wearing something that rightfully belongs to me," Georgiana said steadily. "And I think I know how you came by it."

Erica shrugged—Claes had sold her the necklace long ago, but not till she confronted him with Nicolas's story had he told her where it came from. She was in a mood to taunt and there was a lazy malice in her amber glance that was in no way diminished by her fragile black lace mask. "I think you have something that belongs to *me*, Georgiana, and I care not a whit how you came by him—I want him back."

For a long minute the two women stared at each other, with measuring glances.

Then, "You will never have him," said Georgiana, but her voice was unsteady.

"We will see," said Erica with careless confidence. "Life has many strange turnings. Perhaps I will win in the end."

Perhaps she will, thought Georgiana, and felt all the joy go out of the evening. "If you marry Govert Steendam," she warned Erica, "you will have to cease your pursuit of Brett. Steendam will never stand for it. He has a stern face."

Erica's laughter rippled. "I think I have frightened you," she said softly. "But do not worry, little Bermuda bride. I am not ready to take him away from you—not yet."

She swept on by and the implications of that remark swirled through Georgiana's brain as she hurried up the stairs to join Linnet. She felt humiliated—and glad no one had been in the hall at the time to hear the exchange between Erica and herself. She did not really know what to do about Erica, whose pattern, she could now divine, was to misbehave scandalously and then to repent and apologize gracefully—and expect to be forgiven. She was beginning to see what Brett must have gone through with Erica. What a chase she must have led him!

Perhaps, she thought, the situation would resolve itself. Perhaps Erica in her present reckless mood would become so incensed over the ice dancing that she would do something so rash and so irrevocable that it would wreck her with Brett.

Certainly it was to be hoped!

She found Linnet waiting for her in her bedchamber, where they both hastily changed into their rag doll costumes. Then they parted, Linnet creeping unobserved down the back stairs to make her way into the forested area and wait for Georgiana behind the big bush near the pond.

Georgiana meanwhile strolled down the front stairs unmasked, carrying her headdress with its thick yellow woolen braids and attached mobcap and mask in one hand, and with her skates slung negligently over her shoulder.

Those skates were the problem. They were rather strikingly made, there was only one pair like them, and they must be given to Linnet in the woods.

Numerous faces looked up as Georgiana moved down the stairs, for word that the ice dancing was about to commence had spread about and the guests had milled out into the hall. Brett was among them, and Erica, and Katrina ten Haer. Halfway down the flight, Georgiana paused and smiled down upon them all.

"I have promised you ice dancing," she cried merrily. "And to lead the way, I shall be first upon the ice. If you will all wait five minutes before you come out, I will be ready for you." While they watched, she fitted the headdress smoothly over her own burnished gold hair. "You shall see what a rag doll can do!" she promised them blithely.

Although the headdress with its long woolen braids was now firmly in place, she was still holding up with both hands the attached mask of loose white silk that was to come down over her face and be fitted into her collar, as she reached the bottom of the stairs.

She looked about her. "Here, will someone help me pin down this mask so that I will look like a *real* rag doll—and so that it will not blow up into my face when I skate and blind me when I execute a difficult turn? Or when I fly over something—for I warn you, I intend to close my little skating exhibition by leaping over three barrels, which are already in place; they were placed on the pond this afternoon."

A little murmur went through the onlookers. This Bermuda bride was going to leap *over three barrels*?

Georgiana was enjoying herself. "Perhaps you would help me pin down this mask, Katrina?" she asked sweetly. "Or you, Erica—I am sure you are very adept at handling sharp things!"

Brett stepped forward, barring their way. "*I* will pin down your mask," he said. She could see the concern in his face as he bent his big head down toward hers, but he pinned the white silk mask with its appliqued rosy cheeks of pink silk quite competently to her collar.

"Are you mad?" he muttered.

"Perhaps." He could feel her shoulders shrug.

He was still working with the pins. His lips were very close to her ear; nothing he said could carry to the assembled company about them. "Let me join you, Georgiana," he murmured. "We will dance together. I will whirl you about as I skate so that your skates barely graze the ice. I have often leaped over six barrels—I can easily carry you over three."

Georgiana soood there regarding him for a moment.

It was a handsome offer—but it had come too late. Her plans were already made and Linnet was out there waiting.

"I can do this by myself, thank you," she told him crisply and brushed past him. The guests parted to let her pass.

Hoping desperately that Brett would not follow her, she went out the door and out into the white moonlight, made her way into the trees. Behind her the crowd muttered, but she felt they would wait the allotted time if only to see what their surprising hostess had in store for them.

In the trees she met Linnet and handed over the skates.

"Make Erica Hulft wish she were dead!" she told Linnet breathlessly. "It is all I ask of you—and if you do it, I will give you not only the skates but your choice of my petticoats!"

That was a grand offer indeed, for in New Netherland a girl's fortune was often counted by the number of petticoats she owned. They were of the richest materials, hand-worked and embroidered, and Georgiana's were remarkably handsome.

"I'll do you proud," promised Linnet warmly. "They won't never have seen nothing like me on the ice!" She told herself that while she might have played the mistress false by giving Nicolas the packet, at least she could do *this* for her—and hadn't Nicolas said this would make up for it?

Georgiana settled herself in the big bush as near to the frozen pond as she could. She'd have a poor view from here but she dared go no closer. And from this vantage point she could quickly rise up and change places with Linnet when the girl finished her ice dance.

Everyone was pouring out of the house now. They came by a slightly different and more accessible route, as Georgiana had anticipated, so they did not pass by her hiding place. Instead they were congregated on the other side of the pond. There was a lot of noise and laughter and some clinking of carried skates coming across the ice to her, but Georgiana ignored them. Her gaze, peering through the snow-covered bushes, was riveted on the place where Linnet, now seated on the snowy bank, was fastening on her skates.

She had no inkling at all that anything was wrong. Concentrating on Linnet, with noise and laughter floating to her across the ice, Georgiana never heard the soft footsteps in the snow behind her.

She only knew that a strong hand suddenly closed over her throat, choking her, and a soft tauntingly familiar voice murmured in her ear, "If you scream I'll send a knife through your ribs."

With fear striking through her head like a great gong, she felt a gag thrust into her gasping open mouth. She saw his face then, for the first time: the black enveloping hood, with narrow slits for a pair of glittering eyes.

Georgiana felt blackness stealing over her; she was near to fainting.

It was the executioner.

Then a dark cloak was thrown over her and she was lifted up and carried away.

Gathered merrily around the icy pond, the guests in their masquerade costumes had no hint of what had happened.

CHAPTER 32

All the way upriver, Mattie saw not a bit of scenery. The majestic Palisades slipped by unnoticed, the high rounded hills, the meadow valleys, the forested shores. Mattie saw—for that was where her gaze was focused—only Nicolas's broad shoulders as he stood in the prow of the sloop, only Nicolas's brilliant smile as he turned to regard her. She heard, she thought, she dreamed only of Nicolas.

For the moment, back in his spellbinding presence, she had forgotten her immortal soul and thought only of the man—winning, desirable.

"We must be careful, Mathilde, "he whispered, when he managed to catch her alone on the deck. "For your husband may grow suspicious if you follow me about with your eyes."

"I will—be more careful," Mattie choked, wondering if he could hear her heart thumping.

A flight of birds streamed by. Mattie did not see them. She was staring up into Nicolas's face—and she had her heart in her worshipful brown eyes.

Nicolas was looking down at her. Her small pale face disturbed him. Connoisseur of women that he was, he was only too aware that Mattie was not really beautiful. And he knew himself for a man who loved beauty only too well. Many a wench gained fleeting beauty by night, he knew, but—this was day. What was it that he saw in this frail waif? he asked himself by morning's light—and could not answer. Yet something about her tore at him, made him feel shame for what he was doing, and a protectiveness he had always felt foreign to his nature. He wrenched himself away from these dangerous thoughts. Kincaid should not have brought her along, he told himself irritably. There was danger to the venture. And yet—he looked down into those brown eyes and knew that while he lived Mattie would have at least one protector.

Mattie, almost afraid to breathe, sensed the turmoil in him. She kept waiting for him to say something, make some declaration but he did not.

"Why are we going upriver so furtively and in such haste?" she asked, troubled, for she had noted that they did not pull in at any of the landings nor hail any of the passing river traffic.

"Your husband goes to collect his bondswoman and I my rightful inheritance," Nicolas told her with his caressing smile.

"Anna?" cried Mattie. "We are going to seize Anna?" Her alarm mounted—and it was an unselfish alarm: for Anna, her friend, for Nicolas, her lover. She seized Nicolas's tawny velvet sleeve. "Oh, do let us go back," she beseeched. "Try to make Arthur see that he is mad to do this. Brett Danforth will never allow Anna to be taken. And besides, he has papers to prove—''

"You are not to concern yourself about these matters, Mathilde," Nicolas cut in soothingly. "I give you my word that I will not harm the lady of Windgate. All will be well, you'll see."

Used to being subservient to men, Mattie fell silent. But in her heart she doubted it. All would not be well—all was never well where Arthur was concerned. She felt he would bring the world down on their heads. Shivering, she drew her red woolen shawl about her and thanked in her heart the Leighton sisters of Philadelphia who had forced upon her this woolen petticoat when she had made them handsome gifts. It was plain and sensible but—hidden under a brave pink taffeta one, for with Nicolas aboard Mattie had elected to wear her best dress for the voyage—at least it was keeping her warm!

Arthur came out and engaged Nicolas in conversation. They moved away from her. Left to her own devices, Mattie fell to gloomily watching the shore. She was imagining swordplay and perhaps pistol shots if Arthur made good his effort to take Anna from her husband.

She grew even more alarmed when, as they approached Haerwyck, she was ordered abruptly to her cabin.

"But why?" cried Mattie.

Arthur, who was of no mind to explain anything to his despised young bride, stepped forward to drag her there by force, but Nicolas stepped smoothly between them.

"We do not want you to be seen at either Haerwyck or Wey Gat," he explained. "We are nearing the domain of the English patroon, and he and his bride could be out prowling the river."

"But—Anna would be glad to see me!" protested Mattie in bewilderment.

"Even so, Mathilde. 'Tis best you not be seen with us. Trust us in this small matter." He smiled down at her and Mattie, who gave him all her trust, meekly submitted and went into her cabin.

And there she remained as they sailed first by Haerwyck and then past the frowning mansion of Windgate.

They tied up at dusk on the river's eastern bank and Mattie came out of her cabin to see from the deck a small stone farmhouse, built low in the Dutch style and with a thatched roof. It was Jack Belter's *bouwerie* but Mattie was not to know that. Jack came out and walked down to the river. Silently he greeted Nicolas, who went ashore with Arthur, and there was some conversation she could not hear, nor did she see the gold coins change hands, for big Jack was a man who believed in getting payment in advance.

On shore the three of them talked for a while. Then Belter led out the two horses he was lending them for this venture and Arthur and Nicolas went to get Mattie. Without introduction they brought her into the cottage, where big Jack Belter gave her an indifferent nod—slender Mattie was not his type; he liked big blowsy women with breasts like cantaloupes.

"Ye'll wait for us here," directed Arthur.

"I thought ye'd be warmer in the cottage," explained Nicolas. "Ye'd near freeze on the sloop, and there's a fire here."

Mattie gave him a grateful look and moved toward the stone hearth where flames were shooting up into the stone chimney. She was not used to consideration, and by itself that was enough to warm her. Silent now, she looked around her with apprehensive eyes at the neglected room, at the battered gumwood *kas*, the sagging cupboard doors. Obviously, this cottager did not have a wife. She wondered glumly what they were doing here.

Nicolas and Arthur changed into gloomy black clothing and Nicolas tied a black silk scarf around the lower part of his face while Arthur put on an enveloping black hood with narrow slits for the eyes that made him look for all the world like an executioner.

Mattie shivered. She was afraid to ask where they were going dressed like that.

On the torchlit pond at Windgate, Linnet, having fastened her skates, and completely unaware of Georgiana's abduction, stood and faced the crowd. She felt wildly excited for Nicolas was in that crowd and she so wanted to shine before him.

She glided out upon the smooth ice—surefooted now as she never was in her awkward leather shoes, once again the best skater in her village—and perhaps the best skater in all of Yorkshire, many had told her so.

With light dance steps to tantalize her audience she circled the pond, then raced around it gathering speed. Now a fast swing into the center to execute a flawless figure eight and then another, and then she was gliding backward like a swan, with one leg and both arms extended. Now she was racing toward the crowd again and effortlessly whirled into a spin that brought gasps from the assembled group on the bank. Linnet spun like a top and then suddenly she was moving closer to the ice, still spinning, crouching with one leg extended as she whirled about. As she rose from that, she did another turn around the pond, gathering speed, and took a long leap high across the ice that swirled her light skirts up around her hips and displayed the full length of her bright red-and-white stockings. The crowd around the rim of the pond broke into appreciative applause.

Hearing *that* should please the mistress, thought Linnet complacently. And now to give them steps and figures they'd never have seen and wouldn't expect—no, none of them would, for she was the only person she knew who could do them, she'd *invented* them, she had!

Mindful of the effect her rag doll costume must be creating upon the crowd, Linnet seemed to collapse—almost but not quite—upon the ice. She swayed as if she were a willow reed, bending this way and that as she glided on one skate so that her long yellow wool braids sometimes touched the ice—and suddenly she executed a perfect backflip and landed on one skate blade, whirled into a graceful pirouette and swirled into a deep curtsy.

There were gasps from the audience. Men were known to take great dangerous leaps, but for a woman to do so! And to execute intricate steps they had never seen before! They leaned forward in fascination.

"She has learnt this in *Bermuda*?" Rychie ten Haer's big penetrating voice rose harshly over the excited murmurs of approbation. "And I was told there was no ice there!" she cried indignantly.

Linnet heard and laughed inwardly. They'd see what a Yorkshire girl could do, she told herself with a fierce joy. She was born to skate—ah, would that there was money in it! But a prize or two was all she had won, for golden purses were reserved for horse races and archery contests and such—not for girls who flew like butterflies across the ice.

Reveling in her skill, Linnet whirled, she stamped, she pirouetted in the air, she raced across the ice for the sheer joy of it, winging like a bird. She was a wondrous sight out there and the crowd felt it, went along with it, loved her. Only Brett stood frowning and puzzled. And the ten Haer woman looked indignant, Rychie muttering that no one had better ever try to tell *her* that Bermuda was not covered with ice and snow in winter! And Erica Hulft, standing alone in her fox-lavished fur cloak for Govert had elected not to join her in the ice dancing, looked as if she could bite through a nail at that moment quite effortlessly.

Flying along on her skates, Linnet was entirely carried away by the excitement, the flickering light of the torches, this dazzling crowd of costumed aristocrats who watched her performance and shouted encouragement and applauded wildly. She could not see Nicolas but she was sure he was there among them—and proud of her.

One person was not applauding. Erica Hulft stood frowning on the bank. Like the rest she never doubted that it was Georgiana who whirled and swooped before them—for had she not seen that headdress adjusted with her own eyes? That snip from Bermuda—how had she learned to skate like that? She flashed a look at Brett, saw amazement written upon his face—so the child bride had surprised him too!

And she had his full attention!

That was what hurt. She had counted on the ice dancing, at which she was adept, to bring Brett's wandering attention back to her—but that was not likely, for when this was over she knew everyone would crowd around that rag doll, marveling, congratulating her.

Erica, who had never doubted that she could command everyone's attention above all others on the ice, clenched her white kerchief in her hand and ground her teeth and wished the girl from Bermuda would end up with two broken legs.

Suddenly her face cleared. The cold bracing night air had cleared her head and set her wits to working. She was looking at those three barrels, which Wouter, under protest, had set up on the ice this afternoon. *Georgiana had said that at the end of her performance she would leap over those barrels!* Head on one side, with the instincts of an expert skater, Erica calculated the angle from which that flying rag doll would leap over them, exactly where she would land.

With her gaze never wavering from the figure now skating on the opposite side of the pond, Erica reached down and picked up a handful of snow, made it unobtrusively into a snowball, which she then wadded up into her kerchief—that would give it body so she could fling it where she wanted. Narrow-eyed, she considered the path the skater now must take. Erica was rather nearer the barrels than the others. Liking to stand out, she had sought one end of the straggling crowd rather than the middle. And Erica, who had seen the trick of barrel leaping before although she had never herself attempted it, never doubted that for a wild finale, that skimming rag doll would leap across the barrels. The torchlight cast a shadow across the ice where it touched the barrels—at just the point where the flying skater should be skating her fastest, gaining speed to become airborne. While all eyes were riveted on Linnet, who was just then executing a difficult maneuver that caused her to whirl in the air before landing triumphantly on one flying skate, Erica tossed out the white kerchief.

Propelled forward by the snowball's weight, it landed just where Erica meant it to and spread out innocuously upon the ice—death trap for a skate blade.

Now the rag doll was skating fast, gaining speed. She would need all her power to carry her in her relatively awkward costume over that row of barrels.

Erica saw Brett start forward as he guessed the skater's intention to jump over the barrels, but it was too late to stop her. The crowd on the bank roared hoarsely as the rag doll, skimming now in the torchlight, made her last mad dash toward the waiting barrels.

Too late Linnet saw her danger. She had already checked out the ice before going out on it. The barrels were positioned exactly where she wanted them. Her gaze was riveted on the barrels as she sped forward. She must fly aloft exactly—here.

The wind whipped her woolen braids about wildly and her mask was creeping up over her eyes. She gave it a violent jerk downward and—felt something snatch her foot. Her skate had tangled in the unseen kerchief in the shadow of the barrels.

With a wild scream Linnet tripped and plummeted directly toward the barrels, plowed into them headfirst. With her first contact with the barrels she lost consciousness, flying rag-doll limber across the ice, while the barrels rolled and tumbled every which way.

The shouts had taken on a different timbre now, cries of alarm from the men, screams of horror from the women. As one, the revelers rushed forward but it was Brett who reached the rag doll first, bending over her unconscious form as she lay in a crumpled heap. Erica glided forward, but as she bent to snatch up the kerchief, which had tangled around one of Linnet's skate blades, a big hand came down upon hers and pulled her away.

Erica looked up angrily. The big hand belonged to Govert Steendam, who had changed his mind about watching the ice dancing and arrived just in time to watch Linnet crash into the barrels.

"Come away," he said harshly. "We cannot help. Stay out of the way."

Erica knew she could not allow herself to be pulled away before she had the kerchief—but Govert's grip was too firm to break. As Govert urged her back a pace or two she cast a worried look down at the handkerchief tangled into Linnet's skate blade, for she knew it bore her initials and—knowing her former relationship with Brett—few would doubt who had managed to get it tangled up with the bride's skates.

Nobody watched Erica's enforced retreat, or indeed was even aware of it, because something new had been added.

Brett Danforth, his face ashen, had snatched the silken mask from the rag doll's face. Now he looked up accusingly. "This is not Georgiana!" he cried. "This is her serving maid, Linnet! Dr. Pos—where is that doctor?"

A deep sigh went over the group, to be supplanted by a speculative muttering. *What was going on? Why this spectacular charade on the ice? Where was the patroon's bride?*

Tugging off his somewhat shabby mask, the doctor in his black bearskin hobbled up on his cane—for Dr. Pos had a bad habit of tasting all of his own nostrums and medical concoctions and this mixture of unknown and often near-deadly chemicals had eventually crippled him.

"One side, one side," he gasped, pushing his furry way through the throng. "Let me see how the wench fares." He laid down his cane and went down awkwardly on one knee beside the fallen Linnet. Bending over, he peered at her head wound, felt of her pulse. "She is alive," he announced, as if he had made an important discovery.

"Of course she is alive," snapped Brett impatiently. "How badly is she hurt?"

As the doctor continued his examination, Brett reached down and freed the kerchief from the skate.

"This is what caused her to fall," he said, holding up the kerchief so that the crowd could see. His eyes caught the initials E. H. embroidered on a corner of that kerchief—Erica Hulft. Erica, standing with Govert a little distance away and watching every move, shrank back as Brett's stern accusing gaze transfixed her. She half expected to be denounced on the spot, but Brett's gaze turned to Govert, who stood anxiously by with the others, and without comment he stuffed the kerchief into his pocket.

Erica, weak with relief, almost collapsed against Govert.

"I asked you, how badly is she hurt?" Brett turned again to Dr. Pos.

"I cannot tell," sighed the doctor. "She may have cracked her skull. Her heart seems to be beating regularly enough." He winced suddenly. "What's this?" In trying to listen to Linnet's heartbeat, he had hastily torn aside her bodice and chemise—and caught his ear on the necklace. He grasped the thing that was tugging at his ear and the delicate gold chain came out glittering into the light, showy in the torchlight, with its teardrop diamond pendant winking at them.

"Why—why, she's wearing my necklace!" cried Katrina, springing forward to get a better look. "The one Nicolas gave me! However did she get it?"

Brett fingered the necklace and a muscle in his jaw jerked as he recognized the pendant and chain he had wrenched from his bride's throat all too recently.

"Are you saying the wench stole this necklace?" the doctor demanded.

"It matters not at the moment how she came by it," growled Brett. "The important thing is to bring her inside so that when she comes to she may speak to us and tell us what cursed folly led her into this."

Fear was beginning to gnaw at him—fear for Georgiana. She must have been watching this performance—faith, she could hardly have resisted watching! Why had she not rushed forward the moment she saw Linnet was hurt? Why was she not even now trying to save her maid's reputation by volunteering some reasonable explanation as to how Linnet had got the necklace? *Where was she?*

Katrina would have rushed up and snatched the necklace from the unconscious girl's neck, but her mother held her back. "Let Nicolas explain it," Rychie muttered. "Where *is* Nicolas?" She turned her head alertly to look about her.

"I don't see him," said Katrina sullenly. She had torn off her glittering black mask and her expression boded ill for Nicolas when she did find him.

Huygens ten Haer shouldered his way through the crowd. "What are the girl's chances?" he asked the doctor bluntly. As a magistrate he was aware that he might have to try this woman for theft; he was wondering if she'd make it to the trial.

Dr. Pos shook his head. "I cannot tell yet," he insisted. "But she should be wrapped well in blankets and kept warm and fed hot broth and her wound sponged. And"—he brightened—"if she does not come round soon, I have a new nostrum, a remedy, that I think may work!" Indeed, he had been eager to try this latest creation on someone—and here a golden opportunity had been presented, an unconscious victim who could not protest the concoction's foul smell or bitter taste.

Modern medicine would have feared his "remedy" more than the bone-cracking blow the girl had taken!

By now the servants had arrived, out of breath and slipping in the snow, for none had taken time to put on boots or pattens.

"Carry the wench in," Brett ordered tersely, "and do for her as the doctor tells you. I must look for Georgiana. Have any of you seen her?"

Open mouths gaped back at him; it was answer enough.

But a search of the vast rooms and echoing corridors of the entire house, even though it took a long while for it was thorough, did not discover the English patroon's missing bride.

It did turn up something else.

Lying on the blue and white coverlet of the big square featherbed in Georgiana's bedchamber, with one of Georgiana's white satin dancing slippers anchoring it down, was a scrawled note addressed to Brett.

A tremor went through Brett's big frame as he read the note. He crumpled it in one big hand and threw it at the fireplace as he stormed out.

The guests, who had crowded along to help search for the missing bride, parted to let him past—shrank back indeed, for the black scowl on his face seemed to spell doom for anyone fool enough to stand in his way.

He had hardly swept through the door before Katrina ten Haer, who had been following Brett about, as curiously as the other guests, ran forward. Almost igniting the lace ruffles that spilled from her black and saffron domino sleeves in her haste, she pounced upon the crumpled paper lying a hair's breath from the hot coals. She smoothed it out, scanned it and turned to her mother with a wail.

"Oh, why am I so unlucky? Georgiana has taken Nicolas away from me now!"

As alarmed as her daughter, Rychie snatched the note and gasped as she read it.

I am running away with Nicolas, the note read. *Windgate will not see me again.* It was signed with a flourish *Anna*.

But even as Rychie was exhibiting the note to those who crowded around, Brett was racing to the servants' quarters where Dr. Pos was ministering to Linnet in her rag doll costume. He brushed past the bearskin-clad doctor and seized the girl by the shoulders. Linnet had just opened her eyes and now she quailed to find herself looking up into the dark and furious face of her employer.

"Linnet," Brett growled, his fingers tightening meaningfully on her shoulders, "you will tell me *now* all that you know of this charade—and quickly before I decide to crack your head like an egg, injured or no!"

"Awr-r-r-r!" Linnet gave a choked wail that caused the bearskin-clad doctor to leap forward, expostulating with Brett.

Impatiently Brett pushed him aside. "This is between Linnet and me," he said coldly. "There's a note on my wife's bed saying she's run away with Nicolas van Rappard. Where has he taken her, Linnet? *Where*?"

Before him Linnet's young face seemed to break up and regroup into a mask of pain. She gave a low keening cry that pierced their eardrums, then shuddered away into a moan. "'Twas *her* he wanted," she lamented. "'Twas her all the time and not me. Oh, I should have known—the moment I saw him in that red cloak, *I should have known*!"

Reminding himself sternly that she'd been hurt, Brett fought back an urge to shake the truth from her. "*Where*, Linnet?" he demanded harshly.

But the girl seemed not to hear him. She was wrestling with her own private grief. "He told me he wanted to marry me," she mourned. "And that I'd be mistress of Windgate." Her voice broke. "I'd have been glad just to marry him and forget Windgate, I would." She came back to the present and her eyes filled with tears. "I've done a terrible thing, I have—helping him," she whispered. "I don't doubt ye'll have me whipped for it and 'tis right that you should but—oh, sir, I'll tell you everything, and if she's gone, I know where he's taken her!"

CHAPTER 33

For a long time, after Nicolas and Arthur had gone, Mattie sat apprehensively on a bench near the hearth across the room from Jack Belter, who lounged on his cotlike bed smoking a long clay pipe. At first she was so cold from her long river journey that she just sat and shivered; then as she got warm she relaxed. She looked around the room with its big stone hearth and roaring fire. Against that stone fireplace leaned a poker. If that big black-bearded creature who never spoke, just watched her silently from those evil slits of eyes, tried to rape her, she told herself she would pick up that poker and try to give a good account of herself.

Mattie need not have worried. She was not Belter's type. Although he was looking in her direction, he barely saw her. In his mind he was already spending the gold Nicolas had given him, spending it in a Dutch brothel in New Orange on a girl with big legs and a high shrieking laugh who had last time told him scornfully he "wasn't man enough for her." "I'll learn her," he was muttering to himself. Mattie heard and edged a little nearer the poker.

She seemed to spend hours like that, sitting cramped and frightened, and she was concentrating so desperately on Jack Belter's mumbled words that when the door of the cottage did at last swing open, she jumped up with a shriek that brought Belter to his feet with a curse.

Arthur came in glaring at her and dumped what looked to be a large black bundle with striped legs and black felt boots sticking out, into a chair. A moment later he snatched off the dark cloak he had thrown over Georgiana's head. With it came the silken mask and the long yellow braids and mobcap—and Georgiana's own burnished gold hair, shaken loose from its pins, spilled out over the shoulders of her rag doll costume.

"Mattie!" she cried, as the gag was pulled out of her mouth. "What are you doing here?"

But Mattie, when she saw what Arthur had brought back with him, had staggered back a step. She looked about to faint.

The worst moment of the evening for Georgiana had come when she had realized that it was Arthur Kincaid who had her. At first it had seemed a wild nightmare from which she soon must wake—a man garbed as an executioner had seized her, gagged her, and was carrying her off. But the freezing truth that this particular nightmare was all too real had filtered in to her shatteringly through the thickness of the wool cloak that covered her head, for the voice that reached her, muffled by the wool, was that of Arthur Kincaid. Jolting along on his horse, Arthur had kept up a running one-sided conversation with her—sneering, contemptuous, triumphant. He had punctuated his remarks by taking unpleasant liberties with her body that had made her writhe in fury—pinching or cuddling her breasts or thighs, suddenly giving her a rough hug that took her breath—even shaking her so that she bounced on the saddle before him. How she wished she could have answered his tirade! What an earful she would have given him this night! It was as well that she hadn't been able to, for he might have responded by doing her an injury.

Now her gaze fled past pale, speechless Mattie to dour Jack Belter, standing impassively by and handing Arthur another rope to tie her to the chair she had been dumped upon.

"You, Jack," she said warningly, "are in real trouble, for Brett will not forgive any injury to me."

"We won't injure you," smirked Arthur. "I am but taking you back—my escaped bond servant!"

"I'm not your bond servant!" snapped Georgiana and turned with a last wild appeal to the big black-bearded man. "Jack, turn back from this mad venture before it's too late. Throw this man from your house and take me back to my husband and I promise you a rich reward."

"No use talking to Belter here," snickered Arthur. "He's already bought and paid for, aren't you Jack? Don't bother to deny it—I know to the guilder what van Rappard paid you, for 'twas my gold that financed this venture, the sloop, your services, everything." When Belter's expression did not change, Arthur's voice grew grim. "And well you know the kind of reward you'd get from Danforth for your part in this night's work—a length of steel, if he didn't have you hanged!"

"That's not true," cried Georgiana heatedly. "You know my husband for an honorable man, Jack Belter. Whatever Nicolas has paid you, Brett will pay more! I promise it, and my husband will honor my promises!"

For a moment Jack Belter's dark eyes gleamed and Georgiana thought she had him. She held her breath, waiting.

Arthur too thought Belter might be wavering.

"We'll put the woman aboard the sloop," he decided.

Jack Belter shook his big head. He looked uneasy. "We'll wait for Mr. van Rappard," he said tonelessly.

"Who did you say? whispered Georgiana, her turquoise eyes dilating.

Across from her, Mattie found her voice. "It's true," she said miserably. "They're waiting for Nicolas."

If Arthur Kincaid noticed his wife's surprising use of the golden Dutchman's first name, that fact assumed a secondary importance in his mind. Of first importance was getting Georgiana away from Jack Belter's sphere of influence before the black-bearded devil could change his mind and take her back to Danforth and claim a reward!

"Mattie." Arthur seemed not to have heard Belter. He spoke with a voice of authority. "Take this rope, Mattie, and tie it around Georgiana's waist and tie the other end around your own, so that I may keep track of you both." He turned again to Belter. "You may stay here if you like, but van Rappard may arrive on the run with muskets firing at his heels and I had best get the women aboard now."

Without putting down his long clay pipe, Jack Belter moved over and eased his tall figure in front of the cottage's only door. "We wait," he said laconically.

"Very well." Arthur shrugged. "Could I have a pipe of tobacco while we wait?"

"Over there." Jack nodded toward the broken-hinged cupboard.

"I don't see it," Arthur said when he opened the cupboard door.

"In the cupboard," directed Jack.

Arthur rummaged about futilely. A pewter tankard came tumbling out, rolled along the floor. "I can't find it, Jack."

With a grunt, Belter moved toward the cupboard, bent over to get the tobacco. With a catlike quickness, Arthur moved. He seized the poker Mattie had considered using and brought it down with all his force on the back of Jack Belter's neck. Belter fell face forward with his head in the cupboard. They could hear his chin crash against the wood. Then his body seemed to relax and he slid down the front of the cupboard and ended up lying against it on the floor.

"You've killed him," breathed Georgiana, staring in fascination at the crazy angle of the fallen man's neck, as Mattie covered up her eyes. Her gaze turned accusingly to Arthur. "Now you've done murder!"

"Here maybe—but not in Boston." Arthur gave a short mirthless laugh. He nudged Belter with his foot to make sure he was dead, gave him a sharp kick in the groin that would have been sure to elicit a groan.

Georgiana could not bear the sight; she turned her face away.

"On your feet," commanded Arthur.

"I can't," she whispered. "I'm tied to this chair."

"Then I'll untie you." He swaggered toward her, confident now that he had the situation under control. Jack Belter had been a powerful antagonist, but these two women—he could herd them along, they would be afraid to stand against him.

"They'll hunt you down," she panted, looking up at him with hatred. "Wherever you go, they'll find you. No place will be safe for you ever again.'

The malice in his laugh licked at her, as did the mockery in his voice. "They will not be looking for *me*, Anna. 'Tis Nicolas van Rappard they will be looking for. When Nicolas told me his plan—for me to seize you whilst he stayed on at the ball so that he would not be implicated, I penned a note and signed your name to it.

And 'tis a fair copy of your handwritting if I do say so, for your signature from the Articles of Indenture which you signed was burned into my brain."

Georgiana was afraid to ask. Somehow she kept her voice steady. "And what did you say in this note, Arthur?"

He stood over her, gloating, making no move to untie her. "That you were running away with Nicolas. You will be gone by tomorrow, Nicolas will be blamed, we will get away scot-free."

"And what makes you think I will go with you, Arthur?" she asked steadily. "You have not got Floss to hold over my head this time! You cannot threaten to burn her alive, for she is safe with Brett!"

Arthur's countenance took on an expression so diabolical, so gleeful, that she flinched back instinctively.

"I have something better than Floss," he said softly. *"I have Mattie."*

Georgiana felt her throat go dry. *"You would not,"* she whispered. "She is your *wife!*"

Standing there like a waxen doll, Mattie heard her husband say, "Would I not? You will come with me, Georgiana. We will be far away downriver while your husband scours these hills for you and Nicolas van Rappard. But he will not find van Rappard, for I will be waiting here to kill him. When van Rappard opens that door, he will be met with a musket ball. I will drag his body to the river—but you will not see that; you will already be aboard the sloop that is even now waiting for us at the riverside."

"I will tell them what you have done!" cried Georgiana through clenched teeth.

Arthur's smile was terrible. "You will have no chance, for you will be once again bound and gagged with Mattie to guard you. *She* will know better than to defy me. The crew of the sloop is bought and paid for—they will take my word that van Rappard took a bullet from the pursuing patroon and cast off. Down the river you will go, unseen inside my cabin. In New Orange you will be carried on shipboard bound and gagged in a trunk as part of my 'luggage.' Don't worry, I will not let you smother!" Arthur was obviously enjoying this, swaggering before her, letting her see what a great man he was, driving in the hard fact that she was in his power. "And once in Boston, these Articles of Indenture—" he patted his doublet where the papers resided—"will bind you to me. I will spread the word that you suffered an accident when you fell in front of a carriage wheel in Philadelphia and that your mind wanders; nothing you say will be believed. You will live in my house, do my bidding. If you run away, I will find you and bring you back and strip Mattie naked and whip her with a cat-o'-nine-tails until she bleeds." He was smiling fiercely into Georgiana's eyes, ignoring Mattie's little horrified cry. "And you will come to my bed, Anna—willingly with smiles, or fainting from the sight of Mattie's pain, it matters not to me. For I have sworn that I will break you." He seized her suddenly by her thick burnished gold hair and bent her head back so far that she gasped from pain. *'And break you, I will!'*

Gazing raptly at Georgiana's beautiful white face as he outlined his terrible plans, one by one, Arthur had given no thought at all to his young wife. He considered her cowed, spiritless, to be kicked out of the way like a piece of furniture.

But Mattie had been gazing, dazed, from Georgiana's shrinking bound body to the dead man who lay sprawled on the floor. She was unaware that she was whimpering like a hurt animal caught in a trap from which there was no escape. Screaming nightmares that hurtled at her from a hellish future galloped wildly through her brain. And prime among them was a vision of Georgiana, silently stripping that Arthur might bear her to his bed—and casting a last despairing glance at Mattie, who sagged to her knees, held upright only by a rope suspended from the ceiling dangling her by wrists bound cruelly tight. She could feel blood drip down her naked body, running along her back and buttocks, from the welts of the lash— welts Arthur would inflict.

In that terrible future that Arthur had invented for them she heard herself crying in heartbroken fashion, and wailing at last, "Oh, Anna, don't do it—don't let him!" on a note of despair—and she could feel Arthur's hard fish smashing into her face, and then merciful unconsciousness.

An unconsciousness from which she would wake, dizzy and sick, to see her husband in bed with another woman, a woman who hated and despised him, a woman who had gone to his arms solely out of pity—for *her*.

Now in that shabby Hudson River farmhouse, as she sidled away from her husband, shuffling her feet like a sleepwalker, in a trance from her terrible dreams, her gaze riveted on the pistol that had fallen out of Jack Belter's belt as he dropped, brought down by Arthur's poker. Almost without volition, she reached down and picked up the pistol. She looked down at it in an almost detached way, with a little demented smile. *Here* was a way out. She would not have to go to Boston or endure what Arthur had in store for her. She would remove herself from this hateful triangle. She would turn this gun toward her breastbone and pull the trigger. She studied it dreamily—and cocked it.

At the sound of the gun being cocked, Arthur whirled—and stiffened in shock as he saw Mattie turning it toward herself with that little secret smile on her face.

"Mattie!" he cried. "Are ye mad?" And lunged toward her.

It was sheer instinct that made Mattie turn the gun toward him to fend him off, for it had never occurred to her in her wildest dreams that she could best Arthur in anything. It was sheer reflex action that caused her finger to tighten on the trigger just as Arthur loomed over her, reaching out to wrest this dangerous toy from her slender fingers.

There was a deafening explosion.

Shot through the heart, Arthur's arms closed spasmodically about his wife and he teetered there. To Georgiana's horrified gaze, it seemed as if they were executing some macabre dance.

Then Arthur's hold relaxed. He fell away from Mattie and slumped to the floor, to sprawl at the feet of the man he had killed but minutes before.

Mattie stood staring down at him, her face growing more pinched, more ashen by the moment. The smoking pistol dropped from her nerveless fingers. She took a faltering step backward and her hands went up to cover her face. "Oh, God," she whispered. "I've killed him—I've killed Arthur."

Georgiana, breathless from the swift passage of events, found her voice.

"So you have," she said briskly. "And well he deserved it!" She gave Arthur's fallen body a grim look. "Now cut me free from these bonds before the crew from the sloop come in to investigate that shot and decide to make off with us or drown us in the river to save their skins!"

Mattie's gaze, fixed and horrified, was still riveted on the man before her. He had once been *her husband*.

"I didn't mean to do it," she whispered. "I meant to shoot *myself*. But when Arthur came at me, I thought only to fend him off. The gun went off. . . . " Her voice dwindled away.

"Nobody will blame you, Mattie. *I* will be your witness. Had I had the pistol, *I'd* have shot him without a second throught. Now cut me free."

Mattie's feet still refused to move. She stood there swaying in her pink dress.

"Oh, Mattie, please don't swoon," pleaded Georgiana. "Set me free or it will all have been for nothing—we'll die anyway. Use one of the kitchen knives—there's one on the table there."

Before Mattie could move to do her bidding there was a noise at the door. Both their heads turned as it swung open.

Nicolas stood there, a dark figure against the moon-washed snow. As he took in the scene before him, he gave a low whistle.

"Mathilde," he said with respect, looking at the pistol at Mattie's feet and noting that Georgiana was still bound, "don't tell me that you have killed two men this night!"

Mattie had begun to shake—uncontrollably. Her voice seemed to rattle in her throat. "No," she quavered. "Only one. Arthur struck down this cottager—" she indicated Belter—"with a poker and said he was dead. And when Arthur began telling us the horrible things he was going to do to us, I picked up the gun and—and—"

"And you shot him," Nicolas said sympathetically. "Thereby saving me the trouble."

"You—*you* were going to shoot Arthur?" whispered Mattie uncertainly.

"Of course, Mathilde. And rescue you from an impossible marriage—and incidentally rescue this lady, whose husband would be glad to turn over the deed to Windgate just to get her back from Arthur Kincaid!"

"You were going to—save us?" Mattie's head whirled.

"Don't listen to him, Mattie," said Georgiana in disgust. "Your plan has been found out, Nicolas. Arthur left a note saying I had run away with you—and signed my name to it!"

Nicolas frowned. Even with her wrists bound, he felt that Georgiana was capable of pulling off a tremendous bluff. He turned to Mattie. "Is this true, Mathilde?" he asked severely.

"Oh, it's true, it's true." Mattie burst into tears. "Arthur told us so—he bragged about it."

"He was sneering at your culpability, Nicolas," said Georgiana calmly.

Nicolas gave her a nettled look.

"You may as well untie me, Nicolas," she sighed. "Brett and any number of others will be here any minute."

Nicolas looked disturbed. He moved to the door, threw it open and looked out. It had never been any part of his plan to involve himself in Georgiana's kidnapping as other than a "go-between." He had meant to take them all—excepting Jack Belter, who had been well paid and knew he could expect more—to an isolated place downriver and there quarrel with Arthur and shoot him—something he had been yearning to do ever since Mattie had told him her story. Mattie, he had intended to put on a ship bound for Boston with a promise—not meant to be kept—to join her later and a stern admonition to keep her mouth shut about what had really happened, for she would not stand to inherit her husband's fortune if it could be claimed that she had been party to his murder. Georgiana—ah, his plans toward Georgiana had never been certain, just as his feelings toward her even now were mixed. If she seemed to respond to him, now that he had made his move, he would have been tempted to let her stand beside him as they seized Windgate. If she did not—

He stiffened as he heard in the clear cold air the distant but unmistakable thudding of hooves. Georgiana had not lied. Danforth *was* out there—and seeking him! And doubtless he had a force at his back.

He turned to see that Mattie had seized the kitchen knife and run over to Georgiana and cut free her bonds.

Now as he advanced on Georgiana, she snatched the knife from Mattie's hand.

"I will not let you take me!" she cried in a ringing voice and brought up the knife to defend herself. "And you have not much time, Nicolas, for I can hear them coming. All the forces of Windgate are gathered in pursuit of me at this very moment!"

She was right, this was no time to tarry. He had not the time to subdue her, for they would be on him. He thought fast.

"Georgiana," he said. "You have just killed a man."

"No," cried Mattie. "Arthur killed the cottager and *I* killed Arthur—"

"Ah, yes, you said so." A charming smile curved his lips. "But it will be *believed* of Georgiana," he said softly.

Georgiana watched him warily. What trick was this? She kept the knife poised like a dagger, half expecting him to spring upon her to wrest it away.

Nicolas was gazing at her steadily, still with that smile on his lips. "So I would make a bargain with you. To save both your fair skins, you will say I had no part in this—and I will back you up, saying that I saw the deed. I will say that I arrived too late to stop them, but that I guessed where Kincaid had taken you, knowing Belter for a rogue, and that I had come in haste to save you. I will say that as I flung open the door, Kincaid struck Belter down and from the floor Belter shot him. Are we agreed?"

"Oh, do say yes, Georgiana," cried Mattie, wringing her hands. "Say yes or they will hang me! For as badly as Arthur treated me—and too many know of it—who will believe that I killed him by accident?"

"Why do you do this, Nicolas?" Georgiana demanded.

"I want no further smears against my reputation when my case comes up in court," he said frankly.

"So you are still determined to have Windgate?"

"As firmly as ever." He started for the door and from the entrance cast an uneasy look at the low ridge over which at any moment now help would come. "I will take my leave of you, ladies," he flung over his shoulder and trotted down the slope toward the sloop, which was tied up to a tree. He whipped out his sword to cut the ropes. "Who knows?" he called merrily to the women watching from the doorway. "I may yet find some comfort in the packet of papers ye kept secreted!"

At the word "packet" Georgiana broke into a run, following him.

"Wait!" she cried. "What packet is this?"

"The one you kept in your bedroom." He had leaped aboard and now he hacked through the ropes and was telling the *schipper* to cast off.

Over the rise a number of horsemen were streaming, but foremost among them and some distance ahead, leading the pack on a lathered horse, was Brett Danforth.

He saw Mattie standing appalled at the cottage door. He saw Georgiana running down the slope toward Nicolas who was just leaping aboard the sloop. He saw Georgiana in her rag doll costume running after him.

He could not see her face. He could not know what was in her mind: *The journal and the affidavit—Nicolas had them!* And those papers would unmask her as a counterfeit heiress, they would reveal her true parentage, *they would ruin Brett*!

CHAPTER 34

Without hesitation, Georgiana made her decision. "Nicolas," she cried. "I must have that packet back. If you will give it back to me unread, I will go with you, Nicolas!"

Brett Danforth, still some distance away but thundering forward, could not hear that. But he could see the surprised stance of the man on the sloop.

Had Brett and the other pursuers not been so close, Nicolas might have got the *schipper* to turn the sloop around and go back for Georgiana but—pursuit was too near.

"Too late!" he called.

But Georgiana, hands twisted together, was locked in agony in her private world. She had visions of Brett ruined—and she would have *caused* that ruin by not destroying the packet while she had the chance. "Give them back!" she entreated. "Oh, Nicolas, give them back—and take me with you!" And as the sloop slipped away from the shore, was taken by the current, she slipped, went down in the snow. "Come back, Nicolas! *Come back!*"

Her voice was a blend of heartbreak and entreaty—and Brett heard it. Not the first part, only "—take me with you!" And then as she slipped in the snow and went down on her knees, he heard her calling raggedly, "Come back, Nicolas! *Come back!*"

His face turned gray and he spurred forward like a madman and brought his horse to so sudden a halt that it almost catapulted him over the beast's head, just short of his fallen wife. He vaulted off, dragged out his sword and hurled it with deadly accuracy at the man who stood at the rail of the retreating sloop.

Nicolas, caught unawares, doubled up as the sword pierced him in the thigh. He went down cursing onto the deck of the sloop, which was now some distance from shore, being swept south by the fast current.

Georgiana, hardly aware that there was anyone else in the world at that moment but Nicolas and the stolen papers that meant so much to her, felt long fingers close over her arm in a steely grasp.

"It would seem your lover prefers his life to your embraces," Brett said harshly, and she turned, dazed, to see the deep hard anger in his eyes. "But be that as it may, you are *my* woman—mine to hold or mine to fling away." He jerked her upright and toward him so violently that her feet left the ground and she came up breathless against his hard chest.

"Brett," she cried wildly, realizing with a jolt how the scene must have looked to him, with herself from the shore entreating Nicolas not to leave her! "Brett, I can explain!"

She was suddenly aware that they were surrounded now by a group of silent, staring men, who had arrived shortly after Brett.

"Save your explanations," said Brett brutally and picked her up, tossed her over his saddle in front of him, head dangling, uncaring that her lovely long hair was streaming down and catching in the brush, being wet by snow, or that she was fending off sticks and low branches that slapped at her face and legs as they rode.

"Let me up!" she cried.

He did not answer.

"Brett!" she wailed. "I'm freezing and my hair is getting soaked!"

"Be quiet," he said through his teeth, "or I may be tempted to silence you!"

But he swept her up, righting her so that she rode sidewise before him with her legs dangling over one side of the horse, and he threw his cloak around her shivering body. In the wind her long hair

streamed out and flicked his angry face; he shook it away. She turned
and looked back at him once, her face very close, her eyes full of
entreaty. She intended to speak, but the look in his gray eyes forbade
it. She kept silent, shamed and confused and shivering in her rag
doll costume, for she realized all too well what she had said and how
it must have sounded—as if Nicolas had deserted her and she was
wailing at him to come back. *Half the river must have heard,* she
thought, cringing. Those men who rode behind them now, those men
who had ringed around them and stared at her in wonder, what were
they saying now?

Penitent now—although it was certainly no fault of hers that she
had been kidnapped—she let him take her home. Taken up by one of
the riders who rode behind them, she could hear Mattie sobbing out
that Arthur and that man in the cottage had killed each other—no,
she didn't really know why, some quarrel, she lapsed into incoher-
ence. A pair of riders broke away and went back to investigate
Mattie's story. The patroon rode on in silence.

Georgiana could have spoken up but she felt that Mattie was
doing very well for herself. Later she could corroborate the story
Mattie had told. But for now she was riding home through the
snow to Windgate with her body held against a broad chest
whose deep throbbing rhythm she could feel through her rag doll
costume.

The big frowning mansion had never looked more formidable to
Georgiana than it did when Brett drew up his mount before the open
lighted door. Its dark shape seemed to bulk up enormously, all the
downstairs windows glittering with candlelight, and from the chandelier in the lighted hall, light poured out in a long streamer across
the snow, making a white carpet that they must tread upon to enter.
Guests were crowded into the front hall, craning out—some of the
more venturesome had come outside. She saw men trying to look
elaborately unconcerned, women holding up their satin skirts carefully as they picked their way through the snow on dancing slippers.
Wouter had come out and was standing by anxiously.

Conscious of her disheveled appearance and the fact that her
costume was exactly like Linnet's—she had no way of knowing that
her deception had already been discovered but she divined it from
the knowing faces of her guests—Georgiana felt abject humiliation
as Brett dismounted in that long shaft of light, threw the reins to a

nearby groom and lifted her down. Her awkward black felt boots, stuffed with yarn to make them the same size as Linnet's, sank into the snow.

"Take care of the horse—he's winded," Brett told the groom. "Give him a good rubdown and feed him well. And find a bed for Kincaid's wife," he told Wouter tersely, indicating Mattie with a jerk of his head. "We can sort out her story tomorrow." He paused in that long streamer of light that led inside past his excited guests. "Will ye bid my guests good-bye for me, Govert? I've matters to sort out with my wife."

Silent and dignified and looking more than ever like an elderly liveried servant, Govert Steendam nodded his gray head in grave assent. He looked sorry for Brett, for the story told by the dismounting men was already spreading among the guests like wildfire. They could hear snatches of it buzzing around them now: The patroon's bride had run away with Nicolas, they must have quarreled for he had left her on the riverbank and sailed away—perhaps because he did not wish to be involved in a double murder—and when the patroon and his party had arrived they had found her calling after Nicolas, on her knees in the snow entreating him to come back to her!

That last item, when they heard it, caused Katrina ten Haer's face to contort. She broke her ivory fan in half and hurled it at the mantelpiece. Then in rage she began tearing out her hairpins and then her hair in great saffron tufts, while Rychie, scandalized, tried to soothe her. Erica gasped on hearing it and then sank down and laughed till tears ran down her cheeks and Govert, looking shocked, muttered to her that such mirth was unseemly. But most of the guests reacted with lively interest, for there was much resentment against the "English patroon" and there were many at the ball who yearned to see him humbled.

The word "humble" hardly described the tall man who strode through the whispering throng dragging his strangely costumed wife by the wrist. Up the wide stairway they went, with everybody watching, to disappear from view around a corner of the corridor. Once they were out of sight, excited voices broke loose and there was a general hubbub as everybody, all at once, tried to find out from everybody else the real truth of the perplexing situation at Windgate.

But in Georgiana's big square bedchamber, where a worried Wouter had already lit the candles and ordered a fire built while they were gone, the guests and their speculations were forgotten. Brett almost jerked her off her feet as he strode through it, kicking the door shut behind him. He tossed her onto the bed and stood for a moment glaring down at her. The look on his face was so formidable that she felt a tremor of fear course through her.

"Brett, let me explain!"

"We have no need of explanations," he said contemptuously. "Let us hear no silken lies. You spin your web well, Georgiana—faith, you had me snared in it!" He was tearing off his clothes as he spoke. "Take off that rag doll costume," he snarled. "You look ridiculous!"

In truth she looked lost and bedraggled and pitiful, sitting there on the big featherbed—and he wanted to feel no sympathy for her this night.

Georgiana made haste to get out of the rag doll costume, which she felt bitterly, had brought her the worst of luck. Her fingers were trembling as she undid the hooks, and the forbidding look on Brett's face when he had ordered her to disrobe had made her afraid to speak.

Now as she shuddered away from him, her back was turned to him modestly, but his burning eyes watched the soft white chemise slide down over her smooth lovely back and gently rounded hips, to drift down her dainty legs. As always, the sight of her naked body rocked him, but his blood this night was already stirred to boiling.

Before she could put on the delicate white night rail for which she reached, he grasped her by one white shoulder and spun her around.

"It all went on under my nose and I was too much of a fool to see it," he said thickly. "Never did I think to hear you calling after Nicolas van Rappard, pleading with him to take you with him, begging him to come back!"

"Oh, Brett, you don't understand," she gasped. "There was a reason. If only you will listen—"

"Reason? *Reason?*" He took her by the other shoulder and shook her until she felt her teeth would come loose. His hard laughter fell like stones against her ears. "There can be only one *reason*—strumpet! And tonight I shall use you as no delicate lily whose petals I fear to crush—tonight you shall come to my arms as any other doxy!''

Before she could form an answer, he bore her to the bed, his long naked figure falling upon hers.

Terrified now, for she feared she had lost his love, Georgiana fitted her pliant body to his as closely as he could have chosen. There was a whimper of fright in her throat and her whole body rippled in response to him as he thrust within her—deep and hard, without his usual gentle playful build-up of lovemaking that always drove her to delicious frenzy and bore her along with him to soaring heights.

Tonight he intended to use her for his pleasure and fling her aside—as any bought woman might expect. He would humble the proud beauty who shared his bed, he would punish her for her unfaith!

But—even though his own fury was a roaring in his ears, his rage so bright that it flashed against his closed eyelids, the very silky touch of her, the sweetness of her shivering response to his brutal attack, brought back to him some measure of sanity. He loved this woman—that was the galling fact of it, loved her with all his heart. He wanted to protect her, to keep her safe from harm. In all the world nothing meant more to him than Georgiana.

Some of the tension went out of him and Georgiana sensed it, moved her hips silkily, luxuriously against his, and as he lifted himself upon his elbows that he might not crush her with his weight—an involuntary gesture of compassion, for Brett was a thoughtful lover—she sighed and arched her back and brushed the soft crests of her ardent breasts against his chest.

That little gesture of submission went straight to his heart and he clasped her with all the love that was in him. Those innocent naked upturned breasts—like her sweet half-opened lips, which he could see parted in the candlelight, for in his hurry he had not bothered to extinguish the candles—how they called to him! And as he felt those breasts upflung against him, soft as eiderdown, felt their nipples tingle to hardness against the soft furring of his chest, he felt a groan rising in his throat.

Georgiana, no matter what she did, held him in thrall. He would always love her, always. . . .

And the woman in his arms knew from the way he held her, from the way he stroked her sweet flesh, from the joy he now built in her, from the authority, the very lightness of the way he held her to him—careful not to hurt her but to tease from each moment the last measure of vibrant ecstasy—knew that he had forgiven her.

A great happiness came over her heart, a sense of lightness, of the world well lost. She had been so close to disaster and somehow survived, so close to the fire that she had felt its very flames lick at her face and now suddenly all was right again. She melted into Brett's arms with all her senses singing and winged with him to the very peaks of passion.

And afterward, after she had slid away from him with a luxurious sigh and lay on her back listening to his strong even breathing, she told herself that somehow, *somehow* she would get that packet back from Nicolas. No need to worry Brett about it—for he might go charging out and challenge Nicolas. And when the affair was over, one of them would lie dead in the snow while the other cleaned the blade of his sword.

No—she did not want that. She did not want Brett to risk his life by challenging a dangerous adversary like Nicolas—nor, scoundrel though he was, did she want the golden Dutchman killed.

At last she drifted into a light sleep to be waked by some sound in the next room. She blinked, realizing that pale winter sunshine was pouring in through the small-paned windows. The candles had all guttered out—and Brett was gone.

She would have sat up but that he came striding in through the adjoining door, unsmiling. He was already fully dressed.

"Where are you going?" she asked, for the look on his face told her that there was more afoot than breakfast.

"There are two men dead in a cottage on my land," he said tersely. "The *schout* will be arriving and I will have to piece the story together for him."

"Mattie will tell you about it," she said quickly, remembering Mattie's terrified, *Who will believe that I killed him by accident? They will hang me!*

"I have already spoken to Mattie. What do *you* say?"

"I am sure whatever Mattie has told you is true," she hedged.

Her words had been too glib. Brett was watching her narrowly. "If your friend Mattie is to be believed," he said slowly, "her husband, Arthur, was here seeking you, to carry you away with him—and he forged a note in your handwriting, saying you had run away with Nicolas."

"That is true. It was Arthur who abducted me—not Nicolas. He had infiltrated the ball, dressed as an executioner."

"Yes. I saw the fellow and wondered who he was."

"So did I, but when I tried to find out, he kept slipping away from me. It was Arthur who abducted me—not Nicolas. He seized me as I crouched in the bushes near the lake, having just traded places with Linnet."

"I gathered as much." The lunacy of that impersonation on the ice caused him to shake his head in wonder—it came to him that he would never understand women. "And do you know how Arthur planned to hang on to another man's wife? Especially if the wife was unwilling?"

"Arthur still had my signed Articles of Indenture," she said bitterly. "He had not destroyed them as he told us. He planned to spirit me away to Boston *hidden in a trunk* and pass me off as demented!"

Brett digested this. "Maybe he *was* mad," he murmured in an altered voice. Then abruptly, "It is not to my advantage to have the world know you were ever a bond servant. Far better that they continue to regard you as gently reared. Better for my claim."

"But I *was* gently reared," she protested, flushing.

"Even so, speaking of it—after having given the impression that you were a Bermuda heiress as well as heiress to the van Rappard fortune—would make us seem clandestine, tricky, possibly even fraudulent."

Georgiana winced, for she alone knew that her claim to Windgate was fraudulent—no, now Nicolas shared that knowledge with her. She opened her mouth to make a clean breast of things, but Brett was speaking again.

"I have told your friend Mattie this, and she says she has mentioned to no one Arthur's reasons for spiriting you away."

Good for Mattie, thought Georgiana grimly. At least that was one less worry!

"It seems better to suggest that Arthur had gone mad, assaulted his wife and was seeking you to wreak some insane vengeance for an imagined slight in Bermuda, that Belter tried to dissuade him and they killed each other in the ensuing argument, and that Nicolas van

Rappard, having sailed upriver with the Kincaids, had at last guessed his intentions and come to 'save' you''—his voice was ironic—''and you were entreating him to come back and take you back to Windgate so you could again trade places with Linnet, not knowing that your masquerade had already been discovered.''

"Now they can all be heroes," she said bitterly.

"Have you a better solution?"

"No."

"Then that is the story your friend Mattie will tell. She has already agreed to it. Talk with her, be sure your accounts of what happened are the same. Enough scandal whirls about our heads already—we do not need to add to it."

He had not once asked for the truth, she thought sadly. Well, he would hear it anyway!

"Brett," she said, throwing back the coverlet and starting to rise.

"Stay abed," he ordered. "I will send Mattie in to you. I think all our guests have departed but I do not want you prowling about downstairs, in case they have not. Questions would be awkward at this point. Indeed you would do well to continue to hold your head high and answer nobody's questions. Let them think the worst of you—they will anyway." He reached for his sword and turned to go.

"But Brett," cried Georgiana indignantly. "There *is* an explanation. If you will only wait—"

His head swung around to consider the beauty on the bed and a mirthless smile twisted his lips but found no answering gleam in his cold gray eyes. She had won him again last night with her soft yielding body, the sense of trust he had felt in her—but morning had shown him a beautiful but faithless wife. A woman who, even if her actions at Jack's cottage last night had been entirely innocent and herself a victim of circumstances, had still fallen to her knees in the snow calling out heartbrokenly to Nicolas van Rappard. *He had heard her with his own ears!*

"I will brook no more explanations, Georgiana," he said in a hard voice. "Except for what we must tell the *schout*, we will not speak of this again.' His face was grim as he gave a final jerk to his belt as he buckled on his sword. "But then," he muttered, giving her a look both sad and fond as he heaved a great sigh, "I suppose ye are no better and no worse than Erica Hulft."

No better than Erica Hulft! Indignation made Georgiana leap from the bed and follow him to the door, meaning to plead her case in the hall if necessary. But the door that he opened to let himself out was closed firmly in her face. She could not run after him down the hall naked!

In panic she turned to seize a dressing gown and pursue him but then thought better of it.

And then it came to her that Brett would not believe her, no matter what she said, that he would never believe her again. The bright trust he had had in her was gone, she had destroyed it—forever. Her own folly in baiting him with Nicolas's attentions, in flirting with Nicolas to arouse his jealousy, had written the ending of their love affair—and all the tears in the world would not wash it away.

She pressed her forehead dizzily against the plastered wall. She had thought last night that Brett had forgiven her. But—only his body had forgiven her, not his heart. He considered her now no better than Erica Hulft.

Hot tears scalded her eyelids as she told herself she had broken his heart—and now she must cost him Windgate!

BOOK VII
The Runaway Bride

The wrong she has done him she cannot undo,
For the ink on the parchment is dry,
And to her death she must always rue
What has turned her world awry!

PART ONE
The Flight Downriver

Her back to the past, she looks her last
On the world she used to know
And the future's unclear as she wavers here
Yearning and loath to go.

CHAPTER 35

It humiliated Georgiana to stand there in her own drawing room and tell the sturdy *schout* that she had been pleading with Nicolas to take her back to Windgate to change places with her serving maid so that she might fool her assembled guests as to her prowess upon the ice, but she forced herself to do so. She hoped she sounded believable.

Mattie told her story again—and told it more coherently now that it had been carefully rehearsed. She stuck to it. Arthur and Jack had killed each other, Georgiana corroborated it—after all, what purpose was to be served by bringing the whole ugly story out into the open, how Arthur had shamefully abused his young wife, how she had in terror shot him? And—she dared not make Nicolas look bad, for *he* had the packet!

"But why did Mynheer van Rappard sail away?" demanded the puzzled *schout*. "Did he not realize it would seem that he was fleeing the scene?"

"I suppose he did not think of that. He came to save us—and found us already saved, quite surprisingly, by Arthur and Jack disposing of each other. Mynheer van Rappard has some litigation pending with us here at Windgate. He did not wish to bring down scandal upon all our heads."

Brett was watching her very steadily as she told the *schout* that. He looked big and competent today and very calm, lounging back on a carved high-backed chair with one long booted leg thrown casually across the chair's massive wooden arm. His hawklike face was impassive, the lids over his gray eyes drooped slightly—even though, to Georgiana's penetrating surveillance, they held a wary gleam. His fingers drummed lightly against his knee as the *schout* questioned the two women, and he looked if anything slightly bored with these proceedings. Georgiana could not help but admire him, for who knew better than she that it was all a pose, that Brett was as tense inside as she was, and waiting for who knew what to spring out.

Georgiana held her head high and cast a look at Mattie, sitting there downcast in a plain black dress they had hastily found for her and dabbing at her eyes—as a widow should.

The *schout* scratched his sandy head. It was a very strange story, but—this was a patroon's wife speaking. And a patroon's wife's widowed friend. There was no one to challenge their testimony— indeed they were both more or less corroborating the story that he had just heard from Nicolas van Rappard at Haerwyck! Nicolas had been wearing a large bandage around his thigh at the time and there were some who muttered that he had come by his wound when the patroon of Windgate hurled a sword at him in an attempt to speed him on his way while the patroon's lady called to him wildly from the shore, "Come back, come back!" But Nicolas himself, when the *schout* remarked it, had been vague about his injury. "An accident," he had muttered. He had, it seemed, collided with something.

Ah, well, if the gentry wished to brawl among themselves over a lady—and such a lady!—that was up to them. So long as they did not see fit to call in the law—or kill each other—the *schout* was content to leave well enough alone. There was enough mayhem and quarreling about to keep him occupied!

They walked him to his sloop, Georgiana and Brett, for it had been tacitly agreed between them that whatever their differences, they would present a unified front to the world. They could not have been more affable or seemed more lighthearted as they urged him to stay for tiffin.

The *schout* declined their hospitality with regret. He had urgent business back at Haerwyck, which he had just left—a wife beating, and a violent argument over the ownership of a suckling pig, which had led to blows and broken windows in one of ten Haer's outlying *bouweries*, plus some stolen beaver skins, which he doubted he could ever trace.

Georgiana was half surprised that the *schout* did not seek to take Linnet into custody for theft of the diamond pendant, for he had just left the ten Haers and Katrina, like her mother before her, was a vengeful woman. Earlier this morning a tearful Linnet had told her everything and she had promised to stand by the girl, who was still sojourning in bed after her bad fall on the ice. But the *schout* had said nothing about the pendant and now he was halfway down the slope. She supposed that Rychie had persuaded Katrina that they would only kick up a great scandal if Linnet were brought to trial.

She wondered how Nicolas had squirmed out of *that* escapade, and a wry smile crossed her face for she had no doubt of charming Nicolas's ability to get himself out of practically any scrape.

"I see ye came in Govert Steendam's sloop," observed Brett, raising his eyebrows.

"It was kind of him," said the *schout*. "He is staying the week at Haerwyck and he told me he would have no use for it while there."

"At Haerwyck?" Georgiana said in surprise, for she knew how Rychie and Katrina felt about Erica.

"Yes. I take it he got only as far as Haerwyck before he fell ill and they took him in."

Brett frowned. "Govert ill? And at Haerwyck? What is the matter with him?"

The *schout* shrugged his massive shoulders. "Dr. Pos is also staying at Haerwyck, for he too was en route downriver on the sloop. He calls it only a slight chest cold caught from exposure—it seems Mynheer Steendam and Juffrouw Hulft stood out on the deck in the snow on the way downriver. He was coughing and Juffrouw Hulft felt it best to put in at Haerwyck rather than continue the journey."

At the first sneeze no doubt—as an excuse to put up at Haerwyck! Georgiana felt her lip curl. Erica undoubtedly wanted to stay close to Windgate—in case the patroon there decided to make a change....She felt chilled by more than the whipping wind that lanced along the Hudson.

Brett was frowning as they walked back up the bluff. Absently he steadied Georgiana on her tall pattens. She wondered if he was thinking of Erica.

"I am going upriver," he told her restlessly at the front door. "One of my tenants, Pieter Kolp, has a son of an age to take a wife, and Pieter tells me young Kolp fancies the daughter of one of Huygens ten Haer's tenants, but has no place to take her as she refuses to move in with his family or remain with hers. I will go up to Kolp's *bouwerie* and offer young Kolp Belter's *bouwerie*; 'tis best it be occupied over the winter months even if they choose to set themselves up in some other place in the spring."

"Yes," she agreed mechanically. "That would be best." She wondered if he would then say that he must needs journey down to Haerwyck to apprise the daughter there of her good luck.

"I will be gone two or three days," he said. "For there are other matters that need my attention upriver."

He left without kissing her good-bye, just turned and left without a word. It told her anew how deeply she had hurt him.

Georgiana went inside the house and sat for a long time in the empty drawing room with her head bowed. She was very pale when she reached her decision. Then she went upstairs, opened her little rosewood writing desk and penned a message, walked swiftly down the bluff and gave it to a whistling fellow in a small sailboat, whom she recognized as one of the grooms. "Say the message is urgent," she said crisply, and went back up the grassy bluff.

At the front door she met Mattie, who had come out of the house. A pale, almost ethereal Mattie, who twisted her hands together and jumped at shadows and stared constantly down at her new and unbecoming widow's weeds. "What is the matter?" she demanded anxiously. "I saw you come rushing out and go flying down to the pier and speak to that fellow who is sailing away!"

"Nothing is the matter," said Georgiana, but her set face belied her words. "I have sent word to Erica Hulft at Haerwyck that I must speak to her."

"But why?" cried Mattie, who now knew something of the problems at Windgate. "Why would you want to see *her*?"

"Never mind why now. Go and pack."

"I have nothing to pack except my pink dress. All my luggage went back downriver on the sloop with Nicolas."

"That's right, I forgot," said Georgiana wearily.

Mattie gave her a dazed look but Georgiana was in no mood for questions. Mattie sat down to await developments.

"When Erica comes, Mattie, I will want to speak to her alone. And now I will go up and pack myself—like you, I will be taking very little."

She left a startled Mattie trying to understand what that meant. Could it be that Georgiana was actually going to escort her back to Bermuda? Arthur and his victim, Jack Belter, had both been buried without ceremony at Belter's *bouwerie* where they had met their end. Mattie had pleaded that she was too upset to attend. In the end it was only the gravediggers and the carpenter who had made their rude coffins who had attended them. So Mattie felt she was free to go at any time. Her only regret would be leaving Nicolas.

Evening brought Erica. She was crouched low in the same small sailboat Georgiana had sent, wearing her fur-trimmed velvet cloak and looking about her nervously. She looked surprised when Georgiana hurried down to the pier to meet her.

"Welcome to Windgate," she said with irony.

"I had not expected quite so much civility from you," Erica said frankly, "after I ruined your skating party."

Georgiana gave her a grim smile. "It was not you who ruined my skating party," she said with finality. And, then, because she chose not to discuss that line, "Won't you come in, Erica? I've had a bite of supper left out for us."

Erica walked along beside her, looking about with some curiosity. "Where is Brett?"

"Off inspecting the *bouweries*. He'll be gone overnight. We'll have plenty of time for our discussion."

Erica missed a step. "Our *discussion*? All alone? Should I have come armed?" Her manner was droll but her amber eyes were watchful, uneasy.

"No—although I have no doubt you *are* armed, Erica. Somewhere in the folds of that copper velvet gown there should be a small pistol or at least a dagger."

"How right you are," said Erica coolly. "A pistol. Nicolas urged it on me as I left. He told me I might find Windgate a dangerous place just now. I took it he meant that *you* were dangerous."

"Oh, I am." Georgiana's voice was rueful as she ushered her guest into the great hall. "But only to myself. Nicolas should have told you that also."

"If you choose to speak in riddles, I suppose I must be content." Erica let Georgiana take her cloak. "What, no servants about?"

"I did not want them to see you. The one who brought you I tipped well to keep his mouth shut. The others have been packed off on duties that would keep them well away from the front of the house."

"I am almost afraid to eat," Erica complained, her amber eyes gleaming as they reached the dining room where a handsome repast had been set out. "It would seem you have used all the silver at Windgate's command," she murmured, studying the forest of silver that encrusted the long table and the big sideboard and cupboard.

"I wished to impress you with Windgate's wealth," said Georgiana crisply. "And all that might await you here." With a graceful gesture she pulled out a chair for her guest and Erica and her velvets sank into it.

"And just *what* might await me here?" wondered Erica. "Except possibly some poisoned wine?"

"Do not judge me as you would yourself. I am well aware that you tried to kill me there on the ice. Linnet has told me everything."

"I would Linnet had told *me* everything," sighed Erica. "Else I would not have lost Govert! It seems he has sharp eyes too—he saw me throw the handkerchief. I think that is what made him ill. He confronted me with my 'wicked mischief,' as he called it on the sloop's deck after we pulled away from the pier. It had begun to snow then and he stood there with the snow frosting his hair, berating me—it was then he began to cough."

So Erica had lost Govert!

"Perhaps you can have him back," she said. "Some cold meat? A glass of wine?"

"Both, if you please. I am expected back at Haerwyck—and they will marvel at my loss of appetite. But I am chilled to the marrow. It was freezing coming up here on that sailboat. Thank heaven for that fire." She stamped her numbed feet softly on the Turkey carpet beneath her chair and watched as Georgiana lifted slices of cold meat onto her plate from the big silver charger.

"It is possible"—Georgiana took her time in offering her guest rolls and filling her goblet—"that you may have both Brett and Govert back."

Erica's eyes sparkled wickedly. "While you run away with Nicolas, I suppose?"

Georgiana gave her a cold look. "That is what I want the world to think."

With a roll poised halfway to her mouth, Erica sat considering her. "You are mad," she said finally. "What could that bring you but ruin?"

Georgiana moistened her lips. Once she said what she had to say, the die would have been cast. If Erica did not agree to her terms, there would be another disastrous scandal on the river. "Everyone knows I left a note for Brett that I was running away with Nicolas."

"Yes, and everyone knows the note was fraudulent and that Nicolas bears the scars of his folly! His leg is bandaged."

"I hope he was not badly hurt?"

"Who can tell? He complains so! No, I do not think he is badly hurt else he would not be walking around."

No, he wouldn't be, thought Georgiana in a detached way. Nicolas had the devil's own luck. The sword could as easily have pierced his chest.

"Could you persuade Nicolas to leave Haerwyck tonight on some pretext? Say, to meet you downriver?"

"Probably," said Erica in a careless voice. "If I furnished him a sloop. But why would I do that?"

"You have access to Govert Steendam's sloop. You could send him downriver in that."

"Of course. I could tell Govert that I had forgotten something of great importance, something that must be brought to me instantly— but you have forgotten that he is at the outs with me."

"Yes, but you are only temporarily out of favor with him—and well you know it."

"Possibly." Erica's smile was complacent.

"So you could order out Steendam's sloop yourself. The *schipper* would take your orders—indeed, he is *used* to taking your orders!

And Nicolas could go downriver with a cabin door mysteriously locked.''

Erica was beginning to look interested. "All this could happen, yes. But—"

"The note, you said, was fraudulent—but suppose the note was *not* fraudulent and that Nicolas and I really had run away together?"

"I don't understand."

Georgiana leaned forward, spacing her words. "Suppose I penned such a note *now*. Suppose I was seen to run away with Nicolas? *Now—tonight*?"

Erica bit into the roll thoughtfully. "Brett would come and take you back—as he did before.''

"Suppose he did not know where we had gone?"

"You interest me, but it is all moonbeams and smoke because Nicolas has no intention of disappearing—he means to have Windgate!"

"Yes, but suppose I was seen to leave with Nicolas and then I disappeared? Might it not be thought that he had done away with me?"

"I think Brett would manage to wring the truth out of him," said Erica slowly. "At the point of a rapier! I have seen him fight."

"But Nicolas could not tell him the truth if he did not know it."

A frown drew Erica's fox-colored brows together. "What are you suggesting, Georgiana? Be specific."

"I am suggesting that the whole world knows you are my sworn enemy. If you spread the word that you had seen me leave with Nicolas—of my own free will—and I was not found, then everyone would believe that Nicolas had lured me away from Brett and when he found that I would not further his claim, that he had killed me."

"If I said that, I think they might drag the river for your body," agreed Erica coolly. "But why would either of us do it?"

"Your enlightened self-interest will make you do what I ask, Erica." Georgiana's words were blunt; her voice had an edge to it. "You want Govert and you want Brett and you want Windgate. I am telling you that you can have all three—if you will only help me to escape."

It was Erica's turn to lean forward. "I am listening."

"Mattie and I need a sloop to take us downriver."

"Mattie? Oh, yes, Kincaid's widow."

"*You* will arrange for that sloop. *You* will be my witness that I left with Nicolas."

"I would need two sloops for that," objected Erica. "One to transport you and this Mattie person, and one to transport Nicolas."

"I don't doubt you can arrange that too."

"Yes, there is a trader's sloop presently tied up at Haerwyck. He goes downriver tomorrow. I don't doubt a few guilders would persuade him to cast off tonight and keep his mouth shut about it later."

"There, you see? I said you could arrange it."

Erica was staring at her. "And tomorrow, when you change your mind? What will happen to poor little Erica Hulft then? They will hang her!"

Georgiana sounded tired. "I will not change my mind, Erica. Indeed, I cannot. I have thought it all out. Nicolas has—has certain information that can destroy me, destroy Brett. I—I cannot let this information be brought out in court. If word has it that I ran away with him and *he disposed of me*, public sentiment would go against him. Any evidence he brought would be suspect, thought possibly to be fraudulent. Men like Huygens ten Haer may object to my husband because he is English but they are not men who would stomach a wife being snatched from her husband's arms and killed so that another man might profit!"

"I follow your line of reasoning," said Erica. "You will destroy Nicolas's reputation—whatever reputation he has left—but you will destroy yourself as well."

"Unfortunately, the two deeds are indissoluble. To contrive the one, I must endure the other."

Erica gave her hostess a keen look across her goblet. "And why would you do this, Georgiana?"

"That Brett may have Windgate, for I will not have him lose it through me."

Those brilliant amber eyes studied her. "You realize of course that you may be consigning him to me?"

Georgiana nodded. She could not trust herself to speak just now. Her throat was dry, for she knew the truth of Erica's words. What more likely than that Brett, abandoned, would return to his former mistress? *Indeed, that was what she was offering Erica—another chance at Brett, without a wife in the way.*

"You must love him very much, to do that," murmured Erica, toying with her glass.

"With all my heart," whispered Georgiana, clenching her hands till the knuckles were white, and managing to keep a sob from her voice.

"And this evidence must be very damning," said Erica softly.

"Very."

Erica looked disturbed. "There are different kinds of love," she told Georgiana. "Mine is real enough but it is not so self-sacrificing. I love Brett too but—"

"But you would not give him up to save Windgate for him—even knowing how much it means to him?"

"No."

"Then we are very different, you and I."

"Yes." Erica studied Georgiana's lovely tormented face. "I can see that. I can see that I ought not to have called you the child bride—you are a woman grown, to have thought of this." When Georgiana was silent, she got up and began to pace about the room, sipping her wine. "My feet are still frozen," she complained. "If I were mistress of Windgate"—she turned to Georgiana with a mocking look—"*when* I am mistress of Windgate," she corrected herself, "I will have the fires kept burning high." Her laughter rippled. "That shakes you, doesn't it? The thought of me here . . . with Brett, in the firelight. Come now, can you endure it?"

"I can endure it," said Georgiana steadily. "For Brett's sake." *For if I do not endure it, all that Brett has worked for for so long will be sacrificed, Nicolas will win and Brett will have nothing, nothing. . . .*

Erica paused and leaned on one hand on the long table. She was an appealing figure in her copper velvet, thought Georgiana bitterly. Brett would soon forgive her, and all would be as before at Windgate.

"I must admit I find your proposition fascinating." Delicately, Erica spun her wine goblet around in her hand, but her thoughtful gaze was not on the goblet but fixed somewhere in the middle distance. Her beautiful face had taken on a wily, scheming expression. "And I am sure that you—because you are, after all, very young—at this moment are expecting me to be noble. You are expecting me to say, 'Georgiana, I cannot accept this sacrifice on your part. I realize Brett loves you and so I will aid you in your magnificent charade until Windgate's ownership is unchallenged—and then you may return to your husband's waiting arms. Of course, you may care to toss me a few baubles, but the main prize will be yours.' That is what you expect me to say, isn't it, Georgiana?''

Georgiana shook her head. She was facing up to all that she would lose—lose forever. She could not trust herself to speak just now, her voice might break.

''Because if it is, put it from your mind. I play for keeps, Georgiana. If Brett's fortune is to be saved—and I agree, this *will* save him because he will now become a tragic figure in everyone's eyes, a valorous cuckholded husband fighting a foe who would stoop to anything, even to murdering Brett's wife. No, Nicolas for all his jauntiness could not stand up to that, it would destroy him.''

''Will you do it?''

''Only if you will swear to me that you will not write to Brett or seek to get in touch with him or let him know where you are. And''—the amber eyes flashed—''if you cross me in this, I will know how to make at least part of the story come true, and you will indeed float beneath the Hudson down to the sea.''

A chill ripple went down Georgiana's spine. Erica was cool—she would not hesitate to carry out her threat. But that very coolness was the reason Erica would make such a good witness to Nicolas's ''crime''—she would be believed.

''Actually, it would amuse me to see Nicolas tangled in his own web!'' Erica's laughter rippled maliciously. ''I enjoy watching him struggle. The battle is always so intense—and so unorthodox!'' She became businesslike again. ''You and your friend Mattie can sail back to Haerwyck with me tonight. You can be let off just north of Haerwyck. I just remembered—there is a sailboat, it is small and will not be missed right away, but you could handle it easily yourself and it would take you and your friend downriver in absolute secrecy to New Orange. Coming from Bermuda, I am sure you know how to sail a boat.''

''Yes, I know how to sail, but I have no mind that Mattie and I shall be set adrift in some leaky boat to perish,'' said Georgiana evenly. ''*You* will accompany us, Erica. You will see that we make shore in New Orange safely.''

"I see you do not trust me?" The amber eyes flashed gold. "Very well, then, we will take some other, larger boat—together."

Again that chill feeling. Erica could well have intended to send both the sailboat and its occupants to the bottom of the river. Georgiana realized that she would have to stay awake, to watch Erica all the time.

"If I hear that you have tricked me," she told Erica coldly, "I will come back and say that you and Nicolas together conspired my death but that I escaped you."

Erica's white teeth flashed in the candlelight. "I am beginning to admire you, Georgiana. But you see, my one desire is to get you gone. That has been my *only* desire from the beginning."

"Yes, I remember—you did not tell Brett that you had seen me in Bermuda."

"No, but I foolishly told my brother and he later sold the information to Brett. Claes was ever a fool—I would have paid him more to keep the news from Brett!"

"And perhaps poisoned his wine into the bargain," suggested Georgiana morosely.

"Come now, don't judge me so harshly. I never poisoned anyone!"

It was on the tip of Georgiana's tongue to add harshly "Not yet!" but she needed Erica. Instead she said sweetly, "Would you like more wine, Erica?"

Erica caught her breath and set her glass down hastily, considered it with some trepidation. She had just noticed that her hostess's goblet sat untouched.

"The wine is neither drugged nor poisoned," said Georgiana irritably. "I need your help, Erica—cool-headed and awake—if we are to get away tonight."

Erica gave her an uneasy smile. She drummed her fingers on the table. "I do not think I can manage it tonight," she admitted. "Nicolas could prove troublesome—or Govert. But by tomorrow I can arrange it. But then you said Brett would only be gone overnight. It would not do to have him overtake you on the river."

No, that would not do at all!

"Brett will be gone two or three days," Georgiana admitted. "I am eager to—"

"To be off?" Erica gave her a little slanted smile.

"To make my move before Nicolas can make his. For this I need your help."

"And you shall have it," promised Erica. "I will send word to you tomorrow how I have arranged it."

"Do not sent word. Come yourself."

Erica's fox-brush head bowed in assent. "Very well. Be ready—you and your friend."

New Orange, New Netherland, 1673

CHAPTER 36

"Oh, I do hope Flan hasn't gone!" Mattie said anxiously for the tenth time, as she and Georgiana hurried toward the dock in New Orange. Both of them were heavily cloaked and with shawls pulled up over their heads—ostensibly against the cold but actually that their faces might be hidden from view as they made their way down the quaint narrow street past rows of steep-roofed yellow brick houses with picturesque weathervanes flying aloft, distinctive divided Dutch doors and spotlessly clean front stoops.

Their luggage—such as it was, for Georgiana had elected to take very little with her—resided at the Green Lion, where they had registered as the Bessemer sisters, Pentience and Abigail. Georgiana had done the talking—pretending to have a bad cold and to be perpetually coughing into a handkerchief, which had caused the innkeeper to keep his distance and kept him from having too good a look at her shawl-shaded face.

Their trip downriver had been uneventful. The weather mercifully had held. Erica had indeed accompanied them but she had left them

immediately upon arrival in New Orange and taken a sloop back
upriver. Her story was already prepared. She had ridden away from
Haerwyck on horseback "for a little exercise" right after a limping
Nicolas had been packed off on Govert Steendam's sloop to retrieve
from Erica's house in New Orange the gifts Erica had purchased for
the ten Haer ladies and "forgotten" to bring upriver with her. "My
best petticoats," she had said regretfully to Georgiana. "Such a
sacrifice." She sighed.

"Just think," said Georgiana in a new hard voice, "you will have
all of mine to replace them!"

Erica brightened. "I had heard you found a real trove when you
moved the big wardrobe in my—in the bedchamber next to Brett's,"
she said.

A pang went through Georgiana. Those were her mother's things—
and now they would belong to Erica Hulft, just as her mother's
journal in which she had poured out her secret thoughts now
belonged to Nicolas. "Yes," she said in a colorless voice. "How
will you explain being gone so long, Erica?"

Erica laughed. It was a buoyant, confident laugh, full of excitement. This was the sort of dangerous game Erica loved to play—and
at which she was a marvelous player. "Well, my horse has already
been found riderless—and I am sure they are searching the forest for
me right now. I have bribed the *schipper* well to take me upriver and
drop me at just the right spot along the shore near one of Haerwyck's
bouweries. I will stagger into the *bouwerie* and gasp out my story,
how I was brushed off my horse by a low limb in the forest and lost
my sense of direction and have been wandering around ever since
and have only just found the river!"

"Do you think you will be believed?"

"Of course! After all this harrowing running about, back and
forth by sloop, these days past, I must look worn enough to have
actually done it! And"— she gave Georgiana a wicked smile—"I
will have given Govert time to miss me and realize what life would
be like without me."

"So you think you will have him eating out of your hand again?"

Erica shrugged. "Perhaps." Enjoying Georgiana as an audience
for things she would never be able to admit later, she regaled
Georgiana with how she would entrap Nicolas: When Georgiana's
disappearance became general knowledge, she said, she would say

that when she first rode out the day she became lost—and before Nicolas left on his errand to New Orange—that she had seen Georgiana sail up alone in a small boat. That would not be too surprising, since it was known after all that Georgiana was from Bermuda and a good sailor. But what *was* surprising was that Nicolas had met her on the riverbank and they had strolled away arm in arm toward that old deserted hut that had once been the Larson *bouwerie* before its wooden chimney had ignited and burned the low cottage to the ground with the Larsons in it. She would say that she had sat her horse, very still and concealed by the underbrush, and she had heard words of love pass between Nicolas and Georgiana, that she had heard him promise to take her away from Brett, away from New Netherland.

And to make that more credible, she would greet Nicolas when he returned from New Orange with a surprised "What have you done with her?" which would go unexplained at the time but would later assume a terrible significance.

Georgiana told herself grimly that Nicolas had brought it all on himself but she felt, when they arrived in New Orange, and she watched Erica embark for her return voyage upriver, that she had loosed seven devils on Nicolas in the person of Erica. She wondered if Govert Steendam would survive a year with her, or if before twelve months was out Erica Hulft would have become the richest widow in all New Netherland—and once again mistress of the patroon of Windgate.

She wondered about it, but all she could see through a rain of tears in her heart, was Brett's face, wondering where she had gone—and why.

He would discover the note of course. It would not be too easy to find, she had not wanted him to find it right away, so she had left it stuffed into the toe of one of her shoes, knowing that eventually Linnet, who was always trying to force her feet into Georgiana's smaller slippers, would find it and bring it to Brett to read.

The note would say, *Do not try to find me. I have run away with Nicolas.* And it would be signed *Georgiana.*

And Brett would go looking for Nicolas and she could only hope that they would not kill each other. Or Nicolas might realize how neatly he had been tricked and perhaps take to his heels before the *schout* could come to question him. And Brett would keep Windgate, and Nicolas would be loosed on the world again.

Parting with Floss had been the worst moment. She had spent a long time in the stable, stroking that silver mane while the gentle mare nuzzled her. She had even taken Floss for a short exhilarating ride across the snowy meadow and Floss had danced and made clouds of steam with her hot breath in the cold air that blew down the Hudson out of Canada.

"I cannot take you, Floss," she had whispered into that silken gray ear that had cocked alertly at her voice. "It would be too easy to trace a beauty like you."

Floss, of course, had not understood. She would be confidently expecting her mistress back . . . Georgiana's heart bled. But she knew that Brett would be good to the sweet-tempered horse, and instinctively she knew that he would never sell her.

About Brett she had tried not to think. He would recover from his blow in time, she told herself gloomily. He would forget her, he would turn to Erica—or to some other woman.

Her own life was shattered, of course. She must accept that. Nor would she brood about it. At least Arthur was gone, and with him the Articles of Indenture, which Brett had fortunately found in Arthur's doublet the morning he had ridden out to Jack Belter's *bouwerie*—and had destroyed. Nobody had any claim on her now; she could go where she liked.

Now, in New Orange at last, she paused in front of a little tobacco shop. "Are you sure you wouldn't rather go to Boston?" she asked Mattie. "We could settle Arthur's estate there and you could return to Bermuda a rich woman."

"No." Mattie shivered. "After having lived with Arthur, I'm afraid of everything Bostonian." She gave a little laugh. "I'd rather let Father make arrangements to handle things for me after I get home."

Well, she would take Mattie home and then—who knew? The world was wide. But for herself, she had no plans to stay in Bermuda.

"Why didn't you let that woman who brought us here arrange for our passage?" wondered Mattie. "She seemed so competent!"

"Oh, she's competent enough—and if she'd made our travel

arrangements for us, very likely we'd have been kidnapped and sold into slavery in Barbary!''

Mattie blanched. "Oh, to be out of this terrible country," she whimpered.

"You soon will be. And it isn't terrible—it's beautiful."

"Not to me!"

"There—I see the *Swan* lying at anchor. Just keep looking around for Flan."

It was an hour before they found him, somewhat the worse for drink, reeling out of a waterfront tavern with a girl on each arm.

"Flan!" Mattie was standing directly in front of him and Flan's step wavered. He tried to focus his bloodshot eyes on her.

"Mattie," he said thickly.

"I must speak to you. Privately." Mattie gave his two blowsy companions a look of distaste.

"All right, Mattie." Flan disengaged his arms and gave his two laughing protesting companions a spank each on the rump, promising them warmly he'd see them later.

Georgiana, with the gloved fingers of her right hand holding her shawl almost closed about her face, had no doubt he would. Flan, adorned with cutlasses and a gold earring, seemed to have come into his own. She could picture him in any seaport in the world, swaggering into a tavern and banging his fist down hard enough to make the tankards rattle as he jovially set up the house.

"I—we have something for you. At the inn. In a box," muttered Mattie.

"Oh—the passage money." Flan managed to get his wits together. "We'll have to hurry, for the ship sails in two hours. I'd given ye up, Mattie."

"I need passage for two, Flan. Anna's going with me."

"Anna?" Flan turned sharply to look at her companion. "Why, it is you!" he cried as he peered beneath her shawl. "Mattie told me you were married!"

"I'm leaving my husband," said Anna briefly. "You're not to noise it about, Flan. I'm taking Mattie back to Bermuda. She's afraid to make the trip alone."

Flan whistled. He gave the shadowed face beneath the shawl a lascivious look. "Come and have a drink with me," he offered genially. "Plenty of time before the ship sails. You've brought the money, of course?"

Georgiana frowned. Her money had all been given to the sloop's *schipper* to buy his silence. "I have a pair of candlesticks," she said shortly. "Solid silver. They're worth a dozen passages to Bermuda."

Flan's brows lifted and he gave her what she could only categorize as a sly look. "Whether the captain will take candlesticks, I don't know. Sure you've got no gold coins about you?"

Both women shook their heads.

He left them inside a smoky tavern's common room with tankards of ale set up in front of them. The place reeked from the constant puffing of long clay pipes but mercifully most of the customers were groggy from last night's carousing and gave the two women little difficulty.

Flan came back in a surprisingly short time. "He'll not have the candlesticks," he reported. "Because later they might be called stolen and he'd be caught in the middle. So I'll have to take the candlesticks and sell them for what I can get. Meantime, I had to give him all the coin I had on me, all I've got from this venture, but at least you two shall both have passage to Bermuda aboard the *Gudrun*, and I've heard Captain Maarlandt is a man to be trusted."

Georgiana hesitated. The candlesticks were all she had. She'd arrive in Bermuda destitute save for the clothes on her back and the light valise she'd left at the inn. "What did the passage cost you, Flan?"

"Enough," he said, a cold note creeping into his voice.

Her heart sank and she tried to keep the contempt out of her face as she looked at him. He was cheating her, that much was clear. The passage had cost only a fraction of what the candlesticks would bring but she could not afford to press the point—nor to wait, for the ship was sailing within the hour.

"See that you do not sell the candlesticks in New Orange," she cautioned.

"Oh, that I will not," agreed Flan instantly, and went along with them to the inn to pick up the candlesticks. He grunted as he picked up the long box. "Heavy," he muttered. "Must be made of thick boards."

"Heavy silver," said Georgiana dryly.

Unable to resist checking out his loot, Flan stopped in an alley and behind a pile of boxes peeked at the candlesticks with their fat molded cupids and entwining leaves. Georgiana could see him run his tongue over his lips at the sight. She wondered how she could ever have liked him.

He looked up at her with a bright insincere smile. "These ought to take care of what I had to put out for the passage," he said brightly.

"I thought they would," said Georgiana on a note of irony.

Flan escorted them aboard the *Gudrun*, introduced them to the captain and left. He had learned a lot on this voyage, he told himself, as he waved good-bye to Mattie and Georgiana from the dock. Once, he'd considered marrying that mocking wench. Now he realized there were plenty of women in the world to suit his needs—and they could be had for the price of a few dollars. Bought smiles, bought kisses—it was enough. And—he patted the long box fondly—there'd be enough left out of this lot to buy him all the whores in New Orange!

Georgiana, knowing she'd been cheated, turned her back on Flan's wave and thought about their accommodations. It would be a cramped cabin shared by Mattie, but at least it would be private, not tumbled about in a barrackslike hold with a lot of other women.

"Thank God we're headed for Bermuda," sighed Mattie as they cleared the harbor. "I was sure some Dutch court would hang me for shooting Arthur!"

Georgiana did not answer. She was watching the fort and the big windmill and the skyline of quaint New Orange recede in the distance. She had come here with such high hopes, and now she supposed she would never see it again.

Both of them watched the coast of New Netherland slide away from them, watched until it was a thin slice in the distance and then disappeared over the horizon.

They were going home. Home to Bermuda.

The voyage was a sad one for Georgiana, who saw mirrored in the empty distance an empty life—without Brett. She did not regret her decision but she felt sad and lost without him. He had filled her life more than she had ever realized. And now Erica Hulft would take her place.

But if every scudding sea mile made Georgiana sadder, it had exactly the opposite effect on Mattie.

Now that she was safely away from a place where they might hang her, Mattie was recovering her aplomb—indeed she was possessed of an aplomb she had never had before.

"When you think about it," she breathed confidentially to Georgiana as they stood on the deck looking out into the blue green distance while the sails snapped and cracked overhead, "it was all really very exciting."

Georgiana gave her a resigned but skeptical look. Mattie was basically still a child, she thought.

"Promise you'll never tell a soul," whispered Mattie, "but I let Nicolas seduce me!"

"Mattie, you didn't!"

"I did. I don't know what came over me, but I'll always remember it." Mattie looked dreamy. "It was so wonderful, just the opposite of Arthur, who always told me I did everything all wrong."

Georgiana gave her a helpless look.

"Of course, I realize Nicolas has no character, Georgiana." She looked up. "It seems so strange to call you 'Georgiana' and not 'Anna.'"

"Call me what you like," said Georgiana easily. "Undoubtedly everyone will call me Anna Smith when we reach Bermuda." She was beginning to worry over what she might meet there, but everything in her life there seemed so trivial by comparison with Brett's great affairs in New Netherland, she felt sure she could meet it.

"I know I shouldn't have done it." Mattie pursued her own line of thought. "With Nicolas, I mean. And at first I was sure I'd burn in hell for it." She giggled. "But honestly, Georgiana, do you think it was so terribly wrong?"

Georgiana shrugged. "Don't ask *me*—I've made nothing but mistakes in my life!" *And am paying for them all.*

"Anyway it was loads of fun. I wish"—Mattie blushed—"I wish I had the chance to do it all again!"

Georgiana laughed. It was one of the few occasions she found for laughter on the voyage.

True to his promise, Captain Maarlandt set them ashore on the south side of Bermuda Island—not in St. George but in Smith's Parish. The girls had to hike to the nearest plantation from the isolated cove where he let them off before sailing away. But the first house they came to welcomed them and they stayed the night. The next morning their host sailed them into St. George's harbor and they stepped ashore in St. George in the lazy summerlike weather as if they had never been away.

"Oh, I can't wait to get home," cried Mattie, almost skipping across the familiar dock. "Oh, there's Mistress Maxwell—hello, Mistress Maxwell! And there's—"

Her voice cut off suddenly for a carriage they both recognized was just driving up to the dock. It was coming straight toward them and it had a woman in it dressed in black taffeta with a large amber brooch at her throat. She looked around her in lordly fashion at the barrels and piles of conch shells and bananas and pens of turtles— and then suddenly she sighted Georgiana and her face stiffened in shock.

She shouted at her driver to stop the carriage and she rose in her seat, pointed a trembling hand at Georgiana.

"Constable!" she cried in a strident voice. "Constable, arrest that woman!"

Georgiana would have fled—but she could not. Harsh, work-roughened hands seized her, held her fast.

She knew then. It had been a mistake to come back here. A mistake that could well prove fatal.

Part Two
The Fatal Mistake

The hot swift night of the tropics
Fast is closing down
And she will wish herself anywhere
But in St. George's town!

St. George, Bermuda, 1673

CHAPTER 37

With a crowd gathering to stare and mutter, Georgiana found it hard to maintain her dignity—but she tried. Fighting down a panicky urge to break and run, to hide herself somewhere among the bales and piles of merchandise and produce, and when night fell creep out and stow away on a ship bound for anywhere, she straightened her back and looked Bernice full in the eye.

"Back off!" Her menacing tone surprised those who had seized her. "This woman has no right to order me arrested!"

"That's right, she hasn't!" cried Mattie indignantly. "How dare you touch Anna?"

"Constable. Bernice was standing up in her carriage, beckoning to a big man just now trotting up the street toward them. "Arrest this woman for the theft of a pair of valuable candlesticks. She took them from Mirabelle."

"The candlesticks were mine to take!" shouted Georgiana. "Samantha Jamison had given them to me for my dowry and well you knew it—I told you and the servants backed me up."

"The servants?" Bernice's scornful sniff dismissed them. "They are liars all!"

The burly constable, who had just arrived on the scene, looked in surprise at Anna Smith, who had once been the toast of these islands. "Ye stole this lady's candlesticks, Mistress Anna?" he asked in an awed tone, and those who were holding Georgiana released her to face him.

"Yes!" cried Bernice angrily.

"I took them when I left, but they were mine," cried Anna. 'Mattie, Sue, all the Waites know they were mine!"

"Yes," cried Mattie, trying to step between them. "I do know!"

"I demand you arrest her!" roared Bernice.

"Mistress Anna." The constable looked shamefaced. "I do hate to haul you away to jail to await the magistrate. Could ye perhaps put up collateral so that ye could make restitution if the verdict goes against ye? If so, I think this lady might let ye go along with Mistress Mattie here."

"Well, I—" Georgiana cast a wild look around her. "I do have this valuable ring." She held up her hand and the big sapphire flashed in its heavy gold setting. "And there are the clothes in this valise—they are of some value."

Bernice looked thoughtfully at the ring but sniffed at the mention of the clothes.

"And"—Georgiana drew herself up haughtily—"I am willing to state in writing that should the verdict go against me, I will indenture myself for the rest to anyone who will give me honest employment, and work until the candlesticks are paid for."

"That would take many years," scoffed Bernice. "Pay for them now, Mistress High and Mighty!"

The constable looked upset. "Could ye not do that, Mistress Anna?" he asked anxiously.

Georgiana bit her lip. "I cannot do that," she admitted. "But I will work—"

"You cannot do that either," snapped Bernice, "for you are already indentured to Arthur Kincaid. He has told me so."

"Arthur Kincaid is dead."

"Ah, so you have killed him? I would not put it past you!"

Mattie broke into a wail, there was a gasp from the crowd and even the constable turned to gape at Bernice at this harsh assumption.

"Arthur Kincaid died in New Netherland," said Georgiana with dignity, "as Mattie here would tell you if she was not too upset to do so. His death was none of my doing. I came back to Bermuda to escort his widow."

There was a sudden mutter from the crowd that had gathered. Public opinion, always fickle, was swinging now toward Georgiana.

"That is not all she stole," howled Bernice, glaring at Georgiana. "Where are the clothes you stole from my daughters? *Even the dress she was married in was stolen from me!*"

Married! The constable seized on that. "The girl is married," he cried joyfully. "Her husband will make restitution."

"Don't be a fool, man! Do you see a husband before you? No, you see two bedraggled females and no men at all. Ask the wench where her husband is—ask her!"

"New Netherland," supplied Georgiana.

"And that is a Dutch colony and we are at war with Holland," cried Bernice triumphantly. "So restitution will not be easily come by, will it, Constable? Will it?"

At the news that Anna's husband was at present in a Dutch colony and doubtless trading with the enemy, the constable's mouth had tightened. "Is it true ye stole this lady's clothes, Mistress Anna?" he asked reproachfully.

"They were *my* clothes!" exploded Georgiana, her control breaking at last. "Mine! Which that woman stole from me along with everything else!" She leveled an angry finger at Bernice. "I am amazed that you would pursue me for a pair of candlesticks, Bernice—you who stole all of Mirabelle from me!"

Bernice yelled back something inaudible and the constable sought to intervene in this shouting match. "If Kincaid is dead, Mistress Anna is now free!" he roared. "And if she offers to—"

"Free?" Bernice turned on him, her piercing voice overriding his. "She cannot be free. Her Articles of Indenture will be inherited by Arthur Kincaid's kin—if indeed he be dead!"

"Mattie," cried Georgiana. "Speak! Tell this crazy woman that I am not bound to anyone."

Mattie, who had been standing with her mouth open, watching events that were moving too fast for her, jumped forward. "I am Arthur's widow and therefore his heir—and I renounce all claim to Anna. And if the trial goes against her, *I* will pay for the candlesticks for I am now a rich woman!"

There was a sudden buzz from the crowd as all eyes turned to the small dark girl in pink taffeta. Flushed with indignation, Mattie shrank back from so much attention.

"You have the money *here*?" drawled Bernice.

"No, but I will have it when Arthur's estate is settled."

"But nothing now?" Bernice's brows shot up. "You see the way it is, Constable."

"But Mistress Anna offers to indenture herself, in any case," said the constable eagerly. "So ye see, she can work off the debt."

Bernice's face was a cold mask as she studied the rebellious golden-haired girl before her, standing her ground as she always had. She discounted Mattie's claim to being Arthur's widow and heir, for it seemed more likely that handsome Arthur had deserted her, and that Anna, who had always been surrounded by so *many* men, had run away from the husband she had married in such haste. Her grasping heart yearned to accept Georgiana's offer, for the candlesticks were worth a fortune and it would be good, since she could not have them back, to have their worth in coin. For a moment she toyed with the idea of insisting that Georgiana be indentured to *her*, and then she would sell the girl's Articles to some roving sea captain who could be persuaded to take the girl away somewhere and sell her into a house of prostitution—in Tortuga, perhaps; few women returned from the brothels of Tortuga.

But no . . . that was a lovely face before her, an enticing figure, a persuasive voice. The girl had a dramatic and showy beauty that would make her stand out anywhere. Even if Bernice sold her to some sea captain, how could she be sure that Anna would not win him over during the voyage, tell him her story so winningly that he would end up her champion, and sail back to challenge Bernice's shaky possession of Mirabelle?

No, bad pennies had a way of turning up. Bernice sighed.

"I insist she be arrested," she said righteously. "Even though I take a loss for it. She will be an example to all potential thieves on this island! Constable, do your duty."

"Oh, you *wouldn't* put her in jail?" gasped Mattie, shocked.

"We dare not risk letting her escape," snapped Bernice.

"But *I* will stand good for her," protested Mattie tearfully. "I promise she will not leave the island." She turned to the constable, who was shuffling his feet, with a gesture of appeal.

Georgiana felt panic stealing over her there in the hot Bermuda sun. She had never really considered the possibility of jail. Around her gaped the curious crowd, enjoying the excitement. *Why*, she asked herself, *would grasping Bernice, who cared for nothing but money, refuse to make a deal with her that would pay for the candlesticks?*

She could not know that the will that Bernice had proffered the court had been a sham, that she had written it herself and signed her dead husband's name with a flourish that she had arrogantly expected to hide the fact that she was not an accomplished forger. Tobias Jamison had not been well when he wrote it, she had assured the court with an attempt at tears—his hand was shaky. And she had thoughtfully dated the document three years back, putting in the words *If I should marry again, I hereby instruct that all my belongings, both real and personal, shall be vested in my surviving widow*—Bernice wasn't quite sure what "vested" meant, but it had a fine legal sound. Here in Bermuda, far from London courts, it would hold!

And to give the document the true flavor of authenticity she had hired a fellow to impersonate Christopher Marks, who was known to be Tobias Jamison's London agent, to deliver the will to the court. In reality the man who claimed to be Christopher Marks had not seen London in over fifteen years; he was a disreputable trader in Jamaica who owed Bernice a favor. But he had a powdered wig and a suit of fine clothes and he had tramped around St. George taking snuff and criticizing everything in sight—and since no one in St. George had ever actually seen Christopher Marks, no one doubted his authenticity. Bernice had paid him well; he was gone from her life, and she never expected to see him again.

But although the fictitious "Christopher Marks" had long since departed Bermuda, and Mirabelle Plantation had been adjudged hers and she was now firmly in possession, Bernice knew that she would never feel truly safe while Anna Smith lived.

She wanted the deal Georgiana offered—but she could not afford to take it. Too much was at stake.

She gave Anna a last contemptuous look, then sank back into her carriage and ordered her driver to turn the vehicle around—she was going home. The crowd parted to let the carriage pass and looked after her erect departing back in silence, each one wondering in his heart why this woman was so furiously bent on the destruction of the young sinner who was now being led away by the constable.

Georgiana was cursing herself for having been so foolish as to think she could ever reason with Bernice. She caught up her skirts, which were whirling in the dust as the constable hurried her along, eager to get this embarrassing business over as quickly as possible.

"There's no need to put me in jail," she insisted. "My friends, the Waites, will stand good for my presence at the trial—for I presume there is to be a trial?"

"That's not up to me," muttered the constable, half ashamed that he should be dragging along by her slender arm the girl all the island had believed to be the Jamison heiress. "But I've no authority to put ye anywhere else."

Georgiana turned to Mattie. "Rush home, Mattie, and tell Sue—she'll know what to do."

Big-eyed and frightened, Mattie nodded, gathered up her rustling pink taffeta skirts—and fled.

Sue found her later that day, in the jail. The jailer's wife let Sue into the small cell-like room where Georgiana was pacing about.

"Oh, Anna! How terrible that this should happen to you?" Sue threw her arms protectively around her friend and hugged her. Her hands were grubby, her taffy hair tumbled, and her hat awry, for Sue had been gardening when Mattie stumbled in gasping out the news that Anna had been taken. Sue had thrown down her trowel and had been addressing herself to Georgiana's problems all day. Now her worried blue eyes betrayed her anxiety. "I knew you shouldn't have taken those candlesticks!"

"They were *my* candlesticks," protested Georgiana. "What I shouldn't have done was come back!"

"That's right, you shouldn't have. Why ever did you?"

Georgiana gave her friend a harassed glance. How to explain to Sue that after she had made her deal with Erica she had experienced an almost overpowering yearning for familiar skies and warm sunshine and the big cedars and sea-carved rocks she knew so well. She had needed not some far-off frosty horizon but to come home to lick her wounds and be made whole again by familiar things, familiar places, familiar faces.

"I—don't know why," she said hoarsely.

"Oh, never mind why," cried Sue. "As soon as Mattie told me, I began seeing what I could do about your release."

Georgiana gave her a nervous look. "They *have* agreed to release me to your custody, haven't they?"

The room seemed suddenly very silent. Sue looked as if she were near tears. "Bond has been set," Sue said.

Georgiana's gasp of relief seemed to come up from her toes.

"I had not the bond money to put up—nor had Lance," Sue rushed on. "And Mother refused, because she said she now had Mattie back on her hands again, and no telling if there'd be any money at all from Arthur's estate due to the odd way he died—indeed, she thought Mattie might even be *blamed* for his death and there'd be the additional expense of defending her, not that she in any way doubted Mattie's story but—"

"But surely the bond could not be so large! I'm no great criminal. I but took a pair of candlesticks that belonged to me by right—and a few clothes that were mine also!" She looked suspiciously at Sue. "How much is the bond?"

She hung her head, and the shoulders of her print calico bodice drooped. "A thousand pounds."

Georgiana gasped. "A thousand pounds? Did I hear you aright, Sue? *A thousand pounds?*"

Sue shook her head wearily. "I did try to argue the magistrate out of so great a sum, but Bernice had already been there and convinced him that the candlesticks were of enormous value and that you would surely flee and the bond would be forfeit, and the magistrate is a kinsman of my mother's and he knows how little she can afford—"

"Oh, come, Sue, I wouldn't run away! Not if it was going to cost you a thousand pounds!"

"That is what I told Mother. And Father. But although they feel sad about your plight, Anna, they dare not take the chance—it would ruin them." Her face reddened. "I am sorry, Anna, but all my supplications could not move them."

Georgiana's lovely face hardened. "I suppose that Bernice has been spreading rumors about my bad character?"

"Ever since you left," admitted Sue sadly. "It was as if she anticipated your return and wanted to turn everybody against you."

"And people have listened to her lies?" Georgiana's voice grew sharp. "How could they, Sue? These are people I've known all my life."

"But you were gone and Bernice was here and Mirabelle is the finest plantation in Bermuda and people want to go there, to be entertained there—" Sue made a helpless gesture. "I have certainly tried to refute everything she said, but the candlesticks *were* missing and the servants at Mirabelle are afraid to open their mouths, they live in deathly fear of Bernice—oh, where is your husband, Anna? Brett seemed so able to handle any situation. How could he let you come back here alone?"

"Brett had nothing to say about it," sighed Georgiana. "I have left him, Sue. I am not going back."

Sue's horror was written on her honest face. "But then there'll be nobody to save you!" she blurted.

"Nobody at all." Georgiana turned away to stare at the wall. A spider was running down it, through a break in the plaster. Large and hairy-legged. She shuddered, for she had always had a dread of spiders. She took off her shoe. "Did the magistrate say when the trial would be held?"

"He has set it for Thursday next." Sue winced as Georgiana brought the shoe down against the wall with a slap but missed the big spider, who ran into the crack in the wall and disappeared.

"He'll be back," sighed Georgiana, thinking of the darkness that was on its way. She felt her flesh crawl. "Next Thursday, you say?" It was a long time till Thursday, a lot of sleepless nights.

"Are you sure you don't want us to try and contact Brett?"

"No," said Georgiana. "I left without saying good-bye, Sue." Her lips twisted. "Worse, I left him a note saying I had run away with another man."

It was Sue's turn to gasp. "Then—where is he?" she asked uncertainly. "This other man? Perhaps *he* will help you."

"It wasn't true," said Georgiana. "Oh, Sue, it would take too long to explain. Let's leave it that Brett doesn't know where I've gone—he will never know." She gave Sue a tired look that forbade questions.

Sue shook her head to clear it. Georgiana had seemed so in love. What could have happened in this short time to so change her feelings toward Brett Danforth?

"Would you ask the jailer's wife for some candles, Sue? I don't want that spider running over me in the dark."

"I will." Sue nodded energetically. "And I'll be back to see you every day till the trial. I will bring you any news there is and we will send you your supper so that you will not have to eat jail food—yes, and breakfast too."

Georgiana felt her eyes moisten. "You've always been so good to me, Sue," she murmured huskily.

"The shoe was always on the other foot," said Sue energetically. " 'Twas *you* did a lot for *me*. Indeed"—she gave a little self-conscious laugh—"I think Lance might never have noticed me at all if you hadn't given me that blue dress!"

Half the dinner Sue sent was scraped from the platter by the jailer's wife before she brought it in, but that didn't matter to Georgiana. She wasn't hungry anyway, and at least the jailer's wife had given her a supply of candles. She sat on the one wooden stool her cell afforded, hating the thought of sleeping on that filthy-looking pallet that served for a mattress. She almost wept when just before dark Sue arrived with two servants carrying a wooden bench long enough to lie on and a clean mattress.

"Thank you, Sue," she whispered. "I couldn't imagine sleeping on *that*!"

"Nobody could," muttered Sue. "Although I did have to tip the jailer's wife to let me bring it in. She's out there grumbling now that the culprits they bring in think themselves too good for jail food and jail lodgings. Be careful what you say to her, Anna—she could take both your food and your mattress away and I couldn't do a thing to stop her."

Georgiana grimaced. It seemed to her that she had been a great fool indeed. By returning to Bermuda she had delivered herself not only into Bernice's hands but into the hands of this slattern who ran the jail!

"I'll be careful," she promised, and then to cheer Sue up: "How is Mattie holding up?"

"Oh, she's impossible," laughed Sue. "Mamma does not know what to do with her. Mattie refuses to wear mourning and keeps referring to herself as a 'rich widow' and whispers behind her hand that she had taken a lover! She wanted to come with me, but she's such a rattlebrain I wouldn't let her."

They both laughed. Then Sue gave her friend a compassionate little hug. "I'll be back tomorrow."

But she wasn't. Georgiana sat and worried about that. Had Sue been taken ill? It wasn't like her not to keep her promise. She supposed Mattie was being held back by her mother, and as for Sue's other sisters, Alma had always been indifferent to her and Chloe distinctly hostile—but surely Lance could have brought some word from Sue! She remembered bitterly how many times Lance had urged her to marry him!

The day wore on. Food arrived but the servant who brought it could tell her nothing. He looked blank when she asked him where Sue was.

Not till the next afternoon did Sue arrive. She was dressed in her best, the handsome blue dress Georgiana had given her, and she looked ill.

"Sue," she asked sharply. "What is the matter?"

"Sit down," said Sue tersely. "I have some bad news for you."

Georgiana remained ramrod erect; her whole body stiffened. "What is it?" she cried. "For heaven's sake, don't keep it from me!"

Sue moistened her lips. "The governor himself is going to try your case," she said.

"In heaven's name, *why*?"

"Bernice has set a very great value on the candlesticks. She has been wooing the governor and his wife ever since she came here— indeed, we hear that she is hoping to arrange a marriage between his son and one of her repulsive daughters when he comes back from Cambridge. She has spoken to the governor about you and has his agreement that he will personally preside at your trial." Sue swallowed. "She is charging you with major theft, Anna, and asking that you be hanged."

Hanged? Georgiana took a dizzy step backward. She had never expected so ferocious a vengeance from grasping Bernice; she had always been morally certain that avaricious Bernice would prefer money to blood.

"You must reach the governor somehow," she said hoarsely. "You must explain!"

Sue shook her head sorrowfully. "I have tried, but none of us could get in to see him, his gout was so bad. I sat on his veranda all day yesterday until darkness fell, and his wife came out and told me there was no chance that he would see me." Georgiana knew that the governor had been a semi-invalid from gout for almost two years now. "It seems the governor and his wife are scheduled to go to England next week for his nephew's wedding, which will take place in Nottingham, and he spends all his time cursing his doctor, and his wife can hardly pack for all the excitement. She is frantic and not too much interested in our problems."

"Then we can expect no help there?"

"I am afraid not—although I do promise to keep trying," said Sue hastily. "I have just come from there. That is why I am dressed up like this. I thought you would prefer me to stay and keep trying to see him rather than coming over here to report what had happened and I—I couldn't let anyone else tell you, Anna."

"No, I can see that you couldn't." Georgiana's mind was in turmoil. Her hands were clenched into her skirt, twisting the coarse gray material. For this she had returned to Bermuda! "Is there a chance Bernice might withdraw the charge?" she wondered. "If I were indentured to *her*, she could resell my Articles for a great price to some slaver on his way to Algiers." She gave a jarring laugh.

"Oh, Anna, you are not to think of it!" Sue blanched. "Life must be unimaginable in the harems of Algiers!"

"I would never reach there. I would either escape—or go overboard. Either would be better than hanging." Instinctively her fingers caressed her slender neck and she felt her flesh crawl, felt herself choking, gasping, dying. She dropped her hand. Sue was upset enough. "See what you can do," she told Sue in a firmer voice. "Appeal to her sense of avarice."

"I—I will." Sue gave her a pitying look and fled.

The next afternoon Sue was back with a sober face.

"You saw her? You saw Bernice?" Bernice prodded.

"Yes. Mother and I both went to see her. Separately. I thought we would have a better chance that way." Sue sank down wearily on the bed she had provided for Georgiana. "Mother urged her to relent, insisting the punishment did not fit the crime, but Bernice was adamant. She sneered at Mother and Mother told her she was a vengeful woman and Bernice began shouting at her and ordered her off the property, saying we were all in league with you! I thought Mother would have apoplexy. She came home swearing that Bernice

would never darken our door again—and that we should not go to
Mirabelle either or have Bernice's daughters to any of our parties,
not even if one of them marries the governor's son!"

Just now the social life of Bermuda was remote from Georgiana's
mind. She wished Sue would stick to the subject.

"And then you went to see her yourself?"

"Yes. Right after Mother came back in a rage, I rode over and
found Bernice outside and confronted her. I told her there was no
point in her seeking revenge on you by such a direct method, that
she could have your Articles of Indenture herself—that you would
be glad to give her that—and she could sell them to some sea captain
on a ship bound for Barbary for more than the price of the
candlesticks and a few dresses!"

"And what did she say to that?" asked Georgiana tensely. If she
knew Bernice, the chance to bring an enemy down and profit at the
same time would prove irresistible.

Sue looked bewildered and shook her taffy head in perplexity. "At
first I thought she was going to agree, and then she lifted her head
and balled her fists and swore at me and told me I was no better than
my mother and that we would probably all end up on the gibbet but
that you were going there first!" Sue gulped. Her china blue eyes
begged Georgiana to forgive her, but she felt Georgiana deserved the
truth.

Shock spread through Georgiana's slender frame. Bernice . . . wasn't
going to take the bait after all. . . .

"Then—then you must raise the thousand pounds, Sue!" she
cried.

"Of course. We are going to try. And we will get you on to a
ship—any ship. You can pay us back later."

Georgiana felt weak with relief. "Do you think your father will be
able to do it?" she asked fearfully.

"I don't know," Sue told her honestly. "But he has promised to
try."

They exchanged anxious glances. The trial was only three days
hence.

The next day Sue came back to report defeat. "Father's assets are
too heavily mortgaged," she sighed, looking as if she might burst
into tears at any moment. "He could not raise the money."

So her chance for escape was gone. Instinctively Georgiana

looked up at the tiny barred window set high up in the wall, at the massive door guarded by the jailer and his sturdy wife. No chance that way. If only they could have raised the thousand pounds, Lance would have helped her stow away on some ship if nothing else offered, but now that chance too was gone.

"Then we must seek a continuance," said Georgiana slowly. "I had not bargained on this when I came back to Bermuda. Tell the governor that you intend to contact my husband—" perhaps she could manage to do it so the Hudson River folk would never know about it; and whatever Brett now thought of her, Georgiana was confident that he would not see her hang!—"and he will gladly pay Bernice the value of the candlesticks, yes, and more. Once restitution is made, she will no doubt withdraw the charges and the governor will not be bothered with a trial when he is so ill—he will certainly see the advantages of that."

"Yes," muttered Sue. "A continuance. I do not know why I did not think of it before."

"Because I wouldn't let you think of it," Georgiana told her gently. "I told you Brett was not to know!"

Sue scuttled away. Georgiana thought Sue had lost weight. Her own kirtle, which had been a tight fit, now hung around her waist. It was strange what worry would do to one. The fear of hanging . . . she put the thought away from her and told herself that of course Sue would win the continuance.

Sue came back on Wednesday. It was the day before the trial. Georgiana did not have to ask Sue how things had gone. Two big tears spilled over Sue's lashes and rolled down her cheeks.

"He refused to grant it," she whispered to Georgiana. "He refused even to see me. His wife looked as if she wanted to sweep me off her porch—she was very snippy and said that the governor was in great pain and not to be disturbed, that she had asked him about it and he had said no, he refused to leave the island in a mess, with prisoners awaiting trial in the jail. He said they must be"—her voice quavered—"*disposed of*, brought to justice in some way or he would not rest easy during his voyage. He said—"

"I think I have heard enough to get the drift," said Georgiana quietly, "Sue, you have done all you could. No one could have done more."

"Oh, but it is not enough!" wailed Sue. "Oh, if only we could have contacted Brett, if only we had more time!"

But time was what they lacked. Georgiana sat, wooden-faced. How Erica Hulft would be laughing if she knew! she thought suddenly.

"Bernice is a monster!" Sue burst out. "Hasn't she taken enough from you?"

"Apparently not," sighed Georgiana. "I shall have to throw myself on the mercy of the court."

"There may not be any mercy," wailed Sue. "The governor will sit up there with his leg propped on a pillow in terrible pain from his gout. I could hear his groans from the porch and was told all his servants are afraid to go near him."

"Let us hope he is better tomorrow—before he hears my case."

"I want you to know"—Sue stood up as the jailer came to peer in at them, implying it was time to go "—that we will all of us—Mamma and Papa and Lance and Mattie—do all we can to help you. We will be your character witnesses."

"After the stories Bernice has spread about me, I may need character witnesses," said Georgiana ruefully.

"Yes," said Sue with her usual honesty. "You will need them." She threw her arms around Georgiana impulsively. "If the trial goes against you and you are condemned, Lance and I will somehow manage to break you out of jail," she whispered.

But they both knew that if she were found guilty, the judge was like as not to say, "The prisoner will be taken from this place directly to a place of execution and there hanged by the neck until dead."

Sue could run away and refuse to think about that possibility.

But Georgiana, sitting on that rude bench in her jail cell, staring at the pitiless white beam of sunlight that slanted down from the single high window to penetrate the gloom, was left with the grim truth facing her that tomorrow she would go on trial for her life.

And suddenly the laughing face of that golden woman in the portrait in Windgate's long dining room came back to her, as real as if Imogene herself were standing there gazing at her.

"*Mother*," whispered Georgiana. "*Oh, Mother, what has happened to me? Where did I go wrong?*"

Book VIII
The Landgrave's Lady

The dreams we clung to fiercely
That broke our hearts at last,
They all are gone, forget them—
You cannot change the past.

Longview Plantation,
The Carolinas,
1673

CHAPTER 38

On the Carolina coast, Imogene walked the floor of her bedroom restlessly. Old ghosts haunted her tonight, brought by a little French sea captain they had entertained for dinner. He was a shrewd cheerful little fellow with a waxed black mustache he was fond of tweaking and bright black eyes like buttons. He spoke a dozen languages—and claimed a dozen nationalities at his various ports of call—but to the landgrave of Longview Plantation, a man he both liked and respected, he had admitted that he had been born French. Delighted with the food and wine served graciously in their handsome dining room that looked out over the Cooper River, he had waxed expansive. He had been but recently up and down the coast, calling at various cities, and he was full of gossip.

"So you have been in New Orange as well?" His tall host, who had once been known far and wide as the buccaneer van Ryker, fixed him with a steady gray gaze. "What is the word there? Are the Dutch, now that they have taken New York and turned it into New Orange, planning to pour down the coast upon us? Should we prepare for an invasion?"

"No, no," shrugged the little Frenchman, whose name at the

moment was Valois, but who changed it from port to port as a man might change his hat. "All is quiet there." He contemplated with pleasure the handsome blue delftware plate before him piled high with venison and other game, then looked up with a wicked laugh. "Except for one thing: There is to be a trial in New Netherland over the ownership of one of the great patroonships. It will be held in New Orange sometime in the spring. One of your countrymen bought it while the colony was English, but now that it is Dutch again, a Dutchman claims it."

"Oh?" In a tone polite but bored, for van Ryker had not seen Dutch waters in years and had put behind him all that had to do with his buccaneering past. Politics and the House of Burgesses interested him more now. "And which patroonship is that? Rensselaerwyck? I heard it might be for sale."

"No." Captain Valois shook his head energetically and held out his glass to be refilled. He had been paying for his dinner with gossip at great houses all the way down the North American coast. He paused tó reflect. "A place called—Windgate?"

"Wey Gat?" whispered the beautiful woman across the table from him. Above the deep décolletage of her elegant gold satin gown her face had gone suddenly very pale. "Who—claims it?" she asked with an effort.

The French captain shrugged. "A long-lost cousin of Verhulst van Rappard's, I hear."

His hostess and her tall husband exchanged glances.

"A cousin—oh, I see." Imogene looked down suddenly at her plate. For a moment her world had been swimming before her.

"But to make it more interesting," chuckled the captain, displaying a full set of snuff-yellowed teeth once he had downed his wine at a swallow, "the Englishman who bought the patroonship has—as a countermove—married van Rappard's long-lost daughter."

Imogene's head came up so fast that her gleaming golden curls rippled like the golden satin of her big slashed puffed sleeves. "Verhulst's *daughter*?" she whispered.

The Frenchman, intent on his venison, chewed a moment before giving her an offhand answer. "Yes, some wench he found in Bermuda claims to be the lost Georgiana van Rappard and heiress to all that fortune. Her claim's disputed by Nicolas van Rappard, Verhulst's cousin, who's spent his life wandering about the world

and—gossip has it—is toying with the affections of Huygens ten
Haer's daughter, while trying at the same time to win the wife of
Windgate's patroon away from him!'' He chuckled and cut into the
venison again. "They're talking of nothing else in New Orange, I
can tell you.''

Huygens ten Haer's daughter—that would be Rychie's daughter!
And Verhulst had mentioned a cousin—indeed, in his mad jealousy
he had threatened to send little Georgiana away to Holland to live
with that cousin! *And if she had allowed him to do that, if she had
not been so determined to keep the child by her side, perhaps
Georgiana would be alive today!*

"Imogene!'' Her husband had risen in alarm at the sight of her
white face, fearing she would faint.

"I'm fine.'' Reeling a little, Imogene made it to her feet. She
looked very beautiful standing there in her golden gown, very
fragile. Van Ryker's heart ached for her. Why had this fool of a
Frenchman had to bring it all back? He watched as she made a little
motion as if to brush cobwebs from her eyes.

"If you will excuse me, gentlemen? I just need—a little air. No,
please finish your supper. I'll be back presently.''

Van Ryker would have gone with her, but she shook her head to
dissuade him. Regretfully his long form in his dove gray velvet suit
sank back into his chair, for he knew she must face her ghosts alone.
She had been through so much, this lovely lady of his, and this loss
of her child was the one thing from which he had never been able to
shield her. All the gold he had wrested from the Spanish treasure
fleet in the Antilles could not make up to her the loss of little
Georgiana. Now it would all wash over her again, all the heartache,
all the pain. Silently he cursed himself for having asked the Frenchman
here, while at the same time, like the good host he was, he urged on
his guest more wine.

Imogene made it all the way to the long veranda and leaned her
hot forehead against one of the tall white pillars. Around the
grounds, fog was drifting, making the shrubs appear to be hulking
monstrous shapes and the trees strange dark towering edifices that
might come tumbling down—as her world had when she had lost her
child to the sea.

And now someone was claiming to be Georgiana van Rappard,
someone was claiming to be *her* daughter, when everyone knew

little Georgiana had gone down with the burning *Wilhelmina* off the Great Bahama Bank.

Oh, the things people would stoop to for money! Imogene's knuckles clenched white. She had half a mind to go to New York—no, it was called New Orange now—and unmask this impostor, to remind all the world how the real Georgiana had died and perhaps—her soft lips curled dangerously—she would even enlighten them as to who Georgiana's real father had been!

It took her all of ten minutes before she could calm herself enough to go back to the long dining table and face her garrulous guest, who was unaware that anything untoward had happened and was now launched into a discussion of the fortunes of the buccaneers of Tortuga—another subject that brought back bittersweet memories to the landgrave and his lady.

Now that the Frenchman was gone, back to his coastwise vessel whose lights blinked at her from the dark ribbon of the Cooper River, Imogene could not sleep. She had firmly closed the door between her husband's bedchamber and her own—and van Ryker had left it closed, respecting her grief, for it *was* raw grief that he had seen in her eyes—grief long dormant but now awakened. Barefoot, in a lacy white night rail that barely concealed the naked beauty of her figure against the firelight of the hearth, she paced restlessly back and forth across the carpet, sometimes pausing to stare out the window at vistas that had never graced the Cooper. And after a while she lit a candle and began rummaging through the little cherry writing desk in which she kept her papers.

Somewhere she had—ah, there it was. A bit of parchment on which Barnaby had scrawled some verses. She had confided in Barnaby, the yellow-haired ship's master of their buccaneering days, and to comfort her he had sent her this.

She was in sore need of comfort now. She held up the parchment in the weak flickering light and read:

> *The snows that fell on far Wey Gat*
> *Are melted long ago,*
> *And those who loved—and were loved not*
> *Have gone where all things go.*

Dear Barnaby! He had meant to comfort her for her feelings of guilt over the death of Verhulst. . . .

She bent her golden head and read on:

> *The world is not of your making—*
> *Neither is it mine,*
> *Yet the script for our lives was written*
> *Far back in the pages of time. . . .*

No, her heart rebelled against that! Little Georgiana, her beautiful child, could not have been meant to die before the fury of the Spanish guns, to sink beneath the great green ocean on the deck of a burning ship! She was meant to grow up and become a beauty and tempt men and make mistakes and fall in love and perhaps—if she was very lucky!—to find, like her mother, a last great love that burned brighter than all the rest.

Imogene's beautiful delft blue eyes were filled with unshed tears and the firelight shimmered on her long golden hair as she read the last verse:

> *The dreams we dreamed but yesterday*
> *And cherished to the last. . . .*
> *Weep only for the present—*
> *You cannot change the past.*

Barnaby had penned those lines to comfort her, in the days when she had thought never to be comforted again. Dear kind Barnaby, where was he now?

"I was drunk when I wrote them," he had protested humbly when she had tried to thank him.

"No," she had told him in a soft sad voice. "You wrote them to comfort me—and I thank you for that. I will keep them—always."

Flushed with emotion, Barnaby Swift, that sometime poet, had gone away. The verses had remained. She had locked them away in her writing desk, still damp with her tears, for they had expressed better than she ever could how she felt about Wey Gat and all that had happened to her there on the river.

Now she read and reread Barnaby's verses and remembered what it had been like at that great patroonship along the Hudson. A magnificent countryside of romantic hills and wild lovely dells, a castlelike house rising above the river—and everything had gone wrong there, *everything*. And now a stranger had come to seize Verhulst's property, claiming to be the lost Georgiana. It was too much to bear.

Imogene's golden head bent over the writing desk and the candleshine flickered on its gleaming length. The most beautiful woman in all the Carolinas was weeping for a world she had lost, a daughter she had lost, for all that could never be.

But when she raised her head at last, her beautiful tearstained face was calm and cold.

She had come to a great decision.

She went over and threw open the door that connected her husband's bedchamber with her own and the man lying in the big bed looked up alertly.

"Not sleeping either, van Ryker?" she asked softly.

She could not see his face, for the moonlight shafted in behind him. But he sat up, a dark and massive form with a mighty wingspread of shoulders, against the light. It had been a long time since she had called him "van Ryker" and he knew she must be very disturbed to have done so.

She stood there and he enjoyed looking at her. An enticing figure she was in her long, white, half-transparent night rail in the moonlight. But were those tears glistening on her cheeks? He rather thought so—and fought back an urge immediately to take her in his arms and to his bed, to kiss those tears away, and help her as he so often had—to forget.

But he held himself in check, for this sudden visit in the middle of the night meant that she had something to say to him, and he would let her say it.

But while she hesitated, he could not but wonder at her loveliness, at how lucky he had been to find her, and to marvel that she had found it in her heart to love him, and to ponder briefly on the many times he had so nearly lost her.

"You will think me mad, I know," she said in a soft blurred voice. "But I must go there. If you will not take me, then I will go alone."

He had no need to ask her where she must go—he knew.

He rose from his bed, a tall man, handsome, with thick dark hair that now sported silver wings at the temples. His long arms went around her and he held her close for a long yearning moment—for in this one thing he had never been able to help her. This torment of necessity she had borne alone. His deep, timbred voice reflected his concern.

"I will take you there, Imogene. I knew at supper that what you had heard the Frenchman say would drive you back to that place. Although what you will gain by it. . . ." She felt rather than heard his shrug of helplessness.

"I know—and I am sure you are right, but—" She rested her head against the broad chest she had always loved and a deep sigh went through her delicate body. "It is in God's hands, what I find there but—I must go. I must attend that trial. It is strange but I feel as if—as if something is dragging me back." Her voice was puzzled. "Some great force, dragging me back. . . ."

His arms tightened about her. He understood her so well, this woman of fire and silk and tarnished dreams. She had endured so much, he thought angrily. Must fate deal her yet another blow?

And yet he knew that in her behalf he would set the prow of a tall white ship once again toward Dutch New Netherland—just as he would have sailed to hell and back if she had asked him to.

Imogene, sleeping restlessly at last in van Ryker's strong, comforting arms, never guessed that she was headed for the wrong trial, that the daughter she thought long lost would tomorrow go on trial for her life—but not in the cold Hudson River country—in Bermuda.

BOOK IX
Hang Her High!

Who would have thought her downfall
Would hinge upon a lie?
Through iron bars she stares at stars
And waits ... and waits to die!

St. George, Bermuda, 1673

Chapter 39

The day of the trial had come. All of St. George would be there to ogle and gape and watch Anna Smith, who had once been thought heiress to mighty Mirabelle Plantation, brought down to dust.

The night just passed had been a terrible one for Georgiana. She had tried to sleep, so that she might appear calm and rested and face down the crowd in the courtroom the next day, but every time she had closed her eyes she felt a choking sensation as if even now the hempen rope was tightening around her neck, throttling her. She had pressed her fingers against her throbbing jugular vein and imagined how it would be if they found her guilty.

Shivering in the darkness of her cell, she could hear in her mind the governor's sonorous voice pronounce her guilt, feel strong arms bear her away half-fainting to a tall gibbet that would look down upon the town. There she would be asked to make a last statement— convicted highwaymen were famous for gallows' speeches—some few words of penitence, expatiation.

Imagining it, her head came down on her knees and a dry sob escaped her. She would pay dearly for her foolhardiness in returning to Bermuda.

The rest of the night she spent thinking of Brett. She hoped he would be happy, that he would forget her—no, deep in her heart she hoped he would remember her and that Erica would never satisfy him. It was shameful that she should think that, on this last night of her life, she told herself, but it was so.

Morning found her tired but calm. There were dark circles—the badge of sleeplessness—underneath her eyes, but other than that she was steady as a rock. Somewhere between the dusk and the dawn Georgiana had consigned her fate to God. What would be, would be. Whatever came, she would try to meet it bravely.

It seemed strange to enter the low masonry building that served as a courtroom and take her place in the prisoner's dock, for it was a building she had never before entered when court was in session. Trials had never enchanted Georgiana.

She looked around her at the barren whitewashed walls, at the small-paned thick-silled windows through which bright Bermuda sunlight was pouring. It was a glorious day outside. Nature was in her glory, and cared not that Anna Smith was on trial for her life.

Sue and all the rest of the Waites sat in the front row. They all looked grim and Sue and Mattie had obviously been crying. But Bernice, smiling contemptuously, handsomely outfitted in purple taffetas and flanked on either side by her unattractive daughters, was seated at a table on the other side of the room from where Georgiana stood.

Sue had sent her a dress to wear but the jailer's wife had refused to give it to her. The prisoner, she said, had been insolent to her last night—let her wear the same simple white homespun bodice and gray kirtle she'd been wearing when she arrived at the jail! A servant's garb was good enough for such as her, and she'd be dratted if she was going to let the prisoner mince into court in satin slippers and wearing a silk gown as if she was going to a ball!

But that had not stopped Sue, who had managed to sail in at the last minute wearing the beautiful sky blue ball gown Anna had given her—such a long long time ago, it now seemed.

"You will come to trial looking your best!" Sue had muttered, once the heavy door of Georgiana's cell closed behind her. "This is my lucky dress—and it was made for *you*, so it's bound to fit." She was untying the handsome separate puffed sleeves even as she spoke, and before she began to strip off the gown, she handed Anna a comb. "Work fast," she said, "Your hair's a mess."

Within minutes, they had traded costumes and when the jailer came to take Georgiana away, he was confronted with an elegant lady in a delicate blue silk ball gown with big fashionable puffed sleeves. The bodice was close-fitting and revealed the lines of Georgiana's superb figure to perfection. The full blue silk skirts were divided and caught up carefully on either side into big fluffy panniers, to display a flaring white petticoat handsomely embroidered with blue peacocks. That petticoat was Sue's pride and joy, Georgiana knew, and tears almost spilled off her lashes at Sue's kindness in lending it to her. Georgiana's hair was done as elaborately as time permitted and Sue had even brought along a washcloth so that her friend might scrub off at least the visible filth of the jail. That rubbing with the washcloth had produced a glow in Georgiana's peachbloom skin, the low-cut gown emphasized the pearly loveliness of her bosom and the tops of her round white breasts—and the dark circles under her eyes only made her seem the more ethereal and mysterious. It was a creature of delicate fairylike loveliness who strolled out of her cell at the jailer's insistent cry of, "Ye must hurry now, 'tis time, 'tis time!"

Georgiana would never forget the expression on the face of the jailer's wife as she brushed by. Jaw-dropping amazement, envy, anger and indignation all were blended on her florid countenance and she turned her vindictive glare on Sue, who marched along behind wearing Georgiana's soiled white bodice and limp gray kirtle.

Georgiana knew she would never cease to be grateful to Sue for changing clothes with her—for it allowed her to look every inch the aristocrat she was and to face down her enemies this one last time.

So Georgiana went to her trial in a ball gown, as sumptuous as any in Bermuda. She had no way of knowing that her mother before her had once gone on trial for her life in a sky blue gown.

All those who had known Anna Smith during her short life in Bermuda appeared to have come to the courtroom this day, and those curious who had only heard of her, being denied entrance by the crush, milled about outside. She created a sensation as she moved through them—for her loveliness, for her grace, for the imperious way she held her head even in this extremity. For her part, Georgiana looked on these watchers with a kind of detached wonder. What could there possibly be about her case that would interest so many people?

She did not see it as they did: a young and haughty beauty brought to heel by a woman whose tongue had lashed many of those present—and over the theft of a pair of *candlesticks*! One would think it was murder the girl had done! But they gasped when they heard the figure Bernice had set as the value of the candlesticks—a fortune! No wonder the girl had stolen them.

And now they looked less kindly on Anna Smith.

Georgiana was past caring what any of them thought. She had to convince the governor of her very real ownership of the candlesticks. If she could do so, the case would be thrown out and she would go free.

When she was called to testify, she gave the governor a clear-eyed steady gaze and lifted her head proudly. After all, she had frequently been a guest in his home, she had attended all the balls given in the governor's mansion while she was the heiress apparent to Mirabelle, she had danced with his son—and slapped his face soundly once when he had taken liberties!

The face she looked into seemed not to remember any of those facts. Indeed, it was a crotchety mask of pain.

True to Sue's gloomy prediction, the governor sat half asprawl with one swollen leg stretched out on a red velvet pillow. Occasionally he writhed in pain and gasped and closed his eyes. No one could be sure what he heard or didn't hear.

What was becoming clear was that he had already heard Bernice's story from her own lips and fully believed it. His gasping questions brought out all the hard facts.

To Sue's surprise, she herself was called to testify. Had she not ridden over to Mirabelle and told Bernice of the theft *at the accused's behest*? Reminded that she was under oath, Sue threw Georgiana a look of pure misery. "I did as Anna asked me," she whispered. "She"—her voice rose—"she considered the candlesticks were hers, a gift of Samantha Jamison's for her dowry when she married. We all knew they were hers! Anna felt that Bernice had stolen them from her!"

Georgiana would be forever grateful to Sue for that sparkling defense. Not that it did any good. Sue was soon beaten down by the judge's caustic, "And did she have proof that she had been given the candlesticks? Did she show you any proof? Did Samantha Jamison ever tell you she was giving the candlesticks to Anna Smith? Did she tell anyone else? Or did all your information as to their ownership come from the prisoner in the dock?''

To all these questions except the last, the answer was no, and Sue shrank back, cowed by the governor's furious demeanor and harsh accusing voice.

They had the case well made against her when Georgiana took the stand and swore to tell the truth.

"As God is my witness," she said, leaning forward toward the governor who was this day her judge, "Samantha Jamison told me she would give me the candlesticks for my dowry, as they had been part of *her* dowry."

"And since you were about to marry, you considered them yours already?" demanded the governor.

"I felt they were mine. I *always* felt they were mine," said Georgiana defensively.

"And yet your friend tells me that you were not yet aware of your impending marriage when you took the candlesticks from Mirabelle. You were at her front gate struggling with a gentleman who is no longer with us when Brett Danforth rode up and bought your Articles of Indenture, am I right?"

"Bought them from Arthur Kincaid, yes." Georgiana was about to add more when the governor gave a loud groan and bent over his gouty leg for a few moments.

When he straightened up, he turned a cold suffering face toward her. "Then you were well aware that the candlesticks were not rightfully yours yet, because you took them before you knew you were to be married!"

Georgiana felt trapped. "But that is nit-picking!" she cried. "The candlesticks were mine, promised to me. I was wed that same day in St. George—"

"Under the law," thundered the governor, who had a liking for fine points of law and had prided himself on sending many a protesting culprit to the gallows on small technicalities, "you are guilty! Ordinarily"—he grimaced from pain—"I would take into consideration your youth and lack of any previous criminal record, but in this case—" He winced again—"I feel that since the candlesticks were of such enormous value, that it is necessary to make an example of you, Anna Smith.''

"Georgiana Danforth, if it please the court!" interrupted Georgiana, her own control snapping. "And if you are bound to make an example of me, I beg that before you do it you search your mind and decide whether it is because you think I am guilty of any crime or whether it is because I publicly slapped your son's face and called him a pudgy dwarf when he pulled up my skirts on the dance floor at a ball you gave two years ago!"

In the sudden stir that went over the courtroom, the governor's face went from red to white and back again. He glared at the vivid young beauty who stood so defiantly before him, her hands now on her hips and her head thrown back.

Sue gave a heartbroken gasp and pressed her hands to her mouth. Anna, she realized in terror, had sealed her own fate. Nothing could save her now.

"There being no more witnesses—and no need of character witnesses, as the prisoner's character is well known to all of us—I will now pass sentence on the prisoner," said the governor heavily. He looked about him as if daring anybody to find it amusing that this slip of a girl had dared to defy him. "You will be taken from here, Anna Smith, to a place of execution and there hanged by the neck until dead.''

Georgiana felt the blood leave her face. Her waking nightmare of the night before was coming true, word for word.

"But there ain't no gallows been built yet,'' bawled a voice from the back of the courtroom.

"It will not take a very strong gallows to hang a person as slight as the prisoner,'' observed the governor, rapping for order. "I order the prisoner to be taken forth and she may sit in the sun and wait while the gallows be built. Seeing the bar and crosspiece erected before her eyes may cause this presumptuous prisoner to repent the evil ways that have brought her to this court and she may yet make public confession of her crimes. Court is dismissed!''

It was no great work to build the gallows. There still existed the remains of the last one that had been taken down, for this was a "hanging governor,'' who believed a length of hemp was the best lesson the law could teach.

Georgiana sat in the sun, getting slightly sunburned in her shimmering low-cut blue silk gown, although Sue tried to shade her with a borrowed parasol. Disregarding Sue's low sobbing and Mattie's snuffling howls, she watched in fascination as the gallows went up, board by board. There was the rude wooden ladder by which she would mount it—carried in from a nearby barn; there was the rude platform on which she would stand; there above her the sturdy wooded arch from which she would dangle on a length of hemp, looking her last on life. . . .

At last it was ready, a jerry-built wooden structure but strong enough to support the hangman and those who would assist him in sending Georgiana to the next world.

Sue gave her a last tearful hug and, then, just as she had last night imagined it, she was being urged up the scaffold. She mounted it, slowly, dragging her feet, for she had no desire to leave this life; she could see the sky burning blue and serene above her, feel the heat of the uncaring sun. When she reached the top the wind ruffled her burnished gold hair and she could look out to a lovely vista of turquoise sea. Her anxious gaze combed the ships in the harbor. There was a new one there—but it did not have a Dutch look about it, nor was it any ship she knew.

Help was not coming by sea, obviously.

Down below her in the staring crowd of upturned faces she could see Sue with her handkerchief pressed to her mouth and beside her Lance, looking thoroughly miserable. Help was not coing from that direction either.

Georgiana steadied herself and tried to exhibit a calm she did not feel. She would *not* make a spectacle of herself on the scaffold, she would *not*. She would manage somehow to die with pride—and dignity!

Her hands were tied behind her and she moved her shoulders restively. That slight motion rippled the sky blue silk over her round, delicately molded breasts and brought their contours more sharply into view. From the crowd came a catcall.

Georgiana stiffened, feeling she was being made fun of. She, a woman brought low, standing even now upon the scaffold—who could possibly desire her at this moment? She flashed a look of hot anger at the crowd and her turquoise eyes were still snapping when she was asked if she had anything to say before they hanged her.

"Yes," she said coldly. "And I could say it better if my hands were free."

"You may speak without gestures," was the calm retort.

"But my hair is blowing into my mouth!" cried Georgiana. "It will muffle what I have to say."

"Cut her bonds," came the same dry voice. "But guard her well; she is not to be allowed to escape."

Before her the governor, who had been brought here on a litter and now lay there with his gouty leg outstretched, frowning up at her, motioned to a little black boy to fan him. Georgiana could see every leaf and frond of that palm-leaf fan in elaborate detail. Now that her life was ending, her senses seemed to have sharpened. She seemed to see everything in a clear white light—from the frowning governor and weeping Sue and dejected Lance to the bandy-legged little man who was stumbling up toward them on a path that led from the harbor.

She felt her arms come free as her wrists were unbound, and flexed them with a sigh, massaging them with her hands.

"Well," came that calm voice. "Speak, woman."

But Georgiana's attention was focused on that bandy-legged little man running up to join the crowd—and now fighting to make his way through it.

"I, Georgiana Danforth, whom you knew as Anna Smith," Georgiana began, "having been brought to trial in Bermuda for the crime of taking two candlesticks which were mine already for they had been promised to me by Samantha Jamison before she died—" She broke off, staring. Now she knew where she had seen that little man before. He was Christopher Marks, Tobias Jamison's London agent, and he had been to the island but once, years ago, and on that occasion he had been so ill that he had not left his ship, but Tobias had taken her with him to the ship, she had met him! "Mr. Marks!" she screamed.

The bandy-legged little man, for all that the velvet seat of his trousers was worn smooth from too much sitting and working on account books, for all that he had been seasick for most of the voyage and could feel his lunch rising in his throat even now from all this exertion in the Bermuda heat, had a loud authoritative voice. "Of what crime does this woman stand accused?" he bellowed in a voice that cut through Georgiana's like a knife through butter.

It was the governor who answered, half rising from his litter. "Of the theft of a pair of candlesticks from Tobias Jamison's estate." A numbing shaft of pain went through his leg. "The girl has said enough," he gasped. "Get on with the hanging."

"Wait!" screeched the little man, fairly jumping up and down on his velvet-trousered bandy legs. "She cannot have stolen what is rightfully hers! I have brought with me the will of Tobias Jamison, for I have recently heard that he was dead, and in it he leaves everything he died possessed of to one Anna Smith, who stands here before you on the scaffold!"

All was confusion and shouting as Bernice leaped up from her carriage, choking on the apple she had been unconcernedly taking large bites of as she waited to see Georgiana hanged. The governor shouted "Hold!" in an apoplectic voice and the hangman, who had been about to send Georgiana to oblivion, caught her falling form instead.

Bernice, in rage and bright fear that had struck her like a hammer blow—for here was the real Christopher Marks to disprove her fraud—swallowed whole and unchewed the large bite of apple she had taken and tried to shout a denouncement of the little man. The apple stuck in her throat. She gasped, finding her air supply cut off, and began clawing at her throat, but no one noticed her plight for all eyes, even those of her startled daughters, were riveted on the governor, who was having a shouting match with the bandy-legged agent from London. She staggered forward with an abortive gesture and fell out of her carriage, landing sprawled across the back of a man standing below. He turned with a curse and seeing that he had upended a lady, set the struggling woman on her feet, muttering— but even *his* gaze hardly raked her, for he too was intent on the seeming brawl between the governor and the stranger, for now the stranger had brought out a document and was thrusting it under the governor's nose.

Bernice, choking, gasping, clawing at her throat and at the arm of the nearest person, found herself pushed back against the horse that pulled her carriage. As she reeled against his flank, he shifted his weight and neighed and stepped back. His hoof pinioned her skirt and as Bernice, sure she was dying, fought to get it free, the horse, frightened by the noise and the unseemly pulling at his hoof, reared up and knocked her to the ground.

Now at last she was noticed. A horse had knocked a woman down. That was understandable, something the nearest person could and should do something about.

A tradesman from the town bent to help her up. Above them and to the left the governor, who had been scanning the document that had been thrust upon him, was roaring, "But even if this document is genuine, it says here that the plantation of Mirabelle and all its chattels are to remain with Tobias's wife, should he acquire one, for the duration of her life—and candlesticks are chattels! The girl admits she stole them!"

"I am shocked you could doubt the authenticity of this document!" roared the little man from London, his seasickness forgotten. "For it bears not only Tobias Jamison's signture, clearly and plain to see, but also the signatures of two witnesses who saw him sign it!"

"It matters not!" The governor, half mad with pain and anxious only to get this whole miserable matter over with, shoved back the document at the giver. "There is a more recent will! And *it* left all property, real and personal, of whatsoever nature, to the surviving widow—over here." He turned to indicate the place where Bernice had been sitting in her carriage and frowned at not finding her there.

Bernice meanwhile was writhing against the arms of the man who was trying urgently to lift her up from the ground. She was fighting for air and it was a losing battle. Her face was contorted and her eyes were wide and staring.

"She's hurt, can't you see?" cried the man who had just lost his grip on Bernice as she twitched convulsively away from him. "Somebody help me!"

But his voice was lost in the roar of the London agent. "I cannot believe there is another will. *I* am his London agent, I would know about it! What is the date of this alleged new will?"

In agony from his painful leg, the governor had scarcely looked at the date on the document; he had *assumed* the will Bernice had probated was a later will. Now his wife nudged him. He turned to give her a molten look and she leaned over and muttered something in his ear. "The new will is dated some three years ago and was drawn up in Jamaica," he told Marks with an arrogant gesture. "And Tobias Jamison has not set foot in England these five years past—of that we are all certain.'

"Then *this* will is the more recent!" Christopher Marks waved the document triumphantly. "For it is dated less than two years ago. It was made out in Jamaica, where I met Tobias by chance, for I was but passing through on some other business. He had me draw up this will and have it witnessed, for he was thinking of marrying some woman in Jamaica and wanted his affairs in order in case anything should happen to him—as indeed it did. And you can plainly see my signature affixed—Christopher Marks."

The governor sat silent for a moment. Then, "Can you prove you are Christopher Marks?" he asked in an altered voice. "For if you can, then the man who brought this other will to probate was an imposter, and I don't doubt the legatee will be found to be involved in fraud and worse."

Bernice, being held up now and with a loud whirring in her head, heard this. She lifted an arm in mute appeal but everyone was worried about her knock on the head and nobody at all realized she was choking to death. It came to her dizzily that she was undone, that now there would be an investigation, that the fraudulent "Christopher Marks" would be searched for, seized, the signatures of the two wills compared against other documents Tobias Jamison was known to have signed—the forgery would be all too evident.

And—if only she had not taken these measures, if only she had been willing to wait until the real will could be found—she would have ended up sole proprietress of Mirabelle and all of its chattels for the rest of her life! She would have had full possession, and complete domination over Anna Smith—she could have done what she liked with the girl, marrried her off, gotten rid of her.

Bafflement, anger, regret, confusion, guilt and horror at what might come all warred within Bernice's brain as she fought to swallow the chunk of apple that was more firmly than ever stuck in her throat. She saw them all through a red film now, her lungs were bursting, and the roaring in her head had become an incessant thunder crashing its warning through her brain. She was slipping away, away. . . .

Her head drooped and she collapsed, twitching, a dead weight, into the arms of the man who, now thoroughly alarmed, was calling out for smelling salts to help revive her. Bernice never sniffed the smelling salts. She would never take breath again.

"Bring the girl down from the scaffold," said the governor in a

shaken voice. He groaned as he moved a little. "It would seem—we
may have misjudged her."

But at the top of the scaffold Georgiana was not witness to any of
this. She had fainted dead away.

Mirabelle Plantation, Bermuda
Winter 1674

CHAPTER 40

All Bermuda was talking about Anna Smith. Her name was on
everyone's lips. Indeed they talked about little else. Snatched from
the scaffold, she'd been! The same people who had been so ready to
despise her now eulogized her. From outcast, Georgiana had now
become a folk heroine. In time to come songs would be written
about her and sung throughout the islands—but that time was not
yet.

For now, fresh from her near miss with death on the scaffold, she
was being driven over to Mirabelle with Sue and Lance and
Christopher Marks in a carriage and another carriage was following,
bringing the rest of the Waites.

"I'm surprised you're so eager to take over, Anna," said Sue
frankly. "I'd have thought you'd have wanted to rest the night at
least before tackling Mirabelle."

"Perhaps Mistress Anna wishes to tally up her possessions?"
suggested Christopher Marks smoothly.

"It isn't really for my sake, Sue—it's for the servants," explained
Georgiana. "I want to get rid of that terrible overseer and give
everybody hope. And I want to stop the destruction of our cedar
grove instantly! It isn't"—she gave her friend a level look—"that I

want to crow over Bernice's daughters on the very day of their mother's death. But I do intend"—her brows formed a straight line—"to see that they take away from Mirabelle none of my jewelry and none of my clothes. They were too eager to bring me down," she added dryly.

Sue gave her an understanding look. Naturally Anna wanted to safeguard Mirabelle's valuables. She had been pushed out of her home by Bernice and her daughters and she had every right to take back what was hers. She said as much but Anna wasn't listening. Instead she was listening with joy to the birdsongs, and appreciating anew the glitter of the sea as it broke against the ancient gnarled rocks, the big cedars festooned with sea grapes and vines that edged the road and formed a graceful arch above them, the scented air of freedom. To Georgiana, as the carriage whirled through the front gates of Mirabelle and started up the long drive toward the white cross-shaped house with its flaring "welcoming arms" front steps, the world had never looked more beautiful. She had been snatched from death—she was going to live!

All the servants rushed forward when they saw Georgiana. They had been prevented by Bernice from attending the trial and some of them were crying, for they had thought her already dead. Some of them called her name over and over, prayerfully, as if they could not believe she was really here. "They told us you was sure to be hanged today," said Big Belize, rolling his eyes.

"The report of my hanging was greatly exaggerated," said Georgiana lightly, for she had regained her aplomb since being snatched from the gallows. " 'Tis Bernice who's dead and I'll be coming back here and running things. The place is mine now."

The servants who had crowded around stared at her, not comprehending.

"Bernice is not coming back," repeated Georgiana. "Her daughters will be leaving too—as soon as we've packed their things. In that way"—her voice hardened a little—"I'll be very sure that nothing of mine goes with them."

Sue regarded her friend with new respect. This was not the carefree Anna she had known, but a new and harder version who called herself Georgiana Danforth. Life had tempered her friend and like fine Toledo steel she had been bent—but not broken.

"You're turning them out to starve?" wondered Mattie, coming up just in time to hear that.

"No, not to starve. They've money of their own. Bernice was married before, remember. She still has—had," she corrected herself, "a house in Jamaica that will be theirs now. Her daughters can go back there or"—she shrugged—"to hell if they prefer." She could not forget the sight of their avid faces riveted greedily on her at the trial, or their later smirks as she had viewed them from the scaffold.

Both Bernice's daughters showed up a little later, driving up in a carriage. They had left their mother's body at the church and, having been apprised of how things now stood, had come home to pack. Prue, the older of the two, who had inherited her mother's features and demeanor, was astonished to find their luggage already packed and standing in the driveway, and even more taken aback when Georgiana came out to confront her.

"How do we know everything is there?" cried Prue, standing her ground.

"You will have to take my word for it," said Georgiana coldly, "for you will never enter this house again. And I will have those earbobs, which happen to belong to me." She reached out and snatched them from Prue's ears.

"You would not have dared to do that when my mother was alive," shrilled Pris.

"When your mother was alive," said Georgiana in that new hard voice, "I had to fight back the urge not to tear my clothes from your skinny backs every single day! And that necklace is mine also! It was given me by Papa Jamison." She jerked the coral necklace from Pris's neck with such force that the clasp broke and there was a shower of coral beads on the driveway. Pris gave a little angry cry. "Do not ask me for sympathy," said Georgiana crisply. "For I have none to give you. Your mother drove the people on this plantation past all endurance, she nearly cost me my life. I have ordered round a cart to take your trappings into town. Where you go is no concern of mine. But you have looked your last on Mirabelle, for at your mother's throat today was a large amber pin which all know belonged to Samantha Jamison. If you ever set foot in Bermuda again, I will have you jailed, for I will say that you have stolen it."

"She's turning hard," muttered Chloe, who was watching. "She doesn't sound like the Anna Smith we knew."

"No, no," Sue told her sister. "It's just a reaction to nearly being hanged. Her nerves are still on edge. Give her a few days—you'll see."

They both watched as Prue, looking affronted, took a step backward away from this new avenging Georgiana. "But," she blurted, "Mamma loved that pin. She is to be buried in it."

"Even so," said Georgiana with a gleam in her eye. "Here comes the wagon. Once it is loaded you will both be taken out of my sight and deposited in St. George. I bid you both good day!" She went up the "welcoming arms" front steps, herding the watchers in with her, and slammed the front door with a force that shook the house.

She was trembling.

"A clean cut!" applauded Christopher Marks. "You'll be needing a London agent, will you not?"

"Yes, and I couldn't have a better one than you, sir. I remember Papa Jamison said you collected pipes, as he did. I'd be honored if you'd accept his collection—it will be a small reward for saving my life today."

"Indeed you're generous!" Christopher Marks had long envied Tobias Jamison his beautiful collection of pipes. He rubbed his hands together in anticipation.

Before the weekend Georgiana had overturned Bernice's whole regime at Mirabelle. The staff went about with happy faces, order had been restored, and the hated overseer was looking for work somewhere else. Coral, the cat, was returned by Sue and was happily mousing in all her old haunts.

It occurred to Georgiana that she should give a ball, a sort of homecoming party to herself, but when she thought about Brett and all that she had lost, all that she would never have again, she did not have the heart to plan it. For Mirabelle would never satisfy him. With Brett it was Windgate—or nothing.

Only Sue seemed to understand how she felt. Mattie could think of nothing but her inheritance, which Christopher Marks had sailed to Boston to secure for her. Georgiana, who had suggested to Mattie that Marks would make an admirable manager for her affairs, thought it only just. Mattie had endured much as Arthur's wife—he owed her some happiness! And with a certain future stretching before her, Mattie flowered.

"Walter Meade has told us some of the things Arthur inherited from his parents when they died last year," she confided. "I never dreamed of being so rich!"

"Don't let it go to your head," warned Sue merrily. "Or we won't be able to find a hat to fit you!"

"I am not only a rich widow, I have also become a woman of the world," said Mattie airily. "Well, I must be off to St. George—I've some shopping to do."

"The merchants there have given her credit," explained Sue. "They've heard about her impending windfall and can't wait to get their share. Mattie will have it all spent before she receives it!"

"Perhaps you'd better go along to protect her," suggested Georgiana.

"You're right," Sue laughed. "I will!"

She watched Sue go, riding down the familiar driveway on her mother's favorite riding horse, Jemmy, who had had such a narrow escape when Arthur had set the locked shed on fire. Dear, good Sue, she must find a proper way to reward her. She had considered asking Lance to become her factor. Sue and Lance would have the money to get married then, for they had been postponing and postponing. But that would mean they would be living in the factor's cottage, or alternatively given rooms in the main house. And she wasn't sure Sue would enjoy either cottage life or being a perpetual guest in someone else's house. It was a perplexing problem. She would have to put her mind to solving it.

At least she had been able to stop the felling of Mirabelle's great trees for ship's masts and ship's lumber. The island's vast forests were fast being stripped for the shipping industry, and Mirabelle's trees were dear to her. She had ridden beneath their branches, dismounted to nap in their shade, been thankful for the roof they had provided against sudden rain.

Idly she strolled into the big kitchen where cook and her helpers were contentedly working. And then into the drawing room where once she had thought to stand before that high-flung cedar-paneled fireplace and take her wedding vows. . . . Instead she had taken them in St. Peter's Church in St. George—and again in New Orange . . . to a man she would never see again.

Pensively she moved into the dining room, smiling at the silver, which had all been gotten out and polished yesterday and put back in place, out of the big locked cupboard where Bernice had, miserlike, stored it. Everything was back where it should be—all except the mighty candlesticks with their fat cupids and their twining grape leaves—those candlesticks that she had taken in a moment of madness and which had nearly cost her her life.

She wondered with a little pang where they were. Those candlesticks had meant to her stability, home. Like Mirabelle, they had always been there . . . that was why she had taken them. Unconsciously she had thought of them as a lodestone around which her world turned. She had never really meant to sell them. In a kind of blind, groping way, she had meant to take them to her new home, establish her life around them. And when she had left Windgate, that was the real reason she had taken them with her—not their value. She knew that now. And in a moment of madness she had exchanged them for ship's passage. Now she regretted it.

She walked through the big airy rooms, scanning the familiar furniture, touching a piece here and there. She could almost believe Tobias Jamison would be riding home up the drive from a day in St. George supervising the unloading of cargo bound for Mirabelle. She walked outside and half expected to see frail Samantha Jamison rocking on the big veranda. From out of the past she seemed to hear Doubloon's mocking laughter. All of her youth was tied up with Mirabelle. As a tot, with Elise, she had played along its white beaches, running through the surf, gathering shells. As a young girl she had learned to read and write at that very desk. Outside, on those "welcoming arms" front steps she had held court for any number of suitors.

All her past was bound up in Mirabelle, and once again she was its mistress.

Why, then, did she feel so lonely? So lost?

Her heart and her mind fled north, back to the Hudson River Valley, back to Windgate, back to the tall "English patroon," Brett Danforth, who had swept into her life in Bermuda and taken her north on a tall white ship. She swallowed, remembering Imogene's diary. Another tall gentleman from Devon had broken the heart of another girl from the sunny isles. . . .

She kept walking through the lonely rooms. Those curtains would have to be replaced, they were yellowed. Money-hungry Bernice had been a poor housekeeper. And her wardrobe . . . she looked ruefully through what was left of her clothes, all cut up and altered, and none of it done with any taste at all. There was a lot of work ahead of her in that department.

Hooves were thundering up the driveway and Georgiana hurried to the big front door and threw it open just in time to see Sue leap off a winded Jemmy as the poor beast skidded to a stop at the front steps. Without bothering to tie Jemmy up at the hitching post, Sue tossed the reins aside and ran up the steps, almost colliding with Georgiana.

"He's here!" Sue cried in a hoarse voice. "I saw him just a little while ago. Oh, Georgiana, he's here!"

"Who?" cried Georgiana, shaking Sue in exasperation.

"Brett!" gasped Sue. "He was just stepping onto the dock as I arrived. He didn't see me and I turned around and rode back at a gallop. He'll be here soon—oh, Georgiana, what are you going to wear?"

Brett—here! Joy broke over Georgiana in a bright wave, engulfing her senses. She hugged Sue and for a minute there the two girls spun around ecstatically.

Then Georgiana pushed Sue away. Her face was flushed. It had come to her clearly that it was love that counted—not property. If Brett loved her enough to come for her, he should have her!

"You'll want to wear your best dress, Georgiana—oh, I forgot, those awful women—Bernice had all your clothes cut up!" She brightened. "You still have my blue dress—you can wear it again!"

"No," said Georgiana softly. "I have just the thing to wear." Swiftly she shed her clothes and pulled from her big press the simple white cambric bodice she had worn when she arrived back in Bermuda. "Hand me that gray kirtle, won't you, Sue?" she cried. "And help me get hooked up!"

"But—but those are the clothes you wore in the jail!" Sue was shocked. "I realize they've been washed but—surely you aren't going to greet him in *those*?"

"Yes," panted Georgiana, struggling with her own hooks. She kicked off her shoes. "There—that petticoat, the plain blue cotton one, that will do nicely. And this dark corselet when I get it laced up. Quick, run down and have them take care of Jemmy and saddle two fresh horses for us."

"But you'll look like a goose girl!" wailed Sue.

Georgiana gave her a brilliant smile. "Exactly what I intend!"

Sue left, shaking her head and Georgiana took a quick look at her reflection in the long pier glass. It gave her back a pretty picture of a beaming lass with rumpled golden hair. She reached up and rumpled it some more, for today she did not intend to be a well-groomed beauty whom all might envy—very much the opposite.

Her reflection showed her a pair of bare feet with dainty ankles and a plain clean blue petticoat over which she now tucked up her gray kirtle to give a jaunty effect. The dark corselet with its broad lacing pushed her high bustline up yet a little higher, and the low-cut white bodice with its full puffed sleeves brought into tempting view the smooth white skin atop her rounded breasts. Georgiana loosened the blue riband around the low neckline and gave it a tug that brought it down over one shoulder.

She laughed wickedly. That should be an enticing enough display to tempt even a righteously angry husband!

For a new wisdom had come to Georgiana. Brett—if he saw her as mistress of a great plantation, wealthy, needing no one, might even go back to Windgate without her—back to Erica Hulft! But if she was in dire trouble, Brett would never leave her.

A sweet but very determined expression spread across Georgiana's lovely face. So Eve must have looked in Eden.

She ran out to join Sue, who was standing beside two saddled horses looking mystified.

"Brett is not to know Mirabelle is mine," she told Sue rapidly. "You're to ride on ahead and intercept him and tell him I'm in terrible trouble and there's no time to tell him about it, if he hurries to Mirabelle he may be able to save me!"

Sue gave her a look of pure disapproval.

"Do this for me, Sue," urged Georgiana. "And if it works, if Brett takes me way with him, Lance can become my factor and run the plantation. You and Lance can get married and live in the house—yes, and you can have Mattie with you, if you like. She's going to enjoy being a rich widow but she'll need someone to keep her on the track—and you're steady, Sue."

Sue's face fairly glowed. "Oh, Georgiana," she cried. "I can't thank you enough. Lance and I—"

"May not get the post, if you don't hurry!"

Without pausing to draw breath, Sue was aboard the horse, had wheeled his head about and was galloping down the drive.

Georgiana called to the groom who was watching nearby, "Send someone for this horse. I'll be leaving the animal some distance along the road from the front gates."

And she leaped aboard and was off after Sue.

Riding along with the wind in her hair, she reflected that just wearing these clothes did give her a sense of urgency, of desperation. She had fully meant to give them to the servants but something had impelled her to hang on to them. And now they were ready for just such a moment as this!

She rode through the wide front gates of Mirabelle—and cast a quick look backward. She had the feeling she would not see those "welcoming arm" front steps for a long time.

When she had reached a prudent distance from those gates she dismounted, gave her horse a smart pat on the rump that set him trotting toward home, and set out beneath a canopy of cedars and hanging sea grapes, trudging toward St. George.

Minutes later she heard the soft thud of hooves pounding along the road, saw a rider loom up in the distance.

She began to limp and she reached up and rumpled her hair again. She wished she had thought to rub some of the fireplace soot across her nose but, no, that might have been too much.

With some trepidation she saw the tall rider approach, come to a halt that caused his mount to rear up, and leap off.

"Georgiana!"

"Oh, Brett!" She ran limping toward him like a bird with a broken wing.

"You're hurt," he cried sharply.

"It's nothing." She flung herself into his arms, laughing and crying. Those arms felt so good, enfolding her. She had thought—oh, God, she had thought never to feel them around her again.

After a swift hug during which she could feel a tremor go through his big frame, and reveled in it, he pushed her away from him, held her at arm's length and frowned down into her upturned face.

"Sue said you were in trouble. I thought it might be the candlesticks. If it is, rest easy—I've brought them along."

Georgiana, who'd been about to say she'd nearly been hanged for those candlesticks, gasped. "However did you come by them?"

"When I got home, Linnet had found your note. I'd had time to think and I simply didn't believe you had run away with van Rappard."

Tears shown in Georgiana's eyes. "Thank you for your confidence," she said huskily.

"And when I heard that Mattie had gone too, I guessed where you'd go—Bermuda. I sailed the *Witch* downriver to New Orange and there Govert Steendam told me he'd been offered some candlesticks for sale, recognized them as coming from the long sideboard at Windgate, and had the fellow jailed!"

"But—I gave them to Flan to pay for our passage."

"He cheated you—as he admitted under some persuasion. And returned them to us for the modest price of your passage!"

A quiver of laughter went through Georgiana. Flan had cheated her flagrantly on the sale of the candlesticks; she had let him have them for a pittance when they both knew their worth. How furious Flan must be!

They were both talking and laughing now, words tumbling over each other. Brett was telling her how he'd had to buy a ship to bring him here, no one would sail him into Bermuda waters—and there'd been nothing but storms, he'd thought he'd never get here. And Georgiana was pouring out her "deal" with Erica, ending with a sad little smile. "I only meant to help you, Brett, for I knew how important Windgate is to you."

Brett looked down at her tenderly. God, she looked beautiful, he thought. Golden hair rumpled and in those coarse garments, he was reminded of the night he'd first seen her. Breathtaking she'd been in the moonlight. He remembered how she had swayed like a leaf in the sea wind, how the soft light had caressed her pale gleaming body as he bore her gently to the sand.

"Windgate is important to me, yes, but"—his voice softened and his lips brushed her ear—"the whole of Windgate doesn't hold a candle to you, lass."

Tears rushed to her eyes. She had never thought to hear such an admission from his lips. She was *first*! *First in his heart*.

"So you came to Bermuda to collect a lost waif who might end up on the gallows?" she said with a little catch in her voice.

'Aye—and found her."

"Things are not quite so bad here as you may have thought," she murmured. "Come, let us to Mirabelle and we will talk about it."

"You will be welcomed there?" He sounded astonished.

She shrugged. "Well, now that you have the candlesticks. . . ."

"I see. Well, I do not have them with me, as you can see. They are still aboard ship."

"But can be sent for?"

"Readily."

"That will be good enough."

She was gazing up into his eyes in a way that daunted him. A moment more of this and he'd take her here and now by the roadside! He swung her up on the saddle before him. Feeling her back rest lightly against his strong chest, feeling the slight rasp of his forearm beneath her soft breasts as he handled the reins, Georgiana rode once again up Mirabelle's long driveway—content.

She saw before her the flaring stone steps of the big white cross-shaped house and they seemed to her, indeed, welcoming arms. She slid off the horse and ran up the steps.

"Come!" she called imperiously, opening the front door.

His wide-topped boots clattered up the stone steps after her. "Faith, don't ye announce yourself?" he wondered.

"No, I'm well known here. The servants will not give me away. But hurry!"

Frowning, he followed her into the hall, shot a look around him at the cool dimness, welcome after the sun's brilliant rays.

"Wait here," she said. "If anyone comes—any of the servants—just tell them that you are waiting for me."

"And if the mistress of the house comes?"

"She will not. She has been out all day."

Brett's brows elevated but he held his peace. He did position himself so that he would have a good view of the front door from whence the angry mistress of the house—and who knew how many henchmen—might make their entrance. He was used by now to Georgiana's impulsive reckless ways and would not have put it past her to entertain him by stealth at the scene of her former grandeur—and he did not mean to be caught unawares.

Minutes later he heard a sound behind him and his dark head swung around.

Georgiana stood there, but—a new Georgiana.

Gone were the simple homespun clothes, gone the barefoot lass he had so recently held in his arms, gone the disheveled tumble of the way she'd worn her hair. In their place was an elegant lady, with rustling silk skirts of a lustrous sky blue. It was the gown she'd worn at her trial, the gown she'd borrowed back from Sue, and she looked ravishing in it. The dress was cut shockingly low, and displayed delightfully the curving tops of her round breasts. The shimmering silk outlined breathtakingly her slender waist, billowed out to wide panniers that swayed gracefully above her handsome peacock-embroidered petticoat. Big billowing blue silk puffed sleeves spilled out a cascade of white lace at the elbows and her hair was brushed to a high sheen and caught up fetchingly in the very latest style. The blue lapis necklace—also borrowed back from Sue—was around her neck but the glory of her turquoise eyes put the blue stones to shame.

Brett came to his feet at the sight of her. "My God, Georgiana, are you mad? If Bernice comes home and finds you in that dress—!"

She glided across the polished floor toward him and smiled. "Shall we go in to dinner?"

Automatically he offered her his arm.

"I have a confession to make," she said, as he pulled back her chair at the massive cedar table. "My fortunes have gone round full circle once again—and I am back in my rightful place, mistress once again of Mirabelle!" She waved her arm gaily to include the house, the land, the cedars, the long stretch of coast—and told him how she had come by it all.

Brett sat across the table from her through dinner and listened, taking all this in. "Then you are not a waif and I am not your rescuer?"

"No."

"Why did you deceive me, Georgiana? Why greet me barefoot and let me believe you were in dire straits?"

"Because," she said in a level voice, "I feared you were still angry with me and would leave me—if you felt I was safe."

He looked at her in surprise at this revelation.

"And I was fully prepared to leave all this." She nodded at the opulence about her. "And let you carry me away and forget I ever owned Mirabelle. For I did not intend to lose you, Brett—not a second time." Her gaze was tender and loving. Her heart spoke through her misty turquoise eyes.

"Georgiana." His voice was rich and deep. "I think we need no wine tonight." He rose and walked swiftly around the table, drew back her chair and lifted her up to face him. "I would have followed you to the ends of the earth," he admitted. "Aye, and brought you back with me!"

Georgiana gazed up at him in perfect happiness, and led him from the dining room toward the big bedroom where she had dreamed her girlish dreams.

Tonight those dreams would all be realized—there in that big bed of her girlhood. Tonight she would share that bed with the man who held her heart in keeping.

There, with the Bermuda moonlight streaming in through the big windows, she let him undress her, stand marveling at the beauty of her flawless form, so irresistibly lovely in the pale shaft of light from the windows.

And, then, in leisurely fashion, he undressed too and she smiled at the beauty of his lithe manly frame that towered above her. He reached out for her and she went to him silently, clothed in love and beauty. His hands stroked her slim body tenderly, tingling it to passion, and his voice murmured endearments in her ear, words half heard that yet brought mistiness to her eyes and a tremble to her soft lips.

And then he carried her to the big bed and gently laid her down. And Georgiana told herself she had fought hard for this night of stars and moonbeams, and she was going to enjoy it!

Tomorrow would be time enough to tell him the hard truth about herself, about the packet, her mother's journal. Tomorrow . . . but for tonight her delight at having him back overflowed into boundless joy as she lost herself in his arms.

Morning found them saying good-bye to Sue and all the others amid instructions and tears, and again embarking for the voyage north.

"The candlesticks are still on board," Brett said doubtfully. "Won't you want to leave them here now that Mirabelle is yours?"

Georgiana gave a rich low laugh. "Don't bother to unpack them," she said. "Next to you—and Floss, of course—they're my most treasured possession. They're going home—home to the Hudson, home to Windgate!''

Their voyage north was for them both a golden voyage of rediscovery, but it had about it a sense of desperation too. For both of them were aware that if they lost Windgate, it would change their lives. But it was something that need not be faced—yet. Their nights were wonderful—but then no lovers are ever quite so intense as those who love under the shadow of the sword.

They never discussed the upcoming trial. Time enough to meet that when it came. Instead they seized these golden moments, given to them out of time, with all the fervor and desperation of the condemned. For them, for a little while, the dream would last. . . .

And after that, who knew what lay ahead?

BOOK X
Lady of Legend

They never stop to think, who speak of her
How every lad's hot pulse she seemed to stir
And not a man who looked into her face
But yearned to linger in her sweet embrace!

New Orange, New Netherland
March 1674

CHAPTER 41

The makeshift courtroom—a warehouse commandeered for the occasion—was jammed to capacity on this windy day, but way was made for the lady in amber velvet who strode in with such authority. Partly the crowd gave ground in deference to her obvious aristocracy, for the lady reeked of breeding and money from the sweep of her lemon-plumed hat to her dainty lemon kid gloves encrusted with seed pearls, to the toes of her gold satin slippers. But partly it was in deference to the lady's beauty, which was considerable, even though her face in the main was hidden from view by a scented lemon silk scarf that she had tucked under her wide-brimmed hat, obviously to keep the meticulous coiffure from disintegrating on a windy day like this one, and which shadowed and obscured her face. Several people craned their necks for a better look at her, but gave up and turned away to focus again on the proceedings.

That anonymity was exactly what Imogene wanted. She had come here to weigh, to judge—and then if the wench who posed as Georgiana actually won (which gossip conceded would be unlikely) Imogene meant to rip aside her veil and rise and expose her for what she was—a vile impostor seeking the patrimony of a child long dead.

She settled herself into a seat as close to the front of the room as she could get and bent to arrange her velvet skirts. Heavily cloaked against the cold weather of early March, she hoped to attract little or no attention.

Imogene had been in New Orange two days now, having been rowed into the harbor by night by a burly sailor from the *Sea Rover*, that now lay at anchor, waiting for her out of sight down the coast. For the *Sea Rover* was an English ship and this a Dutch colony and England and Holland were still at war.

Van Ryker had wanted to accompany her, but she had refused. If he were seen—and who could fail to recognize that strong determined visage, that swinging gait, that look of daring strength?—then all would remember Imogene Wells, she who had become disastrously Imogene van Rappard, and she too would be recognized.

No, this was something she must do herself—and alone. So she had given a false name to the innkeeper, kept her hood shadowing her face, and taken all her meals in her room. So far she was safe.

All the great and near great of the river and half New Orange, it seemed, had contrived to get here. People stood packed close together and some had even managed to climb atop two great cupboards that stood against the walls and gazed down upon the long table and the magistrates.

Ownership of mighty Windgate was at stake here and the claimants sat tense on opposite sides of the room.

The lady in amber velvet, now watching over the shoulder of a plump lady in the second row, studied the gathering narrowly. Like the others she craned her neck for a look at the patroon of Windgate and his ravishingly beautiful wife. She had heard by now all the stories that were circulating about them.

The man, Brett Danforth, looked to her to be all that a man should be. She could see him clearly from where she sat and she liked the arrogant way his head rode on his broad shoulders, the confident set of his jaw, the cool steady look in his gray eyes when his dark head swung around to gaze into the crowd. If she had been sixteen and innocent and had met him today, he would have attracted *her*.

But her interest centered more on the woman beside him. Gossip had told Imogene all about the wench's beauty, but nothing had quite prepared her for the fact.

The girl was stunning! Clad in dramatic white with her wide-brimmed gold hat awash with white plumes, white gloves—an elegant effect. And she had a haughty serenity, a defiant lift to her delicate chin that Imogene, under any other circumstances would have approved. Imogene wished she could see her better, but she did not wish to attract attention by finding some pretext to walk up the front of the room as several curious ladies had already done. That burnished gold hair . . . it would be copper in some lights, and now as the girl turned her head there was a flash of turquoise from her eyes. Imogene closed her own eyes for a moment to shut out that sight—those who had arranged this plot had selected a girl who could have been Stephen's daughter! Perhaps she should have told Stephen—no, she would do what needed to be done. *She would strike the blow if the court did not!*

Her interest sharpened as she saw Georgiana rise to settle her wide skirts more comfortably upon the wooden bench. That dress, she knew that dress. It was—anger almost choked Imogene—it was her wedding dress, the dress she had worn when she had married Verhulst. *The strumpet was wearing her gown!*

Georgiana had chosen that dress carefully, so that she would not melt into the general melee of bright colors affected by the Dutch women. She must stand out, she must have . . . stature. She must *seem* for once the wife of a patroon, a woman born to stand above the crowd. The court must view her so, must believe her to be Verhulst van Rappard's daughter, for somehow—she did not know how—she intended to get the journal and Elise's sworn statement away from Nicolas before he ruined her with it. Into the panniers of her handsome satin gown she had thrust a small pistol. There would be a recess, she presumed, and during that recess she meant to approach Nicolas, to sway against him, to press the pistol against his side and murmur to him that he would leave with her—*now*.

She had not thought out what would happen once she had taken him from the courtroom at the point of a gun. That Nicolas would go with her, she had no doubt—if not from fear, from curiosity as to what she would do next.

And once outside, once they reached some private place where they could talk, she intended to make him hand over the journal and the sworn statement that he had duped Linnet into stealing for him. And without it, she was sure he would lose.

Nicolas had made a wonderful entrance—an entrance that had brought a murmur from the crowd and got them with him. With his arm in a white sling made from a silk scarf, he had come in limping—and carrying in his other hand a naked sword. Brett had frowned for he recognized at once that serviceable basket hilt, that excellent grip that fit his hand like a glove.

It was his sword.

The crowd leaned forward, muttering. Nicolas had their full attention.

Smiling, he limped toward Brett and Georgiana. His limp was more pronounced now that every eye was upon him, Georgiana noticed cynically. But for a moment she feared for Brett, whose hand was inching toward the dress sword he was wearing today. Would he be quick enough to counter if Nicolas made a sudden lunge? Her hand reached into her pannier, closed over the gun.

"Do not fear for your husband, Georgiana." Nicolas made her a small courtly bow. "I have come to return in gentler fashion the gift he made me when last we met. This is the sword he flung at me that gave me this wound."

The crowd sucked in its collective breath and craned forward.

Nicolas, ever with a sense of the dramatic, tossed the sword glittering into the air and caught it cleanly by the blade—no mean feat for it was heavy. He held it out to Brett, hilt first.

"I return your weapon, mynheer," he said. "You would have taken my life but you shall not take my inheritance."

There was a little dusting of applause.

Georgiana felt her heart sink to the toes of her satin slippers. Nicolas was outmaneuvering them. And here in this Dutch court in this Dutch land he had these Dutchmen with him! Already—and the trial not yet begun.

"Mountebank!" she grumbled. "He should have been an actor."

Nicolas had won the first round, but there was more to come and—Georgiana had at least chosen her gown well. Some of these women remembered that dress—even now they were muttering to their husbands, wondering how she had got hold of it, for Erica Hulft had plundered all the women's gear she had found at Windgate and she had *never* found anything like this! And now those husbands who remembered the beautiful Imogene were furrowing their brows and noticing a certain likeness to Imogene in Georgiana. She was wearing a ring many recognized and now a gown that had come from nowhere, which their wives had found unforgettable! Circumstantial evidence that this girl was the real Georgiana was mounting up.

There were three judges sitting at a heavy oaken table facing the audience. Imogene knew one of them by sight—Huygens ten Haer, Rychie's husband. The others were strangers to her. They had come in with heavy dignity and their clothing was the somber stuff well-to-do Dutchmen wore which she remembered all too well: rich and black, unrelieved except for gold chains and frosty linen and expensive point lace at throat and cuff. They looked grim and self-important, for were they not deciding today the fate of the most imposing property along the river?

Huygens brought a gavel down upon the table top and the court was in session. They called on Nicolas van Rappard, who had brought this claim, to publicly state its nature—and support it.

Imogene watched intently. So this was Verhulst's cousin, the son no doubt of that cousin in Holland to whom Verhulst had been so determined to send little Georgiana. Her lovely mouth tightened. She had come here today on a mission. She meant to see justice done, perhaps to bring down a dynasty, perhaps to unveil an impostor—she owed it to a man who had loved her and died because of it: Verhulst van Rappard, who slept upriver in a family plot near a frowning mansion that had once been her home—and her prison.

Narrowly she watched Nicolas, gorgeous in scarlet satin, state his claim. Saw the tall frowning English patroon rise to refute it. Like the rest of the crowd she craned to see him better—and found him a sight worthy of her gaze. Dressed casually in leathern doublet and breeches, he stood with his booted legs wide apart. Stood with an air, she thought. His defense was simple:

"I bought Windgate when it was overwhelmed by debt. Now that I am bringing it out of that debt, others seek to claim it."

"The viewpoint of the *English* patroon!" jeered Nicolas.

Even though the proceedings were entirely informal, the judges intending to submit their decision later to the Dutch New Netherland Company in Holland, Huygens ten Haer brought his fist down upon the table.

"Be silent, Nicolas," he growled. "You will be treated justly here—and so will my neighbor, Danforth."

"Thank you, Huygens," said Brett quietly.

Huygens, thought the watching lady. She looked about for Rychie, found a head of hair that could belong to no other—saffron yellow, on a woman dressed in vivid red, whose back she could see some distance away. Beside her, slightly lower, another saffron head. Rychie's daughter, no doubt.

Memories flooded back to her. She cut them off, determined to listen to the arguments of the English patroon. His arguments seemed fair enough to her: Danforth had bought the estate in good faith and Verhulst's cousin was trying to get it away from him.

Witnesses were being called informally at the pleasure of the court. But the watching lady tensed as Georgiana took the stand.

The girl who walked proudly up to stand before the table was young and golden and—now the lady caught her breath—*she had Stephen's eyes!* Brilliant turquoise, they stared defiantly back at the crowd. And that face—with minor alterations that face could almost have been her own!

"I was christened Georgiana van Rappard," Georgiana told the listening judges. "I was born at Windgate—the place you call Wey Gat. And I was transported downriver by Elise Meggs, who took passage under the name Eliza Smith aboard the ship *Wilhelmina* bound for Barbados."

"A ship that burned to the waterline after being attacked by a Spanish warship," interrupted one of the judges. "We all know the story."

The girl seemed to stiffen. "What you perhaps do not know," she said sharply, "was that the *Wilhelmina* put in at Bermuda for fresh water before she was sunk and there Eliza Smith slipped ashore carrying me in her arms"—and she launched into the story of her early life, how Eliza had hidden her, cared for her.

Huygens sat back. But Nicolas was not so easily satisfied.

"How did you come by the ring you wear?" he asked tauntingly. "The sapphire ring set in gold that bears the inscription 'To Imogene, my golden bird of Amsterdam. Verhulst.'"

Georgiana turned and stared him directly in the face. "It was given to me by my husband, Brett Danforth."

A subdued murmur went through the courtroom.

"And where did Danforth get it?" wondered Huygens.

"He had it from Erica Hulft's brother, who blackmailed Elise Meggs out of it in Bermuda, threatening to make her presence known to Verhulst van Rappard if she did not give him money or something of value—poor Elise had no way of knowing Verhulst van Rappard was already dead! I was present when Claes Hulft made his demands, and I remember Elise hurried away that night with the ring, to meet him, and came back without it. She told me it had belonged to my dead mother."

The watching lady in amber velvet passed a hand over her face. There were tears in her delft blue eyes. All this had happened and she had not known, *she had not known*. Dear God, she had thought them all dead and they had been but an ocean sail away. How much blue water she had seen in her life and great waves breaking green across the deck! Why could not the winds of chance have carried her to Bermuda?

Georgiana was speaking again. "I claim Windgate as the acknowledged daughter of Verhulst van Rappard—christened as such."

"May I question this witness?" Nicolas rose.

Huygens nodded.

"Georgiana—or should I call you Anna? You have been very fortunate in your life, have you not?"

"I should not call it fortunate, losing one's parents and being brought up in poverty!"

"Ah, but it was not always poverty, for I understand that you are now possessed of another fair plantation—Mirabelle in Bermuda. And there was some trouble over your inheritance there also? Another claimant, I believe."

"Tobias Jamison named me as his heir. His second wife sought to take all, but the will naming me was found and brought to Bermuda by Tobias Jamison's London agent—and I inherited."

"Papers in *London*." Nicolas's tone made the word "London" sound suspicious. "Strange papers from far away places delivered after the fact have been very fortunante for you, it would seem! Well, here are some papers that will not be so fortunate—indeed they will prove to be your undoing!" He reached into his doublet and drew out a packet.

Georgiana started. She had not expected things to happen this way. She had thought that Nicolas would question her and after she left the witness stand, produce his written evidence. Instead a grinning Nicolas was bringing out the packet!

"I feel faint," she cried. "I request a recess!" And blundered toward Nicolas.

Surprised, the golden Dutchman caught her as she sagged toward him. Her face had fallen onto his shoulder and now he felt from somewhere the hard muzzle of a gun pressed against his side.

"This is a pistol," Georgiana murmured. "If you do not leave with me, I will shoot you now!"

Always wary of excitable women bearing firearms, Nicolas found his voice. "This lady is ill! I will carry her outside where she can get some air." Forgetful of his sling, he scooped up Georgiana and turned to carry her away. His sudden wince as he felt the pistol jab him even more forcefully in the side was proof to the astonished audience that his injured arm and leg—which he was so gallantly using in support of this lady who was wed to his rival—were paining him.

"Hurry!" muttered Georgiana. "Your life depends on it!"

But Brett had already vaulted over the table at which he sat and was shoving his way through to her.

"You'll take her nowhere!" he cried, and reaching out with his long arm, he seized Nicolas by the shoulder.

Nicolas, caught between the devil and the deep, froze.

"In the name of God, Danforth!" sputtered Huygens from the judges' table. "He is but helping your wife to some air!"

"He may help anyone he pleases—save my wife," said Brett grimly. "*She* belongs to me!"

"Your *life*, Nicolas," whispered Georgiana, with closed eyes. She could feel his heart thudding in his chest. She did not know how he would get her out of here but she had the feeling he would manage it somehow. And once outside, once alone, she could put her proposition, and at gunpoint he would be glad to accept it.

It would be an offer he would not care to refuse.

Nicolas surged backward and stumbled. Georgiana, whose finger was not actually on the trigger, almost dropped the pistol. As Nicolas released his grip on her, Brett reached forward to catch her but Nicolas, going down, managed to grasp her wrist and bring it up away from him.

And in her slender hand attached to that wrist was a dueling pistol.

The crowd gasped and fell away from them. Brett was thunderstruck as he set Georgiana, now totally recovered, on her feet.

"Have you some explanation for this?" thundered Huygens ten Haer. "What did you hope to gain by this piece of bravado?"

In silence, Georgiana handed Brett the pistol and he stuck it in his belt. Their eyes met and his were very angry.

She had lost. And in panic she knew that she might have cost him Windgate.

"Answer me!" cried Huygens. "Why were you holding a pistol on Nicolas?"

"I think," said Nicolas, regaining his feet with a push from several onlookers, "the answer is to be found in this packet."

He drew the packet out and held it up for the court to see. With deliberate slowness he drew out a parchment and a journal.

Imogene, who had stood transfixed with the rest of them, watching this little drama play itself out, paled as she recognized the journal—*her* journal. Elise must have taken it with her the night they fled Wey Gat.

"Those are stolen papers!" roared Brett.

Nicolas's wicked grin flashed. "Indeed! Stolen from your wife's bedchamber at Windgate." He swaggered forward to slap them down on the massive oaken table before the judges, and then turned back to Brett. "Don't you want to know how I came by them?" he asked innocently.

It took all Brett's restraint to keep from drawing his sword and slashing blood into that smile. "I *know* how you came by them. You seduced my wife's personal maid and the poor girl stole them for you. Huygens," he turned forcefully to the man who sat in center place at the judges' table, "I demand the return of my wife's stolen papers."

Events were going too fast for Huygens. He sat a minute chewing his lip.

Into that momentary void, Nicolas spoke. His voice was cool, deadly. "Before they are returned, I would have them read before this court and this company. For the letter is a deathbed affidavit of Elise Meggs and the journal is the secret journal of the late Imogene van Rappard, and both documents prove beyond doubt that the lady here who claims to be Georgiana van Rappard is in truth—"

From the door came the report of a pistol and all heads turned to look at a wild-eyed man who stood with a smoking gun in the entrance. For a moment all voices were stilled.

Into that silence, the man—a burgher whom all recognized—spoke.

"I bring news that will change all our lives," he cried. "The war is over! There has been a peace treaty signed at Westminster. Under this treaty New Netherland has been given over to the English! This land is no longer Dutch!"

CHAPTER 42

The courtroom erupted into a scene of confusion. Brett, who had leaped forward and snatched up the letter and the journal from the table, was looking at Georgiana.

English again—not New Netherland, this land was once again New York, this city was no longer New Orange—it was New York City! How could he tell Georgiana how he felt about it? That someday there would be neither Dutch nor English here, but only Americans. He might not live to see it, but his children's children— ah, yes, *they* would unite this land and set it free from European claims. Someday, someday. . . .

"An English court will decide it now," said Brett, pressing Georgiana to him. "Good God, Georgiana, what madness came over you to threaten Nicolas with a pistol in this courtroom?"

"I meant to force him to hand over the documents, even if I had to trade him Mirabelle for them!"

He looked down at her tenderly. She was so fine, so open hearted, so loyal and so headfirst in everything she did . . . he knew he would never cease to love her.

At the head table Huygens was pounding and shouting for order. At last he had it—a semblance of order at least.

"This court"—he said it sadly—"will no longer have jurisdiction in this matter. In any event, we could only have submitted our findings to the New Netherland Company in Holland for final disposition. But now that we are back under English rule—''

The lady in amber velvet had been pushing her way through the crowd. Now her clear voice rang out, interrupting Huygen's last words.

"A Dutch court will do as well as an English one for what I have to say. Nor will there be need to submit any documents. *I wrote that journal.*"

All heads swung toward the lady, who now ripped off her scarf and let her golden curls break free. Her fearless gaze was fixed on Huygens.

"I am Imogene van Rappard. I demand to be heard."

The courtroom was suddenly deathly silent, so still a fly could be heard buzzing angrily among the rafters. Imogene, back from the dead?

Nicolas, ever impressed by feminine beauty, drew in his breath in a silent whistle. This glorious creature standing before them—so like and yet so unlike the young girl whose turquoise eyes had challenged him along with her pistol—was the legendary Imogene, Verhulst's "golden bird of Amsterdam"!

Imogene stepped forward and the light from the rafter chinks where the sky could be seen seemed to gather about her and make her coloring the more brilliant.

"I did not die on the iceboat," she said quietly. "Although for a long time I suffered amnesia. When I recovered, I was told Elise and my child had gone down aboard the *Wilhelmina*, that my lover and Verhulst were both dead. I saw no point in returning—and I never did. But when I heard there was a claimant to Windgate and a girl who claimed to be my daughter, I determined to return and tell my story that justice might be done."

"How do we know you are in truth Imogene van Rappard? Can you prove it?" Nicolas was recovering fast from his initial shock.

Imogene laughed. "You have only to look at Huygen's face—he remembers me from the time he was turned away at Wey Gat by Verhulst on the grounds that I was 'too ill' to receive company—and I dashed downstairs in the midst of the conversation and asked if he could take me on his sloop as far as Haerwyck! And Rychie—ah, Rychie remembers me, I can see that from the consternation on her face. But in case she is still uncertain''—she jerked the silk scarf from around her throat and revealed a white blaze that brought gasps from the crowd—''she will surely remember the van Rappard diamonds, and others will remember this necklace too, for it was the finest necklace seen in New Amsterdam up to that time, and I wore it to Governor Stuyvesant's ball—along with that dress, my wedding gown, which my daughter Georgiana has found somewhere! And Vrouw Berghem''—she turned and her voice softened—''you remember me too. I can see it from your look of shock. You will remember how I went out that night and returned in the dawn to tell you no duel would be fought? That Captain van Ryker had sailed away? And Verhulst came downstairs and we all ate Indian porridge at your table?''

''Ah, it's true, it's true!'' cried Vrouw Berghem. ''It is Imogene herself, returned from the dead!''

Georgiana was stunned by the dazzling radiance of her mother's beauty. She seemed to glow in that crowded room and everyone was watching her with a taut breathlessness. Just looking at her had an effect on the men in the audience—their eyes of a sudden gleamed or dreamed, according to their temperament. And the women looked at her—as they always had—with a kind of inner fear; she was too beautiful—such beauty was disruptive, a menace.

''Then if you now admit my identity, you must also admit that I am the woman Verhulst named in his will. Those 'documents' that have been produced may refute my daughter's claim but never mine! *I* am sole heiress to Windgate.''

Huygens bent his head to confer briefly with the other judges. He rose.

''We are of one mind,'' he said heavily. ''We have all read the will and you are indeed named as sole legatee. We find you the heiress to Windgate—but we also find Brett Danforth purchased the property in good faith. We can only submit your claim to—''

''That will not be necessary,'' cut in Imogene. ''I publicly abandon my claim in favor of my daughter Georgiana, in the hope that she may sometimes remember and think kindly of a mother who missed her young years and has found her perhaps too late ever to claim her affection.''

Georgiana stood up. ''And I abandon my claim in favor of my husband, Brett Danforth, who bought and paid for Windgate. As for my mother"—she turned a radiant face toward Imogene—"my wonderful newly discovered mother—it could never be too late for her to claim me!" She ran forward and impulsively threw herself into Imogene's arms.

Huygens turned to Brett and made him a slightly ironic bow, but his heavy features remained unmoved.

"Then it is the judgment of this court—in the light of all these abandonments—that Windgate belongs to"—he smiled upon his neighbor, whom he had always liked—"the *English* patroon!"

Brett acknowledged Huygen's friendly look with a warm answering smile of his own. He stood up and would have spoken but that from outside came the sudden boom of heavy cannon.

A breathless hush descended on the room, as men sprang to their feet. Those guns—they were not the familiar guns of the fort, they had not the sound of them. In the instant during which that unhappy knowledge sank in, women gasped, some cried out or pressed kerchiefs to mouths gone suddenly pale, and men bethought them of their wives and families and loosened their swords in their scabbards.

"Gentlemen!" Another voice rang out, a voice of pure authority that turned all heads once again.

A tall man stood blocking the entrance—and their exit. Broad of shoulder, he cut a splendid figure in dove gray velvet shot with silver. More importantly, he had a brace of pistols, both drawn and pointed at the crowd. And behind him were some twenty men, armed with cutlasses and pistols.

"I heard a pistol shot and have come to see to the safety of my wife," said the tall man coolly. His gaze flicked over the assembly.

"I am here, van Ryker," said Imogene, and her glorious eyes were wet with tears. "Here—with my daughter."

"'Tis Captain van Ryker!" cried Vrouw Berghem ecstatically. "And we all thought him dead as well for he never came back!" She drew in her breath. "His *wife . . . he has married Imogene*!"

A little of the thrill she felt went through the assemblage. All the old stories were true, then. Scandalous Imogene had run away with one lover and married another! And this one the notorious Captain van Ryker, who had been perhaps the most popular buccaneer ever to visit New Amsterdam!

Huygens ten Haer, who had leaped up at the first sound of heavy bombardment, found his voice. "But the cannon, man? My God, if there's a treaty, the English surely aren't attacking the town?"

Van Ryker's white teeth flashed. "No, that was a salute from the *Sea Rover*'s guns. I'm standing once again on English soil and —since I'm an Englishman—I thought to salute the change of ownership!"

There were indrawn breaths, for up to now, all had thought van Ryker to be Dutch.

"And since there may be some lawlessness tonight because of this change of ownership," van Ryker was saying dryly, "I will collect you now, Imogene. You will come with me and bring your daughter and whoever else belongs to her."

"*I* belong to her," said Brett, stepping out where he could be seen. "Georgiana is mine and I can well protect her without any help from you."

"Be that as it may," was the calm reply, "my help you shall have if you need it. Since we're English again, I realize that the decision of this court—sensible as it was—may have no validity. Having already been challenged under Dutch law, the title to Windgate could now be challenged again under English law. So I leave you with a warning"—his formidable gaze turned to Nicolas—"whatever flag flies above the fort: By right of my wife, I have this day been presented with a son-in-law." He nodded at Brett, who gave him back a stunned look. "My son-in-law's holdings will no longer be at issue in the courts of this colony. Should his title again be challenged, a ship of forty guns will back his claim."

Nearby, numerous eyes widened, for it was well known that a couple of broadsides from a ship like the *Sea Rover* could reduce the town's tottering old fort to rubble.

Van Ryker leaned toward Nicolas. His gaze was very cold. "Do I make myself clear, van Rappard?"

"Very clear," said Nicolas hastily. Never having lacked for wit, he knew when he was beaten. "Indeed, I accept the will of the court"—he gave this dangerous buccaneer a winsome smile—"and herewith renounce all claim to Windgate."

"Before witnesses," added van Ryker dryly.

"Yes! Before all these good folk who have witnessed my renunci- ation!" He was unfastening the silk scarf that had served him as a sling for his "wounded" arm as he spoke. He would no longer need it! Now he stretched that arm and straightened up, moving toward the door with no sign of a limp.

"Van Ryker." Imogene had reached her husband and was smiling brilliantly through her tears. "You have made me notorious again!"

"You have spoiled that martyred effect for your audience, Nicolas," jibed Georgiana as his path led him by her.

"My thorny little rose," he laughed. "I regret I must tell you good-bye."

"Where are you going now?" she could not resist asking.

He shrugged and his golden hair rippled on his broad shoulders. "I need a change of scene. If I can just avoid Katrina ten Haer, who is making her way toward me with battle in her eyes, I think I'll just find me passage on some ship. One bound for Bermuda, I think, now that we're no longer at war with the English. After all, Danforth found a wife there. Yes, I think I'll go down and see Mathilde. Who knows, she may still favor me?"

"Mattie will never have you," she sniffed. "And, anyway, Sue will send you packing if you reach Mirabelle!"

"Thank you," grinned Nicolas, "for telling me where she is." He left them jauntily.

"The likeness is amazing." Brett was gazing on Imogene with wonder. "You could almost be Georgiana's older sister."

"Save that her hair's a shade more copper and she's a breath more slender and—she has her father's eyes. Turquoise." Imogene gazed tenderly upon her offspring. "We have so much to tell each other, Georgiana, so much to make up for, so much time lost."

People swirled around them. Wealthy burghers, losing no time to congratulate Brett on his victory, for they hoped to be trading with him. Neighbors along the river, who wished no rift between themselves and the now firmly established wealthiest patroon in all New Netherland. Curious faces, trying to get a better look at the stunningly beautiful face of Imogene, about whom so many stories swirled. And people gazing in awe at the notorious Captain van Ryker, who had become a legend in his own time.

"You must all have supper with me." Vrouw Berghem bustled up. "For I turn over the key to my home tomorrow and sail back to Holland. And this evening will give me something to talk about all my days!"

Imogene hugged her. "It is wonderful to see you again, Vrouw Bergham!"

"And don't forget, I am expecting to hear all about you and Captain van Ryker, all you have been doing since last we met."

Imogene gave Vrouw Bergham an affectionate look. "That, I am afraid, will be a very long story."

"And one you will have time to tell," chimed in Georgiana. "For I will not let you go so quickly, now that I have found you at last!"

She looked up at Brett and saw him smiling fondly down upon her. *We have won,* she thought. *We will have it all—Windgate, Mirabelle, everything.*

"But now," she said "you must return my mother's journal to her—and Elise's letter, for I think she would like to have them both."

Silently, Brett handed over the documents and Imogene took them.

Her daughter was safe now. Safe from a scoffing world. Safe—surprisingly enough—at Wey Gat! No, she must remember to call it Windgate, as Georgiana did. Windgate.

Windgate. It had a lovely sound—like Eden on the Hudson. A place for lovers.

BOOK XI
The Wedding

You owe me some repayment
For the tears I shed
That in bridal raiment
I would never see you wed....

New York, New York
March, 1674
CHAPTER 43

At the feast that night at Vrouw Berghem's house, mother and daughter exchanged tales, caught between laughter and tears. Imogene listened raptly as Georgiana told her of Bermuda and Arthur—and they both wept over Elise's death.

"If I had only gone to Bermuda instead of all those other places," said Imogene, "how different it would all have been...." Her lovely face was lit by a radiant smile, which rested on Brett with a brilliance that dazzled him. "I thank you," she said softly, "for all that you have done for my daughter. Windgate is yours—it always was yours. I will never trouble you about it, whatever wind may blow."

"You never meant to come back," murmured Georgiana. "And yet it is so beautiful there."

A pensive smile curved Imogene's lips. "No, I never meant to come back, for to me its loveliness was tarnished. To me it is a place of sad memories. I will not visit you there, Georgiana, but you will visit me. And you will bring your children, when you have them— and your grandchildren."

But after dinner she took her daughter aside. Beside a branched

candelabrum she took Georgiana by the shoulders, held her at arm's
length and studied her carefully. "You do not really look like me,"
she said at length. "Or at least the resemblance is superficial. No,
you look more like Stephen—you have his copper hair and turquoise
eyes. I have been watching you and you have handsome ways, like
your father—quick to anger, quick to repent. But you have inherited
my recklessness—I saw that in the courtroom today. It is a dangerous combination." She turned her sunny smile toward Brett across
the room. "I am glad you found him," she said frankly, "because I
think he is just what you may need! And since I find you already a
bride, Georgiana, I have a mind for wedding gifts."

She took from her neck the blaze of diamonds on which Rychie
ten Haer had looked so enviously—that gift from Verhulst so long
ago, in the days when he cherished her and thought her his. *It
belonged at Windgate*, she thought, *for it had the style and richness
of the man whose gift it was.*

"I give you"—she clasped the necklace around her daughter's
neck and stood back—"this little token of my affection." She made
a slight careless gesture. So a queen might have gestured, thought
van Ryker, watching her from across the room with endless pride.
"But like most gifts, it has a condition."

Georgiana gasped at the gift of the necklace. The van Rappard
diamonds—these stones were worth a king's ransom! Her eyes
shone. Her mother too had handsome ways; she could toss away a
fortune with a shrug of her elegant shoulders. She flashed a proud
look at Brett and met a swift smile on his face, for he had seen
Imogene's generous gesture and the happiness that had lit up
Georgiana's face.

"I thank you with all my heart," said Georgiana. "And I accept
your gift—on any condition."

"You have just proved again your recklessness," said Imogene
coolly. "For my condition is—since I was deprived of the opportunity to see you wed, which I had longed to do—that you repeat the
ceremony on board the *Sea Rover*. Now. Tonight."

"But I have already been twice wed to Brett!" gasped Georgiana.

Imogene shrugged her lovely shoulders. "I have been robbed of
your childhood, your girlhood—I refuse to be robbed of your
wedding. It is every mother's right to see her daughter married. It is
true you will not have the wide curving staircase of our Carolina

plantation to walk down—but you will have a swaying deck to walk across. And you will not have a church or candlelight around you—but you will have starlight and white sails floating above you. And you will not have a tinkling virginal—lord, how Verhulst tried to make me learn to play one—but you will have a strumming on the *viola da gamba* and the deep-throated song of the buccaneers. You will walk across the deck with your bridegroom beneath an arch of cutlasses held high and have your health drunk in good Jamaica rum! And the best blade in the Caribbean will perform the ceremony—van Ryker! And I myself will give the bride away!''

"Thrice wed?" murmured Georgiana, shaking her head and laughing.

"And you will wear that very dress you have on—for it was *my* wedding dress when I married Verhulst and that was on shipboard too. God knows it brought me no luck, but it has already brought *you* luck—I could see that in the courtroom today when you swept all before you!'' Her brilliant smile challenged her daughter. ''Come now, Georgiana. Does not every girl yearn to be married in her mother's wedding dress, with her mother standing by, dreaming of white satin and old lace beneath the stars?''

Turquoise eyes met blue ones, locked and held. And suddenly Georgiana was not laughing anymore. It was as if a veil had been lifted and beneath Imogene's lighthearted banter she seemed to see another woman, proud and strong and loving—yearning for her and yet too proud to beg for her esteem.

"Oh, Mother!" Georgiana went into her mother's outstretched arms and Imogene, holding her daughter close after all these years, closed her eyes and fought back tears—for tonight was not a tearful occasion, it was a wedding night, an occasion for merriment, for joy!

"Georgiana," she whispered. "Your father would be proud of you." Tomorrow she would tell Georgiana that her father was alive. Alive and married and living on Barbados. Tomorrow she would tell Georgiana how glad he would be to see her.

But tonight was hers. *Her* triumph. Tonight, this beautiful night of stars that reflected down on quaint New Amsterdam—no, she must remember to call it New York—those stars that sparkled on the North River's dark surface—no, she must remember to call it the Hudson—tonight belonged to her.

And so it was done.

A "buccaneer's wedding" was held that night aboard the *Sea Rover*. Brilliant paper lanterns lit the scene and from the shore a tipsy crowd cheered the bride, for on this night, with the colony "changing ownership," people were too stirred to go to bed and curfew was forgotten. They cheered as Georgiana in her elegant white gown and a necklace of glittering diamonds that put the stars to shame glided across the *Sea Rover*'s deck on van Ryker's arm and took her vows with Brett Danforth—once again. They cheered as van Ryker pronounced them man and wife. They cheered as Brett slipped over her finger once again that gold and sapphire ring that had once been Imogene's and that had such a strange history. They cheered as the bride walked with the "English patroon" beneath an arch of crossed buccaneer cutlasses, and continued cheering as the ship seemed to burst forth with song and the bride and groom were toasted in good Jamaica rum.

On shore this was a night never to be forgotten, for had the crowd not seen with their own eyes a dead woman sail in on a buccaneer ship long ago reported sunk to claim a daughter who was the scandal of New Netherland? And were they not even now celebrating the nuptials of a bride and groom now thrice wed—and this time the ceremony performed by the formidable Captain van Ryker? Such a story to add to the wild saga of the patroons of Wey Gat! It almost capped the change of ownership of the colony!

Now the buccaneers were singing again, deep-throated male voices rising in haunting melody against the creaking of the great ship's timbers as she rode at anchor. They sang of things lost and forgotten, of wasted lives and blasted hopes—but it was to this music that Windgate's patroon led out his ravishing bride to tread the first measure of the dancing that followed the starlit ceremony. He looked very dashing and his white teeth flashed in high good humor.

"Faith, I might have thought twice about marrying you, had I known I would acquire such formidable in-laws! Not content that we are already man and wife, they arrive on a ship of forty guns to insist we be wed again! Thrice wed!" He shook his head in mock dismay as he whirled Georgiana across the deck. "Surely so much has not been asked of one man since the gates slammed shut on Eden!"

Another cheer went up from the shore as Captain van Ryker, resplendent in gray and silver, gave Imogene a sweeping bow and led her, light-footed with amber velvet skirts swirling, across the swaying deck.

Over van Ryker's broad shoulder, Imogene could see the bridal couple looking more than handsome and the bride's diamond necklace rivaling the stars in brilliance. They danced raptly, intent on each other, as if this were the first moment he had held her in his arms. Watching them through misty eyes, Imogene remembered her own "buccaneer's wedding" on Tortuga and smiled at the look of blissful happiness on her daughter's lovely face. All her soul was mirrored there.

Georgiana looked up at Brett. Just as her virginal heart had clutched him to her bosom, now her woman's love—deep and full and true—went out to him. Looking down he met that trusting gaze with tenderness, and their eyes met and held and plighted once again their troth.

"Windgate will be our Eden," she murmured.

And Imogene, who had been swept from the Scilly Isles on the wings of a wish made long ago to two tall standing stones called Adam and Eve, heard her daughter's breathless words and smiled. She had found her own Eden with a tall buccaneer who had chased her across half the world. And now her daughter, her lovely daughter lost so long ago, was returned to her and had found an Eden of her own.

They had both won through!

> *She followed her heart and she rode to the skies,*
> *She never was cautious, she never was wise,*
> *And the truth to be learnt from her life, my fine friend,*
> *Is that love is a story that has no end!*

Epilogue

Across the seas a wayward breeze
Wafted these two together
And firm and fast, true to the last
They'll ride the storm together!

Time changed their story, of course—as it always does.

There were those who protested that the man who showed up in that Dutch courtroom at the head of a band of buccaneers was not van Ryker at all, for it was well known that the real van Ryker had died in a landslide on the Cornish cliffs. And that beautiful woman who had stunned the courtroom with her beauty and her claim of being Imogene van Rappard—she too must have been an impostor, for everyone knew the real Imogene had perished when an iceboat sank into the Hudson. And, as proof, these skeptical souls cited a self-evident fact: Neither van Ryker nor Imogene were ever seen on the Hudson again, nor did the *Sea Rover* sail again into New York harbor.

Indeed, the *Sea Rover* disappeared as if it had never been (no one thought to look for the majestic ship along the Cooper River in Carolina, where she carried the name *Victorious*). And eventually most people persuaded themselves that they had never seen her, that none of it had ever happened, that they had all suffered a kind of mass hysteria due to the strain of learning of the Treaty of Westminster and the English takeover of New Netherland.

Nicolas never doubted what he had seen of course. Married at last to Mattie—a surprising Mattie who bossed him about—he was well aware that van Ryker's ship of forty guns was lurking about somewhere to ensure his good behavior. And Linnet heard about the happenings downriver but she did not really care, because by then she was planning to marry a handsome young schoolteacher and all her energies were bent on learning to read and write.

Vrouw Berghem bragged of that evening all her life—but that was in Holland and she was old and garrulous, so no one believed her.

So in spite of the *Sea Rover*'s last buccaneering venture, the landgrave and his lady were not found out, and the patroon and *his* lady kept their counsel at Windgate on the Hudson and only smiled when questions were asked of them.

Some loves, they say, are everlasting.

> *To fate they are beholden for*
> *This rapture so sublime—*
> *The world is always golden for*
> *True lovers in their prime!*

Exciting Reading from *Valerie Sherwood*

Don't Miss These Other Fantastic Books By HELEN VAN SLYKE!

ROMANCE...ADVENTURE ...DANGER...
by Best-selling author, Aola Vandergriff

Passions For You
from WARNER BOOKS